88 SAINT OLIVER'S ROAD

BY

FRAN O'REILLY

1

DEDICATION

This book is dedicated to the late Joan McCormack, my grandmother, who always encouraged me to write fiction when I was younger.

CONTENTS

This story is set in Dublin, but is entirely fictional. Any similarity in name, description, or events to any actual person, is purely coincidental.

CHAPTER ONE

LEARNING TO SAY GOODBYE

The first thing that would strike anybody who happened to pass number eighty-eight Saint Oliver's Road, was how cold and unfriendly it appeared. Not that the house was dirty, or run-down. It just seemed uncared for and unloved somehow. There was something depressing and unremarkable about the property in the respectable district of Rathmines in south Dublin. Its ivy-covered walls and drab green windows and front door, set it apart from the other brightly-painted houses on the quiet road. The rectangular front garden, with its black painted railings, seemed the dullest of all homes in the well-to-do backwater street. There were no flowers, no rose bushes or colourful plants to adorn the small patch of lawn, despite it being a warm summer's day in mid May. All that decorated the garden of number eighty-eight, was a forlorn-looking dark-green hedge that ran along the railings nearest to the street. This was often left unkempt and overgrown. Then at some stage it would be trimmed hurriedly with a shears. Yet this chore was carried out infrequently, and without any real attention or feeling.

Tony Lee rushed from his front door. Deftly he pulled the heavy green hall door shut behind him, using the large brass doorknob as a lever. The weatherboard slid across the grey hall linoleum, shuddering as the creaking door closed shut. Both the small worn brass letterbox and the weatherboard continued to tremble for a few seconds as Tony made his way down the pathway. He pulled the old gate open. A groaning creak sounded out from the aging black gate. Before the heavy spring could take effect to close it again, Tony wedged his right foot against it. Then, in one swift movement he grabbed his bicycle, which had been lying unevenly against the green hedge. In one well-honed act, he swung the silver racing bike through the front gate, swinging his body across the frame, and cycling away. The metal gate crashed shut seconds later, as Tony adjusted his body on the white saddle.

Fergal Carrie watched from across the street. He had never met Tony Lee in person, but had observed his comings and goings many times. Fergal had an unhealthy interest in the house on St. Oliver's Road, but had not set foot inside the property for over thirty-five years. He eyed the house, his private memories coming flooding back.

Fergal Carrie was in his seventies now. In a certain way he was locked in his own personal time warp, living on the history of his younger days. His flamboyant past had long gone, yet he clung on to certain aspects of his glory days. Although grey and somewhat unkempt in appearance, he still wore his hair long. A well-trimmed, but slight grey beard made him appear somewhat refined. His black fedora hat was still a trademark of his, but it was not in the pristine condition of days past. Fergal still adorned his long black overcoat, sometimes worn loosely across his shoulders in a cape-type manner. He always carried his silver cane. Heads still turned to observe him, but now it was out of curiosity rather than admiration.

Tony Lee was in a desperate hurry. He had only come home to grab a bite to eat, and to have a quick wash. Now he was on his way back to the hospital, where his aging mother lay dying. Tony had spent the previous night at her bedside. Delores Lee had been ill for several years now. She was almost seventy-one. Time after time, doctors had told Tony that there was no hope for her. Yet each time plucky Delores would confound their prognosis and recover. Again, three days earlier, Tony Lee was told to expect the worst. This time there could be no reprieve, the consultant had said. Still Tony refused to give up on his spirited parent. As the hours had ticked by, he again began to believe that she would recover once more and return home. His beloved mother was Tony's world, and each day he prayed for her to get better, promising his God anything for just another tiny miracle.

His mother meant everything to Tony, and he adored her. Delores Lee's ill-health had now been a fact of life for ten years or more. Tony would gladly tend his dear mother for another decade without ever grumbling once. He could not imagine life without her, and refused to contemplate her passing away.

Tony Lee weaved in and out of the traffic as he made his way along the canal on the south side of Dublin City. The streets around him were clogged with cars and trucks, all vying for a precious space on the choked-up city roads. Living and working within easy access of the city centre, Tony had no need of a motor vehicle. In fact, Tony had never learned to drive, and had no wish to do so. Now, aged thirty-six, he was well set in his ways. His mother came first. Everything else was a poor second place.

Tony pedalled harder now, just making the green light at the next bridge. A brief satisfied grin flashed across his handsome face. He looked pleased that he had beaten yet another line of motorists in the never ending race against time. This was a game that Tony played most days. It was a simple battle of wits between the cyclist and the line of domineering cars in the snarling city streets, with no quarter asked or given. On most days, Tony would emerge the victor. He would often target a certain vehicle up ahead in the traffic. His goal was to pass the motorist before either of them turned off the main road. It helped pass the time and get him to his destination faster.

Tony slowed now as a huge articulated truck blocked his path. Lorry drivers had to be treated with the utmost respect. They never gave way to bicycles, and the gush of wind they created as they passed him could easily knock him off his stride. Tony inched along the small gap between the kerb and the high, filthy red truck. He put his left foot on the pavement's edge and scooted along. The traffic lights were red now, and Tony took the opportunity to check his watch. It was almost four o'clock. The lights changed to green, and the truck let out a sneezing sound as it trundled slowly forward. It cut off Tony's path ahead as it inched nearer to the kerb. Tony leaned the silver racing bike inwards and pulled on the breaks.

"Bastard! You did that on purpose! You don't own the road you know!" he yelled. The driver honked his horn as if to admit his intent. Tony shook his head and set off once again. There was no time to lose. Each day he faced the same battle, and in Tony's experience, the buses and trucks usually came out on top. Today he had other things on his mind. Perhaps tomorrow he would win the race, but today his mother needed him. He quickly forgot all about the heavy goods vehicle, and instead focused again on the hospital.

Tony arrived at the gates of the old building and slid from his trusty bicycle. Tony Lee was an athletic-looking man, tanned from his years of cycling. He was clean-shaven, and wore his brown hair tight, as he had always done. Tony styled his own hair, something he had done for years. His piercing blue eyes were arguably his best feature, but in general he was a tall, good-looking man. Tony's one extravagant trait was his tiny gold earring in his right earlobe, which he had had inserted some fourteen years earlier. His beloved mother had always disapproved, but it was Tony's one defiant stance at independence. He had once toyed with the idea of having a tattoo, but his mother would have been horrified, so his tiny earring was the one flamboyant trait to distinguish him from others. His high forehead worried him a little though, and Tony always feared that he might go bald long before old age crept up on him. Tony Lee worked in I.T., servicing computers over the phone for large companies in Ireland. His friendly personality was always on show, and in general he was well-liked wherever he went.

Tony parked the silver bike and locked it to the blue and white railings, with the heavy lock that always hung loosely around the saddle. Walking briskly towards the hospital entrance, he felt in his pocket for his mobile phone. As if on cue, the black and gold phone rang. Tony checked the illuminated screen and saw Stacey's name. He walked away from the main door and pressed the answer button.

"Hello Stace, what's up?" he asked in a casual tone.

"I was just wondering about your Mum. Any change?" asked the soft female voice. Stacey Boyd had been dating Tony Lee for over two years now. Their relationship was more about companionship rather than a huge romance. In a strange way, it was an alliance of two people who had been hurt in the past, and needed a member of the opposite sex in their life for reassurance. Stacey had been badly let down by her former boyfriend. He had called off their wedding just weeks before they were due to marry. In Tony's case, all of his last three girlfriends had broken up because of his reluctance to commit fully. Tony's last girlfriend had grown tired of his inability to see beyond his devotion to his mother. After eight years together, Joan Crilly had issued Tony with an ultimatum. Either they take their relationship to the next level, or she would call it off. Joan had suggested that they should move into a flat together, or at least become engaged. She required a commitment from Tony, fearing that life was passing her by. This had shocked Tony. He could never contemplate leaving his mother to fend for herself. There was simply no choice to be made in Tony's eyes. An exasperated Joan called off their relationship, and Tony soon fell back into a routine. Joan drifted from his life, annoyed and frustrated at Tony's intransigence.

Some months later, Tony had met Stacey through a mutual friend. They had started dating, and Stacey Boyd soon realised the role that Tony played in his mother's life. In An odd way, it suited Stacey. She was not yet ready to leap into another huge romance, having been hurt so badly. And so they began to go out together, whenever it suited them both. A fondness developed, and the two became an accepted couple among their friends. Now, more than two years later, nothing much has changed between them. But what had suited

Stacey at first was now a huge concern to her. Tony's easy-going acceptance of their life together really bothered her. Delores Lee had never made her feel welcome, and so Stacey did her best to avoid calling to their home at St. Oliver's Road. She and Tony would now meet at other venues, or at Stacey's apartment in Ranelagh. Deep down, Tony knew the reason for this, but chose to ignore it. His beloved mother came first, and always would.

"Nah, Stacey, there's no change really. Mam is still the same. I'm on my way back to see her now. I'll have to switch off my phone, so I'll call you later if there is any news. She's gonna be all right Stace. My old Mam is a fighter. I just know that she will get better" he said confidently.

Tony stopped briefly before entering the small room where his mother lay dying. The kindly nurse that he had got to know was still on duty. She offered him a brief smile as he sought some sort of reassurance.

"Is she still the same?" he asked in a whisper. The middle-aged nurse nodded as she slowly ambled closer to him. She was small in stature and wore her dark hair tight. Nurse Nula Sheehan had a warm smile for everyone. She met Tony at the plain white door that led to Delores Lee's room.

"Nothing has changed Tony. I told you that it wouldn't. Delores is a very sick lady" she replied in a clear, but deliberate tone. Tony's blue eyes flashed back at her. He searched her face for some sign of hope. Nula's professionalism had taught her to only deal in bare facts. Tony offered his own prognosis.

"The doctors say that there is no chance of her making a recovery. They don't know my old Mam! Delores Lee is made of stern stuff! You'll see if she doesn't walk out of here again nurse" he said in an assured voice. Nula Sheehan nodded. She looked thoughtful now.

"You say that you live alone with your mother Tony? Have you no other family?" she asked gently.

"Of course I have. I have lots of cousins and such. I also have a sister living in America. I never see her though. She's married to a Yank. They have two kids. I telephoned her to tell her about Mam being sick. Jan lives a hectic life, and can't get home at the moment. Maybe when Mam is home and settled again, she might find the time" Tony said in an upbeat tone.

Nurse Sheehan looked a little startled. She put a comforting hand on Tony's shoulder. It was not really her place to intervene. She had watched his complete devotion to his mother over the past few days, and had thought it most admirable. Perhaps she could offer him some guidance.

"Look Tony, as I said to you before, I think that it's best to prepare for the worst. If I was you, I would insist on my sister coming home. Your poor mother is only breathing with the aid of a respirator. She hasn't really much time left.

9

Delores is a very, very sick lady. I think that you should face the truth. When the doctors sent for you, it was because Delores was facing her final time. I know that she has lasted a few days now, but she cannot go on forever. I really don't know what's keeping her going. Sometimes people's inner strength amazes me, but in the end their bodies just cannot hold out. It would be better for you if you were prepared to let her go when the time comes. Okay?" said Nula gently.

Tony looked down towards the white tiled floor. He nodded slowly. Outwardly he wanted to appear resigned to losing his beloved mother, yet he still clung to the belief that once again his mother would defy all medical logic.

"If the time comes, then I'm ready" he said in a low, barely audible voice. Nurse Sheehan again patted him on the shoulder of his black jacket before turning away. She took a deep breath and sighed aloud. It was always the hardest part of her job. She could never afford to become emotionally involved, but being a mother herself, Nula felt pity for the solitary, devoted man.

Tony Lee opened the door slowly. His mother still lay on her back in the same position. There were no windows in the small, sparse room. A shaded bulb shone its off-yellow light down directly onto the single metal bed frame below. Two grey plastic-seated chairs stood either side of the bed. A plain bedside locker with a vase of yellow flowers atop was the only real form of colour in the drab room. Delores wafer-thin body was barely noticeable on the simple bed. On the other side opposite to where Tony stood, a respirator breathed life into his mother. The clear-plastic mask covered her lined face. Tony tiptoed to the bedside and slid down on one of the chairs. He studied his mother's face now, as if examining it for the first time. Yes, he could see the change all right. She looked older beyond her years, her skin sallow and wrinkled. Her eye sockets were sunken, and her cheeks had all but collapsed inwards. How had he not noticed it before, Tony wondered?

Delores released a slow, steady, even breath. To Tony's trained ear, it did not seem right somehow. It appeared more like the hissing from a tyre, rather than a natural breath of life. It was artificial, forced and lifeless. A single tear ran down Tony's left cheek. He was seeing his brave mother in a different light. Suddenly she seemed vulnerable and in danger. No longer did he feel that his gentle darling mother was invincible. Now a terrible dread engulfed him. Yet still he refused to kowtow to his fear of the inevitable.

"It's okay Mam, I'm here now" he whispered. There was no response, nor had he expected one. Delores Lee had not acknowledged him since she took her last bad turn. He gripped her bony left hand in both of his palms. She felt cold.

Tony rubbed her hand gently. More tears welled up in his eyes. He waited for her to breathe again. Delores duly exhaled once more, but almost without a sound. Tony had become accustomed to it. It was a forced, plastic breath from a machine. He watched as her exhausted frame again lay lifeless on the bed. The seconds of false hope offered by the respirator had again vanished. Tony exhaled himself, almost willing his dear Mam to follow his example. He sat in silence, watching and waiting for the one sound that would prove his mother was still alive. The breaths seemed further apart now, but he could not be sure. The next gasp of air came and Tony patted her hand contently.

His Mam would never give up. She was a fighter, a battler. It was what had always convinced Tony that she would overcome the latest setback. He reached across and gently brushed her grey hair back from her face. Her wrinkled body held a million tales, and Tony guessed that he knew all of them. She had told him of her days of poverty growing up. How she had got her first job at the age of fourteen at the local sewing factory, which now no longer existed. And of the day that she had first set eyes on his late father. On good days, Delores would talk nonstop about the old times. She would tell him tales about his Dad, Sean Lee, a man that Tony could barely recall.

"Remember the picnic Mam? Remember when Dad brought us to Portmarnock and spilled sand all over the food?" he whispered with a forced laugh. Tony could never recall that actual day when he was a mere toddler, but it was always one of his Mam's favourite tales.

"Dad got up to go for a swim, and tripped over the picnic basket. You had just spread out the tablecloth, and you were getting the food ready. Everything was destroyed, the tea, the bread, everything! What was it that Dad said again? Oh yes! "Never mind" he said, "After all, they are sandwiches!" Tony recalled.

Tony looked to his mother, hoping for some sort of response. Nothing. Delores lay with her eyes closed, her face without emotion or any type of expression. He clung to her thin, bony hand, with the violet blue veins protruding through her sallow skin. His mind rambled down memory lane again. All of his mother's tales danced through his brain. Somehow her stories were much more vivid than his own recollections of his younger days. It was almost as if Delores Lee's slant on life overshadowed his. Tony recalled how he would sit entranced by her tales of her hard younger life.

Delores was one of five children. She now had only two living sisters. Both Aunt Ethel and Auntie Mary were senior to Delores. Neither was in good health, and Aunt Ethel was in an old folk's home. Ethel's memory was now on the wane. She suffered with Alzheimer's, and on most days she could not recognise her own family. Auntie Mary lived in England, and she and Delores had not spoken for many years. Tony had never really bothered to ask why. Tony Lee's thoughts drifted on to his teenage years. He recalled his mother's present to him on his sixteenth birthday. It was his first real bicycle, and Tony remembered his Mam's proud face that special morning. Tony recalled setting off down the road on the gleaming blue bike, before returning to wave to his dear mother.

"Don't judge me too harshly" said the voice. Tony wanted to break away from his daydreaming. The voice did not fit the scene. He blinked as he tried to make sense of the distant words. He chewed over the sentence again in his head. Something was wrong. It did not make sense. Tony felt his hand being gripped tighter, but was not sure if he was just imagining it.

"Don't judge me too harshly". The words rang out in his head. It was his mother's voice, yet it was far off. Tony blinked again, shaking himself back to reality. He stared at his mother lying perfectly still on the bed. Tony Lee waited for the next breath, a sign that there was still hope.

Suddenly he sat upright. Something was not quite right. He stood up and leaned over the bed, still clinging to her hand. There was no breath. Her chest was still. Tony waited for what seemed an age. All of his senses were on full alert. Panic spread through his stomach. He watched for some vital sign. His mind now in turmoil, Tony began to question events. Had she gripped his hand so tightly? What about those words? Was it in his head, or had she cried out to him? Logic kicked in as the fear took second place.

"Nurse! Nurse!" he called out in a loud voice. It struck him that there was a different sound now from the respirator. He looked from the machine and back to his mother.

"Nurse!" this time it was almost a scream.

Nula Sheehan opened the door and strode into the room. Without pausing she made for the bed, almost pushing Tony to one side as she sought a pulse. Nula pressed the button to the side of the bed to alert her colleagues. Tony stood helplessly, eyes firmly fixed on his beloved mother.

"No pulse Tony, you are going to have to wait outsider for a moment" Nula said with authority. It was said in a calm, experienced tone, allowing Tony Lee to understand that he had no alternative. Two younger nurses appeared in the doorway, and rushed inside. One ushered Tony away.

"Is ...is she gone?" he asked, looking back over his shoulder.

"Let's just see. Perhaps it's time" said the pretty young nurse. A doctor brushed past him as the door closed. A bewildered Tony Lee flopped down on a chair outside.

In minutes Nula Sheehan came to join him. She put a comforting arm around Tony as he sat in the long, magnolia-coloured corridor. Suddenly he began to blubber incoherently.

"That's my Mam in there. That's my Mam. She can't leave me now" he was murmuring. Nula failed to understand his words, nor did she try to. He buried his head in his hands as the awful truth began to sink in. Minutes later the doctor re-emerged. He nodded to Nula and walked briskly away. Both nurses smiled a nervous smile at Nula as they too went on their way.

"She's gone Tony I'm afraid. You can go in now if you like. Your Mam is at peace" Nula whispered. He did not respond. Tony was lost in his own little world, dreading the future, fearing having to face his dear mother's corpse, wondering where he could gain the strength to carry on.

Nora held a comforting arm around him, talking, urging him to be brave.

He knew that he should have been better prepared. Heaven knows he had plenty of time to come to terms with this inevitable day. Somewhere in the recesses of his brain, Tony Lee felt some sort of logic stirring. It was time to be strong, time to be as man. But still his whole body shook. When he tried to speak, a whining, sloppy, spittle was all that he could produce. His nose seeped, and he was conscious of his sweaty palms.

Tony Lee took a deep breath and tried to speak once more.

"I'm sorry nurse. You have been so kind" he managed to say. He wiped his eyes and face with a paper hankie. Nora smiled back as she released him from her gentle embrace. She gripped his hand in hers and smiled.

"That's okay. Would you like to say goodbye to your mother? Take your time. I'll see about getting you home" Nula replied. Tony wanted to tell her about his bicycle locked up outside. Somehow it seemed important. He decided that it could wait for now. Slowly he climbed to his feet. Still Nula held his hand. A shudder ran down his spine as he prepared for his ordeal. Her hand fell away as he took his first steps towards the small room.

"I'll be here if you need me" Nula said in an assured voice. Tony nodded.

He made his way inside. His mother's face was not covered with a sheet, as he had anticipated. She looked for all the world as though she was simply asleep. The plastic mask was gone now, the respirator disconnected. A serene look was etched on Delores's thin face, and there was a hint of a smile in her curled-up bottom lip. Tony flopped down on the chair and buried his head in his mother's still body. Nula Sheehan watched through the open door. Satisfied that all would be well, she gently pulled the door shut. Everyone deserved their dignity. Death was an everyday occurrence on the ward, and she had learned to detach herself from it. She would do as she had always done. Nula always offered her own brand of sympathy and humanity.

Tony raised his head and pleaded into his mother's face.

"What will I do Mam? What will I do?" he asked, his voice breaking with emotion. This time Delores Lee could offer no response. All through his life she had been there to coax, advise and help her son. Now he was alone. Again he buried his head in the thin light-blue sheet that covered his mother's body.

"Oh Mam, Mam. I'm lost without you. How will I cope?" he whimpered. He could smell the freshly laundered sheet covering his mother's frail body, and Tony sobbed until there were no more tears left.

"Can I get you anything Tony? Maybe a cup of tea?" Nula asked, popping her head around the door some time later. He shook his head vehemently without turning to face her. Nula came and stood next to him. She patted his shoulder.

"I know that it sounds like a cliché Tony, but your Mam is at peace now. Delores was in pain. She had no quality of life without all those tablets and injections. You wouldn't want her to carry on suffering, would you?" Nula said softly. He shook his head quietly and reached for a tissue from the box on the locker. The thin white tissue slipped easily from the pink carton.

"I feel foolish. I'm sorry for getting so upset. You see, we were very close. When my Dad died, I was only very young. Then my sister went to America. My Mam looked after me, and then when she became unwell, I looked after her. We depended on each other. I can't bear to think of life without her. She battled right to the end. It was as if she was clinging to life just to be with me. I still don't know what kept her going. The doctors gave up on her so many times" Tony said in a disjointed way. The tears came intermittently as he tried to control his emotions.

Nula patted his shoulder and spoke again.

"It will sound like yet another cliché I know, but life goes on Tony. You're going to have to pick yourself up and get on with things. You best get in touch with your sister. Then there will be the funeral arrangements. Keep yourself busy. Try to look for positives. Cherish your friends and your job. Have you somebody close, you know, a girlfriend or such?" Nula asked quietly. She herself was married with three children. Tony nodded.

"Yeah, Stacey" he answered, trying hard to offer a smile. Still his voice trembled and his body shook. Nula smiled back at him.

"When you're ready I'll get you a lift home" she said. Tony remembered his bicycle. It seemed important to assert his independence. Tony Lee looked up at her.

"I'm okay nurse. I have my bike outside. I won't be needing a lift thanks" he replied. The thought of the journey home appeared to jolt him back to reality. He was reluctant to leave his mother's side, yet he saw little point in remaining.

"Are you sure Tony? You could always collect the bicycle tomorrow" Nula replied. Tony's mind was clear now. It was time to be practical.

"No. I'm all right. You're right, there are things to do" he answered. Nula Sheehan nodded. She watched as he kissed his mother's left cheek. Tony offered a last lingering glance at his dear mother's body before turning swiftly away.

Nula walked with him along the long corridor.

"You must telephone your sister immediately Tony. She will need to organise flights for her family" Nula said. Tony nodded and thanked her again.

"Don't beat yourself up over this Tony. You've done a tremendous job caring for Delores. It's just nature taking its course" Nula said. He knew that she was correct. Tony Lee shook her hand and hurried outside.

"Hello Jan? It's Tony" he said in a clear voice. He stared out through the window as the sun beamed down on the modest back garden. It seemed surreal to think that his mother had passed away on such a beautiful day. Tony watched as a small sparrow hopped along the patchy green lawn. The grass needed cutting, and now and then the tiny bird would disappear from view. Tony listened for his older sister's voice. They had barely spoken in years. It was not that there was any animosity between them. Jan was always polite when she phoned, and Tony knew well that she really wanted to speak to their mother. It was always a brief greeting between the two. The fourteen year age gap meant that they had little in common. Jan seemed more like a distant aunt rather than his only sibling.

"Hello Tony, It's Mum, isn't it? Is she...?" Jan's voice trailed off. There was an uneasy silence between the two as Tony fought to stay rational. He cleared his throat and composed himself again.

"She...She passed away a while ago. I was with her at the hospital" Tony said, his voice breaking with emotion. Tony began to sob loudly. He had vowed to stay in control, but the occasion became all too much for him. His mind's eye pictured their dear mother lying cold and alone at the hospital which he had left less than one hour ago. He could hear Jan crying softly at the other end of the line.

"Jan, I don't know what to do. I mean, I've never arranged a funeral in my life. There's no one but you to help. When can you get here? I need you home with me now" he sobbed. Jan appeared to compose herself quickly.

"I'll arrange a flight as soon as possible. Look, it's the weekend. Nothing can be done until Monday morning. The undertakers will take care of everything. All we want is a simple funeral. I'll be there as quick as I can. What about Thursday? Would that suit for the burial?" Jan said calmly. Tony tried to think clearly. He did not care when the funeral took place. It was irrelevant. What he needed was Jan by his side, to comfort him and share their grief. He gulped back his tears and spoke again.

"I suppose so, but there are other things to do Jan. What about Aunt Ethel and Auntie Mary? And should I put Mam's death in the newspaper? What about insurance? Look Jan, I'm no good at all of this. I need you here" he pleaded.

Jan Williams chewed on her bottom lip. She had to stay practical and calm.

"Tony, it will be okay. Don't worry about newspapers and insurance. And I'll phone Auntie Mary, but I wouldn't bet on her attending. She and Mum never got on. Aunt Ethel would not know what's going on anyway, so I can see no point in telling her. Listen Tony, just do what you can. I'll sort the rest out when I get there, okay? I have to go now. I have a household to organise and flights to book" Jan said firmly.

Tony realised that the conversation was over as quickly as it had begun. Jan was her usual brusque self. He listened as the line went dead. There was so much that he had wanted to say to her, yet he never got the chance. Jan always sounded to him as though she was more of a business partner rather than an older sister. She never inquired about his life, or how he was coping with their mother. All Tony ever knew of Jan was the hushed telephone calls she held with his mother when she phoned home intermittently. It was as if Jan and his mother had their own little world, and Tony was not welcome in. Always when those hurried phone calls ended, Tony would see that distant look in his mother's eyes. He often felt inadequate after Jan's phone calls. Delores Lee missed her only daughter. She would fall quiet. Delores would sit in her armchair and stare silently into space, lost in her own private thoughts. Occasionally Tony would try to indulge his mother in conversation about Jan, and how she was getting on in America. Instantly he would realise that it was something that Delores would rather not discuss. Tony would put it down to his dear Mam's heart breaking at the distance between mother and daughter. Jan had never returned home, not even on a fleeting visit. He knew that there was always that special bond between his mother and Jan. Jan was a lot older. Unlike Tony, Jan remembered their father. There was bound to be common ground between the two women. He knew that. Tony was never jealous of Jan. Far from it. Apart from those infrequent phone calls, he had had their mother all to himself. Tony's only thought on the subject was how sad his mother looked after those transatlantic calls had ended.

Tony Lee sat lost in his own little world for some time. His tears had dried now, and he reflected on how different his world would be without his Mam. His mind flashed back to the moment of her death. He remembered imagining her gripping his hand so tightly, and those words in his head at that time.

"Don't judge me too harshly". Tony shuddered. How could he possibly judge his dear mother harshly? She had been almost godlike in his eyes. No, he would never judge her. What was there to judge anyway? She had been the perfect parent. Even when his father had died, Delores Lee took on the role of dual parenting. She had encouraged him to join the local football team when he was nine years of age. On Sunday mornings, Delores would stand on the touchline with the other parents, cheering him on. Gradually Tony learned to make his own way in life, but Delores was always there in the background, urging him onwards.

Tony blinked away his daydreaming once again. He realised that Stacey would presume that his mobile phone was still switched off. Stacey had to be told about his mother. Because of his urgency to telephone Jan in Santa Monica, he had forgotten all about Stacey. She would presume that he was still at the hospital, and that his mother was still clinging to life.

"Hello Stacey? Tony. I should have phoned earlier. It's about Mam" he said.

"Is she...alright?" Stacey Boyd asked hesitantly. Silence. Tony exhaled slowly as he sought out the right words.

"She's gone. It happened a short while ago. Mam never regained consciousness. I'm home now. I had to phone Jan in The States. Listen Stace, I'm a little upset. Could you come over? Just for a short while. I need someone to talk to" Tony said, struggling to hold his emotions in check. His faltering voice betrayed him as his utter despair flickered through to Stacey.

"Yes of course Tony. Look, I'm really sorry. Give me a few minutes. I'll be there as soon as I can" she replied. Tony thanked her and slowly ended the call.

He rambled off through the house in no particular direction. The house that had been his home for all of his life was filled with good memories. Each room, every nook and turn held special happy times for him. All involved his mother, and each was a different stepping stone in his life. Some memories involved his teen years; others reminded him of his childhood. Now and then he would remember a conversation or a laugh shared with his Mam. Every room was like an old friend, reassuring, reliable, a promise that things could still continue in a similar vein. Yet he knew in his heart that it would never be quite the same ever again.

Stacey Boyd drove the two miles or so to Tony's home. She felt even more unsure than ever about their relationship now. Although Stacey could not deny her feelings of relief that Delores Lee had finally passed away, she also knew that it would affect Tony badly. How it would alter their relationship in the long term, Stacey could only guess. For now though, she had to be with him. Stacy vowed to be a good listener that evening, whatever her misgivings about Tony's utter devotion to his mother. Idly Stacey wondered if their relationship could now take on a more realistic standing, something that had been virtually impossible while Delores had been alive. A tinge of hope entered her body as she drove on. Of course the next few days would be hard, but maybe, just maybe they could finally move their lives on. It struck Stacy that almost her entire adult life had been put on hold. First there was her relationship with Alex Woods, which had all but dominated her twenties. Stacey always considered those times now to be her wasted years. She had nothing to show for what should have been the best years of her life. Yet since meeting Tony Lee, she still had been unable to move her life onwards. Always lurking in the background had been Delores. She had stood like a giant shadow over Tony, demanding, manipulating, and domineering their lives. In Stacey's eyes, Tony could never see it. Now at last they stood a chance of real happiness. Stacey checked her tight blonde hair in the mirror. Her hazel eyes stared back at her. Stacey Boyd had a pretty, friendly smile, but to her critical eye, she could see her face aging as the months ticked by.

Tony stared out of the window as Stacey's red Nissan Micra drew up outside. Stacey's one-year-old car was her pride and joy. He could never see the attraction. Why someone would want to burden themselves with debts just for the sake of owning a car, was beyond Tony. He knew that it was a struggle for Stacey to make the monthly payments. He had tried to talk her out of committing to the five year contract. Tony had reasoned that she hardly needed a car as she lived within easy distance of her job. With a reliable bus route nearby, it seemed madness to him for Stacey to commit to such an unnecessary undertaking. Stacey however, could not be dissuaded. She dreamed of them making journeys to the seaside, driving through the mountains on hot sunny days, and long summer trips in the countryside. Of course, none of this ever materialised because of Delores Lee's ill-health. Now the car was used mostly to ferry Stacey back and forward to work.

"I'm so sorry Tony, how are you bearing up?" Stacey asked as Tony opened the heavy green door. They greeted each other with the usual peck on the cheek. Their bodies barely touched as they did so.
"I'm okay I suppose" he answered. Stacey brushed by him as he closed the door. She was wearing blue jeans and a white top, covered loosely by a blue open cardigan. Tony followed her inside to the kitchen. This was always where

Stacey would head for on her few infrequent visits to Saint Oliver's Road. Delores had always sat in the living room, and Stacey never liked to face her down. Somehow it was much easier and more practical not to confront Delores. Stacey always found Tony's mothers' remarks cutting and calculating, yet Tony never appeared to notice.

Stacey watched him as he entered the room. Tony appeared tired and drained. His eyed looked red at the rims. She knew that he had been crying. Stacey climbed up on a stool at the small breakfast counter, as she had always done. She casually ran a hand through her short blonde hair again. Sometimes she would allow her hair to grow a little long, but mostly she kept it short and manageable. She was slim, and forever watching her weight. Stacey was just over 5' 5", a fact that she hated. If there was one thing that she would change about herself, it would be her height. She was always attracted to tall men, and wished that she could sprout a few more inches herself.

Tony automatically filled the silver kettle. Stacey sat watching him across the room. She had never known a man so devoted to his mother. At first it had amused her, but she soon realised the effect that it was having on their relationship. It had quickly dawned on Stacey Boyd the threat that Delores posed to her and Tony's future together. In truth, Stacey had soon come to despise the power that Delores held over Tony. But now was not the time to think of the past, or what lay ahead for that matter. Stacey would be compassionate and devoted in the coming days. She would stand by Tony in his time of need, and let nature take its course.

Stacey listened to Tony's ramblings of his life with his mother over a cup of coffee. It was a disjointed, uneven account of their time together. At some junctions, his voice would falter. Stacey remained calm and affable. Tony would quickly recover and carry on. He wanted to talk. It felt good to unburden himself. It was like a form of therapy, easing the weight of his great loss. The evening dragged on, and it was after midnight before Tony noticed the time. "I'm sorry Stace, I didn't realise that it was so late. Do you fancy staying the night?" he asked. Stacey Boyd's brow furrowed. She ran her right hand through her hair thoughtfully. It was an offer that she had not bargained for. The opportunity to stay over at The Lee's home had never arisen before. When Delores was alive, such a thing would have been out of the question. Now Stacey was not so sure that the idea appealed to her. Staying over with Tony at this time did not feel quite right. The spectre of Delores Lee still loomed large. Tony seemed to sense her reluctance. He stood opposite her as she sat at the bar counter in the old-fashioned kitchen. Tony Lee had spent the evening moving about the square room, seemingly unable to settle in any particular spot.

"You've never liked this house, have you Stacey?" he asked suddenly. Instantly she knew that he spoke the truth. Stacey had always felt that Tony's home on St. Oliver's Road was cold and harsh. She had never indicated her dislike for the house and until now, Stacey had always presumed that Tony had not noticed.

"It's not that Tony. You know that it was always awkward when Delores was ill. Parents can be so old-fashioned. Mine would probably be the same if I was to bring you home" she countered. Tony felt that her words rang true. His mother would never have agreed to Stacey spending the night. Not that Tony would have ever suggested it while his mother was alive anyway. Tonight however, he felt vulnerable. He needed Stacey with him.

Tony Lee had never met Stacey's parents, although they had spoken on the phone. They lived in Wolverhampton in the English Midlands. Stacey's father was the managing director of a large stationary company. The Boyd's had emigrated to England almost ten years earlier when Arthur Boyd had secured the position. Since then, Stacey had made several visits to her parents. Tony could never go because of his aging mother.

"Please stay tonight" he whispered. Tony gave her a look that made it impossible for Stacey to say no. She forced a grin and nodded. Stacey Boyd had a magnificent smile that could light up a room. Unfortunately, Stacey's life of late left her little to smile about. She felt apprehensive about sleeping in the old house. But with no work to go to on the following day, it made things so much easier. Stacey shared an apartment with three friends. Her absence would barely raise an eyebrow, yet Stacey seldom stayed away from her third-storey flat in Ranelagh overnight.

Sleeping together had never been high on Tony's and Stacey's list of priorities. Their busy lives had always been too preoccupied with other things. When they did make love, it was always hurried and disjointed. Sometimes they would manage a few moments alone in Stacey's apartment, when she was sure that none of her flatmates would be home. On most nights though, there would be someone home at Stacey's. The "no men staying overnight" rule was strictly enforced by all of the girls. Tony and Stacey had learned to accept that that side of their lives would remain unfulfilled. As their friendship had grown, it seemed to become less and less important.

For some time that night, Stacey slept contently. Having Tony by her side was comforting. He had held her gently until she had fallen asleep. Suddenly Stacey awoke with a start. At first she could make no sense of her surroundings. The grey light around the bedroom doorway was unfamiliar. There was also a stream of yellow light filtering through the thick curtains from the streetlamp outside. The heavy red drapes seemed to almost cling to the window. Only to the far left of the curtains did the light from the tall lamppost outside breach the blackness.

It was only when she heard Tony breathing heavily beside her that Stacey realised where she was. A slight shudder ran down her thin spine. Her naked body felt cold. She pulled the heavy red duvet across her shoulders, forcing a low, stifled moan from Tony. He turned away in the other direction. Stacey followed the heat of his body. She pressed against him for warmth. Although summer, the room felt icy. Stacey buried her head beneath the duvet. For Stacey, there was something unnerving about being in that big house at night. She closed her eyes again and hoped to sleep. At first it seemed like an impossible task, but eventually her body surrendered to tiredness.

Minutes later she awoke in terror. Tony had let out a blood-curdling scream. Stacey sat upright in the bed. She could feel the sweat dripping from Tony's skin. His body shook in uneven spasms as Stacey recoiled in shock. She reached out to rouse him. At first it was a gentle, almost apologetic shake. Now it became more intense as she began to panic. The cold icy air in the room seemed to reach out and touch her, yet Tony's body was in a lather of sweat. She felt threatened by her surroundings. It was as if she was trespassing on another's territory. The need to waken Tony was now a fixation. Stacey shook him violently. Slowly Tony's eyes opened. Despite the blackness of the room, Stacey could clearly see his blue eyes boring into her.

"Mam?" he said, a questioning tone in his voice.

"It's me, Stacey. You were having a nightmare" she whispered. Stacey was shocked that he might confuse her with his mother, yet relieved that he had finally awoken. She could now see his forehead glistening with perspiration.

"Was I? I'm sorry love, I don't remember a thing. God! Did I wake you? I'm in a sweat!" he replied. Stacey flopped back down on her back and stared at the ceiling.

"Phew! I don't usually dream. I can't recall what it was all about" Tony mumbled.

"I suppose that it's understandable after what's happened. Your mind is bound to be troubled" Stacey reasoned. Tony nodded in the darkness.

"You frightened the life out of me!" Stacey giggled in a nervous tone. Tony did not reply straight away. He appeared lost in his thoughts. Stacey turned on her side and cuddled up to him. She placed an arm across his bare chest.

"It's okay Tony; you're bound to have strange dreams for a while. It's a big shock losing your Mam. It will pass, you'll see" she said in an understanding voice.

"Except it wasn't my Mam. There was a baby. I saw a young boy. I remember now. There was a young child crying, a small baby. God! Then there was blood dripping from my hands" Tony whispered. He trailed off as he tried to recall the rest of his dream. Stacey felt scared now, but she tried to make light of it.

"It's all right Tony, my mother used to dream all of the time. After the day that you've had, your mind is probably restless. Come on, let's settle down" she said. Tony continued to search his mind.

"I wish that I could remember. It was like something from my past, but nothing like that has ever happened to me" he said in a faraway tone. Stacey said nothing. She hoped that Tony would forget it and go back to sleep.

"It was something to do with when I was young. Maybe I had an accident or something" he continued. Stacy again remained silent. She wanted the night to pass without further incident. It reminded her of her childhood, and how she tried to wish away the dark nights in her bedroom.

Tony was wide awake now however. He sat up and switched on the bedside lamp. Far from having a reassuring effect on Stacey, the green-shaded lamp seemed to add a certain eeriness to the room. Tony Lee lit a cigarette. He was a light smoker who could stop at will. Sometimes he would give them up for months, only to suddenly fall back on what was one of his few vices. Stacey had never smoked, but never objected to Tony doing so. Her last boyfriend, Alex Woods, had practically being a chain smoker. Stacey watched as the tip of the cigarette turned bright red as Tony inhaled. He blew smoke gently from his nostrils, still in thought about his troubled dream.

"Try not to let it bother you Tony. What time is it anyway?" Stacey said. Tony casually reached out to the bedside locker and glanced at his watch.

"Nearly four-thirty" he replied, tossing the watch back on the dark wooden locker.

"Let's go back to sleep" Stacey said, turning away from him. Tony did not budge. He was still busy trying to piece together his nightmare.

"Do you suppose that dreams mean anything Stacey? I mean, I can still picture that child, yet I'm positive that I have never seen him before in my life" Tony said. Stacey turned back towards him sharply.

"Stop Tony! You're scaring me now. It's hard enough for me to get to sleep in a strange bed" she said crossly. Tony stubbed out the cigarette in the ashtray and turned to face her.

"Sorry Stace, I wasn't thinking. You settle down. I promise to stay awake until you fall asleep" he whispered. Stacey gave him a peck on the cheek and turned away. She felt safe once more as he cuddled in tightly to her.

"You had better get used to this strange bed Stacey Boyd! I plan to see a lot more of you from now on" he said with a grin.

Tony's throwaway line caught Stacey by surprise. She had never considered that their long term future might involve Saint Oliver's Road. Stacey had always assumed that if she and Tony were to have a future together, that they would buy a house or an apartment of their own. Number eighty-eight had belonged to Delores Lee. Surely Tony did not expect her to move in and take his mother's place? It was a sobering thought for Stacey, and suddenly she was wide awake again. The idea nagged at her brain like a toothache, overshadowing her tiredness. She could never move into that house. Tony had to understand this. The scenario refused to leave her head, and Stacey silently vowed that she would never again sleep in Tony Lee's room. One night in that house had been enough. There was something not quite right about the place. It was not a feeling of evil or of the supernatural. It was just something strange that Stacey could not put her finger on. There was a certain coldness, a vacuum, an uneasy stillness that did not seem natural. A certain overpowering, stifling aura appeared to cling to the house like a bad smell.

Stacey's eyes felt heavy now, yet she was wary of falling asleep. She could see the yellow light from the lamp outside filtering through the edge of the dark curtains. Still her weary eyes fought the tiredness. Eventually she felt herself drift away, but just before she did, Stacey Boyd swore again that she would never sleep at number eighty-eight ever again.

CHAPTER TWO

FACING FEARS

Stacey stirred and turned back in towards Tony. His side of the bed was now icy cold. She awoke with a start. Tony was gone. Stacey sat up quickly and glanced around the room. Light streamed in from the side of the red curtains. Stacey got up swiftly. She grabbed her clothes from the solitary wooden chair which stood beside the brown single wardrobe. The red floral carpet felt cold underfoot. Stacey hurried to get dressed. Peeping out through the drawn curtains, she checked that her car was still outside. She smiled with relief on seeing her gleaming red hatchback sparkle back at her in the early morning sunshine. Placing her hand on the white radiator beneath the window, she realised that it was cold to the touch. Stacey shuddered as she wrapped her blue cardigan around her tighter. She hurried downstairs, following the clattering noise to the kitchen. Tony was preparing breakfast and looked up with a smile.

"What's it with this house Tony? It's always bloody freezing!" Stacey moaned as she blew on her hands. Tony gave her a peck on the cheek. He moved back towards the old gas stove

"I don't feel the cold. When Mam was…" Tony stopped to re-phrase his sentence.

"My Mam used to have the heating on all of the time. The only thing that we ever did to this old house was to put in central heating. Mam said that it was the best investment that she had ever made. Since she went into hospital, I haven't really bothered with the heating. Anyway, it's summertime, there's no need" he said chirpily. He was busy cooking scrambled eggs, while keeping a steady eye on some bread in the silver toaster.

"Theirs is a bloody need for heating in this house, I can tell you! Probably the place has never been insulated" Stacey muttered, blowing again on her cold hands. Tony looked around the room. He seemed to consider her words. "Maybe not Stace. That's another job to consider" he said abstractly. A worried-looking Stacey chose to change the subject.

"Don't cook anything for me. I'm not one for eating in the mornings" she said. "It's the most important meal of the day" Tony answered. The aroma of eggs and toast filled the square, magnolia-coloured kitchen, and Stacey plonked down at the tiny round table in the corner. She felt tired and drawn after her fitful night's sleep. Stacey had noted that Tony seemed more upbeat. She decided to ask tactfully about his plans for the day.

"What are you going to do today Tony? Is there anything that I can help with?" she asked. The half-smile disappeared from Tony's face. He pulled thoughtfully on the round gold earring inserted in his right earlobe.

"I dunno really Stace. Jan was right. There's nothing that I can really do until Monday. I was thinking of going to see Aunt Ethel. On good days she knows who I am. If she's well I could explain about Mam" Tony replied. He looked to Stacey for approval.

"Whatever you think. I could go with you if you like" she said. Tony made a face.

"I wouldn't expect you to Stacey. It's a pretty awful place. I'm sure that you would much prefer to hang out with your friends and do some shopping" he answered glumly. Tony was not about to delude himself. Most Saturdays they did their own thing, with Stacey usually heading for the city centre with her flatmates.

Stacey had been sidetracked by something that Tony had said. She inquired what he meant by Jan implying that nothing could be done until Monday. When Tony explained, Stacey was quick to laugh it off.

"It's been a while since Jan was home all right! She must think that Ireland is still in the last century! Sure everywhere opens now on Saturdays! We could go to the undertakers this morning if you like" Stacey said. Tony immediately brightened up. He explained that he was petrified at having to organise a funeral, and would value Stacey's input. She was only too glad to help.

"It's settled then, you have breakfast and I'll drive you there. And while I'm in town, I'll place an obituary in the evening paper for you" she said.

Tony looked relieved as they left the funeral parlour. He had opted for a simple oak coffin for his mother's burial, and seemed satisfied with the arrangements. They sat in Stacey's car, and talked over everything that the funeral director had suggested.

"Yeah, I think Mam would approve. We never discussed her dying, but I know that she would not want a big fuss" Tony said candidly.

"Will you have people back to the house? If so, you should consider getting food and drink in" Stacey suggested. Tony shook his head vehemently.

"Definitely not. Jan said that it should be a low-key affair. Besides, Mam did not really mix with the neighbours. It's mostly flats on my street now anyway. All the old neighbours have gone. Mam's only family are her two older sisters and neither of them might attend. Jan will know what to do for the best" Tony answered. Stacey was busy scribbling on a piece of paper. She listened as he spoke, and vaguely wished that Tony would learn to make his own decisions.

"Here Tony, read this. It's just something for the death notice in the newspaper. What do you think?" Jan said, handing him the piece of paper. Tony read aloud.

"Delores Lee. Died Friday 17th after a long illness. Sadly missed by her loving son, Tony, and daughter Jan, sisters Ethel & Mary, friends & family. Removal to Rathmines Church, Wednesday 22nd at 5:30 pm. Burial at Saint Joseph's Cemetery after 10 o'clock Mass, Thursday 23rd. Rest in peace" he said in a calm voice. Tony sat quietly as he studied the wording. It appeared adequate, but a little cold.

"Could I put a small verse with it? I know people don't usually, but I would like to. And we better say son-in-law and grandchildren, although Jan's family barely knew that Mam existed" Tony said quietly.

"Of course Tony. I should have remembered that Jan has her own family" she replied. Tony said nothing. He was busy composing some words of his own.

"You've gone now Mam, it's time to part.

Wherever I go, you will be in my heart.

You were the dearest person that I ever knew.

I will miss you Mam, in all that I do" he said.

"That's fine Tony, it's a lovely verse. I'll write it down in case I forget" Stacey said with a warm smile. Tony said nothing, again lost in thoughts of his precious mother.

Stacey drove him back the short distance to St. Oliver's Road and parked just outside the house. Tony climbed out and looked back in through the open door.

"Will you be okay Stace? I've a few things to do" he said. Stacey Boyd smiled back at him.

"I'll be fine. You do what you have to and I'll phone you later. Maybe we might go for a drink together tonight? I don't want you cooped up all alone in that house" she replied. There was purpose in her remarks. Stacey was laying down the ground rules for later that evening. She had no intentions of spending another night at Tony's home.

"Oh right Stace. I don't know how I'll feel about going out. Let's just wait and see, eh?" he answered in a subdued tone. Stacey smiled sweetly as she drove away.

Whatever Tony decided to do was entirely up to him. If he settled for staying in that evening, he would be doing so alone. Stacey Boyd had no intention of visiting his house at night. It was spooky enough during the day, she found.

Later that day, Tony set off on his bicycle to visit his Aunt Ethel. On his mother's insistence, Tony would often go to visit his aging aunt at weekends. On some Saturdays past, Ethel would know him instantly. She would smile as he entered the home, and wave to greet him. Now though, those times were few and far between. Aunt Ethel's Alzheimer's was now worsening almost by the day. She would now mostly stare at Tony with a vacant, empty look. At times Tony might try to explain who he was, but the terrified stare on Ethel's face rarely changed. Now he seldom bothered. All Tony could do now was to whisper to his old Aunt that all would soon be okay again.

Today he made the journey out of respect for his late mother. He felt it was what she would have wanted. If Ethel was well enough in herself, he just might try and explain what had happened. If not, so be it.

Tony cycled towards Donnybrook along the canal. He was in no mood today to race cars. Today was a time for reflection. He pedalled along slowly in the warm sunshine, watching as the ripples from the green water flashed back at him. Being the weekend, the traffic was moderate, and Tony Lee drifted onwards at his own pace.

He arrived at St. Alfonse's in the leafy suburb of Donnybrook at about three-thirty. Tony made his way through the heavy cream-coloured wrought iron gates, and up the long driveway. The black tarmac gave way to a grey-pebbled winding entrance. It forced Tony to dismount and walk the final few yards. He crunched his way ever nearer to the huge, imposing doorway, which housed the thirty or so permanent residents. Ethel had lived there for almost eleven years now. Her late husband Henry Langan had admitted her, when he could no longer cope with her failing memory. Henry had himself been fighting cancer for many years, finally succumbing to the disease almost three years ago now. At Henry's funeral, Ethel had cut a sad and lonely figure. She had no idea in the world that her loving husband of forty-seven years of marriage was being laid to rest.

Tony entered the large hall, where most of the residents gathered during the day. A large television flashed images of live sporting events. Nobody appeared to be paying any attention to it, and Tony often wondered why more thought was never given to more suitable programmes for the old folks to enjoy. He noticed Ethel sitting at the large bay windows, which looked out to the spacious gardens. She seemed to be staring out into the distance, lost in a world of her own. Tony feared the worse. It was almost certain that he had had a wasted journey. Ethel was once again most likely to be detached from reality.

"Hi Aunt Ethel, it's Tony. How are you today?" he asked in an upbeat voice. Ethel's wrinkled face half-turned, before slowly returning her gaze to the greenery outside.

"You can't stay, Henry's coming today. He promised that he would bring black grapes. He always knew that they were my favourite" Ethel said crossly. Tony sat down wearily opposite her. He had faced the same scenario many times now. Nothing that he could say or do would get through to his old Aunt. But because of the occasion, Tony vowed to be patient. He reached out and patted her wrinkled hands.

"Who are you again?" she questioned, a confused, faraway look etched on her tired face.

"I'm Tony, Delores's boy" he replied assuredly. Instantly Ethel shook her head, a fearful look on her face.

"No you're not! No you're not! You have to go now! Henry will be angry" she countered in a loud voice. Tony stood up slowly and turned away. He wandered back towards the front desk in the foyer. It was best to leave his aunt for a while. Sometimes she may return to her old self if left alone. He would check on her general health before trying again.

"Ah yes, Ethel Langan. I'm afraid that your aunt is still the same really. She has lost a little weight. As you can imagine, Ethel has her good days and bad days. You won't be surprised to know that her bad ones far outnumber the better ones lately. Oh, her health is fine really for a lady of her age, and she sleeps okay. Lately she has been asking about someone called Delores a lot. I would not worry really. It's probably someone from her past. She is sometimes drawn back to her teenage years also. This is not unusual either for Alzheimer sufferers" said the nurse in the small office, reading largely from notes.

Tony nodded in a courteous way. He saw no sense in explaining who Delores was. Although the lady was always civil with him, Tony reckoned that given the choice, she would prefer if he stayed away. Tony was Ethel's only visitor now. Her only daughter, Carol, lived in Australia. Carol rarely phoned either the nursing home, or Tony's address.

Tony walked back through the foyer, with its thick blue floral-patterned carpet. The cream-coloured walls were peppered with old paintings of rustic landscapes. He strolled slowly back to where Ethel sat. Tony joined her for a time, but did not try to engage her in conversation. He knew that it would be futile. Ethel stared out through the glass at the well-manicured lawns and shrubs. Now and then she would utter some incoherent sentence. Tony was also lost in his own world. His late mother dominated his thoughts, and although Ethel was only feet away, she hardly mattered to him at that moment.

"Henry's late" Ethel said all of a sudden. She seemed upset, and Tony reached out to comfort her. He gently patted her right hand. Ethel recoiled instantly. "Who are you? I don't know you!" she cried, drawing back in fear.

"It's okay Aunt Ether, really. I'm Tony. You don't remember me, do you Aunt Ethel?" Tony replied, going through the motions once again.

"You're not Martin! Martin's gone. I want Henry! He promised that he would come today" Ethel's wavering voice said. Tony Lee stood up wearily. It was pointless to remain.

"Goodbye Aunt Ethel, I will see you next time" he said quietly. Tony turned to walk away. It was silly of him to imagine that Ethel would be well enough to take in news of his mother's sad demise. He stood for a moment and observed the other residents in the large room. Some were happily talking amongst themselves. Others chatted with visiting family or friends. Some sat reading contently alone, while the odd one like Ethel looked totally confused as to their surroundings.

"Tony? Have you come to see me?" said the voice. Tony quickly turned to see Ethel staring in his direction. He flashed a smile and returned to sit by her side. "There you are Ethel! I thought that you had run off with a young fellow!" Tony said chirpily. In her younger days, Ethel and Tony had got on really well. There was always plenty of banter between the two. Now if Tony saw a glimpse of the old Ethel, he would always try and get a rise out of her.

"Divil a bit of it! Sure who would be bothered with an old bag of bones like me!" she smiled. Tony laughed and gripped her hand in his.

"How is poor Delores? Is she still going back and forward to the hospital?" Ethel asked, taking Tony by surprise. The smile quickly disappeared from Tony's handsome face. He briefly considered telling Ethel of his mother's death. It did not seem fair somehow. There seemed little point in adding to the old woman's misery.

"No Ethel, she's over all that now. I can safely say that she's a lot better off than before" he replied. He held his aunt's hand and watched her ageing face.

She asked about her husband, Henry. No matter how well Ethel appeared, she could never come to terms with the fact that Henry was dead.

"Oh Henry's fine Ethel. Really he is. Everyone is doing well" Tony said cheerfully. Ethel glanced out the window and a deep furrow appeared on her forehead.

"You can't stay long. Henry will be here. He promised to come and bring some grapes" Ethel said in a worried tone. Tony sighed slowly and withdrew his hand from hers. Ethel turned to face the lawn once more. It was time to leave. He leaned over and kissed Ethel on the cheek. She neither flinched nor welcomed his kiss as she continued to stare into the mid-distance. Tony again stood up to leave.

"Make it up with Martin. Blood is thicker than water" said Ethel pointedly. Tony glanced back at his old aunt. She was still lost in her own private, strange world. He turned away again. Tony did not know any family member called Martin. He walked outside into the bright sunshine. Ethel was most likely confusing the past with the present. Perhaps Martin was one of the male nurses. Tony reflected on a wasted journey, but took solace in the fact that he had at least tried. Ethel now lived in a different world. In hindsight, to even contemplate telling her about Delores's passing was ridiculous, he thought. Once again, he unlocked the silver bike and wheeled it noisily across the pebbled runway, back towards the heavy cream gates.

Stacey re-emerged from the newspaper offices to rejoin her flatmates. They walked up towards The Ilac Centre, laughing and giggling as they went. Stacey Boyd always thought that there was no better feeling than to walk through Dublin City Centre on a busy sunny Saturday afternoon. There always seemed to be a feel-good factor about the place, as happy shoppers drifted aimlessly around the bustling streets. Some of the streets were pedestrian-only zones. There appeared to be a different atmosphere in such spots, as entire areas became engulfed in a sea of faces. Now and then a street busker could be heard in the distance. Street traders yelled out to sell their goods. Music wafted from the shops and megastores.

"Tell her! Go on!" said Jodie. Jodie looked mischievously towards Angie, who flushed bright red. Angie O'Rourke offered Jodie a withering glare. She planned to tell Stacey her latest titbit of gossip in her own good time. The news of Tony's mother's death had forced Angie to postpone the conversation. Stacey looked quizzically at her best pal Angie O'Rourke.

"Sssh! It's nothing Stace! Ignore her!" Angie said sternly. Angie tugged on her frizzy dark hair, again giving Jodie a look of disapproval.

"What is it Angie? Come on, spill the beans!" an exasperated Stacey giggled. Gina Stynes was the forth flatmate making up their little gang. She looked as mystified as Stacey. Gina was probably the most laid-back of the four and the eldest by two years.

"What are you two up to now? Something must have happened when they were out together last night Stacey! Come on, time for a coffee! We'll winkle it out of them!" Gina grinned.

Stacey linked Angie O'Rourke as they headed for their usual café.

"Come on you! It's my turn to pay. I want to hear all the gossip-and I won't take no for an answer!!" Stacey said with a wry giggle.

Stacey ordered coffee for all four girls, plus the usual plate of apple cake, as they found a seat in the busy but spacious café off Abbey Street. Tina's Coffee Bar was fairly full, as it was most weekends. As soon as all four settled down, Stacey again turned her attention towards her pal Angie. Angie tried to playfully keep her at arm's length, droning on about a pair of black boots which she had earlier decided were not her style.

"I should have bought them there and then. I just pray that they're still there later on. God! I'm always missing out on bargains! Stacey, why did you not insist that I buy them on the spot?" Angie asked with a wicked grin.

"Enough about those damn boots already! What's going on Angie O'Rourke-and how does it concern me?" Stacey demanded with a grin. All eyes fell on Angie. She fiddled nervously with her teaspoon before looking to Jodie for guidance. The tomboy sporty Jodie was not about to help her out.

"Tell her! Go on! You're gonna have to now anyway!" Jodie giggled. Angie looked uncomfortable now. She searched for a way to begin her tale. Stacey looked from Jodie to her best pal Angie with growing impatience.

"For God's sake Angie! What is it?" Stacey said in a snappy tone. All around them customers chatted noisily. Angie finally capitulated.

"It's Alex. We met him last night in a pub. We went for a drink in Temple Bar and bumped into him. He asked about you" Angie blurted out. Stacey Boyd looked shocked. Angie glanced to Jodie for backup. Jodie willingly took her cue.

"He was really nice Stacey. He's off the cigarettes and looks fit and well. He bought us a drink and spent ages chatting to us. I could tell that he still thinks a lot of you. He, er...said that he would like to speak to you-just to clear the air" Jodie said.

All attention was now firmly on Stacey. Gina was sitting next to Stacey and patted her arm. The news of Stacey's ex-boyfriend hit Stacey Boyd hard. She felt a knot in the pit of her stomach as she remembered Alex Woods, the man who she had almost married.

"You didn't give him my mobile number? Tell me you didn't?" Stacey blurted out. She looked from Jodie to Angie again in desperation. Both girls shook their heads in unison. Angie dared to smile a cheeky grin.

"Of course we didn't Stace! But just imagine had you came with us! Had you not stayed with Tony last night, you probably would have been there too. Fate or what?" Angie reasoned.

"Yeah, it makes you wonder" Jodie mused.

Stacey's mind was swimming. She could not follow their logic.

"I don't get it. I might have gone to bed early. Had I gone out with you two, we might have gone somewhere else. What's your point?" Stacey asked. She tried her best to stay composed. The last time that she had seen Alex Woods had been a stormy affair. She had called him some horrible names as he tried to explain why he could not go through with their wedding.

"Yeah, maybe. But had that old woman not died, the chances are that all three of us would have bumped into Alex. What would have happened then?" Angie said in a playful way. Gina Stynes listened with interest. She had worked late the night before and had stayed over at her boyfriend's flat.

"I always miss the good bits! What did he say Jodie?" Gina asked. Gina was the tallest of the four, her red hair worn short and tidy. Jodie leaned in towards Gina, almost ignoring Stacey.

"Oh, he was really nice Gina. He kept asking about Stacey. We hadn't the heart to tell him about Tony Lee. Alex never asked if she was seeing someone, but he probably guessed. He was in really good form. The other chap with him was a bit of a geek. We asked if they were going clubbing, but Alex said that he was in work early this morning" Jodie said. Stacey had heard enough.

"I cannot believe you two! You actually asked my ex to go dancing with you. I can't believe it!" Stacey said forcefully.

"Don't be silly Stace! We never said that we would go with them. We just inquired" Angie replied weakly. She again looked to Jodie to back her up, but Stacey was ready to take control of the conversation.

"Anyway, it really doesn't matter. I'm with Tony now. That bastard had his chance. He humiliated me, and I can never forgive him for that. I wouldn't have him back if he was the last man on earth" Stacey fumed. There was a brief silence, but then Jodie Callaghan felt compelled to speak. She was a girl of strong opinions. Jodie always seemed to have a different perspective to the other three girls, and her strange slant on events and news often amused her three flatmates.

"But you have to see it from Alex's point of view as well Stace. I mean, the fellow wasn't ready to commit, was he? Wouldn't it have been much worse if you got married and then found out that you weren't right for each other?

Maybe he just got cold feet. I wish that you could have seen him last night. He was really back to his old self, Stacey. Come on! If you met him right now, what would you say?" Jodie gushed.

"What would I say Jodie? It would be unprintable! And what would you say if you were practically jilted at the altar?" Stacey retorted. Gina and Angie giggled, but Jodie was not about to give up. Her green eyes widened as she leaned forward on the small square white table. Jodie's blonde ponytail swung from side to side as she spoke. She was truly the tomboy of the group, but occasionally showed her feminine side. Yet Jodie was always most comfortable when wearing jeans and tracksuits. She did date men infrequently, but Jodie Callaghan mostly spent her time partying and enjoying life.

"Yeah, but all of that aside, which of the two did you love the most? I mean, when you were with Alex, you loved him, right? And now that you're with Tony, do you love him just as much?" Jodie reasoned in her own strangely logical way. Again Gina and Angie laughed. Jodie's take on life always fascinated Angie O'Rourke in particular.

Stacey Boyd wanted to say that there was no comparison. She needed to let everyone know that Tony was the best thing that ever happened to her. In her heart Stacey knew that Tony Lee had hardly swept her off her feet. He was hardly romantic, or even attentive. Stacey could feel Angie's eyes boring into her. If anyone knew her true feelings, it was her best pal Angie.

"There's no comparison. It's simple. That swine wrecked my life. I can never forgive him. Tony would never hurt me. We're brilliant together. I hope that I never see that bastard Alex Woods ever again" Stacey replied emphatically. She had a look of thunder, which made it virtually impossible for Jodie to follow up her question. Angie continued to observe her friend quietly. She vividly recalled what Stacey had told her after a few dates with Tony Lee. "He will do for now, but don't go getting your wedding hat out just yet! He definitely won't be the one, that's for sure!" Stacey had confided. Angie O'Rourke knew that Stacey still had feelings for Alex, no matter how much she denied it.

When they had finished their coffee break, the four girls returned to the task in hand. It was Saturday afternoon after all, and while the shops remained open, they would search for bargains, or better still, something spectacular to wear. It was a ritual carried out every weekend without fail. On some Saturdays there might only be two or three of the close flatmates. Nevertheless, the city centre drew them like a magnet. Whether anything substantial was purchased was really beside the point. Shopping was a passion, and each week brought a new enthusiasm.

"I got his mobile number" Angie whispered to Stacey later that day. Both Gina and Jodie were busy looking at handbags at the rear of a large store. Stacey looked aghast.

"What did you say?" she demanded, her trademark squint distorting her pretty looks. Always when Stacey became annoyed, she would squint her eyes and pout her lips.

"You heard!" Angie replied with a grin. It was a catchphrase used by all four girls when they were sure that the other person had understood quite clearly what had been said. Angie continued to speak in a matter-of-fact tone.

"It's in my white bag at home. I'll give it to you later-just in case!" Angie smiled. She studied a black pair of leggings in the shop window, pretending not to notice Stacey's incredulous look.

"What part of this do you not understand Angie? I don't want his bloody number. I don't want anything to do with him" Stacey said, almost spitting out her words. Angie O'Rourke was unperturbed.

"Of course you don't Stace, but I have it anyway. Listen, Jodie doesn't know about it. I'll slip it to you later. Hush, they're coming back" Angie whispered. Stacey glanced around as their two friends came to join them.

"What do you reckon to this chunky handbag Angie? It will go great with my brown jacket!" Gina exclaimed. The moment had passed. Stacey Boyd's brain was swimming. Thoughts of Alex Woods flew through her head. Stacey recalled how she and Alex had laughed together. She remembered all of his good traits and Alex's little annoying habits. All around her the throng of shoppers invaded her privacy. She barely noticed. Her mind in a spin, Stacey was swept along by her three flatmates drive to shop; with all unaware of what she was thinking.

It was late afternoon now, but still the shopping areas were packed. It was as if there was an unwritten rule to uphold. Once the shops remained open, no one dare return home.

Stacey's mind flirted with what Angie had said. Of course she would never dare to telephone Alex Woods. The idea was preposterous. Yet somewhere inside her head he still lurked. It was like unfinished business. Alex Woods had never quite gone away. Somehow Stacey had always known that their paths would cross again. She tried to block him from her mind. Now was not the time to contemplate her past. Perhaps later when she was alone in bed she might consider it. But not now.

Jan Williams replaced the blue telephone receiver on her kitchen wall. Tony had phoned back to confirm that he had arranged their mother's funeral.

"Who was that Mom?" asked her son, Josh. Jan offered a furtive glance at her fifteen-year-old son before turning away to avoid eye contact. Before she could answer, her daughter Amy spoke.

"Was it for me Mom? Tracey said that she might phone. We're going to the mall with Gill and Debs" said Amy. She had just bounded into the spacious kitchen. Amy was a year older than her brother, but looked more like twenty rather than sixteen. Jan Williams bit her bottom lip as she fought to control her emotions. She still had to tell her husband that her mother had died.

"No guys, it was for me. That was your Uncle Tony in Ireland. He just wanted to keep me up to speed on my Mom" Jan said calmly. She busied herself at the sink, avoiding turning to face her children. Amy looked to Josh and shrugged her shoulders. Their mother's family in Ireland was of little interest to either teenager. They had never met their uncle, or their grandmother. Apart from the odd Christmas and birthday card, their mother's past life in Dublin held little appeal. For Josh and Amy, their real grandparents were their father's folks, who lived less than four miles away.

"How is Grandma Mom? Is she still sick?" Amy asked tactfully, trying to show some concern for her mother's feelings. She stood at the large double-door fridge looking for something to eat as she half-heartedly awaited a response. Josh sat in a corner of the light airy room, straddling a high stool. He was vacantly staring at a small television screen, which was transmitting a college basketball game.

Jan Williams swallowed hard as she fought to compose herself. Her mother had just died the day before. The temptation to break down was immense. "Not now" she told herself. She would talk to her husband before telling the children. Howard Williams was still at work. It would be hours yet before he returned home.

"My Mom is not too good love. Don't worry. You go to the mall and have fun. I'll see you later, yeah?" Jan said, managing a smile. Amy shrugged and again turned her attention to the fridge. She reached for a can of Coke and popped the metal ring open. Jan Williams suddenly looked cross.

"Amy! I don't know how you are not the size of a house! You shove so much rubbish inside you, it's untrue! As quickly as I fill the icebox, you empty it!" Jan bellowed. Briefly Amy studied her thin frame. She was not overweight, and as if to prove her point, slipped a hand inside the front of her short blue jeans. Amy gulped down a mouthful of cola and patted her flat stomach over her skimpy yellow top.

"I look after my body Mom! See you later!" Amy replied. She left the room as quickly as she had arrived. Jan watched from the window of the kitchen as her daughters' blond frizzy hair bobbed by outside. Already Amy was phoning friends on her cell-phone. Jan watched until Amy had disappeared from sight. She briefly recalled being the same age. It seemed another world away now. Jan's life had changed beyond all recognition since her teenage years. Now and then she missed Dublin, but her life was now here in California. She lived for her children, her home, her part-time job, and of course her husband, Howard. Her one link with Ireland had been her mother Delores. Now she was gone forever.

"Cool!" Josh yelled as he punched the air. Jan snapped out of her daydreaming and glanced over at the television screen. The basketball game had ended with a victory to Josh's favoured team. He leapt to his feet with a smile on his young face, his dark curly hair bouncing up and down. Josh skipped across the shiny wooden floor of the kitchen-cum-dining room, barely noticing his mother.

"They won then?" Jan asked quietly.

"Sure thing! I'm gonna shoot some hoops Maw!" Josh answered. He scooped up his red-and-black basketball from its usual place behind the back door. In seconds he had followed his sister outside, leaving Jan Williams alone.

Jan could instantly feel the tears well up in her eyes. As the thuds from Josh's basketball hitting the hoop attached to the garage wall echoed outside, Jan's sobbing became more intense. Her mother had finally passed on, and all that that entailed filled Jan with fear. They had gone through so much together. The nightmare came back to haunt her once again, and Jan could feel the dread and anguish from her past returning.

Jan Williams dried her eyes as she sat in the large living room to the front of her house. Normally she would never dream of sitting there during the day. There was always so much to be done around the large four-bedroom house. Now and then she might take a few minutes rest in the kitchen, but to sit in "the evening room" as Howard called it, was almost a forbidden luxury.

When Tony had phoned the previous day with the news, Jan had gone into shock. Howard always worked late on Friday evenings. When he returned home, Jan lay alone in the darkness of their bedroom. Somehow it was easier not to talk to him about her mother. Jan had remained silent until she heard Howard snore lightly. And then the tears came again. She would tell him the news tomorrow.

Howard had left for work early that Saturday morning, still not knowing of Delores Lee's death. Jan knew that she was simply postponing the inevitable. And now as she sat alone that afternoon, Jan Williams realised that the time had come to tell her husband the dreaded news.

Jan's mind raced back to her younger years again. There had been happy times, she told herself. Her mind searched her memory for confirmation. Her

Dad's smiling face came to mind. He had been a handsome man at one time. Jan tried to imagine him standing beside her mother. Somehow the picture did not quite fit. It was as if they were two pieces of a jigsaw that did not interlock. She settled for recalling her parents as separate entities. Jan could see her mother's dear face now, and her father's grin of approval. He had never really laughed out loud, to her knowledge. That was a fact that had just struck her. Jan shuddered. It was best not to torture herself. Perhaps the past was best left alone. She nodded silently. That was it. She would leave things alone, and just remember her lovely Mom as she had always pictured her. Jan Williams rose slowly to her feet. She inadvertently caught a glimpse of herself in the long mirror in the corner of the large room. Jan felt compelled to study her face, to see how cruel that passing of time had been to her.

As she moved closer to the big mahogany-rimmed mirror, Jan saw a thin, bony, middle-aged woman with short dark hair. At best she could describe herself as nondescript. Jan decided that she looked plain. Her once bright hazel-green eyes were now bespectacled. Howard had always advocated contact lenses, but Jan was squeamish about such things. Jan slipped off her gold-rimmed glasses and studied her face critically. Her eyes looked tired and red. Beneath them, her upper face was a web of lines mapping her features. Jan tried to smile in an effort to improve her appearance. It did not really help. She sighed before replacing her spectacles on her tired face and moving away from the large mirror. Somewhere in her subconscious Jan vowed to make more of an effort with her appearance, at least for Howard's sake.

"Howdy folks!" Howard Williams bellowed as he entered his home through the back door. The whole family always used the rear of the house as the entry point. Howard tossed his white Stetson hat on the hanger behind the door. His hat was his trademark at his huge store. He slipped off his matching white jacket and smiled at Jan.

"Sell much today Pop?" asked Josh, as he and his father shared their customary high-five.

"Yeah! Business is fine son. We're doing all right!" Howard replied. He made his way to his wife and planted a kiss on her left cheek. Jan Williams managed a quick smile.

"I'm famished darling. Something smells delicious" he said. Jan tried her best to appear normal. Howard wriggled his nose in a vain attempt to identify what was for dinner.

"Howard, I have something to tell you. Can we have a word in private?" Jan said quietly. Howard Williams looked agitated. By nature he was an impatient man, and he enjoyed his food more than most. Howard was overweight, a paunch steadily growing since he hit his late thirties. His dark hair was slowly receding to the front, creating a large tanned forehead.

"Gee honey sure, but can't it wait? Is it to do with money? Is it the kids?" Howard asked. He mopped his considerable brow with his large white handkerchief. Jan's response was instant.

"No Howard, it's neither, and no it can't wait. Anyway, Amy is not home yet. She phoned from the mall to say she may be a little late" Jan said firmly. Howard nodded, as if to admit defeat. He followed his wife to the living room.

"What is it Jan? Has Josh been acting up again? It's his age honey. Teenagers, eh? When I was Josh's age, my hormones were all over the place! He's most likely got a crush on some girl. Do you want me to..." Howard's words were lost as Jan blurted out her news.

"It's Mom. She passed away. Tony phoned. She never regained consciousness" Jan said in a low, shaky voice. She searched her husband's face for support. The look on Howard's face turned from sudden shock to remorse.

"Oh honey, I'm so sorry. The poor old dear. Do the kids know? Heck! You should have telephoned me" Howard replied. Howard embraced his wife, pulling her close to him. Jan managed to keep her composure. She pulled away to face him.

"I didn't tell them yet. I wanted to tell you first. Look Howard, we're going to have to go to Dublin. I telephoned the airline to book, but then I wasn't sure how many tickets we needed. I mean, should we take the kids? Can you take some time off?" Jan asked, her eyes searching his. Howard turned away and scratched his slowly-balding head. He loosened his white tie from his black shirt collar. It was time to think fast.

"Gee Jan, I really don't know. If you think that we all should go, then okay. It will mean closing the store, and this is my really busy time Jan. But whatever you think is for the best" he replied cautiously. Howard knew how to manipulate his wife. She was a passive lady who would always do as he intended. Without ever realising it, Jan would automatically do what was best for Howard.

"No, no Howard dear, you are right of course. It was silly of me. We can't afford for you to close the business, and Josh and Amy should not miss out on school. No, you're right. I'll go alone. I should be back in a few days. Can you manage without me Howard? I know that it will be a struggle" Jan said, a worried look etched on her face. Howard sighed as if he had been asked a quiz question. He put his right hand to his chin and walked the room. It was time to make his wife feel a little guilty.

"I daresay that the kids will need to rally round Jan. We'll get by honey. You just go and do what you have to do. I'll keep this place ticking over" Howard answered with another long, deep sigh. Howard ran his own shop selling electrical goods, and was a master of verbal rhetoric.

Jan still looked distinctly uncomfortable.

"There is one other thing Howard. I'll have to stay in a hotel. I cannot face sleeping in that house. Will that be okay?" she asked, her dark eyebrows narrowing as she awaited a response. Howard looked relieved. It was a small price to pay for keeping his distance. Returning to Dublin could be avoided after all.

"Of course Jan, I understand. You stay as long as you have to. There will be lots of loose ends to tie up. Besides, you haven't seen Tony for such a long time. You will have lots to discuss, no doubt" Howard said. It was a questioning response. Both knew what he inferred. Jan came to him and embraced him warmly. He cuddled her for a moment as the tears came.

"There, there Jan. Just be brave" he whispered.

"Thank you Howard, you're so kind. I'll tell the children over dinner" she said.

During their meal, Jan tried to pick the right moment to speak to Amy and Josh. Amy was prattling on about some boy from school who had paid a little attention to her at the shopping mall. This was a subject that always left her father on edge. Howard would always inquire about the boy's background, where he lived, and most importantly of all, his parent's nationality.

"Mom, his name is Kevin Lidwinski, and he's absolutely gorgeous. He's on the football team. I cannot believe that he actually spoke to me!" Amy gushed.

"Lidwinski huh? They'll be eastern Europeans. His folks will be Russians or something" Howard said grimly. Amy glanced at her father, mildly annoyed at his interference.

"Dad! You're such a Philistine! The Lidwinski's are American-just like us!" she snapped back.

Howard Williams chuckled as he cut deeper into his huge steak.

"Yeah, but what sort of Americans? Tell her what we are Josh. What type of American citizens are we son?" Howard said, looking to his son for back-up. Josh proudly took up the challenge.

"We're Irish-Americans Pop, the finest that there is! On the rungs of a ladder, we're at the top. Then come the British-Americans, then The Italians" replied Josh, knowing full well the effect it would have on his older sister.

"Oh my God! You are so racist Josh! Everyone in America is equal. This is so old-fashioned! Mom?" Amy retorted, looking for her mother's help. All eyes fell on Jan Williams. It was a discussion that the family had had many times. It was normally a light-hearted affair, with Howard making it clear on how The Williams bloodline should evolve. It always left Amy in no doubt about the type of boy her father expected her to date. Amy Williams was a strong-willed girl however, and would always defend her ground. It usually made for a lively debate over dinner; a time when most of the family's talking was done. Howard's parents hailed from Donegal, and he was fiercely proud of his Irish roots. He enjoyed winding up his only daughter, with his pro-Irish stance. Jan looked silently around the rectangular table for a moment before speaking. "As it happens, I had some bad news from Ireland today. Your grandmother passed away. I'm going to have to fly out early tomorrow. Dad will look after things here. I want you all to help out. I should be back in a few days" Jan said in a muted tone. Amy looked from Josh to her father before jumping to her feet.

"Oh my God Mom, I'm so sorry. You must feel awful!" Amy said as she rushed to her mother's arms. Howard signalled to Josh with his eyes that he should follow suit. Half-heartedly Josh went to his mother and embraced her with a limp hug.

"Sorry Mom" he whispered before returning to his meal. As soon as he sat down, an idea sprang to Josh's young mind.

"Hey! We should all go! I've never been to Ireland. We should go to support Mom! How about it Pop, can we?" Josh asked in a chirpy voice. Howard looked decidedly irked by his son's new-found enthusiasm. He slowly placed his knife and fork on the dinner plate, a sure sign that he was agitated.

"Definitely not. Your poor Mom and I have already discussed what is for the best. It would serve no useful purpose for me to close the store. Besides, your schooling comes first. These are the most important years of your lives, isn't that right Jan?" Howard said tersely. He was always careful to involve Jan when taking a decision which benefited him.

Jan was quick to back up her husband.

"Your Dad is right. I want both of you to rally around while I'm away. Help in any way that you can, and do as you are told" Jan said in a firm tone.

Already Josh had seen another possible windfall from the sudden news.

"Hey! There might be a will! Was Grandma rich?" Josh asked with great enthusiasm. Howard shook his head and laughed. Jan cleared her throat and looked sternly at her son.

"No Josh, there will be no reading of a will. My mother was just a simple working-class lady. Money mattered little to her" Jan said in a quiet, emotional voice. Amy sprang to her mother's defence.

"You're so materialistic!" Amy cried. It was one of her latest crusades in a bid to rid the world of all of its ills. Howard offered a slight grin.

"Hey! Don't knock materialism Amy. That's what puts food on this table!" her father chuckled. Howard winked at Josh, before realising that his wife's demeanour required a more sombre approach.

"Er, sorry Jan darling. Say! Once all this has been tidied up and your poor Mom has been put to rest, maybe we'll grab a few days away together somewhere. Heck, your Mom had no quality of life in the end. She will be smiling down on you from heaven! It was so hard on young Tony too" Howard said with reverence. Jan nodded silently.

"Poor Tony, he's thirty-six now. It's as if he has spent all of his adult life looking after our Mom. He sounded devastated on the phone. Heaven knows what it must be like for him in that old house now" Jan said, almost in a whisper. A moment's silence followed before Josh saw another avenue to pursue.

"What about Grandma's house Mom? Will you sell it? Are houses expensive in Ireland?" Josh asked, his voice attempting to sound tactful. Jan Williams looked horrified. It was something that she had never considered in the short few hours since learning of her mother's death.

"Oh no, that's your Uncle Tony's home. It's the least that he deserves after what he has been through. It's a long-standing agreement between my Mom and me. I promised her that I would never do that on Tony. Where would he go? It's his house now" Jan said firmly. Howard reached out and patted his wife's hand.

"Mom's right. We don't need anything. We're doing pretty well. Uncle Tony needs a break. Heck! He's heading for forty and has barely lived. Do you kids realise that your Uncle Tony has never even owned a car?" Howard said. He sat back in his chair, awaiting the sense of shock which was sure to flow from his children.

"Never! Is it true Mom? What's wrong with him?" Josh asked, a look of horror descending on his young face. For the first time that day, Jan managed to laugh.

"There's nothing the matter with him. Tony is a real pragmatist. He sees no reason to drive. Tony lives real near his job. Dublin is not a huge city, and Tony is hardly adventurous. He has always lived a quiet, settled life. I don't know what he will do now though" Jan replied, her mind drifting off to her younger days in Ireland.

"You lived in Dublin for a while Pop. What was it like?" Amy asked. Howard smiled again and looked knowingly at his wife.

"Yep! That's where I met your Mom. All that I can recall was that it rained every day! But they were great times, eh Jan?" he said, squeezing his wife's hand in his. Jan tried to raise a smile.

"It didn't rain all of the time, but yes, they were good days. Your Dad was working for a large American company back then. We met at a dancehall one Saturday night. At first, my Mom didn't like him, but Howard can be very persuasive, as we all know. He won her around in the end. Anyway, there were lots of tears when I told her that I was emigrating to The States. By then the company had decided to close their Irish operation. Howard was transferred back here. He continued to work for them for a while, before finally breaking out on his own in the electrical business" Jan said in a far-off tone.

Howard nodded and managed a slow chuckle.

"Yep! And what a great decision that was! We have never looked back. The business has gone from strength to strength! Hell, I was just born to sell goods!" Howard grinned. Amy was more intrigued with her Uncle Tony.

"But Mom, why have we never met Tony? I mean, has he never wanted to come over for a visit?" she asked. Jan looked uncomfortable.

"It's complicated Amy dear. There's a huge age gap between Tony and I. We didn't grow up together like you and Josh. I feel that I don't really know Tony all that well. As I say, he has probably never been able to have a holiday while looking after Mom. We have always said that one day we would go back to Ireland to visit, but somehow never got around to it. What with you two at school, and Dad's business, it never seemed viable. Howard would love to visit Donegal, but it simply never happened" Jan concluded, looking to her husband for support.

"Yeah, I guess that we'll do it someday, but by then you guys will probably have your own families. I reckon that I'll be an old man before I get to visit my homeland" Howard sighed. Amy looked irritated at her father's words.

"For heaven's sake Daddy, this is your homeland! You were born right here in California. You can't get any more American than that!" she said mockingly.

For the first time that evening, Howard looked deadly serious. He released his grip on Jan's left hand and pushed his plate inwards on the table.

"Never forget your heritage Amy dear. People sacrificed a lot to come here and start a new life. This great country did not build itself. It was done off the sweat of immigrants from Europe and other parts of the world. Men died making this country what it is today. My Grandad was one of those proud men. I want to go back to Killybegs someday and pay my respects to his family. That's where my roots are-and yours too young lady. We have told you about your Irish history. Don't you feel anything for your ancestry?" Howard said sternly. Amy was surprised by her father's sudden serious tone. She had often listened to his stories of the Irish famine, the dominance of Ireland by Britain, and the struggle for independence. It all seemed so far removed from her cocooned little world. Yet Amy realised its importance to her father.

"I guess so Pop, but I feel American. I'm sure that everyone has roots somewhere, it's just not so significant nowadays" Amy said with a shrug.

In despair, Howard looked to Jan. Jan shook her head and smiled back. It was not worth pursuing. Jan had other concerns. Going back to Ireland at this time was not special for her. Jan had never felt as passionate for her homeland as Howard did. Indeed, returning to Dublin filled Jan with dread. Old memories would be awoken. All those suppressed thoughts would return. Her past would be there, waiting to leap out and ambush her. Yet it was something that Jan realised that she had to face. She always knew that this day was coming. And now it was time. All that she could do was pray for the strength. And still there was poor Tony to consider. If only he knew. He must never find out. The past belonged to another world, another forgotten time. Some things were best left alone. It was after all, how her mother would have wanted it. Jan glanced slowly around the table. Her family could never know of her pain. Her children had to be protected at all costs. No, Howard was right after all. It would be for the best not to bring them to Ireland. It was safer not to tempt fate. The final fragments of her past life were about to be tucked away forever. Only then could she return to her ordinary and contented life.

CHAPTER THREE

REUNION

"Hello Tony, how did you get on?" Stacey asked over the phone. It was a little after six, and she had just returned from her shopping trip. Stacey Boyd sat on her bed in her room. She was in good spirits, despite Angie's news about Alex Woods. Outside her closed bedroom door, her three flatmates talked and jokes boisterously in the shared living area. Each had their own room, but their bedroom doors were almost always open, except when they required some privacy.

"Not great Stace. I went to see Aunt Ethel as I said I might. She wasn't well at all. A wasted journey I'm afraid. Still, never mind. Did you place the advert in the paper?" Tony replied.

"Yes of course. It will be in Monday's edition. Listen Tony, are we going out later? Angie has a date, so she's going with her new fellow. Gina and Harry are off to a show. They asked if we fancied tagging along. What do you think?" Stacey asked. She lay back on her bed and stretched her legs. Tony said nothing for a moment. She listened, guessing that he was weighing up the situation in his head.

"I dunno Stace, I'm not sure if I'm up for company tonight" he replied hesitantly.

"Thank you very much Tony Lee!" Stacey giggled.

"No! You know what I mean Stace! Maybe we should just go for a drink together. I don't reckon that I would be much good company for Harry and Gina" he said, defending himself.

It was as Stacey had expected. The local bar was about as far as Tony's imagination took him. Any other outings were always organised by Stacey or her pals. Tony would enjoy himself at such events, but then the following week it would be back to Madigan's Bar.

"Okay Tony, whatever you like. Tell you what; I can get Harry and Gina to drop me off at the pub. I could meet you there and then grab a taxi home afterwards" Stacey answered. It was a deliberate ploy to let Tony Lee know that she had no intentions of staying over again.

"Yeah, okay love. That's a good idea. Yeah, I'll see you there around nine, say" Tony replied slowly. Stacey said goodbye and listened as the line went dead. She had heard the disappointment in Tony's voice, and she did feel a little guilty. Still, Stacey had no regrets. For her to face another night in that house was impossible. It was best to be firm from the start.

Minutes later, Angie slipped into the room. She closed the door firmly behind her.

"Here, this is Alex's number. Take it Stacey. Please call him soon. Give him a bell and make the peace" Angie whispered with a smile, tossing back her curly dark hair. She pushed the small slip of paper into Stacey's hand before her friend had a chance to object. A look of incredulity spread across Stacey's thin pale face.

"Angie! I told you that I have no wish to talk to him! Make the peace? This is not some trivial falling out among school friends. This man dumped me after years together. I was practically walking down the aisle with him" Stacey protested. She sat up sharply on the bed, tossing the scrap of paper onto the locker beside her.

"Come on, you know that's not entirely true" Angie said, sitting down next to her. Stacey shook her head from side to side in an indignant way. Her familiar squint reappeared.

"Well, nearly then! Anyway, I don't want to speak to that arsehole. Subject closed! Now, what about your new fellow? What's he like? I'm dying to meet him" Stacey said, a smile appearing on her face for the first time.

Angie turned her head away to hide the hurt in her brown eyes. A look of trepidation spread across her round, pretty face. Her dark eyes welled up, but she managed a smile.

"I must be mad Stace. I've been meaning to talk to you about him. His name is Philip Westbourne. He works with me at the office. We get on great together. He's really funny, you know, a great laugh. This will be our first real date tonight" Angie said quietly. She clutched Stacey's hand for support.

"What's the problem? Is he old? Jesus! He's not too young is he? Not that toy-boy who started last month-you know the one that you were telling me about?" Stacey asked, raising her voice a decibel or two. Angie shook her short curly hair and smiled nervously. The truth quickly dawned on Stacey Boyd.

45

"Aw no Angie! Don't say that he's married! Aw please Angie! You always said that you would never get involved in anything like that! Please tell me that it's not true?" Stacey pleaded. Angie's dark eyes could never mask anything from Stacey. She looked downwards on the bed and shook her head in denial.

"It's not as bad as it seems, silly! We're just mates. He's away from his wife. We're just going out together to have a chat. Phil has a lot on his plate at the moment. I'm just going along to lend a sympathetic ear, that's all" Angie replied without conviction. Stacey looked horrified.

"God Angie, please don't get mixed up in that. You know how these things always end up. He'll go back to her, and you will end up broken-hearted. And I'll bet that there are children involved. He's one of those cases where his wife doesn't understand him. Am I right?" Stacey said coldly.

Angie O'Rourke avoided eye contact. She got to her feet and walked across the room.

"I need a smoke" she announced. Angie was a heavy smoker. Her cigarettes were in her handbag outside, and she was reluctant to face Gina and Jodie at that moment.

"Here" said Stacey, reaching inside the small drawer in her bedside locker. "They're Gina's. She left them here the other day" Stacey added. She handed Angie the red pack of opened cigarettes, plus a small pale blue lighter. Angie lit up a tipped cigarette without speaking and paced the room again.

"He has two kids, a boy and a girl. The eldest is six, the youngest four. We haven't really talked about that side of things. He sees them at weekends. Stacey, I'm not sure what to do. He's a really nice guy and I'm sure that he has feelings for me" Angie said, darting glances at her friend now and then. Stacey said nothing, allowing Angie to continue.

"As I said, we like each other. If things were different…"Angie said. Stacey quickly intervened.

"Yeah, but they're not, are they? If things were different, you might have a chance Angie" Stacey said, cutting across her best friend. She had heard enough. It was time to voice her opinion.

"Can't you see Angie? All this will bring is heartache. These kids will be in his life forever. No matter how well the separation goes, they will always be in the picture. He will be forever running back and forth, and you will be caught in the middle. Trust me" Stacey said emphatically. Angie's dark eyes darted at her again.

"I know, I know. Don't think that I haven't been over this a million times. Listen Stace, I'm not getting any younger. I haven't had a serious relationship in over three years. I'm thirty-three on my next birthday. Some mornings I wake up and wonder where my life has gone. I can feel the panic set in. My body-clock is ticking on" Angie said. Stacey Boyd laughed out loud. Angie always made her smile. Her best pal tended to exaggerate everything.

"Get you! We're not past our sell-by date yet!" Stacey giggled. Angie settled on the edge of the bed. She managed a wistful smile while pulling hard on her cigarette.

Before the two could speak again, Jodie bounded into the room, barely knocking on the door. As was the custom with Jodie Callaghan, she wore her favourite blue tracksuit and matching boot-slippers. As soon as Jodie arrived back in the apartment, she would always change into her most comfortable attire. She held her tiny black mobile phone in her right hand and bounced onto Stacey's bed on her knees.

"We're having pizza, is that okay?" Jodie announced. Both girls nodded. Jodie continued her order by phone to the local pizza parlour.

"Yeah, hello? I wanna place an order" Jodie continued. She went into overdrive as she lost herself in ordering the girl's favourite pizza with all the trimmings. They rarely varied from their tried and trusted meal, and Stacey and Angie listened to ensure that their flatmate got it right. As she finished the order, Jodie seemed to sense that she was missing out on something. She looked at both Stacey and Angie, searching their faces for clues.

"What's happening? What are you two talking about?" she asked. Stacey looked to Angie before answering for both of them.

"Oh the usual-men! Angie reckons that we're nearly past our sell-by date!" Stacey laughed. Gina glanced in through the now-open door. She ambled in to join her friends.

"No way! I'm the oldest, but I still feel like I'm only going on for twenty-eight! I've years yet before I'm consigned to the shelf!" Gina grinned. Gina was normally the funniest and quick-witted of the four. She specialised in telling rude jokes, and always saw the funny side in everything.

"Me too! I'm only twenty-seven. I'm practically a baby!" Jodie giggled. All four laughed together, but Angie was in a more philosophical mood.

"Seriously though girls, we're all pushing on in age by modern statistics. Isn't it amazing that we're all still single? I mean, our average age is over thirty, and yet none of us are near to settling down-never mind getting married!" Angie reasoned. It was all a bit too heavy for Gina. It was Saturday evening after all, and usually at this stage of the weekend they would be all in high spirits.

"Come on ladies, we're okay! Anyhow, marriage is not all that it's cracked up to be. Ask Stacey, she had a narrow escape-didn't you love?" Gina cackled mockingly. Jodie and Angie joined in the laughter, and Stacey playfully tossed a pillow in Gina's direction. Stacey offered Angie an apologetic look. Their serious conversation would have to wait for another time. Growing old was not something that any of Angie's flatmates wanted to consider, certainly not on a Saturday evening.

"What have you got planned for tonight Jodie? I suppose that you're going mountaineering or bungee-jumping with your mad pals?" Gina laughed. Jodie giggled again as she continued to bounce rhythmically on Stacey's bed.

"Not tonight Gina. Tonight we're going bowling, and then we're off to a beach party near Brittas Bay. And after that, who knows?" Jodie said indifferently. Angie hit her playfully with the pillow.

"You're mad you! Don't your little gang ever do anything normal?" Angie asked. All three watched Jodie continue to bounce slowly on the bed, as if hypnotised by her. Jodie's blonde pony-tail flicked from side to side as she practiced her neck exercises.

"Like sit in some boring bar holding some boring guy's hand? That's not for me Angie. I like a bit of action. Maybe when I'm your age!" Jodie replied. She jumped to her feet and pranced about the room, half dancing, half high-kicking.

"Ouch that hurt!" Gina grinned, giving Angie a wincing look. Angie grinned and shook her head.

"You'll meet someone soon Jodie. He'll sweep you off your feet, and then you'll descend into a life of drudgery like the rest of us!" Angie smirked, stubbing out her cigarette in an ashtray. Jodie continued to leap about.

"Not me girls! The man has not been born who could tame me! All that lovey-dovey stuff is for suckers! I'm a wild thing!" Jodie purred in a sexy voice, suddenly coming to a standstill. Jodie was from a small village in Kilkenny, to the south of Dublin. She had read an advert by the girls for someone to flat-share many years ago. All three had liked her instantly, and ever since, Jodie had become one of them.

They all laughed at Jodie's antics and continued to joke about. The mood was set for the evening. Later they ate pizza and watched some television.

Much later on, someone noticed the time and panic set in. It was time to prepare for their night out, and battle for the bathroom could begin in earnest.

Tony and Stacey left the busy lounge almost on the stroke of midnight. It had been a nice evening alone together. Tony had made a conscious effort not to dwell on his mother's death. They had talked briefly about the forthcoming funeral, but in general the evening had been cheerful and enjoyable.

"When does your sister get home Tony? Has she given you any indication?" Stacey asked as they stood for a moment outside the popular public house. Tony lit up a cigarette and inhaled sharply. Stacey watched as grey smoke bellowed from his nostrils, disappearing into the cool night air.

"No Stace, Jan will get here when she can. It must be a bit of a headache to organise flights for her family. I presume that they are all coming over. I'm looking forward to meeting Howard and the kids. And Jan of course" Tony said. He forced a smile, but looked uneasy.

"How do you feel about Jan? You hardly know her. It might be a bit strange for you Tony" Stacey said, noting Tony's nervous demeanour. Tony shrugged and drew on his cigarette.

"Nothing would surprise me about Jan. She keeps to herself Stace. It's an odd thing to say, but I barely know my own sister. She left Ireland when I was about six or seven. We hardly got on. I barely recall Howard. Because of the age gap, Jan and I barely talked. Howard appears to be a larger-than-life person. I think that he dominates Jan a little. It's just things that my Mam has said over the years. It's like Howard has some sort of hold on Jan" Tony said with a frown. Stacey linked her arm in his and patted his hand with her free hand as they made their way along the street.

"They are probably just a nice, normal couple. You haven't met either of them since Jan moved to The States. Before that, you cannot really say that you and Jan bonded. So let's just wait and see" Stacey said happily.

They reached the corner, which was always the point where they waited for a taxi. Tony paused just before the junction. He nodded towards an amorous couple up ahead of them.

"Better let them go first!" he said. Stacey observed the young giggling lovers. They were in their early twenties. Both only had eyes for each other. They were kissing and embracing, totally lost in a world of their own.

"I wonder if they are really waiting for a cab?" Stacey asked out loud.

"Huh! I think that it's a bed that they really need!" Tony commented. Stacey stifled a laugh, but it brought something to mind for Tony.

"Speaking of which, you could always come back to my place" Tony added in a more upbeat tone. The grin disappeared instantly from Stacey's face. It was the one suggestion that she had been praying not to hear that night.

"Not tonight Tony, I really do need a good sleep. I barely slept a wink last night. It was probably because I was in a strange bed" she replied defensively. Tony looked disappointed, but changed the topic.

"I don't know what will happen when Jan gets home. The house is rightly half hers. We will probably have to sell it. I might end up in an apartment or something" Tony said quietly. Stacey was surprised by his frankness. She had never really thought about where Tony stood legally regarding his family home. In a way she felt relieved that number 88 Saint Oliver's Road might be out of their lives forever. Then suddenly the thought that Tony could be flat-hunting hit her. Would he want her to move in with him? Could she bear to give up the cosy arrangement of living with her three girlfriends? It was something that Stacey Boyd was not so sure about.

"Jan would never throw you out of your home surely? The two of you would come to some financial arrangement" Stacey said.

"That's just it Stace. I could never afford to buy her out. The house must be worth a fortune on the open market. I realise that it needs a lot doing to it. But it's in a prime location. If we're forced to sell it, I could never afford a home in the same area. I guess that I would end up in some dreary flat on the outskirts of the city" Tony answered sadly.

By now the amorous younger couple had moved on. It appeared that they had changed their mind about hiring a taxi. They now stood in a doorway further up the street, passionately kissing.

Stacey decided to change the subject.

"I reckon that you were right about those two. If they don't get home soon it will be too late!" she said in a jocular tone. Instantly she could tell that her remarks were a bad idea. The look on Tony's face told her that he still harboured hopes that she might join him at his home.

Before Tony had a chance to invite her back again, a taxi screeched to a halt next to them. Stacey quickly jumped into the back seat, closely followed by the reluctant Tony. As he leaned forward to speak to the driver, Stacey suddenly felt guilty. Why would she not want to spend the night with her boyfriend? She put it down to her hatred of Tony Lee's home. But still she knew that there was something else. Guilt-ridden, Stacey reached out in the dark cab and held Tony's hand. Tony had asked the driver to drop Stacey off first. Stacey was relieved that at least she would not have to view his house again in the darkness. Her mind was churning. Tony meant everything to her, she told herself. Yet there was something not quite right. Her mind raced back to something Jodie had asked that afternoon.

Given the choice between Alex Woods and Tony, who had she really loved the most? Stacey Boyd refused to allow herself to answer truthfully. It was something that had never occurred to her before. She hated Alex so much for what he had done to her. Surely that answered the question outright? Or had it blinded her as to how much she had actually loved him? Now she felt her heart thumping as she recalled how much in love she and Alex had been.

"Anyway, by this time next week, it will all be settled. Mam will be laid to rest, and Jan will most likely be on her way back to California" Stacey heard Tony say. His voice seemed far away as she tried to wipe Alex Woods from her mind. She mumbled her agreement, but Alex's image still hung there in her thoughts. Now he was smiling back at her, that boyish, innocent smile that she had always loved. Perhaps it was the drink earlier, but suddenly Stacey felt no bitterness towards her ex-boyfriend. Something had stirred her senses again in favour of Alex Woods. Her brain was swimming with thoughts and mixed emotions. Stacey felt sure that Tony would notice, and yet she felt secure in the darkness of the black taxi.

"Will you come around in the morning Stace? Perhaps we could go for a spin in your car. Then maybe I could cook you dinner?" Tony said. He was looking directly at her in the semi-light from the street outside. Stacey hesitated. The cab rounded the corner to her apartment. She felt that she could not exit the car quickly enough. Feeling that Tony could sense her uneasiness, Stacey began to concoct her story.

"I'm not sure Tony. I think I promised Angie that I would drop her over to her parent's home. She asked me earlier this week before all this happened. Pity. Usually I'm at a loose end on Sunday mornings, looking for something to do. I'll tell you what love, I'll give you a call in the morning, okay?" she replied. Tony half-released his grip on her hand. The taxi drew up outside the three-storey apartment block.

She could feel the relief in her stomach. Still Alex Woods clung to her thoughts. Stacey was confused, amazed at what she was feeling. It was totally wrong, but there was a certain forbidden excitement about the situation. What did Alex feel about her now? What if they could possibly resurrect their life together? She must telephone him, she already knew that. Stacey almost felt that she could not get away from Tony quickly enough, at least to clear her head for a moment. Alex was pulling at her brain like some giant magnet. Almost dreamlike, she felt herself push open the cab door.

"Goodnight Tony, try and get a good night's sleep. I'll call you in the morning, yeah?" she said quietly. She gave him a quick peck on the cheek.

"It's not too late to change your mind" he whispered. Stacey managed a smile, but shook her head firmly.

"I'll phone you in the morning" she repeated. Tony sighed deeply and kissed her on the right cheek.

"Okay, tomorrow" he replied. Stacey Boyd exited the cab and watched as it drove away into the night. She hurried up the six steps to her building and opened the big glass door. Stacey felt like an excitable teenager once more. She felt lighter and alive. The lift stood open in the centre of the hallway ahead of her. She could not get to her apartment quickly enough. And yet, she did not know if she possessed the nerve to phone Alex that night. Could she? Inside the elevator, Stacey pressed the number three button that would take her to her third-floor apartment. Someone would be home, but it hardly mattered. Her room beckoned, at last to be alone with her private thoughts.

"Stacey, this is Philip. Phil, this is my best friend Stacey" Angie O'Rourke said politely. Philip rose from the large blue sofa to shake her hand. He was not how Stacey had pictured him at all. She had imagined Philip Westbourne as a hard, cynical, manipulative man, with a false smile and evasive eyes. In her mind's eye, Stacey had already judged Angie's new beau, but now he seemed gracious, almost the boy-next-door type. Philip was tall, with short blond hair and big brown eyes. He had a ready smile and was well-dressed in casual slacks, shirt and tie. Stacey hated to see men in slip-on shoes. She eyed the floor as she shook his hand. He wore highly polished black laced shoes, which met with her approval.

"I'm making coffee; do you fancy a cup Stacey?" Angie asked as she ambled towards the small kitchen to the left side of the sitting room.

"Yeah, okay Angie" Stacey answered. She would have preferred to go straight to bed, but it seemed impolite somehow. She sat opposite Philip on the large blue armchair and struck up a general conversation. Stacey made sure to keep the chat broad, well away from family and children. When Angie returned Stacey relaxed a little.

"God! Is that the time? It's after one o'clock! I'm off to bed before Jodie and Gina get back! Goodnight you two. Nice meeting you Philip. See you in the morning Angie" Stacey said. She had waited long enough until she felt the time was right. Stacey felt Angie's eyes on her, as if seeking approval for her new boyfriend. Stacey offered no visible sign. Her feeling on married men had not altered. Philip Westbourne seemed a perfectly decent companion for her best friend, but she could only hope that their relationship remained platonic. Stacey would hate to see Angie hurt again. Her best friend seemed to fall in love far too easily, although it had been sometime since Angie had dated a man seriously.

Stacey made her way to her bedroom and closed the door gently behind her. She quickly slipped into her favourite pink and white pyjamas and slid under the pale green duvet. It felt comforting to be back in her bed and smell the freshness from her fluffy white pillow. Now for the first time Stacey realised that there had been no smell or scent in Tony's room, or, for that matter, in the entire house. It was something that had never occurred to Stacey Boyd before.

Stacey shuddered as she recalled the previous night. She still could not come to terms with the strange sense of discomfort that she had felt at The Lee's home. Somehow she had never been at ease in that house, but Stacey had always presumed that it was because of Delores Lee. Now that whole house seemed to bring a certain panic to Stacey's brain.

She reached out to switch off the bedside lamp. It was only then that she remembered Alex Wood's mobile phone number. It was much too late to consider phoning him now. Anyway, she had lost her nerve. That rush that she had felt in the taxi had subsided now. A more sober Stacey picked up the slip of paper from the locker top. She studied the page, torn neatly from Angie's small notebook. Instantly she recognised Alex's writing. The numbers all slanted to the left. He had changed his mobile phone. It was definitely a different number to the one she remembered. Stacey idly wondered if he had done so to prevent her getting in touch. She had said some vile things to him on the phone when they had first split up. It was embarrassing now for her to recall, but at the time she had meant every word. He had jilted her after so many years together, and his feeble excuses had made her feel used and cheated. Now she could look back at those times in a more mature manner. Perhaps it was meant to happen that way. Maybe they had needed time apart to realise what they had together. Stacey recalled how Alex had begged her not to end their relationship. He had stressed that he merely wanted to postpone their wedding, and that he still loved her. Alex told her that his problem was that he was not ready for marriage just then. He had confided that he was scared to death of getting wed, and had only proposed because they had dated for so long. Alex had said that as the big day drew ever nearer, he realised that he could not go through with it. When he finally admitted his feeling just days before the wedding, Stacey Boyd had flipped. Despite his protests, she ended their relationship there and then. Alex would ring her seven or eight times a day, pleading with her to reconsider. It always ended with Stacey hanging up on him.

Stacey tucked the phone number under her pillow. Perhaps she would dream of Alex, something that she had never done since they split up. Momentarily she felt a little guilty about Tony Lee. It quickly evaporated. Alex was now uppermost in her thoughts. She would definitely call him soon. Part of her logic was that it would just be to apologise for the things that she had said. Deep in her soul, Stacey knew that this was not true. If she could rekindle her old romance right at that moment, she would gladly do so. She knew that now, despite quietly wrestling with her conscience.

As she settled down to sleep, it struck Stacey that to get back together with Alex, would mean having to break up with Tony. She tried to picture a scenario in which she would tell Tony that it was all over. The timing could not be worse for Tony Lee, she knew that. Tony had been good for her. He had been there for her when she desperately needed someone. Yet if she was honest, the magic was never really in their relationship. Perhaps both of them knew this all of the time. In the back of Stacey's mind, it seemed reasonable to assume that their romance had run its course. Maybe this was just her looking for an easy way out. Stacey yawned and closed her eyes. All of that was for tomorrow. Right now she needed to sleep.

Tony Lee woke up in a sweat. He leapt upright into a sitting position. Gasping for air, he glanced around in the blackness. He was breathing at a rapid rate, his heart pumped against his perspiring skin. Tony flopped back down and wiped beads of sweat from his forehead. A slow sigh of relief slipped from his dry mouth. It was another bad dream. Yet it seemed to be the same type of nightmare as the one before. He closed his eyes and pictured the child again. He could see the baby clearly. Somehow he knew that it was a boy, although there was nothing to indicate this. It was a clear, vivid image, and Tony felt sure that he had never seen this child before in his life.

"Who the hell is this kid?" he whispered, reaching for his cigarettes. He sat up and switched on the bedside lamp. The alarm clock told him that it was four-fifteen. He idly checked this with his watch. Tony felt wide awake now.

After some time, Tony gave up on any chance of falling back asleep. He threw back the duvet and tossed on some clothes. Perhaps a cup of coffee might help. It was almost five o'clock now and getting light.

Tony sat in the kitchen sipping black coffee from his favourite mug. For a while he thought about his dear mother, but then his mind flashed back to dream about the young child. There was something scary about the scene in his head, but Tony could not quite figure out why. The baby was crying, but was there some sort of weapon involved? He was not sure. Something told him that the child needed help, but how? Tony felt that he had awoken just at the critical time. If only he could recall what had startled him. As he reached the end of his coffee, Tony almost gave up trying to recall specific details. Perhaps Stacey was correct. His mother's death had most likely triggered it off. Maybe the nightmare was meaningless after all and would fade in time. What if it just represented him as a baby, being dependant on his mother?

Tony wondered if he had been a troublesome child. His mother had never indicated so. He stood up and casually walked towards the kitchen window and pulled back the heavy blue drapes. It was a calm morning outside. Tony Lee studied his ramshackle back garden. It was riddled with tall grass and overgrown weeds. The broken yellow lawnmower stood forlornly in the top left hand corner of the garden. It had packed in three months ago, and Tony had never got around to trying to fix it. It would be just another job on his ever-growing list of things to do. When his mother had become very ill, Tony had pushed most things to the back of his mind. Nothing had seemed very pressing, compared to his mother's health. Now he decided that he must pay more attention to jobs that needed doing. And then Tony remembered Jan. Perhaps there was no point. Jan would claim her inheritance, and the house might well be sold off as it was.

The thought of having to find a new home was heartbreaking for Tony, yet he did not begrudge his sister what was rightfully hers. He sat back down at the old kitchen table that had stood in the same position for as long as he could remember.

There seemed little point in returning to bed. Instead Tony settled for lying on the sofa in the sitting room. Eventually he drifted off into an uneven slumber.

Later that morning, Tony was awoken by the sound of his mobile phone's ringtone.

"Hello Tony. Listen, I have to drop Angie off at her folk's house. I'm sorry but we won't be able to meet up after all. I'll call you later today, all right? Did you sleep okay?" Stacey said. Tony smiled dryly and rubbed his eyes with his free hand.

"Not too good Stace. What time is it now?" he replied. She told him that it was after nine o'clock, and that she would phone later. The call was over in seconds, and once again Tony was wide awake.

As they drove to Skerries on the outskirts north of the city, Stacey knew in advance what the talking point would be. Angie was bound to ask Stacey her opinion on Philip Westbourne, and she was also sure to mention Alex Woods again. Stacey knew the route to Angie's family home well. She had driven Angie to her aging parent's house many times before.

"Well, come on Stacey, what's the verdict on Philip?" Angie asked suddenly. Stacey grinned contently to herself.

"Ha! I wondered how long it would take! It went very quiet last night when I went to bed. I hope that you didn't sneak him into your room!" Stacey chuckled.

"No way! You know the house rules! He left about twenty minutes later. I told you Stacey, we're just mates. Don't be avoiding the question. He's a nice guy, isn't he?" Angie replied. Stacey said nothing for a couple of seconds.

"He seems okay Angie, but I won't change my mind. Married men spell trouble. My advice would be to keep it to the confines of the office. Once you start dating this chap, you are bound to become involved. He will end up going back to his wife and kids, mark my words" Stacey concluded. Her eyes never left the road, but her tone left Angie in no doubt about her pal's thoughts on the matter.

There was no more said on the subject and the two made idle conversation for a while.

"So when are you going to give Alex a bell?" Angie asked with a twinkle in her brown eyes. Angie then bit her lip to suppress the laughter. Stacey shook her head wryly.

"You know what Angie O'Rourke? I can read you like a book! You are so predictable. If I ever did get in touch with Alex Woods, it would only be to give him a piece of my mind! Now can we drop the subject?" Stacey said with a playful giggle.

"But you haven't actually said that you won't call him! I know you well Stacey Boyd! Somewhere in the deepest recesses of your heart, a torch still burns for Alex Woods. I won't stop until you admit that you still fancy him!" Angie cackled. Stacey said nothing. She knew well that she could never fool her old pal. All she could do was to take the easy way out.

"I'm not listening!" Stacey replied, reaching for the volume button on the car radio. She hired up her favourite radio station and sang along with whatever song was playing. Angie quickly joined in, as the two friends made light of their respective romantic positions.

By the time that they returned to their apartment later that day, both girls felt extremely tired. Both Gina and Jodie were out, and within minutes Stacey and Angie had fallen asleep in the living room. They slept soundly into the late evening, until a boisterous Jodie disturbed them. The strong aroma of burger and chips wafted under Stacey's nose. Jodie held the open brown bag under Stacey's distorting face. Stacey twitched and grimaced on the propped-up pillow as she tried to avoid the strong smell. Her left hand shot out and tried to shoo the pungent smell away. Stacey could hear giggling in her subconscious and awoke suddenly.

"God Jodie! Take it away-please!" she groaned. Angie was awake opposite her now, and joined in with Jodie's laughter.

"Want a few chips Stace?" Jodie giggled. She plonked down next to Stacey and dangled a chip over her flatmates' mouth.

"No I do not! We had something in Angie's parent's house" Stacey yawned. Jodie shrugged indifferently

"Suit yourself. Shouldn't you be making yourself beautiful for the delectable Tony?" Jodie asked casually, shoving yet more chips into her mouth. Stacey glanced at her watch. It was almost six o'clock.

"God! The whole day is gone! What happened to the weekend?" Stacey said.

"It's not over yet! Angie wants me to go out with her tonight, don't you Ange?" Jodie replied, now chomping on her giant burger. Stacey watched her for a moment, fascinated that such a thin person could eat so much junk food. It seemed to be Jodie's staple diet, and she had often admitted that she could live on such foodstuffs for the rest of her life.

"Yeah, we can go out for a drink, but don't call me Ange. It's Angela or Angie" Angie O'Rourke replied as she struggled to get comfortable again on the armchair. Her name was one of the few things that Angie was sensitive about.

"Whatever, touchy! Where will we go then?" Jodie asked through a mouthful of burger. Suddenly Stacey seemed interested in their plans. All of a sudden a night out with her pals held great appeal. She felt refreshed after her long nap, and now the thought of going out with Tony was not so attractive.

"Hey! Why don't we all go out together? Gina is always up for a night out, and I could do with a good laugh" Stacey said cheerfully. Angie seized on the opportunity for some mischief-making.

"What? You can't go! What about Tony? You can't abandon him at a time like this" Angie said playfully. Stacey made light of her pals remarks.

"Tony will understand. I'll text him now" Stacey said, reaching across the rectangular coffee table for her phone.

Minutes later the three were making plans. Tony had texted back to tell Stacey to enjoy herself. He would be off work that week on compassionate leave, and would be in touch. Tony was not in a fun mood, but saw no purpose in Stacey moping about.

Jan Williams arrived at Dublin Airport early on Monday morning. She had not slept well on the long flight, and had had to endure a stopover at Shannon Airport. Her mind was overactive now, as she struggled with thoughts of her past, and her late mother's burial.

Jan trudged wearily through the terminal and out into the early morning air. It felt good to finally inhale some fresh air. She could not say that she was pleased to set foot on Irish soil once again. Four taxis waited in line. The fact that all four cars were of different colours and makes hit Jan. It was another of the quirky things about Dublin that she had forgotten about.

She set off for Dublin City and her pre-booked hotel room. As the cab driver drove on, Jan watched out of the side window for familiar sights. She reached into her purse and studied the paper money she had acquired before leaving California. The currency was different now from her younger days in Dublin. Jan vacantly wondered how much the cab fare would cost as she gazed out at the bleak landscape of North Dublin. They were well into their journey before the taxi driver spoke.

"I'm guessing that you're home to see the folks. By your accent I would say that you've been in America for some considerable time" said the elderly man. He had been observing Jan in his rear-view mirror.

"Sorry?" said Jan, awaking from her private daydream.

"I was just surmising that you were home for a quick visit to see the family. Sorry. You see, it's a game I play. I'm usually right too. I eye up how much luggage folk have, observe their body language, and listen to their accent" said the grey-haired stocky man in his flat Dublin accent. Jan managed a smile, knowing that she was been watched in the mirror.

"Yeah, I've been away for many years. I live in Santa Monica in California now. My Mom passed away. She had been ill for some time" Jan said without little emotion. The cab driver felt a little uncomfortable. He had not meant to pry, but was merely making conversation.

"Oh I'm so sorry dear. Silly me" he mumbled.

"No, it's okay, really. It's nice to hear a Dublin brogue again" Jan replied, doing her utmost to put him at ease. He nodded back and sat up straight.

"Ah, the old place hasn't changed really. More traffic, that's all. The ol' place is chocker day and night now. Other than that, it's just as you left it. Have you been away long love?" the man said, steering the chat away from Jan's late mother.

"Almost thirty years. We always meant to come back and visit, but the years ticked away. I have two children, you know how it is. Now it's much too late" Jan said, her voice now filled with emotion. It was hitting home that she had missed the chance to say goodbye to her mother. The taxi driver failed to notice. He was busy negotiating a left-hand turn in the early morning traffic.

"Ah well, at least you'll get the chance to catch up with old friends. There must be lots of folk that you would like to see. Are you staying long?" asked the man. He was now only half-listening as the traffic grew more intense.

"Only a few days. I just want to see my brother and lay my Mom to rest. After that I will be heading back" Jan replied. He nodded as if to acknowledge that he understood, but he was really putting an end to the conversation. They were almost at their destination, and already he was planning on which taxi rank he would use in pursuit of his next fare.

Once Jan had settled into her hotel room, she phoned Tony. With the six hour time difference, it was still far too early to call home.

"Hello Tony? This is Jan; I just want to let you know that I've arrived in Dublin. I plan on getting some sleep. It's been a long flight. Perhaps we could meet up later this evening?" she said casually.

"Jan, is that really you? You're here? Where are you staying?" Tony stuttered. He had not been expecting a call from his sister, and was taking completely unawares.

"I'm in The Shelbourne Hotel in the city centre. I booked it before I travelled. It's nice and central for everything" she replied.

"But Jan, I presumed that you would come here. Why not come and stay with me?" a baffled Tony said. A moment's silence ensued before Jan spoke again.

"I don't want to impose Tony. Anyway, I'll be much more comfortable here. Look Tony, I can't face the house at the moment. There are too many memories for me to cope with. Listen, I really need to grab some rest. I'll phone again later when I wake up. We can meet up and sort something out, okay?" Jan said, now in a softer tone.

"I...I suppose so Jan. Do you want my mobile number?" Tony replied.

"What? Sorry, we say cell phone. No, it's okay. I'll phone the house again. You'll be there, won't you?" Jan said. It sounded more like a demand rather than a request.

"Sure Jan, I'll be here" Tony replied. He listened as the line went dead. He replaced the cream telephone receiver and ambled back to the kitchen. It sounded odd that she had booked into a hotel, and Tony now wondered if Jan had come alone. He had not thought to ask if Howard or the children had travelled with her.

Tony tried to rationalise Jan's coldness towards him. Perhaps their mother's death had hit Jan more that he had realised. He would not really be able to tell until they met face to face. Jan's tone was almost furtive and distant on the phone. He decided not to prejudge her. The main thing was that she was finally home, and he needed her by his side now to face this trying time together.

Jan Williams woke with a start in her hotel room. The clank of the cleaner's trolley as it passed in the corridor outside had disturbed her. She sighed as she turned on her side, now facing away from the large window. The heavy floral curtains were drawn tight, yet the light from the early afternoon still somehow managed to seep through. Jan liked routine and order. Sleeping during the day was ridiculous, and yet she needed to catch up on her rest. The days ahead would be a big test of her resolve. Although she already felt mentally strong enough to cope, her physical strength was important also. The noise from the corridor had now abated. Jan tried not to dwell on her mother's death. She searched her brain for other things to focus on. Josh and Amy danced into her mind. They were a more palatable subject rather than her forthcoming meeting with Tony. She again tried to sleep, keeping her children at the forefront of her thoughts. At that moment she needed something more dependable and familiar to cling to. Tony could wait until she was more lucid.

It was Monday evening and Stacey was driving home from work. Her mobile rang on her hands-free set, and she watched as Tony's name flashed up on screen. Jan had phoned Tony back a second time to arrange a meeting.

"Stace? It's Tony. Listen, Jan is home from America. We're meeting up tonight, so I can't call around to you. That is, unless you fancy tagging along with me?" Tony said. He paused to let her know it was an invitation.

"What? Oh no thanks Tony, I would only feel in the way. You two will have lots to catch up on. You go alone. Hey, what do you mean that you are meeting up with her? Did you not say that Jan would be staying at your house?" she replied. There was a brief silence.

"Well no Stacey. You see, Jan felt a little awkward about that. Too many memories and all that. By the way, she's travelling alone. Something about Howard having to work" Tony said in a defensive mode.

"Oh right. Anyway, you don't want me there playing gooseberry. You two will want to discuss the funeral and the house. I can meet her at the Mass on Wednesday evening, okay? If you need me for anything, phone me" Stacey replied. She wanted him to feel that she was there to help, but inside Stacey was rejoicing in the fact that they would not have to meet up that evening.

"No, I think that everything is taken care of. Still, I'll miss seeing you tonight Stace" he said quietly.

"Me too. Listen, you haven't changed your mind about having people back to the house, have you?" she asked. Stacey held her breath.

"No. That is definite. Neither of my aunts will be attending as far as I know. Jan said that she phoned my Auntie Mary in England to tell her that her sister had died. She said that Auntie Mary barely responded. Jan then telephoned back later to ask if she was coming over. She said that Mary practically hung up on her. Cheek! It appears that Auntie Mary is a bitter old woman. Whatever happened between her and my Mam has left a deep scar. I asked Jan about it, but she seemed reluctant to discuss it" Tony said.

"Never mind Tony, you can only do your best. Old people can be very set in their ways. It's probably over something trivial-it usually is. Why not send your aunt something of your Mam's, you know, when the funeral is over? What about a nice ring or broach, a kind of keepsake?" Stacey suggested. Tony liked the idea. He vowed to do so, and then the conversation turned to idle chat.

"Yeah, we had a great giggle last night. The Jodie one is nuts! She's a real tomboy. When I met her first I was a bit sceptical about her. She gets up to such weird stuff. Now I realise that she's just a ball of energy. We got home at all hours. How I got up for work today, I don't know. Anyhow, how did you sleep?" Stacey said.

Tony told her about his second nightmare. Stacey felt her blood run cold. It was as if she was again back in Tony's bed, reliving his horrible dream.

"Stop Tony, I don't want to hear about it. It's creepy" Stacey replied. Tony laughed and said that he would be in touch.

"Oh, give Jan my love. Tell her that I'm looking forward to meeting her" Stacey said. The line went dead, and Stacey Boyd breathed a sigh of relief. She felt a little guilty, but the bottom line was that she did not have to meet up with Tony that evening.

"Hiya Jan, you're looking very well" Tony said as they met up. The setting was outside a city centre pub, with Jan arriving thirty minutes after the agreed time. She had deliberately come late, not wanting to stand outside alone. Tony embraced her, but felt awkward in doing so. Jan barely responded. For her it felt inappropriate to hug. They were practically strangers, and a simple handshake would feel much more natural. It felt surreal to be back in Dublin, meeting up with Tony again. He felt and looked like a complete stranger.

Tony led the way inside, and they sat at a small out-of-the-way corner table. A young lounge boy approached them as they made themselves comfortable. Almost as an afterthought they ordered drinks.

"Well Tony, how are you keeping?" she asked politely.

"Great, yeah, I'm still working away. How are the family?" he replied. The conversation continued in the same way for some time. It was similar to the opening round in a boxing match, with both contestants testing out the other. Both knew that soon they would have to get down to business, but for now they were content to spar.

It was a dull Monday evening, and they were seated in The Oak Tavern in Dame Street, a venue suggested by Tony. Jan was hardly in a position to bargain. Dublin was a stranger to her now. She could barely remember streets, never mind restaurants or bars. Jan's suggestion to rendezvous at her hotel had been countered with Tony's bid to meet up at the family home. The Oak was a compromise, reluctantly accepted by Jan.

Eight square beer mats stood like sentries guarding each area of the shiny brown rectangular table. Tony picked up one of the green and red cardboard mats and played with it haphazardly. The young lounge boy reappeared with their drinks. Tony fished in his wallet to pay, but Jan beat him to it. More idle chat followed, with Jan describing life in California, and how Dublin had changed for the worse.

After some five minutes or so, Tony Lee finally gave up the charade. They were there to discuss their late mother. There was no point in avoiding the topic.

"She battled right to the end Jan" Tony said. Jan felt compelled to respond.

"Yeah, Mom was a fighter okay. You did a great job looking after her Tony. I want to thank you for that. I will always be grateful" she said. Her eyes flicked nervously in his direction, refusing to make complete eye contact. Jan was wearing a smart grey trouser suit and simple white blouse.

"I only did what anyone would do. The house is so empty without her Jan" he replied, his voice almost breaking. Tony was wearing black casual slacks and a white shirt and black tie. Jan Williams glanced at him uncomfortably. She hoped that he could hold it together. It would not be easy to cradle him in her arms if he broke down. Tony did not feel like her baby brother now. Time and distance had eroded any bond that she might have felt for him.

"Hush Tony, don't go upsetting yourself" Jan whispered. Tony swallowed hard and nodded.

"I'm okay, really I am" he whispered. The attentive lounge boy hovered in the background, buoyed up by the fact that Jan had given him a big tip earlier. Tony was halfway through his pint of lager, but noticed that Jan had almost finished her drink.

"I'll get the next drink" Tony said.

"Tony dear, I wasn't planning on making a night of it. We'll just have one or two drinks and leave it at that. I'm still exhausted after the long flight. I really do need a good night's sleep. The jet lag and the time difference really do take it out of you" she said, stifling a yawn. Tony looked surprised.

"But things need sorting Jan. I brought Mam's insurance policy with me. The funeral will be expensive, Then there's the house-not to mention Mam's jewellery" Tony said in a hurried voice. Jan appeared agitated.

"I know, I know. I'll take the insurance policy with me and phone them myself. The funeral will be fine. You and Stacey did well to organise it. We can pay for it out of Mam's bank account. The rest will take care of itself. Regarding Mom's jewellery, all I want is to keep Mom's wedding and engagement rings" she replied. Her eyes questioned him. Tony shrugged and sipped on his drink.

"Whatever Jan, I don't mind. I was thinking that we might send Auntie Mary some jewellery. You know, as a keepsake" Tony said. He looked to Jan for approval.

"I'm not sure that that's a good idea. I telephoned Mary again this evening. I even offered to pay her fare to come over for Mom's funeral. She refused point blank" Jan replied, clearly miffed at the mention of Mary's name.

"Jan, whatever happened between Mam and Auntie Mary? They used to be close years ago, weren't they?"Tony said. Jan squirmed in her seat. Her lined face told Tony that she would rather not discuss it.

"They were close Tony, but they fell out over something silly. I think that it had something to do with Aunt Ethel. It's best forgotten really. The longer it went on, the harder it was for either of them to back down" Jan said tersely. Tony felt like talking. He sat back in his seat and began to open up to his sister. "Sometimes Mam would begin to tell me things from the past. Suddenly she would clam up, as if she had already said too much. We were so close, right until the end of her life. Yet there was something odd, something that I cannot quite put my finger on" Tony said. He looked to his sister as if half expecting an explanation. Jan's eyes had already moved away to avert his gaze.

"It's not best to dwell on Auntie Mary, Tony. Every family has a black sheep. She's just a bitter old lady. Let's just make sure that Mom has a nice send off, eh?" Jan said, at last managing a forced smile. Tony nodded with a grin. His expression changed as he brought up the subject that occupied his mind most. "Jan, about the house. I wish that you would stay on and deal with the sale. I am absolutely useless at anything like this. I mean, what would be its current value? Should I just wait and see what an estate agent says?" Tony said. It was a plain innocent request, yet Jan looked at him as if he had committed a heinous crime.

"What are you saying Tony? You must never sell the house. Didn't Mom tell you? That's your home, for God's sake! Where would you go if we sold it? I promised Mom that the house would be yours. Gee! We discussed it several times over the phone. She should have told you Tony" Jan said with a tone of disbelief. Her voice was shaky now as she digested his words. Without her spectacles on, Jan appeared older than her years. Her forehead was now furrowed with lines, and her old-fashioned hairstyle did her no favours. Her aging face struck Tony Lee too. He noticed the pained expression on his sister, and the web of lines around her eyes. Jan was fourteen years older than him, yet her demeanour seemed to almost double the tally. Jan's voice sounded almost incredulous at having to explain the situation to him.

"I, I don't understand Jan. The house must be worth quite a bit. I mean, what does Howard think? Look Jan, unless we sell the house, I won't be able to pay you your share. I haven't got that sort of money. I'm not even sure how much money Mam had. We never talked about things like that" Tony replied. His voice was trembling now, realising the magnitude of the conversation. It seemed inconceivable that his mother had never told him the house was his inheritance, yet Jan sounded so convincing. Perhaps his dear mother could never face talking about leaving him all alone. He stared again at his sister. He barely knew her, yet she appeared to know their mother better than he did.

"Listen Tony, it's simple. Howard and I have already talked about this several times. His business is doing fine, so are we. Mom wanted you to stay in the family home, in fact she insisted. There will be no payment by you to us-that's final! Regarding Mom's cash, well, I suppose that I'll have to pay a visit to the house and look things over. But once that's sorted out, the place is yours. I'm amazed Mom never told you. I'm hardly going to put my own brother out on the street, now am I?" she said assuredly. Tony Lee managed a sheepish smile. His overriding emotion was one of relief. The news meant that he could stay put. There would be no search for a new apartment after all. It appeared an over-generous act by a sister who he barely knew, but Tony was not about to turn down her kind offer.

"Jeez Jan, that would be great news for me if you really mean it. I can't deny that I was really worried. The price of apartments here are going through the roof-if you pardon the pun! If I had to sell the house and split the proceedings, well, I don't know where I would end up. I'm surprised Mam never said. Still, if that's what she wanted..." Tony concluded.

Jan smiled again and sipped her drink. The ice cubes clinked together in the small glass. She had opted for a gin and tonic. Jan was not a big drinker, and seldom ventured out for social occasions. Her life now was based on her family. There had been a time when a visit to the pubs in Dublin City excited her. Now it left her feeling cold and uncomfortable.

Tony ordered the same drinks again from the attentive lounge boy. The evening was turning out to be a better than expected one for him.

"Let's have no more talk of selling houses. Howard is fine with it, I promise you. It's what Mom would have wanted too, so the matter is closed. It's yours to enjoy for the rest of your life. You have a readymade home for you and Stacey. Hey! On that subject, should you and your girlfriend not be thinking of starting a family? You're not getting any younger either you know!" Jan said with a chuckle.

Tony felt more at ease at last. Finally Jan was opening up.

"How old are Amy and Josh again?" he asked.

"Fourteen and sixteen. You would think at that age I could finally relax, but every day is a struggle" she said with a sigh. It struck Tony that Jan must have had her children while in her thirties.

"I can't imagine having kids now. The chance has probably passed me by" Tony remarked. Jan shook her head.

"Nonsense! I left it very late, I'll admit. At first Howard did not want children. It was only when his business took off that we decided to start a family. I would advise you not to wait too long Tony. My two have me worn out!" she replied. Jan's forthrightness surprised Tony. It struck him that it was the first time he had heard Jan utter a light-hearted remark since he had known her. He thought it necessary to explain about his relationship with Stacey Boyd.

"Thanks Jan for the advice! You see, myself and Stacey are not like a conventional couple. Perhaps it was all that business with Mam being unwell all of the time. My time was preoccupied with taking care of Mam. Stacey and I only saw each other when we could. I was a terrible boyfriend over the last few years. And Stace is such a great girl. You'll love her when you finally meet her Jan" Tony gushed, at last relaxing in the company of his sister.

As if by a secret signal, Jan Williams quickly reverted to type. Her facial expression changed, and her tone of voice became less friendly.

"There won't be time for that really. Remember, I'm only here to lay our Mom to rest. I'm not here to become friendly with your girlfriend. Once the loose ends are tied up, I will be off home again. We can always keep in touch by phone. I dread to think how the children are getting on without me" Jan said tersely. Her tone sounded aloof and distant. She again avoided eye contact. Tony sat to the left of her, but Jan had ensured that there was an acceptable gap between their chairs.

Tony Lee could feel the chill in her voice. For a brief second Jan had let down her guard. Now the shield was firmly back in place. She was once again the cold, unfeeling sister that he had never really known. He felt like grabbing her by the wrists and shaking her. There were so many things unsaid. This was probably his only chance to ever meet her alone. Once the funeral Mass kicked in, they would be surrounded by mourners and strangers. Jan had her family now. It was okay for her. She had her husband and children. Tony felt alone and confused. He wanted to tell her how much he needed to talk to her. To pull at her heartstrings. To pour out his soul to her. Somehow he knew that it would be in vain. He recalled the cold, robotic voice that telephoned the house while his mother was alive. That was the real Jan. In his heart, Tony knew that once his mother's funeral was over, Jan would disappear from his life forever. She would flit out of his life as quickly as she had arrived, leaving him to face his loneliness.

"Have you any photos of the children Jan? I often wonder about them" Tony said gently. Jan seemed to soften slightly. Her lips curled up as she thought of her two beloved children at home. Jan produced some pictures of her family from her handbag and handed them to Tony. Already he had seen snaps of his nephew and niece as young children. He studied each one carefully, taking in their features. One of Amy alone. One of Josh in his basketball gear. A family snap, with Howard in the centre, Jan standing above him, and the two children either side of their father. Tony could not help but feel a pang of jealousy. He had never experienced a real family life, either with his parents or as a father. "Yeah, I would hardly recognise them. Very nice Jan, very nice indeed. You have a lovely family" he whispered, swallowing hard.

"Thanks. You can keep those snaps Tony. I have plenty at home. They grow up so fast. I worry more about them now than I did when they were younger" Jan said, letting her guard down a little.

"And Howard, how is he?" Tony inquired softly. He still desperately hoped that Jan might open up a bit more.

"Oh, Howard is Howard. His work is his life. Howard is the type of man who puts his heart and soul into everything that he does. I barely see him nowadays. If he's not working, he's sleeping. I swear that if his store went belly-up, he would immediately turn his hand to something else. Howard is a workaholic" Jan said.

A brief silence allowed Jan to announce her quick departure.

"Anyway Tony, I really have to go. I need a good night's sleep. I'll telephone you tomorrow and we can run through what needs to be done" Jan said with a yawn.

She gulped down her drink and stood up immediately. Tony looked disappointed. He searched his brain for something to say, but already Jan was placing the insurance documents in her handbag and closing it firmly.

"You're going to have to come around to the house Jan. Mam's financial situation and the funeral bill will need sorting. Then there's her clothes and jewellery, not to mention her life insurance. The deeds of the house will need transferring, and I don't know if there's a will involved. Jan looked irritated.

"Yes, yes, I'm not forgetting Tony. Look, right now I can barely think straight. I'll call around in the morning, is that what you want?" Jan said abruptly. Tony rose to his feet and nodded.

"I'm sorry Jan. I'm useless on my own" he muttered. Jan Williams seemed to relent a little. She buttoned her coat and managed a reassuring smile.

"It will be okay Tony, I promise. Hey, you look like that you could do with a good night's sleep too. Come on, walk me to a taxi, and you get off home as well. I'll phone you in the morning" she said. Tony slipped on his black jacket and rose to his feet. He left the remains of his drink and dutifully followed his sister to the exit.

"I hope that I can sleep Jan. I've been having nightmares lately. It's not like me. Normally I'm a great sleeper. I pray that it's a passing thing" Tony said abstractly.

"I'm sure that it will pass. Once Mom is laid to rest you'll be okay. It's bound to have an effect after looking after Mom for so long" Jan said. She surprised Tony by giving him a kiss on the cheek as they stood for a moment outside the pub doors.

"Oh, it's nothing to do with Mam. No. In these dreams there's a baby. I don't know what the heck it means. Sure I haven't been in contact with a baby for years!" Tony said with a nervous chuckle.

"It will just be the funeral Tony. Don't let it bother you. Hey! There's a cab now! I better dash before someone else grabs it! Call you tomorrow Tony. Sleep tight" Jan said in a hurried voice. Before Tony could reply, she was gone into the night.

He waved until the grey taxi had disappeared from view. Tony turned away. He decided on the spur of the moment to walk home. For him, taxis were a waste of money. Anyway, the walk would help him think.

Ten minutes later, Tony Lee was on the outskirts of the city centre. He considered what life must be like for Jan. It would be something beyond his imagination in his humdrum world. His sister was a conundrum. Even in their first encounter that evening, he had seen many different sides to her. She struck him as a very private person who fiercely guarded her personal life. Tony could never object to that. That was her prerogative. If only she would let him in. Yet Tony Lee decided that it would never be. Once Jan returned to Santa Monica, she would probably never set foot in Ireland again.

Tony considered his own future. He felt relieved that he would not have to move home. Jan's gift of the family home was a welcome bonus. Then he remembered Stacey's dislike of number 88 St. Oliver's Road. If they were to have a life together, it was something that they had to resolve. Perhaps now that the house was rightly his, Stacey might change her mind. They could redecorate. Stacey could put her mark on the old place. Perhaps like him, Stacey Boyd might learn to love the old house in time.

CHAPTER FOUR

MOVING ON

The house phone rang in Tony Lee's hall. In the quiet surrounding of 88 St. Oliver's Road, it gave him a sudden start. He turned and walked briskly towards the cream old-fashioned phone near the front door.

"Hello Tony? It's Jan. Listen, I'm on my way over. Put the kettle on. I should be there in about fifteen minutes" she said in a cheery voice. Tony told his sister that he would have the tea ready when she called. He smiled as he put the phone down. Now at last they could talk. His sister was finally coming home. They could make up for lost time, and speak honestly and openly.

There was a spring in Tony's step as he returned to the kitchen. He filled the old silver electric kettle and switched it on. Now in automatic mode, Tony opened the old-style cupboard and extracted two shiny cups with matching saucers. It was his mother's favourite set of china, reserved for special guests. Normally Tony would prefer his favourite blue mug, but he wanted to make a good impression. He took out the best milk jug and sugar bowl and filled both receptacles, but felt that something was not quite right.

"Biscuits!" he exclaimed in a loud voice with utter disbelief. He had not done his weekly shop because of his mother's passing. There were no cakes or biscuits in the food cupboard.

"I could make sandwiches. No, the bread is not very fresh. Shit!" he mumbled. Tony Lee made for the door, grabbing his keys as he went. He unlocked his bicycle at the end of the garden and made off in double quick time for the local shop. It would only take a few minutes, and he would leave nothing to chance in his mission to impress Jan.

When Tony returned he discovered to his horror that Jan was waiting at the garden gate. An irritable look was etched on her face. Tony began to question the wisdom of his trip to the shop. He leapt from the bike and mounted the pavement, all in one swift movement. Jan opened the gate, allowing him to wheel his silver bicycle through into the garden.

"Sorry Jan. Mrs. Jordan delayed me. She was asking about our Mam's funeral arrangements. I couldn't get away from her. She owns the shop down the road and knew Mam well. Sorry again" Tony said.

Jan said nothing. She followed Tony to the old green front door, her brown handbag dangling unevenly from her shoulder. She wore a matching brown trouser suit, with a simple grey blouse beneath it. Jan stood impassively as Tony fiddled with his small bunch of keys. It was a calm overcast morning, slightly chilly for the time of year. Tony opened the creaky front door and went inside. Jan seemed to freeze for a moment, as if steeling herself before entering her old family home. She had been away for so long, yet nothing had really changed. The front door was still the familiar green colour, and as far as she was aware, the décor in the hallway was still the same. Tony was already in the kitchen, emptying a packet of biscuits onto a plate from his mother's best china.

"Make yourself at home Jan, I'll bring the tea through in a second" he shouted in a loud voice.

"No" said Jan, appearing suddenly in the doorway.

"I would prefer to sit in here. The kitchen will do fine" she said firmly. She tossed her handbag strap across the back of a kitchen chair and took a seat facing the window, avoiding Tony's intrusive stare.

"Sure Jan, we've no need to stand on ceremony, eh? Mam used to like to entertain folk in the living room. Do you remember?" Tony replied chirpily.

"I'm hardly here to be entertained Tony. I just want to get Mom's affairs in order. I felt awful hanging about outside the house. Whatever were you thinking?" she said in a cold, terse voice. Tony was taken aback by her remarks. He had been away for no more than ten minutes. He vowed not to irk his sister any further. Tony apologised again, and explained about the shopkeeper asking a lot of questions.

"I only popped out for a packet of biscuits Jan. That woman would talk for Ireland!" he said, trying to make light of the situation.

"I don't need to be cosseted, and I'm not interested in silly biscuits. Why can't people mind their own business anyway?" Jan snapped. Tony bit his bottom lip. Moments early Jan had seemed so cheerful on the telephone. He hesitantly placed the tea and biscuits down beside her at the table.

"Sorry Jan, but folk will ask questions. Mam only knew a few people around here, but they are bound to want to offer their condolences" he replied as apologetically as he dared. Jan seemed to reconsider her rather petulant stance.

"No, you're right of course Tony. I'm sorry. All this business has made me snappy. You were only doing what you thought was for the best. Look, never mind. Let's start over again. Now, have you got all of Mom's paperwork to hand? She used to keep everything in that box on top of the wardrobe in her bedroom" Jan said, forcing a smile. Tony was still on his feet, fussing about in the kitchen area behind his sister.

"Yep Jan, it's still there! I'll fetch it for you" Tony replied cheerfully. He left the room without waiting for a response.

Jan sighed heavily as she looked around the kitchen for the first time. It had different wallpaper and had been painted, but nothing much had changed. The old blue and white cupboard was still there, and the rough-looking ceiling had had a lick of white emulsion. The memories flooded back. A thousand thoughts danced through her head. Jan flinched. It was time to be strong.

Tony returned with the large white shoebox in double-quick time.

"There we go sis, everything is in there. I had a quick glance through it yesterday. There are lots of old documents, the insurance policy that I gave you last night was in there, bank statements, even Mam's old Prize Bonds. She was always so sure that she would win on those one day!" Tony said with a forced laugh.

"Can you fetch my handbag please Tony? I need my reading glasses" Jan asked dismissively. She pointed at her handbag, hanging on a chair just feet away.

Tony said nothing. He quickly realised the gravity of the situation. It would be hard for Jan to rummage through her mother's personal details. He dutifully took the bag by its long strap and delicately held it before Jan. She took the bag without saying a word and removed her yellow spectacle case from it.

Tony felt surplus to requirements. Jan was spreading papers across the round table now. Tony had planned to join her with his cup of tea. Instead he settled for standing some distance away, sipping from his teacup.

After what seemed like an age to Tony, Jan suddenly placed her reading glasses back in the yellow case and snapped it shut.

"Everything seems in good order, just like Mom said it would be. I phoned the insurance company this morning. Mom's funeral will be well covered, with a bit of cash to spare. There is about forty thousand in the bank. The house insurance and everything else is paid up to date. Once the will is read, the house will be yours Tony. The money in Mom's account will be split between both of us" Jan said in a businesslike tone.

Tony was a little taken aback. He had not heard of a will. Nor did he know the extent of his mother's bank account.

"I don't understand Jan. I never knew about Mam having a will, or a solicitor. I knew she had some money, but I never read her bank details" Tony said with surprise.

"Oh, the details are in that yellow envelope, just as she said on the phone. Her solicitor is John Tomlinson, an old friend of Mom's" Jan said in a matter-of-fact tone. Again Tony looked surprised.

"But surely I would know about him. I mean, I brought Mam everywhere that she needed to go. Most times I did the running around myself" Tony said defensively.

"Well, I expect that Mr. Tomlinson visited Mom during the day, you know, when you were at work. It makes sense Tony. She wouldn't want you worrying about things or about the future" Jan said.

She was now carefully placing the lid back tightly on the old shoebox.

Tony felt a little undermined. He had always thought that he and his mother had discussed everything openly. Now it appeared that his sister knew much more than he did. In a small way, Tony felt betrayed. All of those whispered phone calls had been about his future. His mother and sister had plotted what would happen after his dear mother had died. It appeared that Jan had the upper hand after all. She would lead the way now, and he must follow.

"Will we have to go and visit this...this solicitor chap?" Tony asked. Jan sighed and sipped on her tea. She selected a biscuit and bit into it. The irony was not lost on Tony. Minutes earlier she had berated him for going to buy the "silly things".

"I expect so. I'm sure that Mr. Tomlinson can fit us in before I return home. He was a friend of Mom's after all. Besides, it's no big deal. Mr. Tomlinson deals with matters like this every day" Jan said confidently.

Tony nodded. It sounded bizarre, almost over the top. It appeared that all of those years of hushed calls and hidden details were simply to keep him out of his mother's affairs. He reckoned that his mother could simply have explained what her wishes were to him. Tony felt sure that he could have dealt with everything, rather than rely on Jan.

"What about Mam's jewellery Jan? Will you look through it now? She had lots of trinkets and stuff. I'm sure that some of it is very valuable" Tony said, deciding not to follow up on the matter of their mother's will.

"Yeah, sure. Why not?" Jan said indifferently. Tony reached inside the press to his right. His mother's jewellery box sat on the top shelf in the corner, where it always had. Some evenings Delores Lee would ask him to bring it to her. She would sit for a while, lost in her private memories as she toyed with each piece.

One day Tony came to sit beside his mother and ask about her memories. Delores had firmly closed the jewellery box and told him that it was too difficult to talk about. Since then, Tony had always left her alone with her thoughts.

"I put her wedding and engagement rings with the rest. I took them from her hand at the hospital" Tony said quietly. Jan nodded silently. She opened the small blue velvet box and fished them out. Jan placed the rings on her hand before quickly slipping them off again.

"These are all that I want Tony. You can decide what to do with the rest" Jan said. She shut the jewellery box and stood up. Tony looked perplexed. He had expected his sister to take much longer going through his mother's rings and trinkets.

"But, I... Jan, I would not know where to start. Are they valuable? Surely you want to go through them a bit more?" Tony said. Jan shook her head firmly.

"Too many memories. Best sell them Tony. Keep whatever money you get. Or why not let your girlfriend decide? Maybe there's something there that she might like" Jan replied. Tony looked disappointed, but accepted that it was his sister's final words on the subject.

"What about her clothes and handbags Jan? You know how she loved those bags. I thought that you might like to keep one" Tony said. Jan was unmoved.

"No. I think that the best thing to do is to take them all to a charity shop. There's no hurry Tony. You can do it when I head back to Santa Monica. What about personal items? You know, letters, keepsakes, things like that?" she asked. Tony shook his head.

"No, Mam never kept letters, not that she got many. She collected the ones that you sent all right. She kept them in her white handbag. She kept the snaps that you sent of Josh and Amy when they were babies too. They are all with the other photos in the old mahogany wooden chest upstairs" Tony answered. Jan looked thoughtful for a moment.

"You know what Tony, maybe I will take that white handbag after all. You can leave the letters and stuff in it" Jan said. She stood facing him now. Suddenly Tony realised that Jan expected him to fetch the bag immediately.

"Oh, right. I'll get it" he replied. When Tony returned from the living room he could tell that Jan was ready to leave. Her brown bag was now on her shoulder, and her coat buttoned up.

"Thanks Tony, I had better be on my way. I have things to do. I expect that you have plenty on your plate too" Jan said, taking the white bag with its gold buckles from him. Tony Lee was crestfallen. He desperately wanted to bond with his older sister. He had to speak. It was now or never.

"But Jan, I was hoping that we could spend some time together. You know, get to know each other. You're my only flesh and blood now. I was hoping that we could go and see Mam together at the funeral parlour. I feel that I barely know you Jan" he blurted out.

Jan Williams appeared even more agitated than before.

"Come on Tony, let's be practical. I need to get in touch with Mr. Tomlinson and the insurance company again. I also have errands to run, plus I need to phone home. Haven't you things to look after?" Jan said without emotion.

Tony shook his head.

"I need to be with you sis. Couldn't I tag along? Is it too much to ask?" Tony replied. He was in full flow now. It was time to put an end all of Jan's games. She had to allow him into her private little world before it was too late. A more determined look spread across Jan's face. She wore a steely glare now.

"Frankly Tony, I haven't time for all this. You are not the only one grieving. You are being so unfair. My husband and children are miles away. This is the first time that I have ever left them alone. I'm finding it very hard to cope. I cannot be expected to spend my time babysitting you. People grieve in different ways Tony. I prefer to do it alone" Jan said firmly.

"I...I'm sorry Jan, I just thought..."Tony replied, bowing his head. He wiped away a single tear with the back of his hand.

Jan Williams reached inside her handbag and handed him a tissue.

"Come on Tony, walk me to the door. Let's not fight. If you need to get in touch, I'm in room 304. You can phone the hotel if you need me" she said. Jan sidestepped him and walked down the hallway. She reached the front door and turned the latch.

"The old door still rattles! I remember now" she said, turning back to him. Tony was beaten and he knew it. There was no point in fighting on.

"I know Jan. Someday soon I must get around to fixing this old house up. Lots of jobs were left on the long finger for too long" Tony replied, following his sister out into the hallway.

"You know what Tony? Don't go changing the old place too much. It's kinda quaint. The house has character. I'm sure that Mom would hate it if you suddenly start pulling the place apart! So would I as it happens. I like to remember it just as it is now" Jan said with a smile.

Tony looked around the hallway and up the stairs.

"I suppose. But some things really do need doing" he replied wistfully. Jan wore a faint smile.

"I like to think about this old home when I'm lying in my bed at night. Promise me that you won't do anything too drastic Tony? There's something comforting about keeping things as they are, don't you think?" Jan said with a smile. Tony shrugged his shoulders. He had never really thought about it. Number eighty-eight had always been just as it was. Decorating and refurbishing had never been very high on his mother's agenda over the years. She liked the house to be clean and warm, with everything in its place.

"I guess so Jan. Don't worry, I'm not about to start dismantling the old place! It could do with a lick of paint though, while we're on the subject!" he said with a grin, glancing up at the creamy-yellow ceiling.

"Right! It's agreed. A lick of paint it is!" Jan said. She then surprised Tony by planting a kiss on his left cheek. Tony offered an embarrassed smile by way of reply. He did not quite know how she had turned the conversation around, but she had. Within seconds she was gone. Tony watched as she hauled open the creaky gate with its rusty black heavy springs. Jan waved goodbye as she allowed the gate to slam shut behind her with a shuddering clash. Tony wondered what form of transport she would use to return to the city. Should he have offered to phone a cab? Then he realised that Jan was her own woman. She knew Dublin well enough. Perhaps she would get a bus, or just walk.

Tony sat slouched on the floral patterned sofa in the living room. He was disappointed at how the meeting had gone. Yet in hindsight, he realised that he could have predicted how it would have petered out. Already he had discovered that Jan Williams had a way of manipulating things. It was clear that they had little in common, and that Jan wanted very little to do with him. On the plus side, the house would now be his. Tony lay back and stared up at the faded yellow ceiling. In a way he felt a tinge of excitement that a whole new chapter of his life was about to begin. He was free to do as he pleased. Then the guilt swept over him. It was wrong to think such thoughts while his mother lay dead.

Tony ambled upstairs to his mother's bedroom. There he could feel near her once more. He rubbed his hand along the chest of drawers, his mother's clothes inside. Idly he reached the old dressing table, with its rectangular mirror. The pink hairbrush with its white bristles lay where it always had. Tony picked it up and remembered brushing his mother's grey hair. Of course, Delores Lee's hair had not always been that colour. He cast his mind back further to when his mother went to the hairdressers every Tuesday to have her dark brown hair styled. In her last years though, Tony had become her stylist, her manicurist, and her carer. Tony recalled the day that he had suddenly realised that his world had turned full circle. When he was young his mother would brush and comb his hair, in her dotage, he had returned the favour. Tony opened the old walnut-coloured wardrobe. Ahead of him, his mother's best clothes hung limply on metal hangers. He could smell her familiar perfume. Suddenly he felt her close to him again. Tony swept up a handful of dresses and placed them on the large double bed. Now he lay down beside them and hugged them close to him. It felt comforting. He drew them even closer as the tears inevitability came once again. Tony lay there for some time, quietly falling asleep as the tears subsided.

That night Stacey Boyd returned to her apartment. She had spent the last three hours in the company of Tony Lee. Their date had convinced Stacey that their relationship was coming to an end. Tony's conversation with her that evening had not at all held her attention. Constantly she had felt her thoughts wandering to other things, particularly to Alex Woods. She knew that sooner or later she would contact him. It seemed unavoidable now. The only thing holding her back was the fact that it would be too ill-timed. It was surely reasonable to at least wait until after Delores Lee's funeral.

Stacey turned the key in the door. She could hear the television on loud, as it often was. Voices laughed and chattered boisterously in the distance. Stacey entered to a familiar scene. Jodie, Angie, Gina, and her boyfriend Harry, all sat around the television. Jodie lay sprawled across the armchair in her tracksuit, while Angie, Gina and Harry sat on the sofa. A pizza box containing some residue crusts lay abandoned on the small coffee table.

"Okay Stace? Come on, squeeze in. We're watching a DVD. I'll explain the plot" Angie said, patting the arm of the sofa next to her. Stacey smiled as she slipped off her short grey jacket. Gina casually looked around at Stacey before speaking.

"It's almost over. It's based on a true story Stacey. You can watch it tomorrow night" Gina said quietly.

"Not tomorrow. The funeral Mass is tomorrow evening. Then I'll have to take Thursday off for the funeral" Stacey replied.

"How's Tony bearing up Stacey?" Jodie asked without looking around.

"Oh, so-so. He talked a lot about his mother tonight. It's understandable I suppose. I just wish that it was all over. He will just have to get on with life without her. Sorry Harry, you see Tony and his mother were very close" Stacey said apologetically. She felt the need to explain to Gina's boyfriend in case he thought her insensitive. Jodie suddenly sat up and turned to face Stacey.

"A chap I knew was really close to his father. When his Dad died, he never got over it. His hair fell out and everything" Jodie said in a matter-of-fact tone. Harry chuckled quietly, but Gina nudged him in the ribs. She feared that Stacey would be offended, but Stacey shook her head wistfully and smiled.

"Where do you get these stories from Jodie Callaghan? I swear, you'll go straight to hell!" Angie grinned.

"It's true I tell you! Other things happened to him as well. But it's not polite to talk about that in mixed company!" Jodie retorted. Everybody laughed except Jodie.

"On that note I bid you all goodnight! See you in the morning" Stacey said. She took her jacket and handbag and headed for her bedroom.

On most Tuesday nights the girls usually rented a DVD. It was generally a girl's night in, but occasionally a new boyfriend would be persuaded to join them. Most boys only made that mistake once. The movie was always chosen with the girl's taste in mind, and romantic tales, weepy films, and true stories about lost children, were almost always the flavour of the evening.

Stacey Boyd closed her bedroom door and went straight to bed. She found her mind drifting back through her life. It left her confused and unsure about her future. Life was passing her by, and she felt helpless to intervene. Stacey felt that she was at a crossroads. She simply had to finish with Tony, but would life be any better if she hooked up again with Alex? That evening, Tony had told her about inheriting number eighty-eight St Oliver's Road. She knew well what the implications would be. Although Tony had not hinted at it, Stacey expected that at some stage in the future he would ask her to move in with him. Alarm bells rang instantly at the very thought of such a scenario. She could never face a life in that house, and Stacey wondered if that would be the turning point in their relationship.

"Hello Jan? It's Tony here. I hope I didn't wake you. How are you bearing up?" Tony asked quietly down the phone. He was nervous about how Jan might react to his call.

"Hello Tony. Me? I'm doing all right. I've just phoned Howard. They seem to be coping well without me. I don't know if I should be pleased or vexed! Howard assures me that Josh is helping around the house. Now that's weird!" Jan said, managing a little chuckle. Just as Tony began to feel at ease, Jan again put him on edge.

"Was there something in particular Tony? It's late. Are you worried about the church service tomorrow evening? I've told you, everything will be fine. These things have a way of working themselves out. Get some sleep Tony, it will be okay" Jan replied.

"No, I'm all right. I was worried about you sis, that's all" Tony answered. Jan Williams paused as she chose her words carefully.

"Look Tony, I know that you mean well, but I'm fine, really. I had a nice meal alone earlier, then I had a long soak in the bath before phoning Howard" Jan said without much feeling in her voice.

"You ate alone? Gosh! I never thought! Myself and Stacey could have met up with you. You see sis, it's just for the want of a thought. I hate to think of you all alone" Tony said.

"Listen Tony; don't go getting all mushy on me. I quite enjoy being alone. The last thing that I want is someone fussing over me like a mother hen. This is one of the reasons that I dreaded coming to Dublin. All I'm hoping for is a good night's sleep and the strength to get through the next couple of days" Jan said in a higher pitch.

Tony Lee rubbed his gold earring with his right forefinger.

"Sorry Jan, I didn't mean to come across like that. I'm only concerned for you" he said in an emotional voice.

"Well I appreciate your concern, but it's misplaced I'm afraid. I'll see you tomorrow at the funeral parlour, okay?" Jan replied almost in an ice-cold fashion.

Tony said goodbye and quietly admitted defeat again. Once more Jan had won the joust of words. She had backed him into a cul-de-sac, and Tony Lee felt so alone in the world.

The coffin lay open in the funeral parlour, Delores Lee's frail body on view to all. Once the priest had finished his short prayers, Stacey put a comforting arm around the emotional Tony. Seeing his mother for the last time was proving all too much for him. Stacey tried to lead him away, but Tony refused to budge.

"She's gone Stacey, my poor Mam has gone" Tony cried. Jan approached the couple and put her hand on Tony's shoulder. It had little effect. Stacey's eyes seemed to plead to Jan for help. An embarrassed Jan felt compelled to hug Tony close to her. It was something that she would rather not do. Tony Lee embraced both women. The three stood together for some time, Tony holding on for the strength to face the inevitable.

"Come on Tony, let's go outside" Jan whispered. He nodded and Jan led the way. Tony glanced backwards towards the coffin. He felt utterly helpless and alone.

"Yeah, I need a cigarette" he muttered.

It was almost five o'clock, the start of the evening rush-hour. The street outside was busy and uncaring. The heavy snarling evening traffic trundled by the undertakers within feet of the mourners. Tony gazed ahead, a burning cigarette in his right hand. Life passed by at an unapologetic pace. Cars and trucks fought for every inch of space on one of the main arteries in and out of the city. The stench from the nearby canal blended in with the smell of petrol in the air. Normally Tony Lee would be out there as part of the great dash for home. Tonight he was a bystander.

"Move that friggin washing machine!" a truck driver yelled as the traffic lights suddenly turned green. The lady in the white Fiat Uno ahead of him appeared oblivious to his ranting.

The loud hoot of the truck's horn filled the evening air. The lorry driver had to get back to the depot before the designated time. He was ignorant to Tony's Lee's loss or his surroundings. The funeral parlour on Dolphin's Barn might just as well have been a café, in the driver's eyes.

"Shift your arse! Come on, do you need a bleedin' invitation or what? The lights won't get any greener missus!" the driver screamed. The small white car slowly moved onwards, a steady line of traffic following in its path. Some faces peered out in Tony's direction; others were too focused on the heavy traffic to notice. The noise drowned out any chance of a meaningful conversation. For Jan and Tony it was almost surreal. They realised that their great loss mattered little to anyone else.

"Come on Tony, let's get in the car" Stacey said. She led him gently to the hired big black funeral car, which was parked discreetly in a side street around the corner. Parked ahead of the gleaming car was the hearse. It was awaiting the body of Delores Lee. Tony bowed his head and wiped his tears, recognising the poignancy of what was about to occur. The service, as Jan liked to call it, was imminent.

They watched as the coffin was gently placed inside the black hearse. Stacey sat to Tony's left, with Jan on the other side. Tony watched his mother's coffin pass through the open back door of the car ahead.

Soon the small procession of cars set off for Delores's parish church. Tony stared abstractly out of the window. All the familiar sights of his hometown floated silently by. The distinctive smell of the funeral car filled his nostrils. It reeked of flowers, but not in a pleasant way. For Tony, it was almost as if funeral homes had their own special spray which they used on their vehicles to enhance the occasion. The smell bothered him, and he almost felt compelled to ask the driver what it was. Instead he asked Stacey to open the window a little, allowing some fresh air inside the car.

Outside the church, a small crowd had gathered. Tony scanned the mourners for familiar faces. Some colleagues from work stood out, as did Stacey's flatmates. There was one or two of his mother's old neighbours, including Mr. and Mrs. Jordan who ran the local corner shop.

"That's Mrs Jordan Jan. You know, the lady who delayed me the other day?" Tony said in a hushed voice. He felt compelled to point out Agnes Jordan, as if proof of her existence would somehow vindicate him in some way.

Tony climbed from the car. All eyes stared at the three figures dressed in black. Jan's face was expressionless. Stacey linked Tony's arm in hers. At first his steps were unsteady, but then he seemed to gain confidence. Blank faces stared back at him and Jan. Stacey helped him up the four concrete steps leading into the church. They followed the coffin up the red and black tiles in the centre aisle, taking their place in the front pew to the right of the altar. With no other immediate family, the rest of the front pew lay empty.

"I hoped that Auntie Mary might have made it after all" Tony whispered to Jan. Jan Williams barely raised an eyebrow. She considered her reply before speaking.

"Face it Tony, she's not coming" Jan answered coldly. Tony nodded and sat back in his seat. It seemed insensitive to him that Mary had not travelled over from Walsall. His mother was being laid to rest the following morning, yet neither of her sisters would be present. Tony was distracted as a hand from behind patted his shoulder.

"How are you coping Tony? Sorry to hear about your Mum" the voice said warmly.

Erik Ngombiti was a well-liked colleague from work. Although relatively new to the company, the dark-skinned Erik got on well with everyone.

"I'm okay Erik, thanks for coming. I'll be fine" Tony said quietly. Erik patted his shoulder again.

"Most of the staff are here Tony. I'll talk to you later. Keep your chin up!" Erik said before moving away. He felt that he had intruded enough.

The priest soon appeared and the small congregation clambered noisily to their feet. Mentally, Tony Lee tried to prepare for what lay ahead. As he stood up a voice in his head urged him to be strong.

"Come on, you can get through this" he told himself confidently. But moments later, the truth hit him. The priest spoke warmly of Delores, who he had known slightly. Slowly the tears came for Tony Lee. Suddenly it did not matter anymore. There was little point in holding back. While the congregation stood tall to pray for Delores Lee, Tony collapsed down onto his seat. Stacey's arms trying desperately to comfort him. Tony sobbed fitfully into his hands, totally lost in his grief. Jan stood upright and prayed for her mother, almost detached from Tony's sense of loss.

CHAPTER FIVE

LOVE LETTERS

In a matter of days, Jan had returned to America. The time had passed in a daze for Tony. Jan had promised to keep in touch by phone. It was now the Saturday after the funeral. Tony gazed out through the kitchen window. The back garden was still a project in progress. Tony had made a small start by repairing the yellow lawnmower. There was still plenty to be done, such as cutting the overgrown lawn. Somehow he just did not have the stomach for it. Tony Lee wandered upstairs.

The only comfort that he found now was to lie on the big double bed in his mother's old bedroom. Somehow doing so made him feel close to Delores Lee again. On the landing, Tony glanced up at the attic door in the flaky yellowish ceiling.

"Another job for the list. That attic hasn't been cleaned out for as long as I can remember" he muttered. Tony climbed onto the bed and thought pleasant thoughts of his mother. His mind rambled back to his childhood, to carefree days when his dear Mam had good health. Eventually he drifted off to sleep, still dreaming of days gone by.

Tony woke with a start. His heart was thumping and he was in a sweat. The unfamiliar surroundings startled him for a moment. He then realised that he was in his mother's room.

"That dream again. Jesus! That crying child!" he mumbled. Tony wiped his face and rolled from the bed, still fully dressed. He drew in a sharp breath as he reached the doorway.

"Phew! That's the first time that I ever had a nightmare during the day!" he whispered ruefully.

Still somehow, he felt better after his short doze. Sometimes he needed a nap in the daytime to ward off the tiredness. His nightly sleep patterns were now fractured and uneven. The bad dreams came regularly, but Tony had stopped telling Stacey about them, knowing that it upset her.

Tony went to the bathroom and splashed some cold water on his face. He eyed himself in the mirror. His face looked older than his thirty-six years.

"God, look at me! I'll have to snap out of this!" he whispered. Tony Lee silently vowed to stop moping around his home. Normally on a Saturday he would be out and about on his bike. Since his mother's death, he had barely bothered. The previous day he had attended the family solicitor with Jan. Once the meeting was over, Jan had informed Tony that she would fly home early the following morning. There would be no more discussions or visits.

Jan had got her way, and instead of a long chat with his older sister that evening, Tony had settled for taking Stacey out for a meal. Tony felt that he owed her that for all her patience.

Tony reflected on the uneventful trip to his local restaurant.

"It's hardly fair on Stace. I'm awful company lately. I should phone and apologise" he thought. Tony bounded downstairs and picked up the house phone.

"Hello Stace? Fancy doing something? We could go for a drive if you like?" he said cheerfully.

"Can't. I'm dropping Gina and Harry off in town. Call me later, yeah?" she replied. Tony said goodbye and slowly put the receiver down. He noted that ever since Stacey had bought her small car, it was used mostly for work and to chauffeur her flatmates around. Tony contemplated ringing Jan. His hand hovered over the cream telephone. He calculated that she would barely be home. What would he say, he wondered? He could ask how her family were, and had she got home safely.

"Don't be stupid Tony; of course she got home okay. She would bite my head off for phoning" he muttered. Tony rambled into the kitchen and stared outside into the overgrown garden once more. He would definitely make a start on the house soon. But just not today.

That night, Tony met up with Stacey for a drink. They were alone, and on the way to their local pub. Earlier that evening, Stacey had toyed with the idea of breaking up with Tony Lee. It was merely an exercise of the mind, rather than a serious objective. She had not contacted Alex Woods, but considered that it would be easier to do so if Tony was no longer in the picture. Somehow it seemed unthinkable to break it off with Tony. She could offer no reason to either him or herself. They never argued or fought. Yet she knew that if the chance presented it, she would certainly be ready. Stacey knew that eventually

Tony would ask her about them moving in together. This was bound to cause a difference of opinion, for she could never agree to live at Saint Oliver's Road.

"So you see Stace, I'm gonna have to start clearing out the old place from top to bottom. The house badly needs updating, although I promised Jan that I would not do too much" Tony said as they sat in a corner of the busy lounge. Stacey was barely listening, but she did recognise the opportunity to put Tony straight.

"Be brave" Stacey told herself before speaking.

"Well Tony, whatever you think best. But whatever you do, do it for yourself. Don't do it for Jan-or me for that matter. It's you that has to live there" Stacey said. She tried to make it sound as though she had his best interests at heart. Tony nodded. Stacey observed his demeanour. He seemed to be picking his reply carefully in his head. Before Tony could speak, Jodie breezed up behind Stacey and covered her pal's eyes with both hands.

"Guess who?" Jodie giggled.

"Jodie Callaghan! She's the only one that I know who would do anything that childish!" Stacey giggled. Jodie drew her hands away disappointingly.

"Aw! Hiya Stace, hiya Tony. I was in town at a gig. Just popped in to see who's here" Jodie said, glancing around the busy pub.

"I swear Jodie, you certainly get about! Doesn't she Tony?" Stacey laughed. Tony smiled politely. He liked Jodie. She was always full of energy and in good humour.

"Nah! Don't fancy this tonight. The gang are outside in a big taxi. I'll tell them that we'll go somewhere else" Jodie sighed. In seconds she had vanished once more.

"That girl had boundless energy. She never stays still!" Stacey remarked. The topic of eighty-eight St. Oliver's Road had slipped away again.

As they walked home later that night, Tony suggested that Stacey stay over with him.

"Not just yet Tony, eh? It will take a while for me to get used to that house" Stacey said quietly. Tony did not argue. It was late and both were tired. They caught a cab home, with Tony dropping Stacey off first. He kissed her gently on the lips as she climbed from the taxi.

"Love you" he whispered.

"Me too" Stacey replied, caught off guard by his unexpected words. Tony had told her that he loved her before, but not for a long time now. Stacey hurried inside the small apartment block. She considered his hushed words as she entered the lift. Perhaps it was his mother's death that had prompted his remark, or maybe it was simply because he had not told her for such a long while. Either way, Stacey felt sure that the feeling was not reciprocal. She certainly liked Tony, but doubted that she actually loved him. The fact had been gnawing away at her for days now. She had to tell him soon.

It was Monday morning and Tony had planned to return to work. The alarm clock rang loudly and he instantly jumped across the bed to knock it off. It was something that he had always done to save waking his mother. Now he realised that it did not matter anymore. Tony flopped back down on the bed. Somehow work did not seem so important today. He lit a cigarette and considered reasons why he should start back at his desk job. He had always loved his work in I.T. Yet today his heart was not in it.

"I know, I'll take just one more day off. It will shorten the week, and I can make a start on cleaning up the house" he told himself weakly. Tony drew on his cigarette and lay staring at the ceiling. Minutes passed. He continued to puff on the cigarette, mulling over all the jobs that he planned on doing in the house. Eventually he stubbed out the cigarette and lay back down. He told himself that later he would phone his boss Charles Carrington and make his excuses. Tony drifted off to sleep as the traffic outside grew steadily heavier.

Tony Lee woke with a scream. This time it the nightmare was worse than ever. A lather of sweat enveloped his body. He sat erect in the bed, a startled look on his face. The sheets were soaking wet.

"Jesus, what was that?" Tony said in a loud voice. Just then he realised that it was he who had screamed out.

"Christ! That dream about that infant again. Sweet Jesus!" he whispered, wiping the perspiration from his forehead. He sank back onto the mattress and threw back the duvet.

"I remember now. That baby was clawing at me. Its hands, his fingernails were digging into my face. God almighty, the child was actually chasing me, and I was running away! What a weird dream" Tony said with a shudder. He was wide awake now and scrambled from the bed to get dressed.

After breakfast, Tony telephoned his office. He explained to Mr. Carrington that he could not face work today, but would definitely return the following morning.

Tony was determined not to waste the day. Soon he was outside, tidying up the back garden and cleaning out the shed.

"I'll have to hire a skip for all of this waste" he muttered. All day long Tony laboured on, gradually improving the months of neglect in the rear garden. It was almost three o'clock in the afternoon before Tony stopped for a coffee. He stood in the old kitchen, staring out at the result of his hard work. Tony was happy that at last he had made some progress.

That evening, Stacey Boyd lay alone in her bedroom. Surprisingly, all of her flatmates were in bed, yet it was just gone eleven-thirty. The weekend's exertions had caught up with all four girls, and they had resolved to have an early night.

Stacey idly played with her mobile phone. She thought of Alex. Should she key his new number into her phone, she wondered? Why not? No one would know. Tony never checked her mobile. Anyway, the name of Alex Woods would scarcely ring alarm bells with him. Tony knew of her old boyfriend, but never inquired about him. They rarely talked about their past loves. Idly she retrieved the scrap of paper from under her pillow. Stacey carefully typed in the name, followed by the ten-digit number.

"There!" she whispered with a smile, examining the new entry in her contacts. Then Stacey began to consider doing the unthinkable.

"What if I text him? What if I just say hi?" she thought. It seemed wrong, and yet she typed in the simple word.

"Hi"

Stacey's forefinger hovered over the "send" button. It felt like a dare from her teenage years. Her heart thumped now at the very thought of simply pressing send on the green button. It felt like an adrenalin rush in her fingers as she lay quietly on the bed.

"Do it!" her brain told her. Her finger hovered again. Suddenly it was done. Stacey's head was in a spin. What if he phoned her? What if Angie heard the tone and rushed in? Stacey switched off her phone instantly. She buried her head beneath the duvet.

"Oh God, what have I done?" she whispered. And then she thought of Tony. What if Tony was with her during the week when Alex phoned her? He would surely phone back at some stage now. She thought of Alex Woods, his beaming smile looking back at her. Then there was Tony, who had given her the will to live again. Suddenly she realised that the decision had to be made. She had to decide between the two. Tomorrow. That was it. She would decide tomorrow. Meanwhile tonight she would leave her mobile phone switched off.

By eleven o'clock that same evening, Tony Lee was exhausted. He had cleared out most of his mother's room, bagging off lots of her old clothes. Her handbags and hats were packed away in boxes. Tony eyed the attic door again. If it was a little earlier he just might tackle such a big job. Yet he was back at work the following day.

Suddenly the phone rang in the hallway. Tony skipped down the stairs. He was in good spirits despite his physical tiredness.

"Hello, is that you Stace?" he asked. Stacey was the most likely person to ring at such a late hour. Tony often referred to her apartment as "the place that never sleeps".

"No Tony, this is Jan. I'm phoning to let you know that I arrived home safe and well. I should have phoned sooner. Also, I telephoned Mr. Tomlinson, you know, Mom's solicitor? He will have some paperwork for you to sign on Thursday. After that, the house will be yours" Jan said in a cheery voice.

"Well that's great news Jan, thanks. Speaking of the old house Jan, I've been really busy. The place is neat and tidy. I even straightened out the back garden and shed. I've packed away Mom's clothes. You wouldn't know the place!" Tony replied proudly.

There was a long silence before Jan answered.

"Tony, remember what we agreed? I don't want you wrecking Mom's old home. Just a lick of paint we said, okay?" Jan said deliberately.

"Sure Jan, sure. I haven't got to the painting yet, but it will be just a touch up job, I promise" he said. Jan paused again.

"Right Tony, that's settled. You just sign for the house and relax. It's a sturdy old place, big enough for both you and Stacey. You'll have many happy years there" Jan replied, sounding more confident now. Tony wanted to tell her about Stacey's reservations about number eighty-eight, but thought better of it.

"I haven't asked Stace to move in yet Jan. I expect that she always thought that we would get a place of our own in time" Tony said quietly.

"Well you have a place of your own now Tony! It's my present to you" Jan said happily.

"Yeah, thanks Jan, I really appreciate it. Thanks again sis" he answered, striving to sound as grateful as possible.

"Good. Now all you have to do is enjoy life. Have a good holiday this summer; get out and about a bit. Goodness knows that you deserve it" Jan said.

"Hey, that's an idea Jan. Why don't we go and visit you?" Tony said cheerfully. The telephone line fell silent for a few seconds.

"No Tony. Look, that's not a very good idea really. You see, we always take the kids off. Then I have my job, and Howard is seldom here. It wouldn't be fair on you and Stacey. No, maybe next year when we have more free time, but not this summer, okay?" Jan replied firmly.

"Sure Jan, whatever you say" Tony replied slowly.

"Listen Tony, I have to go. Howard will be home soon. Remember what we agreed, just a lick of paint" Jan said, doing her best to make light of her remarks.

"Yeah, sis, just a lick of paint" he answered. The words were barely off his lips when the line went dead. Tony shook his head and walked slowly away.

The next morning Stacey Boyd woke up with that awful, guilty feeling. She knew that she had done something wrong the night before. Her brain began to search for possibilities. She was not drinking, as her clear head plainly told her. Okay. What about her flatmates? Had she argued with anybody? No, that was not it. How about Tony Lee? Had she said the wrong thing? It struck her in a flash. Tony's name led her to Alex Woods. God, that text message! Maybe she had not sent it after all. Stacey switched on her mobile phone. Her eyes were fixed on the illuminated screen as she waited. There were no messages or missed calls. Stacey reasoned that that had to be a good thing. She checked her sent messages. There it was, plain to see. Alex's new number was in her list of contacts. Message sent at 11:39pm.

"Oh God, I'm mortified" she whispered.

Stacey got up and threw on her housecoat. There would be a queue for the bathroom as usual. She knew that it was important to put on a brave face. Angie must never know. Again she switched off her phone, fearing Alex might ring.

Once out of sight of her flatmates that morning, Stacey again turned on her phone. There were still no messages. She could breathe easily. By lunchtime Stacey had almost forgotten the infamous text message. Suddenly the phone rang. A startled Stacey reached for it in the busy work's canteen. She sat with two workmates from her department. Tony Lee's name flashed up on the screen.

"Hi Stace, I'm back at work from today. I'm bored already. Fancy going out tonight for a while?" Tony said. Automatically Stacey tried to think of an excuse.

"It's Tuesday, we never go out on Tuesdays. Besides, it's girlie night in tonight! I was really looking forward to a lazy night in with the telly" Stacey replied.

"I know, I know Stace. There are things that I need to discuss with you. Come on, please? I promise that I'll have you home early, and I won't ask you to stay over. Please?" Tony said.

Stacey felt trapped. Tony was being so nice. She searched again for a way out. Then she remembered the text message. At least she should meet Tony face to face. Perhaps he was about to discuss moving in together. She could put her foot down tonight. Stacey reasoned that if she told him exactly where she stood, perhaps Tony might even break off their relationship.

"Okay then, if we meet up early. What if I collect you in the car about eight? Once I have the car with me I'll only have one drink, or maybe a coke or two. That way I won't stay out too late. You know me on a weekday night Tony" Stacey answered.

When the conversation ended, Tony slipped his phone back inside his pocket. It was not what he had hoped for, but at least they were meeting up. He was slowly realising how lonely his home was without his mother there. Not seeing much of Stacey was beginning to impact. Tony knew that he was being selfish. While his mother was alive, seeing Stacey during the week did not seem to matter so much. Now he needed some impetus to get him through the lonely week.

At ten-past-eight that evening, Tony stood ready to leave. He heard Stacey's car horn toot loudly outside on the street. Tony rushed out, locking up behind him.

"Stacey, I asked you before not to do that! Why wake the whole street?" Tony said crossly.

"It's only just gone eight! Who would be in bed at this hour?" Stacey grinned. She quickly realised that Delores Lee always used to go to bed early, and so she changed the subject. Tony was probably still a little edgy, she thought.

She drove away, trying to avoid looking directly at Tony's home.

"I thought that we might try that new pub, you know, McCaul's or McCann's or whatever it's called" Stacey said.

"It's McKeon's. Why not go to the local pub? I like Madigan's" Tony replied.

Stacey bit her bottom lip. Tony was nothing if not predictable. Angie once said that he was like an old pair of slippers. Stacey's flatmate always maintained that Tony was dependable and comfy. Angie said that she never met anyone so set in his ways as Tony Lee.

"I thought that you might like a change Tony. Besides, it's Tuesday, and we can always go to Madigan's Bar on Saturday. Anyway, the parking is great at the new pub" she countered. Tony seemed to accept his fate. He agreed to the new venue against his better judgement.

They sat alone under the large window of the quiet pub. Several lounge girls toured the carpeted area with large trays in hand. It appeared that there was far too many staff for a midweek night. Tony studied his new surroundings.

"Not much life in here, is there? Look at the lounge staff! They're almost bumping into each other!" he grinned.

"I daresay that Madigan's is empty tonight as well" Stacey replied dryly. Tony did not wish to get into a war of words, so he quickly changed the topic. "Anyway Stace, what I wanted to discuss was our holidays. Something that Jan said last night put it in my mind. We can finally plan a nice holiday together- just the two of us" Tony said with a beaming smile.

Stacey was caught by surprise. She had planned going over to visit her parents in England for her two-week summer break. Now she had to think fast.

"You phoned Jan? You never said" she replied in an effort to gain valuable thinking time.

"She phoned me actually, but that doesn't matter. It was only a quick call. Anyway, what about it?" he said sharply.

"God Tony, I have not even thought about it. My holidays are the last two weeks in July. What about you?" she answered thoughtfully.

"I can easily get the same weeks. I asked my boss to leave my holiday weeks open this year, you know, with Mam being so poorly" he said. Stacey patted his hand.

"Well, let's not plan anything hasty. I had thought of going to my folks again this year, but we can get some holiday brochures and have a look" Stacey suggested. Tony looked disappointed.

"I don't mind where we go Stace. We could even tour Ireland in the car if you like. I just want us to be together. I know that I haven't been great over the last few months. I want to make it up to you" Tony said, slipping his arm around her waist. Stacey was about to answer when her phone rang. She sat frozen for a moment, watching her mobile vibrate on the small table on front of them.

"Shouldn't you get that?" Tony asked. The phone was turned to its side, away from Tony. Stacey could clearly see the name flash up on screen. Alex Woods.

"Let it ring. I think its Angie O'Rourke messing about! They'll be watching a weepy movie at home! Angie will be telling me what a great film I'm missing!" Stacey said, quickly regaining her composure. Her heart was beating fast, and she could feel her hands sweating.

Tony was talking about holidays now, but she could barely take in what he was saying.

"Here are we planning trips away, and we've barely had a night alone together" Tony said in an upbeat tone. Stacey smiled back innocently.

"Yeah, you're right I suppose" she replied lamely.

"Don't worry; there will be plenty of time together from now on. I suppose that I'll get used to all of your little annoying habits!" Tony laughed.

"What annoying habits? I don't have any, do I?" she said innocently. Stacey's mind was swimming. All she could think of was Alex Woods. What if he phoned Angie? Did he have Angie's number? She recalled telling Angie that they might try out the new pub tonight. Stacey imagined both Alex and Angie marching into the lounge and demanding an explanation.

Tony continued to tease her.

"Oh, you have some good ones all right! There's the way you scratch your head when you're thinking, or squint up your eyes when you're annoyed, and fiddle with your nails when you don't get your own way. You wriggle up your nose too sometimes! Oh, and the way you shake the ice in your glass when you're nervous" Tony replied with a chuckle.

"I do not!" Stacey countered. She quickly realised that she was doing exactly that. Stacey put the glass of Coke and ice back onto the small round table. She wondered if Tony was joking, or if he had noticed that she appeared nervous. She decided to bluff it out.

"Anyway, so do you have annoying habits. You always wind down the car window, even in the winter. And you wipe the windscreen with your hands, marking the glass" she replied.

The two looked at each other and laughed. Stacey could never be angry with him. Tony was just too sweet. Yet in her heart she knew that their romance had to end.

Her mobile phone bleeped to indicate a text message. Stacey knew that it must be from Alex Woods.

Now Tony was talking about foreign holidays away together. Stacey felt as though she was slowly being backed into a corner. And now there was Alex. He had actually phoned her. Had she been alone, they might now be talking about getting back together right now. Stacey felt light-headed. She wished that she could speak to Alex right at that moment. And still Tony talked about holidays.

"I suggested going to visit Jan in The States. Of course, she made her excuses. I guess that I knew she would, but I hoped..." Tony trailed off, lost in his thoughts. Despite everything, Stacey felt so sorry for him.

"Tony love, why can't you simply accept it? Jan really doesn't want to know you. You said so yourself. Jan has her own family now. Don't embarrass yourself by running after her" Stacey replied.

"I know, I know. You're right of course. That's just it though Stace. I'm her family too. Wouldn't you think that she would like to keep in touch?" Tony answered quietly.

"Well, she phoned you last night, didn't she? That must mean something" Stacey said. Tony nodded wryly.

"Yeah, only because she was afraid that I was going to take a sledgehammer to Mam's old house!" he grinned. Stacey felt a shiver run up her spine. They were back on the topic of number eighty-eight again. It was time to change the subject.

"I think that Angie is getting serious with a married man at her job. I don't know how to stop her" Stacey said, again shaking her glass of Coke and ice. Tony looked quizzically at her.

"Stop her? How could you stop her? People have to do what they think is right for them. Angie will make her own decisions Stace. Don't get in the middle of it. She won't thank you either way" Tony said firmly.

His words struck a chord with Stacey Boyd. People do make their own decisions in the end, just as she must do. Now all that she wanted was to get the evening over with, and see what Alex Woods had said in his text message to her.

Later, Stacey dropped Tony off at St. Oliver's Road. She could feel the relief as she drove away. She tried to not look directly at number eighty-eight, fearing that she might have nightmares. Only as she turned the corner at the top of the road did she feel totally at ease. The compulsion to pull over and read Alex's text message was strong. Stacey decided to save it for her bed later on. It was still early. The girls would probably all still be up watching a movie. She thought of Tony. He had been there for her when she needed someone. After splitting with Alex Woods, Tony was the one who picked up the pieces. Without him, Stacey knew that she might never have survived. Alex jilting her had left her devastated. Today she was a much more assured woman. A lot of that was thanks to Tony, and she knew it.

Back at her flat, Stacey made her excuses and went to bed. Gina and Angie were still up, while Jodie had gone out late to meet a friend. Only when she was safely in bed with the light out did Stacey dare to read her messages on her phone.

"Tanx 4 calling Stacey. Tried to call u. want to say sorry again. Alex x".

She read the message over several times. What caught her eye was the kiss at the end of the message. Stacey lay back on her pillow and thought of old times. Had they married, they might have had a child by now. She had always wanted a boy and a girl. She and Alex had never discussed having a family, nor had she really done so with Tony either. With Tony it had been so different. There was always the spectre of his mother in the background. Starting a family was never an option. Stacey realised that that barrier was not there now. Yet somehow a union with Tony Lee had lost its appeal.

"Should I reply to Alex right away or should I leave it until tomorrow?" she thought. Stacey did not want to appear desperate. She hoped that Alex did not see her as some neurotic girl who would go to any lengths to get back with him.

"Of course he doesn't think that! He phoned me, didn't he? I'll text him now" she told herself. Stacey began to compose what she would say in her head. "Sorry I missed you. Out with the girls. How r u? Maybe call u 2 morrow?" she texted. Her finger wavered as she read the message back before sending. "That sounds okay. Not too forward. Send" she whispered. Stacey pressed on the "send" button and waited for the tone. She tried to cough to drown out the bleep, fearful that her flatmates might hear. If Angie thought that she was still awake, she might come in for a heart-to-heart chat. Stacey hid her phone beneath the duvet to muffle out the tone, should Alex text back. She lay awake awaiting a return message. She was not to be disappointed.

"Sounds good. Looking 4 ward 2 that. Love Alex xxx". Stacey smiled and tucked her phone under her pillow. It was time to sleep. Perhaps she might dream of Alex Woods and happier times.

The following evening, Tony Lee dragged the two heavy black bin-liners upstairs to the landing. The bags contained his mother's best hats and handbags, plus some other personal belongings that he could not bring himself to throw away. His plan was to store them in the attic for the time being. Tony knew that the roof space was littered with old junk from years gone by. It would all have to be cleared out, but not just yet. Tonight he would simply pack his mother's belongings next to the big box of Christmas decorations. That particular old wooden box stood just inside the attic door for convenience. Every year Tony would reach up for it when Delores Lee deemed that the time was right. Then in early January he would return it to its designated spot, trying to ignore the rest of the tatty items hidden there.

"Right then, here we go" Tony muttered. He climbed onto the small silver-coloured aluminium stepladder and carefully negotiated the four steps upwards towards the attic door in the ceiling. Tony pushed the old faded white trapdoor backwards, and it fell inwards with a heavy thump. He could see the dust floating about in the blackness above. Boxes and an old tattered suitcase were visible near the entrance overhead. The only way into the loft was for Tony to hoist his body upwards, using the wooden doorframe of his bedroom door for leverage. Tony pulled a torch from his pocket and switched it on. He then rested it just inside the attic door and climbed back down the ladder. Despite the warm summer evening, he could feel a distinct chill coming from the un-insulated attic. Tony Lee then scaled the ladder with the first plastic black bag and deftly slung it inside the loft space. He repeated the act with the second bag before catching his breath.

"Now for the tricky bit!" he sighed. Tony knew he had to climb up and put some order in the clustered loft. There could be no more practice of putting things on the long finger.

"Start as you mean to go on!" he sighed, hoisting his nimble body upwards into the semi-darkness.

Tony groaned as he surveyed the mess of junk, unwanted items, and broken furniture. The large roof space was chock-a-block with abandoned stuff from The Lee's past life.

"Where to begin?" Tony gasped as he shone the small torch in every direction. He had to achieve some order, and Tony quickly came up with a plan. By moving things that might be needed in the future, such as Christmas decorations, he might attain some semblance of normality. Items that he deemed as junk would be placed nearest to the door. At some time in the future he would hire a skip and dispose of them. Sentimental stuff belonging to his mother and himself would be placed in another section.

Tony stuck to his plan and began to clear away. There was not a great deal of headspace, but he gradually began to create some sort of passage. After almost one hour, Tony stumbled across one of his mother's old handbags.

"Huh! Another one!" he grinned. It seemed heavy, and rather than examine the contents in the darkness, Tony dropped it carefully out onto the landing floor.

It was almost midnight when Tony emerged from the shower. He wandered back outside of the bathroom with a yellow towel tied around his waist. The old black handbag caught his eye.

"God! I thought that I was finally finished! I forgot about you!" he said, picking up his mother's old bag from the landing floor. Tony went to his bedroom and slipped on a pair of blue and white pyjama bottoms. He wiped the dusty handbag with the towel and flopped down on the bed.

"Now what have we here?" he said, unzipping the battered handbag. He spilled the contents onto the blue bedspread. Envelopes tumbled out of various colours. Tony picked up a handful and read the name and address. They were all addressed to his mother. Casually he opened one and perused the pages.

"Well, well, well!" he laughed. Tony opened another and read a few lines. He smiled and placed the pages back inside the faded yellow envelope. Tony grinned contently and shoved the letters back into the tattered handbag. He zipped it up again and shoved it under his bed. It was late. The examination could wait for another day. It was time to grab some much-needed rest.

CHAPTER SIX

REDUNDANT ENGAGEMENT

On Saturday afternoon, Tony Lee was disturbed by the sound of the house phone ringing. He looked at the old mahogany clock on the kitchen mantelpiece.

"Just gone four o'clock. This will be Stacey. She will be out shopping with the girls and has spotted something that she thinks I might like" he muttered to himself. Tony picked up the receiver with a smile on his face.

"No Stace, I don't need new shoes-or a shirt for that matter!" he said. There was a brief silence before the female voice spoke.

"Hello, this is Jan. Is that you Tony?" said the voice in a concerned tone. Tony gulped back air. He cringed as he cleared his throat.

"Sorry Jan, sorry. I thought that it was Stacey. She's always trying to dress me over the phone on a Saturday afternoon! She's out with her flatmates, you see" Tony said apologetically.

"Yes, I see. You're a lucky man to have such a caring girl Tony. Anyway, how are you getting on? Have you been to see Mr. Tomlinson?" she asked.

"Yes, that's all sorted Jan. I went to see him during the week. Thanks again Jan. I signed all of the forms and the house is now in my name.

"That's fine Tony, no need to thank me. Just remember what we agreed. No mad renovations or huge attic conversions" Jan replied glibly.

"No Jan, I promise. Hey, as we speak I'm doing some painting. Just the kitchen mind. I thought it could do with a bit of cheering up" Tony answered. Jan seemed pensive as she took in his words.

94

"Yeah, I suppose that it was a bit drab" she replied.

"Oh Jan, speaking of the attic-you'll never guess what I found up there" Tony said at a quicker pace.

"What Tony? What were you doing up there for heaven's sake? God almighty! I'm only home a matter of days and you're already tearing Mom's house apart" Jan said. She sounded very agitated now, and Tony went on the defensive.

"Honestly Jan, I wasn't. All I was doing was storing away some of Mam's old hats and things. I haven't the heart to throw them out yet. Guess what? I came across another of Mam's old handbags in the attic. It was so funny! Inside I found a pile of old love letters from Dad! How corny is that? I had a good laugh I can tell you!" Tony said with a chuckle. There was silence on the line as Jan digested his words.

"I can't believe you Tony Lee! Did you actually read Mom's private correspondence? Gee whizz! I don't know what to say" Jan replied.

It was only now and then that Tony noticed any Americanism's about his sister. Mostly her accent was Irish, but sometimes he would hear the odd twang of an American tone, or a word or two that Irish people seldom use.

"Whoa sis, don't go off on a bender, will you? For God's sake, it's only a bunch of letters from my Dad to our mother! It's not as if I've revealed the third secret of Fatima or something!" Tony retorted.

It was the first time that he had allowed himself to speak frankly to Jan. Previously he had always watched what he had said to his older sister. However, her constant picking at him now seemed grossly unfair, and Tony Lee felt as though he had to make a stand.

"Look Tony, I'm not going off on one, as you so quaintly put it. But these are Mom's private things. They should be destroyed once she has passed away. I specifically asked you about her private belongings when I visited the house, didn't I? All of this is very upsetting for me" Jan said in an almost tearful tone.

"Yes Jan, it's upsetting for me too-to have my only flesh and blood ranting at me every time I do anything. I just told you that I only discovered the letters myself on Wednesday evening in the attic. Now had you stayed on long enough to help me clean away Mam's things, perhaps we might have found them together, okay?" Tony snapped. Jan went quiet as she considered his words. Immediately Tony regretted his outburst.

"Listen Jan, I'm sorry. I didn't mean to upset you. I actually thought that you would be amused by my find. Look, let's forget it and start again. How are my niece and nephew? How is Howard getting along?" Tony said quietly.

"Everyone's fine Tony. You're right of course. I am being too harsh with you. I guess that I'm still in mourning really. You know what would really cheer me up Tony? I want you to burn all of those silly letters. They are from so long ago.

I would hate to think of anybody reading dear Mom's private correspondence. Promise me that you will do that for me today. Promise?" Jan said in a more conciliatory voice.

Tony had no wish to fight with his only sibling.

"If that's what you want Jan, then sure, no problem. I owe you big time for what you've done for me. I'll do it as soon as I put down the phone. Now, is there any other reason why you called? Is there anything that you need me to do?" Tony answered in a light-hearted tone.

"What colour are you painting the kitchen Tony?" Jan asked.

"White and terracotta. I thought some wallpaper too" he answered.

"That sounds lovely. Take each room gradually. You have your whole life to enjoy it. I'm sure that Mom is smiling down on you" Jan said emotionally.

"Thanks Jan. Tell everybody that I said hello" Tony replied.

"I will. Take care Tony, I have to go. I only really telephoned to make sure that you signed for the house. Best of luck with it, and remember our promise" Jan said happily.

"Which one sis? The lick of paint, or burning Dad's letters?" Tony chuckled.

"Both!" Jan laughed.

Tony Lee replaced the creamy receiver. He glanced upstairs towards his bedroom where the old stack of letters lay in the handbag under his bed. Then he noticed the white paint on his arms and fingers.

"Later" he whispered as he returned to the kitchen. The letters could wait for the time being. He wanted to get the painting finished first.

As he again stirred the pot of white paint, Tony reflected on Jan's words. He smiled contently as he realised it was the first time that he had stood up to his much older sister. There was something satisfying and reassuring about flexing his muscles against the domineering Jan. Tony went back to work, painting the kitchen walls and skirting boards. He thought about his Dad, wishing he could remember some more about the father that he had never really known. Tony had always felt cheated at not having a real father, despite his wonderful mother's efforts at being both. He whistled now as he moved on to the wall surrounding the window. It was nice to look out at the now tidy back garden. Tony admired his handiwork on both inside and outside of the old house. Then he thought of Stacey. He hoped to win her over with his efforts over the next few weeks. In reality, all the hard work around the house was for her. If left to Tony, he could easily have left number eighty-eight just as it was.

Stacey linked Angie along Henry Street as they made their way towards The Jervis Centre, another large shopping mall in Dublin City Centre. Ahead of them Jodie and Gina chatted away.

"Did you phone Alex?" Angie whispered.

"No I did not!" Stacey answered indignantly. She nudged her pal in the side with her elbow.

"Ouch! I only asked!" Angie replied with a smile.

"Well don't! How are you getting on with Philip?" Stacey retorted.

"We're just good friends" Angie countered, the smile vanishing instantly.

"Yeah, and I'm the Queen of Sheba!" Stacey cackled. Jodie turned to face the two.

"What's the joke Stace?" Jodie asked.

"Nothing Jodie, we just wondered what mad caper you are up to tonight. Is it bungee jumping or abseiling?" Angie laughed. Jodie Callaghan stuck out her tongue and waited for her flatmates to catch up.

"As it happens, I might stay in and wash my hair" she said haughtily. All three of her flatmates burst into laughter. As long as they had known Jodie, she had never missed a Saturday night out.

"And I'm definitely the Queen of Sheba!" Stacey said.

"And what about you Stace? Will you be out with the delectable Tony again? Another night in that awful pub?" Jodie said cuttingly. The smile vanished from Stacey's pale face. As the days had passed, she felt that she wanted to spend less and less time with Tony. Text messages to Alex Woods were now her preferred choice of fun.

"Yes, that's where you'll find me, once you've done your hair!" Stacey said with a smirky grin.

"Oh, I wouldn't possibly intrude on the two love birds! After all, you two are together longer than any couple that I know! When is the wedding Stacey?" Jodie giggled. Both Gina and Angie joined in the laughter. Talk of wedding was always a sore point for Stacey.

Stacey struggled to remain nonchalant.

"You're just jealous Jodie! Isn't it about time that you found a man? I'm beginning to think that you're turning gay on us!" Stacey said with a serious frown. Gina gasped in mock-horror.

"Stacey Boyd! That's an awful thing to say! Didn't Jodie date that guy five years ago? Now, what was his name?" Gina sniggered. All four girls continued to battle their way through the afternoon crowd. Sometimes they would break into twos or a threesome to allow people to pass. Gina linked Jodie's arm in hers.

"I remember that fellow you dated. You two were very close at the time" Gina said. Jodie looked distant for the first time.

"His name was Michael, Michael Downey, he was nice. Then I found out that he was married" Jodie sighed. A faraway look developed in her eyes, and Gina put a playful arm around her shoulder.

"Sorry Jodie, you never said. Come on, forget him" Gina said with a smile. Jodie grinned back at her.

"I'm okay Gina. It's just… I thought that he was the one, you know?" Jodie replied.

"Come on, time for a coffee, we've earned it" Gina said, hugging Jodie close to her. As Jodie again went to talk to Gina, Stacey paired up with her best pal Angie. Stacey offered Angie O'Rourke a questioning glance.

"I know, I know. I heard what Jodie said" Angie whispered.

That evening, Stacey sat with Tony at their local bar. They knew most of the folk around them, either to see or to talk to.

"How was shopping? Buy anything nice? I thought that you were phoning me with news of a bargain, but it was just my big sister worrying about me!" Tony quipped. He went on to explain about Jan's phone call and the letters in the attic.

"Seriously? And you read them? That's gross Tony Lee!" Stacey said, pulling a face.

"No I did not Stacey! I just opened one or two to make sure that they were all from my Dad. Anyway, Jan says that I have to burn the lot" Tony answered. He broke off to sip on his pint of lager.

"I want to say something to you Tony. Now don't take this the wrong way, okay?" Stacey said. Her expression was stern, and Tony looked directly at her.

"Go on, I won't mind" he replied with a shrug.

"Well, it's just that you always seem to do whatever people tell you to do. I mean, I could understand with your Mam, but Jan? You barely know her, and since you met her she has been shouting the odds. I know that she left you the house, but don't let her walk all over you. You've signed for the house now, so you're not beholden to her in any way. She's probably rolling in money anyway, that's why she can't be bothered to sell that old house of yours. I reckon that it's like conscious money. You know, with you looking after her mother for all of those years" Stacey said forcefully.

Tony looked aghast. Normally Stacey never voiced an opinion on anything of any depth.

"You know me Stace, anything for a quiet life. Besides, I did say a few things to her on the phone today" Tony replied defensively.

"Oh poppycock! She can wrap you around her finger. I saw her when she came home for the funeral. She couldn't get back to The States quick enough.

Honestly Tony, you see good in everyone. Imagine for a minute that Jan was not your sister. What do you really think of her as a person?" Stacey said. Perhaps it was because her new blossoming romance with Alex Woods that Stacey was feeling brave. Normally she would sit placidly with Tony, only discussing mundane matters in a broad way.

"I know that Jan hasn't a very nice personality Stace, but she's all that I have. I don't want to cut her out of my life just in case..." Tony trailed off as he often did, leaving things unsaid.

Stacey knew what he meant. Tony still hoped that Jan might allow him into the bosom of her little family. Stacey understood that he was lonely and missing his mother. She wanted to tell him that Jan was not all that he had. That she was there too. Stacey also knew that that would not be strictly true. For already she was waiting for the right time to end their fragile relationship.

"She was never really part of your life Tony. Let's face it; Jan was always just a person on the end of the phone. Had Delores not been alive, would she have bothered to phone at all?" Stacey reasoned.

Tony again sipped on his lager. He knew that Stacey was probably correct.

"Well, she phones me now" he countered weakly.

"Guilt. You wait a week or two. You'll be lucky to get a Christmas card from her!" Stacey said with a chuckle. She wanted to lighten her remarks, but really meant every word.

"I suppose. Look, let's change the subject Stace. This is depressing! Did you think any more about a holiday?" Tony said, realising that Stacey probably had all of the answers.

Stacey bit her lip. It was time to go into defensive mode again.

Tony Lee poured the letters out on the bed again. Somehow touching them made him feel closer to his parents. Jan's words bounced about inside his head. He would burn the love letters as he promised to do, but not just yet. Tony wondered where his father was when he wrote to his mother. So much of his father's life was clouded in mystery. Tony knew that he was very young when his Dad had died. He remembered nothing of the funeral, although his mother had later shown him the grave in Dean's Grange Cemetery in Blackrock.

Tony opened the first letter that came to hand. It felt wrong, but yet he felt compelled to read the first paragraph.

"My Dearest Delores,
          It has only been a short while since I last saw you, yet it feels like an eternity. I cannot wait to be close to you again, to hold you in my

arms. Each day that I spend without you is so empty, and so very lonely. I long to kiss your lips, to see your pretty smile"

Tony stopped reading. He felt his hand tremble. It was as if he was intruding between his mother and father's most intimate thoughts. Tony pushed the sheets of blue writing paper back inside the blue envelope carefully.

"He had the gift of the gab, my old man, that's for sure!" he muttered with a nervous laugh.

Tony studied the date on the envelope. He worked out that he would have been a few months old at the time.

Tony sighed as he put the love letters away. Stacey was right of course. He must never read his Mam's personal mail. Stacey had said that it would be like reading someone's diary. By now he tended to agree. Tony again considered burning them, as Jan had asked him to. Somehow it seemed a little drastic. Perhaps when his mother's death was not so prominent in his mind, he might consider it. Then he thought of Stacey's words. She was right. Why should he always do as Jan told him? He decided that he would wait until the time suited him.

"Can we meet up? I know that it still hurts, but let's meet and talk" the text message from Alex read. It was Sunday afternoon. Stacey was on her way to Walkinstown on the south side of Dublin to collect Jodie from a friend's house. The traffic lights turned red, and Stacey pushed the text message to the back of her brain. Her mind was filled with a mixture of doubt and excitement. She had led Alex along now for over two weeks. He had not asked if she was in a relationship, but she imagined that he had guessed. Neither had she asked about his personal life. By the way that he spoke to her, Stacey presumed that Alex was free.

Stacey saw a petrol station further down the street. Her fuel was low and it would give her a chance to answer his text message. Stacey pulled over and filled up.

As she sat back in the car, Stacey picked up the phone. She was feeling in a good mood. The sun shone down brightly, and a young toddler smiled at her as she passed Stacey's car with her parents. Stacey grinned back at the little girl and she began to compose her message in her head. It was time to see just how serious Alex Woods was.

"What about 2 nite? I'm passing a pub called The Highway Bar just outside Walkinstown. It's out of the way. We could meet there 2 nite about 8:30?" she typed. Stacey pressed "send" and giggled quietly. The big public house was just minutes from Alex's place of work. Her phone beeped, and within seconds beeped again. Alex had replied instantly.

"See u then. Don't b late!" it said. Stacey gasped. She had only been testing the waters, but it had backfired. Her hand trembled as she wondered what she should do. To back out was the sensible thing. But her heart fluttered at the thought of seeing Alex again. She wondered if it was just curiosity. Maybe somewhat, she reasoned, but there was also the sense that they had unfinished business together. And then she thought of Tony Lee. Tony was a safe bet, dependable, a rock for her over the past few years. How could she possibly hurt him? Stacey's brain came up with an alternative plan. She would meet up with Alex, but only for a short while. If she felt that he had not changed, nobody would get hurt. She would know then that Tony was the right one for her after all.

Jodie Callaghan stood outside her pal's house talking animatedly with three girls. Stacey smiled as she saw her flatmate. It seemed that Jodie was never alone. As ever, Jodie wore clothes that suited her boyish style. Her hair was tied back and she wore denim jeans and a casual grey jacket. Stacey shook her head and grinned. She wound down her window, managing to catch the last snippets of conversation.

"And I say that I didn't Jean. I wouldn't do that. I was outside at the time talking to three chaps from Templeogue" Jodie said.

"Well someone did. My head is still spinning" the small, dark-haired girl replied. Within minutes they were hugging each other. Jodie climbed into the passenger seat of Stacey's car and waved goodbye to her friends.

"You live quite an active life Jodie! What are you doing out here? I was about to have a long soak in the bath when you phoned" Stacey said with a smile.

"Oh, I came back with Jean and her pals last night. Someone spiked her drink in a nightclub. For some reason she suspects me. The nerve!" Jodie said haughtily.

"And did you?" Stacey asked flippantly. Jodie thought for a minute.

"No I didn't! But now I wish that I had now, the suspicious cow!" she replied. Both girls laughed out loud.

"Jodie Callaghan! You lead a mad life, I swear! How do you meet all of these people? I never saw you with any of those girls before!" Stacey said with the shake of her head. Jodie considered the question.

"I really don't know Stace. I met Jean somewhere a few years ago. She contacted me on Facebook last Tuesday and asked if I fancied going to a club" Jodie answered with a shrug.

"You have friends all over the place, and you're not even from Dublin!" Stacey said with a disbelieving sigh. Jodie thought quietly for a moment.

"They're not really friends, Stace. These guys are just people to hang around with. You and the girls at the apartment are my real friends. Friends forever, eh?" she said. Her forthrightness struck Stacey immediately. Jodie seldom took anything seriously.

Stacey smiled. It was a nice thing for Jodie to say.

"Yeah mates forever-or until one of us gets hitched!" Stacey laughed.

They drove on, and then an idea popped into Stacey's head.

"Jodie, you were with Angie when you bumped into Alex Woods, right? How did he seem to you? You know Angie, she exaggerates everything. I bet he's still the same" Stacey said in a matter-of-fact tone. Jodie eyed her pal's profile for a moment.

"Why do you ask Stace? You're not thinking of breaking up with the delectable Tony are you?" Jodie countered. Stacey shook her head vehemently.

"Of course not, silly! I'm just curious" she replied. Jodie seemed to accept the answer.

"Oh, he was okay. He was all smiles with bells on! He couldn't do enough for us. His pal was a geek though. I felt that he was undressing us with his eyes, you know the type? I guess the fellow was married" Jodie said. She gave an exaggerated shudder for effect.

"Yeah, but what did Alex say about me?" Stacey asked. Jodie fidgeted with the car radio, bored already with the conversation.

"Oh, this and that. He was all apologies about breaking up with you. He said that he made a big mistake, something like that. Gee Stacey, I can't remember really. You're better off with Tony though. I like him, he's...well, he's Tony!" she concluded. Stacey nodded. Her mind was racing. Could she really go and meet Alex the once, just for her peace of mind, she wondered? Stacey convinced herself that she would be simply putting her mind at rest. She even told her brain that she would give Alex Woods a piece of her mind before walking away. Her heart knew that that was never going to be the case.

That evening, Stacey drew up in her car in the pub car park. She was nervous now. It crossed her mind that she could quite easily bump into someone that knew both she and Tony. Having told her flatmates that she was going to see Tony, Stacey had counterbalanced her alibi by also telling Tony that she was going out with the girls. It was a simple plan, the logic being that Tony would not discover her scheme because he had no reason to phone her apartment. Most times they phoned each other on their mobiles, but sometimes if either had little or no credit, they might use their landlines.

Stacey entered the dimly-lit pub and glanced around. Immediately Alex came to greet her.

"Hi Stacey, I just got here. Can I get you a drink?" Alex said, cheerfully. He gave her a peck on the cheek, catching her by surprise.

"Er, just a Coke for me, I'm driving" she replied. Alex offered his beaming smile. It was always one of his best features. He was taller than Stacey, with jet black curly hair, cut tight at the sides.

"Yeah, Angie said that you bought a car. Pity that! I could have put a good deal your way! I never had you down for a motorist! Remember all those late nights when you would run to catch the last bus home?" the clean-shaven Alex grinned. Suddenly Stacey felt nervous.

"Can we sit down Alex? Let's not stand here talking" she said in a low voice. Alex shrugged and led her to a quiet part of the lounge. He ordered their drinks from an attentive lounge girl and then sat next to Stacey. Their seats were facing away from the busy lounge bar, which suited Stacey fine. Already she felt uncomfortable.

"I don't know why I'm here" she mumbled. Alex laughed heartily.

"I do! You want to give me a piece of your mind!" he said. Stacey grinned back at him.

"Yes I do! You let me down Alex Woods. I can never forgive you" Stacey said crossly. Alex looked chastened.

"I know sweetheart, I was stupid. What can I say? I've grown up a lot since...since... then" he said, a look of embarrassment etched on his boyish face.

"What were you going to say? Since our wedding day?" Stacey replied sternly. He nodded again, looking deep in thought.

"Yeah, since what should have been our wedding day, precious" Alex answered quietly. Stacey smiled to herself. So far he was saying all of the right things. Alex had always used terms of endearment when talking to her, either privately or when they were with friends. Precious, sweetheart, pet or darling were always added to a sentence.

"When you left me I was devastated sweetheart. My Mum never forgave me. She couldn't believe that I did what I did" Alex sighed.

"I heard about your Mum dying. Sorry. I couldn't make the funeral. So soon after our split too. How is your father bearing up these days?" she replied. Alex shrugged

"It hit him hard. We don't talk about it, you know? I still work for him, but it's different" he said. Stacey nodded. His mother had passed away less than two months after she and Alex had split up.

"Where are you living now Alex?" Stacey asked.

"Oh, I moved out of the flat for a while when Mum died. I went back to look after the old man. Turns out, he didn't need me after all. He more or less said so. Now I'm back in the apartment again. I'm glad that I never sold it, precious" he replied.

"Yeah, I liked that flat. It was cosy and spacious. Still, eventually you'll sell it and move back to Blackrock, eh?" Stacey said.

"Yeah, I guess. A house is much more, well, homely I suppose! I prefer a house to an apartment any day, sweetheart" Alex answered.

"It must be catching!" Stacey said without thinking.

"Sorry? I don't understand pet" a baffled Alex said. Stacey flushed slightly.

"Oh nothing, just someone that I know has just inherited the family home" she said quickly. There was a brief pause between the two.

"Look Stacey darling, I messed up, I know that. You were always the one for me. It was just that at the time, marriage seemed such a huge step. I suppose that I panicked" Alex said.

"Charming! The thought of marrying me caused that, did it?" Stacey said, pretending to be hurt.

"Tich! You know that I didn't mean it that way love. I'm so sorry" Alex said. Stacey paused before asking the question which bothered her the most.

"And has there been anybody else? You know, since we broke up?" she asked. Alex took a sip of his pint of ale.

"Nobody serious, I promise you that. Oh, I've been out on dates all right, I won't lie. The girls that I liked weren't interested in me. Funnily enough, the ones that I didn't like were!" he said with a nervous laugh. Stacey laughed too.

"And what about you Stacey pet? Is there anybody in your life at the moment?" Alex asked. Stacey rattled the ice in her glass of Coke. It was time to come clean.

"Yes, actually. His name is Tony. He's very sweet and caring, but..." Stacey stopped and tried to find the right words.

"But what Stacey?" Alex persisted.

"I'm not sure that I'm in love with him. It's complicated. Tony's just buried his mother. They were really close. I can't just walk away" Stacey said quietly.

"So, if this Tony chap wasn't around, would you have me back?" Alex asked. His dark eyes searched hers for an answer. Stacey smiled and sipped on her drink.

"Maybe. Yes I would Alex. That is, if you want me. I need time though. I can't finish with Tony right now" she said in a barely audible voice. Alex Woods afforded himself a self-satisfied grin. It was all that he needed to know.

"I can wait precious. I'll wait until the time is right for you" he whispered. Alex took her right hand and kissed it. He then held her hand in his. For Stacey it suddenly felt right. They kissed before she quickly pulled away.

"Wait, just for a bit Alex, eh? My head is all over the place" she whispered. Alex Woods nodded. He still held her hand in his.

"I never stopped loving you babe" he replied. Stacey felt a warm glow. She felt good about herself again. All of those times with Tony Lee when she was second best to his mother began to suddenly fade away. She felt wanted, important. It felt good. Suddenly she could not wait to finish with Tony. She had to be with Alex. It felt so natural.

Tony Lee shoved the letters belonging to his late mother back inside the old handbag. He was determined to resist the chance to read any more of the personal details. Twice now he had opened a letter and read a few lines. Resolutely he climbed up towards the attic door. Tony threw the bag back as far as he could into the darkness.

"There! Stay there until I'm ready to get rid of you!" he muttered. Although anxious to avoid temptation, Tonty still could not bring himself to burn the letters. They were his only link with his late father, and that still fascinated him.

Three nights later, Tony met up with Stacey. Far from spending more time together as Tony had expected after his mother's funeral, he and Stacey seemed to be seeing less and less of each other. Tony blamed himself. He had been busy doing up the house. Painting was now his form of therapy. He had tried to involve Stacey, but she still refused point blank to go anywhere near number eighty-eight. Tonight he would be extra nice to her. Tony wanted to impress her with news of his hard work, and planned to spring a surprise on her.

As they sat chatting in their local pub, Tony swung the conversation around to his home improvements.

"I've done wonders with the place Stacey. All three bedrooms are like new. I hired a skip and tossed out all of the old furniture in Mam's room. I even decorated the spare bedroom so that you could have your friends over. You know, if Angie wanted to hang out overnight or something" Tony said cheerfully.

Stacey Boyd was barely listening. She had some news of her own to tell Tony about. Stacey looked at him blankly as his words sank in.

"What? Are you mad Tony? I could never sleep there again. Never. As for asking Angie to stay over, forget it. That's not going to happen" she replied sharply. Tony looked disappointed, but tried to brave it out.

"No, I know not straight away, but in time Stace. We have to move on. I'm trying really hard. I even dumped those love letters that I was telling you about" he said proudly.

"Oh please! Not that again. That gives me the creeps. I can't believe you sometimes Tony! Honestly! What makes you think that I want to hear about all of this? I mean, we're supposed to be dating! All that I ever get is stories about that creepy house of yours. I mean, don't you ever think about making me feel special? A guy should do things for a girl. You know, nice things" Stacey said haughtily. It was all part of her master plan. Tony was bound to get annoyed with her. Then she could blurt out her true feelings.

Tony Lee reached inside his inside pocket. His lips parted into a smile as he pulled the envelope from his jacket.

"I do want to do nice things for you Stacey. You'll see. Things will get better and better between us, really they will. Here, read this. I've book us a sunshine holiday in Portugal for July. It's a five star hotel. You can get time off then, can't you? God Stace, I was bricking it in the travel agency. I've never booked a holiday in my life. The girl was so helpful though. She went through everything..."

"Stop! Just stop will you?" Stacey said in a loud voice, interrupting Tony's ramblings. The tears streamed down her face. Tony looked bewildered. People near to their table tried to avert their gaze. Stacey pulled a tissue from her white handbag and dabbed her eyes.

"What's up Stace? What did I do?" Tony whispered. Stacey shook her head. She tried to speak through her gentle sobbing.

"You did nothing Tony, it's me. Listen, there's no easy way to say this, but I want to finish it. I've been thinking about it for a long time now. Tony, we're not cut out for a relationship. We're more like pals, or brother and sister. I don't want to hurt you further down the line. It's best if we end it now" she said. Her crying was subsiding now as she took control of her emotions. Tony stared back in shock. He tried to speak, but nothing came out. His mouth opened and closed as Stacey spoke again.

"You see, I want you to be happy. You're a good man Tony, but I just can't be with you anymore. I'm so sorry" Stacey said in a barely audible voice.

"I...I don't understand Stace. You and me, well, we get on fine. All of that business with my Mam, well, that's behind us now. As for the house, it's a completely different place. If you want though, we can always move. I'll get an apartment. We could get one together" Tony said. His tone was pleading now, and Stacey shook her head.

"Stop Tony, don't make it worse. My mind is made up. I didn't just decide this lightly. We can still be friends" Stacey said. Tony managed a nervous laugh.

"Oh that old chestnut! Don't be daft!" he replied. Suddenly Tony's mind was racing.

"Is, is there someone else? Have you met someone Stacey?" he asked quietly. She could not lie. Tony's blue piercing eyes were boring into her. Stacey had hoped that it would not come to this. She cleared her throat and pushed the wet tissue back inside her handbag.

"Not really. Alex phoned me. We talked. It made me realise what I wanted in life" she answered slowly. Her eyes glanced downwards as she fiddled with her red-painted nails. Tony nodded his head several times.

"Alex Woods. This is the same fellow that practically dumped you at the altar! This is the guy who you hate more than any other in the world! I can't believe you Stacey. I was there to pick up the pieces. Remember what you were like when we started dating? You could barely talk without bursting into tears. I helped you to get a life again Stace" Tony said.

Stacey could barely look at him now. It was much tougher than she had imagined. She could see the devastation on his face, and the hurt in his eyes.

"I know Tony, and for that I will be always grateful. I'm not saying that I want to get back with Alex. We only talked, nothing more" she said defensively.

"Oh please Stacey, spare me!" Tony said sarcastically.

"I think that I should leave. Will you be all right?" Stacey asked. She stood up hesitantly. Tony looked at her. He tried to hold back the tears, but was forced to wipe them away.

"Yeah, sure Stacey, I'll be just fine" he whispered.

She turned away briskly, wiping her face as she left. Tony sat for a moment alone. He wanted to run after her, to beg her for one last chance. Stacey was already outside, opening the car door. Soon she would text Alex to tell him the news.

Tony Lee picked up the envelope from the table containing his holiday itinerary. He fished in his pocket for the small velvet-covered box. His plan to go down on one knee in the crowded local bar would never happen now. Tony Lee slipped away hoping that no one had noticed. They had of course, and several pairs of eyes followed him all the way to the exit.

CHAPTER SEVEN

ERIK'S STORY

It was now six weeks later. Tony Lee stared absentmindedly out of the office window. Situated on the fourth floor, the company building gave a panoramic view of Dublin City. It was a beautiful sunny day and Tony was on his lunch hour. Normally he would be out enjoying the weather, or cycling around the streets, but since his split with Stacey, Tony barely felt like doing anything.

"A penny for your thoughts" said Erik Ngombiti. Tony glanced sideways at his workmate without speaking. He stared out into the sunshine through the giant glass panel, which ran from ceiling to floor, with a large window sandwiched between. It was next to his desk at the I.T. company, and Tony would often gaze out pensively most days. Erik nodded as he sipped on his paper cup of cool water.

"You know Tony; I've been observing you a lot lately. It appears to me that you're not your old self. It seems to me that it's since about the time of your mother's funeral. Oh, I know that I shouldn't be saying this to you, but someone has to. You were in a bit of a daze that day. Do you recall me wishing you well? I know that I didn't hang around afterwards like the other mourners to shake your hand, but I was there. Y'know this Irish thing about lining up in the church? Well I never quite got used to that! I don't like to intrude, you know?" said Erik. He was a big tall bespectacled man in his late thirties. Erik was always chatty with everyone, and well liked among the staff. He could be deadly serious and straightforward, with strong opinions on world politics. However, Erik Ngombiti could also be surprisingly funny. Although not born in Ireland, he could speak the Irish language very well, and would often use phrases to baffle his Dublin workmates who were not as proficient in their native tongue.

Tony Lee did not feel much like chatting, but did not want to be abrupt or rude to Erik.

"I understand Erik, thanks for being there. It's a shitty world, you know?" Tony answered.

"Yeah, but you gotta make the best of it. You've been under the weather lately, and it ain't just the funeral, am I right?" Erik asked. Tony nodded, staring straight into the middle distance.

"You know what I was thinking just then before you spoke? I was thinking how simple it would be to jump off the roof of this building and end it all. Now there's a thought for you to pontificate on Erik! You always have an opinion on everything, so what do you reckon on that?" Tony replied wistfully.

Erik looked a little startled. He tried to speak but Tony cut him dead.

"Oh just forget it Erik. I know that you mean well, but I just want to be left alone, okay?" Tony said coldly. He attempted to walk away towards the toilets, but Erik managed to grab his arm.

"Hey! I'm not the enemy here. I was looking out for you, that's all. Something else is up, isn't it? It's not just the loss of your Ma, is it?" said Erik. Tony laughed out loud at Erik's attempt at a flat Dublin accent. He was always caught by surprise when his dark-skinned friend used a word normally associated with Dublin or Irish folk.

"My Ma? Jesus Erik, what did you call your mother in London? Mother? Mum? Why do you insist on using Irish words? It sounds so funny" Tony said with a grin. Erik smiled back and gripped Tony by the shoulders.

"Come into my office and talk, yeah?" Erik said. He led Tony around to his desk, just feet away from where Tony worked. Each worker's desk was referred to as their office, a private joke among the staff. Their bosses had huge offices on the floor below. It was space that they hardly needed, while the I.T. staff's booths were fairly crammed together on the floor above them in pod-like curved work stations.

Tony and Erik sat in the semi-secluded workspace on two swivel chairs. The floor was devoid of staff now, all enjoying the lunchtime break. After some moments, Tony spilled out his story on his split with Stacey.

"You see Erik, she was my world. I never got to tell her that really. I was too preoccupied looking after my Mam. I'm totally lost without Stacey. I leave here in the evening, wondering why the hell I'm going home to an empty house. Sometimes I take off on the bike, just to kill some time. I've even cycled past her apartment slowly, hoping that she might come out. I see her car parked outside. One evening I nearly left a letter on her car windscreen, begging her to take me back. I had the words written down in a letter in my pocket. How sad is that Erik? I feel desperate at the moment. Who knows what I will be like when the winter sets in. At least now I can get out of the house and clear my head. Honestly Erik, if this is my life, I don't think that I can go on" Tony said in a whisper.

Erik nodded. His cup of water was empty now. He tossed the white plastic cup in the litter bin beside his desk. Erik looked in thoughtful mood as he rose to his feet.

"I sympathise Tony, really I do. But with respect, you don't know what you are talking about. Don't get me wrong, love is a powerful emotion. I met my wife in London. As you know, we have two beautiful kids. I showed you the photos, right?" Erik said. Tony nodded back. Erik strolled to the large window, turning his back on Tony. For a moment there was complete silence in the giant building. Erik turned back quickly and eyed Tony Lee.

"I'm going to tell you a story my friend. I have never told anybody here at this company, but I will share it with you today" Erik said sternly.

Stacey Boyd sat in her car with her mobile phone in hand. She was on her lunch break, and was busy sharing text messages with Alex. Sometimes she did this from the canteen, but found the car was much more private.

"I know we met last nite, but why not 2 nite as well?" Alex texted. Stacey grinned as she read the message.

"Washing my hair" she replied.

"Can I watch?" he replied rapidly.

The two had been inseparable since her split with Tony Lee. Most nights they met up, even for a short while. Sometimes Alex would wait for her after work. One day he arrived with a bunch of red roses at the entrance to her job in the Revenue Office. Although highly embarrassed, Stacey still loved the idea that he would do such a thing.

"Why not go out in a foursome this weekend? Maybe Angie and her new guy?" Alex's message read. The smile vanished from Stacey's face. Thoughts of Angie O'Rourke shattered her happy mode. She tried to make light of the idea.

"Not sharing u with anyone!" Stacey typed quickly. It was almost time to return to her office job at the Government-run income tax department. She glanced at her watch as she awaited a reply. A man cycled by on a silver bicycle, not unlike Tony's. Again Stacey's happy disposition waned.

"Poor Tony" she whispered. She wondered briefly about the man who had helped put her life back together again. Then Stacey thought of number eighty-eight. A shiver ran down her spine. The bleep of her mobile phone put her mind back on Alex Woods. There was still time for one or two more messages.

Erik Ngombiti strolled back across the floor and sat down next to Tony. He looked him in the eyes and sighed loudly.

"Do you know where I was born Tony?" he asked quietly. Tony Lee shrugged his shoulders.

"London I suppose" he replied indifferently. Erik nodded. It was the answer that he had expected. He had come to work with Tony at the I.T. specialist company almost two years ago. Erik had met an Irish girl in London. He had told Tony that Eileen had persuaded him that their young children would have a better and safer life in Dublin.

"Wrong! Oh, I lived there for many years okay. I even thought of it as home. Then I met this mad Irish lady..." Erik burst into laughter at his own little joke. His deep, distinctive husky laughter could always be heard along the busy floor. Almost every member of staff would mimic Erik's laughter. But today there was no one except Tony to appreciate it.

"You have a lovely wife and two nice children Erik. Me? I guess that it was never meant to be. I'm just boring I suppose. What do you think?" Tony said, interrupting his workmate's flow. Erik took it in his stride.

"Well, maybe just a bit! It depends on what you want out of life, you know? When I was young, all I wanted to do was to find something to eat. I can still remember those hunger pains. My stomach would ache all night. I could not sleep" Erik said quietly.

"Because you came to us from England, we all presumed that you were born in London. Where were you born Erik?" Tony asked. Erik Ngombiti stood up again and walked to the window. The back of his dark trousers and white shirt, with its rolled up sleeves, faced Tony Lee once more.

"A long way from here my friend. It seems like another world now. Do you know that I have family members that I still don't know if they are dead or alive?" he said. Erik turned to face Tony again. His brown sparkling eyes were usually full of life and fun. Now they looked downcast as he relived his private torment. Tony Lee said nothing. He knew that Erik was about to enlighten him further. To ask a question now seemed impolite somehow.

"I was born on the western side of Africa, a country called Mauritania. We have a bloody history, ruled by the French for many years. I lived in a small village. When I was just twelve, the whole country was ravaged by civil war, drought and disease. Both my mother and father died of typhoid. I was left to care for my baby sister and my sick brother. He was soon to die too. That meant that I had to care for this little girl, who was just six. I could barely look after myself at the time. By now most of the villagers were either dead or were dying. The women had fled with their babies, and most of the men folk had gone off to fight. We hid in the bushes, afraid to go back inside the village. Anyway, soon my baby sister died. I buried her there and then, putting some stones over the soft clay. Can you imagine?" Erik said, his voice almost breaking.

"Erik, please don't. It's not worth it" Tony protested. Erik Ngombiti offered a rueful smile. He had barely started his tale.

"After a few more days, this older man befriended me. His name was Saldo, and he said that some of them planned to get to France by boat. He made it sound like heaven. There would be food, work, all that your heart desired. I was young and I believed him. I felt honoured that he had chosen me to accompany him. There would be a price to pay of course. We set off through the jungle, along the coast, several of us. I became his special friend. He made me do things to him. My God! You would never believe what I had to do for this man. I had nobody you see. I was the youngest of our group. I lay there at night dreaming of France, and what it would mean if we ever got there. I lost track of time. We inched our way north. There were about twenty-five of us. Days were like years, always climbing further and further north in the direction of The Mediterranean Sea. We went through Morocco, terrified that we would be slaughtered. By now we only travelled by night. I lost track of time completely. We must have travelled for months, but I was determined to carry on. I had nothing to go back to. One day I remember looking out across the water in the direction of Europe. We had lost many men along the way. Somehow I was still alive. Saldo fed me as best he could. He hunted, stole food, fished, anything to stay alive. Always he promised me that we would eventually make it. I had to believe him" Erik said quietly.

Tony Lee sat uncomfortably listening to his workmate torment himself with thoughts of his younger days. Erik ploughed on with his story.

"Some time later we set off on this ramshackle boat. We stole it one night and set to sea. I say boat, but it was more like a mass of wood just hammered together! No one knew how to steer. All we had to eat was some fruit and some rotting vegetables. Four more men died on the crossing, but we just tossed them into the sea. We drifted between consciousness and semi-awareness of what was going on. Then we ran out of drinking water. It was terrifying, but all of the time Saldo kept telling me that it would be okay. Some ships even came into our view, but quickly disappeared. Either they did not see us, or they simply did not want to know. One morning I woke up to the sounds of Saldo screaming with delight. By then there was only eight of us. We stumbled ashore to what we thought was France. It was really either Spain or possibly Italy, I don't really know. We split up, thinking that it would give us a better chance. Saldo had a good understanding of the law. He said that we would be turned back if captured. He and two other men led me onwards for days, maybe weeks. We stole food, clothes. One night they mugged a couple and stole the man's wallet. And still Saldo kept abusing me. Even as my very soul screamed out for mercy, he continued to do it. I was too scared to protest. All that I cared about was getting to somewhere safe. I knew that I still needed Saldo, and never planned on escaping from him. When we got to France eventually, it was not at all as I had imagined. The people did not want to know us, even though we could speak their language. Saldo pushed onwards, driving on further north in the direction of The English Channel. By now there was just the two of us. We had split from the other two men. Saldo said that we should try to get across The Channel to Britain. We tried to hide on trucks, but were always found. And then one night we got lucky. I could scarcely believe it. When we reached England we were discovered by the customs men. Somehow it did not matter. We were prepared to take our chances. Saldo had taught me what to say. I was a refugee. He drummed it into my head day and night. We would be detained as illegal immigrants. As the customs people separated us, I could see Saldo's eyes. I still can to this day. He nodded to me as if to say "I can do no more for you. You are on your own now".

"When I was put into detention, I never saw Saldo again after that. For years I fought my deportation. I told them that I was an orphan, and how my family had been wiped out. After many years I was finally granted British citizenship. By now I had been educated. I could speak English and French, and took a course in computer diplomacy" Erik said impassively. Tony Lee felt at a loss for words.

"I...I'm sorry Erik, I never knew" he muttered weakly. Erik nodded his acceptance and sat down next to him.

I always wanted to go back to Africa, but to this day I never have. I probably won't now. The reason that I'm telling you this story my friend is because even now there is never a morning when I don't wake up and thank God that I'm alive. Life is precious Tony. Suicide is such a waste" Erik said. There was total silence for some seconds. Tony felt compelled to speak, but was at a loss as to what to say.

"It must have been horrific" Tony mumbled. Erik managed a token grin before strolling to the large window again.

"A problem is only as big as you allow it to be Tony. That's why I wanted to tell you my story. But there's much more. I cannot explain the fear, the stench of death, the loneliness. I saw some horrific sights. Poverty and death were everywhere. Sometimes you get to look into your very soul, you know? Yet somehow I survived, and here I am" Erik said.

"I'm sorry Erik. You must think me a selfish idiot. I bet that you must hate this man Saldo. He was an animal" Tony replied.

Erik turned away from the sunny scene outside.

"I should, but then Saldo saved my life. Without him I would never have made it. I would never have met my wife, or seen my beautiful children. I still recall that look in his eyes when we were caught. It was as if he was saying, "Okay, it's over. I used you Erik, but here you are. I delivered you to freedom".

"From that day I learned to stand on my own two feet. I became single-minded. I had to survive in my new world" Erik said.

"And you met Eileen in London?" Tony asked, trying to lighten the conversation. A huge smile beamed from Erik's face.

"Yeah, many years later. I saw her sitting outside a café with friends. I noticed her smile and walked straight up to her" Erik grinned.

"Never!" Tony gasped. Erik nodded several times.

"I did! I just knew that she was the one. Life is for living my friend. I asked her out and she gave me her phone number. And the rest my friend is history! Now, about your own little problems. Whatever happens Tony, promise me that you will never consider such a cowardly way out" Erik said quietly, nodding towards the window. Tony felt humble. Compared to what his work colleague had been through, his troubles were minute.

"Don't mind me Erik; it's just this business with Stacey and my sister in The States. I'll get over it" he replied.

"Ah families! What I wouldn't give to have family problems! I go through it with my wife Eileen all of the time! One day her sister in Canada is a bitch, the next day she's an angel! If I say anything about her sister, I'm the worst in the world! Tell, me, what is the big deal with your sister Tony? I saw her at the funeral. She looks serene enough!" Erik said with a glib laugh.

"Oh, Jan is okay I suppose. There's a big age gap between us. Fourteen years. Jan is a bit bossy, that's all. She snaps at me for no reason. Like when I found my Dad's love letters to my Mam. She made me promise never to read them, and to burn them right away" Tony said sheepishly.

"And did you?" Erik asked with a bemused grin.

"Burn them?" Naw, I couldn't Erik. I didn't read them either, well, maybe just a few lines!" Tony answered with a grin. It seemed to strike a chord with Erik.

"I have nothing from my past, just bad memories. Yet someday I want to go back to Africa, to my country. Each year I promise myself that I will return, but with the kids..."Erik trailed off as his mind drifted away.

"Someday you will Erik, someday you will" Tony smiled. The sound of workers returning from their lunchtime break shattered their moment of openness. The two men smiled at each other, and Tony silently returned to his work pod.

As the office filled again with bustle and noise, Tony vowed that he would never give in to weakness. He would soldier on with life, even if he was destined to live it alone.

On Sunday afternoon, the house phone rang. It startled Tony for a second as he sat lost in his Sunday newspaper. Tony tossed the paper aside and went to answer the ringing tone.

"Hello?" Tony said in a friendly tone.

"Hi Tony, it's Jan. How are you keeping?" said the voice. It caught Tony a little by surprise. He had not thought of his sister for a while. Tony quickly composed himself before answering.

"Oh hello Jan, how are all of the family? What's the weather like there?" he asked idly.

"Everyone's well. Oh, it's sunny as usual. Too warm to do anything. To tell you the truth, I miss the rain" Jan answered. There was a moment's pause as Tony tried to think of something to say.

"I split up with Stacey. There was no row or anything. We just went our separate ways" Tony said weakly.

"Oh? Never mind Tony, you'll soon meet someone else. Pity, Stacey seemed nice. Anyway, you haven't knocked down the house or anything, have you?" Jan said with a forced chuckle. Tony could not help but think how cold and self-centred his sister sounded.

"No, I've done nothing Jan. Since splitting with Stacey I've felt a little down to be honest. All I do is work, then come home to cook my meal" Tony said.

"Dear, dear. You need a holiday Tony. Why not head off to Spain or somewhere? You must be due some time off?" Jan said. Tony thought about inviting himself over to see her. He quickly changed his mind. Tony knew instantly that he would not be made welcome. A loud knock on the front door changed his focus.

"Sorry Jan, was there something specific you wanted? Someone's at the front door" he said lamely. Tony felt that he was already running out of things to say.

"No no, you go ahead. I was just concerned about my little brother, that's all" Jan said, again forcing an obligatory chuckle.

"I'm fine Jan, tell Howard and the kids that I was asking for them" Tony replied.

"Bye" said Jan. Instantly the line went dead.

"Yeah right! A conscience call more likely!" Tony muttered. A second knock on the door reminded Tony why he had ended the call abruptly.

Tony opened the old front door. A girl stood with her back to him. As she turned towards him, Tony got a surprise.

"Jodie?" What brings you around here?" he said. A beaming Jodie Callaghan stood in her blue tracksuit and white trainers. Tony's brain was now in overdrive. He scanned the street outside for Stacey's car. His mind was racing. Perhaps it had not worked out with Alex and Stacey after all. Maybe she had sent Jodie around to clear a way back. Tony could feel his heart thumping with anticipation. Then Jodie unzipped her tracksuit top and produced an old green and black iPod. Tony's heart sank as he recognised the item.

"Here, Stacey asked me to return this Tony. She found it in a drawer" Jodie said.

"Oh thanks. Sorry Jodie, would you like to come in?" Tony answered, trying hard to mask his disappointment.

They sat drinking coffee as both steered around the topic of Stacey Boyd.

"I see that you've painted the old place. Pity that you stuck to the green outside. I noticed the front door" Jodie said in her usual direct way.

"No, it's just temporary. I'll do a proper job outside later. Everything has always been green at the front of the house. My mother liked it that way. Soon I'll get around to doing a full paint job, something bright maybe. What would you suggest Jodie?" Tony said defensively. Jodie was caught out by him seeking her opinion.

"Oh, white maybe, I dunno. Listen, about Stacey. She's moved in with Alex. I thought that you should know. In a way I feel partly responsible" Jodie said. She went on to explain about how she and Angie had met Alex on a night out together.

"Oh I see. Never mind Jodie, it's not your fault. I'm okay now" Tony said.

"There's nobody else then?" Jodie asked. Tony shook his head. He wanted to put on a brave face for his unexpected guest.

"Well, I haven't really got the time. What with work and trying to do a bit with the house…" Tony replied in a less than convincing tone. Jodie nodded quietly.

"It's not the same around at the flat either. We don't see you, and with Stacey and Angie gone, myself and Gina are lost" Jodie said with a shrug of her lean shoulders.

"Angie's moved out too?" Tony asked.

"Oh yeah, I should have said. She's moved in with her fellow Philip. He's married with kids, but they seem to be getting on well. Phil's nice, but I can't say that I trust him. Something tells me that he will end up back with his wife" Jodie said abstractly. Tony giggled as he listened. Stacey had always admired Jodie's straightforwardness and opinions. He had to agree. There was something refreshing and endearing about Jodie.

"If Stacey's moved out, how come you have my iPod? She didn't ask you to bring it around, did she?" Tony said suddenly. The theory had quickly dawned on him as he fiddled with the old iPod in his hand. For a second Jodie looked startled.

"Well, no, not really. When she was moving out she tossed it on my bed, along with some other stuff. She said that you had lent it to her before she bought her car. She used to wear it when she went jogging with me. Remember? Okay, the truth is that I was just being nosey! You don't mind, do you Tony?" Jodie asked with an embarrassing grin. Tony chuckled and shook his head.

"Nah, I don't mind Jodie, not at all. But you've had a wasted journey I'm afraid. There's nothing to report here! I have no new girlfriend hiding upstairs! My pal at work thinks that I'm quite boring" Tony answered with a flippant grin. Jodie jumped to her feet suddenly.

"Well, why don't we go and do something together? We could go bowling, or maybe just hang out?" she suggested. A look of horror spread across Tony's face.

"Er, what? You mean me and you?" Tony stuttered. He looked directly at the thin fragile-looking girl with her blonde pony-tail as if she was suggesting some suicide pact.

"Sure, why not? We're mates aren't we? Are you afraid to let a girl beat you at bowling?" Jodie asked with a daring frown.

"No, no, well, it's just that... Well, what would Stacey say if she found out? I mean, you and she are still mates. It doesn't seem fair..."

Tony Lee's words were drowned out as Jodie threw her arms around him. She kissed him full on the lips. At first Tony stood with his arms hanging limply by his sides. Then he felt himself respond. His arms engulfed Jodie's thin body. They clung to each other, planting kisses on each other's lips.

"Sorry, I got a bit carried away" Jodie said.

"Me too! This is a bad idea though" Tony replied.

"Why Tony? I always fancied you. I never told Stacey, but now that she's gone..." Jodie replied. They were still locked in an embrace, and Jodie moved her lips again in Tony's direction. Tony Lee pulled his head back and resisted.

"No, this is silly. I mean, we barely know each other Jodie" Tony protested.

"Well, come on then, let's go bowling! We can talk between shots as I destroy you!" she replied. Jodie grabbed him by the arm with both hands and dragged him towards the kitchen door. Her body strength surprised Tony. He laughed at her determination, and quickly found himself agreeing to go.

"Okay, okay, but let me get changed!" Tony said.

Howard Williams sat on his favourite armchair reading the newspaper. Now and then he would cast a furtive glance in the direction of Jan. The children were out and the house was quiet. Jan sat watching television, although she was barely taking in the home makeover programme.

"I'm still not sure about it Jan. I've been searching my mind for another way to deal with this" he said. Jan looked over her spectacles at him.

"What other way? We've been over this a million times Howard. We always knew that this time would come. Things will be just fine as long as Tony stays where he is" she replied.

"That's just it Jan. Now that he's broken up with that girl, who knows what he will decide to do? I tell you, we should both go over there and sort out this mess" Howard replied with a worried scowl.

"Tich! You're been over-dramatic Howard love. What could we do anyway? Let's just get on with our lives and forget all about it. It's behind us now. Tony is a real home bird. He will find another girl soon. Don't forget, with Mom gone, he has a free rein. He will be making up for lost time. You'll see Howard, it will be just dandy" Jan answered with a reassuring smile. Howard returned to his newspaper, but still cast a series of worried glances at his wife every now and then.

Tony Lee lay on his bed with the lights out. It had been a strange type of day. Firstly Jan had phoned for no apparent reason, and then Jodie had called on him. It was Jodie Callaghan who preoccupied his mind. They had gone bowling and had a drink together at a nearby bar. Tony had always liked Jodie, but never in a romantic way. Her boyish adventurous ways had always amused him. Tony had never seen her with a steady boyfriend, and in fact had often wondered if she might be gay. Friends seemed to flit in and out of Jodie's life for as long as he had known Stacey. They had got on extremely well that afternoon, and Tony wondered if he should put it down to being lonely.

"The way I am lately, any girl would be good company!" he mused. Yet Jodie Callaghan had not tried to push their new friendship. She had not suggested that they date, or tried to ask how he felt. In fact Jodie had talked mostly about herself, and her hopes and wishes in life. It appeared that Jodie was gradually ditching her adventurous pals in favour of a quieter lifestyle. She still went jogging a lot, but claimed that she spent most evenings at home. They had parted with one simple straightforward kiss, having earlier exchanged phone numbers.

"Keep in touch Tony. I'll be there if you need me" Jodie had said. Then she was gone into the evening air, leaving Tony at a bus stop near the city centre.

Tony turned on his side and tried to sleep. He wondered what Stacey might make of it all. Somehow he cared. He had no wish to hurt his ex-girlfriend. It seemed in bad taste to date a friend of Stacey's. Still, he was somehow drawn to Jodie. He felt confused. Certainly Jodie was not as glamorous as Stacey. Tony tried to picture her in a designer skirt with her hair expensively styled. Somehow it was impossible. That sporty Jodie Callaghan refused to go away. Tony decided to sleep on the matter. Perhaps he really was lonely. Maybe tomorrow he would see things in their proper prospective.

CHAPTER EIGHT

A PROBLEM FOR ALEX

It was now one week later. Tony had talked on the phone to Jodie most days. They had met briefly one evening for a drink. On Tony's lunch break the previous day, the two had met for a chat. Their relationship was now very close. The only thing holding Tony back was his perceived view of how others might judge his morals. There was really only Stacey and her friends to consider, yet Tony still felt awkward around Jodie. Today Jodie was visiting Tony at his home. It was Saturday afternoon, a bright summer's day.

"Shouldn't you be off shopping with your pals?" Tony asked half-jokingly as they sat in his newly-decorated kitchen. Jodie looked a little embarrassed.

"I told you yesterday that I would call around. I can go shopping anytime" she countered.

Tony smiled. It felt nice to have someone care about him. During the last few weeks he had felt so alone and isolated.

"Thanks Jodie, I know how much you girls like your Saturday afternoons in town. I appreciate you calling, I really do" Tony replied. Jodie looked a little uneasy.

"Listen Tony, I'm not gonna lie to you. Last night I told Gina that I was seeing you. I told her that it was no big deal. Anyway, she didn't see it that way. Gina was a bit miffed. So to clear the air I phoned Angie and Stacey. I just told both of them that we were friends, that's all. Stacey sounded very hurt. Angie said that I was betraying a pal. So, to be honest, I don't think that I would be very welcome on today's shopping trip! My ears are burning as we speak!!" Jodie said.

Tony looked worried. Jodie's forthrightness surprised him.

"You told them? I see. I was hoping that they might understand when they found out. Still, what can we do? I'm sorry Jodie. I didn't want to drive a wedge between you and your pals. I kind of agree with them to be truthful. If someone asked me if I approved of someone else in our circumstances, I would have to say no. But what can we do? It just happened" Tony said quietly.

"Well, I'm not sorry. No one will tell me what to do" Jodie said defiantly. Tony Lee laughed out loud. Jodie's fiery attitude amused him. It was something that he had begun to admire in her lately. Jodie eyed him up and down.

"What would you normally do on Saturday afternoons Tony?" she asked.

"Oh cycle mostly. I used to just talk with Mam and look after her. Lately I've been using the weekends for doing up the house" Tony answered abstractly. Jodie walked towards him and took his hand.

"Well, why don't we go to bed and really give everyone something to talk about?" she whispered. Tony kissed her slowly on the mouth. He led her upstairs to his room and pulled the heavy dark curtains. It never crossed Jodie's mind that she was about to share the same bed with Tony as Stacey Boyd had once slept in.

Later downstairs, Tony and Jodie Callaghan sat chatting on the sofa. It was now early evening, and Tony picked his words carefully.

"Will you go back to the apartment tonight Jodie? If so, what will Gina say?" he asked. Jodie frowned as she considered his words.

"Of course I'll go back. I live there! Anyway, since Angie and Stacey left, we're barely able to pay the rent. We're looking for someone else to share. So Gina is in no position to throw me out! She wouldn't do that anyway. Gina is okay really. Actually, she even hinted at moving her boyfriend in to help with the rent. I'm not sure that I would be comfortable with that arrangement though. Harry's okay, but I never shared with a fellow" Jodie said with a heavy sigh.

"And Stacey, what will happen there? Can you still be friends?" Tony asked. Jodie shrugged her shoulders.

"Who knows? Anyway, let's not dwell on dreary things. I fancy doing a bit of painting! Come on, let's do up a room! I hate sitting around!" Jodie said, immediately leaping to her feet. Tony looked surprised. Already he had noticed that Jodie's energy was limitless. Stacey had often remarked on this fact before. It appeared that Jodie could barely sit still for five minutes. Stacey had told Tony that even while watching a movie, Jodie Callaghan would constantly be on the go, making tea, tidying up, or doing simple keep-fit exercises.

"I wasn't planning on doing anymore decorating for a while Jodie" a worried-looking Tony replied. He glanced around the sitting room at the freshly-painted walls.

"Rubbish! Your bedroom is in a right state! I couldn't help noticing the bedroom ceiling...!" Jodie said with a knowing smile. Tony Lee flushed as he realised the implication of what she was saying.

"Well, I suppose that I have enough paint" Tony answered slowly.

"Goody! Get me some old clothes, will you? I fancy getting stuck in!" she said chirpily.

It was almost two hours later when Tony's bedroom room had had a complete makeover. Jodie examined their handiwork critically.

"It's okay I suppose. Those curtains will have to go though. There gross Tony Lee! How long have you had those awful-looking things for?" she inquired. Tony laughed as he thought for a moment.

"Forever I should think! I think that I inherited them from the spare room!" Tony replied. Jodie continued to study the room.

"What about this wall here Tony? It juts out about four foot for no reason at all. I looked in the back bedroom behind it. That wall in the other bedroom is flat. Why would a wall come out like that? Was there ever a fireplace or something there once?" Jodie asked. Tony glanced at the old wall to the right of his bed. It stuck out for more than a yard, all of the way up to the ceiling. It was about two yards in width, but it had always been like that as long as Tony could recall.

"Maybe, I'm sure that there was a fireplace in the room at some stage. I really don't remember" he replied.

"It looks ridiculous! Let's knock it down!" Jodie said in an upbeat voice. Tony looked horrified.

"Are you mad? It could be holding up the roof! Anyway, we've only just done up the room!" he answered.

"Relax! I was joking!" Jodie beamed. Tony playfully jabbed the small paintbrush at her face, leaving a white mark on the tip of her nose. Jodie looked startled as she brushed the mark away with her sleeve.

"Right! Its war!" she squealed. Tony put up his hands in mock defence. Jodie launched at him with her paintbrush protruding sword-like on front of her. Tony made a grab for the brush and the two fell onto the bed. They struggled for a minute before falling into an embrace. Suddenly they were in the throes of passion once more.

"Hello Jodie? It's Stacey" said the voice. Jodie sighed as she lay on her bed. It was late in the evening and she had just returned from eighty-eight St Oliver's Road. Gina was out, and so Jodie was alone in the apartment. She prepared herself mentally for the onslaught which was sure to follow.

"Yeah Stacey, what's up?" Jodie replied casually.

"What's up? What the hell do you think is up? I can't believe you, really I can't! There are thousands of men out there Jodie, why Tony Lee, for God's sake?" Stacey said in a heated tone. Jodie Callaghan sighed again in resignation. She had suspected that her three friends would discuss her and Tony's relationship that afternoon. A call from Stacey had seemed imminent. Jodie desperately did not want to fight with her friend, yet she was obstinate by nature.

"What's your problem Stacey? You didn't want him, so what's the harm? We get on really well together. I always told you that I liked Tony" Jodie answered calmly. Stacey paused before replying. She sat in her car outside Alex Woods's home, where she was now staying.

"Listen Jodie, I never knew that you meant in that way. Anyhow, there are certain things that you don't do on friends, and that's definitely one of them. You must have known that it would upset me. Come on!" Stacey countered.

"I'm sorry Stacey; I honestly never meant to hurt you. It just sort of happened" Jodie replied weakly.

"Yeah, it happened 'cos you instigated it. Tony would never have come on to you. Angie told me how you went around to his creepy house. Talk about throwing yourself at him!" Stacey answered.

Jodie cringed. It was just as she had feared. Stacey was really angry. The phone call that Jodie had made to her pal explaining how she was friends with Tony had failed to smooth the path.

"Well, you were hardly whiter than white Stacey Boyd. What about you seeing Alex behind Tony's back? And that just after his mother had died" Jodie countered. There was a moment's silence before the line went dead. Jodie looked at her black mobile phone before shrugging her shoulders.

"Ha! The truth hurts!" Jodie muttered. She heard the door open outside and then voices. It would be Gina with her boyfriend. She listened as the two crept silently into Gina's bedroom. The number one rule of the shared apartment was now broken. Boys staying over had always been taboo. Now it hardly seemed to matter to Jodie. In a matter of weeks everything had changed completely.

Jodie closed her eyes and wondered what the future held. She could not imagine living at the apartment for much longer. It was not the same anymore without Stacey and Angie. It seemed as if a chapter of her life was coming to an end.

Tony Lee awoke early the following morning. The smell of fresh paint filled his nostrils. He blinked as he surveyed the room around him. A flicker of a smile crossed his lips as he remembered the paint fight with Jodie. Tony reached for a cigarette and then flopped back onto his pale blue pillow. For a second he considered not lighting up. Smoking would eventually ruin the new paintwork. Instantly he dismissed his reservations.

Tony drew hard on the tipped cigarette as he reflected on his new relationship. He was now smitten with Jodie. She was much more affectionate that Stacey. The way she dressed was amusing, but she was certainly very feminine in bed. Tony wondered if Stacey would ever forgive him for hooking up with her friend. Suddenly it mattered less that Sunday morning. Stacey had abandoned him for her old fiancé. Why should he too not get on with his life?

Tony stubbed out the half-smoked cigarette. He watched as the grey smoke drifted aimlessly towards the newly-painted ceiling. Tony smiled as he tossed the duvet back. He looked towards the wall where he presumed the old fireplace once stood. Jan would probably go berserk if he stared knocking holes in the old place.

Tony wandered to the bathroom in just his black boxer shorts. He examined his face in the mirror. Apart from his unkempt hair, Tony considered that he was bearing up well for his age. He studied his teeth. Perhaps they were a bit dull, he thought.

"That's it. What with the paintwork and my teeth, I'm definitely giving up the ciggies for a while!" he decided.

"Listen Isobel, I can't come up with that kind of money. Be reasonable" Alex Woods said to his wife. It was a terse phone call, something that was becoming increasingly regular lately.

"Well you had better find it somewhere, dickhead. It's mine by right. We're still married don't forget Alex. Any court in the land will find in favour of me" Isobel Woods said angrily.

"Yes, yes, I know. As I keep explaining to you though, the business is still in my father's name. I cannot just go into the bank and withdraw that sort of cash. Look, meet me halfway here Isobel. What if I can get say, €10,000 for now? Then in about six months time I could maybe get another €10,000. Then when I take over the company from my father, I could let you have the rest. What about that Isobel?" Alex said. For a moment the line went silent. After some thought Isobel Woods spoke again.

"Okay Alex, that would do for now. You better not fucking mess me about though. If you do, I will have a solicitor involved so quick that you won't believe what's happening. I'm tired of all your Mickey Mouse excuses" Isobel said forcefully.

A wry smile spread across Alex Woods's face.

"No Isobel, everything will go smoothly. Now, when did you say that you're moving?" he asked. Isobel sighed as she looked to the sky.

"Fuck sake Alex! I told you that I've to be out of the apartment by tomorrow. I'll be in Dublin tomorrow evening. Then I'm off to London to start a new life. I won't be sorry to see the back of this lousy country-and you" she replied tersely.

"Okay, okay sweetheart. Listen, you're gonna have to meet me somewhere. I can't risk the old man finding out. You're getting the bus up to Dublin, right? What about getting off at Naas? I happen to be working out that way tomorrow. I could collect you just outside Naas, give you the money, and then drive you to the airport. How's that?" Alex said confidently.

"Jesus Christ! Can't you just do as I asked and meet me at the bus depot in town? Why the fuck has it always got to be your way? And don't call me fucking sweetheart. I'm not your sweetheart, thank fuck!" she replied. Alex switched his mobile phone from his right ear to his left. Again he afforded himself a smirk.

"Sorry sweetheart, but that's the way it has to be if you want the cash. I could never make it back to Dublin on time. From The Naas Road, I could have you at the airport in less than an hour. Get off at Ryland's Garage. It's about a mile past Naas. The bus driver will know it. Now what do you say darling?" he said cockily.

"Fuck off Alex, just fuck off! Okay, okay, I'll get off at this poxy garage. You better be there. I swear, if this is another of your games, I'll rip your fucking head off, I mean it" Isobel replied.

"Right. It's a date. About eight-thirty at the bus stop opposite Ryland's. I know it well. See you there pet" Alex said. He listened as the line went dead.

Alex strolled across the showroom floor of the giant garage. He glanced around at the shiny new cars on display. There was a fortune tied up in the business on The Long Mile Road, yet his miserly father insisted on running the company himself. Each penny had to be accounted for. Alex was paid a basic salary at Wood's Motors. Every expense he applied for was questioned. The carrot to keeping him going was that one day he would inherit the business. His father was still a sprightly man in his early sixties. Alex was his only child, yet his father treated him more like an employee rather than his heir. Tom Woods's wife was now dead for over two years. He never spoke to Alex about her now, nor did Alex try to discuss his late mother with his Dad. All of their dealings were done in a businesslike manner.

Alex wandered into his small office. He looked at the yellow memo stuck to his desk.

"Collect the contract for the cars at Winsome Motors Naas tomorrow. 6:30pm. Dad" said the note. Alex crumpled it up and tossed it in the silver waste bin. "Fecking notes. That's how we correspond! Fecking yellow sticky-notes!" he muttered.

Alex flopped down on his black leather swivel chair. He was a fit strong man. Although not the sporting type, Alex was an excellent swimmer and had played rugby in his younger days at college. Once a chain smoker, he was now off the cigarettes. The athletic-looking Alex had several things on his mind. He sat deep in thought for a moment.

Now he had to consider his wife, Isobel. She had been a pain since they had split up less than one year ago. Although Isobel was the one who had had the affair, he was now the person under threat.

Alex had met and married Isobel in London four years earlier. He was still seeing Stacey at the time, but fell under the spell of the sexy-looking dancer while on a stag trip. Once smitten, Alex then made several trips back to see Isobel at weekends. Working for the garage made things so easy. He would tell Stacey Boyd that he was away on business. One drunken weekend he married Isobel at a registry office in London. By that stage, they were practically living together at her flat on weekends. Alex knew that his father would never approve of Isobel, and feared being denied his inheritance. Even now his father still did not know of Isobel's existence. Unfortunately for Alex, Isobel now knew all about his wealthy father, and the profitable company that they ran. She was now demanding her divorce settlement before moving back to England.

Isobel originally came from a tough part of Middlesbrough, in the north-east of England. Her dubious past included being a hostess in a seedy London club, a stripper, and a lap dancer. Her refreshing attitude to sex was what first attracted Alex to her. Having then married her, Alex lured her to Ireland, where he managed to conceal her from his father. They set up home in an apartment in Wexford Town, some eighty miles from Dublin, and about a two-hour drive to where Alex worked. Alex would return to their cosy little flat each evening. They kept to themselves, drinking in a local bar when the mood took them. Isobel had even got a job in a large supermarket, to keep herself busy while he was at work. Alex somehow succeeded in operating a balancing act between Stacey and Isobel. His work as a rep for his father's company helped to conceal both women from each other. Everything went fine for a while, until Alex returned home unexpectedly and caught Isobel in bed with a local guy. Isobel shrugged it off as a bit of fun, but Alex could not forgive her. He moved back to Dublin, yet continued to pay Isobel's rent and utility bills.

In fact, this was what raised Isobel's suspicions. She feared that Alex was already married. Why else would he be so generous with his cash, she wondered? Using a water leak in the apartment as an excuse to lure Alex there to repair it, Isobel took the opportunity to search his jacket pockets. While Alex struggled beneath the kitchen sink with a wrench, she found a letter from his father's company in his inside pocket. Further investigations told Isobel all that she needed to know. She quickly realised that there was money to be made. Isobel was bored with life in Ireland, and fancied returning to London with a handsome profit. If Alex did not agree to her demands, there was always the legal route to pursue. Either way, Isobel Woods felt confident that she was on a winner. Soon she could be back in London, enjoying life among the bright lights again.

Alex stood up and paced the office. There was no alternative. He would have to go through with his plan. He would dispose of Isobel's body just as he had plotted many times in his head. There was no one in Ireland that he knew of who would miss her. Even if she had made friends, she was scheduled to return to England anyway. As far as he was aware, nobody in England was due to meet Isobel on her return. That would be a chance that he had to take. Alex's brain was now in overdrive. He reckoned that the best way to get away with murder was to plan meticulously. His second rule was to hide the body somewhere where it would never be discovered. Already he had plotted that avenue. Once Isobel was out of the way, he could settle back down with Stacey. The only reason that he had not married Stacey in the beginning was because he was already married to Isobel. In those heady days, Stacey thought him a single man. Back then, he could still lead a double life. But had he also married Stacey Boyd, things would have been very difficult indeed. He could hardly divide his life between the two women, much as he would have liked to. The only way out had been to jilt Stacey at the last moment. At the time, Alex had hoped that Stacey would forgive him, but that was not to be. And so he had returned to a life with Isobel, only for her to cheat on him.

That evening, Alex set off towards The Dublin Mountains. He knew the exact spot that he wanted to use to dispose of the body. Long drives through the rugged landscape with Isobel's murder in mind had led him to the very place. A secluded off-road glen appeared the ideal setting for Isobel's final resting place. Alex would make sure that her body was never found. It always amazed him at how easily dead bodies were discovered, especially in gang-related deaths. It struck Alex that preparation was important. By readying the burial spot first, the odds were stacked in the murderer's favour, Alex reckoned.

Alex began to dig as dusk fell. His white Mondeo car was parked some distance away. If it took hours to dig deep enough, then so be it. His selected spot was amid some wild bushes. The foliage around him was considerable. The chances of anybody wandering through the area were minimal. Once Alex broke the surface, the clay was surprisingly soft. His biggest fear had been that the ground would be difficult to penetrate. As he made good progress, Alex listened out for any noise. The only sound noticeable was the trickling of a nearby stream. He mused over the condition of the soft soil and came to the conclusion that it was down to the Irish climate. The rain was bound to run down from the mountains towards his chosen spot, thus softening the clay. Two hours later and Alex was almost four feet down. The steady clank of his sharp spade echoed through the late evening. Now and then he would stop for breath. The eerie surroundings kept him on edge. He could hear birds overhead, and the odd rodent scurrying through the bushes. And of course the stream, which he would make good use of later.

Once five foot down, Alex clambered out of the rectangular hole. He surveyed his handiwork with a small green torch.

"That should hold her, the money-grabbing bitch" he muttered with a smug smile. He had no time to waste. Alex quickly covered the hole over with branches and some bushes. He then began to shovel the dirt into strong heavy plastic bags. He hid five of these in the bushes. The plan was that he would use the soft clay to cover the body the following night. The rest of the soil was then shovelled into more bags, for disposal of.

One by one Alex dragged the spare bags downhill towards the running stream. He walked along the bank scattering in huge amounts of earth into the water. Time after time he repeated this act, until there was no more clay to dispose of. Exhausted, Alex sat on the bank of the stream to catch his breath.

"This manual work is tough going. If only you knew what I am going through just to be with you Stacey darling" he smirked.

Alex sat in his car, high in the mountain overlooking his native Dublin. His spade and shovel were safely in the boot. He considered what the future might hold. Once Isobel was out of the way, he would propose to Stacey. This time he would marry her. They could live happily together. An added bonus was that his father approved of Stacey Boyd, not that it really mattered to Alex. Still, it could help his father to finally transfer the business to Alex. Once the prosperous company was in his hands, Alex had grand plans. He did not see his long-term future as a businessman. When the time was right and his father was safely either packed away in a nursing home, or dead, Alex vowed to sell the thriving firm and retire. He saw no sense in working for a living when he could easily live off the sale of a successful business. Alex reckoned that his father's company was worth in excess of four million euro's. It would do him nicely, and he would also inherit his father's house, which was probably worth another two million. Tom Woods also had a large bank account, and Alex had grand plans to get his hands on that also.

"Fuck you Alex; you said that you would be waiting at the bus stop. Where the fuck were you?" Isobel yelled. The bus had departed almost five minutes earlier, leaving Isobel on a lonely country road. Alex had purposely arrived late to ensure that he was not seen collecting her.

The pretty 26-year-old was caked in make-up. Her white blouse was opened at the front, barely concealing her large bosom. Isobel wore her black hair tied up above her head. Her denim jeans clung to her long legs, and her black stiletto heels were ridiculously high. Her short denim jacket was worn casually across her shoulders.

"Shut up and get in Isobel. Throw that suitcase on the back seat. I'm having trouble with this car all day. I got a puncture, and the spare wheel is a bit dodgy" he replied angrily. Isobel cackled at his response.

"Fucking hell! You own a garage and you haven't got a decent motor! Once this heap of shit gets me to the airport though, I couldn't care less" she said in her English twang.

"Oh, it will get you where you're going all right, never fear" he answered.

"Have you got my money? Tell me that you have that fucking ten grand" she hissed. Alex looked sideways at her as he drove off.

"Yep, I have it. It's in my pocket here. But I want you to sign something to say that you agree to our arrangement. As soon as we arrive at the airport we can do that. Okay?" Alex replied.

"Fine, fucking fine. I'll sign your stupid shit. Don't worry, you pox, I won't be coming back here. Unless you renege on the deal, that is! By fuck, then I'll be back all right! You won't know what hit you Alex, trust me" Isobel answered. She lit up a cigarette in an agitated state. Because Alex had recently quit smoking, he thought to object. The smell of tobacco still gave him the urge to light up. He then decided against complaining. It was a small price to pay for a little peace.

"Which fucking way are you going Alex? Stick to the main roads for Christ sake!" Isobel said suddenly. Alex had turned off a side road, heading away from the direction of Dublin Airport.

"It's quicker this way. You don't want to miss your flight, do you?" he replied casually. A bewildered Isobel glanced around at the isolated area.

"No, I suppose not. Fuck me! What is it with this country? Half of the roads have no lamplights, and the other half are covered in pot-holes! I can't wait to get back to London, I can tell you! What possessed me to move to this God-forsaken country, I'll never know!" she muttered. Isobel drew heavily on her cigarette and blew smoke out through the open window.

"You moved here because we loved each other. Remember? I took you out of that rat-hole of a job. I brought you here so that we could have a nice life" Alex replied.

"Huh! Yeah, whatever! You never told me that you owned a motor car company, or that your stinking old man was rolling in it, did you? Or that he would never approve of a low-life bitch like me for his precious son!" she countered. Alex shook his head wryly. It was useless to argue. Since they had split up, Isobel had all of the answers. She could see no good in him at all. He had to go through with his plan; otherwise she would destroy his life.

"Shit! There goes the front wheel! I think it's punctured" Alex said suddenly. Isobel looked startled.

"What? Tell me that you have a fucking spare! Jesus H Christ! What did I tell you about these fucking roads?" You stupid bastard Alex Woods" she shrieked. Alex climbed from the car and opened the boot. He pulled out the wheel jack and rambled towards the front of the vehicle, bending down to examine the imaginary damage. Just as he knew that she would, Isobel climbed out to join him. She pulled her blue denim jacket around her as she crouched down beside him.

"Well, can you fix it? Tell me that you can fix it Alex?" she said. Alex stood up straight. Isobel followed suit, standing tall once again. Alex looked her calmly in the eyes.

"I can fix you Isobel, you tramp" he said deliberately. With one swing of the jack, he knocked her backwards, her head crashing on the road. Purposely he strode towards her. Three more blows rained down, rendering Isobel lifeless. The clunk of metal hitting bone reverberated in the cool evening air. Alex's brain was now in overdrive. He had to do things exactly as he had planned. Alex swept Isobel up in his arms and carried her body towards the open car boot. The deserted country lane was unnervingly silent. He slammed the boot shut with both Isobel and the bloodied wheel jack inside. Next he checked the roadside to ensure that she had not dropped any of her personal belongings. Alex climbed back inside and drove off slowly. Isobel's handbag lay on the passenger seat beside him.

"I told you that those cigarettes would kill you in the end Isobel! I gave them up months ago!" he sneered. Alex fiddled in her bag for her passport. He had to ensure that she had not dropped it.

"Good. Passport, money, flight tickets! Always important when going somewhere!" he sniggered. Alex drove on towards the mountains. He knew that he could never have brought Isobel any further along their journey while she was alive. She was bound to have suspected something was amiss.

Alex parked his white car off road as he had done the previous evening. Once sure that there was no one around, he dragged Isobel's battered body from the boot and heaved her over his left shoulder. Alex's mind was lucid. His plan was vivid in his head. He grabbed the shovel from the boot and then slammed it shut. The noise echoed in the stillness. Alex set off, striding onwards towards the bushes and trees. His footsteps broke the silence of the late evening. It was dull and cloudy, but now and then a half-moon peeped through the trees. Isobel's arms swung rhythmically behind his back, sometimes crashing off his side and the back of his legs. Alex crossed a small field, getting ever closer to his destination.

When he reached his chosen burial spot, Alex let her limp body tumble untidily to the damp ground. He uncovered the makeshift grave and then lowered her in face first. Quickly he went to retrieve the clay from the nearby bushes. One by one he tumbled the contents in on top of Isobel's prostrate body. Then he patted down the fresh clay with the shovel, packing it hard inside the grave. It was important that wild animals would not unearth Isobel's body. When he felt that he could not fit any more soil inside the grave, Alex began to cover the spot with sods of grass, shrubs and stones. He wedged the greenery deep into the fresh clay, covering the grave entirely. Once he was happy that the surroundings looked authentic, Alex Woods stood back to admire his handiwork with his small torch.

"There! You would swear that it was like that for years!" he muttered. Alex checked everything again with his silver torch. With luck, Isobel's body would never be discovered. He headed back to his car, still listening for noise all around him. It was pitch black now, and he strode on relentlessly, carrying just the shovel and empty bags. Alex threw them into the boot of his car and then went to fetch Isobel's suitcase from the rear seat. He tossed it in on top of the bloodied wheel jack and shovel in the car boot. Alex then shoved her handbag underneath the front seat. Lastly he pulled a plastic bag from inside the boot. This contained a fresh pair of jeans and a light t-shirt. He quickly got changed and placed his clothes inside the white plastic shopping bag. His last action was to pour some water from a plastic bottle over his hands, to wash away any blood that might be there. Even then he thought to throw the empty bottle back into the boot. Nothing could be left to chance. Once the boot was closed firmly, Alex set off slowly back towards home. Stacey would be waiting, and things could return to normal once more.

CHAPTER NINE

THE OTHER SIDE OF ALEX WOODS

Tony arrived at work early on Monday morning. He was feeling good about himself. Slowly he was falling in love with Jodie. Her quirky mannerisms and mad text messages kept his spirits up. Tony could now find himself going hours without thinking about his late mother, or indeed Stacey Boyd.

"What's up man?" asked Erik Ngombiti as he sidled up to Tony's desk.

"Oh hi Erik. Nothing much really? You?" Tony answered. Erik's beaming smile appeared from nowhere.

"All's good in the world man, everything is cool" replied the tall, bespectacled man.

"Good! How is the family?" Tony said. Erik released his infectious laugh, which seemed to start somewhere in the pit of his stomach.

"Huh, huh, huh! You see, that's what I want to talk to you about. We're having a very special dinner tomorrow night, and we would like you to come along. I spoke with Eileen and she insists on inviting you" Erik grinned. Tony was taken aback. He had briefly met Eileen Ngombiti at a company dinner about a year earlier. There was no reason whatsoever why she should invite Tony to her home.

"Ah no Erik, I'm not into all that formal dinner party and stuff. Besides, why me? I barely know your wife" Tony replied quickly. The smile disappeared from Erik's face.

"You're right, I should explain. You see, tomorrow we celebrate my real African birthday. You realise that I don't actually know when my proper birthday is? We do this every year on this date, but usually it's just me and Eileen and the children. I told her about me telling you about my life in Africa. We would really love it if you came along. It's nothing formal, so don't be scared! Wear jeans if you like! Hey yeah, that's what we'll do! We'll all wear denim! A symbol of the working class, eh?" Erik beamed.

Tony looked even more confused.

"But Erik, I wouldn't know what to say or do. I mean, I'm no good at this sort of thing, really. Oh, and I'm supposed to be meeting a friend tomorrow night" he said, the excuse coming out of nowhere.

"Well, bring your friend along! Seriously Tony, don't let me down. I've told Eileen that you would come. Gee man, it's my birthday. I have no one to celebrate it with. I'm embarrassed to tell the other guys about having no real birthday. Come on, spare me a few hours, eh?" Erik pleaded.

Tony felt that he could hardly refuse. And neither could he tell Erik about falling in love with Stacey's flatmate. He was not sure that Erik would understand, and did not want his workmate to think him weird.

"Okay, I'll be there-at least for a while! I can't promise that my friend will join us, but we'll see" Tony replied with a smile. Erik Ngombiti clapped his hands with joy.

"Superb! I'll phone Eileen later. One thing though; promise me that you'll grab a taxi. I don't want you showing up on that old bicycle of yours!" Erik said with a broad grin. Tony laughed out loud.

"Sure! It's a deal-but I wear my jeans-okay?" Tony countered.

At lunchtime, Tony phoned Jodie on his mobile phone. He explained about Erik's invite and asked her if she fancied tagging along.

"No way! You two will be all chat about work! I'll be sitting there like a lemon, asking Mrs. Mumsey about her kitchen curtains and her kid's school! No chance Tony! Sorry, but I'm washing my hair!" Jodie scoffed. Tony could understand her logic. Why should Jodie want to spend an evening with two people who she did not know? He accepted Jodie's refusal and resigned himself to a dinner date with Erik's family alone. Perhaps it would be easier that way anyhow. At least now he would not have to explain his relationship with Jodie Callaghan. It might have proven all too much for Erik, the family man, Tony reasoned.

When Tony showed up at Erik Ngombiti's house, he had grave reservations about the evening. He was never one for socialising in other people's homes anyway. Dinner parties in particular left him cold. His mother had never held a dinner party to his knowledge, and Tony struggled to remember the last people that they had over for a meal. He had on occasions had something to eat at Stacey's flat, but that was hardly dinner. A take-away at the local chip shop or pizza parlour was about as far as that had stretched.

Tony carried a small bunch of flowers for Eileen, and the customary bottle of wine for the meal.

The Ngombiti's home from the outside looked like every other house on the well-manicured street. Each house had a nice lawn, freshly-painted garage to the side of the oak hall doors, and of course, double-glazed windows.

"No character! Wooden boxes erected in the boom for blue-collar families" Tony muttered. It was a pet hate of his, as Dublin City continued to spread its wings in every direction into the surrounding countryside.

He politely rang the door bell and took a step backwards off the tiled step. A beaming Erik opened the door and quickly shook Tony's hand. Erik followed up his handshake by hugging his workmate. He then peered up and down the street as if searching for someone.

"Are you expecting many more guests?" Tony asked anxiously. Erik looked surprised at the question.

"No, just you. I was searching for that silver bicycle!" Erik replied with his customary booming laugh.

"Come in, come in. No standing on ceremony at my home!" Erik grinned. Tony followed his workmate through into the living room. Erik's children were already in pyjamas and playing together on the laminated floor.

"The little ones are soon off to bed. Sit down Tony, make yourself at home. I see that you wore the jeans" Erik said. His laugh erupted again, starting somewhere low in his abdomen. Tony did a double-take. Erik was wearing neat black slacks and a white shirt and blue tie.

"You swine! You set me up! I feel awful now!" Tony said in a somewhat embarrassed tone.

"Huh, huh, huh! I like to look nice for my birthday!" Erik said with continued amusement. There was always something child-like and innocent in Erik's sense of fun.

Eileen came to join them, quickly followed by another younger lady. Tony stood and kissed Eileen on the cheek, presenting her with his bunch of flowers as he did so.

"Thanks Tony, I'll put them in water. Erik, get Tony a drink. Oh, by the way, this is Tricia" Eileen said. Eileen was a tall slender lady with short dark hair and brown eyes. She vanished back into the kitchen as Tony politely shook the girl's hand. Erik followed his wife outside to fetch Tony a drink, forcing his workmate to make small talk with the smiling brunette.

"So, you're a friend of Eileen's? Do you live around here?" he asked. The girl nodded, forcing her shoulder-length hair to suddenly dance up and down. Her twinkling dark eyes caught Tony's attention.

"Yeah, I live just across the road. Eileen and I hit it off when I moved in. She babysits for me sometimes" Tricia explained. A brief silence ensues as Tony tried to think of something worthwhile to say.

"I work with Erik. He's a great chap" Tony said weakly. Tricia nodded. She sat opposite him on the big grey sofa, Tony sitting on the armchair.

Tricia Sherry continued the fractured conversation.

"Yeah, Eileen and Erik told me all about you. I'm sorry about your girlfriend" Tricia said casually. A startled Tony looked nervously back at her. An alarm bell rang in his brain. He hoped that he was wrong, but something told him that he had been set up.

"Oh? Sorry, you have the advantage of me. I didn't think Erik told you anything about me" he stuttered. Tricia flushed slightly, but offered him a reassuring grin.

"Oh, it's okay. I broke up with my fellow over a year ago. I caught him with another girl. We have a little boy between us. It was all very messy at the time. I blame her, you know? She threw herself at him. You see, my Mikey was a good-looking man. Well, he still is" she said in a rapid tone. Tony nodded, but wondered what he had got himself into. The evening ahead was looking more and more like a blind date, designed by Erik and Eileen.

"Er, well, we have to move on, don't we?" Tony replied diplomatically.

"Oh I agree Tone. You don't mind me calling you Tone, do you? It's so much friendlier. That's why I christened my Michael, Mikey. It's much cosier. But it's hard to move on when you have a little child to care for. I mean, it's not his fault that Mikey is such a pig. I mean, Mikey has his freedom, but what have I got?" Tricia asked. Tony shook his head. Already he knew more about Tricia than he did about Erik and Eileen.

"Will there be other people here tonight?" Tony asked meekly. Tricia immediately shook her head, but looked annoyed at the interruption.

"Oh no! I prefer intimate meals, don't you? It's not the same with a lot of folk around the table. One tends to be swamped, don't you think Tone?" she gushed.

Erik came to join them, a knowing smile etched on his face.

He handed Tony a beer.

"And how are you two getting on?" he asked, his rowdy laugh already rumbling in his chest.

"Just fine" Tony replied without emotion. It was going to be a long evening.

Later on, Tony managed to catch Erik alone in the hallway.

"Jesus Erik, what's going on? This is like a blind date from hell! What's with this Tricia woman? She natters on at a hundred miles an hour. It's as if she's sifting through all mankind for the perfect partner! It's like a fatal attraction job or something. This woman has a screw loose" Tony whispered. Erik's boisterous laugh came to the fore.

"Huh, huh, huh! Does she scare you Tone? Have you gone off women then Tone? I heard her pet name for you! Very cute" he laughed. Tony Lee looked annoyed.

"That's just it Erik, I've just met someone. I didn't like to say anything 'cos it's a bit early in the relationship. Myself and Jodie are kind of finding our way together, you know?" Tony said quietly. His face almost pleaded for understanding. Erik's laugh ended abruptly.

"Oh, sorry my friend, I genuinely did not know. You should have said something. You see, I was telling Eileen how lonely you seemed, and she told me about Tricia breaking up…" Erik's narrative was quickly interrupted by his workmate.

"Yeah, I understand Erik. But I need to get out of this without hurting anybody. Please don't encourage Tricia, all right?" Tony said. Erik's smile returned, but he promised not to cause any mischief.

Later after a nice dinner, Eileen proposed a toast to Erik. Tony had noticed that she sometimes referred to him as Erikamzina, which Tony presumed was Erik's full name.

"Tonight is my husband's birthday. He has an official birthday according to his English birth certificate, but tonight we celebrate his African roots" Eileen said. Everyone raised their glasses to toast Erik, who then insisted on saying a few words. Erik Ngombiti rose slowly to his feet, his eyes filled with emotion.

"Every year myself and Eileen commemorate this day. It's a celebration, but also an acknowledgement of where I come from. It's been a long journey both mentally and physically to arrive at where I am today. In my darkest days on the road to survival, I never suspected that I would find such peace in my soul. I still grieve for my lost family. I suppose that I always will. Every year I vow to go back to Africa, but the task overwhelms me. Where would I start? How long would it take? Would what I find devastate me? Might it break me mentally? I just don't know. Today I have a lovely wife, two beautiful children, and good friends. I have a great job and a good life. Some people might ask, "what else do you require?" I'll tell you my friends. You need to close your eyes at night and see the darkness. Not the images that I recall. No one should have to suffer that. But tonight I celebrate happiness. Tonight I am a contented man. Life is never perfect. We should all enjoy it while we can! Happy birthday, Erik Ngombiti!" said Erik. Everybody cheered.

Tony could see the tears in his friend's eyes. He wondered how a man could suffer such things and yet come out the other side. Erik was indeed a remarkable man, and Tony felt humbled in his presence.

"Alex? Where's Alex, Vivian?" Tom Woods asked impatiently. He prowled the corridor which led from the showrooms to the offices.

"He was here a minute ago Mr. Woods. Shall I ring his mobile or page him?" Vivian Agnew replied in her best telephone voice. Tom Woods did not answer her directly.

"What is it with that boy? He's never around when you need him. Off gallivanting again I'll wager. Up to no good, that's what! I can't rely on him Vivian. Can you imagine if I ever left him to run the business? What?" Tom Woods said absentmindedly. He did not require a reply, and Vivian knew this. She had worked for Woods Motors for over twenty years as Mr. Wood's personal secretary, and knew instantly when her opinion was required.

"I have to go out on business Vivian. I'll leave a note on his desk. How anything ever gets done, I'll never know" Tom Woods muttered.

Vivian wavered for a moment. She owed her loyalty to her boss.

"There was one thing Mr. Woods. A girl phoned for Alex earlier. He happened to be in here at the time. He took the call and arranged to meet her for lunch. I think it was Frasier's Bistro. It's somewhere off Dame Street I think" Vivian said.

Tom Woods seemed to brighten up slightly.

"Right! I can drop by there on my way. I know it well Vivian. Thanks" he answered.

Alex Woods sat with Stacey in the corner of the small café. He was having an early lunch break to coincide with hers.

"You look beautiful today Stacey pet. How did I ever manage without you? You coming back into my life was heaven sent. I mean it! I bet that God intervened. He realised that we were meant for each other, and put us back together again darling" Alex cooed. Stacey flushed a little.

"Aw, that's sweet. God didn't do it though, Angie O'Rourke did! If she had not given me your mobile number it would never have happened" Stacey said with a smile. Inside Alex was a little miffed. His poetic words had fallen on deaf ears. Today he was in good form though, and decided to try again.

"Yeah sweetheart, but you know what I mean. You and I are special. We have the world at our feet. I'm sure that other couples must envy us. I mean, here am I, a successful businessman, about to inherit my Dad's company, and then there's you love. A very special beautiful lady" he gushed. Stacey smiled sweetly.

"Steady on Alex, its only lunchtime! Anyway, your Dad is not about to pop his clogs just yet-thankfully!" Stacey answered. Alex looked a little crestfallen. He had noticed a subtle difference in Stacy since they had got back together. She was more quick-witted and flippant than before. Perhaps it was down to her affair with that Tony Lee chap. Alex did not like to think about what she did while they had been apart. Stacey had poured her heart out to him one night about her romance with Tony. Once she had explained everything, Alex had never brought up the topic again.

"I'm not talking about him dying, Stacey pet. He's bound to want to retire soon. It stands to reason. I'm practically running the company now anyway. I'm sure that my Dad will realise that he's no longer needed and drive off into the sunset!" Alex said with a smug grin.

"Shit! Look at the time Alex! Listen, I really have to go. If I'm late again this week, Mr. Redmond will sack me! I swear! I was back late from lunch twice in the last six days" Stacey said. She gulped down her coffee and rose to her feet. Alex glanced at his watch wearily.

"When I own the business, you can come and work for me. I could chase you around the desk all day, precious!" he said as he stood up.

"No thanks! I like it fine where I am!" Stacey grinned. Once again Alex's manly pride was hurt, but he masked it from Stacey.

"We'll see" he thought to himself.

Outside in the sunshine, Stacey stopped to give him a kiss. They were heading in different directions, and she was anxious to get away.

"See you later baby" Alex whispered. Just then a car tooted loudly. Stacey looked over towards the red vehicle on the far side of the street.

"Isn't...Isn't that your father?" she asked. Alex turned sharply to witness Tom Woods striding deliberately towards him. Tom Woods looked like thunder as he strode purposely across the busy street.

"Jesus Christ Alex, I asked you to telephone Michael J. Thomas Motor Supplies this morning. Where the hell is your brain son? He phoned me twenty minutes ago like a madman. We could lose the contract you know. What sort of a way is this to run a business? Have you shit for brains or what? Well?" Tom Woods yelled.

People seated outside the busy café stopped and stared as Alex tried to compose himself. There were customers dining outside in the lunchtime sunshine. Tom Woods and his son had everyone's full attention. Stacey released Alex from her embrace and moved slightly away.

"I was on my lunch break Dad. It slipped my mind. Sorry" A chastened Alex replied.

"Slipped your mind? What fecking mind? A chimpanzee has a better grasp on things than you! A lunch break is it? I'll give you a permanent lunch break! You can have your p45 if this sort of thing keeps up. You're useless to me, absolutely useless" Tom Woods ranted.

Alex could hear the sniggering nearby. People all around the small café were taking in every word uttered by Tom Woods. Inside Alex's blood was boiling. He was almost on the verge of letting rip into his father when he remembered Stacey.

"Sorry again Dad, my fault. I'll get on it right away" he muttered.

"Will you? Too late for that now. I'm off to see Michael this minute. This will cost me a hefty lunch no doubt, and probably a case of wine. How many times have I told you that you must look after the smaller firms? That's what holds my company together. I'm going. Get back to the office and do something useful" Tom said abruptly.

He turned on his heels and made for his car. Four guys at a table outside the café began to clap rhythmically. Alex offered them a threatening glare. Stacey grabbed his arm and wheeled him away.

"I really have to go. See you tonight" she said. Alex nodded. He felt totally humiliated. Alex was sure that his father had barely noticed Stacey, or indeed the watching public. All that mattered to Tom Woods was the beloved business, as far as Alex was concerned. There and then Alex vowed to sell the company as soon as he gained control. He promised himself that he would have the last laugh.

Tony Lee hauled himself up into the attic again. He had a skip outside of the front garden. Already he had managed to load the junk from the back garden into it.

"It's gonna be messy, but it has to be done" he muttered. It was Saturday morning, and Tony was determined to go to the next level of his refurbishment. It meant parting with lots of old furniture and broken household goods, but he was prepared for the inevitable.

"I've put it off long enough. We can't cling to the past" he told himself.

Dating Jodie had given him a new prospective on life. Secretly Tony hoped to woo Jodie enough to have her move in with him. The old house had failed to impress Stacey Boyd, but already Jodie was showing favourable signs. She was forever suggesting things that he might do with number eighty-eight. Besides, Tony knew how difficult Jodie was finding it at her apartment, both financially and mentally. With Gina's new boyfriend already staying there and contributing to the hefty rent, it was almost as if she was being squeezed out. For Tony it made sense for Jodie to move in with him. It was too early to consider anything more serious, but by living together they could decide if their relationship had a long-term future. His biggest fear was that Jodie would turn him down. It would leave their relationship in limbo. He considered his best option was to have the house looking nice. Even if it meant Jodie taking a separate room to his, it would be better than living alone.

Bit by bit he lowered the attic contents down to the landing floor. The amount of junk took him by surprise. Old radios, pictures, clocks and general paraphernalia appeared limitless. No sooner had he cleared a path along the attic floor when more items tumbled into his view. An old pram caught his eye. Somehow it appeared familiar. Tony opened it up using the old levers on each side of the handle.

"This had to be mine! God! I think that I remember sitting in this. And Mam kept it! The thing is falling apart. Only two rickety wheels left on it! What a laugh" Tony grinned. He folded it back up again and lowered it down to the floor outside. He surveyed the tangled mess below on the landing.

"That will have to do for now. I'm going to need another skip" he muttered. He clambered down, standing on top of several items unsteadily. One by one he dragged everything outside to the yellow skip.

"There! Now I just have time to clean up before Jodie gets here" he thought to himself.

Fergal Carrie watched from across the street. A tear rolled down his cheek as he recognised the old blue pram lying on top of the yellow skip. It was like a flash from the past, reminding him, probing at his very soul. His heady days as a man about town flashed back through his head. It was all too much. Fergal scurried away, hailing a taxi back to his home. His eyes fixed on the giant skip as the cab drove on. Fergal sat in the black cab, pulling gently on his neatly-trimmed grey beard. His promise all of those years ago was sacrosanct, and yet he questioned it now. What if Tony Lee had decided to move house, now that his mother had died? Yet Fergal had sworn to Delores to obey her wishes. No. He would bide his time for now. Only if he was certain that Tony Lee was about to move home, would he put his plan into operation.

Tony glanced out of the window as Jodie arrived. He watched as she did a double-take at the sight of the big yellow skip.

"Been busy I see?" she remarked. They kissed briefly in the hallway as he led her inside.

"Yeah. The attic is so full of shit that you wouldn't believe. I'll have to hire at least another skip-maybe two!" he replied. Jodie nodded thoughtfully.

"There's so much that you could do with this old house Tony. I mean, see that long back garden? You could build a conservatory, or a new kitchen extension. Oh, and that bedroom of yours? Why not put in big bay windows upstairs? Thing of all of the natural light that would flow in" Jodie said enthusiastically. Tony shook his head dismissively.

"Who needs all of that? You forget Jodie, I live here alone. What would I need with a conservatory? When would I get a chance to sit in it for God's sake?" he sniggered. Jodie bounced down on the old armchair in the kitchen. It was out of place among the other furniture, but was put there some time ago in order that Tony's mother might look out onto the rear garden.

"What about as an investment then? Any work that you do is bound to add to the value of the house if you sell it" Jodie reasoned. Tony picked his words carefully.

"I can never sell it Jodie. It was part of my deal with Jan. I promised her that I would never sell the property on, no matter what" he said. A huge grin appeared on Jodie's thin, pretty face. She jumped to her feet in her white tracksuit and went to hug Tony.

"You mean, you wrote that into a contract just to please your sister? Aw, that's so sweet!" Jodie beamed. She kissed Tony on the lips as they stood locked in an embrace.

"Well no, not exactly Jodie. I sort of just promised. She has this thing about preserving her memories or something. This place is like a shrine to her youth and my Mam's life" he said defensively. Jodie released him from her grip.

"I can't believe how vulnerable you are Tony Lee! No, vulnerable is not the right word. Gullible, maybe. Innocent and trustworthy, certainly! Imagine if you told Jan that she could never redesign her home in Santa Monica? I know what she would tell you!" Jodie giggled. Tony was on the defensive now.

"Ah, that's different Jodie, be fair. I never lived at Jan's. But this was her home, and Mam's. I don't want to disrespect either of them" he said in a voice that was almost pleading for understanding.

"Come here you! What will ever become of you Tony? This is your home now. You can do what you please with it. What's Jan going to do? Send in the fashion police? The chances are that she will never stay here again anyway. She might not even return to Ireland! But please yourself" Jodie said with a chuckle.

Tony cleared his throat. He had not wanted to bring up the subject, but now seemed as good a time as any.

"Well, I don't just want to please myself. I want to please you too. The thing is Jodie, I know we're only together a short time, but maybe in the future you might consider moving in here. Now, don't answer right away, just think about it, yeah? Financially it makes sense. Why should you be struggling with that huge rent? And as you say, you're not comfortable there anyway with Gina's fellow roaming around in his underwear!" Tony said.

Jodie looked surprised. Her light brown eyebrows shot upwards as she took in his words.

"Well, I never considered it, but..." she struggled to answer him for a moment.

"Think about it, that's all. Now, I have to phone that skip company. I want that rubbish out of here before the day is over" Tony said, brushing the conversation aside.

Alex Woods watched from afar as the four guys outside the café rose to their feet. It was a couple of days since his father had confronted him outside the popular café. Just as Alex Woods had suspected, the four lads who had sneered at him, were there again.

"Okay, about time. Now let's see where these big men are off to" Alex muttered. He followed them at a distance as the four strolled away from the busy lunchtime area. Soon, one chap split from the rest and headed down a side street.

"You'll do, Mr. Bigshot!" Alex thought quietly to himself. He trailed the tall younger man until he arrived at a small car park. Alex watched as the man briefly sat inside a blue Ford Focus. The dark-haired man with a light beard then retrieved some documents from the boot before heading for a nearby office building.

"Hmm. Nice car, the Focus, but I never liked its interior" Alex sneered. As the man entered the tall glass offices, Alex donned a white baseball cap and slipped inside the car park. He watched around him for visible signs of CCTV in the area. Alex could see none, and quickly bent down, as if to tie his shoelace. Pulling his penknife from his pocket he quickly slashed all four tyres on the Focus car. Within seconds he was back outside the open gates.

"No one laughs at me mate! Have a lovely drive home Mr. Bigshot. I wish that I could be here to clap!" he grinned.

Jodie listened from her bedroom as Gina and Harry laughed at a comedy show on the television. By nature, Jodie was an extrovert. She had tried to mix with Harry and Gina, but now felt distinctively unwelcome in the apartment she had called home for many years. On the few occasions that she did go to sit with them, Jodie could almost hear a silent groan welcoming her. Things could never be the same without Stacey and Angie. She knew that. But now she felt that she was always one step away from an argument with either Harry or Gina. Harry Brand had now acquired Stacey's old bedroom, although he openly slept in Gina's room with her. Within days of him moving in, the couple had acquired a double bed for Gina's room. Stacey's old room was now Harry's dressing area. Jodie felt that she could hardly object. Harry had a decent job and paid more than his share of the rent. Tony's offer of a new place to stay was looking more and more tempting by the hour.

Two things prevented Jodie from accepting Tony's offer. One was the short amount of time that she and Tony had been together, and the other was Stacey Boyd's feelings. She still considered Stacey a friend, although they were now seeing less and less of each other. Another thing had struck Jodie lately. Sometimes when he was sure that Gina was not looking, Harry might offer Jodie a leering grin. He seemed to be ogling her body at every chance, making her feel distinctly uncomfortable. At first Jodie thought that it might be her imagination, but by now she knew differently. There was something not quite right about Harry, she figured.

Jodie thought of the nice touches that she could add to Tony's house. It needed modernisation, plus a woman's touch. Jodie Callaghan was always thought of as the wild one among her flatmates and friends. Personally she had never felt that the image suited her. Events over the last few months had made her look closely at herself. Now she considered that she might like to take her life in a new direction. Her sporting friends were merely acquaintances in her mind, used by her to socialise with. Already she was distancing herself from her so-called pals who she had always hung out with. Jodie desperately wanted a normal relationship. She clung to the idea that Tony Lee was her future. One day perhaps, they might even raise a family together. She could scarcely believe her good fortune, and nothing was going to jeopardise her and Tony's life together. Most evenings after work she went out jogging, or for a long walk. Then she would return to the apartment and stay in her room, listening to music. If Gina and Harry were out, she might watch some television. Her wild days were now a thing of the past as far as she was concerned.

Jodie always considered Gina, Stacey and Angie as her real pals.

Angie O'Rourke flashed through her mind. Jodie grinned as she recalled idyllic days out shopping with her pals. Then there was the mad evenings when she and Angie might decide to hit the clubs on the spur of the moment. Angie had always liked a drink, and Jodie had been only too happy to tag along. Now Angie had Phillip, and Jodie genuinely hoped that they might find happiness together. Jodie had her doubts however. She had watched Phillip Westbourne close up. A certain look in his eyes told Jodie that he would never settle with Angie. Jodie feared that once again her old flatmate might end up broken-hearted.

Alex Woods sat watching television in his swish apartment. He heard the key turn in the front door and instantly rose to his feet. Stacey walked in with a beaming smile. She carried two plastic shopping bags and her black handbag. "Hi. Everything okay?" Stacey asked. Alex kissed her gently on the lips.
"Sure, why wouldn't it be darling?" he answered. Stacey shrugged and dropped her bags on the floor.
"Oh nothing. How did you get on with your Dad? Did he say anything?" she asked. Alex turned and flopped back down on the red couch.
"Huh! I haven't seen him, precious. On Mondays he's usually hanging about the place looking for someone to pick on. It's normally me! But today he was off wheeling and dealing with some clients. He never thought to ask me along. Meanwhile, I'm left to run the business single-handed. But as soon as anything goes wrong, guess who's to blame?" Alex said tight-lipped. Stacey slipped off her white coat while continuing to observe her boyfriend.
"Let's not be uptight tonight Alex, eh? Hey, why don't we go out for something to eat? I don't feel much like cooking" she said cheerfully. Alex fiddled with the remote control.
"May as well, there's nothing on the telly. Monday is such a boring day, don't you think pet?" he replied. Stacey smiled with amusement.
"Oh, everybody says that, but it's just like any other day-once you get out of bed in the morning! Still, if you say so" she laughed. Alex eyed her up and down for a moment, as if judging what his response should be. He decided against a cutting reply.
"What did you buy? Anything nice?" he asked. Stacey shrugged her shoulders as she glanced at her shopping bags.
"Oh, just some tops. Now will we go out or not?" she said. Alex looked back towards the television.
"I know! Why don't we go and call on somebody? I feel like going on a visit! Will we go and see my old man? Then we can grab a takeaway on the way home" Alex grinned. Stacey looked stunned. She had not been to visit Alex's parental home since they had got back together. The idea appalled her.
"That's not a good idea Alex. Leave it, eh? Wait until he has cooled down" she answered.

"Maybe you're right darling. Okay, why not go and see your pals? I always liked Gina and the girls. Let's pop in on them" Alex said with a huge smile.

"Aw Alex, let's not eh?" she replied. Stacey felt the blood drain from her face. She had not yet told Alex about Jodie and Tony. Alex however was adamant. He rose to his feet quickly.

"Yeah, let's drop over and say hello. Maybe we can go for a drink later. I fancy getting out of here for a while" Alex said with an upbeat tone.

"I dunno. Should we phone first?" she asked.

"Naw, come on, let's surprise them! It will be a laugh. Don't be so stuffy, sweetheart. Let's go, I'll drive" he said.

Stacey pressed the doorbell. It felt weird to be visiting her old flat. Her head was in a spin. She could barely believe that she had agreed to such a venture. Her main hope was that Jodie would be out. Jodie was always off somewhere, Stacey told herself.

Behind Stacey, Alex stood whistling merrily. Stacey realised how quiet the apartment now was. Usually she could hear voices from outside the front door. Perhaps both Gina and Jodie were out. She dared to hope that such was the case. Suddenly the front door swung open.

Gina's face broke into a smile on seeing her friend. The two screeched as they clung to each other.

"Oh my God! Oh my God!" Gina spluttered as they embraced. Harry appeared, wondering what the fuss was. He and Alex nodded to each other.

"Come in, come in" Gina Stynes said.

All four sat in the living room over coffee. Alex glanced around the flat. It had barely changed since he and Stacey first went out together.

"Is there no one else in?" he asked. Gina looked to Stacey before answering.

"Well, Angie's moved out as you know Alex. She rarely visits during the week. Jodie's in her room. She's probably sleeping" Gina answered tactfully. Harry Brand looked troubled. He knew all about Jodie and Tony. Harry had never met Alex before, and wondered how he might react. Alex looked a little surprised at the news.

"What? Little Jodie? She was always a ball of energy, that one! She's never asleep!" he said with a hearty laugh. As if to prove his point, Alex quickly jumped to his feet and ran towards the bedroom doors.

"Which one?" he asked, poised just outside the living room. Stacey tried to remain in control.

"The first one on your left Alex, but leave her be, eh?" Stacey replied. Alex rapped hard on the plain white door.

"Jodie, Oh Jodie!" he sang out melodically. His fist pounded on the door a second time.

Jodie opened her bedroom door and stared back at the faces eyeballing her. She looked startled at the sight of Alex Woods, but tried to offer a friendly smile. Jodie had been listening to some music using her earphones while lying on her bed.

"Come here! Give me a hug!" Alex said. Jodie automatically fell into his strong arms.

"I haven't seen you in years. You haven't changed a bit" he said with a chuckle. Jodie was quick to correct him.

"We met in that pub, remember? I was with Angie" she said in a quiet voice. Alex threw back his head in laughter.

"Of course! I had a few drinks that night, but I do remember. Sure! That was fate in a way. You and Angie got Stacey and me back together. I'll never forget you for that Jodie. Thanks" Alex said, hugging her for a second time. To Jodie it all seemed staged somehow. She said nothing and made her way across the room. Jodie felt compelled to offer Stacey a customary peck on the cheek, unsure if it might be welcomed or not. Stacey reached out and embraced her old pal. Jodie felt relieved. Stacey gave a convincing impression that all was well between them. Alex returned to sit amongst them again.

"This is cosy! It's like old times. Harry, wasn't it?" Alex said. Harry nodded and smiled back.

"Well Harry, when myself and Stacey were first going out together, these girls wanted a place of their own. They were so exited on the night that they moved in here. They scraped the deposit together and we all had a housewarming party here. Jodie, you were only about twelve back then!" Alex said with a loud laugh. He shook his head at the memory. Jodie managed a faint smile.

"I was probably about nineteen! I didn't know any of them back then. I moved in years later Harry" Jodie explained, trying to involve Gina's boyfriend. Harry took up the challenge.

"And did you meet them at your job or something Jodie?" he asked. Jodie shook her head.

"No! I answered an advert in the newspaper. They needed another flatmate to help pay the rent. Things were tough at home for me in Kilkenny, and I was glad to get away. I had just moved to Dublin and was crashing out on a friends' floor. I was delighted to finally get a room of my own!" Jodie replied. Alex laughed again, trying hard to take control of the conversation.

"Yeah, anyway, Angie was with... What was his name Stacey love?" Alex said, clicking his fingers together. Stacey struggled to take in the question. The whole evening seemed surreal to her.

Gina seemed to sense her friend's uneasiness and intervened.

"Who can recall? Angie has been with so many guys!" Gina said. She quickly covered her mouth, realising what she had just said.

"Oops! I didn't mean that the way it sounded! It was so long ago, that's what I meant to say!" Gina added quickly. Everyone laughed. Stacey sat back a little in her seat. Perhaps the evening would be okay after all.

Moments later, Alex was back with a suggestion.

"I know, hey Harry, why don't we go and buy some beers? We can have a few drinks for old time sake" Alex said. Stacey frowned at the idea. She looked to Gina for support.

"I... I don't know. We're all in work in the morning" Gina said tamely.

"Jeezz! We are getting old! Come on, just two beers each" Alex pleaded. Stacey decided to take control.

"No Alex, besides you're driving. Leave it love. We can do this another time" she said with a forced smile. Before Alex could react, Harry was on his feet.

"Yeah, I fancy a few beers, Come on Alex, there's an off-licence around the corner" Harry said. Alex grinned back at Stacey.

"We can grab a taxi pet. After all, I have a whole showroom full of cars!" Alex beamed.

While the two men were gone, Stacey took the time to explain the circumstances to her friends. She told them that it was not her idea to turn up unannounced, and that Alex knew nothing of Jodie's romance with Tony.

"Right, let's leave it that way. I don't fancy an argument" Jodie said quietly. Stacey felt obliged to offer her opinion.

"I still don't approve of what you've done Jodie, but I agree. It's not worth the hassle" Stacey said. They talked about old times until Alex and Harry returned.

"So how are things with you Jodie? Still as mad as ever?" Alex asked later that evening. Jodie smiled sweetly. She sat with her legs tucked up beneath her, wearing her favourite blue tracksuit and fluffy pink slippers.

"No Alex, I've mellowed over the years. I only go mountain climbing five nights a week now!" she replied.

"Touché! And what about romance? Anybody on the horizon?" he asked with a grin. Jodie could feel the eyes upon her. She chose to remain focussed and stared straight back at Alex.

"Oh, no one special. If Mr. Right comes along, you'll be the first to know!" she answered casually. Harry laughed and the others duly followed. Alex seemed untroubled by Jodie's witty attitude. He changed the subject, turning his attention to Harry.

"And what do you do Harry boy? What game are you in?" Alex asked.

"Oh, I'm an office clerk for a big engineering company. Boring stuff I'm afraid Alex. Nine to six behind a desk" Harry replied dismissively.

"Don't knock it mate, once there's money to be made, that's what I say!" Alex said with a huge grin. The mischievous side of Jodie surfaced. She could not help but respond.

"And what about job satisfaction, or the pleasure you get from helping someone? You must enjoy that Alex when you sell someone a new car?" Jodie said. Alex sipped on his beer can and glanced in Jodie's direction.

"You're having a laugh, aren't you? Suckers the lot of them! If only they knew the mark-up price on a new car-or a second-hand car, come to that. Not that I deal with that side of the business, you understand. No. We have a staff of sales people for that kind of stuff. I deal more with administration, you see. Not that I couldn't sell a few Beamer's if the humour took me! But job satisfaction? Naw! A mug's game!" he said dismissively.

Stacey Boyd looked a little embarrassed. It struck her that Alex had become much brasher since they had got back together. In their last relationship, Alex had been almost insecure about himself. In particular, he had always felt a little embarrassed that he worked for his father. Alex would go out of his way rather than mention Wood's Motors.

Jodie however, was far from finished offering her slant on life.

"Well, I still work at a helpdesk for the internet company. I enjoy talking to people over the phone and helping folk online" she said. Alex studied her for a moment.

"And that's job satisfaction? Give me a break Jodie dear!" Alex replied in a patronising tone.

Harry sneered almost silently. Gina nudged her boyfriend. Jodie was on the defensive now. She sought to claw back some pride.

"Well, it gives me a decent wage. I can pay my way and shop till I drop!" she said with a grin. Alex was quick to reply.

"Oh please Jodie! Shop till you drop? You are to fashion what I am to safari hunting! Look at you in that tracksuit! Even after all of these years you still haven't copped on!" Alex sneered. Jodie felt as if she was caught in the headlights of a car. The focus was firmly back on her. No one else said a word.

"I don't wear this to work Alex. It's just what I'm comfortable in" Jodie replied weakly.

"Yeah, whatever!" Alex laughed, again sipping on his beer. Gina looked to Stacey, but her friend seemed unwilling to interfere. Gina Stynes took it on herself to stand up to Alex Woods's domineering attitude.

"Alex, I think that's unfair. You should apologise to Jodie" she said quietly. Jodie rose to her feet quickly.

"There's no need. I'm off to bed. Goodnight folks, it's been really enlightening" she said in a sarcastic tone.

Stacey felt compelled to go to her friend. She hugged Jodie close to her and wished her goodnight.

"Yeah, goodnight Stacey, see you soon. Goodnight all" Jodie said before closing her bedroom door.

CHAPTER TEN

INVITATION TO A WEDDING

Alex Woods lay awake in bed in his apartment. He had lived there now on and off for twelve years. After the first time he and Stacey had split up, Alex had turned it into a bachelor pad. He had had the place redecorated from head to toe, with new furnishings and fittings. Now Stacey was slowly putting her mark back on the second-storey, two-bedroom flat.

Beside him, Stacey lay sleeping quietly. Alex lay on his back staring at the snow-white ceiling.

It had been fun tonight testing the waters with Jodie Callaghan. Sure, Stacey did not approve. He did not expect her to. What a fool they all took him for. Everyone was in on the little secret except Alex. What did they take him for? Well, Alex Woods was no one's fool. He knew all about Jodie's little romance with Tony Lee. He first suspected something was amiss when he checked Stacey's text messages on her phone. This was something he had done regularly since they had got back together. At first it was in case Tony Lee was pestering her. But a particular message sent to Angie O'Rourke had caught his attention. In it Stacey had more or less told Angie what she thought of Jodie. After that, it was simply a matter of following Jodie in the evening to see where she ended up.

Sure enough, on the second night of surveillance, Jodie arrived at Tony Lee's ugly old house.

Stacey had already told Alex where Tony lived. Now it was easy to see why she was mad at Jodie. Stacey was certainly right about one thing. That house was definitely in need of some hard work. Alex lay in the darkness deep in thought. His mind was awash with plots and different scenarios.

Alex turned on his side away from Stacey. She moved a little in the king-sized bed, but Alex barely noticed. He had things on his mind, things that simply would not go away. Looming large was his father's angry face. It was easy to be dismissive of the old man, comforting himself that his father would soon be out of the picture. Yet Alex had to face facts. His father had never spoken about retirement to him. Had he at least set a date somewhere in the future, then at least Alex would have some goal to aim at. His father was in good health too and had seldom had any medical problems, apart from his angina. Alex felt that he was in limbo, waiting for what was rightfully his to bear fruit. He thought of an old saying that his dear grandmother used to use.

"Live horse and you'll get grass" she would say. Alex sighed as he recalled his dear old Nan. His life had never been the same since she had passed away. She had been more of a parent to him than anyone. Alex considered that his Nan Ward was the only one who ever understood him. It was always she who he had gone to with his problems. While his mother worked hard to help his Dad run the business, Nan Ward was the person who looked after him. Alex's world fell apart when Nan suddenly died of a heart attack while babysitting him. His mother then gave up work to care for him, but things could never be the same again. His mother turned their home into an office. Julie Woods never had time for Alex's questions. There were no hugs or kisses any more. Alex learned to be a solitary young man. Now his Mum was gone too. Alex found himself wishing that his Dad would disappear also.

It suddenly dawned on him that that was the solution to all of his problems. He wanted his father dead.

Alex was wide awake now. He slipped from the bed and silently left the bedroom. Alex sat in the living room scribbling on a note pad. He would gladly murder his father at that very moment. But Alex knew that that was not the solution. His mind was suddenly abuzz with thoughts and plots. He was wide awake now, his mind running away with every little idea. It had to be done perfectly, just like Isobel's death. Unless it was foolproof, the police would come and ask questions. Alex scribbled every possible means of death down in a tidy list. He then dismissed each one because of the obvious flaws. Suicide was out of the question. He could never fix it so that it was believable. Poison was too easily traceable to him. Strangulation was ruled out for similar reasons. And so he ticked off each method as he meticulously examined each way of dismissing his father from his life. When Alex reached heart attack, his pen stopped dead on the page. His father suffered with a mild form of angina. The very thing that had killed his dear Nan might just be the answer to his prayers.

"That's it" he thought.

"If only he was to have a heart attack, all my problems would be solved" Alex whispered quietly.

Alex sat back on the red sofa in his red and blue check dressing-gown and considered the matter further. His brain was in overdrive now. Imaginary thoughts of a botched break-in at the family home, where his father lived alone, raced through his mind. But therein lay the problem. While this was happening, Alex would need a watertight alibi. And he dare not have outsiders involved who might mess up the plan. As he considered his conundrum, Alex heard Stacey stir in the bedroom. She came to the door looked tired and worried.

"What are you doing up Alex? I woke and you weren't there. It's only half-three" she said, scratching her short blonde hair. Stacey's wore her white and pink nightie and stood staring at Alex, awaiting an explanation.

He smiled and picked up his small note book.

"It's just a bit of office work for the morning sweetheart. I forgot all about it" he said casually. Stacey smiled back at him.

"You're such a caring man Alex. Your Dad should be so proud of you. If only he knew you the way I do" she said. Alex blew her a kiss.

"You go back to bed darling. Sweet dreams. I'll see you in a bit" he smiled. Stacey returned the imaginary kiss and closed the door behind her. Alex Woods tossed the notebook back onto the coffee table. He would find a solution. He just had to. There was always an answer to every problem.

"Hello?" Tony said as he picked up the house phone. It was late evening and he had been watching television alone.

"Hi Tony, Jan here. How are things with you now? I was worried about you when you told me that you had broken up with Stacey. You are always in our prayers Tony. How are you bearing up?" Jan said. Tony Lee sighed and gathered his thoughts. He was in no mood to be cross-examined by Jan, not tonight.

"I'm okay Jan, how are tricks with you?" he replied in a calculated way.

"Er, things are not too bad I suppose. Listen Tony, Howard has suggested that you might like to come over for a holiday. Unfortunately we would be working most of the time, but you could do some sightseeing, and of course stay here with us" Jan said.

It caught Tony by surprise. He had hinted a couple of times that he might like to meet Jan's family. Each time it had been met with a rebuff.

"Eh, that's very kind of you Jan. When were you suggesting? I might be able to take my holidays soon" He answered thoughtfully. Tony had cancelled the holiday that he had booked for him and Stacey to Portugal.

"Well, as soon as you please. The children are off school. Josh might show you around. Come and stay for as long as you want. We have plenty of room" Jan said. Tony thought immediately about Jodie. It would be pushing it to ask for a double invite. Instantly he realised that Jodie would not be welcome. His sister was old–fashioned. In a family environment she was hardly going to allow an unmarried couple stay under the same roof with Josh and Amy present. Tony was very tempted to accept the offer, if only to see how Jan reacted. There were bound to be a set of rules to follow. On the other hand, he would like to consult with Jodie first.

"It sounds very tempting Jan. Of course, I would have to check with my job first" he replied diplomatically.

"Sure Tony. I'll phone back at the weekend and you can let me know. How's that?" Jan replied cheerfully.

"Sounds good. Thank Howard for me Jan, and say hello to Amy and Josh" Tony said. He said his goodbyes and hung up.

"How did he sound?" Howard asked. Jan looked thoughtful.

"He sounded a bit down at first. He seemed to perk up when I invited him over" she answered.

"There honey, I told you. It's for the best, you'll see. If we can get him away from that old house, we can ensure that he doesn't mess up. We can put any stupid ideas that he might have out of his head. Before he returns to Ireland, Tony will be just as we want him. I can have a few man to man talks with him. You'll see. It will help you sleep better at night, knowing that he's not up to anything silly" Howard added. Jan nodded slowly in agreement.

"I guess you're right Howard. We'll have to watch what we say around him though" she replied. Howard shook his head and laughed out loud.

"I'm a salesman Jan. Lying comes as second nature to me!" he laughed.

Tony discussed his proposed holiday in America with Jodie the following night.

"So you see, they want me to come over there for a while. What do you think?" he said. Jodie looked a little puzzled.

"But you told me that you and your sister don't really get on. Why put yourself through that? And then there's us. I was hoping that we might get away together. Aw! But if you really want to go, I won't stand in your way. You could do with a bit of colour in your cheeks!" Jodie said with a cheeky grin.

Tony examined his bare arms.

"Here! I'm healthy looking! I never put on weight, and all the cycling keeps me fit and tanned" he countered.

"Ha! Tanned in this country? That's a laugh! No, I think that you should go for it. You need a break from all this decorating" Jodie said in an upbeat tone.

Tony surveyed his surroundings. He had put a lot of work into the house. There were still lots to do, and he had barely tackled the exterior of the house.

"Yeah, I kinda hoped to have the place finished before the winter" he replied thoughtfully.

"It can wait. It's been like this long enough, another few months won't make a difference" Jodie countered. Tony stood up and walked towards the kitchen window.

"And would it put you off moving in Jodie? You know, if the house wasn't to your liking?" he asked with his back to her. Jodie followed him to the window and hugged him from behind.

"Of course not silly! I just want it to perfect between us. My biggest fear is that I move in here and we end up hating each other!" Jodie answered. Tony turned to face her. He gave her a reassuring hug.

"That won't happen, I promise" he whispered. Tony ran his hand through Jodie's blonde hair. They kissed for a moment before Jodie broke away. She smiled up at him and led him back to the sofa.

"I have something to tell you too" she said.

Jodie explained about Stacey's visit to the flat with Alex Woods.

"Phew! That must have been awkward for you. What was he like? He obviously knows about us" Tony replied.

"That's just it Tony, he doesn't. Stacey hasn't told him. And yet he appeared to be picking on me. Alex used to be really sweet. Something in him has changed. I can't put my finger on it. When he looked at me I felt really uncomfortable. His eyes looked pure evil" Jodie said quietly. Tony laughed out loud.

"Do you want me to go over there and stick a wooden stake through his heart?" he said. Jodie forced a smile, but looked troubled.

"I can stand up for myself thanks. Normally I would give as good as I got, but I felt that he wanted to goad me into an argument, so I went to bed early" she said. Tony held her close for a moment.

"Well, do you fancy an early night again tonight?" he asked. Jodie smiled back. She took his hand and led him upstairs.

"You know what would really improve this room?" Jodie asked later. The two lay on their backs in Tony's bed.

"What? Another woman?" Tony asked playfully. Jodie thumped him hard in the upper arm.

"Ouch! I was joking! What do you want to do with my room? I'm listening!" he added.

155

"A real fireplace! It would add character. And I know just the spot!" she replied. Tony followed her gaze to the protruding wall in the corner of the room.

"Phew! That will be a big job love. We couldn't do that ourselves. We would need the builders in. Besides, think about the breeze blowing down that chimney at night time! This old place is chilly enough already" Tony reasoned. He felt Jodie's head nodding against his skin.

"Yeah, I noticed. But it doesn't have to be a working fire. We could just find an old fireplace, something stylish, and fit it. Then we could block it off to keep out the draught, providing there's a chimney there to begin with" she suggested. Tony sighed as he considered the idea.

"It sounds like a lot of effort for nothing to me, not to mention a waste of money" Tony said.

"Well, it was just a thought. You did ask me what I would like done to the house!" she said.

"Most women want an extension, or a conservatory. You want a fireplace! Stacey always said…" Tony broke off, realising he had broken one of the great taboos.

"It's okay, you can say her name. I don't mind. Stacey and I are still good friends. What did she want to do?" Jodie asked. Tony took a deep breath.

"No, sorry, I wasn't thinking. Stacey would never have moved in here. She hated the place. She complained of the cold. No matter what time of the year, Stacey was always freezing in this house. A fireplace in the corner would definitely be out!" Tony said. The two laughed as they thought of Stacey Boyd.

"Yeah, she told me often enough about this house. She didn't particularly get on with your mother either, did she?" Jodie remarked. Tony shook his head.

"No, but to be fair, my Mam was a difficult woman. Jan says that she was never the same after my Dad died. Mam was stuck in her ways. No woman would have been good enough for her beloved son!" Tony laughed. Jodie jumped up into a kneeling position. She grabbed her white pillow and began hitting Tony playfully with it.

"She never met me! I would have converted her! We could have gone mountain climbing together, or gone canoeing!" Jodie said with a smile. Tony pretended to defend himself, and then made a grab for Jodie.

"Come here you! I can think of better things to do than canoeing!" he said.

Alex Woods had already booked a table at his favourite restaurant for later that evening. He phoned Stacey at lunch time and casually asked if she fancied dining out that evening.

"Is it a special occasion? It's only Tuesday, we never go out on Tuesday evenings" she said.

"Oh, I just thought my special lady might enjoy a break. But if you would rather stay in..." he replied.

"No, no, I'd love to go! Right, I'll get home as soon as I can. See you later Alex" she said.

"I can't wait darling" Alex replied with a kiss.

They arrived at The Olde City Grill off Lower Leeson Street at around eight o'clock. Stacey looked radiant in a shapely blue dress and white shoes and handbag. Alex wore one of his many black suits, with a white shirt and colourful tie. They enjoyed a nice meal and were soon into their second bottle of red wine.

"I hope my head is clear for work in the morning!" Stacey joked.

"Why not take the day off? We can afford it" Alex said. Stacey looked slightly put out. She liked her office job and seldom took time off.

"You know I don't like doing that. No, I'll be okay" she said.

"Well, it is a special occasion after all" Alex replied. Stacey looked baffled.

"You said that it wasn't. You said..."

Alex interrupted her.

"I know what I said. That was then, this is now precious" he smiled.

"Alex! What are you on about? You have me confused" Stacey laughed.

Alex pulled a sparkling gold ring from his pocket and knelt down on one knee.

"I know that I messed up before Stacey, but please say yes. I promise to make you the happiest girl in the world" Alex said. Stacey's eyes opened wider as she stared at the huge engagement ring. It had a big diamond in the centre, with five smaller glittering diamonds around it. Stacey held both hands to her face in shock. Alex grasped her left hand and held the engagement ring almost hovering above her fingers.

"Well?" he said. All around them couples nudged each other. Soon all eyes in the popular restaurant were on Alex and Stacey.

"Yes, yes I will! Thank you Alex, thank you" Stacey said emotionally. People began to applaud, and Stacey began to sob with tears of happiness. A somewhat embarrassed Alex climbed to his feet and kissed her on the lips. She slid the ring onto her hand and examined it while wearing a great smile. Alex sat down again opposite Stacey. They held hands across the table. She leaned forward to speak in a hushed voice. By now the genteel applause had died away.

"I still have the other engagement ring at home" she whispered. Alex laughed.

"I know! It's probably bad luck or something to use the same one! Sell it, or give it to one of your friends. Hey! Why not give it to Jodie? Let's face it, who would ever marry that tomboy?" Alex grinned. Stacey's expression changed. Her smile faded and her forehead furrowed a little.

"Let's not be nasty Alex. I want us to be happy-especially tonight" she said. Alex continued to snigger away, amused by his remarks.

"I was just kidding precious. I'll be nice, I promise!" he replied.

"Oh Alex, I just love this ring! It must have cost a fortune! I can't wait to show it off!" Stacey gushed. Alex gripped both of her hands in his.

"Better make it snappy! I plan on a short engagement. We should set the wedding date soon. What do you say?" Alex said.

Stacey was still on a high. She tried to take in what he was saying.

"Soon? When? Oh my God! I'm so excited!" She squealed.

I want to get married before Christmas. We don't need a big church wedding. Anyway, we're already living together. What's to stop us tying the knot soon?" Alex answered with a smile.

"My parents! I have to phone them!" Stacey said. The smile vanished from Alex's face.

"Really? Won't your Dad be fuming after the last time? At least hold off until tomorrow, and preferably when I'm not around!" Alex scoffed.

"Okay, I'll ring tomorrow. My folks will be okay though. They know that we're back together. Dad was a bit miffed the last time, but it was not as if he had already travelled over to Ireland for the big day. All he was annoyed about was because how upset I was back then. He's all right with it now. Don't worry, everything will be just brilliant" Stacey said.

"I hope that you're right darling" Alex said quietly.

Jodie met up with Tony at their usual bar for a drink. It was Friday night. They had discovered the small lounge bar while out walking one night. Both were keen to avoid places where they might bump into either Stacey or her friends.

"I have some news for you Tony" Jodie said. Tony examined the tense look on her face.

"You're not...pregnant are you?" he asked, gulping down air. Jodie gave him an irritated look.

"Of course not silly, I'm on the pill. No, it's Stacey. She's just got engaged to Alex Woods" Jodie said. Tony nodded as he took in the information.

"Oh, second time lucky then!" he said quietly.

"That's not all Tony. She's invited us to the wedding. Well, me really, but she said that she had no problem if I want to invite you" Jodie said. Tony looked bemused.

"What? That's sick! Naw! I don't want to go Jodie. You go with Angie and Gina, eh?" he replied.

"But they'll be with their boyfriends. Either you come with me, or I won't go either" she said in an agitated tone.

"Christ! Okay, look, we don't have to decide right away, do we? I mean, they can't be getting hitched tomorrow" he replied.

"Eight weeks. It seems Alex has already booked the reception. It's in one of those posh castles in Meath or somewhere" Jodie answered.

"A posh castle? Aren't all castles posh?" Tony joked.

"Well, you know what I mean! The point is, what do we say to Stacey? If we don't go it will look like I'm snubbing her, and Stacey is still a mate" Jodie said. Her eyes searched Tony's face for a way out.

"Christ! This is tricky! Hey! I know! I could go and stay at Jan's house! That way you would have to go alone!" Tony said cheerfully.

"Thanks Tony, thanks a bunch!" Jodie said, folding her arms.

"I'm joking! I have already made up my mind about the holiday. When Jan phones I'll tell her no thanks. I'll explain about meeting you. Unless by a miracle she invites both of us, I won't go" Tony replied with certainty.

Jodie reached out and kissed him gently on the cheek.

"Tony, we simply have to go to this wedding. There's no other way out" Jodie said.

"Fine. Let's hope that he doesn't show up for the second time!" Tony sighed.

"Hello Jan, thanks for phoning back. Listen, I don't think that I can come over after all. You see, I've met this great girl. I didn't want to say anything when you called, because I wasn't sure how serious it was between me and her. I realise now that I can't leave her" Tony said.

"That's too bad Tony. Still, if you're sure" Jan replied. She sounded genuinely sad at the news that Tony would not be travelling.

"Yeah, she's been great. She even helped me decorate the house. I haven't told anyone this Jan, but I think that Jodie is the one. And here's some news that you might find hard to believe. Stacey's getting married to her old boyfriend, and she's invited myself and Jodie along. Isn't that something?" Tony said with a chuckle. Immediately Jan's mood seemed to change.

"And why would she do that? Does she want to rub your nose in it or something? Tony, you are far too soft. I don't want you to attend that wedding. That Stacey is only mischief-making. I knew that I was right about her. I got this sense of evil when I met her. I didn't like to say at the time. You are well rid of her Tony, well rid" Jan said, almost spitting out the words.

Tony bit his lip. He could not tell Jan that Jodie was Stacey's friend. It would not sound right, and somehow Tony cared what Jan thought of him.

"Thanks Jan, I know that you have my best interests at heart. Myself and Jodie will talk it over" Tony said. Jan paused and seemed to be considering what Tony had said earlier.

"What was that about decorating the house Tony? I thought that you were all through with that?" she asked.

"Oh, I decided to do a better job. The painting was fairly cosmetic. I want to modernise it a little. I've already cleared out the attic and..."

Tony's casual words were quickly interrupted by Jan.

"We agreed. I only allowed you to have that house on the specific understanding that nothing would be touched. That was Mom's house. Have you no sense of decency Tony? Mom is barely cold in her grave and you're already pulling the place apart" she fumed. Tony was caught unaware. He had momentarily forgotten how volatile Jan could be.

"Listen Jan, please listen, I've barely done a thing with it, honestly. I've cleared out all the old stuff in the attic, painted all of the rooms, got rid of all of Mam's old clothes, and smashed up some old furniture. Now is that wrecking the house? Come on!" he reasoned. Jan went quiet for a few seconds.

"Okay, maybe I was over-reacting. Mom's death is still very raw with me. I feel very protective about her memory. I'm sorry Tony" she replied.

"That's okay sis. Oh, I'll tell you what I did find though. I found the old battered pram in the attic. You know, my old blue one? Can you believe Mam kept it? It only has two wheels. God! Mam was really sentimental, wasn't she?" Tony said with a chuckle.

"Yeah, she was. That was fit for the scrap heap all right. No, on reflection Tony, you were right to clear out the attic after all. Well done" Jan said quietly.

"Thanks. The place is looking very well now. I plan to decorate outside soon. Jodie said that it needs brightening up. Mam always liked it kept traditional. You know, with the green front door and ivy walls? The trouble is, I don't get enough time off work to do things. Maybe we'll hire a decorator. Jodie has a million great ideas. She's always coming up with suggestions to improve the house. We talked about a new kitchen too. What do you think Jan?" he asked.

"God Tony! I've already told you a thousand times what I think! Leave the goddamn place as it is for Christsake! This young bimbo is just filling your head with rubbish. Soon she'll tire of you too, and you'll be left to pick up the pieces again. You're so naïve Tony, you really are" Jan said in a cross voice.

"Jodie's not like that Jan, really she's not" Tony replied sharply.

"Look, I have to go now Tony. Howard's just come home. Remember what you promised me. That's all that I ask. Okay?" Jan said tersely.

Before Tony could reply, the line went dead. He stared down the receiver before slowly putting it back on the hook.

Alex was working in the showrooms of his father's business on The Long Mile Road. The radio played in the background. As the eleven o'clock news came on, Alex listened subliminally. Suddenly his blood ran cold. He had caught something on the radio, but was not quite sure if he had heard correctly. Alex stood up erect, straining his ears to their fullest. It was too late. Already the newscaster had moved on to the next item. Alex rushed to the reception area near the doorway.

"Did you catch that Michelle? What was that on the news?" he asked impatiently. The young redhead looked puzzled.

"Sorry Alex, I wasn't paying attention. I've just put down the phone" she said.

"It was something about a body found in the Dublin Mountains. Did you hear it?" he asked again. Michelle shook her head.

"Maybe...sort of...I heard something..." Michelle stammered. Alex rushed away to the office where the radio was located. The speakers were all over the showrooms, but the actual radio was situated down the corridor in a small stores room. Alex stared wildly at the silver and black radio before moving swiftly to his office. He leaned over and switched on his small personal radio. Alex fiddled with the dial, searching other radio stations for the news bulletins.

"Shit, shit, shit!!" he screamed. No other station appeared to be carrying the item. Either he had misheard, or the news item had already been broadcast.

"Fuck! I'll have to wait for the next bulletin" he muttered. Alex paced the office, running through things again in his head.

"It can't be. I buried her almost six foot down. It can't be. Maybe dogs...wild animals...who knows? If they've found Isobel, I'm done for. It won't take a genius to link her to me. Come on, just in case, get your story straight in your head. Okay. I haven't seen Isobel for years. Stacey can give me an alibi..." Alex trailed off as he realised that Stacey would discover that he had been married to Isobel.

"Shit! This is all that I need!" he muttered through clenched teeth. Alex thumped hard on the partitioned wall dividing the office from the corridor outside. He then wandered back outside. Alex glanced out through the huge glass panes, half-expecting the police to appear. A worried-looking Michelle stared across at him.

"Was it important Alex? You could try the internet" she said in her best office voice. Alex barely glanced at her, but took in her words.

He rushed away again to his own small office once more. His computer was always left switched on. Alex tried various sites, but came up with nothing.

"Stay calm. The next news will be on at eleven-thirty" he told himself. He paced the floor again, desperately trying to convince himself that it would be all right.

At eleven-thirty Alex tuned in again. He hired the volume so as not to miss a word.

"In other news, a body was discovered early this morning in The Dublin Mountains. The victim had been shot in the head, and was known to police. The man's body was discovered by a couple out walking their dogs. It is believed that this is the latest gangland killing in the ever escalating drugs war on the south side of the city" said the newsreader.

Alex exhaled slowly. A flicker of a smile soon turned into a huge grin.

"Easy boy, easy. You're far too clever to be caught like that! It was the perfect murder. That old cow's body will never be found" he thought quietly. Alex lowered the radio and stood up again. The scare had taught him one thing. He had let his guard down. From now on he would be more pokerfaced when something happened. Anyone other than Michelle might have wondered what all the fuss was. Alex strolled out to reception and walked casually up to Michelle's high desk.

"Did you hear that Michelle? Another drug-pusher shot dead. It always fascinates me how these criminals live. They take their lives in their hands every time that they go out" he said casually.

"Yeah, it gives me the creeps. Still Alex, he was someone's son" Michelle answered.

"The world is a better place without him Michelle" Alex replied coldly.

CHAPTER ELEVEN

FATHER & SON

"Alex, you know the way you said that I can invite who I like to the wedding?" Stacey asked tactically. It was late evening and the two were sitting together at home watching a movie.

Already Alex Woods knew where she was going with the conversation.

"Yeah, of course sweetheart, but we don't want half of your office staff there. Let's keep it fairly intimate. Don't forget, each guest will bring their partner, so fifty guests also means another fifty strangers" Alex replied.

"Well, yes, but not necessarily so" Stacey said in a faltering tone. Alex turned to face her on the couch.

"I don't get it darling, what's going on in that pretty little head of yours?" he asked. Stacey forced a smile and began again to explain herself.

"Okay, it goes without saying that I should invite Gina and Harry, and of course Angie and Phil. Angie is my bridesmaid anyway" she started.

"And Jodie and a friend" Alex interrupted, trying to sound helpful.

"Yes...well, that's the problem. I've something to tell you about Jodie. You see, I've just found out that my ex, Tony, is seeing Jodie. I was shocked of course when I found out. At first I didn't think it was serious, but Angie seems to think that it is" Stacey said.

"Well, well, that is a shocker all right pet! Poor you, you must feel so betrayed by both of them" Alex replied, stroking her arm in sympathy with her.

"Yeah, I did in a way. I suppose that I have to get over it. Anyhow, Jodie is still a mate, so I really would like her at our wedding. It means her bringing Tony of course. That is if you don't mind Alex" she said. Her eyes questioned him, unsure how he would react.

"Phew! That's a tough one pet. Your ex-boyfriend watching my every move! A chap wouldn't want to have a complex, would he? How can I say no to you darling? If that's the way it has to be, well then, it's okay by me" Alex said in an anguished tone. Stacey hugged him close and thanked him.

"I love you Alex, you're so kind and accepting" she whispered.

"I still think that's it's a despicable thing for Jodie's to do. I'm not sure that I could forgive a friend if they did that to me" Alex replied.

"I know love, but let's just tolerate it for the day, eh?" Stacey said.

"Anything for you, precious. Anything" Alex answered.

During the night, Alex rose quietly from bed. Stacey was sleeping soundly. Alex took her mobile phone and slipped out to the bathroom. He filled the sink and casually dropped the phone into the cold water.

"There! That will teach you never to lie to me Stacey. You've only just found out about Jodie, have you? You knew a lot longer than I did, you little liar. You will have to learn Stacey, that for every action, there is a reaction" he whispered.

After some moments Alex retrieved the silver and black phone from the water. He carefully dried it with the white towel, shaking any surplus water from inside the phone. The screen was now blank, and Alex checked to ensure that it was not working.

"Perfect! No calls for you tomorrow my darling!" Alex sneered. He placed the phone back where he had found it and climbed back into bed.

"Goodnight princess, sleep tight" he whispered.

Tony Lee shifted the last of the attic junk, moving it gradually towards the loft door and then down onto the landing. The yellow skip outside was half full, and Tony reckoned he would just about manage to fit everything in. In the corner of the attic, Tony had amassed all of his mother's personal belongings, including handbags, old clothing, and some old framed photographs and paintings.

"Now, what to do with this little lot?" he mused.

Tony paused for breath. The temptation to have a cigarette loomed large in his head. He had not smoked since repainting his bedroom.

"I suppose I should give the lot to a charity shop. There's not much point in keeping a load of old handbags" Tony muttered. There were at least twelve ladies bags of varying colours and styles. They were hardly fashionable, as his mother had not purchased a new one for many years before her death.

Tony lowered the last of the junk down onto the landing. He swung his body downwards, resting his feet on the tall banisters. Tony then began to lower the rectangular door. He glanced back at the pile of his mother's belongings. "Another day's work" he whispered with a sigh.

Jodie and Tony were out shopping for clothes for the upcoming wedding. Tony had not actually agreed to attend. Given the choice he would stay away, but he knew that Jodie was keen to go.
"What about trying in there for a nice suit?" Jodie said, stopping at an upmarket men's shop.
"Do I have to? I mean, I would rather just wear something casual Jodie" he replied.
"Don't be silly! That's okay if we were just going to the afters. We don't want people talking" Jodie said. Tony laughed loudly at the irony of her statement.
"Jodie, they're gonna be talking anyway! Don't forget, both Stacey's and his family will be there. Everyone is bound to know who we are" Tony replied.
Jodie had not really thought about this. She had only considered Stacey and Alex.
"All the more reason to look good. Come on, your having a new suit!" Jodie replied in a determined voice.

Howard paced the large kitchen, which was the hub of his family's home life. Jan sat on a high stool watching him.
"You're right honey, we'll have to get over there and talk sense to him" Howard said. He stopped pacing and looked to his wife for agreement.
"I think it's for the best Howard, otherwise we will go out of our minds" Jan replied.
"It might mean closing the shop, and then there are the children to consider" Howard said, pacing the room once more.
"I'm sure that your folks would take them" Jan said quietly. Howard nodded.
"I daresay. The business is my main concern. When you lose customers, they rarely return" Howard added.
"What's more important?" Jan said quietly. Howard gave her a furtive glance.
"I know, I know. Don't worry honey, we'll sort this out once and for all" he said in a determined tone.

Alex Woods called to his father's home on the upmarket Hollytree Road. Tom Woods' home, "Hillcrest", was a large, detached Georgian house in the leafy suburb of Blackrock, on the outskirts on Dublin. Alex sat in his car for some moments, observing the home where he had grown up.

"If only my Nan was still here" he whispered to himself. The house was set in about an acre of landscaped garden, with a well-tended lawn to the left of the grey-coloured house.

"Soon this place will be mine. Stacey will stay at home and bring up my children. I will have the life of a gent, once I sell the business. It will be golf days, weekends away, holidays and fast cars. What a fool the old man is to work his butt off, all for nothing. I just might have to speed up his lifespan, depending on what he says today" Alex thought quietly.

He climbed from his car onto the white gravel and strode purposefully towards the front door. Eight wide concrete steps led up to the imposing black front door. Although Alex still had a key to his father's home, he politely rang the doorbell. He knew that his father was home because of his red Jaguar car parked in the broad driveway.

"Hello" his father said in an almost begrudging tone. He held the door wide open to admit his son.

"Something wrong at work?" his father asked. Alex shook his head as he passed.

His father followed Alex inside to the living room. Alex turned to face him.

"Just to let you know that I'm getting married next month. I'll probably need some time off" Alex said casually.

Tom Woods looked a little surprised.

"Oh, congratulations. Stacey is it? I always liked that girl. Very sensible" his father replied.

"Yeah, well the date is set. I hope you'll be there. It's a small wedding at a registry office. We don't want a fuss" Alex said.

"Pity that! I always feel that it's not a real wedding unless it's in a church" Tom Woods said. Alex bit hard on his lip. He had not come for a row, but his father's continual sniping was irking him.

"Well, we can't have everything in life, can we?" Alex said in his barbed way.

"Er, no indeed. Well, the best of luck anyhow" his father answered.

"The other thing I came to see you about was my position at work. Now that I have responsibilities, I was hoping that you might promote me. Stacey will want to raise a family, so in time she will have to give up her job" Alex said in a matter-of-fact tone. His father looked puzzled.

"Promotion? What promotion? You're the manager as it is, and on a damn fine wage at that. When I was your age I was earning buttons. I had to drag my way up. You've had it easy lad. You don't know what side your bread is buttered on! Promotion indeed! What position had you in mind?" Tom Woods sneered.

It was time for Alex to finally confront his father. For years he had lived in fear of his over-bearing parent.

"Well, yours I suppose. I mean, should you not be thinking of retiring? Should you not be finally enjoying life?" Alex said. His father threw back his head and laughed.

"Retiring? Ha! That's a good one! As long as I'm fit, I will never retire. As for enjoying life, that's what I'm doing every day. I love the cut and thrust of business. Since your mother passed away, my company is what keeps me going. Don't worry, Stacey and yourself will be fine. Besides, if I'm honest, I don't think that you have what it takes to make the really big decisions. No, I will continue at the helm son. You should be thankful for what you have" Tom Woods concluded. Alex immediately saw red.

"Thankful? Thankful for what? I've gone to college, spent my time learning the ropes, did your bidding, and travelled the length and breadth of the country, gone abroad for you, worked long hours without overtime. What have I to be thankful for?" Alex fumed.

A faint smile crept onto the lips of Tom Woods.

"You still don't get it, do you? You came in at the top, straight from college to the management side of the company. Do you know how many young men would give their right arm for what you have? And now you want my job? If it wasn't so pathetic it would be funny!" Tom said with a patronising smile. Alex took a deep breath.

"You know what? I've tried, I really have tried to get on with you, but you're just a bitter old man. Life has passed you by, and what are you left with? This empty house and a business that you will eventually leave behind. So who's the pathetic one?" Alex scoffed.

The smile vanished immediately from Tom Wood's wrinkled face.

"Get out! Get out of my home. I have a good mind to call my solicitor and disinherit you. Don't push me any further lad, I'm telling you now" Tom said in a snarling tone.

"Right, I'll go, but this is not finished. I need to know where I stand. I can't go on working as a general dogsbody at my stage of life" Alex yelled.

"You have a choice so. Why not collect your p45? I usually insist on a week's notice from my employees, but in your case I'll waive that" Tom said, the veiled smile returning to his lips. Alex went straight to the front door without speaking again. He stormed his way to his car, slamming the heavy black door behind him.

Alex Woods sat in the driver's seat, cursing everything about his father.

"You'll get yours, old man. Don't worry; I'm coming for you now. See if I don't. I always win in the end" he muttered. Alex banged his right hand on the steering wheel several times in temper. Then the more subtle, calculating side took over.

"No, I have to plan this properly. I have to have a watertight alibi. He has to die. Die bastard, die" he thought. Alex sped off, his wheels spinning wildly on the white gravel.

Just as he was about to exit the black-painted wrought iron gates, Alex suddenly drew to a halt. He had spotted the family cat creeping from the bushes on the passenger side of the car.

"Here kitty-kitty!" he called in a friendly tone. The ginger-and-white cat's ears pricked up. Alex reached over and opened the passenger door. He called the tomcat again, patting the empty front seat as he did so.

The old cat slowly made his way over to the open door, perhaps recognising Alex's friendly voice. Alex's father had always kept a cat, and Whiskey had been with him for eleven years.

Alex scooped up the cat onto his lap. He petted the old feline, stroking its fur and scratching under its chin.

"Good fellow! Good boy! There, there" Alex said, smiling pleasantly. Suddenly his facial expression changed to a scowl. In one swift movement his hand moved up to the cat's neck. He twisted violently on old Whiskey's neck, snapping it in two. The cat's body fell limp. Without a word, Alex climbed from the car. He carried the lifeless cat to the dense bushes to the side of the driveway, which was out of view from the house, and tossed it high in the air into the heavy overgrown shrubbery.

Alex climbed back inside his car, smiling smugly to himself.

"Oh dear, poor Whiskey! Now you're really alone old man!" Alex said quietly with a chuckle. He drove away, now in better spirits than when he had left his father.

Tony Lee cycled along the canal at a relaxed pace. He was on his way to see his old aunt at Saint Alfonse's Nursing Home. It was a bright sunny day with a minimal breeze blowing in his face. Tony had not been to see his Aunt Ethel in weeks. Today he was going out of a sense of duty, rather than in hope of any meaningful dialogue.

Tony locked his silver bike against the railings and took a deep breath. His wish was that Ethel was in good health, and at least mildly aware of her surroundings. He steeled himself and headed towards the entrance.

"Hello Aunt Ethel, how are you feeling today? I've brought you some sweets" Tony said with a smile. Ethel sat by the large bay window and strained to identify him.

"I, I'm fine...I know the voice but my old eyes..."Ethel said in a wheezing tone. Tony sat down beside her and squeezed her hand.

"It's Tony, Delores's son. You look great Aunt Ethel" he said.

"Ah, I'm okay. My breathing is terrible son, but I'm all right. Who did you say that you were again?" Ethel answered. Tony bit his lip. That vacant, faraway look stared back at him.

"I'm Tony, your nephew" he said.

"Not Martin?" Ethel said, a puzzled look etched on her thin, lined face. Tony did not know any Martin associated with the family. He shook his head at the old woman and smiled again. Tony patted her bony left hand and sat closer to her.

"It's me, Aunt Ethel, it's Tony. Remember when you used to tell me stories about your younger days. Remember the toffee apples?" Tony said.

A flicker of a smile flashed across Ethel's lips.

"I do! And the bull's eyes! Henry will be here later. I must ask him to bring bull's eyes. They still sell them, don't they?" Ethel said. Tony felt guilty. He brought Ethel a simple box of chocolates as a treat. Sometimes he would stop off and buy some old-fashioned sweets or grapes. Today it had taken the easy way out.

"They still sell them Ethel, yes. I'll bring some the next time" He replied gently. Once again, Ethel looked unsure.

"How is Delores? She never comes to see me. Henry comes most days. He will be here soon" Ethel said in a faraway voice.

"Delores can't come Auntie, she's...she's not well" Tony said, trying hard to mask his emotion. The expression on Ethel's face changed dramatically.

"Apples and oranges, apples and oranges!" Ethel whispered. Ethel was again back in her own private world. Tony suppressed a smile at the woman's meaningless, childish words. He would wait patiently in hope that Ethel soon returned to reality. It was almost fifteen minutes before Ethel Langan spoke once more.

"Evil she is, evil. How can she live with herself? She turns my stomach. I hate her...hate her" Ethel said, the words suddenly tumbling from her mouth. Tony looked around, fearing that his Aunt was talking about a fellow patient.

"Who is Ethel? Who's evil?" he whispered. Ethel's blue eyes stared back at him.

"Delores Lee. Delores is pure evil" Ethel replied with conviction. Tony felt the hairs on his neck stand up. Obviously the old woman was raving, but there was such purpose in her tone that it disturbed him.

Tony sat quietly holding Ethel's hand for some moments. Her eyes had that distant look, and Tony wondered what she was thinking. Suddenly Ethel turned to stare at him again.

"You should go mister. My husband Henry will be here soon. He will be angry. I asked him to bring grapes, black grapes. My Harry is always so attentive, so kind" Ethel said, a glimpse of a smile appearing on her quivering lips. Tony nodded and rose to his feet. There was little point in arguing. Ethel's mind was somewhere else once more.

"Goodbye Aunt Ethel, you take care of yourself" he said, squeezing her hand in his.

"Say a prayer for Martin" Ethel whispered. She mumbled the same sentence over and over again. Tony nodded and smiled. He walked slowly away, his head bowed in sadness. It was pointless to go on visiting the dear old lady, although he was certain that his mother would want him to.

Tony made his way outside, still unsure if it would be his final visit to the home. He unlocked his bike and turned again to view the old red-bricked home. Tony wondered if he would ever see his poor Aunt Ethel again. It was torment to see the old lady's mind in such confusion. And yet she had no one else in the world to care about her.

Tony set off in sombre mood for home. Today there would be no racing cars along the canal. His mind was troubled as he thought about his mother and her two sisters. The three Goulding girls had once been close. Of that Tony had no doubt. Slowly their lives had drifted apart as they had married and started a family of their own. Ethel's dementia meant she could never be told about Delores dying, whereas his Auntie Mary either could not be bothered, or was too frail to travel to Ireland. Tony wondered what would become of him when he grew old. Would he too end up in a home? Would he have children to care for him? Would he still be with Jodie? It seemed like a million years off, and yet it troubled him. He thought of Erik Ngombiti and how his life had turned around. Then Tony thought of Tricia and Erik's birthday meal from hell. A wry smile quickly replaced his worried expression as he cycled casually along the leafy suburb of Blackrock.

"Huh! Imagine ending up with her! Now that would be a fate worse than death!" he thought.

Alex Woods lay in bed thinking of ways to be rid of his father. Stacey lay sleeping quietly beside him. Most nights now he stayed awake into the early hours, quietly contemplating a master-plan on ways to dispose of his father. Alex was now obsessed with the murder, but needed to establish a foolproof method. His thinking mostly concerned on how he could have an alibi while carrying out the crime. The actual thought of murdering his father did not trouble him; it was the concern of getting away with the crime that sat heavily on his mind. Alex was the one who would benefit from Tom Wood's untimely death, and the police were bound to ask questions. He was loathe to involve anybody else. Alex felt that it might leave him open to blackmail in the future. He would have no problem in paying some criminal to carry out the murder, but knew how dangerous such an alliance might prove.

Alex tiptoed from the bed. He glanced at the bedside clock. It was just gone one-thirty. He threw on his dressing gown and crept silently outside to the kitchen. This room was furthest away from the bedroom, which meant that there was less chance of disturbing Stacey. It would allow him the chance to think straight.

Alex's brain was now overactive. He found that he did his best thinking in the early hours of the morning. As the months had slipped by, Alex found that needed less and less sleep.

"He has to die soon. I have to be somewhere else, preferably here with Stacey. A break in at the house seems the most plausible, yet the old man always sets the house alarm. He must leave a window open though, because that old cat is always coming and going. Oops! There is no cat now!" Alex thought as he paced the small rectangular kitchen. He continued to consider all possibilities as he dug his hands into the pockets of his check dressing gown.

"Now, night-time is ideal, but it could be during the day too. What if I set off the alarm at the house, would a neighbour phone him at work to come home I wonder? I could be waiting and get him then. It would look like a botched robbery. But then there's the alibi thing again. Fuck! Fuck! Fuck!" he thought. Suddenly Alex heard Stacey's phone ringing. She had had to purchase a new one after he had soaked her old mobile in water. Stacey had lost most of her personal phone numbers, but was slowly acquiring her friend's contact details again. Alex hurried back to the bedroom. Stacey was already stirring. Alex tossed off his dressing gown and handed Stacey her phone.

"Here darling, you better see who it is" he said with a stifled yawn.

"Sorry Alex. Who would be phoning me at this hour?" Stacey mumbled, now barely awake.

"Only one way to find out! Pity! I was in a lovely sleep!" Alex sighed. Stacey apologised again as she pressed the green button on her new pink phone.

"Hello, Angie? Hush! What's the matter?" Stacey said. The concern in her voice alerted Alex. He listened intently as Stacey threw question after question at her best friend.

"He said what? Oh my God! Stop crying Angie, I can't make out what you're saying" Stacey said. Alex patted her shoulder.

"What's going on pet?" he asked. Stacey covered the phone as she turned to him.

"It's Angie. She's had a row with Philip. She said that he told her that he doesn't love her. He wants to get back with his wife and kids. They had an almighty row and he slapped her face" Stacey whispered. Alex reached out and switched on the bedside lamp. Stacey continued the fractured conversation. "Where will you go Angie, it's nearly two o'clock in the morning?" Stacey said. Again she covered the small pink phone and turned to Alex.

"She has nowhere to go Alex. Her folks live miles away. Could we fetch her and let her stay for a few nights? Just until she gets sorted" Stacey asked with a frown. Alex scratched his head. Already he was thinking ahead. With Angie O'Rourke also staying at his flat, the possibilities of an alibi might increase.

"I suppose so love. Tell her to hang on. I'll drive. She can have the spare room" he said. Alex climbed wearily from his bed and got dressed. Stacey continued to comfort her friend as Alex left the room. His thoughts again turned to his father. Perhaps this windfall might give him the opportunity to carry out his plan.

"I'm sorry Alex. This is all we need!" Stacey said. Alex drove on along the quiet streets of south Dublin. He managed a smile as he reassured Stacey.

"It's no problem precious. You know what they say; a friend in need is a bloody nuisance! You know what this means though? We'll have to be extra quiet in the bedroom!" he chuckled. Stacey grinned but looked embarrassed. She continued to offer directions, but Alex already had a fair idea where he was going.

"I can't believe that he hit her. What a bastard!" Stacey said

"Yeah, big brave man. He used to work with Angie, what happened? What does he do for a living anyway?" Alex replied. Stacey thought for a moment.

"Oh, he left to become a manager in a bakery. More money I think. I remember Angie saying that he goes to work early in the mornings. I hear that he has to leave home at some godforsaken hour" she answered.

They pulled up outside a small flats complex at the end of a street. Alex glanced around the area.

"It's not the best of neighbourhoods, is it?" he observed.

"No, but it was all that they could afford. They live on the ground floor flat over there. He's still paying his wife maintenance money. It doesn't leave them with much" Stacey said, pointing to an old artisan block of flats.

"Well now he can go back to his wife and live happily ever after" Alex muttered.

Angie came into view on the far side of the dimly-lit street. She crossed the road carrying just her handbag and a small black suitcase. Her face was tearstained and her eyes had noticeable black smudges from her crying. "Thanks Alex. I'm so sorry Stacey" she mumbled as she climbed into the back of the car.

"It will be okay Angie. Come on, let's go home" Stacey replied.

Back at Alex's apartment, Stacey made coffee while Angie unburdened herself. "I can understand him missing his children, but then to tell me that he didn't love me…" she blubbered. Stacey came and put a comforting arm around her. "Sssh! Try not and think about it Angie" she whispered. Angie needed to talk. Her whole body was awake and in need of understanding.

"I tried to reason with him. I said to give it more time. I promised that I would make him happy. How pathetic do I sound Stacey?" Angie said, trying to smile her way through her ordeal. Alex leaned forward in his armchair. He was sitting opposite both Angie and Stacey who were on the red couch.

"Is this the first time that he hit you Angie love?" Alex asked. Angie went quiet for a few seconds before answering.

"Well, he pushed me once before. He said that it was an accident. But this time it was a full-blooded slap. I was in shock. He just drew out and hit me. I was pleading with him to see reason. He told me to stop talking. Then, whack!" she replied, trying to make light of the incident. Stacey wrapped her arm around her pal once more.

"You can never go back Angie. Once he's done that, he will do it again" she said. Alex nodded as he stood up.

"Stacey's right Angie. Stay as long as you like. He's just a bully. I'm going to bed. I have to be up early. Stacey will look after you. Goodnight Angie, goodnight Stacey" he said.

Alex lay in bed considering the implications of Angie O'Rourke's stay. There had to be a benefit in it. He began to plan for every possibility that might arise. Alex ran through the girls' job routines. Both Stacey and Angie worked similar hours. They would probably arrive home at the same time, and they would go out together in the mornings. It struck Alex that they both liked similar movies and television programmes. Now his brain was again working hard on every eventuality. He saw a small window of opportunity.

"Yes, it just might work" he thought.

Outside, Stacey was at last talking Angie around.

"You'll see Angie, you'll be better off without that animal" Stacey smiled. Angie's dark features looked unsure. Her weepy brown eyes searched her pal's face.

"Do you really think so Stacey? Every time I glance in the mirror I seem to look older. I really hoped that Phillip was the one. Maybe my age is making me desperate! What do you think? Perhaps I'm destined to end up an old spinster!" Angie joked, managing to force a smile.

"Stop, you're grand! There are plenty of decent fellows out there. Look at me. I'm back with Alex. It's the best move that I ever made, and that's thanks to you" Stacey said.

"And Jodie" Angie replied mischievously. Stacey frowned back at her friend, her familiar squint reappearing.

"Okay, and Jodie. I still like her you know. It's just sick for her to be with Tony. I mean, she never let on that she fancied him, did she?" Stacey replied sternly. Angie paused before she spoke.

"Well, no, not really. Listen Stacey, I do remember her telling me how lucky she thought you were. She said that Tony was a fine-looking man, well fit were the words that she used" Angie said quietly. Stacey eyeballed her friend.

"Well fit? I suppose he was, but so is Alex" she replied defensively. Angie was feeling more talkative now.

"Looking back, I do remember her looking at Tony. You know, in the flat together? She would eye him across the room. I don't suppose that Tony ever noticed. He was too into you at the time" Angie said. Stacey took in her friend's thoughts before replying.

"Tony was too into his mother at the time. I came a poor second" she said quietly.

"It was understandable back then Stacey, to be fair. I liked Tony. Besides being fit, he had a good sense of humour. Oh, and a great bum!" Angie said. Stacey pushed her friend in a playful manner.

"Angie O'Rourke!" she said. The two pals laughed out loud together. For a moment it was like old times.

In the bedroom, Alex Woods listened quietly. He had a lot on his mind, but he was genuinely pleased to hear Angie happy once more. She would feature in his plans, unwittingly helping with his alibi.

"This the new phone then?" Angie asked, picking up the small compact pink phone from the coffee table.

"Yeah, my old one got wet. Alex thinks that I left it down in water in the bathroom. I honestly don't remember" Stacey said abstractly.

"So he bought you a new one?" Angie asked. Stacey giggled again. She leaned forward to whisper in Angie's ear.

"No. God knows that I hinted enough though! Alex is usually so generous, but he wouldn't take the hint! I had to buy it myself, worse luck!" Stacey said.

Angie examined the phone again before placing it back on the circular table. "It's a bit flimsy, isn't it? Wait until near your birthday and drop it in the bath! Then you can hit him for an Iphone!" Angie grinned.

"By then I'll be an old married woman" Stacey answered with a deliberate sigh.

"And I'll be an old spinster!" Angie giggled.

Alex lay in bed putting his revised plan together. His mind was awash with details and plotting. Buoyed by his success with Isobel's murder, Alex felt almost invincible. With great planning to detail, Alex now considered himself a match for the most formidable of police officers. Nothing would stop him from reaching his goals in life. First he would marry Stacey Boyd, and then he would eventually take over his father's empire and sit back to soak up the good life.

CHAPTER TWELVE

FIXING PHILIP

It was three days later when Alex decided to pay a visit to his father's house. He needed to patch things up, if only for cosmetic reasons. It would not do for people at work to sense an atmosphere between them. As he drove through the ever-opened black giant gates in his white Ford Mondeo, Alex paused to examine the place where he had killed Whiskey, the old family cat. The heavy bushes looked undisturbed, just as he had hoped.

Alex rang the doorbell and stepped back. The gleaming red Jaguar car was in the driveway. It was now almost eight years old, but still one of Tom Woods's favourite models.

His father looked surprised to see Alex. He opened the door wide and invited him in.

"Two visits in two weeks! Now there's a novelty! But it's hardly a social call, is it? What demands have you this time lad?" Tom Woods asked.

Alex appeared edgy, but managed a wry smile.

"Listen Dad, I don't want us rowing. I have the wedding on my mind a lot. Can't we just call a truce, at least until after I'm married?" Alex said.

Tom Woods eyed his son. He looked thoughtful as he casually put his right hand inside his trouser pocket.

"Okay then, Remember lad, I didn't start it. But think on son, I'll run the business my way. I won't be retiring anytime soon, so get that idea out of you head lad" Tom said emphatically. Alex nodded and sat down on the old-fashioned leather sofa. He ran his hand along the brown material before speaking.

"Well, I've been thinking about that Dad. You're right; I'm far from ready to take over. I'm still learning the trade really. I only want to do my best for you"

Alex said. His father watched him from a standing position, nodding in agreement.

"At last! Common sense! Now, about the wedding, I've been giving your present some thought. What about a nice Mediterranean holiday? I could book a ten day cruise for you and Stacey. You could take the two weeks off, and then return to work. Frank McKenzie is due his holidays for that week, so you could help out there when you return" Tom said in a businesslike tone.

Alex could feel his blood boil. His father was offering a miserable cheap cruise as a wedding gift. He had hoped for at least a new car. Alex had always considered cruises were for retired folk. He had also planned on taking at least a month off work. Now the idea was for him to do the foreman's work after just two weeks holidays. Once again, Tom Woods had put the company first.

"A cruise eh? I'm sure that Stacey would love that. We had talked about travelling to The States, but we could do that another time. Okay Dad, we'll do what you suggest. I'll cover for Frank when I get back" Alex said. Inside he was absolutely fuming, but he managed somehow to mask his feelings with a smile.

"Fine, fine. Now, about the company, I plan on looking over premises out in Foxrock this very minute. I can see the possibilities of having an outlet over in that direction. Nothing major, you understand. Just somewhere to take the pressure off our current workload" Tom said. Alex tried to sound enthusiastic, but deep down he hated the idea.

"Oh, like a repair garage with a small showroom?" Alex asked. Tom Woods looked a little evasive.

"Well, maybe more than that. It's an upmarket area. We will need something substantial to let people know that we mean business. There's no point in setting up a backstreet garage" he answered.

"Okay, would you like me to go with you?" Alex asked, half-rising to his feet. His father suddenly looked irritated by the conversation. Tom Woods shook his head.

"There will be no need for all that. I'm well able to judge what's required. Oh, when you go into work, scrap that old blue Volkswagen Golf. The engine is shot on it. It's leaking oil all over the goddamn place. Frank McKenzie took it in as part exchange. I think we lost money on that deal" Tom said with a frown on his high forehead. Alex stood up and nodded.

"Okay. Yeah, I saw that car all right. The body looks in pretty good shape, apart from a few dents. Pity. I'll look after that" Alex said. His father walked with him towards the door.

"The body can be deceiving lad. It's the engine that counts, just like me. My old engine will do another twenty years, please God!" Tom Woods said with a chuckle.

"If you say so Dad. Okay, I'm off. I'll see you later" Alex replied. Tom looked deep in thought. There was something he was forgetting. Suddenly it came to him.

"You haven't seen old Whiskey the cat around, have you? He's been missing for a good few days now" Tom said. Alex turned and looked him directly in the eyes.

"No Dad, I haven't, but you know what cats are like. They eventually come home" he said. Tom Woods looked at him dismissively.

"Whiskey has never stayed away before. He's an old cat now. He prefers to lie by the fire. The furthest he goes now is out to the gate. I hope that he hasn't been hit by a car. Anyway, I leave the back window open at night in case he comes back" Tom said. This was useful information for Alex. His father now had his full attention.

"The downstairs window? Isn't that a bit dangerous? I hope that you set the alarm at night" Alex said. Tom looked agitated.

"Oh stop fussing Alex! Most of the time I do. Listen lad, since your mother died, I sleep very lightly. I would hear a pin drop when I'm in bed. Don't worry about me. Anyway, I never keep cash at home, so what is there to steal?" Tom answered.

"The thieves don't know that. You take care Dad. Look after yourself. I would hate if anything happened to you" Alex said, a concerned look on his face. He offered his father a smile before heading off.

Tom watched from the doorway as his son drove away. It had been a long time since Alex had shown any interest in his wellbeing. It was nice to know that he cared. Tom put it down to his son rekindling his relationship with Stacey Boyd. "A good girl that Stacey. She'll make a man of that boy yet" he grinned.

As Alex drove on towards his job, two plans were forming in his head. The one regarding his father might take a few days. The first plan he could implement the following morning.

Already he knew enough about Phillip Westbourne's movements to go ahead. The blue Volkswagen was a welcome bonus.

That evening, Alex returned home around seven o'clock. He had already phoned Stacey to tell her what time to expect him. Angie usually disappeared into the spare room when Alex came home. She liked to give the couple time to themselves. Angie stood up quickly as Alex entered the sitting room.

"Don't go just yet Angie. Sit down for a minute" Alex said. Stacey smiled back at her friend to let her know that she approved.

Stacey went to fetch his meal as Alex sat down at the table in the corner of the room.

"About the wedding Angie, do you plan on bringing a guest? My best man is Terry Thompson. We're old friends from school. I did best man for him a few years back. You see, he's married, so you really need to have someone with you" Alex said. Stacey heard the tail end of his remarks as she re-entered the room.

"Alex! That's so hurtful! Angie will be with us and our friends. It really doesn't matter one iota if she brings a guest or not!" Stacey said with an embarrassed laugh. Before Angie could reply, Alex spoke again.

"No, no, I understand that, but just in case she wants to invite another chap along. I mean, the invitation said "Angie and Phillip". We don't want her feeling that she can't bring a different friend, that's all that I'm saying" he reasoned. Stacey smiled and went to kiss him. She gave him a peck on the cheek.

"You're so thoughtful Alex! Isn't he kind Angie? I never considered that you might want to bring someone else. Is there anyone from work?" Stacey asked. Angie shook her head.

"No. I haven't really given it much thought. I think I would be better off on my own. Anyway, Gina and Harry will be there, and there's Jodie and…" Angie stopped herself from finishing the sentence. Alex gave a little chuckle.

"And Tony. You can say his name Angie. I'm not paranoid!" Alex said with a forced laugh. Stacey was keen to move the conversation on.

"Yeah, there will be lots of people there that we know. I can't wait to see my folks again. It's been ages" Stacey said. Alex had already planned how the conversation would go. Stacey's little interjections were a mere slight distraction.

"And this Phillip Westbourne, was he looking forward to the wedding?" Alex asked. It seemed a curious question to both Stacey and Angie. Angie O'Rourke looked a little rattled by it.

"We…we didn't talk much about it Alex. Phillip was a private sort of man. He disliked social events I suppose. Being separated could prove difficult in conversation, you know? People tend to prejudge you. They think that there is something wrong with you" Angie said.

"And they would be right where that pig is concerned, wouldn't they?" Alex grinned. Angie squirmed on the sofa. She did not like to be reminded of what had happened to her.

"He wasn't all bad Alex. We had some good times" she said slowly.

"But he's back with his wife now?" Alex inquired. Angie shook her head.

"I don't think so. A pal at work said that they are having counselling. They're trying to work things out. Meanwhile, Phil is staying at the flat" she said in a low voice.

"That's good. He definitely needs help" Alex said.

It was all that he needed to know. It meant that Phillip Westbourne was still residing at their old run-down apartment, just as Alex had hoped. Alex had already seen photographs of him when he had had a quick look through Angie's handbag. Angie also had some pictures of Philip on her phone.

"I won't stay up late tonight Stacey sweetheart. I've a very early start in the morning. The old man has me running errands for him" Alex said with a sigh. He pushed his half-eaten dinner towards the centre of the table.

"Not hungry?" Stacey asked.

"I had something in work darling. I'm going to have a shower and an early night. Why don't you girls go out for a drink?" he said. Angie and Stacey looked at each other, an instant smile slowly breaking out jointly on their faces.

"Will we? Come on, let's!" Stacey said.

"I'll grab a shower and then the bathroom's all yours!" Alex said. It was all part of his plan. With a few drinks inside of them, the girls would not hear him leave early in the morning. Anything that gave him an advantage had to be good.

Alex Woods set off at 4:10am for his workplace. Stacey and Angie had come home late the night before. They were both sound asleep in the apartment when Alex left.

Alex arrived at the deserted premises and opened up the big sturdy rear gates. He parked his white car inside and then set about driving the old blue Volkswagen Golf out onto the street outside. Alex quickly locked up again, checking that he had everything. The car would be scrapped all right, but not until it had served its purpose.

Alex drove off in the semi-darkness for his planned destination. Once there, he parked up some distance from his intended target. It was still dark, and was a cloudy, windy morning. Once he was sure that the coast was clear, Alex slipped out with his black marker. He doctored the rear number plate, altering a number five so that it read as an eight. Alex did the same with a number six so that if spotted, the witness would give a false number. He hoped that it would not matter, but thought it better to cover his tracks.

Alex waited some fifteen minutes, constantly checking his watch. In the early morning gloom, Alex quickly identified his target. He checked his mirrors and took a good look around. There was nobody about on the murky Tuesday morning. Alex shoved on his baseball cap and wrapped a black scarf around his lower face. He hired the radio to full blast and then set off at a slow pace before quickly accelerating.

Phillip Westbourne was now almost in the centre of the road. Alex drove at him at full speed. Phillip wavered. He wanted to turn back, but was caught in two minds. He put out his left hand to protect himself, mentally pleading with the speeding car to halt. The yellow headlights appeared to hold him spellbound. Alex aimed the old Golf car straight for him, grinning beneath the woollen scarf. He hit Phillip at such pace that the man somersaulted over the bonnet, hitting the windscreen and then onto the roof.

"Whoa! What a shot! Bull's-eye!" Alex laughed as he witnessed the body cascade like a rag doll over the car. Alex watched through his rear-view mirror as the limp body hit the road like a wet sack of clay. He slowed to see if Phillip moved. The body lay motionless and so Alex sped off again.

"Whee! Brilliant, absolutely brilliant! Hit women do you? Let's see you hit someone now!" Alex screamed, the adrenalin flowing through his body. He lowered the radio and pulled away the scarf before tossing the baseball cap over to the passenger seat.

"What a high that was! I would nearly go back and run over the bastard again!" he sniggered. Alex drove slower now, careful not to draw attention to the Volkswagen car. The garage was now about fifteen minutes away. He did not know if Phillip Westbourne was dead or alive, nor did he care.

Alex parked the car exactly where he had found it and pulled both number plates from the vehicle. He then examined the dents to the front of the car and to the roof.

"Amazing. He hit that windscreen with such force, and yet not a single crack! They don't make windscreens like they used to!" Alex exclaimed with a sneering tone. Alex locked the old car and walked away whistling. He put the keys back in the office, where he had taken them from the night before. Alex then tossed the number plates into the big brown metal bin, which was used to scrap old metal car parts.

"Time for breakfast. A man needs to keep his strength up!" he thought.

That evening when Alex came home, Stacey and Angie were awaiting with the news.

"You'll never guess Alex! Phillip Westbourne was knocked down by a hit-and-run driver" Stacey said in an excitable voice. Alex tried to look surprised.

"Oh? And when did this happen?" he asked, looking from Stacey to Angie. Angie took over events.

"We think it was when he was on his way to work. Details are still sketchy. They think that it was some boy racers, or some drunk on his way home.

Phillip's in a bad way in hospital" Angie said. Her voice was full of remorse. The news that Phillip Westbourne was not dead surprised Alex.

"So he's alive then? He's a lucky chap so" Alex said. Stacey took over the storytelling again.

"I wouldn't say lucky. He has two broken legs and a fractured arm. They say that his face is in an awful state. His skull is fractured, and he's bleeding internally. He has cracked ribs and a host of other injuries. The doctors don't know if he will make it or not" Stacey said as if reading out a shopping list.

"Who told you all of this?" Alex asked, trying his best to look concerned. It was Angie's turn to take command.

"It's all over my office. Phillip used to work there as you know. It was even mentioned on the radio news. I would nearly go and see him except that his wife is probably there with him" Angie said. Alex looked aghast.

"What? After what he did? You must be mad!" Alex said.

"Well, I won't go now of course, but still..." Angie replied. Stacey put a comforting arm around her friend. Alex could see the tears in Angie's eyes. Stacey looked to Alex.

"I'm sorry Alex; I didn't feel much like cooking. Angie's a bit upset. How about a takeaway?" Stacey said.

"Yeah, okay, I'll go" he replied. Stacey looked surprised.

"No love, we can phone it in" she said. Alex managed a courteous smile.

"It's all right, I'll leave you girls to set the table and make coffee" he answered.

Alex sat in his car outside the local Chinese takeaway. He hammered his palms hard on the steering wheel several times.

"Ungrateful bitch! Stupid, stupid silly cow! I risk jail for the airhead bitch, and what does she do? She wants to visit the bastard, that's what! Silly stupid fucker! I've a good mind to fuck her out of the flat. No, Alex, think. The wedding is coming up. Wait until after the honeymoon, and then we can do something. Yeah. Wait, always wait. Plot things out. Don't rush in. Smart people plan ahead. Yeah" he thought. Alex Woods climbed from his car and ordered his meal. While waiting, he considered the evidence surrounding Phillip Westbourne's hit-and-run.

The Golf car used was already crushed since earlier that morning, so all evidence was already destroyed. His face had been covered anyway, so there could never be a positive identification. Alex had altered the rear number plate. Even if a witness had got a clear view, the number plate would not tally with a blue Volkswagen. And Phillip Westbourne was hardly in a position to read the front number plate. That thought made Alex smile. He sat grinning in the busy takeaway as he pictured Phillip's face. It was an image that would live with him for a long time.

On Saturday morning, Tony took the opportunity to do some shopping. His plan was to cycle to town and buy some socks and underwear. He needed a new lamp for his bicycle, and some odds and ends for the house. Later he would meet up with Jodie.

Tony strolled around the city centre aimlessly. He loved Dublin on quiet mornings, when the shopping was not quite so intense. As he turned a corner onto Mary Street, Tony suddenly stopped in his tracks. He almost walked straight into Stacey Boyd. She looked as shocked as he did. The two stood gaping at each other, both unsure what to say or do.

"Hi. Shopping?" Tony managed to stammer. Stacey nodded.

"The wedding. Lots of bits to organise" she said quietly. Tony nodded and smiled back at her, hiding his hurt.

"I can imagine! Best of luck with it. I hope it goes well" he said, forcing out a nervous laugh.

"Thanks. You'll be there, won't you?" Stacey replied. Some people pushed by, forcing them closer together.

"Sorry. Yes, we'll be there thanks. Looking forward to it" Tony said.

"I...I should go" Stacey said, avoiding eye contact now.

"Listen Stace, about before. I'm sorry. I should have been more....With my Mam and all I wasn't very..." Stacey held out a hand apologetically and interrupted him.

"Please don't Tony, it's in the past. I hope that you and Jodie can be as happy as Alex and I" she said. Stacey forced a smile and looked him in the eyes once again. Tony Lee gulped hard as he searched his mind for a sensible reply.

"I did love you, you know" he whispered. Stacey looked embarrassed.

"It's in the past Tony. Leave it, eh?" she replied.

"Sure, no hard feelings, eh?" I know, let's grab a coffee together?" he said, showing a beaming smile. Stacey shook her head and frowned.

"No, better not. I have lots of things to do. You take care Tony. See you soon" she replied, stepping to one side.

"Yeah, okay. You look after yourself too. You're looking as beautiful as ever" he whispered, swallowing hard again.

"You still look good too Tony. See you at the wedding" Stacey replied.

Tony stood and watched as she disappeared into the early morning shoppers. He pulled thoughtfully on the round earring in his earlobe as he stared into the mid-distance. Stacey was slowly vanishing into the thin crowds. Sometimes she would reappear further up the street. The sun beamed down, highlighting her short blonde hair. He waited until he was sure she was gone and then turned away.

"That was stupid Tony, telling her that she looked beautiful" he thought, annoyed with himself.

Stacey Boyd's heart thumped hard against her chest. She was not sure if it was the shock of seeing Tony, or if she still felt something for him. It had all been so unexpected. Her mind was racing with all sorts of thoughts and feelings. Then there were the doubts. Should she tell Angie, or even Alex about seeing Tony? What would have happened if they had gone for coffee together? Did she still like Tony? There were no answers, just mixed-up feelings. Stacey told herself that it was due to the pressure of the wedding. She wanted everything to be just right. It simply had to be.

Alex arrived home on Monday evening carrying a huge cardboard box. He struggled inside the front door before lowering it gently to the floor.

"What did you buy Alex? Is it to do with the wedding?" an excited Stacey asked. Alex shook his head.

"No darling, it's a new telly. I'm going to erect it on the bedroom wall. I should have done this ages ago. It's ideal when you think about it. When you want to watch your girlie stuff and soaps, I can go to bed and watch sport. It's the ideal solution all round" he said chirpily. Angie looked amused.

"And can you do that? Erect it on the wall?" she asked coyly. Alex offered her a cheeky grin.

"Now, now! None of that smutty talk here! Of course I can Angie. There are two strong brackets in the box. My trusty drill will have it done in no time!" Alex replied.

"Boys and their toys!" Stacey grinned. Alex kissed her gently on the lips.

"You'll thank me when you two want to watch weepy movies!" he said.

As the nights followed, Alex would often retire to the bedroom. Sometimes he might sit with the girls all evening. It was sporadic, and never in a pattern. This was all part of Alex's second plan. Unwittingly, both girls were going to form an alibi for him without ever realising it.

Jodie knocked on Tony's door.

"Quick! Open up!" she squealed. Tony rushed to answer her call. He laughed out loud on seeing her.

"Come in! You look like a drowned rat! I'll get a towel" Tony said. Outside the rain teamed down. The sudden cloudburst had caught Jodie out. As usual, she was wearing trainers and a tracksuit. Tony returned with two large bathroom towels.

"Here, dry yourself off. Maybe you should slip out of those clothes. We could dry them on the radiator. You could wear some of my things" he said.

"I know what you're up to Tony Lee! Okay then, but no funny business!" Jodie said with a knowing smile. Tony held up his hands in mock surrender.

"Promise! But on a serious note Jodie, why not just move in here? All this going backwards and forwards is so silly. And I worry about you when you get the bus home alone. Would it not be easier all round if you just agree?" he asked. Jodie continued to dry off, tossing her wet jacket onto the back of a nearby chair. She looked deep in thought as she considered his words.

"I have thought about it Tony. Hold on 'till I change and we'll talk" she said.

Tony fetched some clothes for her, an old pair of white shorts that he hardly wore, and a shirt that was a little tight on him. He threw in a pair of white woolly socks to keep her feet warm. Tony then went downstairs to make some tea.

When Jodie Callaghan arrived in the kitchen some moments later, Tony was visibly surprised. He had never seen Jodie with her hair down. She had always given the appearance of a somewhat tomboy character, but tonight she looked positively feminine.

"You, you look fantastic!" he whispered.

"Stop! I do not!" she laughed. Tony went to her and kissed her.

"You do you know. Your hair suits you that way. You look stunning" he said. Jodie kissed him back, and then planted several kisses on his face.

"I think I'm falling in love with you Tony Lee" she whispered.

"So when can you move in?" he grinned. Jodie broke away. The smile quickly vanished from her lips.

"I want to, I really do. I'm just afraid" she said.

"Afraid? Afraid of what?" he asked. Jodie rambled to the table where Tony had poured tea.

"Everything. I haven't been very lucky in love Tony. Before I met you I sort of gave up. It was easier to go out and have fun. I pretended that I wasn't interested in dating. I put on a front for Gina and the girls. The truth was that inside my heart was breaking. I threw myself into all sorts of mad activities. In reality, I hated being around Gina and Harry. And I especially dreaded being around Stacey and you. I was jealous, and I was terrified that it might show. Sometimes I looked at you and Stacey together and wished that it was me. It was easier to find new friends and disappear. So that's what I did" she said. Tony kissed her across the table and held her hand.

"So why are you afraid? We're together now" he asked gently. She smiled back at him.

"I've always messed everything up, ever since my first date. If I move in and it doesn't work…" she answered. Tony clasped both of her hands in his.

"The only way to find out is to try. I promise that I will do everything to make you happy" he said. Jodie nodded and smiled back at him.

"Okay then, but let me give Gina two week's notice first. I have to make sure that she's all right with it. The rent is a pain, and she might need to get someone else in" Jodie replied.

"Sure! Two weeks it is then! If you don't agree in a fortnight, I'll come looking for you!" Tony grinned. Jodie shivered and stood up.

"Come on, take me to bed. I need someone to warm me up!" she smiled.

Stacey's and Alex's wedding was now just over two weeks away. All the arrangements were made, and Stacey's parents were due to fly in from England on the morning of the wedding. Stacey's Dad phoned her to confirm that everything was going to plan.

"He won't let you down again dear, will he?" Arthur Boyd asked.

"No Dad, Alex has been as good as gold. This time he's sure. Don't worry, you and Mom will have a great time" Stacey said.

"And what about you dear, are you happy? No last minute worries?" her father asked. Stacey smiled as she replied.

"I told you to stop fretting. I couldn't be happier, honestly. Alex has done all the arrangement for the reception. He won't let me lift a finger. You should see the place Alex booked for the reception Dad; it's like something out of a fairytale. I don't know how he got it at such short notice. He knows someone in the motor trade who managed to pull a few strings. Oh, and having Angie around is a great comfort. She's been such a pal, despite everything" Stacey said happily.

"Despite everything? What do you mean? Stacey, are you hiding something from me?" Arthur Boyd asked, a worried tone now in his voice. Stacey laughed again.

"No Dad, I promise. It was just that her ex-boyfriend was in a hit-and-run accident. He's still in hospital in a bad way. Angie was a bit upset about it. She even blamed herself. She wondered if she had not split up with him if it might not have happened. I told her not to be so silly, but you know how it is" Stacey said.

"I see, fate and all that. The wrong place at the wrong time?" her father said.

"Exactly Dad. Listen, I have to go now, Alex is taking me out. I'll see you soon yeah? And stop worrying! Say hello to Mom for me" Stacey said.

Alex Woods sat in the bedroom listening to the conversation. He had used their bedroom as a place of sanctuary a lot since Angie had come to stay. It was news to him about Angie blaming herself for Phillip Westbourne's troubles. The news made him seethe with rage.

"That stupid bitch. What an ungrateful cow. She doesn't deserve to have friends like Stacey and me. As soon as this wedding is over, I'll fix her. Maybe something similar might happen to her" he thought quietly.

Stacey bounded into the room as Alex lay on the bed watching television.

"Guess what? Dad just phoned. I can't wait to see Mom and him again" she gushed. Alex lay in a pair of shorts and an old t-shirt.

"For Fuck sake Stacey, what do I keep telling you? Don't keep bursting in here every few minutes with stupid shit. I'm lying here half naked, and you swan in here leaving the door open. Can I have some privacy?" he yelled. Stacey looked shocked. She stood motionless for a few moments, unsure how to react. Alex had never spoken to her like that before.

"I'm sorry Alex, I didn't think…" she stammered.

"That's the trouble, you never fucking think. I've moved in here to get some peace. It's you and Angie that I did this for. At least show a little respect" he fumed. Stacey's hands were visibly shaking. She searched her mind for something to say. Alex beat her to it.

"Where is Angie anyway? Close the door, will you?" Alex said crossly.

"She's…she's in the bathroom showering. I told her to go first so that we could get ready. She's having an early night" Stacey said.

"Right, in future knock before coming in here when Angie is at home. In fact, I would prefer if you only came in when it was really important. I've given up two thirds of my home for you two. At least leave me one room" he said. Stacey nodded. There were no words that sprung to mind to help the situation.

"I'm sorry Alex, really I am. It won't happen again, I promise" she said in a barely audible voice.

"Good. I'm sorry for raising my voice honey. Maybe it's everything getting on top of me" Alex said, managing a half-hearted smile. Stacey nodded again and she too forced a slight grin.

"I'll try and be a bit more considerate Alex" she said. He smiled again and reached out his arms.

"Come here, give me a kiss, precious" he said. Stacey bent over and kissed him on the lips. She then slipped away leaving him alone.

Alex smiled contently. Everything was going as he had perceived. In just a few more days he would implement his next plan, this one much more intricate than the last. His staged confrontation with Stacey had gone exactly as he had hoped. His privacy masked an alibi for Alex. Soon his master plan would come into force, and Stacey and Angie would be his perfect cover.

CHAPTER THIRTEEN

A BOTCHED BREAK-IN

When Tony took the call from Jan on the Friday evening, he was dumbfounded. Jan was telling him that she was back in Dublin, this time with Howard. She said that they had managed a few days off, and on the spur of the moment had decided to fly to Ireland.

"But you always said that Howard was so busy, and that you had family and work commitments. How did you manage it so suddenly? I genuinely thought that it would be years before we met up again" Tony said. He had just come home from work when the telephone had sounded.

Jan had booked into the same hotel as before. Howard sat beside her on the bed, listening to the planned phone call.

"Yeah, me too Tony, isn't it super? Howard surprised me with the trip. I was over the moon when he told me. He has a friend looking after the store while we're away. I had some holidays coming, so here we are" Jan explained.

"Well, it's great news anyway. Should we meet up? I mean, would you like to go out for a meal tonight?" Tony asked. Jan answered immediately.

"Maybe tomorrow night Tony. We slept on the plane. We just need to freshen up. What we really wanted to do was to go and see you at the house this evening. Howard would love to look over the old place. We just want to have a cosy chat with you, oh, and with your new girlfriend of course, if she's there" Jan said.

Tony was at a loss for words. The whole thing seemed unnatural, yet he was pleased that they had come so far to see him. It would not do to be unfriendly.

"Yeah, I would like that too. Say around seven? I can ring Jodie. I'm sure that she would love to meet you" Tony said in a faltering voice.

"About seven it is Tony. Now don't go doing anything special. Howard and I have eaten at the hotel. Just tea and sandwiches will suffice" Jan replied.

"Fine, and would you like to stay over Jan? You're more than welcome. I have decorated the spare bedroom. There's plenty of space" Tony said.

"Oh definitely not Tony, we will be returning to the hotel. Thanks all the same" Jan replied quickly. They said goodbye and Tony slowly put down the receiver. He sat on the stairs in the hallway and tried to make sense of it all. It seemed implausible that Jan would fly halfway round the world just to see him. And now she had Howard with her. Perhaps she had changed her mind about allowing him to keep the house.

Tony quickly decided that such was the case. His brain began to dissect everything that Jan had ever said to him. Suddenly it all made sense. The house was meant for him and Stacey. Jan had asked that his new girlfriend would be there to meet them that evening. Everything fitted perfectly. Jan had brought Howard along to persuade him to rescind his possession of the house.

Tony began to question his legal standing on the matter. Sure, he had signed all of the paperwork presented to him by the solicitor, but Mr. Tomlinson was the family solicitor. For all Tony knew, there might be a clause that Jan could evoke.

Tony rose wearily to his feet. He looked around at all of his hard work in decorating the old house.

"What a waste of time" he muttered. Tony made coffee and slumped down on a chair by the kitchen window. He had to phone Jodie, but not just yet. Tony felt that he needed to get everything right in his head first. For weeks now he had begged Jodie to move in. She had continued to postpone it, for one reason or another. Now it seemed that it was never destined to happen. Tony thought back to his last conversation with Jodie Callaghan on the subject.

"You keep saying you will, but still all of your stuff is still at the flat" he had said.

"I told you Tony, I will move in. Just give me more time. Gina and Harry will really struggle with the rent. I want to give them every chance to find some flatmates, maybe another couple. Harry knows a chap at his job that might be interested" Jodie had replied.

"Excuses, excuses!" Tony had answered in a joking tone.

"I will, I promise. I love you Tony Lee" Jodie said, grinning back at him.

Tony's daydreaming was shattered by the sound of his mobile phone's ringing tone. He looked at his watch. It was five-thirty. Jodie was on her way home from work.

"Hi love, what's up?" he said cheerfully. Jodie asked if they should meet up in town later, or if she should call over after she had eaten. Tony explained what had happened, and told her of his fears.

"Wow! This sounds heavy! I'll just have a shower and grab a taxi. We'll need to talk before they get there. Let's not say anything about me moving in. Let them do all of the talking" Jodie suggested. Tony agreed that it might be for the best. As he ended the call, Tony slowly looked around the kitchen. He decided that it was best to clean up as best he could, although he could not help feeling that he was wasting his time with houshold chores.

Jodie arrived within the hour. She had abandoned her customary tracksuit and was wearing smart white jeans and a blue casual top. For a change her long blonde hair was not tied back, and she wore just enough make-up to look casually pretty.

"You look well Jodie, what's the occasion?" Tony joked. She gave him a playful push as they kissed.

"Well, you always say that you like my hair down. I want to impress the family!" she answered with a cheeky grin. Tony looked more serious now.

"What do you think? They haven't come all this way for nothing" he said.

"Well, I was considering everything that you said on the way here. Have you got the deeds to the house?" Jodie asked. Tony appeared startled. He put his hands to his face.

"Well no, I asked Mr. Tomlinson to hold them for safe-keeping. Isn't that what you are supposed to do?" he replied.

"Well usually yes, but this doesn't sound normal. All I can say is that if the worst happens; insist on getting half of any resale. You are at least entitled to that" Jodie reasoned. Tony nodded as he took in her words.

"God! I'm mortified! What will I say if she suggests selling up? I mean, it could come down to fighting a court case with my own sister" Tony said. Jodie patted him on the back.

"Let them do all of the running. Let's hear what she has to say first. Maybe it's as she said. Perhaps it's just a social visit" Jodie said. Tony immediately shook his head several times.

"No Jodie, you don't know her. Jan would rather visit the dentist than meet me socially. There's something up, I can just feel it" he answered.

The police came to visit Phillip Westbourne. They had been to see him several times, but Phillip had been too ill to speak. Although still on the critical list, Phillip was now at least conscious.

"We have a few questions Phillip. Take your time and do your best, okay?" said Garda Steven Lennox. Phillip barely nodded. His wife Karen sat by his bedside. She had been to visit constantly since the accident.

"Now, can you remember anything about the car? For example, what colour or make it was?" the policeman asked gently. Phillip cleared his throat.

"Not really. It happened so fast. The car was green I think, a small car. It might have been an Opel Corsa. It was barely light that morning" he said, his voice straining to get the words out. The policeman nodded and smiled. His colleague stood next to him, writing in his black notebook. Garda Lennox continued with his gentle probing.

"Very good Phillip. Now, did you get a look at the driver? Can you say how many people were in the car?" the red-haired policeman asked. Phillip Westbourne half-closed his eyes. He had been through the scenario in his head many times since the incident.

"It was dark. I had only just woken up. I'm sure that there were two, one in the front and one in the rear. I couldn't really make out the driver. I think he had a dark beard; in fact I'm sure of it. There was music playing, loud thumping music. I'm sorry, it happened so fast" Phillip said in a slow, considerate voice. His wife looked at both policemen.

"Can't this wait? He's been through a lot" she pleaded. She was a small lady with tight dark hair. Phillip's face was bandaged heavily around the forehead and chin. Both his legs were in traction, and his left arm was totally covered in white plaster

"Yes Ma'am, we understand. Just one or two more questions and we'll leave it at that, okay Philip?" the taller policeman said with a degree of sympathy.

"Now, you didn't have any enemies Philip, did you?" he said quietly. Karen Westbourne immediately looked infuriated.

"What sort of a stupid question is that? Why don't you go and arrest these so-called joyriders? You meet them in court every day. You probably know them by name" she said angrily. Phillip closed his eyes impassively.

"It's all right Karen. No Garda, I have no enemies. No one who would want to kill me anyway. No, it wasn't anybody that I know" he said softly. The questioning policeman nodded. He glanced from Karen Westbourne to his colleague, as if seeking the correct words.

"We have to ask these questions, just to eliminate any possibilities. Please be patient, we're almost done" he said. He turned his attention back to Phillip Westbourne.

"Now Phillip, when you say that you had no real enemies, what did you mean? I understand that you recently broke up with a girl. Did she have a jealous boyfriend perhaps?" he said, his eyes fixed on the hospital patient. Karen Westbourne looked up to the ceiling and sighed heavily, but said nothing.

"No. Positively not. And Angela O'Rourke would never have anything to do with something like that. It was a stranger. I was probably in the wrong place at the wrong time" he replied.

"Did you and Angela fight?" the policeman asked. Again Phillip closed his eyes. "Sort of. I told her that I loved my wife and wanted to go back to her. Angie got angry and I hit her. It was over in a second. She went to stay with friends that night. I don't know the address" Philip said.

"And you worked together for a while?" the policeman queried. Karen Westbourne became annoyed once more.

"Jee-zus! You lot have been busy! If only you put as much work into locking up drunks and car robbers!" she fumed. The policeman turned to her again.

"These things are easily researched Mrs. Westbourne. We talked to some of Phillip's neighbours at the apartment where he lived. They heard screaming that night in question. Miss O'Rourke was seen leaving the flat in the early hours. We have to follow these things up, if only to eliminate them from our enquiries" the policeman said in a calm voice.

"She's just a silly misguided girl. I have more reason than most to dislike her, but this was nothing to do with her, I guarantee that" Karen sneered.

"Let them do what they have to do Karen. I know what happened. Two young punks probably out of their heads on drugs. They will never be arrested. The cops have no control over them" Phillip Westbourne sighed. His eyes fixed on the ceiling again, a sight that he had become so familiar with over the last few weeks.

Outside the two policemen compared notes on the incident.

"What do you reckon then William?" said the ginger-haired policeman.

"Oh, he's probably right. My guess is local joyriders. There's an outside chance that it was some drunk on his way home from a late night somewhere, but yeah, a stolen car seems the most likely thing. The loud music is a giveaway" replied the younger man.

"The car will be burned-out somewhere so, or in the canal. We better talk to that Angie O'Rourke anyway, just to cover ourselves" the older policeman concluded.

Howard and Jan knocked politely on the green door using the heavy metal knocker.

"That'll be them! Now remember Tony, let them do all of the talking" Jodie said in a hushed voice. Tony nodded and went to answer the door. He was dressed casually in black slacks and a pale blue shirt.

Howard's hand immediately thrust into Tony's, surprising him somewhat.

193

"Tony! Good to finally meet you! You look fine, just fine! You were only about five or six when I last saw you" Howard beamed. Tony nodded, managing a smile. The handshake seemed to last an eternity. Almost unnoticed, Jan crept ahead of both men. They followed her inside, Tony keen to keep pace with his sister. He managed to enter the sitting room just a step behind her.

"Howard, Jan, this is Jodie. Jodie, this is my sister and her husband Howard" Tony announced. Jodie smiled politely and went to shake hands.

All four sat drinking coffee. They talked about America, Ireland, and the weather, almost anything rather than what was on their minds. Finally Jodie broke the ice.

"So you left all of that sunshine to come here. I would never leave! What drags you back here Jan after such a recent visit? I can't say that Ireland holds any fascination for me. If I could emigrate I would be gone tomorrow!" she said.

Tony Lee bit his lip. Somehow Jodie's remarks had not come out quite right. He looked to Jan for a reaction.

Instead Howard interjected.

"It's never easy for me to get away Jodie. I work long hours, sometimes seven days a week. We got the opportunity of a short break because business is slow at the moment. I have a great manager who will keep an eye on things, plus my Pop is on hand to help out" Howard said in a stern, but firm tone. Jan looked slightly uneasy.

"Yes, we decided that I left rather hurriedly after the funeral. I love Ireland. If I had my wish I would live here again. Unfortunately, our children are really settled in The States now. There's no way we could ever dream of returning. The next best thing is a holiday" Jan said, rather unconvincingly. A moment's silence ensued before Howard spoke again.

"Jan tells me that you've been busy decorating Tony. I must say, the old house looks great from what I can recall, although it's been over thirty years since I was here" he said. Tony's defence mechanism kicked in. His brain ran Howard's words through a filtering process and out the other side.

"What he's really saying is that he can't see much difference in the house. Jodie's right. There here to take my home away. Why not just spit it out?" Tony's brain told him.

"So Jan, how long are you staying for? It would be great if you could hang around for a while" Tony said diplomatically. His sole objective was to determine if they had any definite timeline. Or perhaps they might stay for as long as it took. Jan looked a little shifty.

"Oh, just a few days. It's not really fair on Howard's folks. My two are a handful, even if they are growing up fast" she answered. It felt like a game of chess to Tony. He was waiting for Jan to suddenly claim back her house, and to shout checkmate.

They talked generally for a bit longer, with Jan now admiring Tony's handiwork around the house.

"The hallway is lovely, and I especially like what you've done in here. It used to be so dull and dingy" she said. Tony nodded, still unsure how to reply. Howard casually asked to see the rest of the house, and Tony led the way upstairs. He left his mother's room until last, feeling that it might be a bit much for Jan to take in. She surveyed the freshly-painted room with its new furniture, almost coldly.

"Very nice indeed Tony. You've done very well. It must have cost a bit. Howard and I would love to pay something towards it. Of course, if you have other things planned, we can wait and settle up when you're finished" Jan said in a calculating tone.

Jodie and Tony's eyes locked. Neither could quite believe what they were hearing.

"I...I'm sorry Jan, I don't quite get what you mean. I don't expect you to pay anything. You've already done enough by allowing me to keep the house" Tony blurted out. He waited for the bombshell to hit. Jan was bound to tell him that she had changed her mind. Instead, Howard put a playful arm around Tony's shoulder.

"You are such a fine fellow Tony, you really are! We're all family now! It can't be easy on your salary managing all of this alone. Let me help. Once you're sure that the work is finished, I'll write you a cheque. We want you to enjoy your life, and not spend your time pulling this old place apart. When you're sure that this old house is just the way you want, I will gladly reimburse you. Why should you scrimp and save to update the house? Life is too short" Howard said with a huge grin on his face. Jan too forced a smile.

"Howard's right Tony. Don't spend any more of your precious time updating Mom's old home. I worry that this place will come tumbling down around you! I really wish that you could see our point of view. We left this house to you in good faith. I see new skirting boards, furniture, fixtures and fittings, and God knows what else! You'll throw all of your savings away if you're not careful. Remember your promise to me before you signed for Mom's old house?" Jan said.

"I just want to make it habitable for the future. That's all Jan" Tony said weakly.

"And you've done great! What we're saying is, if you're sure that the work is complete, we would love to ease the financial burden. Let Howard write a cheque and leave it at that. I hate to talk financial matters, it's so personal, don't you think?" Jan said.

Jodie was about to speak, but managed to stop herself. Tony gulped in air. He had to ask the most pertinent question.

"So now you want to pay me off and sell the house, is that it?" he asked. Jan stared back at him, Tony's words washing around her brain. She looked to Howard, who looked as confused as she did. Jan shook her head and spoke again.

"No Tony, I would never do that. All I want is for you to be happy here. Not to spend your life wrecking the house. These walls are ancient. The roof and ceilings are older than I am. It won't take much to bring the whole place down around you. Look, you can do all that to a new house. Conservatories, extensions, that sort of thing. Not with these places. I'm sorry, but you can't" Jan said forcefully.

"I just want to make it nice Jan. Jodie is about to move in. We want something cosy, somewhere homely, that's all" Tony said. He immediately realised that he had revealed his hand. Earlier he and Jodie had decided against telling Jan about their plans. Jan Williams took his words in her stride. She managed a smile before replying.

"And that's what you have now. It's beautiful. You've done marvellously well. You've turned the place into a cosy home. I want both of you to be happy here" she said.

They made their way back downstairs. Nothing had really been resolved, and Tony suggested that they might go out together to talk. Howard looked to Jan to speak on their behalf. She gripped Tony's arm as they stood in the hallway. "It's a nice idea Tony. Look, both of us are a little tired. We need a good night's rest. Why not meet up tomorrow night in town? Wouldn't that be a better idea?" Jan said with a smile. Tony knew that it was pointless to disagree. The meeting was arranged, and Howard and Jan were soon on their way.

"Well, what do you make of it all?" Tony asked Jodie.

"Weird! Are they some sort of conservationists or something? She seems to care more for the house than she does for you!" Jodie said with an amused grin. Tony frowned and nodded his head.

"Something doesn't add up Jodie. I don't feel that those two are here on holiday" Tony replied.

"I agree. Let's watch what we say tomorrow night. Sooner or later they will have to spit out what their intentions are" Jodie said.

"That's the first sensible thing you've said all evening!" he grinned. Jodie gave him a playful dig in the arm before skipping into the kitchen to make coffee.

"How did you think that went Jan?" Howard asked on the taxi journey back to their hotel.
"As expected I suppose. At least we know the true extent now. I think that everything should be fine" she replied. Howard looked thoughtful.
"Yeah, we were worried about nothing really. Tony's not very ambitious. He seems to respect you though. Maybe if you have another serious chat with him, huh?" Howard said. Jan nodded; she too was deep in thought.
"Yeah, I'll put the fear of God in him, just when he least expects it" she replied.

The same day, Angie O'Rourke noticed the tall gentleman standing talking to her supervisor in the hallway, which led to the offices on the third floor of the building. In all there were six floors, and visitors were rare to the communications network company's administration headquarters. Angie's section dealt mostly with staff's wages. They employed about three thousand people, and Angie O'Rourke spent most of her day with paperwork and computer data.
"Who's the tall guy outside?" Bernie Collins asked. Angie shrugged her shoulders.
"He must be a bigwig. That's the only guys who come to see us!" Angie grinned. Almost immediately, Angie's boss, Mrs. Whitehaven, popped her head back inside the glass door.
"Angie, have you got a minute?" she asked, looking concerned. Angie's nodded and rambled to the door. The eyes of the rest of the staff followed her. Seventeen people worked there, mostly females. The novelty of a visitor intrigued them, especially one who would wish to speak to a member of staff. Detective Timothy Gilchrest identified himself and Mrs. Whitehaven made herself scarce. He explained why he was there, and Angie told him she knew about Phillip Westbourne's accident.
"We haven't got your home address Miss O'Rourke. Are you staying with friends?" he asked.
"Yes. Look, what's this all about? It's a little embarrassing" Angie replied.
"It's just routine Miss O'Rourke, I assure you. Now, on the morning in question, where exactly were you?" Detective Gilchrest asked. Angie gave him a curious look.
"I was in bed at the flat where I'm staying. You don't think that I had anything to do with this, do you?" she replied. The tall policeman pulled a notebook from his breast pocket and began to write.

"As I say it's purely routine. We suspect it was a joyrider, but we just need to eliminate you from the inquiry" he said in a matter-of-fact tone.

"Eliminate me? Christ! Look, I was in bed. I have two witnesses" Angie said. She quickly realised the implication of what she had just said.

"Sorry, I don't mean that I had two people in bed with me, just in the apartment. I'm staying with a couple. They're friends of mine, due to be married next week as it happens" she added, hoping to add some respectability to her alibi.

"Quite. So you left the apartment at the normal time to come to work?" Detective Gilchrest asked. Angie looked to the glass door separating her from her colleagues. She could feel all eyes upon her.

"Yes. My friend Stacey drove me to work around eight o'clock. It was only when I got here that I heard about Phillip. Listen, we had a row and I left him, but I would never do anything like that" Angie said, almost pleading to be believed.

"I understand. We heard about the altercation. He assaulted you?" the dark-haired policeman asked. Angie looked to the ceiling and folded her arms.

"What is this? Why are you using words like that? Altercation. Assault. He wanted to go back to his wife, for God's sake! We argued, he slapped me, end of!" Angie said tersely.

Timothy Gilchrest leaned forward and lowered his voice.

"Angela, I'm not here to antagonise you. I just need your side of things for the record. Trust me; I'm only doing my job. For what it's worth, I don't condone what Phillip Westbourne did to you, but at the end of the day, a man almost died. I have to cover all angles. I doubt if we will need to speak to you again, but I will need the address of where you're staying" he said quietly. Angie nodded and gave Alex Woods's address. Detective Gilchrest wrote it down and then closed his notebook. He offered Angie a reassuring smile.

"That's everything Miss O'Rourke, thank you for your co-operation" he said. Angie looked thoughtful as she nodded back at him.

"There was one thing. If you hadn't got my address, how did you know where I worked?" she asked. The policeman smiled again.

"Er, you forget that Philip once worked here. If only all of my detective work was that easy!" he replied with a grin.

Angie pushed open the glass door as the policeman quickly stepped into the lift.

Bernie Collins was first over to inquire about the tall visitor. Angie explained as best she could that it was routine, but could not help at feeling a little embarrassed. She hoped that none of the staff might think that she had something to hide. By lunchtime, everyone in the office was talking about it.

Angie's biggest fear was that she might somehow jeopardise her position at her well-paying job.

That evening, Angie explained to Stacey and Alex about her interview with the police.

"I didn't know where to put myself. I'm sure at least one of the guys thinks I had something to do with it. Can you imagine? John Vernon is a bit of a geek. I could feel his eyes watching me all afternoon. He knew Philip well" Angie said. Alex was more interested in what the policeman had to say. He ran over what Angie had told him again.

"It must mean that they haven't caught anybody for it yet. They are looking into every possibility" he concluded. Angie was bemused by the whole thing.

"Well, they can rule me out! I was tucked up in bed, still drunk from the night before!" she laughed. It immediately struck a chord with Stacey.

"Oh yeah, that was the morning after our night out! I was still groggy driving you to work! Hey, don't say anything about that to the cops! I was probably still over the legal limit!" Stacey cackled. Angie grinned before informing Stacey that she had already done just that.

"Oh, mortified! They'll come and arrest the two of us now!" Stacey replied. She held both hands to her face in mock horror.

Just then the doorbell rang three times in quick succession. All three looked to each other.

"Are we expecting anybody?" Stacey asked. The other two shook their heads simultaneously. Stacey made her way to the front door as both Alex and Angie fell silent.

She returned minutes later looking pale and concerned.

"Alex, it's for you. It's two policemen" she whispered. Alex stared back at her, a million things running through his mind.

"Did you show them in?" he asked, trying to gain valuable thinking time. Stacey nodded.

"They're in the hallway" she answered. Alex rose slowly from the armchair. His first thoughts were of Isobel's murder, and secondly Phillip Westbourne. He took a deep breath, striving hard to gather some credible tale in his head. He could feel the panic in his stomach, and his head was fit to burst with fear and worry.

"It's okay. Probably nothing. Something to do with an unpaid speeding fine, I'll bet" he said to Stacey unconvincingly.

Alex opened the door to the hall and was surprised to see two plain clothes policemen awaiting him. He had expected them to be in uniform. Again he sucked in air and tried to smile.

"Alex Woods, how can I help you?" he said, sticking out his right hand. Both policemen avoided his attempted handshake. The first man nodded slightly before speaking.

"I'm sorry Mr. Woods, we have some bad news. Earlier this evening there was an attempted robbery at your father's home. Your father's okay. He's in hospital though, and a bit shook up. He confronted two youths trying to break in through a rear window of his house. He fought them off, but received a few blows to the face. He had a bit of a fall also. It's just some minor cuts and bruising. He will most likely be kept in hospital overnight for observation" the policeman said.

Alex felt relief, mixed with shock. The first think that struck him was how ironic the whole thing was. In different circumstances he might consider bursting into laughter. He had planned his movements over the next forty-eight hours meticulously. He was about to break into the family home in two days time. The image of the concerned son quickly took over.

"Oh my God! Poor Dad! How bad is he? I've told him a thousand times about locking up that house. He leaves that window open for the cat. I've pleaded with him time and time again" Alex said, displaying an almost tearful façade.

"We can drop you off at the hospital if you feel that you are too upset to drive" said the second policeman. Alex shook his head.

"No no, I'll be okay. Just a little shaken. Just tell me which hospital and I'll go. I will need to drive to the house anyway, maybe sleep there tonight" Alex replied.

"That might be for the best. The two lads involved got away. They will hardly return, but it's best to be on the safe side" the first policeman said.

The policemen left, leaving Alex to explain events to the two girls.

"My God! We're having a day of it, aren't we?" Angie sighed.

"Your poor Dad! Alex, I better go with you. You shouldn't drive" Stacey said. Alex shook his head.

"No, I'm really okay. You stay here Stacey. I will probably have to check over the house, maybe even the garage, depending if the keys are missing. I don't know if anything was stolen. Look, I suppose that I'll sleep at Dad's place tonight. I'll phone you later anyway. Don't wait up for me" Alex said, all in one breath. Stacey nodded and Angie wished him good luck. Stacey followed him to the door, ensuring that he had everything he needed.

"Yes Stacey, keys phone, garage keys. I have everything. Don't be worrying. I'll call you if there's any news" he said before waving a hasty goodbye.

Alex parked inside the hospital grounds and stared out into the darkness. He reflected on his plot for Wednesday evening, which was now defunct. It had been planned to such lengths that it was almost heartbreaking. All of those nights spent alone in the bedroom to glean an alibi. The hidden knotted rope that would allow him in and out of the apartment. The fake row with Stacey to stop her bursting into the bedroom unannounced. The immaculate timing to allow him to travel to his father's house and back. It was all now redundant. Alex thumped hard on the steering wheel several times.

"Fuck! Fuck! Fuck!" he screamed. It was perfect. Just as the football match would start on the television, Alex would shout to Stacey that he did not want to be disturbed. He then planned to slip out through the bedroom window by way of the knotted rope he had concealed in their bedroom. Although on the second floor, the rope would be long enough to reach at a jump. He would leave it dangling from the bedroom until he returned from his father's home. Alex planned to smother his father that evening and hoped to make it look like a heart attack. His father took tablets for his angina, and Alex planned to spill them on the bed. He would then slip back out through the open window and return to his flat, via the knotted rope. By then it would he half-time in the football. Alex would slip out to the toilet, making sure both Angie and Stacey noted his presence. He would then return to watch the football in the bedroom, making sure to put in an appearance again once the match had ended. The body would not be discovered until the following day at the earliest, when Tom Woods's solicitor was due to visit his client at the family home. By then Alex would have disposed of the rope and his clothes from the night before, just as a precaution. Weeks of plotting were now in vain.

"Bastard! A fucking break-in of all things. What are the odds?" Alex fumed. He climbed from the car and walked slowly towards the main entrance. Alex afforded himself one more wry thought before entering the hospital.

"Why could they not have finished the job, the dopey little bastards?" he thought.

"How are you Dad? How are you bearing up?" Alex asked in a deeply concerned tone. Tom Woods lay on his back in a private room. His face was a mesh of bruises and stitches and his eyes were puffed and remained closed.

"Alex? I'm okay lad. Make sure that the business keeps ticking over. I should be home soon. It's not as bad as it looks son. My breathing is the trouble. It took a lot out of me" Tom said, his breath uneven as he spoke.

"What happened Dad? Did you disturb them?" Alex asked. His father slowly opened one of his swollen eyes. He blinked as he focused on Alex's face.

"I was watching a movie. I rarely turn on the lamp downstairs in the evening. The bathroom light was on upstairs. I thought that I heard a noise in the kitchen. I lowered the telly, but there was nothing. I began watching the film again, and minutes later I heard it again. I hoped it was Whiskey coming home at last, so I crept out to greet him. Low and behold this thug is halfway in the window! Well, I grabbed him and dragged him to the ground. That was probably my mistake. I thought that he was alone. I had him on the kitchen floor, about to knock seven bells out of him, when his mate came from behind the door on top of me. Between them they beat the shit out of me, if you'll pardon the expression! I managed to crawl to the phone and call the cops. I must have passed out, because the next thing I know I'm in the hospital. I presume the police came around to the back of the house and saw the open window" Tom explained.

"Don't worry Dad, they'll get them. You have a good description, yeah?" Alex replied, patting his father's hand. His father pulled his hand away sharply.

"Jesus my knuckles! I must have whacked him all right! Description? Sure what difference will that make? These little thugs could buy and sell the legal system! Sure they'll be out in no time, that's if they ever caught them in the first place! No lad, put it down to experience. Next time I'll lock up properly" Tom sighed.

Alex saw a quick opportunity to score some favourable points.

"Listen Dad, I'm not so sure about you returning to that old house. Why not come and stay with Stacey and me for a while? In fact, why not sell up and buy somewhere smaller?" he said. His father began to laugh, silently at first. As the laughter became audible, Tom felt his ribs ache in pain. The smile vanished and he grimaced in agony.

"My ribs hurt. Don't make me laugh again lad! Stay with you? Sure we would kill each other in days! Listen, I'll die in that house, and that's how I want it to be. When I get out of this godforsaken hospital, I will be straight back to work. No two little shits are gonna change my outlook on life. You get nothing if you don't work for it. My father told me that, and it's served me well. Remember that lad, nothing" his father said.

Alex wanted to argue with his father. He wanted to tell him that he had enough money to live on to cover another six lives. Alex also knew that it was useless to say anymore on the topic.

"I had better go and check the house. Are you sure that they got nothing in the break-in? What about the keys to the job? I should go and check out the place anyway" Alex said. His father nodded.

"The keys are safe in the jacket that I was wearing. I often leave my coat on in the evening. It saves me turning on the heating. I asked the nurse to check when I woke up. The keys are safe. No, they got nothing, the little bastards. Both of them were only about eighteen or so. They were as scared as I was! No, check the premises anyway, but sure it's alarmed. There's a policeman at the house I was told. Go and identify yourself there and lock up" Tom Woods said. His voice wheezed a little now, and he closed his eyes once again.

The thought that his father wore a jacket to save on heating amused Alex. It was typical of the man. Alex could not help but consider how easy it might be to cover his father's face with a pillow right at that moment. The man's death might well be attributed to the young thugs who had put him in hospital in the first place. If he was sure that he would get away with it, Alex would definitely do it right there and then. The lack of planning put him off the idea. What if he was disturbed? What if he did not manage to complete the act? With so many doctors around, what if they diagnosed his father's death as suffocation? Alex watched his father for a moment, the older man's eyes closed in a semi-conscious state. He looked down at the man's grazed knuckles, and then back to his bruised and bloodied face. Alex Woods felt no sympathy, just annoyance at having to plot the murder all over again. He trudged away from the bedside without saying goodbye.

Outside, Alex identified himself to a nurse on call at a desk at the top of the corridor.

"He had a bunch of keys with him. It's important that I retrieve them tonight or else no one will go to work in the morning!" Alex said in a jocular way. The young nurse smiled pleasantly and asked him to wait. She returned with his father's jacket and handed it over to Alex.

"How is he nurse? Will he be discharged tomorrow?" Alex asked. The slim dark-haired girl looked surprised at the question.

"I doubt it very much Mr. Woods. Your father's breathing is abnormal. I see that he suffers from angina? Doctor is not happy with him at all. Has he been on those prescribed tablets for long?" she asked. Alex thought for a moment.

"Yeah, years. At least since my mother died. I can't remember how long exactly. But he's as strong as an ox. He still works every day, maybe six days a week" Alex replied. The young nurse smiled and shook her head in dismay.

"I'm not sure that's such a good idea really. We might have to persuade him to slow down a little!" she said. Alex grinned back at her and shook his head.

"I wish you well on that score!" Alex replied.

He said goodbye and headed outside.

Alex sat in his car and considered what the young nurse had said. Perhaps by a twist of fate he might get what he felt that he was rightly entitled to after all. It would be ironic indeed if a botched burglary brought about his father's early retirement. It would allow Alex to run the company after all, and without the messy job of having to carry out a murder. Alex smiled at the lunacy of events that evening. The night had gone from fearing arrest when the police called, to possibly attaining his ultimate aim in life by default. And earlier Angie O'Rourke had more or less informed him that he had got away with ploughing down Phillip Westbourne. If anyone was a suspect, she was! Alex grinned and turned the key in the engine. Suddenly the scowl appeared again on his face as he thought of his father.

"It's still not ideal. Once he's still alive, he will prevent me doing as I want. I would much prefer him dead, the miserable old swine" he muttered.

CHAPTER FOURTEEN

BARTO'S OFFER

It was Saturday evening, and Jodie and Tony were on their way to the pub where they were due to meet up with Howard and Jan.

"We have to push them on what their plans are Tony. No one travels all this way to protect an old house. They have to be trying to buy it back. My guess is that they went to see that solicitor Mr. Tomlinson today. It stands to reason. They want to find a loophole or something. Why else would they offer you cash?" Jodie said. Tony turned to face her. They were within yards of the quiet pub that Tony had selected the night before.

"Everything that you say makes sense Jodie. I just don't want to burn my bridges with Jan. She's the only flesh and blood I have in this world. Please don't jump in when we go inside, eh? Sooner or later they will spell out what they want" he reasoned. Jodie sighed and agreed to be patient.

"I don't want her messing you around Tony. You give in far too easily. I'm a fighter by nature. I'll stand up to Jan for you" Jodie replied. Tony smiled and kissed her.

"You're nuts you! You wanna fight with everyone!" he grinned. Jodie hugged him close to her. She looked up to him with admiration.

"I love you Tony Lee, and I just want what's best for you" she said, kissing him again on the lips.

They soon met up with Jan and Howard, who arrived about fifteen minutes later. Both seemed in good spirits, and Howard in particular wanted to let his hair down. His trade mark hat which he wore in The States had been left behind, and both Howard and Jan were dressed casually. Howard was in a particular jocular mood, and every time something serious cropped up,

Howard quickly swung the chat back to Dublin's night life. It was clear that he viewed the night ahead as a chance to have fun.

For a while, Tony and Jan discussed their late mother. Jodie tried to listen with compassion, but Howard seemed uncomfortable and detached from the conversation. He glanced around the quiet pub looking bored. Later, the conversation became fractured, with neither couple prepared to say exactly what was on their minds.

As the evening wore on, Howard constantly urged everyone to move to a livelier venue.

"Gee, this crumby place is lifeless. Jan, show me around this town, will you? We're on vacation honey!" he said. Jan finally agreed, and all four stood up to leave. Tony looked worried. He had selected the quiet pub specifically so that they could talk. A lot of things had been left unsaid. Tony managed to have a word with his sister as Howard led the way outside.

"Don't you want to talk about the house Jan? I thought that was why we were here?" he whispered. Jan fixed him with a stare.

"And I thought that we agreed last night to leave things alone. Can't you concede that the work on the house is finished Tony? It looks fine. We've travelled all of this way to make the peace. Can't you just accept the house the way it is? It would put Howard's and my mind at ease so much. All we want is to write a cheque and move on, okay?" Jan whispered.

"I agree Jan, but I don't want your cash. All I ever wanted was somewhere nice to live" Tony countered.

"Finally! A bit of logic at last! That's exactly what you've created Tony. The house is perfect. Now, I don't want to hear another word on the subject so. Let's enjoy tonight, okay?" she said. Tony smiled back at her.

"Yeah sis, you're right, let's have a nice evening. I'm so happy that the old place is mine" he said. Jan glanced around. Howard and Jodie were already walking towards the exit. She turned back to Tony and leaned closer to him.

"I'll tell you this though. If you touch another brick of my mother's home, there will be hell to pay. Mark my words Tony; you don't want to cross myself or Howard. If you do, it will be the sorriest day of your life. Remember what I'm saying to you" she said. Jan then turned abruptly and walked away.

Tony Lee stood rooted to the spot. Her words sank in, yet Tony found it hard to digest them. Had she just threatened him? Had he misinterpreted what she had meant? Tony did not think so. He turned and followed Jan outside. Jodie stood smiling as he exited the quiet premises.

"They seem okay this evening Tony. Perhaps they are just here for a holiday after all! Come on, let's have some fun!" Jodie whispered. Tony had not got the heart to tell her what had just occurred. He smiled back at Jodie and gripped her hand.

On Sunday morning, Tony woke in a sweat. He shot upright in the bed. The shock of the bad dream had roused him from a deep sleep. Tony felt his light-blue pillow. It was soaked from his perspiration. He turned it over and flopped back down on it.

"Shit! It's been weeks since I had one of those horrible dreams. I was having such a nice sleep as well. Me and Jodie were on holidays..." Tony's train of thought suddenly rewound the scene. It was not Jodie in the picture, but Stacey. The thought that he was suddenly happy again with Stacey confused Tony Lee. He was over her. Why would she flash into his dreams? And then that crying child reminded him of the nightmare.

Tony lay staring at the white ceiling. Was the child somehow linked with Stacey, he wondered? It always came into his head either when Stacey was around, or when he thought about her, he reasoned. Tony knew that this was not strictly true. He had had these dreams while he was dating Jodie as well. Lately the nightmares had not been so prominent. Tony then remembered Jan and Howard. They had had a good time the night before, yet Jan's words still haunted him. They had parted on good terms, with all four of them sharing a taxi home. Jan and Howard were first to be dropped off. On the way to Jodie's apartment, Tony had tried to explain what Jan had said to him. Jodie had been a little tipsy, and Tony was not sure that she understood what he was implying. Tony turned on his side and tried to sleep. The under sheet was still damp with sweat from his body. Tony tried to think of a pleasant life ahead with Jodie. He closed his eyes and drifted away once again.

Tony awoke suddenly to the sound of the house phone ringing. It was light now, and he looked at the bedside alarm clock. It was just gone nine-thirty. He threw on his dressing gown and hurried downstairs.

"Hello Tony? Jan. Listen, a change of plan. Howard has hired a car and wants to travel north. He has a hankering to see Donegal, where his folks are from. If it was left to me I would stay right here in Dublin. Still, I can't be selfish, can I? I'll either phone you later in the week or when I get home. Now, I insist on you sending me an estimate for all of the work that you have done. Howard and I will pay in full, understood? Oh, and tell Jodie that we said hello. I have too dash Tony, Howard is like a two-year-old at Christmas! Good luck, talk to you soon" Jan said. Tony barely had a chance to speak before the phone line went dead. He lowered the receiver looking dejected and confused.

"Why would she do that? They come all of this way and leave after two days. I don't know what to think anymore" he whispered.

"Are you sure about this Jan honey?" Howard asked. Jan smiled at him as she replaced the receiver.

"Yeah, let's go and enjoy our vacation in Donegal, Howard. Tony knows his place. I'm convinced that he finally sees things our way" she replied.

Alex Woods sat in his office studying figures on his computer. He heard his name being paged on the intercom system.

"Alex Woods to reception, Alex Woods to reception please" said Michelle's voice. Alex peered out through the glass. He could not see anybody except a salesman talking to some customers. Alex ambled outside. At Michelle's reception desk, a shifty-looking man in jeans and a casual green jacket stood alone.

"This gentleman wishes to see you Alex. He asked for you by name" Michelle said, ensuring that she could not get the blame for Alex being disturbed.

"Thanks Michelle. How can I help sir?" Alex asked, turning to face the unshaven man.

"Er, in private" the man said, daring to look Alex in the face for the first time. Alex studied the man's features. He was in his early twenties, sporting a thin moustache and heavy dark eyebrows. He wore his black hair fairly tight, but brushed to the side. The man's eyes were jet black. Alex decided there and then that he was not to be trusted. In Alex's mind, the man was either a petty criminal, or an unemployed man looking for work. Alex could tell at a glance that the man had no experience in the motor trade. His hands looked soft and unused to manual work. The company were not hiring anyway, but Alex would never employ someone who came for an interview dressed as casually as this man.

"If you're looking for work I'm afraid that you've had a wasted journey. Whoever gave you my name led you astray. Sorry" Alex said with a shrug. The man shook his head and leaned forward.

"No Mr. Woods, you've got it wrong. It's a personal matter" he said. Alex tried to weigh up what it might be about. Michelle pretended to busy herself, but Alex knew that she would be taking in every word.

"Okay, follow me" Alex said. He led the man down the corridor and into his small private office. Alex pointed to a chair on the near side of the desk, and slipped around the other side to his modest leather swivel chair.

"Now Mr...? What can I do for you?" he asked. The younger man sat down and opened the zip on his green jacket.

"My name doesn't matter. I'm here on business. I understand that your father had a bit of bother the other night" he said, his dark eyes narrowing slightly. Alex shot forward in his chair. Both men looked to the phone on Alex's desk.

"I wouldn't if I were you. Hear me out first" said the man.

Alex exhaled slowly. He sat back just a slight bit, leaning an elbow on the desk. Alex then rested his chin in his hand.

"Go on, I'm listening" Alex said.

"Well, the other night I was in this pub. I heard these two young toe-rags discussing a robbery that they had committed. I was on my own at the bar, so I became interested. Anyway, the bottom line is that I heard the house name "Hillcrest" mentioned, then I heard Hollytree Road. They were going on and on about how much they should have come away with, if it wasn't for the old man being home that particular evening. They were talking about the Blackrock area, and rattling on about house burglaries. I followed these two guys out of curiosity, and tailed them to their homes. Some criminals, eh? Anyway, I looked up the house on the internet. It was easy to check out your father's address. So I did a bit of detective work. Then I discovered your father's identity, so I Googled the name "Tom Woods". It was easy to find him. I then used the phone book to check out that his address tallied. I found Woods Motors and guessed it might belong to him. It only took me minutes to trace him to this place. Then I looked up the yellow pages to check out the garage. Very impressive! I phoned here and asked who was running the company while Mr. Woods was in hospital. Just as I hoped, it was one of the family. You're doing very well for yourselves Alex, very nice indeed" The young man said, looking around the office.

Alex Woods was no fool. He could already guess where the conversation was going. However, he played along with the game just to be sure.

"You have been busy! A nice bit of detective work indeed! So, out of the goodness of your heart you want to give me this information, yeah?" Alex asked with a stern poker face. The man in the green jacket smiled again.

"I won't mess you about Alex. I'm off to England to do a bit of work in the next week. You pay me €800 today, and I will lead you straight to those two dirtbags. Take it or leave it" the man replied. Alex knew that he had to weigh up the situation quickly. It could be a scam. This guy could even be in league with the two people who burgled his father's home. He might even be one of them.

"What's to stop me from calling the police right now? This is blackmail that you're trying on here" Alex said. The younger man raised his dark eyebrows and smiled.

"I prefer to think of it as a good deed. Call the cops, go on. I'll be gone in two seconds. And where will that leave you? Nowhere! The cops will never find those two, but I can deliver them to you right now. What you do with this info is down to you. You could have them kneecapped; shot dead, battered, or even give the names to the police. I really don't care. Listen Alex, pay me and I walk away. You will never hear from me again" the stranger said.

Alex had to think fast. He certainly was not about to hand over that amount of money to a perfect stranger. Yet the temptation of finding those two thugs who ruined his plans was very attractive indeed.

"I'm interested, very interested. But I wouldn't have that type of money on me. We don't carry lots of cash on the premises, for obvious reasons. I don't suppose a cheque would be acceptable?" Alex said, half reaching for his inside pocket. The other man laughed out loud. His eyebrows narrowed again as he leaned forward.

"What do you think? Look Alex, don't mess me about here. Either you're going to pay up or you're not. Now, I'll tell you what I'll do. Here's my mobile number. If you change your mind over the next day or two, phone me. If not, forget it. After that, I will be on the boat to England" the man said. He scribbled down his phone number on a piece of paper on Alex's desk and stood up.

"I'll need a name, just so you'll know that it's me" Alex replied. The man walked towards the door of the small office.

"Call me Barto. It may me my real name, it might not be. What difference does it make?" he said with a cocky smile. In a second he was gone, leaving Alex with a dilemma.

Alex paced the office back and forth.

"It's too good a chance to miss. Fuck! €800! I can't miss this chance though. I would love to knock the shit out of those two little pricks! Fuck!" he muttered.

It was Monday evening. With just days to go to the wedding, Alex wanted the business with Barto settled soon. He and Stacey were to be married Thursday morning at a city centre registry office, with the reception at Ashton Castle Lodge that afternoon. The couple, along with some guests, would stay overnight. The cruise was booked for the Saturday, departing from southern England, which did not leave Alex a lot of time to make plans regarding the break-in at his father's home. Alex could not leave it any longer. With Stacey and Angie in the bedroom together, Alex made a quick phone call.

"Barto? Alex. I have your money, but it has to be tonight. Can we meet?" he said in a low voice. Barto seemed to hesitate before answering.

"Okay, tonight. But don't try anything stupid. I'm doing you a favour here. The first sign that things are not right and I'm off. I want the money in cash, fifties will do" Barto said in a cold, determined voice.

"That's not a problem Barto, where's convenient?" Alex replied.

"Do you know Morgan's Bar, just around the corner from your garage? Meet me there at nine. Don't be late. Any messing and I'm off" Barto answered.

"Gotcha. I'll see you then" Alex said. He finished the call and slipped his phone back inside his pocket.

Stacey Boyd was looking forward to her hen's night out with her friends and work colleagues. With just three days to the wedding, a tour of city centre pubs in the Temple Bar area of Dublin was planned, followed by a trip to a popular nightclub. She and Angie were in Stacey's bedroom getting dressed, while Alex had retired to the sitting room. He felt that there was little sense in moping in the bedroom, now that his master plan had been scuttled. Still, as he sat staring blankly at the television, Alex continued to critically run over his murder plot in his head. He felt sure that it would have worked, and cursed the two young thugs for spoiling it. His father was still in hospital with breathing problems, and Alex had already been to visit him that afternoon.

Angie eyed Stacey as her best friend tried on yet another top.

"Well, nearly there at last Stacey. Any last minute thoughts?" Angie asked. It was a tongue-in-cheek query with reference to the wedding, but Angie knew Stacey would never twig what she had meant.

"Thoughts? Yeah! I hope that you lot behave yourselves! Don't tie me to a lamppost or anything silly! Promise me Angie that you'll look out for me. I don't want to be made to drink mad concoctions of spirits. I'll be sick everywhere!" Stacey said, making a face.

"Of course I'll watch you, but I can't promise anything! That's not what I meant though. I mean, this is the second time. What if Alex gets cold feet again?" Angie asked with a mischievous grin on her lips. Stacey's shoulders immediately drooped from her erect pose. She turned from the mirror to face her pal.

"I know that he will be there Angie. Last time I should have read the signs. Looking back, he had hinted so many times that he could not go through with it. I wouldn't listen. I just wanted to get married. You know how it is. I can see the difference this time. Alex wants to do this as much as I do" Stacey replied confidently. Angie barely nodded and continued to probe her friend.

"And what about Tony? I have to ask this, Stacey. Does any part of you wish it was him marrying you?" Angie asked. Stacey's brow furrowed a little. Her worried squint reappeared. She half-turned to face the mirror again, thoughts racing through her mind.

"I can't believe that you've just asked me that Angie. You've lived with us for God's sake! You above everyone can see that we're in love" Stacey replied coldly. Angie smiled at her best friend and went to hug her.

"I'm so happy for you. I just want to be sure that there are no doubts" she whispered.

"Thanks Angie. No doubts. I'm finally going to live happily ever after. Remember you always said that we were past our sell-by date? Well I'm living proof that we're not! Your turn will come too, you'll see" Stacey said. Her eyes were almost tearful now, and Angie noticed this.

"Don't start me off you! Come on, no tears!" Angie smiled. Angie wafted the air between them rapidly with her left hand. Stacey shook her head several times.

"No, I'm all right. From now on I'm only going to be happy" she said with a beaming smile.

Angie and Stacey were almost ready to leave. It was about eight o'clock, and the two presented themselves to Alex for inspection.

"Will I do?" Stacey asked.

"You look lovely Stacey pet-too lovely if you ask me!" Alex grinned.

"Thanks Alex. I'm raging that you're not having a stag. Won't you change your mind? You could still have one" Stacey said. Alex shook his head as he got to his feet.

"No, I'm fine. I put some cash behind the bar at the local pub for the chaps in work last Friday. I popped my head in the door and had a quick drink with them. Then I got the hell out of there before they realised that I had left! It's different when your management and they are the staff you see" Alex boasted.

"But what about friends, and your best man?" Angie enquired. A look on Alex's face said that he would rather not discuss it, but he smiled politely and carried on.

"Well Terry Thompson is my best man. He's the type of guy who I can call on anytime. We might even have a pint together tomorrow night. I've sort of lost track of all of my other mates. You see Angie, running around after Dad has not been easy. Over the years I've been like his general dogsbody. My social life was put on the backburner. Success doesn't come easy in this game. There are a lot of sacrifices to be made" Alex said.

If it was anybody other than Alex, Angie might have been tempted to laugh at his self-importance and egotism. She thought better of it and changed the subject.

"Stacey, we had better be going. There are drinks waiting with our names on them! Come on, we'll grab a taxi outside!" she said.

Alex kissed Stacey goodbye and walked them to the door.

"Enjoy, but not too much! Remember that you have to come back here tonight!" he said.

Once they were out of sight, Alex began to get ready to leave. He shoved the envelope with the €800 into his back pocket and threw on his jacket. He then pulled his old flick knife from a drawer, well aware that the meeting could be a set up for a mugging.

Alex drew up alongside Barto, who stood on the pavement alone outside Morgan's Bar. Barto eyed him through the window on the passenger's side before climbing in.

"Where's the cash?" he asked.

"You'll get it. Which way?" Alex countered. Barto looked annoyed.

"Fuck this! I'm not playing games here! Pay up front or forget it pal!" he yelled.

"What's to stop you taking the money and legging it?" Alex said in a loud voice.

"And what's to stop you keeping the cash once I show you where these toe-rags live?" Barto replied. Alex grinned back at him and nodded his head several times.

"I like you Barto! You're like me! Trust nobody. I'll tell you what; I'll pay you half now and half later, how's that?" Alex said, reaching for his back pocket. Barto mumbled something under his breath before agreeing.

"Fuck it, okay then" he said. Alex counted out the cash and shoved the remainder back into his back pocket. They set off with Barto giving directions.

Stacey's and Angie's high-heeled shoes clicked their way along the streets of Temple Bar in the city centre.

"I can't believe that you asked Alex about having a stag night out" Angie said.

"Why? He should have a night out with his pals" Stacey replied.

"Yeah, but don't forget he already had a stag night a few years ago! He's probably too embarrassed to have another one after what happened" Angie reasoned. Stacey stopped in her tracks and held both hands to her face.

"Oh-my-God! What was I thinking? Mortified! Oh My God Angie, why didn't you stop me?" she gasped in mock-horror. The two burst into laughter as they continued on their way.

"What about the night before the wedding Stacey? It's bad luck to stay in the same house as the groom" Angie said with a gentle nudge to her friend. Stacey pushed her back. The two were in fine spirits as they neared their first port of call. The girls from Stacey's job would be there, along with Jodie, Gina and some other pals.

"That's already sorted Miss Smarty –pants! Alex's father is still in hospital, so Alex will stay at his Dad's house overnight. He will leave for the registry office from there" Stacey replied.

"Wow! That leaves us with an empty flat that night! We could get up to all sorts of mischief! We could invite a few guys around, get some booze in!" Angie laughed.

"Huh! We never did that when we lived together! We're hardly gonna do it now!" Stacey replied with a smirk. Angie stared at her friend for a few seconds. "You could always phone Tony that night. You know, have a nice talk with him. See what he has to say" Angie said. Stacey looked irritated now.

"Angie O'Rourke! You are such a trouble-maker! You fixed me up with Alex in the first place! Now you're trying to break us up at the last minute!" Stacey giggled.

"No, I set you up in the second place! The first time around, the two of you blew it! And Stacey, here's another point. Alex will be alone at his father's place. How do you know for sure that he will show up for the wedding?" Angie asked.

The question was lost in the evening air as loud screams sounded out across the road. Some of Stacey's friends had spotted her, and came running to greet her with outstretched arms.

"Here we go Angie, remember that I'm counting on you to get me home" Stacey said with great trepidation.

"There, see that house there? One of them lived in there, the other lives in that house a few doors up. The first fellow is called Burrener or something like that. The other guy has a mad nickname. Muggser I think, possible Buggser. The pub was noisy that night, but I distinctly heard a name similar to that" Barto said with conviction.

"Well, why don't we just sit here for a while and wait for them?" Alex replied calmly. Barto banged his fist on the passenger door in temper.

"Fuck sake man! What is this? Am I your fucking guardian angel or something? Pay me and I'm out of here!" he said in a rage. Alex felt for the flick knife in his jacket pocket.

"What do you take me for Barto? You could pick out any house in Dublin. Who's to say two innocent blokes don't live here?" he said, tossing his head in the direction of both houses.

Barto seemed to consider his words. He stared across the street at the red-bricked terraced houses which ran the length of the street. The hall doors led directly onto the streets in the old Dublin homes. There were no front gardens, with just a small yard to the rear of the ancient properties.

"Look Alex, we could sit here all night and not see them. These weasels only show up when they feel like it-and that's mostly in the dead of night" he replied. Alex nodded.

"I agree. But I have to be sure. These scumbags have left my Dad in hospital. They're gonna pay for that. Now if you want to fuck off for a while, then go ahead. But I'm staying here until I see some proof" Alex said firmly.

Barto looked to the white roof of the Mondeo car. He sighed and cursed under his breath again.

"Fifteen minutes, fifteen minutes and I'm out of here pal" he muttered.

They sat in silence for a while, both lost in their thoughts. The radio played low in the background. Alex's eyes remained fixed on both houses. The lights were on in each of the nondescript homes, but no one either came in or out.

"Shag this for a joke! Listen Alex, I'm out of here. I thought that I was doing you a favour. Are you paying up or what?" Barto said some minutes later, his dark eyes fixing on Alex Woods. Again Alex felt for the knife.

"I'm a man of my word. When I see proof, the rest of the cash is yours" Alex answered in a calm, collected tone. Barto opened the car door and leapt out.

"Fuck this; I'm going for a walk. If I'm not back in a while, I'll be looking for you pal" he said in a threatening voice. He slammed the door and disappeared into the darkness.

Alex smirked and sat back in his seat. He was prepared to wait into the early hours if necessary. Angie and Stacey would be home very late. He had plenty of time.

About twenty minutes later, the car door suddenly opened. Alex jumped in surprise, and turned sideways. Barto looked out of breath, but had a flicker of a smile on his face.

"There here. Fuck me Alex; I nearly walked straight into the two pricks! They were around at the chipper buying food. They're on their way" Barto said, panting hard.

Alex nodded calmly and sat up straight. He was alert, the adrenalin rushing through his veins. He would gladly get out of the car and maim both of the worthless thugs there and then. His brain told him to be calm, to think things through.

"There, right over there!" Barto said, nodding to his left. Alex followed his line of vision. He saw the two figures, one in a grey hoodie, the other in a light casual black bomber jacket.

Alex leapt from the car. He could hear Barto's voice, but it seemed to be coming from miles away. Alex slammed the door behind him.

"What the fuck are you doing? Jee-zus! Not now you gobshite! Don't touch them now!" Barto pleaded. Alex never heard a word. He strode forward, getting nearer and nearer to the two younger men.

Alex Woods marched towards the two until he was within feet of them. Both looked at him suspiciously as they ate their takeaway meal from open brown paper bags.

"Hey lads, you haven't seen a small brown and white terrier dog have you?" Alex asked in an innocent tone. The slightly smaller youth appeared to wear a permanent grin. He was the lippier of the two, and was quick with a retort.

"Naw, but if he went anywhere near the bleedin' curry shop he's a gonner!" he sneered. Both youths cackled mockingly without looking at Alex a second time. The two kept walking, ignoring Alex completely. It did not matter to Alex Woods. As their laughter blended into the cool night air, a smugness descended on Alex. He had achieved what he needed to do. All he had wanted was to get a good look at their faces. He turned and strolled back to the car, reaching into his back pocket on the way.

"Here's your money, you've earned it" he said to Barto. Barto fixed him with a glare.

"Jeezus! I thought that you were going to take those muppets on there and then! I have to tell you mate, you would have been on your own!" Barto said with a grin. Alex raised his eyebrows and shrugged.

"I can fight my own battles. I'll tell you this though, when the time comes, those two little bastards won't know what hit them" he said. Barto shoved the cash into his inside jacket pocket and zipped up his coat.

"Whatever mate, I'll be long gone. You can drop me off where you collected me" he muttered.

"No problem Barto, no trouble at all" Alex replied dryly.

Tony Lee sat at home watching television. Jodie was out at Stacey's hen night. The irony of it was not lost on him. A few months ago the scenario would have sounded ridiculous.

Jan's visit to Ireland still baffled Tony. She had not phoned since, and Tony was unsure if they were still in the country, or had returned to America already. He wondered if Jan was paranoid about their mother's home, or if she just liked to get her own way. Tony also wondered about Howard's role in all of this. What husband would fly all that distance just to please his wife on some trivial matter, he wondered? Perhaps Howard's only real intention was to finally visit Donegal, Tony mused.

Tony tried to block Jan from his thoughts, but time and again she returned. She always seemed to be there, questioning him, bossing him about and mothering him.

It struck Tony that this summed up Jan entirely. It appeared that she wanted to take his mother's place. Instead of being the sister that he had hoped for, Jan Williams had turned into a sort of maternal figure. Both Stacey and Jodie had remarked that he should stand up to her. Somehow as of yet he had not had the strength or mental courage to do so. Tony would like to believe that he might do so in the future, but Jan appeared to have some sort of hold over him.

He stood up and wandered around the big empty house. The décor had improved almost beyond recognition, yet there was so much more that he wanted to do to make it habitable for Jodie. It definitely needed a woman's touch, but it also required a lot of money spent on it. To achieve the things that Jodie wanted required lots of cash. She had talked about an attic conversation, a conservatory, even a wet room. While Tony could afford some of these things, it might leave his finances stretched. He recalled Howard's strange offer to pay for the refurbishments. Idly Tony wondered what would have occurred if he had accepted.

It was immaterial really. He could never take their money. It would leave him totally beholden to his sister and her husband.

Tony lay on his bed with both hands behind his head. His life had turned topsy-turvy over the past few months. In a few days he was going to witness his ex-girlfriend getting married. Tony was a little insecure at the thought of it all. If he could avoid going, he certainly would. Stacey's fiancé had a much better job than he had. Alex Woods could easily offer Stacey a much more comfortable lifestyle than he ever could.

"She'll be much better off with him, that's for sure!" Tony muttered flippantly. His feelings for Stacey were confused. When they were together, they barely had time for each other. It was only when she left him that he realised how much he had loved her. At that time, Tony also understood how badly he had treated Stacey. And then Jodie came into his life, just when he was at his lowest ebb. Slowly he had fallen for her, and now they planned a life together. A fear, almost a panic crept over him. What if he was to lose Jodie? It did not bear thinking about. If such a calamity happened, Tony felt that he might never recover.

"A guy can only handle so many setbacks!" he thought. Meeting Jodie had been wonderful for him. It had given him renewed confidence and belief in himself. Tony vowed there and then to try even harder at their relationship. His laid-back approach to the women in his life had cost him dearly over the years. This time he would make sure that Jodie Callaghan did not slip through the net. He would persuade her to move in with him, and when the time was right he would propose. They were not too old to have children, and perhaps he could finally settle down and be as happy as his good friend Erik Ngombiti. He felt that he owed something to Erik also. When Tony was at his weakest point, it was Erik who convinced him to carry on.

It was late in the night when Tony awoke with a start. In his drowsy condition, Tony feared that it was yet another nightmare. Something told him that that was not the case. There was a banging, somewhere in the distance. He heard it again.

"Christ! That's the front door" he muttered. Tony switched on the bedside lamp and peered at the small square alarm clock. It was almost one-forty-five. His first thought was that it was Jan and Howard. They might have travelled back from Donegal with nowhere to stay. Tony jumped from the bed and grabbed his dressing gown to cover his white boxer shorts. The knocking began again, a slow repetitive tapping.

"All right, all right, I'm coming!" Tony yelled. He opened the hall door to find Jodie standing alone, looking a little the worse for wear. He quickly remembered Stacey's hen night.

"I'm sorry Tony, quick, I need the bathroom!" Jodie squealed. He stood back allowing her in. Tony closed the front door quietly as Jodie scampered upstairs. He smiled as he followed her up to the landing.

"That drinking is a terrible habit! You'll end up an alcoholic" he called out with a chuckle.

Moments later Jodie came to his bedroom. Jodie explained that Gina was still out with Stacey and her friends, and that she had decided earlier to go home alone.

"I wasn't feeling too clever, and I'm working in the morning, but then I discovered that I had forgotten my key. Harry's alone at the apartment, and I didn't fancy getting him out of bed. To be honest Tony, he's been giving me peculiar looks lately. He's become a bit creepy. I don't feel comfortable around him anymore" Jodie said.

Tony looked concerned. He barely knew Harry Brand, but had thought of the man as a pretty ordinary decent chap.

"Has he said anything?" Tony asked. He was still in his dressing gown and sitting on the end of the bed. Jodie inched down beside him.

"No, nothing, but I know by the way he looks at me that sooner or later he's going to try something. I'm mortified for Gina. I mean, if I say anything, she'll think that I'm making it up. Then the two of them will gang up on me" Jodie reasoned. Tony smiled and put an arm around her.

"There's only one thing for it. You're gonna have to move in here" he whispered.

"Yes. Yes please" she replied, kissing him hard on the lips.

CHAPTER FIFTEEN

THE WEDDING

It was the night before the wedding. Alex was spending the evening socialising with Terry, his best man. Purposely Alex had ditched any other friends associated with his frequent trips to see Isobel during his first ill-fated romance with Stacey. Although Terry knew of the affair, he never realised that Alex had in fact married Isobel, or that they had set up home in Ireland. Terry's and Alex's friendship was open-ended. One could pick up the phone and talk to the other without having seen each other for months. They might then stay in contact for days or weeks before cooling their friendship again.

Alex had ruled against doing anything about the two thugs who broke into his father's house, at least until after his wedding had taken place. He had decided that he needed a comprehensive plan, and would give the matter his full attention while on honeymoon.

"So this is it Alex, my old mate! You're really going through with it this time?" Terry said with a smile. Alex lifted the bottle of Budweiser to his mouth and swallowed hard.

"Yep! Stacey's the one after all. The last time I just wasn't sure, but we've lived together now and I'm positive" Alex replied confidently.

Terry Thompson was not quite as tall as Alex. He was a fairly good-looking man with a heavy well-trimmed black moustache. Terry liked to keep in shape, but his habit of attending his local gym was now a thing of the past. His wife Margaret, had persuaded Terry that it was more money wasted, and so Terry was now limited to one hobby. His love of fishing had been with him since his childhood, and Terry enjoyed nothing better than sloping off on a quiet morning to a local river or a lake.

"Pity your old man won't be there" Terry mused. Alex raised his dark eyebrows.

"Yeah, he will be in that hospital for another while yet. His heart is not as strong as he thought after all! Do you know what mate? He was always banging on about how he could do the work of men half his age. Old age comes to us all!" Alex grinned. Terry sipped on his gin and tonic.

"I take it that you and he still don't see eye to eye?" Terry said. Alex looked to his pal sitting next to him at the long bar. He needed to reassure Terry that there was no bad blood between him and his father. Alex still considered his Dad as unfinished business.

"We get on all right Terry, it's just that he won't let go of the reins. I want to take over. God knows that I've waited long enough. It was all right learning the ropes when I was a teenager, but for fuck sake..." Alex trailed off.

"I can see your point mate. Still, with your Dad laid up, it will give you a feel for what the future holds" Terry replied.

"I'm relishing it pal, really I am. I could run that place blindfolded! The old man makes the job out to be complicated. It isn't really" Alex said.

Terry again turned his thoughts to the wedding.

"Will there be any spare talent there tomorrow?" he asked with a grin. Alex threw back his head and laughed out loud.

"Easy, easy old mate! You're a married man now! Nah! The registry office is just for close friends and family. Maybe afterwards at the reception, but you watch yourself; Margaret will have her beady eye on you!" Alex said. The smile vanished from Terry's face.

"You're not joking Alex. We're not really getting on at the minute. Ever since she had the second child, things have gone a bit pear-shaped" Terry mused. A thought suddenly entered Alex's head.

"Oh, I never told you! Guess what? Stacey's ex-boyfriend will be at the wedding with one of her old flatmates! Unreal or what? She invited both of them along! Is that creepy or what?" Alex chuckled. He went on to explain about Jodie and Tony Lee.

"Man, that's heavy! I wouldn't put up with that, no way!" Terry said, slowly shaking his head. Alex laughed again. He threw a friendly arm around Terry.

"Ah, you see, that's where you and I differ! I'm more mature you see. A modern man can face this kind of thing head on. I have no insecurities about some silly little ponce who dated Stacey for a while" he said.

"Well, I'm the best man, so I'll keep an eye on this gobshite-just in case he gets jealous!" Terry said with a sniggering chuckle. Both men laughed together and Alex ordered another couple of drinks.

Back at Alex's apartment, Angie and Stacey were having a few drinks together. Stacey had wanted to stay sober on the eve of her big day, but Angie had arrived home with a shopping bag full of booze.

"The hen night went well I thought?" Stacey said. She was on her third short, having had two bottles of cider beforehand.

"Yeah, it was a great night. I still can't remember getting home" Angie said.

"Jodie was nice. I thought that it might have been awkward, but everything was cool" Stacey replied. Angie smiled sweetly, her mind abuzz with mischief.

"Yeah, Jodie's great, but where did she disappear to? She never came to the nightclub with us" Angie said. She watched Stacey for a reaction, but Stacey merely shrugged.

"She went home I suppose" Stacey replied nonchalantly.

"Yeah, that's what I thought, but then I realised that Harry was back at the flat on his own" Angie said with a wicked grin.

Stacey stared back at her pal with a puzzled look.

"So? What's that got to do with anything?" Stacey asked.

"Don't you see? Gina was out with us. There's her fellow, who lives with Jodie, back there at the flat all alone. Why would Jodie leave early? Do I have to spell it out girl?" Angie said with a wide grin. Stacey's facial expression slowly changed from puzzlement to shock.

"You don't think... You're not saying that their having an affair?" Stacey stammered. Angie nodded slowly.

"Poor Gina" Stacey said in a faraway voice.

"Poor Tony. Someone should tell him" Angie replied casually. Stacey shrieked at the idea.

"Not me! It's nothing to do with us Angie, besides, we're probably way off the mark" she said. Angie bit her lip and looked back at her best friend.

"If it was me, I would like to know. You could call Tony and say that you were just checking if they were okay about going to the wedding" Angie suggested. Stacey shook her head.

"No. Come on, let's just enjoy tonight" she said.

Much later, Angie was about to troop off to bed. She was feeling the worse for wear, having downed one vodka too many.

"See you in the morning Stacey. You should get some beauty sleep too. You want to look your best, don't you?" Angie said, slurring her words.

"I'm going in a while. Alex promised that he would phone. As soon as he does, I'll hit the hay!" Stacey replied cheerfully.

It was almost thirty minutes later when Alex finally called.

"Hiya babe, how's things?" Alex said. Stacey explained that she was all alone, and that she and Angle had been drinking.

"Yeah, that's cool honey. Terry and I are just gonna have one more beer and then I'm off to the old man's house for the night. I can't wait to see your beautiful face tomorrow darling" he said. Stacey smiled and kissed him goodnight down the phone.

"Goodnight princess. Our life together starts for real tomorrow" Alex whispered.

Stacey lay in bed considering what Angie had said. She found it hard to believe that Jodie would do such a thing, but accepted that there was always a bit of daring in her former flatmate. Stacey glanced to her phone on the bedside locker. The drink had made her head a little woozy. She reached for her phone and played with it for a while. When she came to Tony Lee's number, Stacey paused. In her semi-drunken state, Stacey began to consider what Angie had said earlier. Suddenly the temptation was too great. She would use the pretext that Angie had suggested and ring Tony.

"Hello Tony? This is Stacey, can you talk?" she said in a low voice. Tony Lee sounded baffled.

"Yeah, sure Stacey, what's on your mind?" he replied.

"Are you alone? Is Jodie there with you now?" Stacey asked. Tony Lee fell silent for a moment.

Look, I'm gonna level with you Stace. Jodie has just gone over to Gina's to collect some of her belongings. Things are awkward at the apartment with Harry there. Jodie is going to move in here for a while. The night of your hen party she came here and stayed. She forgot her key. That sort of started the ball rolling, so she's moving in" Tony replied.

"Oh, I see. Well, I was really calling to make sure that both of you will be there tomorrow. I hope that you don't feel out of place or anything. Jodie and I go back a long way, and you..." Stacey stopped mid-sentence.

"No, we'll be there Stacey. We have the day off work. Listen, I want to wish you all of the best. I might not get a chance to speak to you again" Tony said. The thought hit Stacey. She might never meet up with Tony again in life.

"Don't say that! Dublin is not so big! Anyway, I'll see Jodie. We'll still be mates" Stacey reasoned. Tony chuckled down the phone.

"Really? You'll be married; maybe soon you might have a few kids. With Alex being such a high-profiled businessman, I'm sure that your life will be too busy for the likes of us! You'll live in some posh house, well away from us ordinary folk!" he said in a jocular tone. Stacey considered his remarks.

"I would hate to end up like that Tony. I want to enjoy my life, not hide away behind some door, washing snotty children!" she laughed. Tony laughed too. For a second or two it was like old times.

"I miss you sometimes Tony" Stacey blurted out suddenly. Tony fell quiet. "Have you been drinking? Where's Alex?" he asked. Stacey explained her evening to him.

"I see. Well, I miss you too sometimes Stace. But what can we do? Life goes on" he whispered.

"Don't mind me Tony, I'm just feeling sorry for myself" a now-drowsy Stacey said. Tony heard the garden gate slam and then footsteps on the pathway.

"Stace, I have to go. Jodie has just come back by taxi. I'll see you tomorrow. Don't worry about anything, you'll look amazing. Goodnight love" he said.

"Goodnight Tony. Thanks for being so nice" Stacey replied.

On the morning of the wedding, Alex went to visit his father in hospital. His father sat upright in bed, reading a newspaper.

"How are you today Dad?" Alex asked tactfully. Tom Woods looked at him over his reading glasses.

"I'll bet that you're loving this, aren't you? Bloody hospitals! I'll soon be out of here, never fear. They've pulled me this way and that way, all because my breathing is a bit off. Bloody quacks!" Tom complained.

"Don't be silly Dad; I want you back at the garage with me. The doctors are only concerned for your health. There is an irregularity in your heartbeat. Once they find out what's causing it, they'll release you. Those damn tablets that you were taking did more harm than good. Listen, today is my wedding day. I don't want to fight with you, okay?" Alex replied, managing a smile of sorts.

Tom Woods dropped the newspaper slowly onto the blue bedspread. He removed his gold-coloured spectacles and chewed thoughtfully on the earpiece.

"I actually forgot about it Alex. You lose track of the days in here. Sorry, you go and enjoy the day and your honeymoon. Kiss Stacey for me. She's a lovely girl. I hope you appreciate her. She will be the makings of you, trust me" Tom said. There was a slight wheezing in his voice, noticeable when he spoke more than a few words. At the end of each sentence he sounded tired.

"I do appreciate her Dad. Stacey is one in a million. You take care now. I will be up to see you before we go away, we both will" Alex replied.

Alex headed back to his car, texting Stacey as he went.

"Been 2 see Dad. Seems ok. Asking after u" he said.

Stacey read the message. She was relieved that it was from Alex and not Tony.

"Whatever was I thinking last night?" she wondered quietly. Stacey was sitting alone in the kitchen. She began to text back to Alex. Just then a bleary-eyed Angie peered around the door. Stacey laughed on seeing her best friend.

"The state of you Angie O'Rourke! You're not walking up the aisle with me in that condition!" Stacey chuckled. Angie exhaled slowly and trudged towards the cooker.

"Any coffee? I'm in bits! I'll never touch another vodka again! Anyway, you're not walking up the aisle today anyhow!" she replied. The smile vanished from Stacey's face, trying to take in what Angie had said.

"Why are you saying that Angie? Don't joke about things like that" Stacey said crossly. It was Angie's turn to laugh.

"Don't be so touchy! It's a registry office, silly! There won't be any walking up the aisle today, thank God!" Angie replied sharply. She held her hands to her head in a vain attempt to stop her thumping headache. Stacey sighed with relief.

"Phew! Sorry Angie, I'm a bag of nerves. For a minute there I thought that Alex had phoned you. Sit down, I'll get your coffee" Stacey said with a smile.

The two sat sipping coffee, discussing the day ahead.

"Who were you texting?" Angie asked, casually picking up Stacey's pink phone. Stacey looked startled.

"Shit! My head's all over the place! I was texting Alex when you came in, and there's me fearing that he had phoned you!" Stacey exclaimed. She explained about her worries that Alex might get cold feet again.

"Nonsense! He's the luckiest man in the world, and he knows it!" Come on, I'll run you a bath and you can have a nice long soak. First though, where are those aspirin?" Angie said.

Later that morning, Stacey parents phoned. They had come in on an early flight. Stacey made arrangements to meet them at the registry office. They were booked in to stay at Ashton Castle Lodge, along with the rest of the wedding party for a couple of days. Stacey and Alex, Terry and his wife, Angie, Gina and Harry were the other guests booked in. Jodie and Tony had been invited to stay over, but had declined the offer, much to the relief of most.

Jodie and Tony arrived at the registry office. They were one of the first couples to get there. Jodie wore a neat matching navy skirt and jacket, with a white blouse beneath. She topped off her outfit with a wide-brimmed navy hat, with a white ribbon around it. Tony wore a grey suit, white shirt and red tie. Both looked immaculate, with a single red rose in their lapels. Tony lit up a cigarette and inhaled hard.

"I thought that you had given them up?" Jodie said with a deep frown.
"I have, I mean I did. It's just for today Jodie. Please don't go on at me. I'm nervous as it is" Tony said. Jodie giggled and cuddled up to him.
"And what have you to be nervous of? You're not getting married!" she replied.
"I know, but this is a bit surreal, don't you think? I mean, what do I say to this Alex chap? And Stacey, I mean, do I kiss her, shake her hand, what?" he said nervously. Jodie giggled again.
"Just wish them well, that's all. You can kiss Stacey on the cheek, but remember I'll be watching!" Jodie grinned.
Slowly the guests began to turn up. Tony recognised Stacey's parents as they arrived by taxi. Arthur Boyd pretended as if Tony was an old friend. Both had spoken on the phone many times. They shook hands warmly, and Tony introduced Jodie to Arthur and his wife, Rose. Rose was a slight, timid-looking lady, much smaller than her husband. Arthur Boyd stood almost six foot tall; the final wisps of his once-blond hair blew about in the gentle breeze. He was almost bald now, his shiny scalp well bronzed from a recent foreign holiday. His once fair heavy moustache was now distinctly grey, yet Arthur barely noticed. He had worn a moustache since his teen years.
"Yes, hello Jodie, we spoke on the phone when Stacey lived at the apartment" Rose said without thinking. There was an awkward silence for a moment until Gina and Harry appeared, climbing from a cab. The group talked among themselves for some time. Slowly more guests arrived, swelling the gathering bit by bit. Tony felt more relaxed now. Perhaps the day would not be so tense after all. Suddenly Jodie nudged Tony.
"Here he is. That's Alex there, the taller one" she whispered. Tony had seen pictures of Alex Woods, but had never seen him in the flesh. As Alex stepped out of a black taxi with his best man, Terry, he seemed to glance in Tony's direction.
"Oh, he spotted you all right! If looks could kill!" Gina whispered. Tony lit another cigarette and tried not to make eye contact.
Twenty minutes later, a white taxi pulled up decked in pink ribbons and honking loudly. Alex had booked the cab especially for Angie and Stacey. Everyone watched as Stacey's father went to open the rear door. Stacey was dressed in white, but it was not a wedding dress per -se. She wore a white midi-length skirt with a white jacket and matching shoes. Her hair was styled immaculately, with a small simple white hat for effect.
As she stepped out of the car, her eyes locked on both Jodie and Tony. Stacey seemed to waver a little, before gripping her father's arm. Arthur Boyd and his

daughter led the way inside, with Alex and Rose following close behind. Jodie spoke to Angie, who looking stunning in a long purple dress and matching hat. "How was she this morning?" Jodie asked. Angie fixed her hair as she picked her way up the stairs in her white stilettos.

"She's fine. Honestly, I never saw anyone so relaxed, Jodie. She's as cool as a cucumber!" Angie replied.

Inside the upstairs room, people chatted openly while the registrar introduced herself to Alex and Stacey. Tony watched from afar. Jodie moved about, talking to some of Stacey's friends, but avoiding Stacey's parents. Once or twice Stacey's and Tony's eyes met. He tried to look away, but her eyes were like a magnet, drawing him ever closer.

When everybody had taken their places, the ceremony quickly began. The registrar was a middle-aged lady with a solemn-looking face. Tony sat next to Jodie on the edge of a second row of seats. Ahead of him sat Rose and Arthur Boyd, Angie, Gina, Harry and Alex's best man, Terry and his wife Margaret.

As the ceremony wore on, Tony's mind began to wander. He wondered where Jan was now. Her menacing words still haunted him, and Tony ran over them again in his head. It definitely amounted to a threat, and he searched his brain for a possible reason for Jan's aggressive behaviour. He felt Jodie nudge him, and snapped out of his daydreaming.

"She didn't answer" Jodie whispered. Tony blinked and stared up towards Alex and Stacey.

"Do you take this man, Alex Thomas Woods, to be your lawful wedded husband?" the solemn-looking lady asked Stacey for a second time. Tony could tell that Stacey was now visibly trembling. He feared that she might pass out. Her father rose tentatively to his feet.

"No...I can't!" Stacey whispered in a barely audible voice. Gasps filled the room, followed my loud murmurings. Tony strained to hear above the noisy backdrop.

"Do you need a moment to gather your thoughts?" the poker-faced registrar asked, leaning forward. Alex grabbed on to Stacey's arm, a look of disbelief etched on his face. Arthur Boyd strode forward and put a comforting arm around his daughter.

"I'm sorry Alex; I can't go through with it. I'm so sorry" Stacey said through her gentle sobbing. More gasps filled the room. Some people stood up, other told the person beside them what they already knew.

Tony watched on with shock. He wondered if Stacey was doing it out of revenge. There seemed little other possibility. Yet, if she had not wanted to marry Alex, why not call off the wedding before arriving at the registry office, he wondered?

Arthur Boyd took his daughter to one side. Terry spoke to Alex Woods, who looked totally shattered by what was going on. Amid it all, the lady registrar strove to keep order.

"Ladies and gents, can we resume our seats please? Let's show some decorum please" the registrar said in a loud voice. Most people ignored her. They continued to chat noisily among themselves.

"What the hell is Stacey playing at?" a bewildered Angie asked, turning around to face Jodie.

"Was there any inkling back at Alex's apartment?" Jodie asked, her eyes wide with amazement. Angie shook her head several times.

"Nothing! They exchanged a few text messages. Her parents phoned twice, once to say that they had arrived, the next to make sure that she was okay. This is totally out of the blue" Angie replied. She looked to Tony, but he was still fixated with what was going on before him. Stacey's father led his daughter outside, quickly followed by Alex and Terry.

"Are you okay love, what happened in there?" Stacey's father asked.

"I don't know, I just couldn't go through with it. I'm sorry Dad" she sobbed.

Alex bounded up to the two. Terry stood behind him, watching anxiously.

"Stacey darling, what's going on? Don't do this to me pet. You know that I love you. Please, just take a minute. Compose yourself. You mean everything to me sweetheart" he pleaded. Stacey buried her head in her father's shoulder.

"I can't Alex, I can't do it. I thought that I could, but it's too soon. When I saw Tony with Jodie..." she sobbed.

The blood drained from Alex's face. He looked visibly stunned. Alex took a step backwards, not wanting to believe what he was hearing.

Terry Thompson stepped forward, perhaps thinking that he was doing his part as best man.

"Come on Stacey, it's just nerves. Every girl goes through this. My Margaret was..."

Arthur Boyd cut him off.

"Just leave her, will you? Stacey can make up her own mind. Come on Stacey, let's get some air" Arthur said. He put a comforting arm around her shoulders and led her downstairs. Terry turned back to face Alex.

"Hang on in there mate. She'll be okay in a bit" Terry said in an unconvincing tone. Alex shook his head. His brain now felt almost disconnected from his body.

"No, she won't do it, I just know it. That bastard Tony Lee has poisoned her against me. What am I going to do Terry? I'll be a laughing stock" Alex said. He began to weep openly. Terry put an arm around him and patted his back.

"Come on, don't lose the plot now mate. There are people in there from the garage. Keep it together for now, okay?" Terry whispered. Alex nodded, but continued to sob into his fist.

Angie came to the door, unsure if she should be there or not.

"Alex? What's happening? Where is she?" Angie asked. Terry looked to the bridesmaid who he had never met.

"Give us a minute love, eh? We're just sorting it" he said with a quick smile. The registrar followed Angie out, closing the door behind her.

"We'll have to move on soon. I have another wedding party in twenty minutes" she said in Alex's direction. By now Alex had totally lost it. He was sobbing into Terry's chest like a baby.

Arthur ran back upstairs to the landing to where Alex and the others stood. He called Alex aside and whispered to him.

"Come downstairs son. Stacey wants to talk to you" he said. Alex Woods dared to hope. He stopped crying momentarily and looked to the older man.

"Has she...? Will she go through with it?" he stuttered. Arthur put his right arm around him and led him away. He looked back towards the registrar and spoke.

"I'm sorry; can you give us two minutes please?" Arthur asked. Thelma Baird looked impatiently at her watch. She tutted loudly and began to mutter.

"Most irregular...no consideration...schedules to be kept..." she whispered under her breath.

Angie crept back inside. She took her seat ahead of Jodie and Tony.

"What's happening Angie? Where's Stacey?" Jodie asked, poking her pal in the back. Angie half-turned once more.

"Your guess is as good as mine Jodie. I'm as baffled as you. I think that she's downstairs with her father" Angie O'Rourke whispered. Tony Lee sat quietly beside Jodie. He could not help but feel that somehow he was involved. He recalled the phone call from the night before, and the chance meeting in town. Perhaps Stacey had only been putting on a brave face. Jodie was now chatting to the people to the other side of her. Tony had not told her about either event regarding Stacey. Now he feared that somehow Jodie might learn about his late night phone call.

"Here's Alex love, tell him in your own words. I'll just wait over there" Arthur said to his daughter. He walked away, leaving a little distance between himself and the couple.

"Stacey darling, whatever is the matter?" a tearful Alex whispered. Stacey's eyes were now red from crying. She looked up at him and tried to speak.

"I'm so sorry, so very sorry. I do love you Alex, but I just can't do it. I thought that I was well over Tony Lee, but the truth is that I'm not, not really. I wanted

229

to be strong today. I honestly tried. When I woke up this morning this feeling came over me. I can't explain. I somehow knew that I couldn't marry you today. Maybe in the future…We can still live together, I just can't marry you yet" she said in a whimper. Tears began to roll down Alex's cheeks again. He could scarcely believe what he was hearing.

"No Stacey, no. We can't do that. Either you marry me now, or forget it. I mean it. Either we become man and wife today, or we split. Don't make a fool out of me this morning, please, I beg you. Everything is arranged, the honeymoon the castle, the reception, the music. Come on precious, you'll be all right. Let's do it, please" he sobbed. Stacey began to shake her head from side to side.

"I'm sorry, I'm so sorry" she repeated over and over again. Her father came to comfort her again. He led her away, leaving Alex standing alone in his sorrow. Arthur placed Stacey in a taxi and asked the driver to wait. He then marched back upstairs and told the registrar the news. Thelma Baird nodded and sighed in a loud manner.

"Right. I suppose that I should tell the witnesses" she said with pursed lips. She went back inside the room and all eyes fell on her. Terry Thompson was again sitting next to his wife, explaining what he already knew of events.

"I'm afraid that I have to inform you that the wedding is off. Thank you for your patience" Thelma said in a cold, unfeeling voice. Again the murmuring started. Thelma Baird looked cross now.

"If you could kindly vacate the room as quick as possible, we have another wedding scheduled" she said. Slowly people got up to leave. Angie turned anxiously to face Jodie.

"Where will I stay tonight? I thought that I was going to a castle! Now I'm homeless!" she said, her sense of fun surfacing for a moment.

"It looks like it's back to the apartment for both you and Stacey!" Jodie said with a wicked grin.

Stacey sat in the rear of the taxi between her parents.

"Where are we going?" she asked in a faltering voice.

"We'll book into a hotel Stacey" her father replied in an upbeat tone. He patted her shoulder, his arm around her, resting on the back of the rear seat. Rose Boyd was weeping gently to Stacey's left. The ordeal was only hitting home to her now. They had left their luggage at the Ashton Castle Lodge, and would have to have it forwarded to them by taxi.

"We'll have to buy you some clothes Stacey. You can't go out in what you're wearing now" Rose Boyd said quietly.

Stacey was barely listening. All she could think about was Tony Lee. She had quickly realised that she was still in love with him. But now there was Jodie.

Her head was spinning, and the taxi journey through the city was almost like watching someone else's life pass by.

The cab drew to a halt in the Clonskeagh area, a place well-known to Arthur Boyd. It was here that he had lived as a young man, and he and Rose had bought their first home together in the vicinity when they had first married.

"Come on Stacey, I know the manager here. We'll get a couple of rooms and we can start to put today behind us" Arthur said softly. He helped his daughter from the taxi and paid the fare.

"What about my future Dad? Where will I live? How can I possibly face people again?" Stacey said, the tears welling up in her eyes again.

"You'll manage love. And you can always come back with us to England" he answered. Stacey said nothing. She followed her father up the ten white steps to the hotel entrance, her mother linking her arm for support.

Tony and Jodie shuffled outside of the registry office. Angie was ahead of them, hastily making arrangements with Gina to stay indefinitely at the apartment. Alex Woods sat in a taxi on the far side of the street. Already he had dismissed the large white taxi which was to be used to ferry him and Stacey to the reception. He observed the last of the wedding party leave the building in silence. Terry and his wife sat in the rear of the cab.

"Can we go now Alex? There's no more that we can do" Terry asked gently, leaning forward in his seat. Alex's eyes never left Tony Lee. A million thoughts flashed through his mind. He wanted to hurt Tony Lee much more than he ever thought possible. Across the road, Stacey's friends gathered in a huddle.

"What happens now? Poor Stacey" Angie said. Gina linked Harry's arm in hers.

"I spoke to Rose; she thinks Stacey is on the verge of a breakdown. They want to bring her home to England" Gina revealed. Angie disagreed.

"I can't see that. Her job is here, plus all of her pals. She loves living in Dublin" Angie reasoned. Jodie offered her opinion.

"Yeah, but it has bad memories for her now. Maybe she might be better off to get out of Dublin for a while" Jodie said. Angie tried to phone Stacey again on her mobile phone.

"She's still switched off. I'll try again later. What a day! Who would have seen this coming?" Angie said, managing a smile. Gina put an arm around her.

"Nobody would Angie. Come on, let's get you home and get settled" Gina said. Angie hugged her former flatmate and again turned to speak to Jodie.

"All of my clothes are at Alex's place. What am I going to do?" she said with a worried frown. Tony Lee had been listening quietly, barely able to take in the morning's events.

"Why not do what you lot always do-go shopping!" he suggested. Everybody laughed. It felt good and lightened the mood.

"I have a better idea, why don't we all go for a drink?" Harry said.

"I could do with a vodka. Okay, let's" Angie replied. They set off for the nearest pub, oblivious to the parked taxi across the street.

"Okay driver, you can go now. Take these good people home" Alex said quietly. The driver moved off, and Alex Woods's eyes were gradually drawn away from Tony Lee. Already Alex was making plans on how he might do maximum damage to Stacey's former boyfriend.

CHAPTER SIXTEEN

BACK AT THE OLD APARTMENT

Stacey finally switched her phone back on. She was alone in her hotel room, her parents resting next door. She scanned through her messages. There were several from her work colleagues wishing her good luck on her big day. There were missed calls too, but none from Alex. Three missed calls from Angie caught her eye. Stacey sighed as she realised she must steel herself for what lay ahead. People deserved an explanation. Angie would do her apologies for her. Right now she just wanted to be left alone.

"Hello Angie? It's Stacey, can you talk?" Stacey asked. Angie looked to Gina. She was back at her old apartment. Gina gave her a knowing nod and pointed her towards her old bedroom.
"Yeah, Stacey, it's all clear now. I'm back at Gina's apartment. How are you now?" Angie asked in a concerned voice.
"I feel terrible Angie. I'm so sorry about everything. And I let you down too. You have nowhere to stay. I forgot about that" Stacey said quietly.
"Don't be daft, I'm all right here. More importantly, where are you, and how are you bearing up? What came over you Stacey, I never expected that?" Angie replied.
"Oh, I'm in some hotel with my folks. They've been great. Listen Angie, I want you to apologise to everybody for me. I can't face them at the moment. I'll probably go back to England with my parents for a while. I'm off work anyway, but I don't know if I can ever go back to my job. I'm so mortified about everything" Stacey said.
"And that castle was booked for a couple of days too. Gosh Stacey, what happened?" Angie asked, repeating her question. Stacey stayed silent for a few moments.

"It was Tony. Just seeing him with Jodie brought it all back. I spoke to him the night before..." Angie cut across her friend.

"You what? You phoned him?" she said in an incredulous tone.

"Well, you told me to!" Stacey countered.

"Did I? Well I didn't really mean for you to actually do it! It was only a dare" Angie replied defensively.

"Well I did. When I heard his voice I just sort of melted. This morning in Alex's flat I knew that I could never go through with the wedding. I kept telling myself that it would be all right. I thought that it was nerves. But when I saw Tony there I knew that it was him that I wanted to marry. Angie, I'm so confused" Stacey said. She began to weep again.

"Hush, come on, we'll get through this. Do you want me to meet you?" Angie said.

"No. it's okay. I'll be fine" Stacey whispered.

"Stacey love, listen to me. Tony is with Jodie now. They seem to be getting on fine. If you really want him back though I could..." This time Stacey interrupted her best pal.

"No, no, I would never do that! God no! I want them to be happy together Angie, really I do. Listen, I messed up, it's up to me to pick up the pieces" Stacey said forcefully.

"And Alex, what about Alex?" Angie asked. Stacey went quiet once more. She then explained about his ultimatum to her, and told Angie that he had not phoned her.

"I could call him for you?" Angie suggested.

"No, it's pointless. He hates me now for what I did. He will never forgive me" Stacey replied.

"Stacey, on a more practical point, I need my clothes and stuff. Everything is at Alex's flat, including all of your things" Angie said.

"Shit! I've really fucked up, haven't I? Look Angie, you're gonna have to phone him later yourself. Could you take my things to Gina's for now? I hate to put you on the spot. God knows what Alex will do to our stuff if we don't get it out of there!" Stacey said, trying hard to laugh at the situation.

"Okay, I'll do that. Funny, we might all end up living back together here. Your room is still empty. It's used as a dressing room by Harry and Gina" Angie said with a smile.

"It could never be the same again, especially without Jodie. I don't really fancy moving back in. There will be boxer shorts and smelly socks everywhere!" Stacey joked.

"Once he covers up, I'll manage!" Angie laughed.

They talked further for a while before Stacey said that she had to go. Her mother was insisting on bringing her shopping for clothes.

The following day, Angie telephoned Alex. His mobile rang for some time before he answered.

"Yes?" he said tersely. Angie realised that her name would have flashed up on his phone.

"Alex, it's Angie. I know how upset you must be. I'm truly sorry for everything. Listen, I need to get my clothes and things. I was wondering when might be convenient for me to call around. I can get Harry to come with me" Angie said. Alex Woods seemed to pick his words before replying.

"Sure Angie, it's not your fault. I dunno, I'm in most evenings. Why not call around tonight? I suppose you'll want to take her stuff as well?" Alex replied, deliberately omitting Stacey's name from the conversation.

"Er, yes I suppose. I think that Stacey's going back to England for a while, but yes, we can store her things" Angie replied, doing her utmost to sound as businesslike as possible.

"Okay Angie, say about eight?" Alex replied. Angie agreed and said goodbye.

"How was he?" Gina asked. Angie shrugged her shoulders.

"He seemed all right, considering what he's been through. God Gina, it must have cost him a fortune! And that cruise has gone to waste too! You and me could have sailed away into the sunset!" Angie said with a giggle.

"I think Harry might have something to say about that! I better get his grub, he will be home soon" Gina said, rising to her feet. Angie followed her friend towards the kitchen area.

"Listen Gina, about Harry. I'm not in the way or anything, am I? Only, I have nowhere else to go. We'll have to work out rent. I have a few bob behind me. Alex wouldn't take any money from me, so I can easily pay my way" Angie said. Gina turned and smiled at her. She hugged her old friend close to her.

"Of course you can stay. This place is as much yours as mine. And if Stacey needs to come home, she's welcome too! I've already discussed it with Harry. Now, I don't know about the old rules on not having men stay over...!" Gina laughed.

"I think Stacey and myself have already forgotten that rule!" Angie replied with a loud, coarse laugh.

Tony explained again to Jodie what Jan had said to him exactly. He had not brought it up before the wedding, fearing it might spoil their day. Now as they sat watching television, he was in a talkative mood.

"The whole thing sounds bizarre! Is she going through a midlife crisis or something?" Jodie sneered. Tony feared that Jodie was not taking the matter seriously.

"Jodie, she actually threatened me, don't you see? If it wasn't my own sister, I would be thinking of going to the police. I have to see my solicitor to make sure that she has no grounds legally regarding this house" he replied. Jodie jumped to her feet. She could never stay still for long.

"Oh, she's just flexing her muscles! You know, the big sister thing! Hey, why not take them up on their offer to pay for everything? We could build that wet room, and a nice big conservatory!" Jodie grinned. Tony Lee smirked at her mischief-making.

"I can't take their cash. It would give them a real hold on me" he sighed.

"If we had the money I would build a little bar in the corner over here. We could do with a downstairs loo as well" she suggested. Tony looked appalled.

"Ugh! So tacky! Anyway, I have some money, but I don't want to waste it. We might need it in the future. And I was thinking that we could have a holiday later in the year" he said.

"What about a nice cruise?" Jodie grinned. She began to laugh. Tony could see the funny side too. He joined in and the two had a good belly laugh together.

"Seriously though, poor Stacey" Tony said.

"She'll be okay. Angie texted me earlier. Stacey's going over to England with her folks. They'll spoil her rotten. She'll meet a rich Englishman over there and live happily ever after" Jodie said. She was now practising her kung-fu kicks. Tony Lee had become accustomed to her constant energetic stunts around the house. It appeared to Tony that Jodie was always a bundle of energy, and regularly became bored when sitting around.

"A rich Brit, eh? Let's hope that they don't set up home in a castle!" Tony chuckled.

Harry Brand and Angie arrived at Alex's apartment. Before they rang the doorbell, Angie laid down a few last minute rules.

"Now, don't mention Stacey by name, unless he asks about her. Don't try to joke with him, and if he offers us coffee, refuse point blank. We want to be in and out as quickly as possible" she said. Harry nodded and rang the doorbell.

"Ah, Angie and Harry! Good to see you!" Alex said, over-exaggerating the welcome. Both smiled politely back at him as he showed them in.

"I have everything packed up in boxes for you. Oh, and a few bags of clothes too" Alex said in a friendly voice. He pointed to some cardboard boxes stacked just inside his bedroom door. Alongside them were three black bin-liner bags. Angie was surprised at the neatness of everything. She had visualised having to rummage around the flat for her personal belongings, and was not sure that she liked the idea of Alex handling her most private items.

"Oh, that's great Alex, thanks, thanks for everything" she mumbled.

"No problem. I'll give you a hand to carry them to the car" he replied. Each took as much as they could carry and set off. Two trips later and everything was loaded up.

"That's a nice car Harry. Toyota's a great make. Three years old? I could do you a great deal on a new model, if you're interested?" Alex said. Harry was unsure how to reply. He stared back at his Toyota Avensis, trying to think of something acceptable to say.

"Er, thanks Alex, that's something to bear in mind. The old finances are a bit tight at the minute though" he stammered.

"There's always the old hire-purchase. I know that nobody really wants to go down that road, but I'll make sure that the repayments are very manageable. Anything for a mate" Alex replied quickly. Harry tried to think of a way out.

"Er, yeah, that sounds very attractive Alex. I'll tell you what, Angie has your number, I'll give you a call, okay?" he said. Harry could not wait to get into his silver-coloured car and drive away.

"Thanks again Alex. Take care" Angie said, forcing a painted smile. Alex smiled back and patted the roof of the car. The two drove off into the night, with Angie breathing a sigh of relief.

Later that evening, Alex Woods drove to the small housing estate where Barto had directed him to the previous week. It was nearing eleven o'clock, and Alex was unsure if he would encounter the two youths or not. He sat quietly for a while, staring out at the two terraced houses in question. The radio was on low, but Alex's mind was miles away. He thought about his father, Stacey Boyd, Tony Lee and about Harry and Angie calling.

"A deal on a car? I know the deal I would give him! Twat! As for Angie, ungrateful bitch. She'll get hers all right, no question about that!" he muttered. Suddenly he heard voices. Ahead of him, a youth was banging on the door of one of the houses he had been watching. The young man had come from around the corner, and Alex identified him as the smaller of the two thugs that he was interested in.

"I'm back Burrener, are you ready or what? You and that bleedin' X-box!" the youth bellowed up towards the bedroom window. Alex followed the youth's eye line up towards the yellow light emitting from the small bedroom window. Suddenly the flimsy blue curtains shot back and a face appeared at the window.

"Me Ma says will you leave out the banging. I'll be with you in two bleedin' seconds Muggser, for Jaysus sake" the other youth said, opening the window wide.

Alex noted both names. He recognised "Burrener" as a Dublin colloquial name for the surname, Byrne. The name Muggser was probably self-explanatory, he decided.

Within minutes the two guys were together on the dimly-lit street. They set off at a casual pace down the narrow road. Once out of sight, Alex Woods leapt into action. He opened the car boot and pulled a wooden baseball bat from inside. Locking the car securely, he then set off at pace on the trail of the two younger men. Now Alex was in automatic mode. He knew exactly what he must do. There could be no other outcome. His single-mindedness drove him on, his pace increasing by the second. Alex could see the two ahead now and was closing in. Muggser pushed his counterpart playfully as they fooled about on the roadway. Alex's hearing was crystal clear. He began to pick up on words between the two.

"I say we go to the park. Some of the lads might be there" Muggser suggested. "Fuck that. Let's do something! Let's rob a gaff" Burrener replied with an evil cackle. Alex quickened his pace even more. By now he was within feet of the two. Muggser looked around curiously at him. He went to speak but Alex lashed out before he could say a word. He smashed the club into Muggser's face, sending the young man reeling backwards. Burrener stood motionless, trying to come to terms with what was happening. Alex turned on him, laying into him with the bat. He pounded it into the man's midriff, and then across his thin face. Burrener crumpled to the ground instantly. By now Muggser was climbing back to his feet. Alex strode forward again with menace. Blows rained down on the youth as he tried in vain to stand up. Muggser pleaded for mercy, blood now pouring from his mouth.

"Who the fuck? What did we do? Stop, enough" he mumbled. Alex paused for a second and gathered his strength. He waded in again with a series of heavy blows until Muggser lay crumpled on the ground. The younger man let out a final loud groan before falling silent. Immediately Alex turned his attention back to Burrener.

"Bastard! Break into houses will you? Hit old people? How do you like a taste of your own medicine?" Alex said in a crazed voice. He stood over Burrener, lashing out at every part of his body with the baseball bat. Burrener groaned in agony. He tried to protect his head with both hands. Only when Alex heard Muggser stir, did he relent. He strode across to his other victim and laid into him with his heavy boots. Muggser screamed in pain as he felt one of his ribs crack. He crumpled up in a ball to protect his body.

"Dirty little scumbag. You attacked my old man, you toe-rag. I'll fix you, once and for all" Alex said. He took it in turns to kick and beat Muggser to a pulp. By now the young man was only semi-conscious. As he lay lifeless, Alex returned to Burrener.

"Call yourself a fucking burglar? A real burglar would have finished the job. Dozy twats. Thanks to you I'm left with a huge fucking problem!" he screamed, his eyes now wide with rage. The youth made one last effort to clamber to his feet. Instantly Alex smashed the club against his head. The thud seemed to reverberate into the night air. Burrener crumpled onto the cold concrete pavement again.

Alex could hear voices in the distance. Still he was not finished. He aimed one last deliberate heavy blow at Burrener's right arm. Then he casually walked across to where Muggser lay and repeated the deed.

"You won't be climbing through any windows in Blackrock for a while lads" he panted, leaning on the bloodied baseball bat for support. Alex stood grinning as he surveyed his victims for a moment. He then walked away, shoving the baseball bat under his arm.

"These clothes will have to go straight into the washing machine. Dear oh dear" he sniggered.

Alex tossed the bat back inside the trunk and drove off. He felt good in himself. Just for a while he had forgotten all about Stacey and Tony Lee. He climbed into his white Mondeo and started the engine. Alex then hired the radio and sang along to the music. It was time to return to his empty flat to ponder his next move.

Two days later Alex received a call from the hospital. His father had had a stroke, and was in a bad way. Alex rushed from his job to be at his father's bedside. Tom Woods was in an induced coma. There was damage to his brain. Alex had a million questions, but it appeared that there was no one to answer them. Eventually later that evening, he managed to speak to a doctor who was treating his father.

"What brought all this on? Was it his angina? Was it the medication? He was fine up until a few weeks ago. Will he be all right?" Alex asked. He sat in the small office at the end of the corridor. Tom Woods was a private patient, and in a room just yards away.

"Your father is a fit man, so hopefully he will respond well to treatment. Alex, we may have to operate. There's swelling to the brain. We can't allow him to remain like that. Several things may have triggered this off. Perhaps Tom should have been on a different tablet. It appears that he hasn't been to a doctor for many years. It seems that he has simply being renewing his prescription. My guess is that he has outgrown that particular pill. He should have had a check-up months ago. It happens a lot with older men. They feel as though they are invincible. This might have happened to him at anytime, who's to say?" Doctor Greene answered.

"He had a break-in some weeks ago. He tackled the burglars himself. Would this have led to his condition?" Alex asked. Doctor Greene looked thoughtful.

"We can't say. It certainly would not have helped. It might have put unnecessary pressure on the heart, but again, I cannot be definite. Alex, we need your permission to operate. There really is no alternative" Doctor Green stressed.

Alex agreed. He signed the necessary papers and wandered slowly from the office.

He had wanted his father dead, but now he was not so sure. The lines between what was right and what he required from life were now blurred. The fear of being totally alone in the world scared him. Yet if his father lived, Tom Woods would surely revert to being the overbearing parent that he had become.

Alex sat in his car and stared ahead at the hospital.

"I wonder did I kill either of those scumbags. I sincerely hope so. If not, I will definitely go back and finish them off" he thought. Alex slouched back in his seat. He considered the matter again.

"No, my old son, that's not the way to go about it. These pups are well used to a beating. They fight among themselves all of the time. Think Alex, think. What else could we do?" he thought. It came to him in a flash.

"That's it, perfect! If the old man dies, why not get them for manslaughter? If not manslaughter, there are a string of offences that they could be done for. There's grievous bodily harm and breaking and entering for a start. I could get those dirtbags locked up for a long time, and when they come out I could have someone shoot them. Better still do it yourself, but you'll have to be careful" Alex reasoned. His brain was alive again, considering every possibility for his adversaries.

Alex drove away, a thin smile on his lips. He had things to think about once again, and that's when he was most content.

"And don't worry Tony Lee. I'm not forgetting you, my old mate" he sneered.

"Tony, I've been thinking about what you told me. Everything that you've said over the last few weeks adds up to one thing" Jodie said. She had just returned from her nightly jog, and was now doing her exercises on the mat in the hallway. This greatly amused Tony. He considered that he got all of the exercise that he needed by cycling. The fact that Jodie was so thin and fit also made Tony question why she needed to go through such an extensive routine every evening.

"And what conclusion have you come to, Doctor Jodie?" he said with a grin.

"There must have been a falling out in your family. Your Aunt Mary in England must have a reason for not responding to Jan's phone calls. Wouldn't you think that she might have at least sent a Mass card? Maybe she fell out with Jan and your mother for a reason. Why not write to her?" Jodie suggested. Tony continued to watch her exercise with great amusement.

"Why put yourself through all of that Jodie? Buy a bicycle and you can come for a cycle with me in the evenings" he said, failing to respond to her question.

"I enjoy running. I've always done it. Cycling is so old-fashioned. Then there are punctures and chains coming loose! No thanks; I'll stick to my runs every night, thank you very much!" Jodie said, panting heavily. She struggled to her feet, straightening out her white tracksuit in the process.

"Well, are you gonna write to her?" Jodie asked. Tony blinked, finally realising that the spectacle was over.

"What? Yeah, maybe. Why don't you go and have your shower and I'll cook us a calorie-free pizza?" he smirked.

"Not for me. I'll have lettuce on rye bread. I'm watching my figure" she laughed as she walked upstairs.

"So am I love, I'm watching your figure too!" he grinned.

Following their beating, Burrener and Muggser had been taken to hospital by ambulance. Their proper names were Joseph Byrne and Bernard Claffey. Claffey was the more seriously injured of the two. He had suffered several cracked ribs, a fractured skull, a shattered arm and a broken nose. Both of his thumbs were broken. Byrne too had cracked ribs and internal bleeding among his several injuries. Both had broken fingers from trying to protect themselves from the blows.

Some days later, the police came to the hospital to interview both youths. The two were well known to the gardai. They had been in and out of juvenile detention for much of their young lives. Already twenty-two-year-old Muggser had been incarcerated in Wheatfield Prison for burglary and a series of muggings. Joseph Byrne had also come to police attention for break-ins and petty crimes, but without concrete proof, Burrener had never been sentenced as an adult.

Who did this to you Claffey? You must have crossed the wrong person this time" Sergeant Ryan asked. Bernard Claffey continued to stare at the ceiling from his hospital bed.

"Why don't you piss off and catch some real criminals? You know, the ones going around selling drugs? The ones with shotguns in the back of their cars? Are you too fuckin' scared? Why are you here bothering innocent law-abiding citizens, such as my good self and Mister Byrne?" Bernard Claffey replied dryly.

"Who did this to you? Did you recognise them? Can you give me a description?" Sergeant Ryan persisted. He sat in a plain chair next to the bed with a small notebook in hand.

"I fell down the stairs. I believe the same fate befell Mister Byrne" Claffey sneered.

"Very well, have it your way. The next time you might not be so lucky" The policeman said abruptly in his country accent. He snapped shut the notebook and put it back in his navy jacket pocket. Sergeant Ryan got to his feet and stood over Bernard Claffey.

"Last chance Muggser lad. Give me a name. They've left you two in a right mess" he said.

"Why don't you get the fuck out of here, you dickhead!" Muggser snarled. The policeman turned on his heels and walked away. He went to see his colleague who had been interviewing Joseph Byrne. The younger policeman shook his head as he approached.

"Nothing?" Sergeant Ryan asked.

"Not a word! Struck dumb overnight!" the fresh-faced policeman replied.

"I'll bet that drugs are involved. It's a natural progression for these yobs. Eventually they'll be found shot in some undergrowth in the mountains" he replied.

The following day, the surgeon operated on Tom Woods. Alex paced the waiting room. He had already been at the hospital for over two hours. It was early afternoon before a doctor came to speak to him.

"He's out of theatre now, but he's very weak. We cannot tell yet how his body will react. The surgeons are hopeful that he will make a good recovery. The next forty-eight hours are critical" Dr. Greene said.

"Can I see him now Doctor?" Alex asked.

"Er, not just yet. He's sleeping. Your father is very weak Mr. Woods. Perhaps he might be strong enough tomorrow. I suggest that you go home and get some rest. There's no more that we can do for now" Doctor Greene replied.

Angie returned from work that evening. Harry sat playing with his Playstation console, plugged into the television.

"Is Gina not in yet?" Angie asked. Harry barely looked up from the screen.

"Naw! She's working late. She said that she would be home about eight" he replied. Angie went to the kitchen to cook her evening meal. Some minutes later Harry followed. At Angie opened the fridge, she felt Harry brush against her black jeans. Angie froze, but said nothing.

"I'm going to have a shower. Do you need to use the bathroom?" he asked. Angie shook her head. She forced a smile, presuming he had rubbed against her by accident.

"No thanks Harry, you work away" she said. Harry walked to the door before turning back to face her.

"You can always join me if you like?" he said with a grin. Angie was stunned. She was not certain if he was joking or deadly serious.

"I...no thanks" she stammered.

"Suit yourself. The offer stands. Follow me in if you like. I'll leave the door open!" he said, continuing to grin back at her. Angie tried to stay composed. She watched as he disappeared into the bathroom. The gush of water from the shower could be heard from the kitchen. Angie O'Rourke tried hard to stay rational and calm. It was the first time that she had been alone with Harry. She cancelled any thought of cooking and opted for a quick sandwich. Harry was singing now, as if he had not got a care in the world. The bathroom door stood open. Angie made a coffee and took her snack to her room. She locked the bedroom door and quietly sat on the bed.

Her mind was in turmoil. The more she considered what he had said, the more convinced she was that Harry Brand had meant every word. Angie felt trapped. With nowhere else to go, she had to think quickly. Moving back to her parents was hardly an option. They lived miles away, making it virtually impossible to travel to and from work.

Angie reasoned that she had never given Harry any encouragement to come on to her. She tried to make sense of what happened, but to no avail. As she finished her sandwich, she heard a low tapping on her door.

"What's wrong Harry, I'm tired" she said in a quiet voice.

"You don't want to be speaking to Gina about this. There's only one person that she will believe anyway. Think before you open your mouth" he said. Angie listened for further sounds outside. Eventually she heard the Playstation start up again. Angie put her head in her hands and began to cry softly. Harry was right of course. Gina would never believe her. She lay down on the bed and eventually fell asleep.

When Gina arrived home, Harry had already cooked her something to eat.

"Hiya love, how was your day?" he asked cheerfully. He kissed her on the cheek as she threw off her grey jacket.

"Boring, but we need the money. I'll have to do this overtime once it's on offer. Where's Angie? Is she not in yet?" Gina said. Harry looked about the flat as if missing Angie for the first time.

"Yeah, she's here all right. Oh, I think that she said she was tired. Probably grabbing forty winks!" he said with a chuckle.

Later Gina knocked lightly on Angie's door.

"Are you awake sleepy-head?" she asked in a low voice. Angie opened her eyes and looked around. The truth about what had occurred quickly dawned on her. She simply could not tell Gina. Angie rose from her bed and unlocked the door. "I must have dozed off. Is everything all right?" Angie said. Gina entered the room as she often did. They sat and talked for a while before Harry called Gina. Her favourite programme was starting on the television.

"Come out and join us. We can watch a bit of telly" Gina said.

"In a while. I'm just going to have a quick shower" Angie answered. She closed the door behind Gina and went to get some clothes. When Angie opened the small drawer containing her underwear, she noticed that her clothes were not as she had left them. Tears welled up in her eyes again as she realised that Harry had been in her room. He had been at her underwear, and she could feel goose pimples all over her body. Angie took some items from the drawer and took them to the bathroom with her. She would rinse them and dry them on the bedroom radiator. Angie vowed that from now on, she would keep her room locked at all times. She could never feel safe again alone with Harry.

Muggser silently wheeled his wheelchair into the ward where Burrener lay in bed. Burrener's eyes widened. He had not seen his pal since the beating almost a week ago.

"Fucking hell! You look awful!" Muggser said with a dark grin.

"You're not bad yourself! Burrener replied without emotion. Muggser parked the wheelchair as near as possible to the bed.

"We have to talk. I've been thinking of what that prick said when he gave us the going-over. He knew that we broke into houses. He said that we hit his old man. What did he say to you?" Muggser said quietly. Burrener could barely speak. His face was lined with stitches, and his neck was in a brace. There were bandages around his head and ear.

"Yeah, I've been thinking about that too. He mentioned Blackrock. We only did three jobs out that way. One was that house where the people were away on holidays. The other one was that old dear who set the dogs on us. That only leaves that old geezer with the window open. But we got absolutely nothing at that gaff" Burrener replied.

"But that has to be it, see? All we did was knock his old man to the floor. For Jaysus sake, it was nothing!" Muggser said casually.

"I slapped the old man about a bit" Burrener added dryly. Muggser was deep in thought.

"Yeah, I gave him the digs too. Still, if this swine wants to play games, so can we" he said. Burrener appeared interested for the first time.

"When I get fixed up, I'm going straight back to that gaff to burn it down. With a bit of luck that toe-rag will be inside it at the time" Burrener said with venom. Muggser sighed and closed his eyes for a second.

"You never think, do you? I cased that gaff, remember? It was owed by that old geezer. The old man lived alone. Besides, if you burn it down, the insurance will pay, what's the good in that? No, we need to get that scumbag ourselves. Or maybe batter the old man. That would really piss off our friend!" Muggser replied calmly.

"Yeah, already I feel better. What did you tell the cops?" Burrener said.

"Don't be thick! Tell those bastards nothing! Now, there's something else that that scumbag said that has me baffled. He said something about leaving him with a problem, and he mentioned us not finishing the job properly-something like that" Muggser said quietly.

"You mean, as if he wanted the house robbed? Maybe to get the insurance money?" Burrener reasoned with a sly grin on his battered face.

"No, there was something else, something that I can't put my finger on. It's as if he wanted us to get away with it or something. Don't worry, it will come to me" Muggser replied.

"Jaysus Muggser, by body is in bits. Even going to the loo is an episode!" Burrener replied.

"Whatever! I need to go back to the ward before that skinny nurse finds me. I robbed this wheelchair off some old dear! It doesn't half get itchy under these bandages. My knee is busted, and I'm coughing up blood" Muggser said. Burrener offered his pal a sly grin.

"Keep the head up Muggser; we'll soon be back in business!" Burrener said.

CHAPTER SEVENTEEN

HOLD ME

Alex Woods folded up the plain sheet of paper and put it in an envelope. The note contained the nicknames and the addresses of the two men that he had beaten up. He addressed the envelope to the police station which was dealing with the break-in at his father's home. Alex had not signed the note. He had merely stated that this was a tip-off, and that he had information that these youths had been involved in several burglaries in the Blackrock area. Alex put the letter with the rest of the outgoing mail and left it with Michelle at reception.

"If the cops follow that through, it might fix those little bastards" he thought quietly.

At Tony Lee's house, Jodie was preparing for her evening run. Tony was busy putting up shelving in the kitchen.

"Why not give that run a miss and help me out here?" Tony said. Jodie laughed back at him as she did some warm-up exercises.

"My only night off from running is Saturday. You know that. You decided on shelving, so you finish it! If I'm honest Tony, I would prefer a totally new kitchen. That unit is so dated!" Jodie said. Tony stopped what he was doing and stood back to examine the old presses.

"I dunno Jodie, we should get a few more years out of it" he said thoughtfully. Jodie sighed and looked to the ceiling.

"You have the cash Tony, splash out a bit. Life is for living!" Jodie remarked. Tony released a long sigh as he considered his response.

"I have the money okay Jodie, but I don't want to blow it. I'm afraid that I might need it in the future" he replied. Jodie shook her head in dismay.

"We have the money coming in for God's sake! Both of us are working. This house could be lovely if we spent a few bob on it. Painting and shelving are all very well, but it's only cosmetic. The place needs a major overhaul. And don't use Jan as an excuse" Jodie said forcefully.

Tony grinned and looked at her.

"Is this our first argument?" he chuckled. Jodie shook her head in frustration.

"I'm going for my run. It will help me to calm down" she sighed.

Outside, Alex Woods watched from a distance. He sat in his car on the far side of the street, a few doors down from number eighty-eight. Alex had observed the house many times now. Sometimes he watched in the morning before heading off to work, other times he sat outside Tony's house in the evening. He had also spent some weekend time viewing the comings and goings at Tony Lee's home.

Alex watched as Jodie Callaghan jogged by on the far side of the road.

"Bang on time again little Jodie. The dark evenings are closing in. Wearing those earphones can be very dangerous when crossing the road!" he sniggered. Alex's mobile phone rang. He answered immediately on his hands-free set.

Alex's face turned pale. It was the hospital on the phone. His father had taken a bad turn.

"I'll be right there" Alex said quietly. Alex drove away at speed.

When Alex arrived at the hospital, he was ushered to a small administration room.

"I'm afraid that your father didn't make it Mr. Woods" Doctor Greene told him. Alex sat on the plain black chair staring back at the middle-aged doctor. The doctor offered a long narrative of why Tom Woods's heart could not hold out. It was just a jumbled load of words to Alex. Nothing was sinking in. He felt numb, and yet his father's passing was something that he had wished for months now.

"Did he regain consciousness? Did he speak to anybody?" Alex asked the doctor.

The grey-haired man peered over his black spectacles at him. He shook his head.

"Sadly not. He was on strong medication. Your father would not have felt any pain. I know that is little consolation for you" Doctor Greene replied.

"This all happened because of that break-in at the house. That's what triggered all of this" Alex said crossly. The doctor looked uneasy.

"Well, that's a matter for the police, I'm afraid" he said.

Alex went to the room where his father had passed away. The room was darkened, and Tom Woods looked as though he was sleeping peacefully. Alex stood at the end of the bed for a moment. He felt nothing for his father. Apart from working together, they had never really been close. When Alex was younger, his father had always been too busy working to pay Alex much attention. Alex stood staring at the corpse, his young life flashing before him. "Well, I'm gonna enjoy my life from now on, old man. You had your chance, and look at you now! I have a few scores to settle, and then I'll sell the business and live the high life! What a fool you were!" he thought.

Alex then turned on his heels and walked away. It was as if a chapter of his life had ended. He felt no emotion or guilt. It was time to move on.

Tony Lee admired the new shelving over the kitchen units. It would do for now. Privately he had decided that Jodie was right after all. The house definitely needed revamping. He would not tell her of his re-thinking just yet. It would be a surprise for her, he decided. Tony vowed that he would get an estimate for a new kitchen while Jodie was not around. He might even stretch to a conservatory and a few other touches. Jodie had stuck by him, and she deserved at least the basic comforts of life. The cosmetic attempt at decorating over the past months had only proved to him that he was merely papering over the cracks. If he and Jodie were to spend their lives together at number eighty-eight, then he owed it to her to make the house as comfortable as possible. Jodie's birthday was fast approaching, and although Tony Lee was not great at committing, he was seriously considering proposing to her on that special day.

Tom Woods was buried a few days later. The man was well-known in the motor trade, and was a popular businessman around the Dublin scene. His funeral was well-attended, but with no other close relatives, Alex Woods stood with Terry Thompson. Most of Alex's work colleagues attended, with the garage closed for two days. People offered their condolences, but Alex was barely listening. His brain was awash with ideas and plans for the future.

The following day, Alex received a call from the police. It was regarding the break-in at his father's house, which Alex was now considering moving back in to.

The police confirmed to him that they were aware that his father had died, and that they were still investigating the burglary.

"Well, have you any fresh leads? I mean, this is almost a murder now" Alex replied impatiently. The policeman informed Alex that the matter could never be treated as murder. At best it would be aggravated assault. Even a case of manslaughter was out of the question, he said.

"What about fingerprints? I saw the police search for prints at the house. If the criminals are on record, can't you match them up or something?" Alex asked.

"Yes sir, I understand your frustration, but this takes time. Let's say that we are giving this our full attention at the moment. We expect to make some progress in the coming days" the officer stated.

Alex put down the receiver, a smug grin appearing on his lips.

"Those two boyos are going to jail. And when they get out, I'll smash them again!" he grinned.

Alex Woods was now a very busy man. Already he had paid for a state-of-the-arts alarm to be installed at the house in Blackrock. H e was implementing new work practices at the garage, taking a closer look at the stock, and eyeing anyone who he considered a slack worker. Behind his back, some of the staff still joked about him being jilted on his wedding day, but to his face everyone appeared polite and friendly. Everyone knew all about Alex's bad moods.
Alex was planning a long holiday, but as of yet had not decided where he should go. His priority was to ensure that the business was on a sound footing, in order to obtain the best possible price for any future sale.

Three nights later, Alex again sat outside number eighty-eight St. Oliver's Road. The evenings were gradually getting darker. Alex watched as Jodie set off on her hour-long jog. By now he knew her exact course, having parked in different locations over the past weeks. Alex had drawn a map of her usual route, marking the best spot for any possible attack. He had pinpointed any area that might have a security camera, such as local business's or shops. One area in particular interested Alex. Jodie ran by a park on a straight stretch of road. The area was shaded by trees, both on the pavement and from within the park. Jodie crossed the street at the corner, and turned for home, heading back down the far side of the road. Alex had almost perfected his plan. To be doubly-sure that his plan passed without a hitch, all he needed was for the spot to be devoid of witnesses.

He watched as Tony Lee set off on his silver bicycle. Tony's pattern was not as straightforward as Jodie's. His bicycle outings were sporadic, venturing out in the evenings only when the humour took him.

"There you go Tony, enjoy your little trip. Soon you'll be coming home to an empty house again, just as I do. I asked myself what would hurt you worst? I could have given you a good kicking, but what's the sense in that? I could have run you off the road, but then you would have just presumed it was some nutcase driver. No. This way you will suffer maximum pain. You'll face all of those lonely evenings without your precious Jodie, just as I have had to do without Stacey" he thought.

Tony passed Jodie on his journey towards The Dublin Mountains. Once he left early enough, he would reach his favourite spot before dark. It was nice to look out over his native city for a short while before turning for home. It was a regular destination for him when he ventured out either at weekend or in the summer evenings.

"Get the lead out! Come on, faster!" he yelled. Jodie offered him a smile. She barely heard him above the din of her music on her iphone. Jodie always played her music loud while out jogging, another detail noted by Alex Woods. "See you later! Don't get a puncture!" Jodie called back without breaking her stride.

The following day, Stacey Boyd phoned Angie O'Rourke. It was just after one o'clock, and Angie was on her lunch break.

"How's things now with you Stacey? How are you coping?" Angie asked.

"I'm good Angie, I'm getting there. How are things in Dublin?" Stacey replied. Angie decided not to burden her friend regarding her encounter with Harry. "We're all fine. I'm back at the apartment as you know. Jodie's doing well. She's still living with Tony" Angie said.

"In that creepy house? She's welcome to it! Listen Angie, I need to get back to Dublin. My job is still open. I've been on to my boss this morning. If I don't resume by Monday I could be in trouble. Can you ask Gina about me moving back in to my old room? I feel awful for asking, but it might sound better coming from you" Stacey replied. Angie O'Rourke laughed gently down her mobile phone.

"It's already sorted, silly! I'll mention it to Gina, but she has already said that it's not a problem" Angie assured her.

"Great! It will be like old times-well, maybe not quite, but still..." Stacey said. She sounded more upbeat than Angie had expected, and Angie questioned her pal on how she was getting on at home with her parents.

"Oh, that part is okay. Mum is fussing all over me, and Dad keeps asking if I'm okay, but I don't know anyone over here. When I go out in the evening, it's with my parents, and I think that they only go out to please me. I'm sure that if I was back in Dublin, they would happily stay in and watch television at the weekend. That's why I have to come home Angie. I'll lose my reason if I don't get away" Stacey said.

Angie smiled contently. It would be great to have her old pal back in her life. She would feel safer at the apartment too. Lately Angie had avoided contact with Harry as much as possible. With Stacey around, it would feel much like old times.

"Okay, when will you get back? I can hardly wait! And the extra rent will help too, so Gina will be pleased!" Angie said.

"And Harry, I suppose" Stacey replied.

"Yes, and Harry" Angie said, the very name almost sticking in her throat.

Muggser and Burrener were now discharged from hospital. They sat at the corner of the street on the edge of the kerb. Muggser's left arm was still in plaster, and both had to continue to attend the hospital as out-patients.

"I've been thinking about that scumbag who battered us. There's something really fishy about that night" Muggser said with an evil stare.

"I agree pal. It's as if he wished that we had stabbed the old man to death or something" Burrener replied flippantly. In a flash Muggser homed in on the idea.

"That's it! It has to be! What if that bloke wanted his old man out of the way? What if he stood to inherit a fortune or something?" Muggser said, his smile growing by the second.

Burrener seemed less convinced.

"You're watching too much bleedin' telly. That lunatic was no toff. He sounded like an ordinary working class bloke. Fucking millionaire indeed!"Burrener sneered. Muggser seemed to re-think his reasoning.

"Well, maybe not a millionaire, but maybe he was due to come into cash if the old man died. Jaysus, that has to be it! What if the old fellow owns a shop or something?" Muggser said. Burrener thought about it for a minute.

"You know what Muggser; you could be on to something. It sounds a bit far-fetched, but yeah, it would make sense. The trouble is, we'll never know, but it makes me feel good that we fucked up his plans!" Burrener laughed.

Two nights later, Alex sat parked up on St. Oliver's Road. He had made up his mind that tonight was the night to carry out his plan. The car he was driving that night belonged to the garage. It was due to be resprayed the following day. He watched as Jodie set off in her white tracksuit and trainers.

"Bang on time again! Jodie, you'll be the fittest corpse in the graveyard!" he chuckled under his breath. The evening was overcast, and night was already closing in. Alex eyed up Tony's house in the distance.

"You're in for a troublesome long night, Mister Lee!" he thought quietly.

Minutes later, Alex Woods turned the key in the ignition. The red Ford Fiesta started up first time. Alex set off at a moderate pace on the quiet street. He could almost guess the exact spot where Jodie Callaghan would be.

Tony Lee left his house on his bicycle. His journey to The Phoenix Park had almost been cancelled because of the rain forecast for later that evening. At the last minute Tony had decided to take a chance. Tonight a trip to the mountains was out of the question because of the weather. Tony had his green rain gear folded up neatly on the carrier over the rear wheel. He cast a furtive glance skywards as he slipped deftly out through the old green gate with its tense spring. The slamming noise barely registered with Tony as he mounted his bike. He would catch up with Jodie further along the way. Tony cycled off, still unsure if his trip was a wise move or not.

Alex Woods pulled in alongside the park. He had already passed Jodie. All he had to do now was watch until she was further up the street. The overhanging trees made the pavement area appear almost as a train tunnel. Alex checked his mirrors and had a good look around. The spot was perfect. There was no one around, apart from a man walking his dog well inside the park. Jodie jogged by across the road, her blue earphone wire dangling across her tracksuit. Alex waited until she was further up the perfectly straight road.

Tony cycled around the corner onto the tree-lined road. He kept an eye out for any sighting of Jodie. It was difficult to spot anyone among the heavy foliage of the trees. Jodie's obsession with running and exercising amused him. Her slim, fit body was perfectly honed, and Tony considered her jogging passion a total waste of time. She was as fit as he was. Tony never gained weight because of his cycling, and had never been a member of a gym.

Jodie Callaghan neared the corner of the street. She was halfway along her regular route now. The clouds were slowly gathering overhead. Jodie always felt better once she reached the corner of Mayhew Road, and knew that she was heading for home. Sometimes if there was traffic coming, Jodie would jog on the spot until it was clear to cross the road. This evening there was nothing approaching from either direction. The traffic was always light anyway. Mayhew Road was well off the main roads and mainly used by pedestrians. Jodie stepped out onto the quiet road. Her favourite band, Queen, were blasting out their hit, "Radio Gaga" through her headphones. Jodie glanced down the street from where she had come. There was a red car approaching, but she should easily cross the road before it reached the corner. The car appeared to be accelerating faster and faster by the second, but Jodie was already on the road by now.

Tony was further down the street. He caught a glimpse of Jodie's white tracksuit up ahead. There was a red car between him and her, and so his view was obstructed somewhat. Tony looked to the heavy sky. Perhaps The Phoenix Park was not such a good idea after all. He considered curtailing his trip. Before he could decide, Tony looked on in shock at events further up the street.

Alex Woods drove straight at Jodie as she tried to reach the far side of the street. She was three-quarters of the way across when he veered straight at her. The right side of the car caught her full force. The headlight and wing of the car smashed into her body sending her reeling towards the kerb. Jodie's head crashed against the edge of the kerb as her body flopped lifelessly to the ground. In seconds, Alex Woods had turned the corner to the left and sped away. He checked his mirrors again before slowing down. Now all he had to do was make the ten minute journey back to the garage, and exchange the Ford Fiesta for his own car.

"Yiihaa!" he screamed at the top of his voice, delighted with what he had done.

"Let's hope that the little bitch is dead" he laughed as he drove on.

The awful truth dawned on Tony Lee as he saw Jodie's limp body lying to the side of the road.

"Jesus no, please no!" he screamed. He pedalled faster now, praying that she was not too badly injured. When he reached the corner Tony flung his silver bicycle to the kerb. He could see the blood dripping from Jodie's head and mouth.

"Oh shit, shit! Jodie, hang on love, hang on!" he yelled. A black car slowly turned the corner and crawled to a halt. Tony pulled his mobile phone from his jacket and phoned an ambulance. The elderly man rushed from his car and ran to Jodie's side.

"It was a red car, a small one. It was a hit and run. Did you see him?" Tony asked in a panic. The bewildered gent scratched his head.

"A red car did pass me, I think. I'm not sure though. No son, I'm sorry" the grey-haired man said.

Tony whipped off his jacket and knelt down beside Jodie's still body.

"It's okay love, help is on the way. Hang on. Please hang on" he whispered.

Tony stroked her hair, pushing her pony-tail away from her face. Jodie lay on her side, her eyes opening and closing. She tried to speak, but nothing came out. Tony slipped his jacket under her head.

"It's okay, really it is Jodie. Try to stay conscious. The ambulance will be here in a second" Tony said. He was starting to panic inside. The blood still trickled slowly from Jodie's mouth, and her hair was now soaked in sticky red blood. "Don't move her son, it's best to leave it to the experts" the old man said. Tony barely heard him. His eyes tried to take in the scene. A young couple out walking sprinted up to the corner. They looked unsure at how to help. The man took off his brown coat and spread it over Jodie's body. Tony noticed that the left knee was ripped open on Jodie's tracksuit bottoms. Her knee was cut, and he also saw a graze along her cheek. But the huge gash to the back of Jodie's head was his real worry.

"We'll soon have you fixed up Jodie, it will be all right" Tony said.

"That's it, keep talking to her" the young woman said, leaning across Tony and patting him on the shoulder.

Alex Woods parked the red Fiesta in the garage to the rear of the showrooms. He went immediately to the front of the car and examined it.

"Dear oh dear! The headlight is shattered. Well, that will have to be replaced for a start! Those dents will have to be pulled out too. Add that to the respray job, and there won't be much profit in this one" he sneered. Alex casually looked at the passenger door. It was badly scraped from an earlier accident, which was the real reason for the car needing to be resprayed. It was to be sprayed black the following morning.

Alex went to the stores and quickly located a new headlight for the Fiesta. Within minutes he had replaced the old one, tossing it into the large metal bin.

"Good as new! Sorry we can't say the same for Jodie!" he grinned.

Jodie spluttered as she tried to breathe through the blood. In the distance, Tony could hear the ambulance's siren. Jodie tried to speak again. Tony put his ear to her mouth.

"Hold me" she said in a gulping, faint voice. Tears streamed down Tony's face. He lay beside her, his arms around her. The rain began to fall, softly at first. Tony could smell the freshly cut grass from the nearby park. The siren tone was louder now. He looked around helplessly as he cradled her in his arms. Still the rain poured down.

"Hang on Jodie, the ambulance is here, it's gonna be okay" he said through his tears. Her eyes rolled back in her head. She coughed again spitting out blood. Her body convulsed suddenly. Tony held on to her tighter.

The ambulance screeched to a halt just yards away. The couple and the elderly man drew back to allow both paramedics through. A police car turned the corner slowly and pulled up at the opposite pavement. One paramedic gently moved Tony aside and knelt down beside Jodie. The lady beside him pulled Tony to her.

"Let them do their job son" she said, embracing him.

Alex Woods took a last look around the garage. Everything was as it should be. He switched off the lights and set the alarm. It was dark outside now. He strode to his car and set off for home. On the way he checked on his appearance in the rear-view mirror. Alex felt smug about what he had just done. He basked in what he perceived as his cleverness. For Alex it was a game. It was all about the plotting and attention to detail. Soon he would be home and could check the news. If Jodie was dead, it would feature either on the internet, or on the radio or television. If she was just injured, Alex would have to re-think his next move.

The younger paramedic shook his head as he looked to the ambulance driver. They could do no more. They had carried out C.P.R, and tried to open Jodie's air ways. Her head injuries had been too severe. Jodie Callaghan was dead. The rain cascaded down now. Tony barely noticed it. Already the police were talking to the elderly man and to the young couple. Neither had seen anything of note. Tony was too distraught to speak. He insisted on travelling in the ambulance with Jodie's body. Another police vehicle arrived, this time a white box van. They would check the scene for clues, examine tyre marks, and speak to residents in nearby houses. This was just a formality. Any homes in the vicinity were too far away from the scene to have witnessed anything of note. Eventually the white van would leave with Tony's bicycle. Alex Woods had judged well. There would be no evidence.

People had gathered by the side of the road. As the ambulance pulled away, the small crowd gradually lost interest. The elderly man got into his car and the young couple drifted away. All that remained was Tony's bicycle and the two police vehicles. The police examined the collision spot for any evidence. They found nothing of note at the scene. Jodie had died from the impact of her head against the pavement, rather than from the blow from the car driven by Alex Woods.

At the hospital, Tony wandered around A&E in a daze. He would slump down on a seat, only to get up again and pace the room. He fiddled with his mobile phone, but could not think who to phone. Eventually the name of Erik Ngombiti caught his eye. Tony rang his work colleague and slowly explained what had happened. Erik told him that he was on his way to the hospital. The tears came again to Tony's eyes. He was inconsolable. A young nurse led him away. She directed him to a room where Jodie's body was laid out. Tony flopped down beside her body and cried like never before.

When Tony eventually drifted outside into the corridor, a policeman stood some yards away with his hands behind his back. He wandered slowly towards Tony.

"I understand that it was your girlfriend that died this evening? My condolences to you. Would you be up to making a short statement just yet?" the policeman asked. He was a giant of a man, well over six foot six, and broad in the shoulders. Tony felt like talking.

"Sure, I don't know what I can tell you. It happened so fast" Tony said.

"Did you manage to see the vehicle involved?" the policeman asked.

"I didn't see the make. It was red, maybe an Astra or a Mini. It was travelling at speed. It looked like he lost control for a minute. He turned left at the top of Mayhew Road, and sped off. The wing of the car caught Jodie. I guess she hit the pavement. There was blood on the edge of the kerb" Tony said quietly.

"Aye lad, we saw that. Is there anything else that you can tell me? Did the car actually pass you on the street?" The policeman asked. Tony thought about it for a few seconds.

"Well, no, I don't think that it did" he said, realising the fact for the first time.

"That's a long straight road lad; the chances are that he passed you at some stage. It may come to you later. You can make an official statement sometime in the future. In the meantime, try and recall the make of the car, and if the driver overtook you. You may have caught a glimpse of him without realising it. The only alternative is that the car was already parked on the street and pulled out before you got to him. We will be making house to house inquiries anyway, but take your time and see does anything come to mind" the policeman said. Tony nodded. In his emotional state, it was hard to remember the exact details. The policeman wished him well once again and left. Tony stood alone, unsure where to go or what to do. The following day Tony would make a statement. It would leave the police with nothing more to go on.

Moments later Erik Ngombiti appeared. Tony had forgotten that he had called him. The tears came again for Tony. Erik put an arm around his shoulders and led him away to his car.

Jodie's parents decided that their daughter would be buried in the small village that she had grown up in. Angie and Tony phoned each other regularly over the next few days. Everyone was stunned by what had occurred to the young likeable girl. Angie was also in touch with Jodie's parents. She knew of the funeral arrangements, and was anxious to attend. It would mean Stacey driving the long distance to Kilkenny, something that Stacey was hardly keen on. She had never actually driven outside of Dublin, but was resigned to chauffeuring both Gina and Angie to the funeral. Then Angie dropped the bombshell.

"I promised Tony Lee that I would try to arrange a lift for him. I don't suppose..." Angie left the question hanging in mid air.

Gina and Harry sat watching a movie, but both turned quickly to gauge Stacey's response.

"Ah come on Angie, what do you take me for?" Stacey said with incredulity. Angie smiled her wicked smile.

"Okay, it was just a question. I don't know how he'll manage. I can't think of anyone else to ask" Angie sighed.

"Aw Angie, don't make me feel any worse than I do already" Stacey said with a frown. They were interrupted by the ringing of the doorbell. Angie went to answer it, but returned quickly with a look of shock on her face.

"You won't believe it, but it's Alex Woods at the door! I saw him through the peephole. What will I do?" Angie asked. Stacey gasped in disbelief.

"Get rid of him! I'm not here! I'm going to my bedroom Angie, and I'm locking the door. Under no circumstances say that I'm here. He will presume that I'm still in England" Stacey pleaded. Angie nodded. She waited until Stacey had vanished and went to the front door again.

"Alex, what a nice surprise!" Angie said with a false welcoming grin.

"I only wish that it was in different circumstances Angie. I've only just heard about poor Jodie. Naturally I could not call at Tony's home. I don't know where he lives anyway. Look, this is just a Mass card. I'm still in shock about this awful news. Jodie was such a nice girl, so full of life" he said. Alex looked genuinely upset, and Angie saw no alternative but to invite him in.

"Yes, we're all devastated Alex. Won't you come in for a minute? Jodie is to be buried in her home town" Angie said.

Alex entered the flat and greeted both Harry and Gina. He sat down without being invited to do so and quickly struck up a conversation.

"Yes, I couldn't believe it when I heard it. A hit-and-run I believe? He should be locked up for life. How do these people live with themselves?" Alex said, shaking his head in a mock show of grief.

Harry felt obliged to reply.

"The details are still sketchy. It seems that Tony Lee saw the whole thing" he said. Alex Woods felt his stomach churn over. This was news to him.

"Oh really? My goodness, how terrible" he managed to reply without losing his composure.

Angie then interjected.

"Unfortunately, Tony saw nothing to help the police. He was too far away" she said. Alex could feel the relief immediately.

"What a pity. Still, with a bit of luck the cops will catch that animal" he said with conviction. Angie nodded. Gina paused the movie on the television screen. It seemed to trigger a response in Alex Woods's mind.

"I had better be off. Don't let me spoil your film. I just felt compelled to offer my condolences. The last thing that I want is to interrupt your evening. I'm deeply sorry again folks for poor Jodie. God bless her" Alex said. He stood up and walked to the door. Angie saw him out as they all said goodbye. Stacey listened from her bedroom.

"He never even mentioned you" Angie said later to Stacey.

"Good! He obviously thinks that I'm still in England" Stacey said.

"The nerve of him calling anyway!" Gina remarked.

"Well, he did know Jodie, I suppose. As he said, he could hardly call on Tony!" Angie grinned mischievously. Stacey raised her light eyebrows. It made sense in a way, she realised.

"Speaking of Tony, what will I tell him?" Angie continued. Stacey looked to Gina for support. Perhaps Gina might see that Angie was being unreasonable. Gina, however, was keen to side with Angie O'Rourke.

"It's only out of respect for Jodie, and it's not as if you'll be alone with him Stacey" Gina reasoned. In despair, Stacey turned to Harry.

"Could you not drive Harry? That way Tony could go with you and Gina" she said. Harry Brand shook his head.

"Sorry Stacey, I already told you, I can't get the time off work. Anyway, I barely know Tony Lee" he replied. Angie fixed Stacey with a gaze.

"Well?" she asked. Stacey looked to the ceiling.

"I suppose it will be okay, but you sit in the front with me. I don't want any awkward moments with him" Stacey replied.

"Good, I'll text Tony now" Angie said with a smile.

Outside, Alex Woods looked back at the apartment block. He grinned smugly at having carried out his daring visit.

"What a laugh, and Stacey hiding in one of the bedrooms! Do they think that I'm stupid?" he thought. Alex had been watching the flat periodically since Jodie's death. He had seen Stacey enter the apartment after work. His sole purpose in calling was to glean any information about the hit-and-run. It was as he had hoped. Jodie's death had not been witnessed. The fact that Tony Lee was nearby was an added bonus for Alex. He could not have hoped for a better outcome. His only disappointment was that he did not see Tony Lee's face as Jodie lay dying.

CHAPTER EIGHTEEN

GIVING LOVE A HELPING HAND

The police swooped on the homes of Muggser and his friend Burrener. The two
were taken in for questioning at the local police station. Muggser put up a
stubborn defence. After about one hour of stalemate, he demanded to be
either charged or released, refusing to answer any further questions.
Detective Maguire continued to press the petty criminal for a confession.
"Leave it out Claffey; we have your fingerprints all over the houses. Both you
and Byrne are going down for a long time" the detective said in an assured
manner. Bernard Claffey had to think fast. He decided to call Detective
Maguire's bluff.
"That's bollocks! I was nowhere near Blackrock on those dates. You better get
out there and pick up the right guys. We're totally innocent" he said with a
confident laugh.
"Muggser, you are nailed down on this one. You had better get a good
solicitor. That old man died in hospital a few weeks ago. We're looking at
possibly manslaughter, maybe even murder" the elderly detective said.
The severity of the crime quickly registered with Muggser. However, the old
man's death was news to him. Muggser doubted that they could pin such a
serious crime on him Muggser reverted again to his earlier stance. He could tell
by the detective's face that the information was probably true.
"I have nothing more to say. From now on it's no comment-and that's to any
question! Now, either release me or let me have a solicitor" Muggser replied
abruptly.
"Sure it's best to just admit everything. If you co-operate with us we will do our
best to reduce the charges. Aggravated burglary or breaking and entry could
be agreed on. We could take a few other break-ins into consideration that we
might charge you with further down the line. That way, we can wipe them off

the books, and you can start again with a clean slate. The game is up for now Muggser. See sense and admit everything" Detective Maguire said in a persuasive voice.

"No comment" Muggser replied curtly. Detective Maguire pressed on regardless.

"Joseph Byrne has already confessed. He said that you were the one who pushed the old man" the detective continued.

"No comment" Muggser replied coldly. He knew that the detective was lying. Burrener would never admit to anything. It was just a ruse to get him to talk. The seasoned detective decided to try one more time.

"Admit to this one charge Muggser and I'll do my best to scrap the other charges" the detective said.

"No comment" Muggser replied.

Burrener was being questioned in another room by Detective Myles Forde. He too was having little joy.

"Bernard Claffey has already made a partial confession. He claims that you two were just snooping around when you spotted the open window. He claims that you suggested that you break-in, and that you pushed the old man to the ground" Detective Forde said.

Burrener was quick to dismiss his claims.

"What sort of a twat do you bleedin' take me for? Look, I was nowhere near that gaff that night. I was at home watching "The Bill!" Burrener cackled.

"I can see that you're not taking the matter seriously Joseph. A man lost his life because of that burglary. Think about that" Detective Forde said.

"I've already told you, I had nothing to do with it. Now either charge me, or let me get the fuck out of here" Burrener said forcefully.

"You're going to need a very good solicitor for this one Burrener!" the policeman said with a wry grin.

"I'll get free legal aid. I couldn't give a toss!" Burrener replied coldly.

As both Muggser and Burrener sat in the park some time later, they discussed their situation regarding the impending charges.

"We're going down for that bleedin' botched job Muggser, I just know it" Burrener said. He kicked violently at a nearby bush as the wandered through the deserted local park. It was dusk now, and a calm muggy evening.

"I'll tell you this, if I go down, I'll take that bastard with me-that swine who battered us" Muggser replied. They reached a park bench and slumped down. The wooden brown slats on the park seat were covered in graffiti, and had many names carved into it by penknife, including both Muggser's and Burrener's.

"We don't know where he lives or where he works" Burrener replied dryly. Muggser was already a step ahead of him.

"That's gonna be the easy part. We check out the old man's death. It has to have been in the newspapers in the last few weeks. We can check it on the internet. Already we have his address. That bastard has to be his son. Once we establish who the old man is, we can easily find out the rest" Muggser reasoned.

"We better do it fast Muggser. You heard those coppers. There bound to charge us in the next few days. They just want to be sure that they have all of their facts right" Burrener replied.

Muggser and Burrener sat across the road from Wood's Motors on a low wall. It was now a few days later.

"What did I tell you? There's the bastard driving off!" Muggser grinned. Burrener nodded as he watched Alex Woods' white Mondeo drive into the heavy afternoon traffic.

"Yep! You were right. That's him okay. I'd love to punch the fucker in the face right now!" Burrener snarled. Muggser shook his head in dismay and laughed out loud.

"That's why I do all of the thinking! Listen, if we touch him, the first thing he would do is call the police. Who are they gonna believe? The garage owner or us? Now, we either blackmail that bastard, or we make sure that he gets what's coming to him" Muggser said.

He outlined his plan to his less intelligent friend. They went over it several times until they were sure that they had got their story straight.

"I already know his address. You and me will pay him a visit soon. The only thing that bothers me is how he knew that we did the burglary. I hope that you haven't been shooting your mouth off to anybody" Muggser said in a grim voice.

"You know me Muggser. We never tell anybody anything, that's how we operate" Burrener replied. Muggser nodded quietly. He still could not understand how Alex Woods had traced them to the very street that they lived on. It was the one worry that Muggser could not figure out.

Stacey's car drew up outside number eight-eight St. Oliver's Road. Angie sat in the passenger seat, with Gina in the backseat alone.

"I'll get him" Angie said cheerfully. She climbed from the red Micra car and opened the gate. Stacey heard the gate groan and then slam shut again. It was all coming back to her again. She eyes the old house. Nothing had changed too much with Tony's home.

The green faded door still looked the same, albeit sporting a fresh coat of green paint. The only notable thing was that all of the windows had new curtains on show.

Tony opened the front door. Immediately Stacey noticed that the hallway was freshly decorated. Gone was the dreary paintwork and musty-looking decor. Stacey watched as Angie hugged her former boyfriend.

"What are you thinking Stacey? Gina asked. Stacey snapped out of her daydreaming.

"That house gives me the shivers. I never felt comfortable in that place" she said. Gina eyed Tony's home.

"It's a fine big place. It must be worth a few bob. All the houses around here are converted into flats. I bet that a developer would pay a right few quid for that old house" Gina remarked. Stacey laughed an uneasy laugh.

"Tell that to Tony! He will live there until he dies!" Stacey replied.

"Sssh! Here he is! Try and be nice Stacey, remember where we're going" Gina whispered.

Tony looked uncomfortable as he climbed into the back of the Micra.

"Thanks for doing this Stacey, I appreciate it very much. I don't know how I would have managed" Tony said, his voice filled with emotion.

"No bother Tony" Stacey replied. Gina patted him on the knee.

"How are you bearing up Tony?" she asked. Tony Lee gulped down some air.

"I'm all right Gina I suppose. Some days are better than others. It's crazy. Jodie was so full of life" he said in a quiet tone.

"We all miss her" Angie said.

The four were on their way back from Jodie's funeral. They sat in the same positions in Stacey's car as they had travelled down in. The mood was sombre now, a contrast from the more jocular one on the way to Kilkenny.

"It was nice of her family to ask us to stay over" Gina said, breaking the silence. Angie reached out and lowered the volume on the car radio. All were dressed mostly in black, with only Gina's navy-blue jacket standing out.

"Yes, we couldn't impose though. Besides, we all have work in the morning" Stacey replied. Angie nodded, but seemed deep in thought.

"Of course, but we should have gone for a drink. I know that you're driving Stacey, but I thought that was a bit rude" Angie said. Stacey shook her head in despair.

"We went back to the house for sandwiches and tea, didn't we? It's a long drive home Angie, I don't want to be driving home in the dark" Stacey answered. Angie said nothing for a moment, but her brain was working away quietly.

"Well, what about having a drink together when we get back to Dublin? The four of us will probably never be together again. Just for Jodie's sake, can't we raise a glass to her?" Angie suggested.

Stacey did not like the idea at all. Sitting down in a pub with Tony would feel awkward at best. Yet she did not want to appear as the wet blanket. Stacey hoped that Gina might disagree with Angie's suggestion. Tony Lee sat beside Gina, lost in his private thoughts. Stacey raised her eyebrows and looked in the rear-view mirror at Gina. Immediately Gina took up the subject.

"That's a brilliant idea Angie! I didn't want to say anything, but I felt bad too at not going for a drink with her parents" Gina said. Stacey's heart sank. Tony said nothing. He was still devastated by Jodie's death.

As they arrived back on the outskirts of Dublin, Stacey asked where she should park up.

"Just drive back to our apartment. We can have a drink locally. You don't mind that Tony, do you?" Angie said. Tony shook his head. He was not even sure if he liked the idea of going for a drink, but because the three girls had been so good to him, he felt obliged to tag along.

"No, that's fine, anywhere will do" he answered.

They sat in a quiet corner of a Madigan's Bar, a pub that they had often socialised in at the weekends. Angie had noticed how subdued Tony was.

"Do you want to talk about it Tony?" she asked gently. Tony shrugged his shoulders.

"What's there to say? We all knew Jodie. She was always messing about and joking. She was a ball of energy. Even now when I think of her doing her exercises, I smile to myself. The day of the accident, I asked her not to go running, but then I often did. She was so slim; I wondered why she exercised so much. She enjoyed jogging, pure and simple, just as I enjoy cycling. You never think that you might not come back home that evening. But that's what happened to poor Jodie. One idiot driver, not looking where he was going. He probably was on his mobile phone at the time. Then he just panicked and shot off" Tony said.

"Oh my God, and for you to be there and see it happening. That's just the worst thing!" Gina said in sympathy. Tony raised his eyebrows and sighed.

"In a way I am glad about being there. It meant that I got to hold her one last time before she died. They were her final words. "Hold me" she said. I told her parents this" Tony said. It all became too much for him. The tears came again, as they had done at the graveside. Stacey sat next to him to his left. The seating arrangement had been cleverly concocted by Angie, without raising anyone's suspicions. Stacey reached out and hugged him.

"It's okay Tony, it's okay" she whispered.

Later, Gina and Angie met up in the ladies' room.

"How do you think it's going out there?" Angie said with a cunning grin. Gina Stynes arched her thin ginger eyebrows and looked at her friend suspiciously.

"Well, their talking, but why wouldn't they? They never really fell out" Gina said.

"Yeah, but they're getting on really well. I wonder if the old spark is still there." Angie said with a grin. Gina gave her friend a suspicious glare.

"Angie O'Rourke! You planned this whole thing! This drinking session was your idea-and giving Tony Lee a lift to the funeral!" Gina exclaimed.

"Well, sometimes you have to give love a helping hand. Those two were meant to be together. I only saw that when Stacey arrived at her wedding. You should have seen the way she looked at Tony that morning" Angie said. Gina shook her head in bewilderment.

"It's too soon Angie. Stacey's wedding was only a few months ago, and Tony's hardly over Jodie yet" Gina replied.

"I know. I'm just sewing the seed for the future" Angie said with a satisfied smile. Gina shook her head again and walked towards the door.

"Where do you think that you're going?" Angie asked. Gina looked bemused.

"Outside, why, what's wrong?" Gina asked.

"What's the hurry? Fix your hair again. Give them a little more time alone" Angie said with a knowing smile.

Muggser and Burrener knocked on Alex Wood's apartment. Alex had been staying mostly at his father's home, but tonight he was at his flat. Muggser and Burrener had watched the upmarket building for two evenings now. The previous night they had wondered if they had made a mistake, but tonight Alex's gleaming white car stood in the car park.

"If he doesn't answer, I'm gonna smash that car to bits!" Burrener whispered. Muggser sniggered cynically at his pal's reaction.

"There are CCTV cameras everywhere! You'll be arrested in about three minutes" Muggser replied in a low voice. They heard footsteps approaching the front door. Both stood away from view of the peephole. Alex opened the white front door in a cautious way. He was not expecting anybody, and guessed that it might be someone selling something.

"Whatever you're selling, I'm not interes…" Alex's words stopped on recognising both Muggser and Burrener.

"Ah Alex, we just dropped by to say hello" Muggser said with a threatening grin. Alex went to slam the door, but Burrener wedged his foot on the doorstep. Alarm spread across Alex's face. He was unarmed, and his phone was in the living room.

"Can we come in?" Muggser asked, raising his dark eyebrows skywards.

"I'm calling the police" Alex said firmly. Burrener grinned and shook his head.

"There will be no need Alex, no need at all. We're here to talk business" Burrener said. Alex still had a firm grip on the white door. He stood slightly behind it, Burrener's heavy boot planted in the hallway inside the threshold. Muggser stepped forward.

"He's right Alex; this is purely a social call. By the way, sorry to hear about your old man. In a way though, that benefited you. You're now the sole heir to the business. So in a funny way, you owe Burrener and myself a nice little nest egg. I would say, oh, maybe €2,000 each should do it" Muggser said confidently. Alex Woods steeled himself.

"You two scumbags are off your head. You won't be getting a penny from me, not a fucking penny. You don't realise who you're messing with here. What you got the last time was nothing compared to what I will do to you if you don't just fuck off out of here. I don't know who you think you are. And for the record, I never clapped eyes on you two in my life" Alex said. He afforded himself a wicked grin, feeling that he had the upper hand on the two petty criminals. Muggser stepped up onto the doorstep, raising his frame to its maximum.

"Listen Alex, the cops are already on to us about the burglary. If we go down for this, so do you. It makes little difference to us. I can do a stretch inside standing on my bleedin' head. But you…"Muggser said, sucking in air at the end of the unfinished sentence.

"The cops would never believe anything that you two wankers say. I'm a respectable businessman. Go and tell them what you want. I'm looking forward to their visit already" Alex said with a grin. He was growing more confident by the minute. Burrener made a strong push against the door. Muggser put out an arm to restrain him.

"Last chance Alex. €1,500 each and that's it. We won't bother you again" he said quietly. Alex shook his head vehemently.

"Fuck off now, I mean it. One call from me to the cops and they will lock you up. Imagine how it will look. You two have killed my father, and now you're around at my home trying to blackmail me! Your feet wouldn't touch the floor!" Alex said.

Muggser stepped back onto the walkway.

"Ah, but Alex my friend, you let slip when you jumped on us. You told us how you wanted the old man out of the way. How will that sound to the cops? You cocked up Alex. You better rethink your attitude mate!" Muggser said determinedly.

"You two scumbags can say all you want. Who's gonna believe you?" Alex countered. Muggser looked sideways to his accomplice.

"Come on Burrener, let's go. We'll see you soon Alex, real soon!" Muggser said with a cackle.

Reluctantly, Burrener moved his foot slowly back onto the walkway outside of Alex's home. Muggser backed away from the door, his dark eyes still fixed on Alex Woods. Alex continued to eyeball the two men until they had vanished from sight. His heart was thumping, but he was sure that he had won the battle.

Alex stood with his back to the closed white door. He had to think fast. Should he phone the police? No. How would he explain knowing who the two thugs were? They would tell the police of the beating he gave them.

He had to get his story straight. Alex poured himself a whiskey and downed it in one go. He flopped down on the expensive red couch. Were those two thugs just chancing an arm, he wondered? Yes, that had to be it. They were small-time crooks trying to extract a few quid cheaply. He had stood up to them, and they had backed down. Alex convinced himself that he would never see them again. But if so, he would phone the police immediately. Alex vowed to carry a weapon with him from now on. He had been caught unawares. Selling his apartment would now move to the top of his list. He had no need for it now. It held bad memories anyway, now that Stacey had left.

Why did we not bust his face open?" Burrener asked menacingly. Muggser cackled his evil laugh into the night air.

"Because he would go to the bleedin' cops, you arsehole! If we even laid one finger on him, they would have us. I didn't expect to get anywhere tonight with him, not really. But when he thinks about it, he might just come across with some cash" Muggser said determinedly.

"And if not?" Burrener grinned. Muggser shook his head in abject frustration.

"No, you gobshite, there will be no violence with the Alex fellow, we have too much to lose. That would be like admitting the burglary charge! We bash up the son of the man whose house we broke into? Are you nuts? No Burrener, its plan B, the idea we plotted before. If we get done for these robberies, then Alex Woods goes down with us" Muggser replied.

It had taken Muggser days of painstakingly following Alex Woods home from work to find out where he lived. He had had to borrow an old Honda 50 motorcycle and trail Alex from the garage on The Long mile Road to his apartment in Terenure. Twice he had lost Alex's white Mondeo in the traffic. Finally on the third evening he had managed to track Alex all the way to his plush apartment.

Alex was packing the last of his belongings. A permanent move back to the family home felt like his best option. Although he realised that both addresses were now known to the two thugs, he would feel a lot safer at his father's former home. The house in Blackrock was now fitted with CCTV cameras, and a state-of-the-art security alarm. Even if Muggser and Burrener were to appear at his new home, Alex vowed that he would phone for the police immediately. As the removal van left with the last of his furniture, Alex walked back inside the apartment. It was on the property market, and he hoped for a quick sale. All he had to do now was to collect the last of his belongings, and drive to Blackrock. Alex took his briefcase and laptop from the now-empty bedroom and left them by the front door. He had a last look around. A small bag of clothing had already been placed in the boot of his car. Alex spotted his heavy winter coat hanging behind the white front door.
"Nearly missed that. This will come in handy for those cold nights..." Alex stopped his muttering in mid-sentence. Beneath his heavy black coat was a more flimsy navy jacket, and it did not belong to him.
"What have we here?" he whispered. Alex held up the short jacket and examined it. It was clearly a ladies coat, and Alex presumed that it might belong to Stacey. On further inspection he realised that it was in fact Angie O'Rourke's. He delved in the pockets and his eyes lit up at his discovery.
"Well, well! A key! I don't suppose that it would be the key to her old apartment? What a nice little bonus!" he sneered.

The police picked up both Muggser and Burrener at seven-thirty the following morning. They were charged with three burglaries in the Blackrock area, including the home of Tom Woods. They were also charged jointly with aggravated assault on Mr. Woods.
"By you two admitting to these charges, we could ask for leniency on your behalf. If you make it difficult for us, there are a host of other charges that we can put your way. For example, there are at least twenty other burglaries in the nearby district that have all the hallmarks of your dirty little work. Make no mistake Muggser, your going down for this one" said Detective Forde. Muggser

was unmoved. He had listened to the tall detective trying to pry an admission from him for almost an hour now.

"We didn't do it. You have nothing on us. Where's the proof?" Muggser repeated for the fifth time. He yawned again, highlighting his contempt for the policeman.

"Oh, we have plenty of proof, don't you worry. Your filthy little prints are all over those houses. We will nail you for this, mark my words" the detective said confidently. He sat opposite Muggser in the small square room, the white venetian blinds firmly closed on the small barred window behind him.

"You raided my house and found nothing. You did the same at Burrener's. Not a shred of evidence, not a sausage! If we robbed all of these homes, where's the goods? This is a stitch-up job, just to get these cases off the books. Now, that's it, no more talking. I want a solicitor in here-now!" Muggser said. His mood had changed in seconds, as it was prone to do. He folded his arms and sat back on his seat.

"Muggser, just admit to this one break-in and I'll see what I can do about the others" Detective Forde said.

"Solicitor-now!" Muggser repeated.

Alex Woods turned the key to Stacey's apartment. He realised that all four occupants would be at work. As he opened the front door with Angela's spare key, he listened for any sound. Nothing. Alex crept inside. He was not after anything in particular; it was just the novelty of being able to gain access.

It was early afternoon. Alex had told Michelle that he had to go out on some business. He had decided to travel to the apartment on a whim, unsure how long he would stay. The first room that Alex tried was locked. He could not know that it was Angie's bedroom. Undeterred, he carried on. The next room had a double bed. Instantly he knew it was Gina's and Harry's. Alex only spent moments there. It held little interest for him.

He sought out Stacey's room. He could smell her distinct perfume, and all the good times jumped back to greet him. Alex lay down on Stacey's bed. He stared at the ceiling, recalling times when Stacey lived with him. They were the happiest days of his life, he concluded. Conveniently he overlooked the bad times; including the time he had jilted Stacey during their first romance. Alex lay there for some time, basking in the memory of his ideal relationship. Suddenly his wedding day flashed before him. He remembered the embarrassment at having to phone the venue of The Ashton Castle Lodge to inform them that the reception was cancelled. Alex recalled having to return to work to face his colleagues, realising that they knew he had been jilted. Unknown to Alex, Frank McKenzie had warned all members of staff to act as if nothing had occurred. The entire embarrassing morning played back to Alex Woods in slow motion, and he rose from the bed in a simmering rage.

"Bitch, fucking bitch! How could she do that to me?" he screamed. He flung open Stacey's single wardrobe in the corner of the room. Her scent invaded his nostrils once more. It seemed to calm Alex down.

"It's not Stacey's fault, it was that Tony Lee. He's to blame, but I fixed him! Oh yes, I fixed him good and proper!" he muttered. Alex Woods spent another hour wandering from room to room. He delved in drawers, looked in cupboards, and examined pictures of the girls on the walls and in photo albums. Gina was the one keen on taking snaps. She had always done so at social events, either with her camera, or on her mobile phone. As a result, there was no shortage of happy pictures of the girls dotted around the apartment.

"Ah, Jodie, what a pretty girl you were!" Alex said, picking up a framed photo of the four girls together. He wandered out into the hallway with the picture in his hands. Something caught his eye. Alex looked to the ceiling. There was a small trapdoor leading to the loft. He had not considered that the flat might also have an attic space.

"Now this is interesting. I wonder what lies up there?" he thought. Alex stood on a chair near the door and pushed the small white door upwards. He peered inside. There was a switch to his left. Alex clicked on the light and glanced around. All that he could see was suitcases and some broken kitchen chairs. Another thought crossed his mind. He had noticed an air duct behind a grill in Stacey's room.

"I wonder" he whispered. Alex's mind was racing. What his brain was proposing was preposterous, and yet it filled him with delight. He began to plan things in his mind.

Muggser and Burrener talked with their solicitor. He listened to what they were telling him with great interest.

"So, how did this Mister Woods find you?" Mr. Hinchcliffe asked.

"Well that's just it, we don't know. Maybe through a friend in the police, we're not really sure. He offered to pay us if we broke in and gave the old man a heart attack or something" Burrener said in an animated state. Mr. Hinchcliffe looked unconvinced.

"What were his exact words? Think now. Did he actually say that you must give him a coronary? This evidence is crucial" Mr. Hinchcliffe said. Muggser took over the story.

"Well, what he said was that he wanted his father out of the way. He told us that the old man had a bad heart, and that any sudden shock might kill him.

They were his very words. Of course, we're only small time; we don't go in for violence. When we saw the old man downstairs, we just panicked. We ran away and never looked back" Muggser concluded.

"I see, and this Mister Woods, did he actually pay you? You know, after his father had died?" Mister Hinchcliffe asked.

Burrener looked to Muggser for guidance. His friend again gave their account of events.

"No, you see, that's what we went to talk to him about. We went to his apartment out in Terenure. That's when he denied the whole thing. That's when he threatened us you see. Then he said that he would call the police" Muggser replied.

"These are grave charges gentlemen. Are both of you positive that it happened as you have outlined?" Mr. Hinchcliffe asked. He pushed his brown spectacles further up the bridge of his nose, which was a trait of the silver-haired solicitor.

"Cross my heart" Muggser said, a look of pure innocence etched on his thin face.

"Yeah, definitely" Burrener replied.

Alex Woods searched the kitchen drawer for a screwdriver or a strong pointed knife. He needed something to force a small hole in the ceiling of Stacey's bedroom. He came across a spare key to Harry's Toyota car.

"This might come in handy, you never know!" he grinned. Alex shoved the key into his pocket and then managed to find a small green screwdriver.

"Just the job! Now for some provisions!" he thought.

Alex punched a small hole in the white ceiling, just to the right of Stacey's bed. He then raided the fridge and cupboard for some food. His final mission was to find a container in case he was met with the call of nature. An empty plastic milk container from the kitchen bin came to hand. Alex studied the small hole in the high bedroom ceiling before heading for the loft.

"Tiny, you would barely notice!" he decided. Alex put things back the way he found them as best as he could. He then hauled himself up into the loft and crawled to where he had drilled through the ceiling with the small screwdriver. The tall ceiling gave him an almost panoramic view of Stacey's room.

"Brilliant, and with this food and a can of Coke, it will like watching television!" he grinned. Alex found an old mat and used it as a type of mattress. He used his coat as a pillow, and settled down for a nap until the residents below arrived home.

Tony sat in work talking to his friend, Erik Ngombiti. He confided about how he had wanted to propose to Jodie on her birthday.

"And was she the one, Tony?" Erik asked. Tony Lee looked baffled by the question.

"Well of course she was! Why do you think that I wanted to marry her?" he asked. Erik shrugged his shoulders.

"I don't know. Loneliness, doing the right thing, wanting to settle down, who knows?" Erik replied. Tony looked a little irate.

"I don't know where you're going with this Erik. I loved Jodie very much" he replied.

"I know you did Tony, I know. But why such a rush to get wed? I saw how devastated you were when you split with Stacey. Remember that you wanted to ask her to marry you too? To me it looks like you've been given a second chance. You tell me that Stacey has broken up with her boyfriend. Well why not go and see if she will have you back? I don't mean that the two of you should jump into a big romance. It's maybe too soon for that, probably for both of you. But why not be there for each other? You know, a shoulder to cry on? You don't know until you try. You spoke to her at Jodie's funeral. How did that go?" Erik asked. Tony looked uneasy at Erik's probing observations.

"Okay I suppose, it felt a bit strange. Neither of us could really relax. It was as if we had to watch what we said to each other" Tony replied.

"Both of you are probably afraid to hurt the other. You've got to go to Stacey and pour your heart out. Tell her how you feel about her, before someone else does. I know by the way that you talk about her that Stacey's still in your heart. I think that it's meant to be" Erik said with a smile. Tony Lee looked unconvinced.

"It's a bit soon. Jodie's only gone a couple of weeks" he said. Erik nodded knowingly.

"Of course, respect and all of that, of course. But phone Stacey, talk to her. Stay in touch. How would you feel if she met someone new? Would you be doing your nut, as they say in Dublin?" Erik asked. Tony laughed out loud. There was always something amusing about the way Erik Ngombiti used phrases or Irish sayings.

"Yeah Erik, maybe I would be kicking myself. We'll see. I'll give it some thought. Right now I don't feel very romantic. I wake every morning and see Jodie's face before me. It's an effort just to get through the day" Tony said.

"Remember what I said Tony, Stacey is a beautiful-looking girl. If I noticed, so will some other guy! Don't leave it too long" Erik replied.

Alex Woods lay on his stomach peering down into Stacey's room. He could hear voices in the apartment below, and guessed that it was Gina and Harry. They usually came home around the same time, as he had observed while watching the building on a few occasions. It was during one of those evenings that he had seen Stacey go inside. That was the first night that Alex had realised that she had come home from England.

Suddenly the light went on in Stacey's room. Alex watched as the top of her blonde head came into view. Stacey's coat dropped onto the bed. She slipped out of her working clothes and into pyjamas. Within minutes she had vanished again, switching off the light as she went. Alex sat up and sipped on the can of Coke which he had stolen from the fridge. He ate a chocolate snack bar and waited once more.

Almost one hour later the light in Stacey's room flashed on again. Alex gave the room below his full attention. The sounds below were almost crystal clear as they drifted up through the air duct. He could hear the television, the sound of cooking, and even made out a hairdryer being used in another room. The smell of fried onions and steak wafted up to the attic space. This time there were two females in Stacey's bedroom. Angie O'Rourke had joined her friend and the two were sitting on the bed.

"Angie, something's wrong. That's why I called you in here" Stacey said in a quiet voice.

"What do you mean Stacey? Has something happened at work?" a concerned Angie replied.

"No, something is wrong here in the flat. Somebody's been at my stuff. I went to get some clothes earlier, and they've been moved. Even my underwear drawer is not how I left it" Stacey said. Her eyes darted from the chest of drawers and back to her pal.

Above, Alex Woods felt his heart beat hard against his chest. It felt as though it might explode. All it would take was for someone to grow suspicious and search the apartment. He had endeavoured to leave everything as it was, yet already Stacey had noticed something odd. Alex could hear every word clearly. Angie stood up and walked to the door. She checked that it was closed tight.

"Oh Stacey, I didn't want to say anything. You seemed so sad when you moved back in. I thought it best to keep it to myself" Angie said, her brow furrowed.

"What? Tell me what you mean?" Stacey asked, her eyes pleading for an explanation. Angie again sat on the bed. She gripped Stacey's hands in hers.

"Soon after I moved in, something happened" Angie said. She went on to explain about Harry's behaviour, and little innuendos that she had noticed in his speech.

"So you see, since that day I try never to be on my own with him. I always lock my door when I'm out, and especially at night. I remember Jodie saying something about how creepy he was, but I never paid any attention until it happened to me" Angie concluded. Stacey looked terrified.

"And you think that he's been in here too? He's been searching through my private things? Ugh! That's sick! I've never noticed anything strange until tonight. I'm definitely locking my room from now on" Stacey said in a hushed tone.

Above them, Alex listened intently. He was taking in every word.

Outside in the living room, Gina was searching for her phone charger.

"It was definitely here this morning. Everything vanishes in this flat! Someone robbed my can of Coke too. And the chocolate biscuits are gone. Those two never buy any food, yet they steal my stuff" Gina said with purpose. Harry looked shifty.

"I took the biscuits. I hadn't time to have breakfast, so I grabbed something from the press. Sorry" an embarrassed Harry said. Gina made light of his response.

"Still, it's always happening. And that doesn't explain my charger. I have a spare one somewhere. It's from my old phone. It works on my new one too. I know, I brought it on holiday with me. Oh! It's in the suitcase in the loft. Harry, be a dear and grab it for me" she said. Harry rose wearily from the sofa.

"Sure. It's the yellow suitcase, yeah?" he asked.

"Yes, It's just inside the attic door" she replied.

Harry stood up on the chair in the hallway and pushed back the small square door. It fell back with a thud, startling Alex Woods. The light from the hallway seemed to fill the attic space. Alex waited for Harry to flick on the light switch. He pulled his coat around his head and lay as still as possible.

"Found it Harry! It was down behind the armchair. I'm sure that I left it on the table" Gina called. In an instant, Harry closed the white door and the light vanished from the loft once again. Alex Woods exhaled with relief.

Gradually the apartment fell silent. One by one the residents below went to bed. Alex Woods watched as Stacey turned on her side. She reached out and switched out her bedside lamp. Moments later she was fast asleep.

"Goodnight precious. Alex is watching over you" he whispered. Alex took another sip from his can. He sniffed under his arms. The hot attic had caused him to perspire. Soon he too would sleep. He promised himself that in the morning when everyone had left, he would have a shower before going on his way.

CHAPTER NINETEEN

SUICIDE NOTE

Alex Woods woke up from a restless sleep. He lay for a while as the residents below him prepared for work. Alex was calm and thoughtful. Harry Brand was uppermost in his mind. Anyone who threatened his fixation with Stacey Boyd was at odds with him. Alex listened as the noise below slowly abated. Harry and Gina left first, quickly followed by Stacey and Angie. Alex climbed down cautiously from the attic and stretched his body. By now he had decided that Harry Brand was his sworn enemy. He paced the flat trying to come up with a plan of action.

"It can't be another hit and run. They might tie it in with Jodie's death. Too much of a coincidence. No. I need something different for that, that pervert. Anybody who does that is sick. How can he live with himself?" he mumbled. It came to him in a flash. His own words had dictated a plan of action.

"Yeah, he definitely can't live with himself! Okay, now where does he work? Let's do it sooner rather than later. Those poor girls have been through enough" Alex said, his mind abuzz with thoughts and plans. He began to search the sitting room and Gina's bedroom for an address for Harry's workplace. Along the way, he checked that both Stacey's and Angie's doors were locked. "Good girls! Don't worry, he won't bother you again. I'll see to that" Alex thought quietly.

Tony Lee sat quietly in his office. His eyes were tired, and he felt a bit drowsy. Erik passed by and seemed to notice.

"Out late again last night? Too many pints?" Erik said in his pretend Dublin accent. A small laugh erupted deep in his torso and spread upwards through his body. It exploded from his lips, causing Tony to join in. Several passing workmates also got the bug. When the laughter finally subsided, Tony answered his pal.

"No! For your information I was in bed early. I was tidying the gardens well into the evening and felt worn out, so I had an early night" Tony replied.

"Still working on that old house? Why not knock it down and build a new one? Those old shacks are money-pits. I'll bet when the roof comes off, they will find all sorts of problems" Erik reasoned. Tony looked at him with astonishment.

"The roof won't be coming off! Those houses are sturdy, not like your Lego box! Slapped up in a day that was! If you must know, I'm still having those dreams that I told you about. I woke up and couldn't get back to sleep" Tony replied. Erik sat down on Tony's desk.

"Yeah? Is it still that mystery child?" he asked. Tony nodded.

"Yeah, but now I see Jodie too. She's covered in blood and walking towards me. Her arms are outstretched begging me to help her. Her white tracksuit is soaked in blood. It's awful" Tony said tersely. Erik patted him on the shoulder.

"It will pass my friend. Hey, why not come over for dinner some night?" he said, changing the subject. Tony gave him a withering look.

"No thanks! That Tricia woman might be waiting in a cupboard to ambush me!" Tony chuckled. He still had not got over the night of Erik's birthday party. It set Erik off once more.

"Huh, huh, huh!" his grumbling laughter boomed from the depths of his stomach. Once again guys in the nearby office stations joined in, mimicking Erik's deep laughter.

"Seriously Erik, what were you thinking of that evening?" he asked. Erik's infectious laughter continued to reverberate around the office.

"I told you-it was Eileen's idea! You know how women are! She wanted to play matchmaker. Anyhow, we've distanced ourselves from Tricia. She was getting too friendly. Every time I opened the front door she was there, wanting to be our friend! Eileen told her politely where she stood!" Erik replied.

"Phew! Thank goodness for that! A fatal attraction waiting to happen!" Tony answered, wiping pretend sweat from his brow. Erik looked thoughtful.

"Okay, maybe not Tricia so, but what about Stacey? Have you phoned her?" Erik asked. Tony made a face.

"It's still too early Erik. I want to, but I can't. I still think of Jodie" he replied in a whisper.

Erik stood up and patted his workmate's shoulder again.

"I understand. Remember what I said though, don't leave it too late. Stacey is a fine-looking lady. She works in a big office with lots of guys, right?" Eric said with a knowing smile.

Alex Woods stood and observed the Toyota Avensis car, parked at the rear of Harry Brand's office. There was just one vehicle there now. Alex had watched the last employee leave. Harry's silver Toyota stood alone in the small unlit tarmacadam patch. To be doubly sure, Alex tried the key, which he had found in the apartment, in the passenger door. The door opened silently. Alex tossed the long heavy rope inside on the floor in the rear of the car and then locked the vehicle again. Silently he tried the door handle of the premises where he had watched the last worker leave from earlier. It was locked from the inside. Alex had expected as much. He had to be positive that Harry was alone, yet was fearful that there may be CCTV on the premises. All that he could do was to wait.

Alex slid into the rear seat of the Toyota and lay down flat on top of the rope on the floor. He pulled the black woollen balaclava over his face. It covered his nose and mouth, with just his eyes visible through the round small holes. His black coat and trousers would blend in well with the dark evening. He lay face down on the floor of the car and waited.

Eventually footsteps in the distance grew louder as they approached the vehicle. The adrenalin rushed through Alex's body again. It was a high that he was becoming all too familiar with. Still the fear was there. It was all part of the attraction for Alex Woods. All he could pray for was that Harry had no need to open the back doors of the car.

Harry Brand climbed into the driver seat and turned the key in the ignition. The car set off at a reasonable speed on Harry's half-hour journey home. Alex raised his head to peer out of the window behind Harry's seat. He had guessed Harry's probable route home, but had to be sure. Once he established that he had estimated correctly, Alex could breathe a little easier. He knew the exact point at which he would implement his plan.

Harry stopped at the traffic lights. He was well away from the city centre and about to turn onto a quiet avenue. Harry used this street every evening to avoid the traffic congestion. It was a well-known rat-run, which linked The Coombe area with Portobello. Once past this traffic black-spot, Harry would be just minutes away from home.

"Turn right, here! Turn fucking right!" Alex roared as Harry set off again. He held the airgun to the back of Harry's neck. Harry leapt in his seat with shock. "Jesus Christ! Fucking hell!" he screamed.

"Don't turn around! Don't speak! Just drive and you'll live!" Alex bellowed. The balaclava masked his voice, distorting it slightly.

"I haven't much cash on me! It's in my wallet. Take it, take it!" Harry stammered.

"Drive the car! Now! Keep both hands on the fucking wheel" Alex yelled. Harry drove on slowly; sweat now dripping from his forehead. The metal barrel was pressed against the back of Harry's skull. Alex lay crouched between the two front seats of the car.

"Straight on. Nothing funny and you will walk away from this. One wrong move and I will blow your fucking brains all over this car!" Alex screamed.

"Please, please, I'll do everything you ask" Harry cried. His body trembled as he clung to the steering wheel with both hands.

Alex directed him towards Memorial Park, which was about fifteen minutes away. They parked up in the rain, and Alex waited for a gap in the traffic.

"Right, into the park now!" he shouted. In one swift movement, Alex leapt from the car and hauled open the driver's door. Before Harry could react, Alex pulled him from the vehicle. He put the small airgun to the rear of Harry's skull again and frogmarched him forward. In his other hand, Alex carried the coiled-up rope. Alex pulled the set of keys from Harry's sweaty right hand and automatically locked the car behind him.

"You're making a mistake! You have the wrong person!" Harry pleaded. His first thought was that he had been mistaken for some petty criminal or underworld figure.

"Shut the fuck up! Through the gates! Down that way!" Alex said, barking orders in a military-style mode.

He pushed Harry deeper and deeper into the wooded area of the park.

"This will do. Get down under that tree" Alex ordered. A giant oak tree shielded both men from the rain. Harry cowered down on the damp grass, trembling with fear. Alex wrapped a red scarf tightly around Harry's mouth to stop him blubbering.

"Write this down. Here's a pen" Alex said. He kept the gun pressed against Harry's head. A single sheet of paper folded in half dropped into Harry's lap. The blue pen shook unevenly in Harry's sweaty palm. Alex stood behind him, dictating each sentence.

"I can't go on like this. I want to end it all" Alex said in a muffled voice. The pen wavered in Harry's right hand, as he realised the implication of the sentence.

"Write it, or so help me I'll shoot you right fucking now!" Alex said forcefully. He could hear Harry's muffled sobbing through the red scarf. Harry began to write. Alex switched on a small torch to check every word.

"I love Angie, but she doesn't want to know. Gina will never forgive me. There's no other way out" Alex said. Harry tried to look around. Alex jabbed the airgun forcefully against his scalp. As the names tumbled from Alex's lips, Harry knew that it had to be someone who knew him personally.

"Do it! Write it down! So help me, I'll fucking blow your brains all over this park!" Alex yelled, ramming the metal barrel hard against Harry's trembling skull. Harry began to sob even louder. His wailing could be heard clearly now. He began to scribble faster. Alex watched each word appear on the clean white page.

"Good! Now sign it-sign it!" he shouted. Harry was distraught. He choked back tears as he scrawled the name Harry at the bottom of the page. In a flash, Alex pulled the paper from his grasp and slipped a noose over Harry's head. He pulled it tight around his neck. Alex was in that special zone now. Nothing could stand in his way. Every movement, every section of his plot, passed through his brain in slow motion. He had planned out what must happen that evening meticulously.

Alex swung the long rope over a heavy branch and yanked it tight. Harry's hands grabbed at the noose. He was now in a standing position. Alex yanked on it again. Harry almost lost consciousness as he gasped for breath. Alex tied the bottom of the rope to the trunk of the tree, dragging Harry's body to a full, erect position, stretching his neck to its limits. He then marched forward and dragged the heavy stone towards Harry's feet. That morning he had walked through the park, selecting the giant flat rock for his mission that night. Alex had then shoved it behind a bush in readiness for tonight.

"Stand up there on the rock, go on! Do it or you're a dead man. I want you to know what fear is. You frightened Angie, now it's your turn" Alex screamed, again jabbing the gun against the back of Harry's head.

For the first time since his ordeal began, Harry Brand started to believe that he might live. He took in the words of his captor. He had said that he only wanted to frighten him. Logic told Harry Brand that he should obey. It was his only chance. The man wanted to scare him. To cross this man would mean certain death, his brain told him. Bu obeying, there was still a chance. Harry gasped for air. His brain was swimming with confusion. He climbed unsteadily onto the big flat rock. His feet wobbled from side to side. Eventually he stood erect, trembling in terror. Alex tightened the rope even further. He then whipped the scarf from around his prisoners' mouth. Alex stood and took in the scene for a moment. He pulled away the balaclava and looked up at Harry.

"You're evil Harry, a pervert. You're gonna go straight to hell. You terrified Jodie and Gina. You probably had Stacey in your sights next. I could never allow that to happen. Not my lovely Stacey. You have to die" Alex said deliberately. Alex could see the incredulous gleam in Harry's eyes as he recognised his tormentor. Alex stepped forward and shoved the piece of paper into Harry's jacket pocket, along with his car keys. Harry tried to kick out at him with his right leg. Alex dodged the swipe, and deftly kicked away the large stone with his left foot. Before Harry could scream, his body dropped downwards. It dangled like a marionette, whose strings had become intertwined.

Momentarily, Harry's feet shook in spasms before falling limp again. Alex watched the spectacle impassively from just feet away. Harry's eyes bulged as his head sunk to the side. The limp body was swaying in the wind now. Alex looked around. Some evenings there might be teenagers about. The park often attracted a bad element, especially in the summertime. With the winter closing in, and the evening's bad weather, Alex's plan had run smoothly. He was taking more risks lately, but he had decided that attending to Harry had to be a top priority.

Alex slipped unnoticed from the park. He walked for some time before hailing a taxi. Alex was covering for all eventualities. His car was parked in a pub car park, so there would be no direct trail from the taxi driver to his home. It was best to be safe. Alex prided himself on his attention to detail, but even by his own particular standards, tonight had been a huge risk. He felt for the black air gun in his pocket as he drove home. He had bought the weapon in a pub in London many years ago as a bit of fun. Alex had never thought that he might one day use it in such a daring fashion.

"Harry's late" Gina remarked to both Stacey and Angie.
"He probably got talking at work" Stacey replied. Gina looked at her watch again. It was not like Harry to miss his evening meal. She tried his mobile phone again.
"It's just ringing. He's not answering" she said. Angie looked at her directly for the first time.
"He'll be in the pub with his mates so! You know men! He will be telling them that it's just the girlfriend phoning, and to let her wait!" Angie said with a wicked grin. Stacey recognised Angie's sense of fun.
"Yeah, they like to act macho! They all think that they're big men. Let her wait! I'll go home when I'm ready!" Stacey said, trying to don a male voice. Gina looked cross.
"Harry would never do that. I'm worried. This is not like him at all" Gina said. Stacey relented a little. She went to sit next to Gina on the sofa.
"Listen Gina, it will be something simple. He most probably got a puncture, or had to go back to the office. Maybe he left his phone back there" Stacey said. Angie liked the theory.
"I'll bet that's it. Men are always forgetting things" she agreed.

By eleven o'clock that evening, Gina was pacing the floor. Both Angie and Stacey were also showing signs of concern, but secretly each felt that there was a simple explanation.

"We have to do something. Let's phone the cops" Gina suggested.

"We can't do that! He's only missing for a few hours. The cops will laugh at us!" Angie replied. Stacey had to agree with her pal.

"Look, let's go to bed. He should be in soon. There's no point in us staying awake all night" Stacey reasoned. Just then, Stacey's phoned bleeped with a message. All eyes fell on the pink mobile phone, lying on the coffee table.

"Answer it, it might be important" Gina said quietly. Stacey looked at the blue screen.

"It's Tony. What does he want at this hour?" Stacey wondered aloud. She read the message for the benefit of the other girls.

"Can't sleep. Fancy chatting?" she giggled. Her smile vanished as she saw Gina's worried face.

"I'll phone Tony. He might have some idea on what to do" she said.

Stacey explained to Tony about Harry not arriving home. All that he could suggest was that they wait until the morning. Stacey wandered off to her bedroom to chat to Tony. Already she had forgotten all about Harry.

The knock came to Gina's door early next morning. She had had a fitful night's sleep on the sofa, and had already decided that she would not be going to work. It was just after seven-thirty. She answered the door as both Stacey and Gina were getting dressed in their rooms. Gina had been awoken by their alarms on their mobile phones, which was the custom in the apartment on weekday mornings. Once Gina saw the two tall men, she immediately knew that something was wrong. Two policemen stood before her, both in full uniform.

"No, please God, no!" Gina mouthed, the words barely leaving her lips.

The senior policeman asked if it was the home address of Harry Brand. By now Stacey and Angie had joined Gina at the front door. Once the policeman had told them why he was there, Gina began screaming. Stacey and Angie half-dragged her inside onto the sofa. The two policemen followed them into the apartment. Gina was now hysterical now, and Stacey led her away to her bedroom.

"Where did this happen? I can't believe it! Are you sure it's him? Harry Brand?" Angie asked all at once.

"As sure as we can be. There will have to be a formal identification of course. We found his car outside Memorial Park. A man out walking his dog discovered the body a couple of hours ago. We have his wallet and photo. Harry left a note. Can we ask you a few question Miss? It won't take long" the first policeman said. He handed Angie a small photo of Harry, plus his driving licence. Angie nodded at the tiny coloured snap.

"That's him, yes. Sorry, what? Questions? Sure, why not?" she stammered, still in shock.

The policeman introduced himself as Sergeant Bob Tillman, and asked Angie's name. He seemed immediately interested when hearing who she was.

"Did Harry seem troubled to you? Has he ever struck you as emotionally disturbed Miss O'Rourke?" he asked. Angie felt trapped. She was unsure how to answer.

"He…seemed okay. I think Gina might have a better idea. She's his girlfriend" Angie replied, anxious not to become too involved.

"Quite, but has he ever said anything to you? You see, there was this note that Harry left. He mentioned you by name. Did he ever have a crush on you Miss O'Rourke? Were you two ever romantically linked?" asked Sergeant Tillman. The words flashed through Angie's brain. She searched for a way out. Again Angie felt cornered. She did not know what Harry had written, yet she recalled his crude suggestions to her.

"I…We were never together, if that's what you mean. Harry did…I don't want to say anymore just now" she said, her voice almost breaking.

"We can come back Miss O'Rourke, that's not a problem. Would you prefer to tell us now? Did Harry have a thing for you, as they say?" the policeman asked gently.

Angie found herself nodding.

"He was very suggestive one evening. I got scared. I think he was in my room one day. Touching my…clothes. After that I locked my door" Angie blurted out. Her dark eyes darted at both policemen. Bob Tillman nodded.

"That's okay, it confirms what we thought. We will call back if we have any more questions" he said. Angie sat shaking on the chair. Her eyes were tearful, but she managed to check her emotions.

"Does Gina have to know? I mean, how can I tell her?" Angie asked, her eyes pleading for guidance. The policeman stood up slowly.

"She will have questions of her own, no doubt. I suggest that you be honest with her. There will be an autopsy and an inquest. It is best to be truthful in the long run, that's my advice" he said.

Angie saw them out. She could hear Gina weeping in the next room. Angie stood with her back to the hall door. How could she face her friend and look her in the eyes, she wondered?

That afternoon, Alex Woods was working in his new office. He had by now taken over his father's bigger office at the garage, and had plans to extend the larger room even further. Vivian, his father's secretary, knocked politely at the door. Alex was engrossed in his computer, searching for any news of a suicide in Dublin. There had been nothing on the news, and as of yet, Alex did not know if Harry Brand was dead or alive.

"I should have checked. I should have waited a bit longer. What if someone came along and cut him down? Fuck! That was most unprofessional of me" Alex thought.

Vivian knocked politely again. Alex called on her to enter.

"There are two gentlemen to see you Alex. They showed me identification. They are policemen. Will I show them in?" she asked. Alex froze for a second.

"Er, yeah, yes, show them in. It's probably something trivial" he replied. Alex turned off the internet page on the work's computer and stood up.

"It will be okay. Don't panic. Let them do the talking" he thought.

Detective Forde shook hands with Alex as he entered the room. He introduced his colleague, Detective Jack Routledge to him.

"How can I help?" Alex asked with a smile. Immediately Detective Forde looked shifty.

"Well, this case regarding the break-in at your father's property has taken a curious turn. We tried to call at your home address, but it appears that you have moved?" the policeman said, leaving Alex in no doubt that it was a question.

"Oh yes, I've moved into my Dad's house. It was the security issue you see. I didn't want another incident at the place. It's still tough to think about what he went through. I'm selling the flat, sorry, maybe I should have told you" Alex replied.

"I have to ask you some questions Alex. Do the names, Bernard Claffey and Joseph Byrne mean anything to you?" Myles Forde asked. Alex breathed a little easier. It had nothing to do with Harry Brand after all.

"No, I can't say that either name rings a bell. Should I know them?" he bluffed. He had already figured out who Joseph Byrne was.

"Well, they claim to know you. Very well in fact. They say that they visited your apartment. They further claim that you sought them out, asking them to do a favour for you" Detective Forde said. He paced the office at a snail's pace, as if studying every inch of the thick grey carpet. Alex thought fast. Already he had in place a story to cover such an eventuality.

"You'll have to explain" Alex said, as if totally lost by the conversation.

"They also are known as Muggser and Burrener. You could say that those are their street names" the tall well-built man added. He watched Alex's face for a reaction.

Alex flopped down on the swivel leather chair.

"I should have phoned you, I know that I should have. It's all been a bit much. I really didn't want to be drawn into a court case, so I ignored the whole thing.

You see, these two toe-rags came to my flat and threatened me. They tried to embezzle money from me if I didn't use my influence to have the charges against them dropped. Of course, I told them that it was a matter for the police. Then they said that they would burn my father's house down. Oh, they threatened to do all sorts, including having me shot. I refused point blank to give in to their demands. I said that I would go to the police. They just laughed. They told me that they would deny everything. Eventually they left, but said that they would be back. That's when I fled to my Dad's house. I suppose that it was silly of me. Still I feel a little safer there. It's where I grew up after all" Alex said, his voice breaking with emotion.

Detective Routledge spoke for the first time.

"It's a peculiar thing, but they seem to know that you benefited financially from your father's death. They claim that you wanted Tom Woods out of the way, and that you asked them to help. When did you first meet Byrne and Claffey?" he asked. Alex had anticipated such a question.

"That's ridiculous! I loved my father; no money in the world could replace him. I was never short of cash, nor is it my motivation in life. I told you, I first met them when they arrived at my flat. That's the only time that I ever laid eyes on them. They had obviously concocted this story to make some easy money. It's what criminals do, isn't it? God! How I wish that I had gone to the police now. It just seemed too fantastic to be true. I took the easy way out and ignored these thugs, fearing I might have to face them in court. I was so naïve" Alex said, putting his head in his hands.

"So you don't deny meeting them?" Forde asked. Alex looked up with an incredulous mask on his face.

"What? I just told you sir! I met them at my apartment. I should have pressed charges, but I was too afraid. I visualised court cases, threats, hidings. I even feared that they might burn down my father's business. The easy way out was to say nothing. I hoped that that brief encounter was the end of things. How stupid I was" Alex said. He began to cry softly into his palms. Both policemen looked at each other.

"I know that this is tough, but we have to ask these questions Mr. Woods. Now, at anytime, did you seek out these two gentlemen before the break-in at your father's home?" Detective Routledge asked. Alex shook his head vehemently.

"No, never. I never saw them until that awful night, believe me. On my life, on my father's life" he wailed.

"We'll be going now Mr. Woods. If we have any further questions, we'll be in touch. You will be required to make a statement. You can phone us when you

feel up to it. I suggest that you contact a solicitor" Detective Forde said quietly.
"Why? What have I done?" Alex asked.
"It's best to seek legal advice sir, that's all that I am saying" Detective Forde replied tersely.
 The two quickly left, and Alex followed them outside to the showrooms and watched through the giant glass panes as they drove away.

"What did you make of him?" Forde asked his colleague.
"Oh, he seems believable enough. A few things troubled me. The natural reaction would be to phone us, if what he says is true, that is. The business about moving to his father's house doesn't seem right either. How would he feel safer at a much larger place? That big house is more isolated. But who do you believe? Those thugs or an ordinary citizen? Then there's the logic of it all. I mean, would you go to either Muggser or Burrener if you wanted a thing like that done? They could barely plan a trip to the supermarket! Come on!" Detective Routledge replied. Both men laughed loudly for a few moments.
"The date tallies. Both admit it happened on the 23rd. I want to believe Woods, the alternative is too frightening. But what if the other two are telling the truth? Woods stands to gain everything from his father's passing" Forde said. Detective Jack Routledge nodded firmly a couple of times.
"Yes, but he would have inherited the lot anyway. And let's look at it from Muggser's and Burrener's point of view. Those two would have needed to visit Alex Woods' flat to make their story credible. I mean, he's not denying that they called. If he had something to hide, he might well have refuted the whole incident" Routledge reasoned. Forde nodded his head.
"We'll make a few more inquiries, but I'm with you on this" Forde replied.

Angie and Stacey sat with Gina in her bedroom. Angie tried to gently explain what the police had said.
"They think that he was depressed. Harry must have just cracked" Angie said.
"But I never saw any signs. I mean, you know him Angie. What was he like?" Gina pleaded. Angie looked away. Stacey put an arm around Gina again, but Gina had seized on Angie's demeanour.
"Is there something that you're not telling me Angie? What did the police say exactly?" she sobbed. Angie looked to Stacey for guidance. Stacey barely nodded.
"In the note Harry mentioned me. I swear Gina, I knew nothing of this. The police think that he fancied me or something. Harry never said anything like that to me. I'm as confused as you are" Angie blurted out. Gina threw herself on the bed and began to wail even louder. Angie got up to leave.

"I'm sorry Gina, really I am" she whispered. Gina suddenly leapt up again. "No, wait! I want to know everything" her tear-stained green eyes begged. She pulled free from Stacey, demanding Angie's full attention. Angie stood in the doorway looking to the floor. Gina spoke once again.

"What did you two get up to behind my back? Did you sleep with my Harry? When did it happen?" she yelled. Angie looked up, startled by her pal's words. "What? Don't talk crazy Gina! Nothing ever happened, I told you!" It was Harry..." As soon as Angie spoke, she regretted it.

"What about him? Gina demanded, her hands held to her face in shock. Angie walked slowly back and sat on the bed. She told Gina everything that had occurred between Harry and her.

"And that's what happened, I swear it Gina" she concluded. Stacey felt obliged to add her own experience to endorse Angie's version of events.

"I found that someone was at my clothes, even my underwear drawer" Stacey told her. Gina eyes welled up again. She looked from one to the other.

"But I never saw any signs. Why did you not say something? Why did nothing happen before you two came back to live here? When Jodie..." Gina stopped herself. She recognised a certain look in Angie's eyes.

"Is there something else?" Gina asked. Angie O'Rourke looked decidedly uneasy.

"Jodie told me that she was scared to be alone with him. I don't think that he ever did anything though. She just didn't like being on her own with him" Angie said. Gina cut her off again. She held both hands to her ears.

"Stop! I don't want to hear anymore!" she sobbed. Stacey cradled her in her arms. Angie slowly stood up and went to her room. She lay on her bed and she too cried until she fell asleep.

Alex drove towards the vicinity of Memorial Park. He slowed as he reached the entrance on the Islandbridge end. The gates were closed, and an unmarked police car blocked the entrance. It was all that Alex needed to know. Sometimes suicides in Ireland were kept away from the media to protect families.

Alex smiled a self-satisfied smug grin as he drove away.

"Mission accomplished!" he sniggered. He could head home to Blackrock. Then he remembered Muggser and Burrener again. Their sheer audacity troubled him. The rage returned as he thumped on the steering wheel.

"Fucking twats, don't they realise who they're dealing with? I could crush them in an instant, the silly arseholes. Oh, I should have finished them that night! If I could live that moment over again..." he thought quietly. He drove on in the traffic. A black BMW cut him up. Alex banged hard on the horn.

"Silly fucking gobshite! Stupid prick!" he screamed, winding down the electric window. Suddenly peace descended on him. Instantly he calmed down again. His brain began to rationalise what really mattered.

"Relax Alex, it's not worth it. Why get involved because of something silly? We have things to do, scores to settle. Now think. We can't touch those two scumbags for now. Wait until after the trial. Let's hope that those two do time for what they done to my poor father. There will be loads of chances in the future to get them. Then there's Tony Lee. He must be getting over Jodie by now. Maybe it's time to fix him good and proper" Alex thought.

Tony Lee called to the apartment in Ranelagh. Stacey had texted him again, telling him about Harry death, and about the police calling. Gina had gone to stay with her parents for a while on the north side of town.

"How are you bearing up Stace? I'm sorry to hear about Harry. How are you Angie? Are you all right?" he asked.

The two went on to explain that Harry might not be as innocent as he appeared. Both told Tony their stories, tactfully omitting any mention of Jodie's experiences.

"Suicide eh?" Holy shit! That's scary stuff. I'm sorry; you girls should have said something. You stayed here with that going on? My god! Look, if you need to get away from this flat, there's always my house. The bedrooms have just been decorated, and you could have a room each" he said. Stacey answered for both of them. She smiled sweetly back at Tony.

"Thanks Tony, you're very kind. No, it's all right; we'll be okay here now. Thanks again" Stacey said. Tony smiled back his friendly grin at her. Angie backed her friend's view.

"Yeah Tony, thanks. We want to be here for Gina when she comes back" Angie added.

After Tony Lee had left, Stacey considered his offer. She would rather live anywhere in the world rather than at that house on St. Oliver's Road. Stacey Boyd still got goose-bumps thinking about it. No matter what Tony did to that place, Stacey always felt that she could never reside there. She shuddered as she remembered her one night in Tony's bedroom. And then she remembered Jodie. Jodie had stayed there happily for a time. Perhaps it was all in Stacey's imagination. It mattered little. She could never face that house again, and that was final.

287

CHAPTER TWENTY

LOSING THE PLOT

As the days went on, Tony and Stacey became more and more friendly. They kept in touch mostly by phone and text message, but they were beginning to joke and have fun again. Jodie Callaghan was never far from either of their thoughts, but slowly they were trying to move on. Tony had imagined asking Stacey out on an official date, but still had not had the courage to do so. Erik Ngombiti continued to push him into a new relationship with Stacey, but Tony still felt that the need to move more slowly.

"She will never really take me back" he would say to his closest friend at work. Or else

"It's still too soon after Jodie" he would state. Erik would shake his head and laugh, always warning that someone else would ask Stacey out. This always scared Tony, and privately he would vow to muster up the courage for another push at becoming Stacey's boyfriend. But as was his custom and his laid-back way, Tony would always postpone the process to a future date.

Alex Woods went to see his solicitor following another visit from the police. They had quizzed him a second time regarding any contact he might have had with Muggser and Burrener. Alex of course had strenuously denied everything, sticking hard to his story.

The family solicitor, Mr Waddington, poured over his story several times.

"The odd thing about this is that these hoodlums apparently have nothing to gain by incriminating you, Alex. This is my only fear. I cannot see what their motivation is. You, on the other hand would have everything to lose if a jury were to believe their story, don't you see?" Mr. Waddington said. He had been Alex's parent's solicitor for years. Mr. Waddington knew that everything in Tom Woods's estate would have naturally gone to Alex anyway. Tom had never sought to alter his will, and so Mr. Waddington could see no possible truth in the proposed testament of the two young thugs.

"I see what you are saying Mr. Waddington, but all that I can do is to tell the truth. I realise of course that I should have gone to the police when those thugs visited my home, but I was terrified. Having buried my dear father, my head was a mess. I simply could not bear the thought of a long drawn out trial just to have these yobs dealt with" Alex answered.

"Yes, yes, quite. I understand. Still, these petty criminals can twist things around. They have nothing to lose, you see Alex. A life of crime stretches out before them. They will lie, manipulate, cheat and steal, anything in fact to beat the legal system. By the way, call me Ronald, your dear father always did" The small rotund solicitor replied.

"So what should I do sir? I mean, do we just wait for the law to run its course, or should I speak to the police privately?" Alex asked. Mr. Waddington looked aghast.

"Dear, dear! No, you must never do that! It might be seen in the wrong light Alex! No, let the police deal with the matter. I doubt if they would ever try and make this matter stick. These two hoodlums may try and use this in their defence, heaven knows why. If I was their solicitor I know what I would be advising them to do. Lying in court never goes down well with a judge. Any reasonable judge will see this for what it is, a blatant attempt to deflect attention away from their crimes. No Alex, we must let nature run its course as I said. Perhaps their legal team will see sense and persuade them to change their statement. Otherwise these two petty gangsters might well do more prison time than they have bargained for" Mr. Waddington said.

Alex left the solicitor's office in the city centre feeling a little more pleased with himself. He was growing in confidence following his staged suicide of Harry. Alex now felt that he could get away with practically anything. He felt he had a superior intellect than most people, and would lie awake at night plotting ways to punish anybody who crossed him. Each day he scoured the newspapers and the internet for potential buyers of his company. But without Stacey Boyd to accompany him in his dream retirement, Alex was now in no immediate hurry to sell up and live the easy life. There always appeared to be other matters to attend to.

In fact, Alex was spending more and more of his days observing other people's lives. His latest fixation was a car salesman at his garage. The flamboyant young man was forever arriving to work in new suits and expensive shirts. Alex was convinced that this confident young man was somehow stealing from the firm. Yet Alex could see no possible way for this to be the case, and George Rae was great at his job. George had only been with the car sales team for a year or so, and was well liked by all. Alex had taken to following the chap everywhere; hoping that he would uncover what George was up to. He had had a fruitless time of it so far, and Alex was becoming more and more agitated by the day. If he could sack George he would, but had no real grounds to do so. Alex was now considering tampering with George's old car, but wondered if he might be pushing his luck to the extreme.

Tony answered the telephone on Saturday evening. Jan greeted him in an over-friendly voice. Tony looked to the ceiling. His infrequent trans-Atlantic phone calls from his sister really irritated him lately. He had telephoned Jan to tell her of Jodie's death when he was at his lowest point. Jan had swung the conversation around to discuss her children's grades at school.

"Hello Tony. Listen, first I want to apologise about the last call. I was so insensitive. It was inexcusable. I honestly don't know what came over me. I'm really am struggling to stay level-headed, but my kids just push me over the edge some days" Jan said.

Tony sighed loudly before replying.

"Whatever. Look Jan, I can't do this anymore. I'm also having a tough time. The difference is, no one died at your end of the phone" Tony replied caustically.

"What a cruel thing to say Tony. I may have been tactless, but I didn't mean any harm..." Jan continued.

Before she had finished speaking, Tony cut across her.

"Here's how it is Jan. I tried to get on with you, I really did. It hasn't worked. Why don't we simply leave each other alone? I won't bother you, and you promise to stay out of my life. You have your cosy little family, and I have no one, but hey! That's life! Now, I'm very busy knocking the shit out of this godforsaken house, so is there anything else?" Tony yelled, his voice decibel rising as his temper reached breaking point.

"What did you just say to me? Goddamn it Tony, don't you ever speak to me like that!" Jan screamed back.

"Why? Because of what you did for me? Is that it? Well, you gave me back my home, so goody for you! Put it down as part payment for looking after our mother for all of those years. Tell me about the Californian sunshine again. Well, while you were fucking soaking it up, I was here practically wiping my mother's backside. Think about that! Now fuck off and leave me alone!" Tony howled. It had all became too much for him suddenly.

Tony slammed down the phone and sank to the floor. He sobbed softly as he clambered onto the bottom step of the stairway. He grieved for Jodie and his dear Mam, but mostly he grieved for himself. Tony Lee wallowed in self-pity, unsure if he could go on with life. There was nothing to drive him, no incentive, nothing whatsoever to look forward to. All he could see was empty nights, lonely evenings, and meaningless days at work. No one in the world seemed to care if he lived or died, least of all Jan. She was his only real blood relative, and yet all she seemed concerned about was her children, and number eighty-eight St Oliver's Road.

The phone continued to ring as Tony lay sobbing into his hands. He knew that it was Jan, phoning back to apologise once again, just like she always did when she messed up. This time it was once too often.

Tony Lee saw a red mist descend. He was at the end of his tether. He had to do something, to strike out. He felt himself rise from the stairs. It was as if he had no control over his thinking.

Tony went to the shed in the back garden. He found the heavy sledgehammer and grabbed it with both hands. Nothing mattered anymore. Hoisting the large wooden handle over his head, Tony Lee threw it through the kitchen window. The metal end crashed into the large pane sending splinters of glass everywhere. Tony could instantly feel the relief. Without stopping, Tony ran inside and grabbed the sledgehammer again from the floor. Still the telephone rang. Tony ran to the hallway and lifted the heavy tool over his head. He aimed for the receiver and the sledgehammer clattered down hard on the phone. The small table holding the old-fashioned cream-coloured phone disintegrated into firewood. Part of the telephone danced across the new wooden floor in the hallway.

"See if you can ring now-bitch!" Tony screamed. He took the wooden-handled hammer and marched into the kitchen. Tony swung haphazardly at the old kitchen units, demolishing them one by one. Foodstuffs and crockery tumbled noisily to the floor. Amid the mayhem, Tony carried on. The shelves that he had spent so much time painstakingly erecting went next. Anything that stood in his way fell foul to his temper. He moved on to the kitchen table, systematically smashing it to shreds.

"You were right Jodie, that shelving was shit!" he yelled. Tony waded into the chairs next, and then the old armchair once used by his mother. Finally he ran out of energy and slumped to the floor again. All around him lay debris, and Tony began to chuckle. Broken white plates and shattered cups littered the floor. Cutlery and groceries lay spilled everywhere.

"All of that racket, and still no one came! I could be dead like Jodie, but still nobody would give a damn!" he laughed. His laughter turned to tears, and Tony lay prostrate on the tiled floor. The sledgehammer lay to his left as he stared upwards at the white ceiling. The bizarre scene amused him somehow, yet his soul cried out for help and company. Tony recalled a line from an old Queen song, Jodie's favourite pop group.

"Nothing really matters, any fool can see. Nothing really matters, nothing really matters...to me".

About a half-hour later Tony stumbled to his feet. He surveyed the damage. A gentle breeze blew in through the shattered window.

"I better call someone" he mumbled. He feared for his mental state, and for what he might do next. Tony then realised that his house phone had also fallen victim to his crazy behaviour. The irony was not lost on him. He smiled as he searched for his mobile phone.

Erik Ngombiti was the first number that came to mind. Erik's number was an easy one, and Tony almost knew it off by heart. He phoned Erik and walked slowly to the sitting room.

"Erik, I'm so sorry to bother you. I feel like shit. I've done a terrible thing. I've smashed up my house. I don't know what happened to me. Can you come over? Please? I'm worried that I might do something...worse" Tony said.

Erik Ngombiti explained that he was out shopping with his family. He said that he would be there as quickly as he could, but that Tony should get in touch with someone else in the meantime. The only other person that Tony could think of was Stacey. Reluctantly he called her and explained what had happened.

"Can you come over Stace, even until Erik gets here?" Tony pleaded. Stacey Boyd tried to think of a way out. Her compassion overcame her misgivings. She left hurriedly, explaining to Gina and Angie what had occurred.

Once Stacey was out of earshot, Angie and Gina began to speculate.

"That's not like Tony Lee. He's always so...so" Gina started.

"So predictable?" Angie asked with a giggle. Gina laughed too. Angie was pleased to see her cheer up a little. Gina had barely stopped crying since Harry's funeral.

Harry Brand had been the youngest of four brothers. He could hardly wait to leave home when he was younger. Gina's flat was the tenth or eleventh home that he had had since leaving his father's house in Palmerstown on the south side of Dublin City. At the funeral, his eldest brother had told of Harry's desire to explore the big wide world. He joked that Harry had not gotten very far, but had at least found happiness for a short time with Gina. Harry Brand's death by suicide would soon pass off as just another statistic in Ireland. His short life would only be remembered by those who knew him well. Perhaps his fixation with girls was because of his sheltered life in a male-dominated environment.

His mother had died when he was very young, and until he left home, all that he had known was his brothers and a father who worked hard to feed his children. Whether or not his suggestive remarks to Angie could have led to anything more sinister, was still open to conjecture. Harry was gone now, and the only person who knew the real truth was Alex Woods.

Stacey braced herself as she drew up outside Tony Lee's house. It was probably the last place on earth that she wished to be, yet out of loyalty to her former boyfriend she felt obliged to help. She knew by the tone of his voice on the phone that there was something seriously wrong.

Stacey knocked on the door. Instead of Tony opening the green front door and clinging on to it as he normally did, this time he merely released the old latch and walked away. The door swung open a few inches.

"Tony? Are you there? Are you okay?" Stacey asked, pushing the heavy door backwards. She saw him walk further down the long hallway towards the kitchen. Stacey called out his name again before following him inside.

"Oh-my-God! What happened?" she exclaimed. Tony smiled and shrugged his shoulders.

"Exactly! What happened? I don't know. I flipped I think Stacey, I just cracked up" Tony said coldly. Stacey surveyed the remnants of the furniture.

"But why? This is not like you Tony. You're usually so passive. What possessed you to ruin your own home?" she asked. Before Tony could reply, there was another knock, this time on the open hall door.

"Hello? Anybody home?" the voice called. Tony recognised the tone as that of Erik Ngombiti.

"Come in Erik, we're in here" he called out. Erik looked startled as he entered the room.

"My! It must have been one hell of a party!" he said with a grin. Stacey and Erik had met briefly at one of Tony's office parties. They nodded politely to each other.

"I think that he's feeling the pressure. He's been through a lot" Stacey said.

"I am here you know" Tony said impassively.

"What happened my friend?" Erik asked. Tony shrugged again.

"Jan phoned. I tried to stay calm, but she just got to me. There's hardly a week goes by when she's not on the goddamn phone preaching about what I can and cannot do. I know she let me stay in the house, but I can't live like this. I feel like putting a match to the place and just leaving" Tony said in a quick, ranting tone. Stacey put a comforting arm around his shoulders. Erik's eyes surveyed the room, focussing on the broken window. He whistled sharply and grinned again.

"Don't you think that you've done enough damage already?" Erik said. Tony managed a smile.

"Yeah, I suppose. All of my hard work down the drain! Still, Jodie always wanted things to be new. Shelving and paint were never her idea of home improvements. Oh, she had grand plans for this old place, and where did it get her? Meeting me was the worst possible thing that could have happened to her" he said. Stacey hugged him close to her.

"Don't say that. Jodie was just in the wrong place that evening. It might have happened to her anyway, whether she was with you or not" she reasoned. Tony shook his head.

"You know that's not true. If she had not left my house that night, she would still be alive today, and that's a fact, whichever way you twist it" he said. Erik picked his way through the debris.

"Look, blaming yourself won't solve anything. Let's get this mess cleared up, and then we can have a coffee and talk" Erik said.

Almost one hour later all three say in the living room. Erik had used the broken shelving to board up the kitchen window. All of the spare wood from the units was now stacked away in the back garden, along with the broken furniture. Tony had calmed a little, having poured out his heart and blaming himself for Jodie's death.

Stacey was already considering a way of making an excuse to leave. Unfortunately for her, Erik beat her to the punch.

"Listen guys, I have to head off. Thanks for the coffee. I left Eileen with the children and the shopping at Liffey Valley Shopping Centre. I have to go back and collect her. We can talk Monday Tony eh? In the meantime, you should be looking up DIY stores on the internet!" he quipped. Tony gave him a look that said "I had that coming!"

"Thanks Erik for everything. Yeah, Monday. I'm sorry about this, and for dragging you away from your family. I didn't know who to call. Thanks again" Tony replied. Erik quickly left leaving Stacey feeling decidedly awkward. She did not want to leave Tony alone, yet she had to get away from that awful house soon.

"Well, Stacey, you should go too. I'll be okay, I'm sorry again" Tony said. Stacey smiled back sweetly at him. Somehow his words made things even more difficult to simply just leave.

"It's all right, I'll make some more coffee" she replied. Stacey went to the dark kitchen with the boarded-up window and put the kettle on. She stood there staring at the bare walls, wondering what Tony must be going through. He had lost his mother and girlfriend within months, and then he had Jan telling him how to live his life. She made some coffee, adding a drop of brandy to each mug and went back to sit with him.

"Well, you only have three mugs left! All of your Mum's best china is broken. This is going to cost a fortune to replace Tony. At least you had the pleasure of telling your sister where to go! She won't bother you again!" Stacey said with a chuckle. Tony grinned and raised his eyebrows.

"You have no idea of Jan. She will be on the phone tomorrow apologising" he answered.

"Not that phone she won't!" Stacey grinned. The two laughed together, and suddenly their eyes locked. They sat next to each other on the sofa in silence. Tony leaned forward and kissed her. For Stacey it felt like the most natural thing in the world. She returned his kiss and they fell into each other's arms.

"Just hold me" she whispered.

Alex Woods watched from the bedroom window as the two shadows dodged up the driveway.

"Yes! Come on bastards, just a little bit more. Come on, come to Daddy!" he muttered. His investment in a new security system was already paying off. He was taping the events on camera, but wanted to witness the situation for himself.

"Now remember, let me do the talking Burrener. We give him a last chance to pay up. I know for a fact that the cops have spoken to him now. Remember what our solicitor said? He's gotta be scared of ending up in court. I think that he will cough up this time. If he doesn't, well then he goes down with us. I can't wait to see his face when we knock on the door! He thought that we wouldn't find him! It's so bleedin' obvious where he has moved to. What a prick!" Muggser said with an evil cackle.

"Sssh! Come on, the light is on downstairs!" Burrener replied in a whisper. Alex sat in the darkness in the front bedroom. He held his mobile in his hand, ready to telephone the police. A camera inside the hallway was pointed straight at the front door. Alex made his way downstairs and waited.

When the doorbell rang, Alex answered it right away, catching the two unaware.

"Yes, what do you want?" Alex asked. Muggser cleared his throat.

"Er, it's about the money, are you gonna pay or what? It's a thousand each, that's the final offer" Muggser said, trying hard to sound menacing.

"Oh, so let's get this straight. I pay you €2,000 for something that never happened, and I never see you again? This blackmail is a handy game, isn't it? And it's getting cheaper all of the time. It was €1,500 each the last time you visited my apartment. Is this cut-price blackmail?" Alex said casually. Burrener looked to his friend to reply. Muggser was not quite sure what to say.

"Listen Alex, we don't want to put you in hospital, but we know people who can deal with you, understand? Look, just pay us and we walk, otherwise things could get very fucking nasty for you, understand?" Muggser said, stepping forward deliberately.

"But you said that I offered to pay you for killing my father. That never happened, did it?" Alex continued. Muggser looked more flustered than ever. "Okay, not exactly, but isn't it worth the money to get rid of us?" Muggser countered. Alex had heard enough. They had fallen into his trap.

"If I was you two, I would start running now. The cops are on their way. I phoned them a few minutes ago when you walked through the gates. Smile lads, you're on Candid Camera!" Alex said. The two ruffians stood at the top of the wide steps staring at each other. Each looked around the grounds, trying to identify a camera in the gardens. Alex spoke again.

"They don't show up so good at night, but you two do! What would you be doing such a long way from home? How will you explain that to the police? Out for an evening stroll, were you?" Alex asked, now enjoying every moment.

"We came by bus" Burrener said lamely. Muggser nudged him slyly in the ribs. The sound of a siren could be heard in the distance. Muggser made a run down the steps, quickly followed by his pal. The garda car was already speeding in through the gates. There was no other way out, and as the headlights trapped them, the two stood still. Two burly policemen climbed menacingly from the squad car.

"We did nothing, we were just talking to him" Burrener protested.

"Shut up Burrener, say nothing" Muggser said quietly.

Back at the police station, the two detectives viewed the CCTV footage. "Well, pretty conclusive, eh? The audio is crystal clear too. Those two fools more or less made a full confession" Detective Forde said to his colleague. Jack Routledge appeared to be not entirely convinced.

"Woods looks a little too confident to me. I mean, here are two thugs trying to blackmail him, and he's as cool as a cucumber. He answers the door without a weapon, knowing full well who is outside. These two have already threatened him in the past. There's no trace of fear or panic in his voice. He speaks to them as if they are the next door neighbours, for God's sake" Detective Routledge replied. Myles Forde laughed out heartily.

"You never change Jack, always the suspicious one! I tackled Woods about that. He said he knew that he had to capture them on tape to prove his innocence. He said that he was concentrating so much that he forgot completely about what might happen to him. It's plausible, I suppose. I tend to believe him" Detective Forde replied.

"I don't like it, not one little bit. It smacks of something. Don't you think that it's a bit too convenient? I mean, the very two people that you want to clear your name just happen to knock on your front door?" Routledge reasoned. Detective Forde smiled and nodded.

"It is a godsend for him all right, but I never thought that there was enough to prosecute anyway. What are you suggesting Jack? A set-up? You hardly think that he paid those two to knock on his door and say what they said?" Detective Forde asked. Routledge shook his head. He shoved his hands deep into his trouser's pockets and paced the room.

"No, I'm not suggesting that at all. Maybe it's just my nature, but it just doesn't feel right" Routledge replied.

"Case over?" Forde asked. Detective Routledge nodded hesitantly.

"I guess, unless Burrener and Muggser stick to their story and walk free in the courts. If that was to be the case, we would have to look at it again" Routledge said.

"You're clutching at straws Jack. Those two are going to jail, mark my words" Forde laughed. Jack Routledge nodded again and hurriedly left the room.

The next morning, Stacey awoke next to Tony. She had had a peaceful sleep and felt totally refreshed. Tony had an arm around her thin waist.

"Sleep well?" he asked softly.

"I slept like a top! That's the best rest I've had for ages. At the apartment there's always someone up early. Harry clatters around as if..." Stacey stopped herself, realising that Harry Brand was no longer with them.

"Thanks for staying over Stacey, I don't know what I would have done without you" Tony whispered. He planted a kiss on her forehead to emphasise his point. Stacey had to think fast. Although last night had been exceptional, she was still reluctant to make some ground rules clear.

"How could I not stay after the way you were Tony? Let's take things slowly for now" she replied. Her head lay on his chest now. It helped somehow, not to have to make eye contact.

"Agreed, but I won't wait forever! I never stopped loving you Stace, you know that. Sooner or later you're gonna have to take me back. I won't take no for an answer!" Tony chuckled. Stacey cocked an eye up to study his face. The implications of what he had just said struck her. Stacey said nothing. Tony quickly realised that Stacey too had been through a lot. Her ruined wedding was probably still very much on her mind. Tony knew that it was time to backtrack.

"Sorry Stace, I didn't mean to push things. How are you coping yourself? Do you ever see Alex?" he asked quietly. He felt her shake her head as she lay back down on his bare chest.

"Only that time that he came to the flat, although I didn't actually see him. It felt weird hearing his voice again. No, I don't want to see him, nor do I suppose he wants to see me. I'm sure that he's glad to see the back of me after what I put him through. When I went to my parents in England, I was terrified that I would meet him while out shopping. I used to stare at faces in the crowds, half-expecting to see his face. I mean, what would he be doing in Wolverhampton, but still I expected him to pop up somewhere. Weird or what? I mean, why would he be in the high street in Wolverhampton Town?" Stacey said.

"Shopping?" Tony replied dryly. Stacey leapt up and grabbed her pillow.

"Fight!" she yelled, pounding him playfully with the white fluffy pillow. Tony Lee easily overpowered her, pinning her to the bed.

"Now, what will I have for breakfast? Let me think!" he said with a grin. He leaned forward and kissed her on the lips.

Alex continued to stake out George Rae. He had decided that George was to be his next victim, but just how he would deal with George had given Alex many sleepless nights. A hit and run was now out of the question. Alex knew that he could only push his luck so far. A car accident seemed an unlikely scenario, but Alex was warming to the idea more and more. He knew how to bleed the brake fluid from a car, and the road outside of George's house was on a steep hill, overlooking a severe drop. Alex had more or less settled on the plan. He could make it look like negligence on George's behalf, leaving the police to believe that George Rae had not maintained his car properly. It might seem strange for someone working in the motor trade, but George's old car had a poor service record.

Alex had acquired a spare key for the old Renault, something not too difficult to do in the car trade. He had viewed the service record, and had had a good look at the engine. George had barely done any maintenance on the old car since buying it. If things went well, Alex might consider tampering with the car that very night.

It was now 2am. Alex had napped in his vehicle until all of the lights had gone out in The Rae's household. His only fear was for the large dog which they kept in the back garden. If his handiwork set off the Alsatian barking, he might have to abandon the job. But even for that eventuality, Alex had a contingency plan.

Alex opened the driver's door and crept from his car. Two other cars were parked in the long driveway, but George's was to the front. Alex popped the bonnet and went to work. Within seconds the dog set off howling. The howling turned to barking. Alex cursed the dog under his breath.

"Fucking mongrel, shut up for Christ sake! This bastard has to be sorted out. Stealing from me-me! And I'm the one employing him. Ungrateful scum!" Alex ranted as he tried to speed up the process. A light went on to the rear of The Rae's home. Alex lowered the bonnet without closing it tight.

"Okay, I didn't want to do this, but fuck it!" Alex raged. He slipped away to his vehicle and waited. Eventually the yellow light to the back of the large house vanished. No one had actually checked the front garden, probably presuming that a cat had upset the dog to the rear of the property.

Once things had quietened down, Alex again silently crept from the driver's seat of his car.

"Right! You won't be howling again doggy" Alex sneered. He took the pork chop laced with rat poison from the plastic bag and set off a second time.

"Here boy, here boy!" he called in a low voice. Alex was to the side of the property, a high wall separating him from the dog. He tossed the meat over the wall and heard the dog scamper in that direction.

"Bon appétit!" he smirked. Within minutes he was back at the Renault engine. He set about bleeding the brakes, whipping off both front wheels. It took him just minutes to complete the process, pumping brake fluid from the old car through the loosened valve. When finished, Alex quietly closed the bonnet and locked the car. He swiftly climbed back inside his white Mondeo with a beaming smile on his face.

"I can safely say that your thieving days are over Georgie boy!" he said with a loud cackle. Alex drove on towards Rathfarnam, leaving him with a half-hour drive to his home in Blackrock. On a weekday, this journey might take over an hour in traffic, but at two-thirty in the morning the streets were quiet. Suddenly Alex noticed a police motorcycle in his rear view mirror.

"Keep calm, nothing to worry about" he told himself. Alex continued on his way, observing the speed limit at all times. The policeman sat in behind him and trailed him at a steady pace along the almost deserted road. Alex continually watched in his rear-view mirror. He slowed at an amber light, just to be certain that he was obeying the law. This seemed to trigger off suspicion in the trailing motorcyclist's head. Alex was being ultra-careful. He could see the policeman on the phone, no doubt checking out the owner of his car.

Alex set off slowly again as the lights turned green. He was on Foster's Avenue, only ten minutes or so from home. Immediately the flashing blue lights lit up the street. Alex began to sweat slightly. He felt confident that he had done nothing wrong, but if George was to be killed the next morning, a clever policeman might tie him in with it.

"What's the trouble officer?" Alex asked with a smile, winding down the electric window.

Where are you off to sir?" the policeman asked, ignoring Alex's question.

"Well, I'm off home to Blackrock. Is there anything that I've done wrong?" Alex countered. The policeman asked Alex for his driving licence and checked that his car insurance and road tax was up to date.

"Your hands are full of oil. Can I inquire what happened?" said the garda. Alex examined his dirty hands. He had wiped them in a cloth, but the oil from George's car was still visible.

"Oh, I got a puncture back there, sorry, I forgot all about it" Alex replied.

"It's a bit late for a drive sir. Can I ask where you've been?" the garda asked, his glass visor on the helmet still covering half of his young face. It was time for Alex to play the sympathy card.

"Nowhere really. You see, my father has just died. I've moved into his house, which can be pretty lonely. I grew up there with my Dad. The house holds some pretty special memories, you know? Sometimes it's hard to get to sleep officer" Alex said, he wiped away a fake tear from his eye.

"I understand. Listen sir, the left indicator on your car is not working, that's why I pulled you over. Perhaps you hit the wiring when taking out the spare wheel from the boot. Have it attended to in the morning. Good night" the policeman said. Within seconds he was gone into the night.

"Fucking twat! Brains up his arse!" Alex cackled. He set off for home and a much needed rest.

"Tomorrow should be interesting, very interesting indeed!" he smirked as he drove in through the large black gates of Hillcrest.

As expected, George Rae did not arrive for work the following morning. Alex looked at his watch as he walked towards reception.

"Are all the staff in Michelle?" he asked innocently.

"Yes, all but George" she replied.

"Oh? That's not like him, he's always so prompt. Perhaps he got a puncture. I'm always telling him about that car. He seems to have money to burn, yet his car is a heap of scrap!" Alex said with a friendly chuckle.

"Well, he won't be in today. Mechanical trouble. His mother phoned" Michelle replied. She was busy on the computer, and barely looked up at Alex. Alarm bells began to ring in Alex's head. It appeared that George Rae was not dead after all.

"Er, how long ago was that? Did she say what happened?" Alex asked. Michelle made eye contact for the first time. Alex did not usually make inquiries about staff at such an early point in the day, certainly not about salesmen. There were eight sales agents on the staff, which was probably more than enough.

"Oh, about thirty minutes ago. No, she never said what happened, just that he would be in work tomorrow" Michelle replied. Alex walked away to his office without another word.

"Fuck! Shit! What happened? I opened the nut to the brake fluid. I pumped those brakes dry. The fucking fluid would have drained out. He had to crash, he just had to" Alex ranted. He paced the office trying to figure out what might have gone wrong.

"The nut was barely on; the vibrations would make it appear that it had happened over a period of time. That shithead should be dead by now-dead!" Alex muttered. Alex was in a rage. He stormed out to the reception desk at the main entrance to the building. The early morning sunshine beamed in through the giant glass windows. Outside, cars and trucks whizzed by on the busy street. Wood's Motors was situated on a main road leading into the city centre.

"Michelle, I want you to get George on the phone now. It's not good enough staff ringing in sick all of the time. Tell him to get his arse in here now! I don't care how. Let him get the bus or get a taxi. I'm trying to run a business here, not a holiday camp!" Alex said. Michelle seemed totally surprised. She picked up the receiver and sought out George's number on the computer.

"Okay sir, if you say so. George is never absent. It had to be something serious" she said. Alex thought twice. He put a finger on the receiver button of the modern white telephone.

"What are you saying Michelle? Do you think that I'm over-reacting?" he asked. The young secretary looked nervous. She did not want her boss thinking that she was going against his better judgement.

"No Alex, not at all. I'll tell him what you said" she replied. Alex took the receiver from her and replaced it on the hook.

"No, maybe you're right Michelle. I'll tell you what. You phone his mother back and tell her that we were concerned for George. Tell him to take an extra day if need be. George's attendance record is exemplary" Alex said quietly. He walked back to his office leaving Michelle looking confused.

The following morning Alex noticed that some of the staff had gathered for a chat in the showrooms. George Rae was in the middle of them, talking in an animated way. It was still five minutes to opening time, and Alex wandered up to see what was going on. The foreman waved to Alex to come over as he approached.

"Quick Alex, listen to this! That old rust-bucket of George's finally packed in! Not only that, but a dead dog saved his life! Tell Alex what happened George!" Frank McKenzie said with a beaming grin.

"It's not funny Frank; some of us are pet-lovers!" Wes Doyle chipped in. Laughter erupted again among the workforce. George Rae began his story again.

"Well, yesterday morning I left for work as normal. I started the old banger up, and as usual, she started first time. Good old Betsy, God be good to her! I had only driven a couple of feet when I saw the Ma waving like mad in the driveway. Of course, I thought that I had forgotten my lunch or something, so I hit the brakes. There was nothing there, not a dickey bird, so I began to pump them like mad! Still nothing! I sailed into Hickey's wall across the street, resting gently against their lovely new red-brick wall! The Ma comes running up to say that she thinks old Hercules the dog is dead. It seems that he ate something he shouldn't have! Hercules was old anyway, but was my elder sister's pet. You could say that Hercules saved my life! We live on a steep hill, a few minutes later and who knows? I could have been wearing the old wooden overcoat!" George said with a chuckle. Alex joined in the laughter, but under his breath he was cursing his bad luck. George continued to hold court.

"I'm not a doggy person myself, but my sister loved old Hercules. She was heartbroken all day yesterday. I expect that she will get over it. Last night the Ma was talking about buying her a new puppy!" George said. Alex walked slowly away, his mind deep in thought.

Later that morning, George managed to have a quiet word with Alex.
"Thanks for the offer of another day off boss, I appreciate it. It wasn't needed after all. I've decided that it's time to scrap that old car. The brakes are shot, and God knows what else is wrong with it. I was wondering if we could do a trade-in deal?" George said. Alex said nothing for a few seconds.

"Leave it with me. I'll have to think about it" Alex said coldly. He walked away leaving George slightly bemused. Alex and his father had always being very approachable to staff regarding scrappage deals. George considered that he had always got on well with both Alex and his late father.

Later that afternoon, Michelle came to Alex's office with some paperwork.
"What do you make of that George Rae fellow?" Alex asked her bluntly. He was seething inside because of his failed mission. Michelle dithered. She was always reluctant to take sides between staff and management.

"He seems okay, but I hardly know him" she said defensively.

"Yeah, but all of those new expensive suits and shoes! He was wearing a shirt last week that must have cost a small fortune! Yet he drives around in an old banger that was hardly fit for the road! I mean, I know that we pay well, but he's only with us a short time. How can he afford all of these new clothes and things?" Alex reasoned. Michelle looked uncomfortable. She waited for Alex to sign the paperwork.

"As I say, I really don't know. Perhaps he makes lots from his music" she said. Alex stopped reading the paperwork and looked up at her.

"What music? What do you mean?" he asked. Michelle smiled as if relieved by the question.

"His adverts! George writes jingles for radio and television advertisements, didn't you know?" she smiled. Alex shook his head.

"Yeah, he played some for me on a disc. They're very good! I recognised some of them from the telly. You know the soap powder one about the sheep? And the one for petrol on the island? They're all Georges, I thought that you knew" Michelle said.

Alex finished signing the paperwork and handed it back to the red-headed receptionist. He was in a daze. Michelle left quickly leaving Alex to his thoughts.

Alex paced the office as he considered what he had done. He had never taken much interest in his staff's hobbies, or what they got up to after hours.

"You fool, stupid fool. You nearly killed an innocent man, Alex. That's not you. That's wrong. From now on you have to be more selective. We can't go around killing folk for no reason. Come on, re-focus! Only the ones who cross you deserve to be punished. A new rule Alex. From now on, we have to consider everything before we make a move. People like Muggser and Burrener deserve it. Tony Lee, he definitely needs sorting. Maybe Angie for her stupidity and ignorance. Even that Gina bitch for taking my Stacey back in to the apartment. Who is she to take sides anyway? Yeah, let's go again, but this time concentrate" Alex told himself.

CHAPTER TWENTY-ONE

THE VISIT TO WALSALL

Tony Lee knew that he had to woo Stacey all over again. While they were now very much an item again, Stacey continued to live at the apartment with her friends. The two dated steadily, mostly at weekends and maybe once or twice during the week. Tony had never brought up the thorny subject of her moving in with him since the night that she had stayed over. He knew how tricky the topic would be. Stacey's dislike for his home was very apparent. When Tony discussed what he planned for the house, Stacey would always quickly change the subject.

Jan had not tried to get in contact since their argument over the phone, and Tony hoped it would stay that way. He had given up on having any meaningful relationship with his sister.

"Why don't we do something this weekend Stace? We could drive somewhere and book into a hotel" Tony suggested. They were sitting in their local bar on a Wednesday evening. The pub was fairly quiet, as it usually was during the week.

"Yeah, that sounds cool; we could head off on Friday evening. What about Wexford? It's not too far, and the roads are great" Stacey replied. Just then, her mobile phone rang. Tony went to the bar to order drinks while she took the call. He returned to see Stacey face appearing pale and drawn.

"Something the matter?" he asked.

"It's Mom, she's taken ill. She's in hospital in Wolverhampton. Alex, Dad thinks that it's cancer. Mom was always a heavy smoker in the past, although she's given up now. I'm gonna have to fly over Tony. Dad is extremely worried. I'm sorry about the weekend" she said. Tony put an arm around her.

"No, that's okay. You have to go. Another time, eh? Your Mom needs you" he replied with a concerned look. They talked for a while, with Stacey saying she would catch a flight the next day. Tony made a subconscious decision that while she was away, he would do some serious work on number eighty-eight. It was the perfect opportunity to refurbish the house, and perhaps finally make Stacey change her mind about his home.

Alex Woods let himself into Stacey's apartment again. It was Thursday morning, just after ten o'clock. He had watched the apartment a few times lately, but had noticed nothing out of the ordinary. All three girls came and went to work as normal. Alex had not seen any male companions for any of the three, and his curiosity was now getting the better of him. Earlier Alex had rung the doorbell before entering, just to be sure. Once there was no answer, he quietly slipped inside.

Alex wandered around checking rooms, making sure that there were no male items on show. At the same time, Stacey Boyd was finishing up at work. She had gone in that day to explain the situation to her boss. Stacey had already used up quite a lot of time off on compassionate leave, but had forfeited her annual holidays in return. Reluctantly she would be given more time off, but this time at her own expense.

Stacey parked her car in the resident's car park outside her apartment. Had she been more observant, she may have noticed Alex's white car further down the car park. The lift doors were closed, and so she bounded upstairs, anxious to pack for her trip. Having taken her suitcase out of the attic earlier that morning, Stacey hoped to be away within the hour. She planned on parking her car back at her workplace for security, not knowing how long that she would be away for. Her plan was then to catch a cab to the airport for her flight at 1:15pm.

Stacey turned the key in the front door. Alex froze in the hallway. He made a grab for the door to Angie's bedroom. It was the one room that he had not yet checked. Subconsciously he remembered that Angie always kept it locked. It was too late. There was no time to hide anywhere else. Luckily for Alex, since Harry Brand's death, Angie had ceased her habit of keeping her room locked. Alex squeezed in the door and closed it over behind him. He watched through the slightly open door to identify who was entering the flat. Once he saw Stacey, Alex made himself scarce. He slid under the bed and listened quietly. Stacey dashed to her bedroom, pulling the pink suitcase down from on top of the wardrobe. She flung it on the bed and began to pack.

"Jeans, jumpers, blouses, underwear" she recited as she emptied some drawers. Her wardrobe was wide open as she picked her preferred clothing for the trip.

"Now, where's that yellow top that Mom bought me? Oh, I lent it to Angie. I'll go and get it!" she said, thinking aloud.

Stacey pushed in Angie's bedroom door. She made straight for Angie's wardrobe and began to flick through her pal's clothes.

"Where is it, come on, I'll miss my flight!" she muttered. Alex took in her words. His mind was racing as he considered where she could be going. Suddenly he felt his car keys slide from his trouser's pocket. He tried to make a grab for them, but they slipped through his grasp and clinked noisily onto the laminated wooden floor. Alex cringed and readied himself to be discovered. His mind was already thinking ahead. He might have to strangle Stacey Boyd if she discovered him. At the same time, Stacey dropped a hanger to the bottom of the wardrobe. It bounced heavily on the floor of the wooden wardrobe, making far more noise than Alex's keys.

"Bugger! I'll have to go without it! That Angie, I'll kill her when I see her!" Stacey muttered once more.

She quickly left the room, slamming the door behind her. Alex Woods exhaled slowly. He picked up his keys and waited. Within a few minutes Stacey had left, and Alex slipped quietly from beneath the bed. He cautiously made his way outside. A note in the sitting room told him all that he needed to know. He picked up the piece of paper and read aloud.

"Angie\Gina, gone to Moms. Will text you with any news. Phoned this morning, Dad says that she's comfortable. She had a restful night. See you when I get back. Who knows when! Love, Stacey".

"Well, so she's off to tend her mother! Phew, that was a close thing! At least I won't have to stake out this place for a while!" Alex thought. He took a last look around the apartment before leaving hurriedly.

Tony Lee had arranged to have the following few weeks off work. He had not used his holidays because of his mother's death earlier in the year. Plans to get away with Jodie had never materialised. This appeared to be the perfect opportunity to do some serious work at home. Reluctantly he would spend some real money on house improvements, despite his misgivings. Jodie's words echoed in his head, and Tony secretly wished that he had listened to her when she was alive. He pictured her face if she could have realised her dreams of a conservative in the back garden, a proper kitchen, and perhaps double-glazed windows.

"Oh, and of course, an artificial fireplace-just to look at!" he thought with a hint of humour.

"Penny for your thoughts!" Erik said as he stood next to him. Tony continued to gaze out of the giant glass window.

"Oh, I'm just thinking about Jodie. I wonder what she would make of me and Stacey getting back together. And now I'm doing what she visualised for the house anyway" Tony said.

"Seize the moment! It's no use looking back Tony. "What ifs" are for dreamers! I'm sure that Jodie would approve. You thought it best at the time to plan for the future. It's all very well holding on to your cash for a rainy day, but the future is now. You get on with your life. Turn that old house into a palace while Stacey is away. I'm sure that when she gets back, she will be well impressed" Erik replied with his usual friendly grin. Tony turned to face his pal.

"And what about you Erik? What does the future hold for you?" Tony asked. Eric sighed and gazed out across the sprawling city.

"I still have ambitions mate, I still have, honestly. But realistically now, my dreams are for my children. Oh, I daydream, of course I do. Going back to London to live, returning to Africa, moving to New York, they are all somewhere in my sub-consciousness. But as time passes, I am less and less restless. My children are growing up fast. Dublin is their home. Why would I uproot them? They like school and have friends here. I cannot be selfish anymore" Erik answered. He smiled at Tony, but Tony Lee could see the doubt in his workmates eyes.

"But Erik, you've always had dreams and plans. London was your home for years. Would you not like to go back there? The Irish economy is still on a downward spiral. If you want the best for your kids, then you must go where your career can earn you the maximum" Tony reasoned. For the first time Erik looked uneasy. He slipped off his heavy-rimmed black spectacles before replying.

"It's complicated Tony. I won't return to London. Eileen and the children must come first now. Let's leave it at that, eh?" Erik said.

By Erik's tone, Tony knew that the topic was over. He returned again to his own plans.

"Okay Erik, I didn't mean to pry. My worry now is that I will blow my life savings on this house, plus the money Mam left me. I could end up with a nice home, but one that Stacey might refuse to live in. What do I do then? I won't be able to afford to move, and Stacey might become restless again" Tony said. Erik managed a chuckle.

"That's the female sex for you Tony my friend! The nest is so important to them! They like to select the home, adorn it with their special choices in furniture and fabrics. The man simply has to supply the cash, and stand well back!" Erik laughed. Tony nodded in agreement. He could sense that Erik was probably correct.

"That's my biggest fear pal. It might be easier to sell up and move on. But I can't. I love that old house you see. I'm gonna have to gamble that I can win Stacey around" Tony said with a long deep sigh.

"Hello Tony? It's Stacey. How are you?" the voice on the other end of the line said. Tony smiled. Stacey had been in England now for over a week. He wanted to tell her all about his big plans to renovate his home, which were well underway, but thought better of it. Tony considered that it might be best to complete the renovations first and hope that they met with Stacey's approval. Anyway, Stacey had much more important things on her mind, he decided. Tony instead asked after her mother.

"She's got to have a serious operation I'm afraid. The specialist reckons that they will catch the cancer before it spreads. They seem very confident, so let's hope that he's right. That's really what I'm phoning you about. You see, I've arranged with my job to take some compassionate leave, without pay of course. I was wondering if you fancied coming over for a few days? Maybe Friday till Monday or something? I would love to see you. I miss you so much Tony, but I simply cannot leave Mom" Stacey replied.

"No, of course not" Tony answered. His mind was in overdrive. Stacey's invitation had sparked off something else in his brain.

"Yes, I want to see you too. Maybe I could get over for the weekend. Yeah, it's not a bad idea" he replied. I'll phone back and let you know" he said.

"Well, there is one thing Tony. Dad would never approve of you staying here at the house. Just so you know. He's such an old-fashioned man!" Stacey said, forcing a laugh.

"No, no. I understand completely. I'll find a B&B or something" Tony answered. They talked some more before saying goodbye, with Tony agreeing to phone back.

As he put down the receiver he began to plot his visit. Stacey was staying in The Midlands. His Auntie Mary lived in Walsall, which was not too far away. He could go and visit his aging aunt, and maybe get to understand why his mother and her older sister had fallen out. The more he considered the idea, the more Tony liked it. And if he could get the work to continue on the house while he was away, so much the better.

Muggser and Burrener asked to see Detective Jack Routledge. They wanted to change their story regarding their meeting with Alex Woods.

"Tell me again boys, and this time in more detail" Routledge replied coldly. His tone was almost one of boredom. Muggser began the tale of the night that

Alex Woods had dished out a hiding to the two young thugs. He described the night in graphic details, almost over-embroidering the fateful evening.

"And now both of you are saying that Mr. Woods did this?" Detective Routledge replied. Both men nodded vigorously in unison, as if to add even more weight to their tale. Routledge sighed and tossed his pen down on the desk. He had been taking brief notes, but the meeting was not an official one. The interview was not being recorded.

"And why are you coming to me now lads? Do you want to plea-bargain or something? And what has your solicitor advised you?" Routledge asked. Burrener looked to his best friend to take up their cause. Muggser cleared his throat.

"We were advised against saying anything, but what does he bleedin' know? Yeah, we could do a deal all right. If you drop all charges against us regarding the break-in at The Woods house, we'll testify against him, and we'll admit to several other burglaries" Muggser said earnestly.

Routledge laughed out loud. He shook his head in disbelief. The wily detective stood up and leaned forward on the wooden, rectangular desk.

"Your solicitor offered you some sound advice there lads. It sound to me that you have it in for Mr. Woods. This story is full of holes. Why would he batter the two of you? For what reason? How would he know where to find you for a start? You say that you had never clapped eyes on him before that night. Last week you said that he had offered to pay you for the break-in. You two have told so many lies, and now no one can believe you. When we asked at the hospital about who smashed you up, all you gave us was abuse. So, even if I wanted to believe you now, what possible motive would Woods have to give you a going over?" Detective Routledge asked. Burrener tried to take up their case.

"He wanted to get us for breaking in, didn't he? He said that we hurt his old man. He wanted to get even" Burrener said.

"Ah! But that's not what you told us! And it comes back to the same old question. How did he know it was you two, and where would he get your addresses from?" Routledge countered. Burrener looked to Muggser again.

"Look, we don't fucking know how he knew. Maybe there's a grass in the police station. Maybe one of your lot slipped him our details. Does it matter? The point is, he did that to us. He shouldn't be allowed get away with it" Muggser responded. Detective Routledge reached for the drawer in his desk.

"Do you want to make a formal statement, boys? It can either be about corrupt police officers, or an assault by Mr. Woods. Either way, both of you are going to look pretty silly" Routledge replied in a tiresome voice. Muggser leaned forward in his chair.

"Are you saying no to a deal then?" he asked.

"You got it in one!" Detective Routledge answered with a grin. Muggser thumped the desk in temper before standing up sharply. Before Routledge could react, the two had vanished again.

Both men walked on aimlessly through the afternoon pedestrians on the busy street.

"We're going down this time Muggser-nothing surer" Burrener rasped.

"Shut up, shut up. Let me think!" Muggser answered.

"Well, I've had enough. I've let you do all of the thinking. I'm gonna make a full confession. Sometimes that works. The judge might give us probation for admitting everything. It's worth a try" Burrener said. In a second Muggser had grabbed him by the coat and shoved him hard against the wall.

"Listen dickhead, there will be no confession, got it? If you open your mouth, I will see to it personally that you never get to speak another word-do you hear me? Jesus help me Burrener, I'm not messing here. Whatever happens, we do this together. Do I have to paint you a fuckin' picture? Now stop whining and let me see if there's another Jaysus way around this, yeah?" Muggser said through gritted teeth. Burrener nodded slowly. Muggser then released his friend from his grip and smoothed out his coat with both hands. The two nodded to each other and set off again at a slow pace.

Alex Woods drove to the home of George Rae. He climbed from his car carrying a small basket. Alex rang the doorbell and waited. It was just gone twelve o'clock on a bright fresh morning. A kindly-looking old lady answered the door, wiping her hands in a floral tea towel.

"Sorry to bother you, Mrs. Rae is it?" Alex asked with a beaming smile. The grey-haired bespectacled lady nodded; unsure to whom she was speaking.

"Ah! I expected a much older woman! George told me all about your dog's tragic death. I was deeply moved by your loss. I'm George's boss at the garage. Look, I know that you can never replace a pet; they're like one of the family. I'm a cat-lover myself. We recently lost our own family tabby-cat. We still miss him dearly. Anyway, I thought that you might like to have this beautiful puppy. Perhaps it might help George's sister get over Hercules" Alex said in a matter-of-fact tone. He held up the khaki-coloured straw basket to display a tiny cream Labrador pup. Mrs. Rae's features brightened up immediately.

"Oh he's lovely! Won't you come in for a moment Mr...?" she exclaimed.

"Thank you, yes. It's Alex, Alex Woods Ma'am" he replied.

Alex returned to the garage and George immediately made his way over to talk to him.

"My Mum's just been on the phone. That was a nice gesture Alex. Thanks a lot. Oh, and by the way, thanks for the deal on that car again. I can't wait to drive it! I'm lost getting buses every day" George smiled.

"No problem George, it was a pleasure to help out. That's what I'm here for. I like to think of this place as one big happy family" he answered.

Alex had set up George with a brand new Seat Ibiza, a car that George had always wanted. The repayments would be stopped out of George's wages, with a modest amount of interest charged.

Later that day, Vivian Agnew came to see Alex. Vivian had been his father's personal secretary for many years. In truth, Alex never saw the need for such a position. One of the office girls now did Alex's secretarial work in an ad-hoc way.

"I can't come in tomorrow Mr. Woods. I have another hospital appointment" Vivian said. It was like a red rag for Alex. He had had to back down with George Rae, something that still rankled with him. Now he was anxiously watching every member of staff.

"I've been looking at your attendance record Mrs. Agnew, it's not pretty reading" Alex said with a deep sigh.

"I haven't been at all well Mr. Woods. It's my asthma you see. It comes and goes" she replied. Alex rose to his feet suddenly, almost springing from his leather chair.

"A bit like you Mrs. Agnew. You seem to come and go a lot. Fifteen days off out of the last six weeks I make it" Alex said, raising his voice.

"It's Vivian, your father always called me Vivian. He understood about my breathing" she said in a nervous tone.

"Well I'm not my father Mrs. Agnew. What are we running here? A garage or a clinic? If everybody took time off like you, we would go out of business. Don't you get it?" he said, leaning forward on his cluttered desk.

"I...I'll try to improve Mr. Woods, but I'm suffering at the minute" Vivian Agnew answered weakly. Alex could not hold back any longer.

"I'll tell you what we'll do Mrs. Agnew. If you can't make tomorrow morning, just don't bother coming in the next day. How is that? It's not that you actually do anything around here anyway. Answering the phone and sending out invoices could be done by any of the staff in the office" he remarked. Vivian looked shell-shocked.

"What are you saying Mr. Woods? I've worked here all of my life. I've served your father..."

Her sentence was punctured by the booming voice of her employer.

"Don't keep bringing my father into it. He's gone. There's no one here to protect you. You either work here or you don't. It's as simple as that" Alex yelled.

Vivian physically leapt at the sound of his loud statement.

"I see, but I need to attend the hospital" she continued.

"Fine! See if they will pay your wages. Call back on Friday. I will have your money ready. I will even pay you two weeks wages extra. Even better, why not finish now Mrs. Agnew? That way you can run straight to your doctor this afternoon" Alex replied tersely. He turned his back on Vivian Agnew and stared out through the small window into the rear of the garage.

Vivian's attendance record was indeed appalling. Alex felt fully justified in letting her go. Only when he heard the door close quietly behind him, did Alex Woods look around again.

Minutes later the foreman knocked sharply on the door. He let himself in, as was Frank McKenzie's custom.

"I've just been talking to Vivian, boss. Is it right that you've sacked her?" Frank asked. Alex swivelled to and fro on his black leather chair, as if considering the question.

"Well, not exactly. Let's just say that I gave her a gentle push in the right direction" Alex replied casually. Frank looked surprised by his employer's candour.

"Vivian's been here longer than any of us. She's in bits out there. We can't just fire her Alex. She's an old dear. Surely the other girls can take up the slack until she's feeling better. We can all muck in Alex, what do you say?" Frank said.

Alex stood up and walked around his desk as if in thoughtful mode.

"What's we? Who are we? Let's get a few things clear Frank. I'm the boss here. There is no we. People who can't put in a week's work will have me to answer to. Got it? Now, that applies to the mechanics, the cleaning lady, and even to you. That old biddy hasn't done a decent week's work in years. My father kept her on out of pity. I've been studying the attendance sheets and I'm not very impressed. You've had some time off too Frank, and you're beginning to arrive late nearly every morning. You're another one who would want to buck up his ideas" Alex said. Frank McKenzie's face paled noticeably.

"I've had a bit of trouble at home with my eldest, Alex. I think that I told you. He's coming home at all hours. My wife is up the wall" Frank replied. Alex nodded as he continued to stroll around the rectangular desk.

"Yeah, I recall you mentioning something. Still, work comes first eh? Unless we're making money, there won't be any wages at the end of the week. That wouldn't do, would it Frank?" Alex asked. Frank shook his dark curly hair. The foreman was six foot five tall, but looked genuinely terrified of his boss for the first time in his life.

"No Alex, you're right of course. I'll make every effort" Frank replied.

"Good show Frank. After all, you are the foreman. It's your job to get the best out of the staff. Sometimes I sense that you're a little too soft with them. You want to kick a few of them up the arse now and then. Know what I mean?" Alex said. He looked the tall thin foreman straight in the eyes before setting off again on his deliberate stride around the desk.

"Yeah Alex, you're right. I'll get a bit more out of them from now on" Frank replied.

"Yeah Frank, and be on time in the morning, okay? It will answer you better to look after your own record. Leave the running of the garage to me" Alex said deliberately.

"Yes Alex, very good" Frank replied, nodding several times.

He left, closing the door quietly behind him.

Tony Lee met up with Stacey at Birmingham Airport. She ran to greet him as he arrived through the gate.

"Come on, I have my Dad's car. Let's go" she said, kissing him on the lips.

"You've booked a hotel. Which one?" she asked, as they drove towards Wolverhampton.

"The Bridlington Arms. Have you heard of it?" Tony replied. Stacey said that she knew of it, but had never actually passed it. It was on the outskirts of the city. Her plan was to bring Tony directly to the hotel, and then on to her parent's home. That night they might go for a drink, depending on how ill her mother was.

"There's something else that I need to do while I'm here" Tony said. He explained about wishing to visit his aging aunt. It surprised Stacey, who considered the idea a strange way to spend his time.

"Shouldn't you just leave the matter alone Tony? I mean, she never even bothered to come to your mother's funeral. As you said, there was bad blood between Delores and your Aunt Mary for some time. Why stir it up again?" Stacey said.

Tony smiled as he listened to her words of wisdom.

"I'm not going to stir things up, as you put it! I just want to see my Auntie Mary. Perhaps she was too ill to get over to us. If that was the case, I should tell her about Mam. I'm sure Auntie Mary would like to know about Mam's final days. Besides, I've brought some of Mam's jewellery for her to keep. I thought that she might like a keepsake. You suggested it after all!" Tony replied. Stacey nodded and smiled back at him.

"Aw! That's lovely! You're so thoughtful Tony Lee. That's why I love you" Stacey said.

"I missed you Stace. It's good to be with you again" Tony replied.

The following day Tony caught a bus to Walsall. He had his aunt's address tucked away in his inside jacket pocket. Before leaving Dublin, Tony had studied the area on the internet. He had printed off a map of the council estate, and was now examining it as he took the bus ride. Now and then he would glance out of the window, but was totally oblivious to his surroundings. The previous evening had been idyllic. He and Stacey had met for a drink. She had told him how much she was looking forward to settling down back in Dublin. However, her mother was still seriously ill, and Stacey was not sure how long she might have to stay in England. Tony's hotel was quite ordinary, but the novelty of it had not been lost on him. He had rarely travelled anywhere outside Ireland. One flitting weekend away at a football match, and another short break away with an old girlfriend was the sum of his experiences abroad. He had continued to renew his passport over the years, always wondering when he might get to use it again.

Tony arrived at his Aunt Mary's address at lunchtime. He felt nervous now. The ordinary-looking terraced house appeared plain but tidy. Tony imagined that the working-class estate might have been a lively place to live in when it was first built. Now it seemed settled and quiet.

He rang the doorbell on the red and white door and stood back. Inside, he could hear the radio or television. A loud English voice was reading the news. Tony looked to the large bay window with its lacy white curtains. He was sure that he had seen them twitch, but tried not to stare.

He pressed on the bell a second time. Presently a small frail lady appeared at the door. She had difficulty in walking and used a heavy brown cane to get about.

"Yes?" she asked in a shaky voice. Tony gulped down hard. It was difficult to judge how his aging aunt might react to him.

"Hello, Auntie Mary? It's me, Tony Lee, Delores's boy" Tony said with a forced smile. The woman held the door barely ajar, but seemed to close it even more on his words. Her mouth opened and closed again without a word. Tony spoke again.

"I've come over from Ireland to see you Auntie Mary. How are you keeping?" he said.

"Tony? Delores's child?" she asked. Tony nodded.

"I have my passport to prove it Auntie. I know that you have to be careful who you answer the door to" Tony said. He pulled his passport from his pocket and held it out towards her. Mary Stoneham nodded solemnly.

"I can see Delores in you all right. I recognise you son. I saw pictures of you when you were younger. Come in, come in" she said in a wheezing voice. She turned very slowly and led him inside.

Tony sat on the floral-coloured armchair sipping tea. Mary sat opposite him on the other chair nearer to the fireplace. Although it was a moderately warm day, the fire blazed away, dancing and crackling behind the black fireguard. It had taking Mary an age to make tea, insisting that she needed no help from her guest.

"So she sent you over to make the peace did she? Huh! After all this time too!" Mary said finally. Tony stopped dead, holding his cup in midair.

"Who Auntie Mary? My Mam?" he asked. She nodded back with a smug expression. Tony's mind began to race backwards. He had never actually phoned or written to his aunt. That task had been entrusted to Jan.

"I'm sorry Aunt, I thought that you knew. You see, well, Delores didn't make it. She was ill for some time. I'm sorry" he replied. Mary Stoneham facial expression slowly changed. She stared back at him, trying desperately to take in his words.

"Delores has died? Dear God! When son, when did she pass away?" Mary whispered. Although living in England for almost a lifetime, Mary still retained a strong Dublin accent.

"Some months ago Auntie Mary. Jan was supposed to phone you. I take it that she never did? Jan lives in America, it must have slipped her mind" Tony replied defensively.

"I'm sorry for your troubles Tony son, it must have been difficult for you" Mary said. Tony nodded and sipped on his tea.

"Yes, we were very close. My Mam was one in a million. I know that you both didn't get on in her final years but..." He left the final words unsaid.

"Blood is thicker than water Tony, but I can be a stubborn old fool sometimes. My old body is shot son, but my mind is as sharp as a tack" Mary said. Tony noticed a certain twinkle in her blue piercing eyes.

"Unlike my Aunt Ethel you mean? I've been to see her a few times. She hardly recognises me now. It's so sad. Ethel's in a home you see. She has nobody at all" Tony explained. Mary nodded.

"I know. I've written a couple of times, but whether or not she gets my mail, only God knows. She probably wouldn't remember me anyway" Mary said quietly.

Tony thought out his next words carefully. He had no wish to upset his aunt any further, but felt compelled to pursue his reason for the visit.

"But you have never written to my Mam?" he asked. He could detect a defensive look on Mary's lined face. She pursed her lips before replying.

"And why would I lad? We both took a stance long ago. Delores would never admit any wrongdoing. After a while, the phone calls turned into screaming matches. We would slam down the receiver on each other. In the end, I simply could not be bothered. I had my own family to rear. I just let Delores get on with things" Mary said.

"And where are my cousins now?" Tony asked, glancing around him. Mary smiled for the first time, displaying two missing teeth at the front of her mouth.

"Oh, Belinda calls to see me every Sunday with my two grandchildren. The other fellow, Raymond, visits when he feels like it. Always on the take he is, and me without a shilling! The day I die he will sell this house. We only bought it off the council before my husband, Jimmy, died. It's all that I have of value" Mary remarked.

Tony wanted to turn the conversation back to his mother, but was mindful of agitating his aunt. He explained that he had come over to see his girlfriend, and was returning to Dublin on Monday.

"Good for you son. I miss Dublin, but these aging bones can never return home now. I daresay that I would have liked to make Delores's funeral though" Auntie Mary said. For a moment Tony left her to her thoughts of home, noting the faraway look in her eyes.

"What ever happened Auntie? It seems such a shame that two sisters should fall out for all of those years" Tony said gently. Mary Stoneham emitted a long, weary sigh. She looked cross for the first time.

"I would rather not say anything Tony, you being her son and all. It's best forgotten" she replied. Tony leaned forward in his chair.

"I really would like to know, if that's all right with you. Jan refuses to speak about it either. Once my Mam died, Jan more or less abandoned me. I'm left with lots of questions about my past, with no real family to turn to" Tony explained.

Mary again refused to speak of the past. They settled for a middle ground, with Mary discussing her children and her younger days in Dublin.

Later, Tony produced some of his mother's jewellery from his pocket and handed it to Mary. She took an instant liking to a Claddagh ring. Mary seemed visibly moved that Tony had thought to visit her, and warmed a little to her nephew.

Tony later noticed that the evening was closing in. He had spent hours with his aunt, and was anxious to head back to Wolverhampton. Mary was telling him how her husband had died, and how her grandchildren made life bearable.

"Jan has two kids, a boy and a girl. I would like to meet them, but I don't think that Jan wants me to. I have photos of them with me Auntie Mary. Here, have a look" Tony said. He produced photos of Josh and Amy, standing alongside Howard and Jan.

Mary Stoneham barely looked at them, citing her fading eyesight as the reason.

Soon Tony stood up to leave.

"I'm sorry that you have had a wasted journey son. Let the past rest eh? Enjoy your life with your girlfriend and forget about us" Mary said. Tony shook his head.

"I can't Auntie Mary. I miss my Mam so much. I can barely recall my Dad. Then I found some letters in the attic that he had written to Mam. It helped me feel closer to both of them. Jan thinks that I've burned them, but I just can't" Tony said.

His words seemed to strike a chord in Mary's heart. Tony was already standing up, ready to leave. She motioned him to sit down once more.

"I swore that I would never speak of it, but I suppose that you do have a right to know. Listen to what I have to say Tony. I don't say this out of malice, or to be hurtful, but what I say now is the Gospel truth. A long time ago, your Dad Sean came to live with me and my husband. He and Delores were having difficulties in their marriage. The poor man was distraught. He was convinced that your mother was seeing someone else. We looked after him for many years. He would return to Dublin, begging Delores to give him another chance. Sometimes she would promise to try again, but nothing ever became of it. He died a broken man did poor Sean. He spent his final days here in Walsall" Mary said, blinking back tears. Tony Lee looked stunned. He digested what the old woman had said, but found it hard to give it any credence.

"But, but my Mam and Dad loved each other. I read the letters. He had to go away on business a lot. No Auntie Mary, you have it wrong. Mam used to bring me to his grave to pray when I was younger. She only ever had good things to say about him" Tony said, a tone of astonishment in his voice. Mary said nothing for some moments.

"Sean said that she had taken up with a handsome man, a few years younger than him. Someone from her job. Sean Lee was disconsolate, beside himself with heartache. He would sob himself to sleep at night. Both Jimmy and myself would hear him from our bedroom. He and Jimmy were always the best of buddies. We tried everything to keep his spirits up. In the end, he died of a broken heart" Mary concluded.

Tony Lee tried hard to take in her words. It was as if Mary was speaking about another couple. To his knowledge, his mother and father had never had a cross word between them.

"I think you might have it wrong Auntie. When I was growing up, everything seemed fine. I don't recall any stories of arguments or fighting. Maybe Dad was exaggerating" Tony replied. Mary Stoneham frowned and let out a deep, impatient sigh.

"I knew that this was how you would react. In truth, I always felt that this day might come. I swore that I would never say a word. I don't know what changed my mind today Tony. Perhaps it was seeing you so desperate for news of your past. Anyway, there it is for your consumption. Do with it as you please. You can choose to ignore what I have to say, or ask Jan. A dark one she is, by the way! I'll say no more on the topic. But don't think of me as the one who fell out with your mother, not that it matters one iota anyway. I phoned her many times begging her to take Sean back. That's why we fell out son" Mary said.

"I...I find it hard to believe. Jan never indicated that anything was wrong between Mam and Dad" Tony replied.

Can I give you a piece of advice Tony?" Mary said. Tony Lee nodded.

"Never believe everything that people tell you. Always hold back, especially if they are speaking about someone else. Judge that person yourself by how they treat you. I'm sure that Jan thinks that I'm a monster. You See, I loved my sister Delores dearly, but she was no angel" Mary said. Tony Lee again cast a furtive glance towards the darkening sky outside. It was time to be on his way.

"I'll write to you Auntie Mary, I promise" he said. Tony leaned forward and kissed the old woman on the left cheek.

"I'd like that Tony, I really would. It might give me something to look forward to" Mary said with a big smile.

On the way back to his hotel, Tony reflected on the visit. Why would Jan lie about telling Mary of Delores's death? Or had old woman simply forgotten? That seemed implausible. Auntie Mary's wits appeared very sharp. Unlike Ethel, Mary was in complete control of her faculties. It appeared to Tony that Jan had once again decided what was best for everyone. Tony had not spoken to his sister since their major row on the telephone.

As Tony sat on the bus, he considered what Mary had told him. It seemed ridiculous that his mother might have had an affair, if indeed that was what Mary was suggesting. Perhaps she had meant that his mother had an infatuation with someone from her job. Tony decided that this was in fact the case. His dear mother could never cheat on his father. For his own peace of mind, Tony Lee allowed himself believe that this was what had happened. But why then would his father flee to Walsall? It was all very puzzling. Tony recalled that his Dad travelled a lot because of work. Maybe he had just happened to be in the area and dropped in on Auntie Mary and her husband. Tony wondered if his father may then have poured his heart out to the couple. It possibly made sense, and Tony was inclined to settle for that also to be the situation. He tried not to dwell on the topic, but it still haunted him throughout the journey back to Wolverhampton.

Later that night he explained to Stacey over dinner what Mary had told him. She seemed quaintly amused by the tale.
"I never thought that people had affairs back in those days! How odd!" she said with a cheeky grin. Tony was far more serious about the matter.
"I don't believe she had an affair, it was probably an infatuation. But of course people had affairs. It's been happening since we were put on this earth. But forty years ago folk stayed married. Affairs were kept secret. Divorce was almost unheard of in Ireland and Britain. Men ruled the roost back then. They could have their affairs and crawl back to their wives. The woman had very little rights. To admit that her husband was cheating on her would bring shame on the family, and mostly on the wife! It was as if she wasn't looking after her husband's needs or something!" Tony said in an upbeat tone.
"It's still a man's world! But your Aunt Mary is saying that it was your mother who had this affair, so that's a little peculiar" Stacey remarked. Tony thought for a moment.
"I still don't believe it went that far. Anyway, the other chap was probably married, so it amounts to the same thing" he replied.
Later on, Stacey changed the subject. She told Tony how she missed home and her friends, and how she could not wait to get back to a normal life.
"Your mother's health comes first love. The doctors appear happy with her progress, from what you tell me. She will soon be home, then you can plan what to do" he said.
"Yeah, I'm hopeful she will make a full recovery. Anyway, what about you? How are you coping?" Stacey asked. Tony shrugged his shoulders.
"I manage. I just look to the future and you getting home. Stacey, if I'm honest, I still worry about our future together. I mean, there will come a time when we have to decide on what's best for us. Can you ever see the day when you will feel at home at my house? To tell you the truth, I cannot see myself ever living anywhere else" Tony said candidly. He did not want to reveal anything about the renovations, fearing it might put even more pressure on Stacey.

For a moment Stacey Boyd looked pensive.

"I have been considering that thorny subject Tony. In fact, I've been giving it a lot of thought lately. I surprised myself last night by actually wishing that I was home with you. I reckon that it was just childish of me to feel uncomfortable in that house. It's probably because it's so old and a little neglected. Let's just wait and see when we get home, eh?" Stacey said. Tony's face immediately brightened up. He was tempted to spill the beans, but then decided that it would be a nice surprise for Stacey. Maybe he might even have all the work done before she did eventually return to Dublin.

Alex Woods watched the house on St. Oliver's Road from across the street. It was Sunday, and he had been there on and off for most of the weekend. With no sign of Tony Lee, Alex was becoming a little frustrated. Knowing that Stacey was away in England, he began to fear the worst. If the two were back together, it would be his worst nightmare. Already he was planning on how to dispose of Tony Lee anyway, and an idea was forming in his head. He knew where Tony worked, and if he could gain access to the high-rise building, he might get a chance to carry through a dramatic-looking finale for Tony Lee. Alex had hatched a plan whereby he could push Tony to his death from a window in the office block. He had seen his adversary gaze from the building while on his lunch-break. Most sunny days the office windows were at least partly opened. Alex had two main worries. One was if security cameras were employed on the floor where Tony worked. His other concern was a suicide note, but Alex reckoned that the latter was less important. Plenty of men had jumped to their deaths without leaving a message. It could look like the pressure of life had finally got to Tony Lee. Alternatively, it might appear that Tony had died in a tragic accident.

As evening fell, the boredom got to Alex. He got out of the car once more to stretch his legs. He was sure that Tony Lee was not at home. He eyed up the old house with the scaffolding poles bedecking the front of the building. Alex decided on the spur of the moment to try and gain access to the house. There was no real reason why, just a bit of bravado on his behalf.

He strode up the straight pathway and knocked politely on the door, using the old green knocker. Alex's plan if Tony answered was to appear friendly. He would say that he had some items belonging to Stacey, which he wished to return. His angle would be that he had called to her flat and had got no reply. Alex's next question would be if Tony knew of her whereabouts.

As Alex suspected, there was no one home. He remembered that some people in such old Dublin houses left a latch door key hanging on a piece of string inside the letterbox. He had a quick look around before proceeding to open the letterbox with his left hand. Alex then delved inside with his free hand, searching for a spare key. It was a long shot, and he accepted defeat after a fruitless foray. Alex then peeped through the letterbox into the hallway. The builders had left the house in a mess. His next thought was if they had actually closed the front door properly. Sometimes workers were not so careful with other folk's property. The door appeared loose, and Alex wondered if a good old-fashioned shoulder nudge might open the aging door. He levered the door hard with his right shoulder. The door rattled, but stood firm. Suddenly Alex felt a firm hand on his left shoulder.

"Can I help you sir?" said the voice. Alex froze for a second. He had to think fast.

"Er, who are you?" he asked. The elderly man with the black hat smiled back at him.

"I'm a friend of the family. Were you trying to gain access?" the grey-haired man asked, the smile vanishing from his lined face. His long dark coat swayed as he removed his hand from Alex's shoulder. Alex Woods looked the ageing man in the face. The old gent looked as if he was caught in some sort of time warp to Alex. His long flowing heavy coat and black hat looked almost Victorian in appearance.

"Oh, I see. Well, I'm here to check on my builders, but they seem to have already left. I suppose that I can call back in the morning. Pity though, I like to stay on top of my staff. I forgot my set of keys you see. Never mind, I've had a wasted journey. I don't suppose that you have a key to Tony's property?" Alex said in a casual manner. Fergal Carrie took in the strangers' words. He shook his head.

"No, I'm afraid that I don't" the older man replied curtly.

"Er, okay then, I won't delay. I'll see those lads tomorrow about locking up early, never fear!" Alex said. He walked away, making sure to head in the opposite direction to where his car was parked. Alex did not want some nosey neighbour scribbling down his licence plate number.

The man with the black hat surveyed the old house for a moment. Fergal Carrie's memory was drawn back to happier days when Delores Lee was alive. He recalled her as a beautiful friendly lady, with a ready smile for all. Mostly he liked to remember her effervescent personality and sense of fun. He was almost tearful now, as he turned away from the old house. It was time for Fergal Carrie to return to his empty home again.

Alex went for a drink and a sandwich in a pub some minutes away. He would collect his car once he had a bite to eat. Inside he felt annoyed that he had allowed himself to be caught out so easily. It was a childish mistake, and Alex prided himself on his attention to detail. As he retired to a quiet corner of the bar, Alex's mind was racing.

"What a stupid thing to do. Idiotic. There was nothing to be achieved by gaining access to that crummy old shithole. What was I up to?" he asked himself.

"You're a stranger here, aren't you?" a voice asked. Alex looked up from his toasted ham sandwich. An elderly man was eyeing him from across the quiet bar. Alex ignored the tiny slight man and continued eating. The pensioner sauntered over to Alex, a half-drunk pint of Guinness in his right hand. To Alex's horror, the man planted himself down next to him.

"Yeah, I can always spot a stranger. I live opposite here, number fifty-six. I've lived here man and boy for over seventy years" the frail-looking man stated.

"Really? How fascinating!" Alex replied in a sarcastic voice. The old man continued as if Alex was an old friend.

"Of course, this old pub is not everyone's cup of tea. No entertainment you see. I come over here to stay warm. It saves me putting on the heat at home, you know? I get a cheap pint here because I'm a pensioner. They're very good like that you see. Of course, I've seen several owners of this place come and go over the years, plus hundreds of barmen" the small-sized man said, as if relaying a tale he had told several times.

"Just who the fuck are you anyway?" Alex asked through gritted teeth. The old man looked taken aback, but quickly composed himself.

"I'm Nobby Clarke. Of course my real name is Robert, but everyone calls me Nobby" the man stated in a proud voice.

"Well Nobby, why don't you take your poxy pint and bugger off back across the bar? I want to be left alone if you don't mind" Alex snarled. Nobby took a swig from his Guinness and looked thoughtful.

"If that's what you want son, then so be it. I was young and petulant once. Sooner or later someone comes along to sort you out" he replied. He then shuffled back to the far side of the room where he spoke quietly to the barman.

Presently the muscular-looking barman came to chat with Alex.

"Listen mate, this is a friendly type of pub. We don't like it when strangers come along and upset our regulars. Old Nobby there meant no harm. He's just a lonely old man trying to pass away an evening. Most nights he's in here until ten or so. Then he will be off to bed without a bad word to anybody. I suggest that you finish your drink and leave, okay?" said the young barman. Alex thought quietly for a moment before replying.

"You know what? You're right of course. I was just having a bad day. Tell you what, get Nobby a few pints on me. There's a tenner. I'm sorry if I caused any offence" Alex said, pulling a crisp €10 from his wallet. Alex finished his drink in one quick gulp and stood up to leave. He smiled at the barman and made for the door.

Once outside, the red mist descended again on Alex.

"Number fifty-six is it Nobby? Well, let's just see what we find" Alex muttered. He strolled across the narrow road and crept up the garden path. The garden was overgrown with bushes, the pathway overshadowed on each side. Alex reached the shabby brown front door and reached inside the letterbox. Just as he had suspected, the single brass key hung loosely on a piece of twine.

"Hah! Old habits die hard, eh Nobby? Well, let's just see how you like to be bothered by a stranger!" Alex smirked. He let himself in quietly and made straight for the kitchen at the back of the house. Alex shoved the black sink plug into the hole in the old chipped white sink and turned the cold tap on full. Within seconds he was outside again, closing the door silently behind him.

"That should be a nice surprise for you at around ten o'clock tonight Nobby!"Alex chuckled. He made his way back to where his car was parked, now in much more cheerful mood than earlier that evening.

That night, Nobby would return to a flooded home. With no house insurance, hundreds of euro's worth of damage to his floors and furniture would take a huge chunk out of the pensioner's life savings. He would presume that he had left the plug in the sink earlier. It would never cross Nobby's mind that the man who bought him a couple of drinks had been anywhere near his old run-down home.

CHAPTER TWENTY-TWO

A PERSON FROM THE PAST

Tony Lee returned from England on Monday afternoon. He smiled as he viewed the builders hard at work as he exited the taxi. Planks were slanted in through the open hall door to accommodate the wheelbarrow. This was transferring cement through to the back garden, where the conservatory was almost complete. The fitted kitchen was in place, well covered up with clear plastic to protect it. Tony went to speak to the foreman.

"How long to finish the job?" he asked. Eddie Harrison took off his yellow hardhat for a second and scratched his black hair.

"Well, we're well on schedule Tony, but at least another week. The double glazing has to go in, and the Velux window in the attic. We should finish off the conservatory tomorrow, and after that there's the two en suites. There are other bits and pieces too on the snag list" Eddie answered.

"I daresay that I can cope until the weekend!" Tony replied.

"Are you planning on staying here or with friends? There's a hell of a lot of dust and muck about!" Eddie warned.

"Oh, I'll manage. Listen Eddie, can I get your advice on something?" Tony asked. Eddie let out a deep sigh. He hated when customers wanted to add jobs on to a project. They would want work adjusted, and probably expect to pay the same price already agreed on.

"Sure, once you haven't changed your mind Tony. Things are progressing nicely. I would hate to have to redo anything on the list" he replied. Tony assured him that that would not be the case. He led the foreman upstairs to his bedroom.

"What do you make of that? I guess it was an old fireplace at one stage" Tony said, pointing to the wall. Eddie surveyed the boxed off square wall.

"It could have been Tony. These old houses have peculiar features all right. Perhaps it was a dumb waiter, or maybe the original staircase ran along there.

Believe it or not, I once came across a loom built into an old cupboard! There it was, blocked off for almost a century in an old tenement house out in Ballsbridge! Yeah, you never know what you'll find, but I would say that an old fireplace is the most likely usage. No need for it with the central heating though" Eddie concluded. Tony had other ideas.

"Well, that's just it you see. I sort of fancy the quaintness of an old Georgian fireplace there, you know, restore a bit of character to the old house" Tony said. Eddie nodded while still studying the wall. He stepped forward and felt the wall, running both hands along its exterior. Eddie then pulled a small screwdriver from his pocket and tapped gently on the plaster with the handle. "Tell you what though, it's no plasterboard job. This wall has been covered over well. My guess is that there's a solid wall there. It's not a matter of just demolishing it with an old hammer. I would get a surveyor in to look at it first. I can't see it holding anything up, but best to be sure" Eddie said.

"Pity that! I fancied tackling it myself, you know, as a small project. I was going to price an old fireplace and take my time to install it. A labour of love if you like" Tony sighed. Eddie dare not tell his latest customer what he was thinking. He hated inexperienced folk having a go at jobs that they did not understand. "Er, yeah, as I say Tony, get it looked at first. Look, it's most likely an old bricked-up fireplace, but best to err on the safe side, yeah?" Eddie replied diplomatically.

Tony Lee returned to work the following day. In a way he felt that he had wasted his holiday, but figured that it had been worth it. It had been great to spend some time with Stacey, and then he had the added bonus of visiting his aging Aunt Mary. He had also done a lot of manual work on the house, including stripping down the old ivy from the exterior walls. The night before returning to work, Tony had toyed with the idea of telephoning Jan. He had wanted to confront her on why she had not invited Mary over to their mother's funeral, if such was the case. In the end, Tony had decided against it. It could only end in an argument, and Tony was enjoying not having his sister pry into his life.

At lunchtime, Tony again stood gazing out through the large office window. It was a beautiful sunny day, and Tony leaned on the open window ledge. Unknown to him, Alex Woods had spotted him from his parked car below. Alex came alive on seeing his adversary. At last Tony Lee had surfaced again. Alex watched, and quietly imagined how easy it would be to sneak up behind him and push him out to his certain death. Already he had studied the building for CCTV. It appeared that the only camera was at the entrance to the tall office block. Alex was fascinated about the internal layout. If he could establish that there was no security cameras on the floor where Tony Lee worked, his daring plan might just work. Alex decided that the following day he would attempt to enter the building, and see what resistance he was met with. He had identified a service door to the side of the building. It was used by janitors and cleaners to empty bins. Alex planned on gaining access through that very door the following day.

At one o'clock the next day, Alex sat in his car watching the building. It usually took Tony Lee about twenty minutes for lunch. The rest of his break was usually spent either going for a short cycle, or viewing the Dublin skyline from his vantage point on the fourth floor. At some point during the hour break, Tony would normally phone Stacey. Today would be no exception.

"Hiya Stace, how is your Mom today?" he asked.

"Yeah, we've got good news back from the hospital. Tests show that there are no sign of the cancer returning. Mom will be in remission, so we're hopeful that she will make a full recovery. It's the answer to our prayers Tony. Dad is over the moon. He hasn't stopped crying since we got the news" Stacey replied. Tony could feel the joy in her voice. He had known that the test results were due, but had feared the worst. Most people that Tony knew who had been operated on for cancer had subsequently succumbed to the deadly disease.

"Brilliant! So what happens now? I mean, do they allow her home?" he asked tentatively.

"Well, I'm not sure. She might need some more treatment, but I suppose that she will be allowed home eventually. This might sound a horrible thing to say Tony, but I can't wait to get back to a normal life in Dublin" she said.

Tony wandered towards the open window, his mobile phone held to his ear in his right hand. He peered out across the city skyline. The bustle down below occupied his vision as he continued to speak to Stacey.

"Yeah, me too love. I miss you so much. It's a beautiful day here in Dublin. I always say that when we get the weather, this is the finest city in the world!" Tony said.

Alex climbed from his car. The adrenalin was pumping. He had seen Tony on the phone and immediately surmised that he was speaking to Stacey. It was something that had played on Alex's mind overnight. With Stacey away, and Tony Lee absent from his home at the weekend, Alex feared that the two were back together again.

Alex homed in on the two big glass doors with their long slender silver handles, which led to the building. He could see the camera overhead. His eyes shot in the direction of the side door. A janitor in a long brown smock casually came out carrying a refuse sack. As the door slammed shut behind him, Alex seized his chance. He strode rapidly to the door and pulled it open. By now the janitor had gone to the rear of the building to where the huge wheelie bins were located. A short passageway led Alex to the foyer. A girl exited the building by the main door barely glanced at Alex. He made for the elevator and pressed the button for the fourth floor.

Stacey continued her conversation with Tony.
"Yeah, like you're an expert on world cities Tony! You are the least qualified person that I know to compare the greatest cities in the world! London has to be up there, and New York. Oh, and what about Paris?" she said, a passionate tone entering her voice.

Alex stood back as the elevator binged to prepare to open its doors. As the silver metal doors slowly drew back, Alex glared out onto the fourth floor, taking in the layout. Again there was no reception area, just another door leading in to the main working area. Alex viewed the walls for cameras. He then studied the ceiling. It appeared that there was no security in place whatsoever. Alex afforded himself a smug grin. Perhaps he might actually get the chance to do away with Tony Lee at his first attempt. His senses were all on full alert. He took in the sounds, the smells and the view. Opening the wooden door with its centre glass panel, Alex entered the main working area of the huge office.

Tony and Stacey continued their light-hearted conversation.
"I know that I haven't travelled very much Stace, but I read all the time. I can guess what these places are like. Mad bustling places the lot of them! Dublin has real soul. It's a place where you can relax and enjoy life" Tony countered.

Alex homed in on Tony Lee. He could see him by the window with his back to him. Alex scanned the quiet office. There was nobody else about. Now he had to decide if he should wait until the phone call had ended. He decided not. Perhaps people might think that Tony had slipped. All Alex had to do was to grab him by the legs and hoist him upwards and out. It would be done in seconds. His brain decided that he had to go for it. There was nothing to consider. He crept closer. The office was deadly silent. All that Alex could hear was the bustling noise from the street outside, and Tony Lee's muted voice.

"I suppose that you have a point. Anyway Tony, I have no plans on settling down anywhere else. Just you and me in our own private world, eh?" Stacey said.

"Yeah, that's all that I want too" Tony Lee replied.

Alex crept forward again. He was now just feet from his target. Tony Lee stood slouched on the lip of the open window. He was peering down nonchalantly to the streets below. Alex took a deep breath. Again he surveyed the ceiling and walls for a camera. There was nothing. His brain told him that it was safe to proceed. In minutes it would be over. He could escape back down the stairs and into the streets outside. Then he would slip away unnoticed as the crowds swarmed around Tony Lee's dead body.

"Can I help you?" asked the voice. Alex turned suddenly to his left. A dark-skinned man stood eyeing him. Again the man spoke.

"Are you lost sir? Can I help?" he asked. Alex composed himself quickly.

"Isn't this the fifth floor? I have an appointment with a Mr. Winston Flood" Alex said. Erik Ngombiti eyed him up and down. The man seemed presentable and genuine, yet Erik felt that there was something furtive about him. Erik shook his head and beckoned him towards the exit. Alex followed reluctantly. Oblivious to the intrusion, Tony continued his phone call to his girlfriend.

"This is the fourth floor sir. Take the elevator to the next floor up" Erik said as he opened the wooden door. Alex smiled politely.

"Thank you for your help. I must have pressed the wrong button. I was about to ask your colleague at the window for directions. He was very wrapped up in his phone call though. Probably in love eh?" Alex replied.

"I guess so. Have a good day" Erik answered. He turned back towards his desk and shook his head.

"The security here is unbelievable! I always said that someone would have to be murdered before anything is done! People simply walk in off the streets without being challenged. Ludicrous!" Erik commented.

Tony finished his call and noticed Erik at his desk. He went to chat to his colleague.

"Go for a walk then Erik?" he asked. Erik nodded.

"Was that the lovely Stacey on the blower again? She can't get enough of you lately! Was I right that you two were meant for each other or what?" Erik said, his deep laugh began to rumble low in his belly. Soon it shot out through his throat, engulfing Tony as it did so. He could not help but to join in the laughter.

"Yeah, you were right Erik, and I do love her. We see so little of each other though. I miss her terribly. That weekend away was a godsend" Tony said.
And the house, how's it coming on?" Erik asked. Tony sat down on Erik's desk.
"Yeah, nearly there. It's costing an arm and a leg! Still, it will be a great surprise for Stacey when she returns" he said.
"Hey, speaking of surprises, some dude just wandered through the building a while ago. He said that he was on the wrong floor, but I wonder! I'm sure that people come in here and pinch things during the lunch break. I had my good pen taken last week" Erik replied, his ready grin vanishing from his friendly face.
"You most likely left it at home. Probably your kids are drawing on the furniture as we speak!" Tony smiled. Erik held his hands to his head in mock horror.

Downstairs, Alex Woods leapt inside his car and slammed the door.
"Fuck! Fuck! Fuck!" he screamed, thumping his hands on the steering wheel.
"I nearly had the bastard. I nearly had him" he shouted. Alex then became aware of a driver next to him watching his fit of temper. The traffic had slowed to a crawl, and the young man stared from his yellow Opel Corsa at Alex's parked car. Alex pressed on the button for the electric windows.
"And what the Jaysus are you looking at, fuckface?" Alex yelled.
"I'm looking at a prick making an utter fool of himself" the blond younger man replied dryly. Alex flung open his door and leapt from his car. The man grinned back at him and drove on. The traffic lights were green now, and the yellow car quickly disappeared from view. Alex spread his hands across the white roof of the car and leaned his forehead onto the roof's edge.
"Calm down Alex, come on, take it easy" he whispered. He then took several deep breaths before returning to the driver's seat.

A few days later, Tony Lee answered a knock on his front door. It was Saturday morning and he was not expecting anybody. His heart leaped as he wondered if Stacey might be making a surprise visit home. The upbeat mood soon vanished as he saw an elderly man standing in the doorway.
"Sorry, whatever your selling, I'm not interested" Tony said in a bored tone. The man was dressed in a long black overcoat and a black fedora hat. He carried a silver, expensive-looking cane in his right hand. His greying hair was long to the back and tumbled out over his upturned collar. His silver-grey hair also jutted out at each side of his hat, which was tilted slightly forward.
"I'm not selling anything, not today" the man replied with a ready smile. His blue twinkling eyes appeared to eat up Tony Lee, who already felt a little

uncomfortable in the older man's presence. Tony was sure that the man had an angle for either some scam, or wanted to sell him some form of insurance. "Look, I don't want to be rude, but I'm in the middle of my meal" Tony lied. The man smiled and tipped his hat in a respectful gesture.

"I won't keep you so Tony. I have something to tell you" the gentleman replied. It quickly registered with Tony Lee that the elderly gent already knew his name. Tony noticed a crisp white shirt and a deep red tie beneath the man's long overcoat.

"How do you know my name? What exactly do you want?" Tony asked.

"What do I want? Acceptance I suppose. This is not easy for me Tony. I swore that I would never do this. Prepare yourself for a shock" The man said, the ready smile disappearing for the first time.

Tony said nothing for a moment. He stared blankly at the man, now unsure what to expect.

"What can I do for you?" Tony said as the man paused. It appeared that the older man was struggling to find the right words.

"I'm from your past Tony. It was a very long time ago. You don't know me directly. You see, myself and Delores, well, there is no easy way to say it. We were lovers. Tony, you are my son" the man said quietly.

It was said in such a matter-of-fact way, yet the words jumped out at Tony Lee. He felt shocked, frightened, unsure and stunned all at once. His first instinct was to slam the front door shut. Yet something was preventing him from doing so. He was curious, mesmerised by the tall, aging man.

"What are you saying? Are you mad?" Tony stuttered. The man nodded his acceptance of the shock of what he was saying.

"Why should you believe me lad? It's preposterous, isn't it? But it's positively true. Can I come in? It's not something that we should discuss outside" the man said quietly.

Tony considered the request. It made sense, yet the fear of being alone inside his home with this person, terrified him somehow.

"No, I don't know you sir. Look, you're obviously making a mistake..." Tony said firmly but politely. The man again shook his head.

"No mistake Tony. My name is Fergal Carrie. I worked with Delores in a shoe shop in the city centre. That's how we met. We were drawn together" the man said bluntly.

Immediately Tony recalled his Auntie Mary's words. She had mentioned that his mother had met her lover at a shop where she had worked. Tony had heard enough. This was not something to discuss on the doorstep. He ushered the stranger inside.

"You had better come in. I'm not sure that I believe a word you say, but this is not something to share with my neighbours" Tony said quietly. He led the man inside to the sitting room and offered him a seat. Fergal Carrie continued his tale.

"I admit that I knew she was married. We were both infatuated by each other. Delores and I became deeply attracted. Your mother was a very beautiful lady. I knew that it was wrong, we both did. Then your father found out about us. He insisted on Delores leaving her job. It hardly mattered by then. We were so in love that we could not bear to be apart" Fergal said.

Tony viewed the elderly man from across the room. He guessed that in his day Fergal Carrie was a very handsome man. There was something suave and sophisticated about him. He was almost bohemian and intriguing in his mannerisms and appearance. Tony could see how women could be drawn to him, yet his words hardly made sense.

Tony did not want to hear anymore, but it was as if he was witnessing a fatal crash. He simply could not look away or stop Fergal Carrie in his tracks. Fergal continued his story.

"When your mother found out that she was pregnant, she was in absolute panic. She knew that Sean would go berserk. They had settled for having just the one daughter, your sister Jan. By then Jan must have been about thirteen. Delores decided that she must have an abortion. I was distraught. I begged her to have our baby. She told me that she could never put her husband through that. In her way she still loved Sean Lee. Days ticked by. Each time we spoke, I pleaded with Delores to go through with the pregnancy. She was resolute in her decision. I had to respect her, but I was heartbroken. I wanted us to be together, although such a liaison was deeply frowned upon back then. Married women seldom left their husbands. I wanted us to go to London. Nothing else mattered to me except being with Delores. And of course to see you born Tony" Fergal Carrie said.

Although Tony Lee was feeling sick to the stomach, he wanted the stranger to continue his story. Tony did not want to believe any of it, but something told him that he must hear it through. He could feel the questions piling up in his brain. Simple questions, peculiar questions. There were things that he needed to know. Fergal Carrie paused and removed his black hat. He looked around for somewhere to put it, and then settled for resting the fedora on his lap. Fergal took in his surroundings.

"The house has changed a lot. Oh, the layout is still the same, but it's not how I remember it at all" Fergal said, his mind clearly somewhere else. Fergal Carrie stroked his well-trimmed slight grey beard, lost in his private thoughts for a moment. Tony looked surprised that the man had visited his home before, despite what Fergal had already told him. Fergal Carrie was now almost tearful. "I never stopped loving her you know" he whispered. Tony Lee felt that there was little that he could say. He watched the elderly man, his grey hair now tumbling down almost to his shirt collar. His wild hair fell across his eyes, and Fergal swept it back with one brush of his right hand.

"Go on, is there more?" Tony asked nervously. Fergal nodded, his mind returning to bygone days.

"One day, Delores came to me with a proposal. She said that she had decided to make a go of her marriage. She and Sean had made things up between them. She said that Sean knew that she was pregnant, and was prepared to keep the baby under certain conditions. Delores made me agree to never bother her again, and never to attempt to see the child when it was born. It broke my heart, but at the same time, I wanted Delores to be happy. After much soul-searching, I finally agreed. Delores even insisted that I put it in writing. She went through with her pregnancy, much to my delight. I still prayed that she would relent and take me back. Sometimes during her pregnancy she did show some encouraging signs. Unfortunately they were always short-lived. I knew that her love for me infuriated Sean Lee, but I could not help myself. It was like a battle between us for Delores's love, and I did all in my power to win Delores over. Alas, once you were born Tony, Delores tried to cut me out of her life forever. Oh, I wrote the odd letter to her, but she never responded" Fergal said.

Tony Lee did not wish to believe him. But somehow there was a certain assuredness to what Fergal Carrie was saying. He had so many questions, and Tony waded right in.

"I don't believe you. Why would you wait this long? I'm almost forty, for God's sake! My mother just asked you to have nothing to do me, and so you obeyed? Anyway, what proof have do you have that you are my father?" Tony said, the emotion in his voice seeping through.

"I have no proof Tony. A blood test will prove who I am. Why did I wait? I waited out of love for Delores. I had given her my word, and my word is my bond. When she died, I thought at first that I could leave everything alone. But it continued to eat away at me. I had to see you Tony. I had to tell you the facts" he said.

Tony Lee tried to take it all in. It was preposterous. Then he began to consider who might know the truth. Who could prove or disprove what this stranger was saying? His mother of course came to mind, and of course the man who Tony perceived to be his real father. Both were dead. Tony then thought of Jan, and perhaps Howard. Also both of his aunts might know. Yet over the years, not one person had as much as hinted that he might not be who he always presumed that he was. His Auntie Mary came to his thoughts. At least she had described how upset that his father had been. Mary had told him of his mother's infidelity. Was it too much of a coincidence, he wondered? Certain things that Fergal Carrie had said suddenly rang true for Tony Lee. His father's unhappiness described by his Auntie Mary, fitted in with what this stranger was telling him. Suddenly his doubting brain started to reluctantly believe what Fergal Carrie was saying.

"Have you spoken to my mother at all over the years? You know, since I was born?" Tony asked nervously. Fergal shook his head.

"Only fleetingly. When you were born I admit that I tried to win her back. At first Delores showed encouraging moments, but then something happened. Delores made it clear that she wanted nothing to do with me. It broke my heart. She shut me off completely. I think that she blamed me for her marriage break-up" Fergal replied.

"But my Mam's marriage never broke up. She had a happy marriage. Mam always talked adoringly about my Dad. He was a brilliant man. He spent all of that time away from home making money for us..." Tony stopped in his tracks. Maybe what Fergal Carrie was saying did make sense. Perhaps the father that he knew had lived apart from his mother.

Fergal stood up and paced the room, leaving his black hat positioned on the chair.

"There's something else that I haven't told you lad" he said. Tony watched the man walk towards the door and back again. Fergal Carrie had obviously been a flamboyant chap in his time. With his silver cane, fedora hat and flowing hair, Tony imagined that Fergal had always led a colourful life.

Fergal Carrie stopped dead and looked Tony in the eyes.

"Before your father died, Delores met someone else. That's what really broke Sean's heart, not me. I think that she fell under the spell of this man. Oh, it spoiled any chance of reconciliation between myself and Delores okay, but it destroyed her marriage completely. Sean returned to England and never came back. I don't know who this chap was, or whatever became of him" Fergal said.

Tony Lee rose quickly to his feet.

"Get out! Get out of this house! Liar! Get out" he bellowed.

Fergal Carrie stared straight at him for a moment, his face expressionless.

"Aye, I suspected that that was how you might react. Still, I can't blame you lad. I'll be going so. I want no quarrel with you" Fergal replied calmly.

Tony Lee stood shaking. His emotions were shot to pieces. He tried to compose himself, to understand what was being said, but his heart felt as though it might explode in his chest, and he felt a sickening pain in the pit of his stomach.

Fergal Carrie reached over to the armchair to reclaim his black hat. He grabbed his silver cane from the side of the chair and stood for a moment facing Tony. "I'll go lad. I want no trouble with you. Here, I've written down my phone number in case you wish to get in touch. I'll understand if you do not want to" Fergal said. He held out a small white card, but Tony Lee declined to accept it. Fergal nodded once again and placed it down gently on the old coffee table. "I'll see myself out" Fergal said, donning his hat as he made for the door.

Tony slumped down on the new blue sofa. He surveyed the room. It contained a mixture of memories and newly acquired furniture. The new surrounding had been put in place in the hope of building a new life. Tony had spent his savings on ridding himself of his mother's past. He felt that it was ironic that her former life would return to haunt him, right in the very room that Delores loved most. Suddenly everything seemed pointless to Tony. If he was to believe this stranger, his entire life had been a lie. Tony heard the front door slam. Curiosity got the better of him, and he arose to secretly peer out of the new double-glazed windows. The laced curtains masked him from the world outside. Tony watched as the older man crossed the quiet road. Fergal Carrie glanced up and down the street. He spotted a taxi and raised his silver cane to hail it. In a moment he was gone, and Tony ambled back to the old coffee table. It was the only item of furniture that remained in the room from his mother's time. Tony had kept the table as it was a favourite of his mothers, although he felt sure that Stacey would want to dispose of it in the future. He picked up the card and read it. Tony Lee had expected a business card, but this was simply a handwritten name and telephone number on a small plain white card. Fergal had prepared it in advance, probably knowing that he would hardly be made to feel welcome.

Tony sat for what seemed like hours, digesting the new information that Fergal Carrie had spewed out. It made little sense, yet there was something believable somewhere in the roots of Fergal's tale. Certain things rang true, such as Sean Lee fleeing to England. Tony's Auntie Mary's account of things also fitted in with Fergal's.

Tony began to question how much Jan Williams knew. She was a lot older than him, and would have been able to take things in back then. He felt that Jan held the key to unlocking the story, but Tony was also reluctant to get in touch with her. Jan would hardly come clean if she knew what had just occurred anyway. Already she had lied to him about the most basic of things. Tony felt that only when Jan was cornered on something, would she then tell the truth.

Anyway, they had had no contact in weeks, and Tony was reluctant to make the first move to patch things up. There was a certain satisfaction in not having Jan dictate to him on how he should live his life. Even with this bombshell of information entering his life, Tony was not sure that he wanted to open the door to Jan Williams again.

His thoughts returned to Auntie Mary. So far, it appeared that she was the one person who had been totally honest with him. Perhaps Mary knew who his biological father was. It seemed plausible if she and her husband were as close to Sean Lee as she claimed. Tony speculated that maybe Fergal Carrie's claims were wishful thinking on the man's behalf. It could be that Fergal and Delores Lee had been nothing more than close friends, and that Fergal had wished to take it further. This was what Tony wanted to believe, really for his own peace of mind.

Tony then considered Fergal's words on his mother's second affair. It was absurd to think that having saved her marriage, his mother would embark on another sordid fling. Even now Tony felt his stomach heave. And then something else struck him. He remembered the pile of coloured envelopes containing all of those old love letters. Something was gnawing at his brain, something he did not wish to contemplate as the truth. What if Fergal Carrie had written all of those special words and phrases to his dear Mam? Worse still, what if this mystery lover that Fergal had spoken of, had been the author? Tony felt compelled to seek out the old pile of envelopes there and then. Armed with the writing on Fergal's card as a comparison, Tony bounded upstairs, his heart thumping even faster. He remembered that none of the letters he had read had been signed at the bottom. At the time it struck him as odd. Now it hit Tony as utterly sickening. He pulled the envelopes from on top of the wardrobe and spilled them onto his new king-size bed. Tony pulled open envelope after envelope until they covered the new white duvet. There was now no way of telling which letter belonged to which brightly coloured envelope now, as he frantically scanned each letter in search of a signature. Tony went to the bottom of each last page. As he had suspected, there was no signature. It was always, "Love always" "Forever yours", or some other term of endearment. Tony compared the writing with that of Fergal Carrie. It was very similar, but not conclusive. Tony realised that the letters were probably written over thirty-five years ago. Fergal Carrie's handwriting might have changed a little.

Tony sank to his knees in despair. He was not sure if his sense of anger was with his mother or Fergal Carrie. Perhaps it might even be with his almost forgotten father. Tony did not know. At that moment he had to release his emotions. His tears dropped gently onto the coloured paper spread across the bed. The tears blurred the ink and smudged the pages which they fell on. Somehow it did not matter anymore. Tony Lee was in a state of utter despair. He felt as though someone had rolled his emotions up in a ball and thrown them in the bin. Tony perched on his knees beside the bed and wept openly against the white duvet. He could smell the freshness, mixed with the musty smell of the writing paper. Tony was overwhelmed with a sense of loss and deceit. He felt abandoned and alone. His world had crumbled overnight, and Tony did not know what to believe anymore.

CHAPTER TWENTY-THREE

DO A FRIEND A GOOD TURN

By late afternoon that same day, Tony Lee had calmed somewhat. The earlier events still dominated his thoughts though, and he now needed someone to share them with. For the moment he had ruled out Jan. Eventually he would have to discuss things with her. He knew that. But for now he needed a friend, someone to rely on and listen with a sympathetic ear. Stacey sprang to mind, but Tony feared that she would be with her mother at the hospital. His next thoughts were Erik Ngombiti, but his friend would most likely be spending time with his family.

By now Tony had gathered up his mother's love letters and put them safely away. He wandered about the newly-refurbished house aimlessly, wondering what he should do. Tony had done some painting and gardening that morning. He had earlier planned out his day so well. In the afternoon he wanted to do some more shopping for the house. New pillows and cushions had been top of his agenda before Stacey's eventual return to Dublin. Now everything seemed so pointless. His world had turned upside down, and Tony had not got the heart to stir outside the door.

On a whim he decided to telephone Stacey. He would only ask how her mother was doing, and vowed not to upset her with the devastating news that he had received.

"Hiya Stace, how is everything? Just thought that I would give you a call" Tony said cheerfully.

"Yeah, Mam's doing fine. I'm just on the way to the hospital now. We hope that she will be allowed home on Monday. If that's the case, I could be home by the weekend. Isn't that great?" Stacey replied. Tony could tell that she was in a good mood. He could not burden her with his problems. They chatted for a while until Stacey reached the hospital.

"Tony, we're there now. Dad says hello. He's just parking the car, so I had better go. Phone me during the week, yeah?" Stacey said. Tony promised to do so and said goodbye. He wandered around the house again, ruling out bothering Erik with his news, at least until Monday.

Then a thought hit Tony Lee. Why not call Fergal Carrie? There were still a million questions left unanswered. Tony decided to make the call. It was the least that the man owed him.

"Can we talk? It's Tony, Tony Lee" he said when Fergal answered the phone. It was a mobile number, and Tony wondered if the man was with his family.

"Certainly Tony. I did not expect you to call back so promptly" Fergal said in a cheerful tone.

"I...I have a lot of things running through my mind" Tony said.

"I can appreciate that. So where do you wish to meet up? Would you like to call to my home?" Fergal asked.

"What about your family? Do they know about me?" Tony replied, startled that he may have some half-brothers or sisters.

Fergal Carrie laughed down the line.

"Goodness me, no! I have no family to speak of, definitely not! You see Tony, when your mother and I split up, there could never be anybody else for me. I live alone, always have done. I threw myself into my work when Delores rebuffed me. When I met your mother she worked as a shop assistant for my father's company. It was then just a large department store in the city. I was a salesman for the firm when I met Delores. I now own a chain of shops, not too extravagant you understand, but it's a thriving business. No, I never married. How could I? I always hoped that one day...Still, never mind. Where shall we meet up Tony?" Fergal said, managing to keep his emotions in check.

"Er, anywhere you like. I'll call to your place if you want" Tony answered.

Fergal gave him the address. It was in the Dublin 4 area, an upmarket part of Dublin on the south side of the city.

Tony set off on his silver bicycle. The address was only twenty minutes away at most. As he pulled out of St. Oliver's Road, Alex Woods slipped in behind him at a respectable distance. He had been watching the house for some time, wondering how to make his next move in his mission to do away with Tony Lee. Perhaps today might provide that very opportunity. Alex recalled how Stacey had told him about Tony's weekend cycling trips to the countryside, or to the Dublin Mountains. She had told Alex about one place in particular, which was a favourite venue of Tony's. Alex recognised the spot, up near

Johnny Fox's pub, which was high in the hills overlooking Dublin City. If Tony was to head off to that isolated area, it would be perfect for Alex.

Yet lately Alex noted that Tony had barely ventured out on his bike. Perhaps it was because of the house refurbishment, Alex was not positive. Either way, Alex had decided that the open countryside may well be the perfect place for Tony Lee to have that fatal accident.

Tony sprinted along the canal, weaving past slow-moving cars. Saturday shoppers dominated the traffic, and Alex Woods soon lost sight of him.

"Shit! Fucking shit!" Alex screamed as an elderly driver dithered ahead of him on an amber light. Alex tooted the horn loudly several times. The older bespectacled man looked startled as he viewed Alex's car in his mirror. Alex continued to toot the horn, holding the button down firmly on the steering wheel.

A policeman on a motorcycle tapped on Alex's window. He beckoned to Alex to roll down the window. Only then did Alex's simmering temper subside a little.

"What seems to be the problem sir? Are we in a hurry somewhere?" the policeman asked. He sat astride the white motorbike, his white and blue helmet glistening in the afternoon sunshine.

"I'm so sorry officer; I own a garage and need to pick up some supplies urgently across town. This old fart thinks that he owns the road. He's driving at ten miles an hour. Just now he stopped before the light had changed from green to amber. People like him should not be on the road. He's probably half-blind anyway" Alex said with a friendly smile.

"Now, now sir, the roads are for everybody's use. I was observing that gentleman. He stopped on amber, which is the correct thing to do, providing it's safe to do so. If anything, you might have been driving too close to the vehicle ahead of you" the cross-looking garda replied. Alex was seething inside.

"I don't agree garda. Look, I'm in the motor trade for years. I deal with these fuddy-duddies everyday of the year. Half of them should be in retirement homes, never mind driving through our city. I know that you're only doing your job, but can't you get him to drive at a reasonable speed so that the rest of Dublin can get home tonight?" Alex said, raising his voice slightly.

The policeman had heard enough. He dismounted from his motorbike as the lights ahead turned green, and wheeled his motorcycle in ahead of Alex's car.

"Can I see you driving licence please sir?" he asked in a bored tone. The traffic behind Alex began to inch past him along the narrow road. Alex punched the passenger seat hard with his fist.

"Fucking hell! Have you nothing better to do? There are criminals out there shooting one and other and selling drugs in open daylight! Jesus Christ! A poxy old age pensioner can do what he likes on the road, and because I toot the horn it's a crime!" Alex fumed.

"Who said anything about a crime sir? I merely asked to see your driving licence" the policeman said calmly. Alex pulled his licence from his wallet and showed it to the young garda. The policeman studied the plastic card, comparing the photograph with Alex's face. Alex took a deep breath. It hardly mattered now. Tony Lee was long gone. It was another opportunity wasted.

Tony Lee knocked on the door of the huge house on Haddington Road. It was an imposing four-storey building with a substantial front garden. The lawn itself was not very well-cared for, but Tony mentally priced the property in the €3 million range. If Fergal Carrie did own the entire estate, Tony wondered why he would live alone in such a huge property.

Fergal Carrie answered the door with his ready smile on view. He had a kindly face, but Tony noticed how sad his eyes looked. Heavy dark bags of skin hung below his sharp blue eyes, a testament to the passing of time. His slim grey beard was well groomed, yet Tony felt that it dated the man somewhat.

"Hello Tony, do come in" Fergal said, holding the giant glossy blue door open. Tony glanced back over his shoulder. Down the four rounded steps below him, his silver bicycle stood chained to the grey railings surrounding the property.

"It will be okay there Tony. It's not such a bad neighbourhood!" Fergal said with a witty chuckle. Tony nodded as he passed him.

"I've had two bicycles stolen in this city, both times in areas like this" he replied coldly. Fergal led him into a large sitting room with a high ceiling. Ornate white cornerstones adorned the elaborate ceiling. Paintings hung on the walls, and a large book stand covered one entire wall. Everywhere in the gigantic room there were antiques and sturdy old furniture. Tony noted that there was neither a television nor radio. He took a seat on an old Queen Anne-style armchair with its red velvet inlayed cushion. Fergal sat opposite him on an identical chair.

"I know that you have many questions Tony. I would prefer to discuss our future rather than my past. We could be good for each other, you see. I could offer you a comfortable future. I'm worth a handsome fortune. Once this is proven, I could write you into my will as my beneficiary" Fergal said with a confident tone in his voice.

"If I'm honest sir, I couldn't care less about your wealth. I have no interest in your money. Mainly my questions are about my mother" he replied quietly. Fergal looked disappointed. He offered him something to drink, but Tony declined.

Fergal began to outline how he and Delores had met.

"I first noticed Delores when I visited the store one day in May. It was a beautiful morning, and she had just started work in our shoe shop in Capel Street. Oh, I should explain that it was the family business. Over the years I have acquired several others. Anyway, I was drawn to her immediately. I must confess that I was disappointed to discover that she was already married with a daughter. I was learning the trade, so to speak, visiting shops abroad and learning what shoes were popular at home and in England. It must have seemed very exciting to others, but I was bored with it. Delores paid me a lot of attention back then, and I admit that I was flattered. Eventually we went out on a date. Soon we were seeing each other at every opportunity, even at your current home" Fergal said frankly. Tony Lee felt a knot in his lower stomach.

"And where was my father at this stage? Was he out of the country?" Tony asked. Fergal thought for a moment. He wanted to be totally honest.

"Sometimes, but not always. At times he might be at work in Dublin" Fergal answered.

"And Jan, did she ever meet you?" Tony asked. Fergal Carrie rose to his feet. He wandered towards the bay window overlooking one of Dublin's more upmarket roads.

"Yes Tony, we met. She was just a child, but Delores introduced us one day. You see, it was the summertime and Jan was off school. Naturally when I came to visit, Jan would be at home. Delores introduced me as an old friend. It was not always easy to meet up in the evening when Sean Lee was home you see. When he was out of town, Delores would ask either of her sisters or friends to babysit" Fergal replied candidly.

"I don't want to know the details, but when did my father find out about you?" Tony asked. With each titbit of news, Tony's vision of his perfect mother was being destroyed. Fergal sighed and returned to sit opposite Tony Lee.

"I suppose that we became careless. Back in those days, having an affair was not easy, unless it was totally away from prying eyes. You see, my parents still lived here in this house. At times we used St. Oliver's Road to see each other, but other times we might meet up in the city, or on the outskirts. Once or twice I booked into a discreet hotel. Anyway, your father became suspicious. By then Delores was already pregnant" Fergal said. His voice was emotional now as the past returned to haunt him.

"What happened?" Tony asked, daring to face the truth once more.

"Well, there was an almighty row between your parents. I use that term for convenience, you understand?" Fergal said, looking Tony in the eyes. It triggered a response in the younger man.

"This is not some bloody game here! My Dad Sean Lee is still my father as far as I'm concerned. This is my life that we're talking about. I've grown up not knowing any of this. I feel cheated, let down and humiliated" Tony yelled. Fergal bowed his head.

"I understand, really I do. Tony, I feel cheated too. Cheated out of a son, cheated out of a relationship. Cheated of life itself. Once Delores decided that she would have nothing to do with me, I gave up on that side of life. Oh, I dated women, but always found myself comparing them to Delores. Of course, none of them measured up. After a few years of trying to replace your mother, I simply gave up. I engrossed myself in work. When my father died, I took the reins at the company. My mother was frail, and she soon passed away too. This house became my office, my home, my prison if I'm honest! It still is to this day. Upstairs is where I work on a daily basis. Above that are the bedrooms. The top floor is empty, except for some old furniture" Fergal replied. Tony Lee quietened inside. He did not wish to be angry, merely to find answers.

"Okay, you say that you persuaded Mam to keep me. Obviously my father knew that I was not his child. Who else knew?" Tony said quietly. Fergal shrugged his shoulders.

"Both of Delores's sisters knew. I told no one in my family. Your sister Jan knew. I found that out later. She was only a child. One day I knocked at your home in despair. All I wanted to do was to see you, just one time. Maybe even to hold you son. Jan came to the door. I think that Delores sent her. She was only a kid as far as I was concerned. She called me some terrible names. I got the shock of my life. She told me to go or Delores would phone the police. I had just been standing there on your street, watching the house that morning. Pathetic, isn't it? Anyway I guessed it might be my last chance to reconcile with Delores. I had heard a rumour that she was planning on moving away to England. That thought terrified me. The idea that I might never see Delores again would have been too much to bear. That never happened of course. Soon Delores met someone else. I continued to write to her. I bought you presents and left them at the door when Sean had left for work, or was away. I even bought you a pram. I was so proud when I saw Delores out wheeling you down the street" Fergal said. He wiped away tears now as he recalled those long ago days.

Tony remembered the old pram from the attic. He recalled the panic in Jan's voice when he had mentioned it. Yet he said nothing to Fergal Carrie. There were still too many doubts, too many questions for him to be sure just yet.

"And who was this guy that you keep on about? This mystery man that conveniently took over where you left off? You must have seen him. You must know his identity?" Tony demanded, holding his emotions in check. Fergal shook his head sadly.

"No Tony, I wish that I did, but I never saw him. You see, around that time my father had died. I was busy working. It was almost a year later before I realised that I was still deeply in love with Delores. When I had some spare time, I would go and watch the house in the hope of seeing you or Delores. I rarely did of course. But God how I tried to. Any spare time at all that I had, I would be across the street; praying that the door would open and either one of you would be there. Delores knew where I lived. Each morning I hoped for a letter from her, but it never came. Then my mother died. Again I took a sabbatical away from begging Delores to take me back. I managed to put her to the back of my mind for a while. It did not last long however. Soon I began writing to her again. Then I was soon back spying on her. I think that by now her mystery man had vanished. You were about five years old by then. Unfortunately Sean Lee had died too. Delores became a loner. She seldom ventured out. I heard that she cut herself off from neighbours and friends. So sad, so very sad" Fergal concluded.

They talked well into the afternoon. Fergal Carrie offered an open and frank account of his younger life. Tony listened with interest, interrupting him when he needed an explanation or to ask a question.

"I took the difficult decision to approach you, with great trepidation and a certain amount of reluctance, Tony. You see, I'm not a young man anymore. I suffer with high blood pressure-among other things! It's all the result of a somewhat unwholesome lifestyle! I still smoke. I eat out a lot nowadays. I cannot be bothered to cook, you understand? Anyway, my unhealthy lifestyle over the years points to the fact that I may not have much time left. I decided that you should know the truth before it's too late. Do with it what you will Tony. Can I just say this? I don't regret for a moment what happened. Some might say that I have wasted my life, living for what might have been. Perhaps. But I was in love with the most beautiful, the most friendly, the most wonderful lady in the world. We produced a fine child, one that I'm so proud of. And there you have it Tony" Fergal said.

"How old were you when you met my mother?" Tony asked. Fergal's face lit up. It was his favourite subject, his best time on earth.

"Oh, I was in my late thirties. Your mother was about thirty-three. I had seen and done things, but was still a man about town with no wish to settle down. You could say that I was a ladies' man. Delores changed all of that! From the day I met her, I never looked at another woman seriously. I suppose that she was fascinated with me at first. I had a million tales to tell, and Delores had married young. She had little experience of the world. Most women back then were the same. They married, had children, and made their homes cosy. It was the done thing. Ladies seldom travelled, except the upper-class. Delores enjoyed my company and vice-versa" Fergal said.

Tony did the maths. His mother might well have been thirty-three or thirty four. He knew that she had married at the age of twenty. At thirty-four, Jan might have been thirteen years old. There was a fourteen year age gap between Tony and his sister. Everything fitted. Tony knew that he had to take Fergal Carrie's claims seriously.

"There will have to be blood tests or DNA tests done" Tony replied warily. Fergal nodded his acceptance.

"Of course, of course! I'll pay. I'm just delighted that you have the foresight to believe me" Fergal answered.

"I never said that I believed you. All I want to do is prove it one way or the other. To be frank, I hope that I can disprove it sir" Tony replied. Again Fergal nodded. He could hardly expect Tony to wish that a perfect stranger was his biological father.

"I'll arrange it then, shall I?" Fergal said. Tony stood up and nodded.

"I'll keep in touch. One thing that I don't believe is that my mother had a second affair. You will never convince me of that" Tony said. Fergal rose to his feet and faced Tony Lee. He looked him straight in the eyes.

"Why would I lie? I only wish that it weren't so. If that was the case, myself and Delores might have stayed together for the rest of our lives. Sadly, we will never know the truth now, nor does it matter Tony. Let's just sort out this mess once and for all, eh?" Fergal replied. He offered Tony a handshake. Reluctantly Tony accepted. He felt the warmth of a firm, friendly hand in his. Somehow it felt right.

Tony Lee sat at home that evening trying to piece together his mother's young life. Only two or three people could confirm or add to the story. Tony ruled out his Aunt Ethel. Her mental state could not be relied on. He decided not to trouble the old woman with his problems. On the other hand, Auntie Mary seemed to have a certain amount of knowledge on the subject. Tony vowed to question her again, and cursed his luck that he had only recently returned from Walsall.

Then there was Jan. His sister, or half-sister as she may now be, definitely knew more than she had told him. The question was, would she ever tell everything that she knew? Tony doubted it, and did not relish getting in contact with her. Lastly there was Fergal Carrie. Could he really believe this man? On the other hand, why would a wealthy man claim such a thing if it was not true? Tony considered if it amounted to wishful thinking on the man's behalf. Maybe. That would make sense. If Fergal Carrie had been in love with his mother and she had rejected his advances, maybe Fergal had invented his own little world. Tony sincerely hoped that such was the case, yet something in the back of his mind told him that Fergal Carrie was sincere.

The trial of Burrener and Muggser took place the following week. Joseph Byrne and Bernard Claffey stood in the dock dressed casually in dark trousers and plain jackets. Byrne wore a red tie over his white shirt, while Claffey wore a blue shirt, open at the collar. Their solicitor had persuaded them to drop their story involving Alex Woods, fearing it might harm their case. He found it unreliable and unrealistic, and considered that the judge would also. Reluctantly both Burrener and Muggser had agreed to plead guilty. They had asked for five more charges to be taken into account, clearing away any further charges that might be brought against them in the future. It was now a case of how long they would spend in prison. Although there seemed little chance of either walking free, their solicitor went through the motions, as he did with most of his criminal cases.

Mr. Fredrick Hinchcliffe outlined the unfortunate lives of both of his charges, depicting his clients as having a life of poor education and of being somewhat social misfits. He told of Claffey's parents being alcoholics, and how Bernard had tried without success to find work. It was a tried and trusted method that the elderly solicitor had used many times, sometimes with limited success. On a good day the judge might take pity on the accused, and reduce the sentencing considerably. Also, by admitting to other outstanding burglaries, the law always looked favourably on the case. Mr. Hinchcliffe droned on as he paced the small courtroom near The North Circular Road.

"My client Mr. Byrne has also had a terrible deal from life. Both his parents also have a problem with alcohol. With a severely handicapped sister at home, his parents could never afford Joseph the time that he deserved. He was left to fend for himself as they struggled to give their daughter a decent standard of living. Alas, young Joseph got in with the wrong crowd, leading to a small amount of petty crimes. But Joseph is not a bad lad. He is most content when wheeling his young sister about in her wheelchair, or spending time with his much beleaguered parents. Without him to take the load off them, I'm not sure how Mr. and Mrs. Byrne might cope. He has expressed his regret for his past misdemeanours, and like Mr. Claffey, he merits a second chance. I feel sure that if your honour deems this acceptable, both men will go on to make a better life for themselves. There is nothing to be gained by sending another two young men into the penal system. In fact, I would argue that the opposite is the case. Prison might only harden these two chaps against society. On the outside, they could assist their families and become decent members of society once more" Mr. Hinchcliffe concluded.

The judge sentenced Bernard Claffey, aka Muggser, to six months in prison, with two months suspended. He sentenced Joseph Byrne to 300 hours of community service, allowing for the fact that it was Burrener's first offence. Although known to the police for his petty crimes, Joseph Byrne had not officially ever being found guilty of anything as an adult. He was free to go.

The following day, Burrener visited Muggser in Wheatfield Prison at three o'clock.
"What's it like in here?" Burrener asked.
"Ah, it's okay really Burrener. I'll do the time standing on me bleedin' head, yeah? Then you and me, on the fuckin' tear again, eh?" Muggser said with a huge grin. Burrener glanced to the floor, a guilty look etched on his face. The smile vanished from Muggser's face.
"Don't go getting fucking soft on me Burrener. What's up?" Muggser asked. Burrener looked shifty. He avoided eye contact with his pal.
"It's the old man, isn't it? Me and him had a heart to heart last night. Then there's Caroline, my sister. You can see how I'm fixed? The Ma and Da need me to help look after her. The old man isn't getting any younger Muggser. He can barely cope" Burrener replied.
"He's only gone Jaysus fifty for fuck sake! If he laid off the funny tobacco he would be okay. He smokes the weed like it's going out of fashion, for Jaysus sake!" Muggser snarled, raising his voice. An incredulous look spread across his scarred face, his eyes widening with astonishment at what he was hearing. Burrener continued to defend his position.
"Still Muggser, I had a narrow escape this time, as the Da said to me last night. I was thinking of lying low for a while" he reasoned. Muggser leapt to his feet. They had been seated at a small table in the big hall, sitting opposite each other.
"Lie low! Who are you? Jesse fucking James?" Muggser bellowed in a mocking tone.
A prison officer craned his neck to observe Muggser. The officer was standing against the wall. Muggser had his back to him. A row of inmates sat along a line of tables in a similar position.
"Sit down there! You! Claffey! Sit back down or lose your privileges!" the officer yelled. Slowly Muggser returned to his seat. Burrener looked amused.

"What privileges do you get inside? Can the girlfriends stay overnight or something?" Burrener asked innocently, leaning forward on his plain, plastic-seated grey chair. Muggser looked agitated.

"Of course not, dickhead! We can play snooker and pool. We have our own telly in the cell, that sort of thing" he replied sharply.

"Sound all right. I haven't even got my own telly at home! I have to borrow the Ma's portable" Burrener said thoughtfully.

"Forget all that. Listen, you have to help me get even with that Alex Woods arsehole. He's the reason that I'm here in the first place" Muggser said. Burrener looked shocked. His thin face paled as he gulped down air.

"Are you mad Muggser? Remember what happened the last time? There are cameras everywhere at his house. He's sold his flat. I can hardly do anything at his garage either. That has CCTV too" Burrener said in a low voice. Muggser was undeterred.

"Don't you see? It would be perfect while I'm banged up! We can get a few of the lads to do it. Set fire to his fucking house. Treadser Tracey is good with the old arson. We can pay him a few quid to burn his bleedin' house down! Old Treadser would probably do it for nothing anyway. He loves a fuckin' good blaze!" Muggser said with a satisfied grin. Burrener looked aghast.

"Are you feckin' crazy? I'm not getting involved with mad Treadser Tracey! He would set fire to his own granny for a laugh. And the other lads won't help us out unless we pay them big bucks up front. Where am I gonna get that sort of cash? Listen Muggser, as I said, I'm gonna lay low for a bit. It's for the best, yeah? Maybe when you get out we can..."

Burrener's words were lost in the noise as Muggser lost his temper. He upturned the small table and began ranting at his friend.

"You fucking cowardly bastard! You shithead! I took this rap for you! You should be in here! It was you who wanted to do that Blackrock job! You chickeny yellow-belly swine!" he screamed.

Muggser was quickly restrained. He was led away back through the giant battle-grey doors behind him. A shaken Burrener hurried away towards the exit, unsure what to say or do next. He would head home on the bus, and do what he always did when troubled. His X-Box beckoned, and he would spend a few hours playing mind-numbing games to pass the time.

In the next few weeks, Joseph Byrne would become the model reformed character. Nothing was too much trouble for Burrener as far as his family was concerned. He helped look after his invalid sister, did chores at home, and did his community service without complaint. Burrener now dreaded the day when Muggser would be due for release. The temptation to return to his old ways would be immense. Burrener would never visit his old friend in prison again. His X-Box occupied his free time, where he could lose himself away from the real world for hours on end.

"Hello Alex? It's Terry. Have you time for a chat?" the voice asked. Alex had been sitting at home trying to come up with a plan to finally be rid of Tony Lee. Only then could he think about wooing Stacey Boyd back into his life. Yet Alex still did not know if he could ever forgive Stacey. He feared that once Tony was out of the way, his next logical move was to dispose of Stacey also. Alex's problem was that the police would surely become suspicious under those circumstances. And so he had to plan his next move with ultra caution.

"Terry old mate! How are you? I haven't seen you for ages. I've been busy with the business, you know? It's taking over my life, this motor trade!" he replied in a jokey tone.

"Yeah, I can imagine. Listen, I haven't been in touch purposely. I wanted to give you a bit of time to organise your life. How have things been?" Terry asked. Alex read between the lines. What Terry really meant was that he was giving him time to get over Stacey. Terry had not wanted to be around to keep him company while he was brooding over being jilted at the registry office. Alex put on his brave face and donned a confident tone.

"Yeah, I appreciate it pal. It's been hectic all right. I told you that I was moving back into the old man's place? Well, I made a handsome profit on the apartment. I'm busy turning this house into the ultimate bachelor pad! When I sell the business, I want to become the most in-demand playboy in Dublin!" Alex chuckled.

"I can well believe it mate! Listen, are you doing anything later on? We could grab a few beers and chat things over" Terry suggested. Alex sensed an undercurrent in his old pal's voice. He felt that there was something troubling Terry Thompson.

"Sure, I'm free as a bird. You on the other hand...What's happening with you and the lovely Margaret?" Alex asked. A moment's silence followed as Terry picked his words.

"Oh, you guessed it Alex mate. Things are rocky between us. I need to talk to someone before she drives me mad. Can we meet up or what?" he replied. Alex laughed out loud again. He was enjoying playing the carefree friend.

"No problem! What about Caffery's Bar on The Quays? We used to have a laugh there a few years ago. I'll meet you, oh, say in an hour?" Alex answered. Terry quickly agreed before hurriedly ending the call.

The two friends sat at the long high bar in the popular pub, just yards from O'Connell Street, the main thoroughfare in Dublin City. They both drank bottles of Budweiser by the neck as they caught up on their latest news.

"And what's going on with you and the missus?" Alex asked pointedly. Terry took a long swig from the brown bottle and sighed.

"Oh, I can barely fart without her becoming suspicious. I've given up most of my social life for her. You know, going to football, the dogs, even the pub on a Friday night" Terry said wearily.

"Yeah! You used to like the old greyhounds, didn't you? What about the fishing? Did you knock that on the head too?" Alex asked with a grin.

"I'm doing that less and less too mate" Terry replied.

"I never got the fascination with that hobby. Sitting for hours in all weather, and you not able to swim a stroke!" Alex laughed.

"I don't need to swim! The fish do that!" Terry laughed.

"And what's Margaret's problem pal? Does she want you to become a monk or something?" Alex asked with a chuckle.

"Something like that Alex! She wants to save money on everything. All of my free time is spent with her and the kids now. You see, she has this idea in her head that I cheated on her. I wouldn't be surprised if she phones you to confirm that I'm sitting beside you!" Terry said with a sneering grin. Alex cackled and slapped his hand on the counter. A worried-looking Terry took another drink from the bottle.

"And did you, cheat I mean?" Alex asked, a roguish smile appearing on his lips. Terry turned to look his friend in the eyes.

"I couldn't resist pal. This young chick from the hotel where I work practically offered it to me on a plate. I dragged her into an empty bedroom and had my wicked way with her, didn't I? Anyway, fool that I am, I gave her my mobile number. Next thing you know, she's phoning me in the middle of the night. Jesus Christ! Margaret heard the female voice and put two and two together. Of course, I told Margaret that it was some kid from work who was infatuated with me, but she won't believe it! I warned off this, this Clonessa, but she won't take no for an answer. She wants second helpings, and is threatening to call to my house. Apparently someone from work gave her my address" Terry said.

Alex could not help but laugh again.

"It's not funny mate, my marriage is at stake here" Terry added.

"Well, you should have thought about that when you were jumping into the sack with this Clonessa sort!" Alex cackled.

"Touché pal, but she has this body to die for. Anyway, you weren't always that innocent yourself! Remember that Isobel one in London? You were all over her like a rash, and there was poor Stacey at home preparing for the wedding!" Terry countered.

For a moment the red mist descended on Alex Woods. Then he realised that Terry's words were spoken in innocence. How was Terry Thompson to know that Isobel's remains were now rotting away in The Dublin Mountains?

"Good shot! You got me there chum! Old Isobel, what? She's probably married to some Hooray Henry by now! Anyway, let's return to your predicament. What do you want to do? What about divorce? Leave the bitch and see how she likes it! Move in with this Clonessa chick. If her body is what you say it is, you'll live happily ever after!" Alex said with a loud guffaw.

Terry looked distinctly uneasy.

"If only it was that simple Alex. If I divorce Margaret she will take me for every penny. Don't forget that I have kids and a mortgage. The courts don't look favourably on the likes of me. No, I'll have to bow and scrape to Eileen for the next few months and hope that she comes around. Women! Who would have them, eh?" Terry said with a grin.

They talked some more in general, but always came back to Terry's problem. "It sounds to me as if the glow has finally gone from your happy little family life" Alex surmised. Terry sat staring ahead. They were now on their sixth beer, and also had had several shots.

"You could say that old pal. I thought that Margaret was the one, but she's just a selfish cow! All she thinks about is those kids and that bleedin' house!" Terry replied, slurring his words. Alex threw his arm around him awkwardly. He too was feeling the worse for wear.

"Why not do away with the bitch? I mean, think of the advantages! There would be the insurance money-providing that you did it right! You would be free to take your pick of other women. No more nagging or fighting. You could go for a pint when you liked, leaving Chloressa to babysit!" Alex cackled.

"It's Clonessa" Terry pointed out, waving a finger unsteadily in the air.

"Yeah, whatever! She can babysit, and me and you can go out drinking! Speaking of which, two more beers here!" Alex said, raising his voice in the bartender's direction. The young fair-haired barman nodded wearily and went to fetch two more bottles from the fridge with its clear glass doors.

"Nah, that won't work, you see pal, in Ireland, no...nobody gets...gets away with murder. It's a fact. They always get caught" Terry reasoned, slurring his words somewhat.

Alex's first instinct was to brag, but he managed to control his ego.

"Aha! But not if you plan it right! What if she drowned in the bath, or slipped in the shower? What about a faulty electrical switch mate? Or how about the car suddenly going out of control?" Alex suggested, leaning closer to his old friend. He continued to hold a comforting arm around Terry's shoulders. Terry Thompson turned to examine his pal's face, trying to take in Alex's wise words. He watched his old friend for any signs of humour, but Alex remained deadly serious.

"It, it would never work my old chum, never. You see, I'm no good at stuff like that. I couldn't lie. When they got me in for questioning, I would crack under pressure. You see, I'm no...no crinaimal... no criminal" Terry said, no doubting his own lips as they poured out words in the oddest way.

"I won't let you suffer old mate, I refuse! We'll sort something out. The best thing is for you to be away when something happens to her. Think about it! You could be on some stag do from work, or away in England at a football match. Before you leave we set up the accident. That way, no one can blame you! Simple!" Alex said, almost toppling over his beer as he reached for it. Terry shook his head vehemently as he flopped forward towards the long shiny bar counter.

"No...no pal. You're bang out of order. You see, I have two young kiddies. What if something was to happen to my little ones? I couldn't forgive myself" Terry murmured, now almost in tears.

Alex strengthened his grip on his friend, pulling him closer to him by the shoulders.

"That's where I step in pal. You're my mate, and I won't let anyone mess with you. Tell you what, I'll get rid of the bitch for you, how's that? I mean it Terry lad, I'll do her in for you. You just make sure that you're out of the country. Those kids will be fine, I promise" Alex said earnestly.

"What?" Terry asked, watching his friend's face for confirmation.

"Sure! It will be easy. I'll make it look like an accident. I'll doctor the car engine, or fix something electrical in the house. Don't worry. There will be no hint of foul play whatsoever" Alex replied confidently.

Terry sat upright again as Alex patted his shoulder. Suddenly the effect of the drink was wearing off for Terry Thompson. Had Alex really offered to murder his wife? He regurgitated his words again in his brain. Terry felt a chill run down his spine. This was not the Alex Woods that he knew and liked. There was something scary and evil in what he was proposing. Joking about things like this was all very well and even amusing in a macho way. It passed an evening and helped him to forget his problems for a while. Yet this was more than black humour. What Alex was saying rang true. Terry felt beads of sweat on his forehead. He wanted to get away from Alex Woods, as far away as possible.

CHAPTER TWENTY-FOUR

SECRETS TO YOUR DEATHBED

The following morning, Tony Lee received a curious phone call from Walsall, England. It was from his cousin, Belinda, a cousin that he had never met. "Is that Tony, Tony Lee?" she asked in her Midland's twang. Tony said it was, and asked who was calling. Belinda gave her full marriage name, and then realised that it would mean little to Tony.

"I'm sorry; this is your Auntie Mary's daughter. I'm Belinda" she explained.

"Oh, hiya Belinda, It's nice to hear your voice after all of these years. I was over visiting Auntie Mary..." Tony's reply was cut short.

"I'm sorry Tony; this is not a social call. You see, my mother died over the weekend. It was her heart. She had already had two minor heart attacks in the last couple of years. She passed away peacefully in her sleep. I'm trying to get in touch with as many relatives as I can think of. I found your address and phone number in Mam's purse. She told me all about your visit. Thank you for calling on her. I know it cheered her up" Belinda said.

Tony offered his condolences and asked about the funeral.

"It will be on Friday morning. Mam wanted to be cremated, so we will abide by her wishes" Belinda said. Tony expressed an interest in travelling over for the funeral, and Belinda offered him her mobile number so that he could keep in touch.

Tony Lee put down the receiver and entered the living room deep in thought. He felt for his Auntie Mary and her immediate family, but also realised that the person best placed to shed some light on his mother's younger life had now also passed away. Tony cursed the timing of her death, and wished that he had pushed the old woman harder on his mother's marriage. Now he only had Fergal Carrie's account of events to rely on.

Once again, Jan Williams entered his thoughts. Could he trust his sister to offer an honest account of what she remembered? Tony was not so sure. Jan seemed to be filled with hate and spite about their mother's passing. She appeared entrenched in her ways, and unable to discuss anything in an adult manner. It was as if she still considered Tony as her little brother, someone who should simply do as he was told.

Tony wandered back out into the hallway. His hand hovered over the new white phone, a replacement from the phone company. He dared himself to ring Jan Williams' number. Right then the phone rang loudly, startling Tony. His heart leapt as his hand recoiled in surprise. He then picked up the receiver and composed himself.

"Hello Tony? Stacey! Glad I caught you in. My credit is low. Great news! Mum is much better. Dad insists on my going home for a break. I'm catching a flight on Friday, just for a couple of days. Is that brill or what?" she gushed.

Tony quickly explained about his aunt's funeral. He asked if Stacey might like to come home anyway and meet up with her friends rather than him. Stacey declined. Hurried arrangements were made for them to meet up in Walsall instead. Stacey would book a hotel for a couple of nights, and they would spend the weekend together in England.

The next day, Tony went to see his Aunt Ethel. He carried a brown paper bag containing some black grapes, and a small box of chocolates. Tony felt that he owed it to his mother to pay his aging aunt a visit out of respect for Mary. It would be pointless to mention Ethel's sister dying. Tony knew that. He just felt as Ethel was the last of the Goulding sisters, it would be appropriate that he spent some time with her.

"Hello Aunt Ethel, It's Tony, Delores's son. How are you today?" he said, going through his tried and trusted routine. That scared, baffling look that Tony hated spread across her thin, lined face. Ethel stared back blankly at him, yet Tony felt that somewhere in the deepest recess of her brain, Ethel knew who he was. That initial panic, that sign that something different was happening around her, made Tony feel so sad. Yet he hoped that somewhere in Ethel's soul she recognised him just a little bit.

He forced back the tears as he held her frail, bony hand. It hung limply between his fingers, neither embracing him nor rejecting his touch.

"Well Ethel, what have you been up to? Chasing all those young doctors, I shouldn't wonder!" Tony said cheerfully. The faintest of smiles touched Ethel's thin pink lips.

"Divil a bit of it son! I'm barely able to stand. My old knees can't support my body anymore!" Ethel said.

A thought entered Tony's head.

"Would you like to walk Aunt Ethel? Would you enjoy a spin around the gardens?" Tony said. Ethel's whole body shook at the very thought.

"What? How could I Tony? It is Tony?" she said, her voice trembling.

"Yes, it's me Ethel. I'll get a wheelchair. It's a beautiful day out there. I'll bring you for a stroll" he whispered. Ethel's head nodded several times. She gripped Tony's hand in hers.

"I'd love it son. Just to smell the flowers. Sometimes I can almost taste their aroma through the open windows, but then the nurses shut the windows tight. They're afraid we might catch cold" Ethel said in a barely audible tone.

Tony rushed up to reception to speak to the nurse.

"Mrs Langan doesn't usually go outside. She's happy to sit indoors. Shall I open another window for her?" the plain-looking nurse asked with a plastic smile. Tony shook his head.

"No. Today she wishes to go out. Just for a short while. I'll see that she's all right" he said in a determined voice. The middle-aged nurse opened her mouth to debate the point, but then seemed to think better of it.

"Very well, just for a little while. I'll arrange a wheelchair from staff" she replied.

After what seemed like an age, a friendly medic came to help Ethel into the sturdy wheelchair.

"Where are we going again son?" Ethel asked, staring worriedly at Tony Lee. He leaned over to talk to her. Ethel had her old heavy black coat on.

"Just out to the garden Aunt Ethel. That is, unless you want to run away to America with me!" Tony grinned.

The medic fixed Ethel's feet on the footrest and left the two alone. Tony set off down the ramp and into the spacious gardens outside. He slowed as they reached the first flower beds, with the scent of roses, carnations and red and white begonias wafting through the early afternoon. They moved on, now the tang of lilac filled the air.

"It's nice here, isn't it Ethel? Remember when we went to The Botanic Gardens in Glasnevin? I was only seven…" Tony's words were interrupted by his frail aunt.

"Where's Henry? Henry! Who are you? Take me home to my husband. He worries about me. Dear Henry, dear, dear Henry" Ethel said, trailing off towards the end of the sentence. Tony stopped pushing the wheelchair and went to attend to Ethel. He crouched down on front of her, smiling at the old lady.

"It's okay Auntie, it's me, Tony" he said with a reassuring grin. Instantly he witnessed the faintest of smiles.

"Smell the flowers Aunt Ethel. Isn't that beautiful?" he said. Ethel's grey head turned towards the flower beds. She inhaled and smiled broadly. It struck Tony that he had not seen her really smile for many, many years.

"It's wonderful, marvellous. I love been in the Botanic Gardens Henry. Thank you for bringing me here" Ethel replied. Tony patted her shoulder through her heavy coat. For a few moments Ethel was back with her husband, at least in her dreams. For Tony Lee, it had all been worth it. They moved onwards through the well-attended lawns and flower beds, halting now and then to take in their surroundings. Sometimes he could hear Ethel mumbling incoherently to herself. Tony forgot his troubles for a while, basking in his old aunt's new-found freedom. Moments later Ethel turned around, expecting to see her dear husband. Immediately the long-lost smile vanished. Tony could see the panic in her eyes. She recoiled back further in her seat.

"I'll take you back inside Ethel. Just in case Henry calls" he said quietly. He turned the wheelchair again, facing it back towards the home. Tony smiled a contented grin. The trip had been worth it, just to see that one smile on his Aunt Ethel's lined face. Ethel Langan sank back in the chair again, relaxing a little. Ahead of her stood the reassuring sight of the nursing home, the building which had been her residence for many years now.

"Of course Henry will call, he always does. He promised to bring black grapes. They're my favourites" Ethel said, almost talking to herself.

Tony took her inside and a medic helped him lift Ethel back onto the armchair by the window. Ethel looked a little reassured once more. Tony said nothing, allowing the old lady to familiarise herself with her surroundings again. Presently he placed the bag of grapes beside her on the small round polished table.

"Look Ethel, Henry's brought you some grapes" he smiled. Ethel snapped out of her daydreaming. She looked to the grapes and then back to Tony.

"I knew that he would. Thank you Tony for taking me outside. The roses smell lovely, don't they?" she said with a satisfied smile.

"Yeah, they smell beautiful Aunt Ethel. We'll go for a walk again sometime, eh?" he replied. Ethel's smile vanished instantly.

"Oh no, I can't go out there again. It's not safe. No. I'm happy now. I just wanted to smell the flowers again. Thank you Martin, thank you. You're a good kid" Ethel replied. Her eyes were drawn towards the window again, back into her own little world of imagination and days gone by.

Tony sat for a while in quietness. Eventually he rose to his feet, ready for the cycle home. He placed the bag of grapes on Ethel's lap and kissed her on the cheek.

"Goodbye Ethel, see you soon" he whispered. The old woman snapped back to life once more.

"Goodbye son, thank you again for walking me around the gardens. Make it up with Martin. Life is too short. Tell Delores that I love her dearly" Ethel said.

Tony sat back down slowly. Perhaps it was worth spending some more time with his aging aunt. Maybe she might mention Fergal Carrie, he thought.

"Look, look, it's Henry! I said that he would come!" Ethel suddenly cried out. She pointed her bony hand to an old man who was wandering aimlessly around the gardens. Tony stood up slowly as Ethel's mind again drifted away.

"Goodbye Aunt Ethel" he whispered, the tears streaming from his eyes.

Alex Woods tiptoed quietly inside the apartment shared by Angie O'Rourke and Gina Stynes. He had watched both girls leave for work. Surmising that Stacey was still away, Alex had nevertheless rung the doorbell a couple of times, just to be sure.

His mission this time was to try and establish if Stacey Boyd had left Ireland for good, or was in fact living elsewhere in Dublin.

Alex systematically searched each room for clues. Gina's room was his first port of call. A portrait of Harry stood on the locker beside her bed. Alex picked up the framed picture and sat on the bed. He studied every detail of the rectangular photograph, with a smiling Harry pictured on a night out.

"What a loser! How easily he gave in. He just did what I told him without question! If that was me, I would fight every inch of the way. Imagine being so scared that you do exactly what you are told. Some people, eh? Well Harry, it looks like Gina still hasn't got over you, but give her time, eh? Sooner or later someone will come along! Me? Nah, she's not my type! Jodie, maybe. Stacey, certainly! Angie, maybe in a moment of weakness! But Gina? Nah. I don't really go for redheads!" Alex said with a callous chuckle. He placed the picture back carefully as he had found it before moving to Angie's room.

Suddenly his mobile phone rang, startling him a little.

"Hello Alex? It's Michelle from the garage. I have a Mr. Deveroux from Windscale Autos here. He wants to talk to you about some business. Mr. Deveroux was in the area and popped in. He's disappointed that he missed you" Michelle said. Alex Woods punched hard into Angie O'Rourke's sky-blue pillow on the bed.

"Jesus Michelle, I told you that I was out on business. Let Frank McKenzie deal with it. That's what we're paying him for. Where's Deveroux now?" Tony said angrily.

"Sorry Alex, Mr. Deveroux is in the main office" Michelle replied.

"Right, get Frank out there now. Deveroux runs a two-bit tiny company. He's probably on the look-out for some cheap deals. My father threw a bit of business his way. They were old pals, and he felt sorry for the old scrounger. Tell Frank to give him nothing, you hear? We're not a charity. Tell Deveroux that I can't be reached today, okay?" Alex snarled. He switched the phone to vibrate and continued his tour of the apartment.

In the living room, Alex found a scrap of paper in a drawer with Stacey's phone number and her parent's address on it.

"Hmm, this might prove useful, that is if she still lives there" Alex said under his breath. He noted that Stacey's clothes and belongings were in her room, leading him to believe that she would eventually return to the apartment. Alex noticed a white handbag in the corner on the floor. His curiosity got the better of him. He opened it and examined the contents. Inside he found a folded up letter. It was addressed to Angie. Alex read the short note aloud.

"Dear Angie, Thank you for the get well card. Of course I still think about you. I miss you lots. I'm so sorry for what happened. It hasn't really worked out with Karen and me, so I still live on my own at the apartment. I'm still not back at work because I have to attend the hospital regularly. I'm on crutches, so can't get about much. Maybe when I'm better we could talk? Take care, Phil xxx" he read. Alex's hand shook with rage. He realised that the letter was from Philip Westbourne.

"What an utter and absolute tosser! Can he not take no for an answer? He just doesn't know when to quit! Well I'll fix him, only this time there will be no way back. He can't get back with Angie. I need her here for when my Stacey gets back. No. He'll have to be silenced" Alex whispered, deep in thought. He calmed down somewhat as he rummaged through the rest of the contents in the small bag.

Content that there was nothing else to find, Alex switched on the television and lay down on the blue couch.

"Let's see how the other half lives-the work-shy half that is!" Alex said with a snigger. He settled back to watch some daytime television, flicking through the stations at will with the TV remote.

Alex heard the key turn in the door. It was almost two hours later, and he had drifted off to sleep. In a panic he rose to his feet, unsure which way to run. He snatched his phone and keys from the coffee table and made for Stacey's room.

Gina Stynes breezed into the apartment, tossing her light pink jacket on the table in the hall. She sauntered into the living room and stopped dead in her tracks. The television was on, and Gina had never watched television in the morning before leaving for work.

"Angie, are you home?" she called.

"Stacey, have you come back from England?" she said, opening the door to Stacey's bedroom. Alex Woods held the wardrobe door shut tight. He listened for approaching footsteps. If necessary, Gina Stynes would become his latest victim. Alex heard the bedroom door close again.

"I know that I didn't leave the TV on. That Angie! Last week it was the cooker. She won't be happy until she burns down this place!" Gina muttered. She ran the shower and stripped off her clothes, idly dropping each item onto her bed. Gina had changed her job, and was now doing shift work. She did three hours in the morning, and then a further four in the afternoon. In between, Gina enjoyed a two-hour break.

Gina stepped into the shower and pulled over the translucent plastic curtain. Alex listened as she hummed one of the latest pop tunes. He climbed silently from the wardrobe and opened the bedroom door. Alex then crept along the hallway, halting at the open bathroom door.

He eyed the silhouette of Gina's body through the shower curtain. She stood sideways, the white froth from the shampoo sliding slowly down her wet body. Alex was suddenly interested. The temptation was too great. Alex was infatuated by the girl's wet naked body. Easy targets like this could only be fantasised about. His earlier dismissal of any physical attraction to Gina Stynes had now evaporated. Suddenly Gina was very desirable indeed. He went to take a step inside the bathroom. Then he felt the mobile phone vibrate in his pocket. Michelle's name leapt into his brain. Instantly Alex forgot about Gina Stynes. Now Michelle had his full attention. His brain was going berserk at his secretary's incompetence. Alex could barely wait to get outside so he could give the girl a piece of his mind. He slipped unnoticed past the bathroom door and deftly opened the front door. Closing it silently with one hand, Alex reached inside his trouser's pocket and pulled out his phone.

Terry Thompson's name flashed up on the blue screen. Instantly Alex's rage quelled a little.

Terry had been giving Alex's proposal a lot of thought over the past few days. It scared him that his best friend would suggest such a thing as murder. It was time to test Alex, to see if it had been some kind of sick drunken joke, or if in fact the man had been deadly serious.

"Alex, is this a bad time? It's Terry" Terry Thompson said. Alex took a deep breath. How could he be angry with his old friend?

"Not at all Terry, I'm just going to lunch. Do you want to meet up?" Alex replied cheerfully. They arranged to rendezvous at a small café which both of them knew.

"The thing is Alex; I've been giving your suggestion some serious thought. As luck would have it, I'm due to go on a fishing trip to Scotland with my workmates next month. Now if something was to happen to Margaret while I was out of the country, I would be totally innocent, wouldn't I?" Terry said, picking his words carefully.

Alex eyed him from across the small white veneer-covered square table. Both were having burger and chips. Alex was enjoying a beer, while Terry opted for a cup of coffee.

"You really want to go ahead with this? Only, the other night you did not seem at all enthusiastic" Alex ventured.

"Yeah, well it's not every day that a mate offers to bump off your wife!" Terry whispered, leaning across the table. Alex grinned satisfactorily.

"Well, that's the type of chap I am! Anything for a friend!" Alex sniggered.

Terry felt his blood run cold. Already he wanted to get away from Alex Woods. Yet he knew that he had to act cool and collected.

"She's really doing my head in Alex. I swear, I can't go on like this" Terry continued. Alex appeared completely at ease. He bit into his cheeseburger and shrugged his shoulders indifferently.

"Well, we'll have to put her out of the picture, won't we pal? It's better in the long run. Why should you have to suffer a life of misery? The kids will soon forget all about her. You'll meet someone nice, and everything will be tickety-boo!" Alex said in a matter-of-fact voice.

Terry Thompson smiled back at him. He wondered just how well he knew his old friend. They had gone to college together, but had only been in and out of each other's lives on a fleeting basis. What Alex got up to away from work had never entered Terry's head. Now he was questioning everything about Alex Woods.

"So what would you like me to do?" Alex asked. Terry was shaken out of his daydreaming.

"Huh? Oh, I don't care Alex. I just want shut of her" he answered.

Alex wiped his hands and mouth with the paper napkin and leaned forward.

"Right. This would be my plan. I gave it some thought last night. We don't want the kids upset, so I would wait until she dropped them off with her family. What if you suggested on her having a night out with friends while you were away? Girls don't usually take that much persuading in my experience! If she was to leave the children with her parents overnight, that would be ideal. I could break in, make it look like a genuine burglary, and strangle the old cow there and then. It would like she disturbed a burglar and that he panicked. Listen, this does not have to be a hard and fast plan Terry. We can change it whenever you like. If you can think of a better way, then I'm very flexible. But this is a good outline idea of how to go about it. What do you think?" Alex asked.

Terry took in his words. Alex Woods might just as well be planning a night out with friends. There was no feeling or anxiety in his tone of voice. It struck Terry how ruthless and cold he appeared.

"Er, yeah, it sounds simple. God Alex! I'm shaking just thinking about it! You act so cool! It's as if you've done this before!" Terry replied. Alex ran his tongue around the inside of his mouth, finding a crumb of his burger and swallowing it. He tapped his nose with his forefinger twice.

"Now now, Terry, best not to ask any awkward questions!" he answered with a grin. It left Terry pondering as to just how much experience Alex had with such things. He looked at Alex Woods in a complete different light now.

"Sure Alex, whatever you say. We can discuss it in real detail in a few days time, yeah?" Terry said quietly. Alex Woods smiled back at him.

"You're the boss on this one mate. Whatever you say, goes!" Alex responded. Terry nodded and looked his friend in the eyes once more.

"Do I have your word on that Alex? I don't want you doing anything without my say-so" Terry said. Alex held both hands up in surrender.

"Like I said Terry, you call the shots. This will be the perfect crime. No one will suspect a thing. The thinking now is for you to be extra nice to Margaret. Make it look like she's the best thing in your life, both around people and when you're alone. Let no one suspect that you two are not getting on. When the topic of you going away for the fishing trip crops up, tell her that she should go out with the girls that particular weekend. Make out that you're not looking forward to going away whatsoever. Tell her how much you are gonna miss her" Alex suggested. Terry nodded again, his mind awash with fear and trepidation. The truth was that there was no actual fishing weekend in Scotland planned. It was a ruse by Terry Thompson to discover just how serious Alex had been by his proposal of murder. To Terry's surprise and shock, his old mate had meant every word, it seemed.

They parted with Terry vowing to phone his friend soon with more details. Even then Alex's attention to detail surfaced.

"You don't want to do that Terry. Phone records and all that. We'll have to speak face to face on this matter" Alex said before leaving.

The gravity of what was involved quickly hit Terry Thompson. He watched Alex disappear from view. It appeared to Terry that there was more of a spring in Alex's step on his departure, as if he had a renewed mission in life. It frightened the hell out of Terry Thompson, and he now feared that Alex might even do something rash without first consulting with him.

Alex watched as Philip Westbourne levered himself along the quiet street. Philip now could easily manage the crutches after weeks of practice. He had been to the local shop to buy bread and a newspaper, as was his custom most mornings. This was Alex's third day in a row to observe Angie's ex-boyfriend. Already a plan had formed in Alex's head. Philip was a creature of habit, it seemed. He did the same things each day. Philip would have a shower when he awoke, before going to the shop. It was not easy to wash with both legs in plaster, but somehow he managed. Philip would then fetch a newspaper from the nearby shop and read it over breakfast. He would then have another stroll to exercise his body before doing some weights.

In the afternoon, Philip's unemployed brother would call, and they would watch the horseracing together on television. Sometimes his brother would sprint to the nearby bookies to do a bet. When his brother went home that evening, Philip would do a little weightlifting, which was his hobby. Then he would go for a short walk before watching television again.

Alex had watched his routine and quickly come up with an idea. Something else caught Alex's eye. Philip always left his latch key in the door until nightfall.

Once Philip had let himself in, Alex sprung into action. He quietly removed the key from the closed door and drove to the hardware shop. He had them make a duplicate key before returning to Philip's apartment. Once sure that there was nobody around, Alex quietly slipped the original key back inside the lock. He would return the next day to carry out his master plan.

Tony Lee walked hand in hand with Stacey towards the crematorium. They had met up that morning. Stacey had been in England now for weeks. Each time she had planned to return home, her mother's health prevented her from doing so. Stacey was positive that she would soon be able to leave her father to take charge of her mother permanently.

It was a fine bright day in Walsall, and Tony tried to recall as much as he had learned about his Auntie Mary, but little came to mind. In her later years, his mother had practically airbrushed her elder sister from her life. Tony knew that whilst growing up, Delores had a great relationship with Mary. He remembered Jan talking about stories that their mother had told her regarding Delores's and Mary's schooldays. Now he only wished that he had paid more attention. He was only a young lad back then, and not very interested in what he perceived as female chat. Tony would create his own fantasy world of war games and Wild West shoot-outs in the then woman-dominated life at eighty-eight St. Oliver's Road.

"Do you fancy being cremated Tony?" Stacey asked, puncturing his carefree thoughts of long ago. Tony squeezed her hand and smiled.

"Not just yet Stace!" he quipped.

"No silly! I mean when the time comes! I have to know what to do with your old bones!" she laughed. Tony took a second to consider the topic.

"Nah! On reflection, I think I would prefer to go down the hole!" he said with a playful grin.

"I quite like the idea. After all, there probably won't be anyone to care once I'm gone" Stacey said thoughtfully. Tony released his grip on her hand and hugged her close to him.

"I'll still be here! I intend outliving you by about twenty years!" he said. Stacey shrugged her shoulders and looked sad.

"Either way, we'll be old folks without any children. One of us might even end up in a home like your Aunt Ethel" she replied.

"This is morbid! I know that we're going to a funeral service, but come on, cheer up a little" Tony said. He sought to change the subject. They reached the doors of the crematorium and Tony again brought up Fergal Carrie. He had earlier outlined what he knew to Stacey, but wanted her opinion on what he should do. Before Stacey had a chance to reply, Tony felt the need to for a smoke. He reached inside his jacket pocket and pulled out his cigarettes.

"Are you back on those horrible things again?" Stacey asked, looking extremely cross. Tony frowned as he examined the gold-coloured box of tipped cigarettes.

"I had to Stace, I miss you so much" he said with great conviction. Stacey's face broke into a smile.

"Liar, Tony Lee! I hate those things now, especially after what happened to my mother" Stacey exclaimed. Tony lit up a cigarette anyway and inhaled.

"I know love. Your Mam had a lucky escape. Anyway, she's on the mend, isn't she?" Tony said. Stacey nodded.

"Yeah, thank God. Still, I see all of those commercials on the telly. It's awful what those cigarettes do" Stacey said. Tony shrugged and inhaled once more. "Something's gonna get you in the end! You drink, don't you? And driving a car, that's far more dangerous!" Tony reasoned. Stacey had heard enough. She was never going to win her battle of words with Tony.

"Anyhow, what are you going to do about this...this Fergal chap? Do you believe him or what?" she asked. Tony looked deep in thought for a moment. "Well, there must be something to it. I mean, he seemed to know my Mam very well. Whether or not they had a passionate affair is open to conjecture. Maybe he's just fantasising, you know? Anyway, I'll have the D.N.A. tests or whatever. One way or the other, we'll find out the truth" Tony answered. Stacey offered him a playful smile.

"So you could be a millionaire. I'll get to shop at lots of shoe shops. You might even give me a shop of my own!" she said with a cheeky smile. Tony stubbed out the half-smoked cigarette as he noticed some members of Auntie Mary's family approaching, dressed all in black.

"I have no interest in his money. I just want the truth Stace. I hope that he's not my father. He makes my mother out to be a bit of a slut really. According to him, my mother had affairs all over the place. I felt like punching him at one stage" Tony said quietly.

"Well, from what you told me, this chap seemed like he was quite the suave, charming lover -boy of his day!" Stacey said.

"I'll bet that he was! But now he's just a lonely sad old man. Imagine wasting his whole life because he lost out on my mother. That's his story anyway" Tony said.

The conversation ended as Tony put out his hand to greet Mary's family. He introduced Stacey, and then Tony slowly made his way inside to say farewell to his old Auntie. He was saying goodbye to another member of his family, knowing well that she had taken her secrets to her deathbed. Secrets from his and his mother's past lives.

Early the next morning, Alex sat in his car outside Philip Westbourne's shabby apartment. Being Saturday, the area was particularly quiet. Alex parked out of sight of the ground floor flat. It was just gone seven o'clock. Alex slipped quietly from his white Mondeo and walked briskly around the corner. He watched as the light suddenly went on in Philip's bathroom, situated at the front of the old tenement flats. Next to the bathroom was the front door. Alex felt for the latch key in his jacket pocket and pulled up his collar. Donning a pair of light black gloves, Alex silently walked casually towards the apartment, glancing around to ensure that he was alone.

Alex could hear the sound of running water. He checked again that the coast was clear. In one quick movement, Alex entered the small flat, careful to place the new key back inside his jacket pocket. The bathroom door was closed over, but not fully shut. Alex could hear Philip humming inside the shower in a carefree tone. He peeped inside the bathroom, inching the door open a little more. A blue shower curtain was half-drawn across the white bath, which housed the shower. Philip's contour could plainly be seen standing back awkwardly from the flow of the water. He clearly wanted to avoid getting the white plaster too wet. Alex crept closer. He was on a high, anticipating his next move. He held his arms apart, ready to carry out his daring plan. Still Philip hummed, oblivious to Alex's presence in the same tiny square room.

At lightning speed, Alex made a grab for Philip Westbourne's feet. He yanked hard, whipping the man's feet away from the bath. Before Philip could react, he was sent flying downwards. His head crashed against the tap handles below, impaling his skull on the brass-coloured metal cold tap. Still the water gushed down from the shower up above. Alex never spoke. He whipped back the blue shower curtain with his gloved hands. Philip lay sideways with his eyes wide open. Alex had to be sure that the man was dead.

"Well there's a nice bonus! A fucking tap stuck right through his head! There will be no more thoughts of Angie O'Rourke now, my son!" he whispered.

Satisfied that Philip Westbourne was dead, Alex carefully pulled the curtain back across to its original position. It would look as if Philip had slipped in the bath. The blood seeped from Philip's head, mixing with the running water. His body lay in a bizarre position, half-turned and crumpled on the bottom of the white bath. For a second Alex took in the macabre scene. He felt no guilt or remorse. It was merely a mission that he felt compelled to carry out.

Alex listened in the hallway before inching the hall door open. Philip's latch door key lay on the small table in the hall. Once he was sure that nobody was about, Alex slipped quietly away towards his car.

"There! Another good deed done, but will Angie appreciate it? Probably not. But she'll thank me in the long run when she meets someone decent. She's well shot of a woman-beater like that scumbag" he muttered before driving off.

It would be later that afternoon before Philip's body would be discovered by his brother. William Westbourne would eventually force the front door open, realising that something was wrong. The sound of the running water from the bathroom, plus the fact that Philip's key was not in the door, would alert him that all was not well with his brother. Although late afternoon, the bathroom light would still on in Philip's apartment. A panicked William would discover his brother's dead body in the tiny bathroom. The police would class Philip's death as a simple accident, just as Alex had always planned.

Tony sat in Stacey's parent's house awaiting the taxi which would take him to the airport. Stacey's father was upstairs tending his wife, and Tony eyed the big clock over the mantelpiece.

"I wish that you were coming home with me. These last few days have been great" he said. Stacey sat next to him on the sofa.

"Yeah, I miss you. I miss everything about home. I talk to Gina and Angie on the phone all of the time, but it's not the same. Don't worry, I'll be back soon, possibly by the weekend" Stacey replied. Tony squeezed her hand.

"And when you do come back, where will you live?" he asked. It was the one question that he had put off asking since he arrived in England. Now he looked at Stacey directly as he awaited his answer.

"At the flat-to begin with. Look, I want to be with you too. I promise, I'm warming to the idea of moving in, honest. Give it a few more weeks and we'll discuss it some more, okay?" she replied with a smile. Tony Lee grinned back at her.

"Yeah, don't mind me, I'm just feeling sorry for myself. We will be together Stacey, won't we? I mean, all of that business with Alex. That's all behind us, isn't it?" Tony said.

He was feeling a bit insecure at returning home, and wanted some sort of reassurance.

"Of course! I told you, it's you that I want to be with. You'll see, when I get back to Dublin, things will be brilliant. No more silly break-ups. We're together forever, okay?" she said, a reassured look on her pretty face. Tony looked thoughtful once again.

"It's funny, you know Erik from work?" he asked. Stacey nodded.

"Well, he reckoned that we were always meant to be together. Even back when I was with...Jodie" Tony said. He looked shifty at having to mention Jodie Callaghan's name. Stacey cuddled up to him.

"That's nice of him to say. Poor Jodie though, I think about her all of the time. They never arrested anybody for her death, did they?" she replied. Tony shook his head.

"No. I hope that he rot's in hell. How can that man sleep at night? I hope he has nightmares for the rest of his life" Tony said forcefully.

"Speaking about nightmares, do you still get those dreams?" Stacey asked.

"Nah! I reckon that you were right. It was probably just the fact of my mother dying" he said. It was a pure lie. Tony still had the same awful dreams, at least once a week. He did not want to say anything that might put Stacey off moving in with him.

Just then there was a knock on the door.

"That will be the cab. Phone me when you get home, yeah?" Stacey said, rising to her feet.

"Yes Mammy, and I'll wash behind my ears before I go to school!" Tony said with a grin. Stacey punched his arm playfully.

"Come on, grab your holdall. See you soon" she said, kissing him gently on the lips.

Terry Thompson sat in his car deep in thought. He was on his lunch break, and Alex Woods occupied his brain. Now, from the moment he awoke until he finally went to sleep, Terry could see his pal's smirking face before him. Terry no longer wondered if Alex could carry out his threat to kill his wife Margaret, now he knew that he could. He had seen it in his eyes, listened to his voice. Yet Terry found it hard to envisage Alex committing such an act. As long as he had known Alex Woods, Terry had never seen a violent side to him. They had spent many months at a time apart since their schooldays, and as Terry searched his head for any subtle changes in his old friend, he could not come up with any solid evidence. Perhaps Stacey jilting him had tipped Alex over the edge, Terry speculated. But Terry considered that Alex had taken things well on the whole. There and then Terry decided to put some distance between him and Alex Woods. He would telephone Alex and announce that everything was now fine in his marriage. Terry vowed that he would say that he and Margaret had had a heart to heart talk and were going to make a fresh start with their relationship. It was best to make a clean break from his friend. Alex appeared to have problems, and Terry felt uncomfortable around him now.

Terry climbed from his car and slammed the door shut. He eyed his old green Corsa. Alex had offered several times to cut him a deal on a new car. Terry had always refused, embarrassed by his financial standing. It was a struggle to pay a mortgage and raise two young children. Margaret was a stay-at-home-Mum, meaning that Terry was the sole breadwinner.

Terry returned to work, wondering why Alex would not simply sit back and enjoy life. His old pal had the world at his feet. He had plenty of money, a thriving business, and a beautiful home. The one thing that Alex had not got was a family, or someone to care for him. The notion hit Terry hard. He stopped in his tracks in the hotel foyer, realising for the first time the simple fact. For all of Alex's wealth and bravado, there was no one to share his life with. Terry blinked back tears as he realised what he had risked with his brief fling with Clonessa. At work he had asked her to cool their friendship, pointing out that he was married with young children. Clonessa did not seem to care. She still let him know that she was available, and maintained her routine of giving him suggestive smiles and encouraging looks.

Terry Thomson had a certain steeliness in his eyes now as he entered the hotel reception area where he worked as the front desk manager. He was going to make his marriage work no matter what. He loved Margaret and his little family. Nothing was going to come between them, not Clonessa, and certainly not Alex Woods.

Tony Lee returned home to Dublin that evening. He took a taxi to St. Oliver's Road as the rain fizzed down. It felt good to be home. He paid the taxi driver and stood looking at his home, as if for the first time. It now fitted in nicely with the rest of the street. The new windows and guttering looked the part. The old creaky gate had a fresh coat of white paint to match the new smart front door. Even in the hazy rain Tony could not help but admire the appearance of his home. Then he noticed the uneven bush behind the railings. "That will have to go. I'll but some nice plants and create a neat flower bed around the garden" he thought quietly.

Tony hurried inside, opening the door with his new set of keys. He could still smell the paint and the new woodwork as he entered the fresh new kitchen. "Well Tony, you've done all you can with the old place! If Stacey does not move in now, she never will!" he muttered. He put on the kettle and sat down, still examining the work carried out on his home. Then he thought of Jodie. Tony considered what might have been had she lived. He wondered would he have been so keen to revamp his house for her. Probably not, he decided. Tony wandered upstairs as he awaited the kettle coming to the boil. He entered his bedroom, now looking tidy and attractive. Tony's gaze fell on the bricked-up fireplace. In a million years he would never have noticed the jutting-out wall. The layout of his bedroom had always been the same for as long as he could remember. It was Jodie who had suggested opening it up to add some character. Perhaps he would carry out her wish after all. He was sure that Stacey would approve too. Tony still had a few days off work the following week. Maybe it would be a nice project to keep him busy until Stacey returned.

CHAPTER TWENTY-FIVE

CROSSING ALEX

"Hello, Alex? Terry here. Listen, I just want to let you know that things have improved between Margaret and me. We sat down and had a chat, and cleared the air. Anyway, the upshot is that we're gonna try and make a go of our marriage" Terry said.

Alex listened quietly for a moment before speaking.

"That's good news then" he replied tersely.

"Yeah, I mean, I've been a bit of a dickhead too. I probably wasn't paying her enough attention, you know how it is" Terry said.

"Oh, I know only too well mate! So, you won't be requiring my help, is that what you're saying?" Alex answered. Terry Thompson laughed nervously.

"Well no, but thanks anyway. You're a real pal Alex, I won't forget it" Terry said.

"Oh, but you must forget it Terry. You see, that's incriminating evidence. Planning to commit a crime is against the law, didn't you know that?" Alex replied. Terry said nothing for a few seconds. Alex laughed out loud.

"I'm joking Terry! Listen, we're old mates; we can say anything to each other. No look, I really hope that it works out for you two. Margaret is a lovely girl. I'll tell you what, why don't we go out for a few drinks some night? You pick the evening and the venue this time" Alex said. It was the one suggestion that Terry had feared most. He fell silent again as he struggled to reply without offending Alex Woods.

"Well, the thing is Alex; the youngest one has not been too well today. I reckon that she's coming down with something. I'll have to get back to you on that, okay?" Terry said.

Alex bit hard on his bottom lip. It sounded like a rejection to him. He never expected it from Stacey Boyd on their wedding day. He certainly never saw it coming from his oldest and closest pal.

"Sure Terry, I understand. You have a good life, you hear?" Alex barked down the phone.

"No Alex really, I will get back to you, promise" Terry said. It was too late. Alex Woods had already turned off his mobile phone. He flung the black phone across onto the new white leather couch in temper. Then Alex jumped to his feet and began to pace the room.

"Bastards, every one of them. The more that I help people, the less grateful they are. It's like my Nan always said, friends are fickle, and family are everything. Well, we'll see Terry lad, we'll see. You'll meet me again one day, you can bet on that. I tried to help Angie O'Rourke, and what did she do? Threw it back in my face, that's what! Well, no more. That it, I'm through with being mister nice guy. From now on, anybody who gets in my way, gets crushed" he ranted as he paced his father's sitting room.

Stacey Boyd was to spend an extra week in England. Her mother was making day visits to the hospital, and Stacey would take an extra couple of days to be with her. It was as much as Tony had expected. There had been many false dawns over the last few weeks. Stacey was worried that she might lose her job, and anxious to get home soon. However, her mother had to come first.

Tony Lee had sourced a nice period fireplace for his bedroom. It would be the final part of his restoration plan for his home, and a job that he would do personally. Knocking out the wall would not be a problem for Tony, but he would take his time installing the old cast iron fireplace and mantelpiece. With his last few days off work, Tony intended to enjoy the project and not rush it. In a way it would be a tribute to Jodie, but he also hoped that the house would now meet with Stacey's approval.

Tony's best pal from work, Erik Ngombiti, was much more of a handyman than Tony. Tony Lee had picked his brains as to the best way to go about the task. With Erik's advice, Tony now felt well able to proceed with installing the old fireplace. He had all the tools that he required, and was all set for a long day of hard labour. A surveyor had assured Tony that structurally it was not a major problem.

Tony swung the sledgehammer with all of his might. It crashed into the wall, cracking the plaster and shattering the cement block beneath it. He swung again, causing a further dent to the bottom of the sturdy wall. The dust spread like a plume of smoke towards Tony's masked face. Erik had warned him to buy an industrial mask to cover his nose and mouth, and Tony now realised how important it was. The room was covered in dustsheets to protect the furniture. Tony had tilted his bed up sideways against the wall to give him more leeway to work.

After ten or so blows, Tony had at last managed to create a small hole about three feet from the ground. He was careful not to go too high, as only the lower end of the wall was to be demolished.

Tony rested his arms for a moment. The weight of the heavy sledgehammer was pulling at his biceps. Tony was hardly used to hard manual work, and stood with both arms resting on the handle of the hammer. He heard the phone ring in the hallway and was glad of the interruption.

"This will be Stacey I suspect" he thought as he made his way hurriedly downstairs. Tony picked up the receiver and heard a familiar voice.

"Hello Tony, this is Jan. How are you keeping?" his sister asked. Tony was silent for a moment. It was early morning, and he quickly calculated that it would be past midnight in America.

"Can't you sleep Jan?" he asked casually, trying to show little emotion.

"Not very well at all lately Tony. I hate that we fell out over nothing really. I honestly want us to get on. It tears at my heart that we can't be civil to each other at the very least" she said, her voice almost breaking with emotion.

"Well Jan, I bear no grudge. All I ever wanted was for to be treated as your equal. From the first time I got in contact, you seem to believe that you could order me about. I want a relationship with you too, but I need to be able to live my own life" he replied.

"I know Tony, I know. God! I realise how it must have sounded. You must have thought that I wanted you to keep the house as a shrine to Mom. Really it was never meant that way. I suppose that I was still in shock over Mam's death. The romantic in me wanted to preserve her memory in some way. I guessed that keeping the old house as it was would be the best way. I'm sorry Tony, honestly I am" Jan said.

Tony considered her words. He wanted to believe her. Tony also hoped to bring up the subject of Fergal Carrie, but waited to pick his moment.

"Well I'm prepared to start again Jan. I bear no malice" he said quietly.

"That's all that I want to hear Tony. I miss our little chats. Howard will tell you, I'm at my wit's end when we don't get on. I hoped to catch you before you went to work this morning. I lie awake all night wondering how I made such a mess of things" Jan said. She began to weep, and Tony felt moved by her emotional state.

"Hush Jan, please. It's okay. Come on, we can start all over again. I want you and your family in my life. It's important to me. Listen, I have some sad news. Auntie Mary died last week. I know, I should have phoned you but..." Tony said, leaving his sentence unfinished. There was a brief silence as Jan took in the news.

"How sad. Did you make the funeral?" she replied quietly. Tony thought hard before replying.

"No Jan, I only heard later through her daughter, Belinda" he lied. Another moment's silence ensued.

"Oh, I see. Well, she and Mam were never close anyway" Jan replied. Tony felt that Jan's cynical side was resurfacing, but he was not about to jeopardise their renewed friendship.

"I suppose so. Anyway, I thought that you would want to know" Tony replied.

"Yes Tony, thanks. Oh, I think that I've woken Howard. I had better hang up. Tony, it's brilliant that we're talking again. I'll phone you at the weekend, okay?" Jan said, her voice gushing down the line.

Tony wanted to say so much more. He needed to lay down some ground rules, to tell Jan that he would do as he pleased to the house. He also needed to quiz her on Fergal Carrie. All in all, Tony decided that it could wait for another day. The important thing was that he and Jan were now back on speaking terms.

Tony returned to his task with a renewed vigour. He felt pleased with himself. Life suddenly felt good. Soon Stacey would come home. They could plan for their future together. If she consented to move in with him, Tony knew that his next step would be to propose to her. And now Jan was coming round. From now on he would have a good relationship with her and her family, which was what he had always wanted. Once Tony was firm with Jan, he reckoned that everything would be fine.

"How did it go Jan?" Howard asked. Jan Williams smiled at her husband.

"He was like putty in my hands. Tony is an old softy really. He needs to be led through life. I'll soon have him back in check again. Tony needs us more than we need him. I can tell by his voice that he needs to feel wanted. Don't worry Howard, we'll soon have him where we want him again before he can do any serious damage" Jan replied. Howard grinned and put his arms around her.

"Things will be fine. You'll be able to get a decent night's sleep again love" he said.

Tony put all of his might into each swing of the heavy sledgehammer. The downwards blows was tough on the arms, but Tony was naturally strong and agile. Dust filled the room, and for a while Tony wondered if he had bitten off too much. As he paused for breath, he considered the wisdom of what he had undertaken.

"Bugger this! Why didn't I pay those builders to carry out this job? A project is it? More like a month's work! It will take me days just to clean up this mess!" he sighed. Just then his mobile rang. Tony picked up the dusty phone from the bedside locker and saw Erik Ngombiti's name light up on the screen. He pulled down the white mask again from his mouth and strolled out to the landing. "God! It's like the stock exchange here today!" he muttered before taking the call.

"Hello Erik, what's up?" he asked.

"Hey! Have you started that job yet? Only I was thinking, if you want to leave it, I'll come around tonight and give you a hand" Erik said in his booming voice. Tony chuckled to himself.

"I'm nearly finished the demolition part Erik. If it wasn't for all of the interruptions, I would have the bloody fireplace in already!" Tony replied, trying his best to sound cross.

"Huh-huh-huh!" Erik laughed, his infectious laugh sounding down the line. Tony chucked back at him.

"No, seriously Erik, I should be all right. We can't go hammering down walls around here in the evening. You have to consider the neighbours. Anyway, I've marked out the measurements. I'll use a metal girder to prop up the wall, and then slip the fireplace in, as you suggested. Once it's in place, a bit of plaster will cover up the edges. I don't intend using the fire as I told you, so it's only for decoration really" Tony said.

"Yeah, I know. Stuff some material up the flue to block the draught, or jam something in it before putting it in place if there is a chimney behind the wall" Erik suggested.

"Yeah, I know, I've already thought of that now, can I please get on with it?" Tony said in a jokey way. Erik laughed again before wishing him well with his task. Tony shook his head wryly and returned to work.

In about another twenty minutes, Tony had fully cleared the bricks away. He was using a metal bin to transport the rubble downstairs. The work was backbreaking, and took several trips to the back garden before Tony had the majority of the rubble outside.

"Now for the sweep-up. There will be layers of dust everywhere. God Almighty! What have I gotten into?" he mumbled as he made his way back upstairs for about the tenth time.

Sometime later, Tony had finally cleared the space away completely. One final bin load of dirt and rubble needed to be dragged downstairs. He admired his handiwork while leaning on the broom. There was little point in cleaning any more. He would fit the fireplace and then worry about the rest of the mess.

Tony removed the white mask. The open bedroom window helped clear the air. He hauled the metal fireplace in from the landing. Once the measurements were right, he could fit it in place there and then.

Tony noticed a heavy, choking smell. At first he presumed that it was coming from the street below. As the stench filled his nostrils, Tony wafted the air ahead of him with his hand in a vain attempt to dispel the stink. It dawned on him that the odour was getting stronger. Tony quickly realised that it was coming from the wall space which he had just cleared. A fearful sickening feeling took over his body. Had he hit an old gas pipe, he wondered? Tony wondered if there was a disused sewer pipe running behind his bedroom. Again he cursed himself for not bringing in the professionals. He bent down to check, but all he could see was darkness.

"I'll get my trusty lamp" he said, again covering his mouth and nose with the white mask.

Tony returned to the bedroom with his black bicycle lamp. He switched it on and knelt down next to the opening.

"Probably a dead mouse or rat" he thought, as he gingerly leant into the open wall.

Tony Lee recoiled in shock. He then tumbled sideways in his effort to get away. He let out a pitiful yell, his heart thumping hard against his chest. Tony scrambled around on his hands and knees, his eyes drawn to his discovery. He staggered backwards as he rose to his feet, the black lamp shining in every direction possible.

"Jesus! Holy fucking Jesus!" Tony screamed. He felt dizzy. Tony reached for his phone on the bedside locker. The room was hazy now. Tony's hand searched in vain through the haze, his trembling hand missing the new white locker completely. He felt his body sink to the floor, a wooziness descending on his mental state. Tony Lee fought with all of his might to stay conscious. It became all too much. He passed out, unable to fathom what he was seeing.

Sometime later, Tony regained consciousness. His eyes opened slightly, wondering if it was in fact another bad dream. Immediately he focused on the open gap at the bottom of the wall. The stench still filled the air. Tony gulped hard. The black lamp lay to his right, still switched on and shining at the ceiling. He reached for it, his hand still shaking. Tony crept forward and aimed the light at what he had seen earlier. Perhaps he was mistaken. He prayed that such was the case. Tony's hand refused to steady itself. Trembling, he pointed the ray of light to the bottom of the open wall.

"Jesus Mary and Joseph!" he screamed, recoiling again. Tony switched off the light, unable to believe what he had just witnessed. He ran from the room to the bathroom, vomiting openly into the toilet.

His instinct was to phone the police. Tony tried to think logically.

"Oh shit! Oh God, oh my God!" he whispered. He felt his stomach heave again.

Tony sat hunched on the bathroom floor. His brain tried hard to digest what he had seen in his bedroom. There could be only one explanation. Jan Williams came to mind. It had to be her. Everything pointed to it. He washed his mouth out under the tap. Still the taste and smell lingered. It seemed to be everywhere. Tony ran downstairs and grabbed the receiver. Then something took over. To phone Jan Williams was the wrong thing to do. No. He had to reconsider. The police should be called, and yet he hesitated. Tony wandered into the kitchen, his whole body shaking with fear.

He sat at the round table, with its four brand new chairs surrounding it. His mind was awash with abstract thoughts and sickening questions. Somehow he had to figure out what had happened and what to do about it. Out through the kitchen, the new glass conservatory seemed a total, bizarre contrast to what lay upstairs in the gloom. He wandered out into the new sparkling sunny room, desperate to do what was right. Tony stood motionless in the centre of the newly erected room, almost oblivious to his surroundings. All his focus was on what he had discovered upstairs.

"Think Tony, think!" he muttered.

Thirty minutes later, Tony had made up his mind what he should do. It was insane, but he felt that he must fly to Jan in Santa Monica and confront her. There was little point in phoning her. It would put her on her guard. Tony Lee had to see her face. He needed to see the guilt in her eyes, to witness her torment. All her bravado about preserving the house for their mother's memory had been a front. Tony made up his mind that the woman was pure evil. He had to get to The States as soon as possible.

Tony managed to book a flight for later that evening. It was one-way, but that barely mattered to him right now. He would tell no one of his discovery, not the police, not Erik, not even Stacey. Suddenly everything made sense. He had a lucid picture in his head about Jan's cover-up, yet he had to hear it from her mouth.

That evening Tony sat in Departures at Dublin Airport in sombre mood. Beside him was his small holdall. He recalled the girl at check-in eyeing him suspiciously when he told her that he had no other luggage. It barely mattered.

He just hoped that he would not face hours of questioning when he reached Los Angeles Airport. He had blocked up the hole in the bedroom wall with a large sheet of wood, yet the vision stayed with him at every moment. His past life flashed before him. How could he not have known? Only now did specks of his childhood flick through his brain. There was a part of him that had wiped an episode of his young days from his mind without even knowing. Tony felt the tears well up in his eyes. His stomach felt sickly again. He needed to use the bathroom to regain his composure.

Tony Lee sat in the cubicle and cried into his hands. He tried to muffle the noise, yet the tears refused to abate. He cried for his past, and for his dear mother. He prayed like he had never prayed before. But still he knew that he must confront Jan. He needed a strategy, something to ensure that he got the whole truth from her. This time she would not fob him off with lies.

Tony washed his hands and face. He wore a smart shirt and tie, and a pair of grey slacks. His casual black jacket lay across the top of his blue holdall, and he decided to put it on before boarding the flight.
Tony began to work out his time of arrival. It would be probably the early hours of the morning when he touched down, U.S. time. He would need to book into a hotel. All sorts of things occupied his mind. What would he say to Stacey if she phoned? Should he ask Erik's advice? How long would he be in America? He needed to get back home soon, to deal with the situation.

Tony arrived at Jan Williams home in the early evening. A taxi driver had brought him to the address. Earlier he had found a nice hotel with ease, and had changed his clothes. To his surprise, Tony had managed a couple of hours rest. He had even had a decent meal at the hotel. But still his mind was abuzz with unanswered questions and sickening visions.

As he surveyed Jan's home, he felt ready for what lay ahead. Two cars sat in the long sloping driveway to the side of the large white house. The sun bore down on him on the leafy well-to-do road on the east side of town. Tony eyed the quiet, affluent street. It was like another world. Nothing he had seen in Dublin could compare to the picture-box scene of sunshine, tranquillity and wealth. Swish cars and impressive houses dotted the wide crescent-shaped road.
Jan's home was a testimony to the American dream. The large porch to the centre of the front of the house looked almost like a room in itself. Six steps led up the high-platform area, with a mass of red rose bushes spilling out on all

four sides. Their scent wafted down towards Tony as he stood taking in the scene. The huge garden had circular flower beds placed carefully around the well-manicured lawn. A paved area led to the rear of the property.

Tony started out up the long driveway. The slightly-sloping garden ran to the far side of the detached home. He felt out of place, but knew that he had no alternative. It was finally time to confront his sister.

Tony took the route up the six wide wooden steps. He could see the gleaming white front door beckoning him. Tony was more than ready for his encounter. The only thing that could hold him back would be Josh and Amy. There was no need to involve them. If they were present, Tony would ask to speak to Jan alone.

Tony Lee rang the bell in a polite manner and stepped back. He could hear nothing inside to indicate life. Then he recalled that Jan had told him about spending her time in the sunny kitchen to the back of the house. He heard footsteps. It sounded like a man approaching. Tony stood tall, a determined look etched on his lean face.

A beaming smile on Howard's face faded away on seeing him. Slowly the ready grin returned. It appeared again, greeting him like a long-lost friend.

"Well, well! Howdy-do old Tony! How are you doing? Jeez! What brings you all this way? Come in, come in! Jan will be so pleased!" he said in a loud, friendly voice. Tony accepted the welcoming handshake and followed him inside. The wide hallway had several doors leading off it, but Howard led on until they reached the spacious kitchen area at the back of the house. All around him Tony could see the trappings of wealth. Expensive ornaments, pricey-looking paintings, and elaborate furniture filled the place. Howard pointed to Jan on the far side of the airy modern room. The kitchen was at least three times the size of Tony's one back home.

"Hey darling, look who's here! Look Mama, it's old Tony, your little brother!" Howard crowed in an over-exuberant way. A startled Jan looked up from her magazine. Her eyes homed in on Tony, her jaw dropping open in surprise.

"Tony? What are you doing here? How did you find the house? What's the occasion? Howard, are you in on this?" Jan asked. Howard shook his head, still managing to wear his beaming smile.

"No honey, I swear! It's entirely Tony's idea! I guess that your heart-to-heart chat had an effect on him after all!" Howard Williams said with a healthy chortle.

Tony eyed his sister across the room.

"Where are the kids? Are Amy and Josh home?" he asked earnestly. Jan shook her head.

"No, why? Amy's at the mall with some friends. She spends her life there lately. Josh has basketball practice, he should be home later. They will be chuffed to finally meet you Tony" Jan said, at last managing a grin of sorts.

"It's not really a social call, I'm afraid" Tony said purposely. Jan's flickering smile quickly vanished.

"Oh? Has something happened? Is it something serious?" she said. She folded away her magazine and gave Tony her full attention.

"I'll make some coffee" Howard said.

"Not for me thanks. Can we sit down? What I've come about can't wait" Tony replied. Jan rose to her feet.

"Sorry Tony, of course. How rude of me. We'll go to the sitting room where we won't be disturbed. Howard can watch out for the children returning" Jan said.

"I think it's important that both of you are there" Tony said deliberately. Howards and Jan looked at each other. The blood drained from Jan's lined, plain face.

"Sure" Howard said slowly.

CHAPTER TWENTY-SIX

CONFRONTING JAN WILLIAMS

They sat together in the huge evening room, as Howard liked to call it. To Tony it was like a giant sitting room, probably the largest room he had ever seen. A worried-looking Jan tried to distance herself from Tony, sitting almost behind Howard on the huge coffee-coloured leather sofa. Tony positioned himself on the big, matching buttoned-back armchair with its brown and tan circular scatter-cushions.

"I found it. Right there in my bedroom. Buried there like some, some ragdoll" Tony blurted out all of a sudden. Jan's face paled significantly. Howard tried to avoid eye contact. He looked to the floor, picking at his fingernails.

"Found what exactly?" Jan asked, her voice trembling. Tony Lee leapt to his feet.

"The baby" he yelled, standing directly on front of his sister. Jan drew back on the sofa.

"I found your child. I found the fucking baby, buried in an old blue blanket. Christ! Its face will haunt me until the day I die. How could you do it? How could the two of you bury a baby, just like that? And in my room. What possessed you? How could my mother agree to it? I presume that she knew. What was going on? Was it before you got married?" Tony said, the questions tumbling from his lips. From the time that he had unearthed the child, his mind had been filled with a million sickening issues.

Jan looked to Howard for support. Tony stood over her, his demeanour demanding a reply. Howard Williams rose slowly to his feet. He paced the floor, eyeing the expensive carpet with his hands buried deep in his white trousers. He knew he must speak to save his wife from totally imploding.

"It was a long time ago Tony. Having a baby out of wedlock was frowned upon back then. The child was never healthy. It only lived for a short while. Four months in fact. It died in its sleep one night" Howard said in a barely audible tone. Tony turned to confront him.

"It? You call your own child it? What was the baby's name? Was it a boy or a girl? That's my niece or nephew that you're talking about there. It was a human being, for Christ sake!" Tony shouted.

"Can we all just stay calm? Tony please, Howard will explain how it was" Jan said, gulping back tears. Tony Lee sank back down on the armchair. His eyes never left Howard. Howard slowly sat back down next to his wife.

"His name was Martin" Howard said. The name jumped out at Tony. It was the same name that his Aunt Ethel had used in her ramblings.

"Dear Christ! Ethel thought that I was Martin sometimes when I visited her. Christ Almighty! Even Ethel knew what was going on, probably Auntie Mary too" Tony gasped.

"Your mother never knew that we buried the child there. I did it when she was in hospital. She thought that I had simply taken out the old fireplace to block up the draught" Howard said quietly. Tony Lee shook his head slowly.

"You're lying. What did she think had happened to the kid? It was four months old you say. Did Mam think that it simply vanished? You better tell me the whole truth or so help me..." Tony said firmly. His eyes darted from Howard to Jan and then back again.

"You haven't been to the police, have you?" Jan asked. Tony shook his head.

"Not yet. I want to know the truth before I do anything" he answered. Howard watched Tony's face for a moment.

"Who else knows Tony?" he asked. Tony had already thought this particular question through.

"Stacey and my friend Erik. All three of us helped demolish the wall" Tony replied. For his own safety he had devised his alibi. He did not trust Howard. It was a serious crime, and Tony feared for his life if Jan and Howard suddenly felt trapped.

"They just let you waltz off to America leaving things as they were?" Jan asked. Tony was well prepared for their probing questions.

"No. I had a hell of a job convincing them to wait. What do you think? Erik is a respectable man. His first reaction was to go straight to the authorities. I asked them for a little time. I told them that if I did not phone them today, that they should contact the police" Tony replied. Jan's eyes fell to the floor. Tony felt that he was back in command. He demanded answers to his questions again.

"Okay, okay. Delores did know. In fact, it was her idea. We emigrated soon after. Delores said that people would presume that we had taken the child back to The States. And up until now, that's the way it worked" Howard said. Tony looked aghast.

"How could you sleep at night? What sort of folk buries their child in a wall and walks away? I saw the baby's face. Christ! It still haunts me. It didn't die naturally, did it? All of those horrible dreams that I had. Jesus! They were nightmares about my dead nephew! And all of those rows about redecorating the house. It was all a cover to protect you two. But I get it, I really do. You couldn't sell the house on in case the new tenants refurbished the place anyway. Your best hope was for poor old Tony to preside over your filthy little secret until the day he died. What a mug I was! Now this time, tell me the truth" Tony said forcibly. His words were met with a stony silence. Tony Lee tried another angle.

"You know who came to see me last month Jan? Have a guess? Only Fergal Carrie! Now there's a name from the past!" Tony said. He watched his sister's face for reaction. He could see the shock in her eyes. Jan's bottom lip trembled.

"What...what did he say?" she asked in a shaky voice. Tony stood up once more.

"Oh, he said quite a lot as it happens. For one thing, he told me that I'm his son. We're having tests to confirm it right now" Tony answered. Jan's eyes welled up instantly. The tears came as she buried her face in her hands.

"Oh my God Howard, he knows everything. Sweet Jesus! That man promised Mam that he would never interfere" Jan sobbed. Tony decided to push his luck further.

"I lied too Jan. You see, I saw Auntie Mary before she died. I was actually at her funeral too. Oh, we had a very long and frank chat weeks before she passed away. Auntie Mary had her wits about her right until the end. Did you know that our father lived with her for a while? Yeah, and she knew lots about Fergal Carrie. And what about Mam's second affair? Do you want to discuss that?" Tony demanded. Jan screamed in torment.

"Stop Tony, please stop! I can't take it. Please!" she sobbed. Howard said nothing. He went to comfort his wife. Tony shook his head in disgust.

"I'm going outside for a cigarette. I'm slowly running out of patience here. Either you two tell me the truth, or I'm going to the police" he said firmly.

Tony returned to the huge room some moments later. Jan had dried her tears, but her lined face still looked tired and distraught. Howard glanced in Tony's direction.

"Here's the deal Tony. I'll tell you everything. The whole nine yards. All that we ask is that you leave your sister in peace. Have we got a deal?" Howard asked. Tony Lee shook his head.

"You're not in a position to cut a deal Howard. I want the truth, that's all. After that we'll decide what to do for the best" Tony said. Howard looked to his wife. Jan nodded slowly, a white handkerchief covering her mouth and nose.

Howard rose to his feet. He again shoved both hands into the pockets of his flamboyant trousers. His bright yellow shirt was now open wide at the neck as he paced the bright blue carpet.

"I was living in Dublin at the time. Jan and I had started dating. She was almost nineteen; I was a few years older. Anyway, I was a young handsome man back then. I suppose that you might describe me as a ladies' man. A Yank in Ireland back then was unusual, but I had kind of settled down with Jan. We had plans to marry and live in Dublin. I knew of Delores's affair with Fergal Carrie. In fact, everyone did, including your father at the time. They tried to save their marriage, and for a while it looked like it could work. However, Fergal Carrie never gave in. He courted Delores relentlessly. They worked together for a while, as you probably know, which did not help the situation. Even back then he was a larger-than-life character. He had the gift of the gab, and was a real womaniser" Howard said. Tony Lee interrupted his flow.

"What has all of this got to do with your child? I want to know why you two buried Martin behind a wall, for God's sake!" Tony demanded. Howard looked to Jan once again. She barely nodded to him.

"I'm coming to that Tony. Bear with me. Anyway, myself and Sean Lee got talking one night over a drink. Oh, it was a stupid, drunken conversation. His hatred for Fergal knew no bounds. Sean suggested to me that it might be an idea to turn Delores's head away from Fergal Carrie if she could meet someone else. He travelled a lot, and asked me to throw some attention Delores's way while he was away. It was a crazy, bizarre idea. Sean was desperate to hold on to Delores. He really despised Fergal Carrie with a passion. What started out as a mad drunken scheme developed into something completely ridiculous over the next few weeks. I went along with your Dad's plan, heaven knows why. I began by complimenting Delores at every turn. I told her how well she looked, how beautiful she was, all of the things that a pretty lady likes to hear. Before I knew where I was, I had fallen head over heels for your mother" Howard said. He looked nervously at Tony Lee.

Tony could barely believe what he was hearing. He prayed that the story was not going the way he feared. In the background, Tony could hear Jan snivelling. It barely mattered. He was fixated with Howard Williams. Tony listened as the words that he dreaded tumbled from his brother-in-laws mouth.

"Sean Lee was away on business. We had a brief affair, and then the unthinkable happened. Delores became pregnant again, this time with Martin. She insisted on keeping him. Delores had considered aborting you Tony, as Fergal Carrie probably told you. However, she delighted at having you, and so she was determined to keep Martin too" Howard said.

Tony felt his stomach heave. It was sordid, sick and beyond him. The hair at the back of his neck stood erect. Suddenly he saw red. He rushed at Howard in a fit of temper. Howard saw it coming and shielded himself, grappling with his attacker. Jan rushed to her husband's aid.

"Stop! Please Tony, stop!" she yelled. Tony ceased struggling as the couple held him back.

He turned his attention to his sister.

"You! How could you allow this? Did you turn a blind eye while this was going on?" he bellowed, breathing hard from his exertions. Jan began to sob again.

"I didn't know about it at first. Howard told me only when Mam became pregnant. I forgave him. I was still a young girl Tony. It was such a long time ago. We had almost forgotten about it until Mam died. We've built a good life together now. Tony, I beg you to put this behind you. It happened so long ago. It was a nightmare for all concerned. The cover up was to protect you too. Can't you see that?" Jan said.

Tony Lee was appalled at her attempt to justify what had occurred.

"Don't you dare use me as an excuse for this; don't even contemplate it for a minute. Now, what happened to Martin? How did that poor child die?" he asked. Jan looked to her husband. By now Howard was composed and calm.

"Martin had this habit of whining constantly. He would cry almost all of the time. Delores could barely cope. You were still young and needed attention, but Martin occupied her every minute. One night... one night Delores shook him violently. It was completely out of character. She phoned me in a panic. Martin was already dead when I got to her house. Delores came up with the idea of hiding the body. Her story would be that Jan and I had taken the baby to The States to live. We were about to emigrate anyway. It fitted in perfectly. Reluctantly we agreed, but it has haunted both of us ever since" Howard said.

Tony shook his head in disbelief. This was not the doting mother that he remembered and loved.

"You're saying that my mother murdered her son? I won't believe it for a minute. Why did you not call the police? It was an accident, if what you are saying is true" Tony countered. Howard sighed and hung his head. Jan took up their story.

"It's all true Tony. I pleaded with Howard to go along with Mam's plan. My mother was devastated. I feared that she would have a nervous breakdown if put into custody. We never told my father. He was living in Walsall at the time. Dad went to his grave believing that we had taken Martin to live with us in The States. You see, Mom could never have Sean Lee back after that, in case he started asking awkward questions. God forgive me" Jan said. She continued to sob intermittently, but Tony was past caring.

"And Dad knew that Howard was the father?" Tony asked.

Jan nodded as she sobbed into the white hankie.

"And what did Auntie Mary think? She must have known about Martin" Tony asked.

"She never forgave Mom for what she put Dad through. She accused Mom of giving her child away. They never spoke again after that" Jan sobbed.

"You could have buried the poor child anywhere. Christ! To put an innocent baby inside a wall..." Tony said coldly. Howard was quick to respond.

"We panicked Tony. That was it pure and simple. By coincidence, Delores was having central heating installed at the time. She wanted the old fireplace pulled out. We were heading off to start a new life. Delores always intended living out the remainder of her life at Saint Oliver's Road. It was only as she came to the end of her days that we began to consider the implications. Delores spoke on the phone frequently to Jan. It was her expressed wish that you would continue to reside at the family home. All we could do was to hope that you left things alone" Howard said quietly. Tony tried to take everything in. It was insane, unbelievable and sad. He turned his attention again to Jan Williams.

"And Fergal Carrie, is he my real father?" Tony asked. Jan refused to look directly at her brother. She weighed up her response before speaking.

"Yes Tony, Mam was sure. When the baby died, Mam went into her shell, despite Fergal wishing to come back into her life. He continued to send those goddamn letters to her. Mam refused point blank to reply. Maybe she was too embarrassed. Fergal never knew anything about Martin. We never brought him outside you see. Our Mom was too ashamed about what the neighbours might say. Mom then devoted her time to raising you. When we settled in California we phoned home every week, but we never discussed Martin. That only came about when Mam fell into ill-health. That's when we started making plans for the future. During all of those years, Mom refused Fergal Carrie permission to speak to you, or to have any contact. It was part of their agreement from when they first broke up. I know that she broke Fergal Carrie's heart, but he deserved it. He wrecked my parent's marriage after all" Jan said. Tony could feel Jan's hatred for Fergal Carrie. It appeared that she blamed Fergal for her mother's unhappiness. Tony appreciated that it must have been so much tougher for Jan at the time. He was young and unaware as to what was going on. Jan had lived through it, and was also a witness to her current husband having an affair with her mother. Yet Tony still felt disgust and a loathing for his sister and her husband. It was beyond his comprehension at what they had done. Other little things started to make sense too. The fact that Jan wanted little to do with their mother's jewellery came to mind. Fergal Carrie probably lavished Dolores with presents. Some of his gifts lay at home in his mother's precious jewellery collection.

Tony felt isolated. Suddenly his very identification was gone. Jan was really his half-sister. Howard's affair with Tony's mother was unforgivable, yet Tony still adored his mother. He could barely fathom as to how Jan could stand by her husband. It smacked of desperation to him. Was she really so in love with Howard that she could overlook anything, he wondered?

"I'm sickened by all of this. My mind is spinning. I can't think straight" Tony said. Howard seized on Tony Lee's dilemma.

"We can get over this Tony, all three of us. We can put it behind us and move on. Everything can be fixed up" Howard said in a pleading voice. Tony eyed him across the room.

"And what should we do about Martin?" Tony asked cynically. Jan and Howard looked at each other again.

"What do you mean? What can we do?" Jan asked. Tony looked terse.

"I don't know. I have to think things over. I'll be in touch tomorrow evening. Make sure that the children are not around" Tony said. He stood up to leave, refusing Howard's offer of a handshake.

"I'll see myself out" Tony said, and walked briskly back the way he had entered the house.

"What will happen now Howard?" Jan asked. Howard looked thoughtful.

"I'm not sure sweetheart. Hopefully when he has time to digest events, he can come to terms with it. He has to realise that it was such a long time ago. We did what we thought was right for Dolores. You see that, don't you Jan dearest?" Howard said.

"Of course Howard. We've made a decent life since those awful days. Tony has to realise that we have a family to consider. After all, Josh and Amy are still his nephew and niece. I'm sure that when he realises that we did what was for the best, he will move on" Jan said. Howard sat with a comforting arm around his wife.

"He never said where he was staying. Pity. I might have been able to meet up with him and talk. Or I could have maybe telephoned him and persuaded him to return home. I mean, what else is there to say?" Howard replied. Jan said nothing for a few seconds.

"Tony has a lot on his mind. That business with Fergal Carrie must have come as a shock. On the upside, Mr. Carrie is a wealthy man. Perhaps Tony could do worse that embrace him with open arms" Jan reasoned.

Howard nodded and stood up again.

"Once he stays away from the police. That's the main thing" Howard said. Jan looked frightened suddenly.

"Do you think that he will Howard? What could we be charged with? I mean, we didn't kill that child after all" Jan said.

"Who knows? We could be charged with accessory to murder, concealing a crime, perverting the course of justice, all sorts I suppose. On the other hand, if Tony was to simply forget this, we could carry on as normal. What if we offered him cash? I mean, in a subtle way. You know, costs for travelling here, money to cover his out-of-pocket expenses? Say around $10,000? What do you think Jan honey?" he asked.

"Can we afford it Howard? We have to consider the children's education" Jan replied.

"I don't want to be an alarmist Jan, but this could well be more important. If we don't handle this properly, who knows where it will end?" Howard said.

Tony lay on his bed in the air-conditioned hotel room. He stared at the ceiling, wondering how he had been so naive. All the signs had pointed to a cover-up by Jan Williams. He felt totally alone in the world, despite his romance with Stacey. How could he ever trust Jan again, he wondered? The mother who he adored had led a life of lies and deceit also. It appeared that Sean Lee was not his real father. The irony that not even his surname was his own was not lost on Tony. This was something else that he must confront. Tony decided that the matter of Fergal Carrie was something for the future. Right now he had to do what was best for his dead half-brother.

In a small corner of his mind, Tony could barely recall his baby brother. Little things like children's toys on the floor, a pram, a baby crying at night surfaced. When Martin had suddenly vanished, Tony had never even noticed. It rankled with him now, yet he was just a child himself at the time. Tony felt the guilt seep into his soul. He should have remembered Martin, but he simply did not. Perhaps when his father died, Tony had begun a new idyllic life with just him and his beloved mother. Maybe that fresh start had blurred his memory. He had quickly forgotten Sean Lee, and certainly baby Martin. His mother had never mentioned a little brother. Now it was all too apparent why.

Tony turned on his side and tried to think of nicer things. He wanted to dream about the future with Stacey at his refurbished home on St. Oliver's Road. Somehow it did not appeal in the same way now. It would always be the place where he had discovered the remains of Martin. Stacey had been correct after all. She never felt comfortable in the old house, and with good reason. The nightmares fitted into place too. Maybe his little brother had been calling to him, pleading for a humane burial. Tony vowed that was the very least that Martin deserved. He would see to it, no matter what it took.

Alex Woods closed up the showrooms and garage for the night. Most evenings his foreman,   Frank McKenzie, would deal with locking up, but now and then Alex liked to take charge. The giant yellow skip outside the glass showrooms caught his eye. Alex was having his Dad's old office renovated. Anything that had belonged to Tom Woods was being disposed of. A wall had been demolished. An old store room had been gutted to enlarge Alex's new office. The hi-spec room would be more befitting of a successful businessman. Alex would impress his clients when they visited his premises. His staff would realise that he was a force to be reckoned with. Tom Woods way of doing things was over forever.
Alex set the alarm and closed the main door. Tonight there would be no trip home to Blackrock. Some evenings Alex felt compelled to spy on his adversaries. He had tired of watching Stacey's apartment. Tonight he would visit St. Oliver's Road. Perhaps Tony Lee might go out for a cycle, he thought. Alex still harboured hopes of an opportunity to kill off Tony Lee, and make it look like an accident. Tonight he was in for a fruitless evening.

Tony Lee arrived back at Jan Williams' home the following evening. The two cars stood outside in the long driveway. Tony reckoned that it meant that both Howard and Jan would be home. He pressed the bell politely and waited. Jan opened the door, a false smile painted on her thin face. Tony said nothing. Jan held the door open and Tony headed for the living room. Howard greeted him with a smile and signalled for him to take a seat.
"Well Tony? What do you think we should do? Howard has had a few ideas. Howard, talk to Tony, will you love?" Jan said. Tony's eyes moved to his brother-in-law as Jan sat down on the huge couch. Howard flashed his customary smile.
"Well, I was thinking that this must have put you out quite a bit Tony. The expense, not to mention the trauma, must be horrific. Jan and I would like to reimburse you for your expenses, plus some cash to deal with the matter at home" Howard said confidently. Tony felt his stomach heave once more. It was blackmail by another name. The pair could not even bring themselves to mention Martin by name. It was Howard's own flesh and blood they were

talking about, yet it might just as well have been a business deal from his electrical goods company. Tony decided to prolong their agony.

"Which matter at home Howard? And how much money are we talking about?" Tony asked innocently. Howard's confidence appeared to grow. He leaned forward on his seat with a swagger to face Tony.

"Well, the matter with the baby's remains. If you could see your way to, er, burying the child, somewhere appropriate of your choice, we would greatly appreciate it. Jan thinks that you deserve $10,000, and I concur" Howard announced.

Tony had already made up his mind as to how things would be done. However, it was refreshing to get an insight into the workings of both Jan's and Howard's minds. Everything in their cosy little world revolved around money. Jan watched Tony's face for any sign of agreement. Tony Lee rose steadily from the big armchair.

"No Howard, that's not what's going to happen at all. You see, the money doesn't interest me whatsoever. I'm not very materialistic, I never have been, I'm afraid. This might be seen in your eyes as a weakness, but I quite like my concept of life. Plenty of fresh air and exercise, a good job, friends that you can trust, and above all, peace of mind are things that I value. I also hold with living a decent life, and never, ever harming anybody" Tony said as he stood in the centre of the large room.

Howard seemed a little taken aback, but quickly regained his composure.

"No, no, that's fine Tony, I can identify with that. Listen, I now that we messed up, but there's nothing that we can do now really. Your sister needs your help with this matter. After all, that's what families are for" Howard said.

"Well Howard, your family needs you too, starting with Martin. He was your flesh and blood, long before Amy and Josh were on the scene. I'll tell you exactly what is going to happen. You and Jan are going to fly back to Ireland and deal with it yourselves. This matter, as you call it, requires your immediate attention, I'm afraid. You two will fly back to Dublin and take Martin's remains to the graveyard. You will then inter him in my mother's grave" Tony said calmly and firmly. Jan looked shocked. She leapt to her feet and moved towards Tony.

"Are you frigging crazy? We can't go digging up a graveyard in broad daylight. What are you suggesting? Listen to yourself Tony, in the name of God!" Jan yelled. Tony stood his ground as Jan moved to within feet of him.

"Maybe not, but you can certainly do it at night-time. It's not that there is much of Martin left anyway. But I want you two to see him, to remember him. It shouldn't take long. You place Martin in a box and just dig a hole large enough at the foot of Mom's grave. Then you cover it over and place some

387

fresh flowers on the grave. Now is that too much to ask?" Tony asked calmly. Howard came to Jan's side and placed an arm around her. He looked Tony in the face and shook his head.

"Do you really want to put your poor sister through this ordeal? Hasn't she been through enough?" Howard said. Somehow Tony Lee managed a smile. "Well that's rich! What about what I've been through? Can you ever comprehend what I felt when I opened up that...that squalid tomb? My stomach still turns when I think about what you bastards did. Christ! And then you have the audacity to order me about as if I'm the guilty one! Do me a favour! Hear this Howard; you will do as I say without question. I will be on a flight out of here tonight. It's already booked. You two had better get on the phone now to the airlines. I want you in Dublin within twenty-four hours. This is not an option" Tony said firmly. Jan seemed to relent.

"Okay Tony, we'll do as you say. Howard, your parents can look after the children. We at least owe Tony that much" Jan said, almost in a whisper.

Within minutes, Tony had left. A passing yellow cab pulled to a halt as he waved it down. Tony sat and looked back towards his sister's immaculate home for a second.

"Where to bud?" the taxi driver asked. Tony was lost in thought. He gave the address of his hotel without taking his eyes off the up-market property.

"They have everything in the world that they want. A beautiful house, a nice family. Relations to babysit and dote on their kids. Howard has his own company, and Jan has a nice little job to keep her occupied. Yet still they don't appreciate the value of life itself. Morons!" Tony thought quietly.

Howard and Jan watched as Tony vanished into the sunny early evening.

"It's morbid what he's asking us to do" Jan said. Howard nodded solemnly.

"Yeah, He wants to punish us honey. Don't worry; we'll get through this together. This is the last chapter of a sorry affair. Once we do this, we can cut Tony Lee from our lives forever. It would be too dangerous to stay in contact. You'll see Jan; it will be for the best. We've built a nice life here. There is no need to look back at our past" Howard said.

There was a sad, faraway look in Jan's eyes

"I suppose so Howard, you know what's for the best" she replied.

Jan Williams had always followed her husband's lead. It was clear to anyone who observed the couple, that she was far more devoted to him than he was to her. Jan tended to take care of Howard's needs. Sometimes he would drop subtle hints or suggestions to his wife on what he required. Obediently Jan would fulfil his wishes. She was the perfect devoted wife and mother, slavishly taking care of her family.

When Jan and Howard had first started dating, Jan could hardly believe her luck. She considered herself plain, and to have an older American boyfriend was exotic beyond her wildest dreams. From that time onwards, Jan could forgive Howard anything. She considered she was somehow below her cleverer spouse.

By now though, Howard's good looks had faded. He was overweight with a sizeable paunch, and rarely brought Jan out anywhere without the children. Jan never complained. She accepted that Howard was the head of the family, and followed him unquestioningly.

When Jan had first learned about Howard's affair with her mother, she was shocked to the core. However, when a tearful Howard expressed his remorse, Jan soon forgave him. It was then that Howard realised that Jan could be easily manipulated. He had dated Jan while in Dublin, but had never considered her as a long-term partner. A scheming Howard quickly saw the benefits of having a dedicated, obedient woman in his life. And so they married and moved to Santa Monica. It took Howard years to establish his company. Only then did he agree to have children. Two children were Howard's ideal family, and although Jan would have liked another two kids, Howard's word on the subject was final. He picked the house where they would live, chose the furniture, and dictated most important aspects of Jan's life. Jan deemed that nothing should upset her husband, and did her utmost to keep problems and petty matters away from Howard.

Alex sat parked in his car discreetly down the street from Terry Thompson's home. He had borrowed the black Honda Civic from the garage stock so as not to be recognised by Terry. Terry lived in a modest terraced house in the Walkinstown area on the south side of Dublin. Today was the third time that Alex had watched his former best friend's house. It was hard for Alex to figure out when Terry's day off would be. Most times Terry had to work at weekends. Such was life in the hotel trade. Today was Wednesday, and Alex could only hope that Terry had some leisure time. Alex had already decided that Terry Thompson was to become his next victim, and considered that his best chance at murdering his old pal was by drowning. His hope now was that Terry might decide to do some fishing, his most passionate hobby by a mile.

Alex waited patiently for almost two hours. Terry's hours were erratic. He might begin work early in the morning, or it might be late in the afternoon. Suddenly Alex shot forward in his seat. At last Terry had emerged from the red-brick house into the late-morning sunshine. Alex watched as Terry placed his fishing case and a black holdall in the boot of the old green Corsa. The case would contain Terry's fishing rods and reels. The black holdall probably had his bait, lures and waterproof clothing.

"Yes my son! Today is the day! Let's hope that we're going somewhere where the water is nice and deep!" Alex exclaimed with a sense of excitement. Alex was not to be disappointed.

He watched as Terry returned to the front door to kiss his wife Margaret goodbye. She held their youngest in her arms while their eldest child clung to Margaret's tight blue jeans. Terry hugged his wife and then kissed the baby. He then bent down to say goodbye to his son.

"Aw! How touching! What a lovely family scene! Let's hope that it's for the final time. With any luck, old Terry won't be coming home tonight!" Alex thought quietly to himself.

Alex trailed Terry's green car as he wound out of Dublin. He hit The Naas Road, a main artery leading to the south of the country. Three lanes of traffic sped onwards on the duel-carriageway. Alex switched lanes and kept his distance.

"Great! This is not some local river that we're off to! Terry means business today. Well so do I! Let's hope for a large lake or somewhere very remote" Alex muttered.

One hour later, and Terry turned off a side road. Alex had a white box van between Terry's Opel Corsa and his black car. The white van rumbled onwards. Alex slowed again and turned down the quiet narrow road after Terry Thompson.

"Lead on Terry. It's a nice dull day now. Perfect for fishing, I would say! But what do I know?" Alex cackled.

About a half-a-mile further on, Alex noticed a clear blue lake appear on his right. Gradually the trees and bushes gave way to a spectacular vista. Now and then Terry's car would vanish from view on the twisting, uneven road. By now Alex was searching for somewhere to park up. Alex guessed that Terry had finally reached his chosen fishing spot. He had no wish to come face to face with Terry Thompson. As he rounded the next bend, Alex got a jolt. Ahead of him Terry was already out of his car. The roadway gave way to a small wooden jetty to the right. There was ample parking space now, but the last thing that Alex wanted to do was to stop. Luckily for Alex, Terry was already preoccupied with his day ahead. Terry opened the boot of his car and ducked his head inside. Alex drove on. There was just Terry's green car stopped at the picturesque spot. Alex drove further on along the bumpy, winding road, his plan clear in his mind. He would park out of view and work his way back, creeping up unexpectedly on his former friend.

A further couple of hundred yards along, Alex came to yet another clearing. The road had wound around to the side of the huge lake, but something else caught Alex's eye. There was a small rowing boat out in the calm water with a two men aboard. They were rowing steadily back towards to where Terry was. Alex peered through his black binoculars in the direction of his latest sworn enemy.

"We'll have to wait until those two old farts vanish, but then Terry old boy… And you're not the only one who has come well prepared today" Alex whispered.

Alex watched from afar as Terry chatted with the two local men.

"Good day for it" the elderly man said with a smile. Terry smiled back.

"Yeah, I only have a few hours. Did you do a bit of fishing yourself?" Terry replied.

"No lad, we just went for a leisurely boat trip. My brother here lives on the other side of the lough. We're just going across to my old farm to look at some cattle" he said, as both men dragged the small brown rowing boat ashore.

"I'll keep an eye on that for you" Terry said, nodding towards the small vessel. The farmer seemed to re-think his position.

"I'll tell you what lad; why not take a loan of it? Sure all of the good fishing is to be had out there in the middle. There's perch and roach as well as the trout, fine big ones too if you're any use!" the balding man said with a friendly grin. His younger brother laughed and then offered his opinion.

"Sure it's the only way man! Once you have it back before dark, no one minds. I have to get off home by boat, otherwise it's a hell of a walk!" he said, displaying a missing tooth to the front of his mouth.

"Well, thanks. Thanks, I will! Er, can I offer you a few bob? How about ten euro's?" Terry said with an embarrassed smile. The two men waved away his offer.

"Not a bit of it son! Just bring it back in one piece!" said the older man.

Alex looked on with glee as Terry loaded his gear into the small boat.

"Oh yes! Even better!" Alex muttered as he watched the elderly men disappear. He was in his special zone now. Alex opened the boot of his car. His back-up supplies had lain in the car for three days now. He was an excellent swimmer, and today he would put it to good use.

Once Terry had stopped rowing and had cast his rod into the water for the first time, Alex swung into action. From his secluded spot to the right of the lake, Alex crept ever closer to the grey-blue water. Already he was stripped to his black swimming shorts and held a snorkel in his hands. He wore old flip-flop shoes to protect his feet from the ground. Alex kicked off his old holiday shoes as he reached the water's edge. Slowly Alex eased himself into the deep water and set off. He had checked around the lake with his binoculars. It appeared that only Terry and he were on the water that day.

Alex swung around so that he was approaching the tiny craft from behind. Terry now had his back to him. Alex took his time, swimming with expert, even strokes through the clear water. Nearer and nearer he got to his old school pal, with only one goal in his mind.

Alex rested as he came within feet of the old rowing boat. He would need his strength for his final part of the mission. Raining the black snorkel from his face, Alex took a final glance around the lakeside. Just then he heard the whirr of the fishing line. It appeared that Terry had got lucky almost immediately. "Wow! This is a big one!" Terry said enthusiastically. Alex watched from the water as Terry rose cautiously from the wooden seat. Terry crouched over the side of the boat as he allowed the line to run away from him. Suddenly he began to reel it in expertly in a stop start manner.

"Jesus! This fellow is a battler all right!" Terry said, as the rod took the strain. He reeled the line in again, both hands gripping tightly to the blue and red rod. Suddenly Alex moved into action. From the opposite side to where Terry was fishing, Alex seized the boat. He rocked it rapidly from side to side. Terry dropped the rod from his grasp. He tried to regain his balance. In one rapid movement, Alex succeeded in capsizing the tiny boat. Terry landed in the water with a loud splash. By now Alex was towing the upturned rowing boat away in the opposite direction. Terry's arms began to flay about in a panic. He screamed for help as his head ducked beneath the clear water. Alex was already swimming silently away. Once well out of reach of his old friend, Alex abandoned the small wooden vessel and sank beneath the grey-blue water. Terry resurfaced again, letting out a sickening, pleading scream. The water swallowed him up for a second time, his arms thrashing about helplessly. Minutes later Alex was getting dried off on the green towel that he had left on the bank. Soon he would be dressed and away back to work, first checking that he had retrieved everything.

"I enjoyed that dip! I always said that he should have learned to swim! Pity that he never listened!" he quipped as he drove back towards Dublin. Later that day the two old farmers would see the upturned boat. They would alert the authorities, but it would be too late for Terry Thompson. He had kissed Margaret and his children goodbye for the final time.

Muggser hammered on Burrener's door. He had spent just under a month in custody. The shortage of space in Irish prisons had conspired to grant him an early release. This was a regular occurrence in the Irish penal system. Petty criminals rarely saw out their full sentence.

"Burrener! Get your arse down here!" Muggser yelled. Joseph Byrne popped his head out of the upstairs window. He had only visited his pal once since Muggser had gone to jail.

"What's up? I'm busy here. You got out early then? I'll catch you later" Burrener said with a disinterested tone. Muggser's short temper quickly surfaced.

"Get down here now, you prick! I want a word" Muggser yelled.

Alice Byrne appeared at her front door. She was a tubby woman with broad shoulders. Both of her flabby biceps featured black inky tattoos.

"What's all the bleedin' racket for? What's your beef Muggser? Why are you coming around here bothering my Joseph?" she roared stepping out onto the pavement outside her home.

"I just want a word Alice. I did my time, now that waster owes me. The tosser barely came to visit me" Muggser said aggressively. Alice shuffled forward, her giant wide frame confronting Muggser.

"Who are you calling a tosser? My Joey owes you nothing, you thick you! And why should he go to see you? Joey's been doing all right lately. He's been as good as gold without your bad influence. Now piss off and leave us in peace" Alice said, her face now only inches from Muggser's. He stepped back reluctantly, giving way to the broader woman.

"Is that how it is now? After all I did for your son Alice" Muggser said. Burrener watched developments from the sanctuary of his bedroom.

"You did nothing for Joey, you waster! All you did was lead him down the road of crime" Alice said, again stepping forward towards the younger man.

"Me? Bleedin' me? He's the fucking burglar, not me!" Muggser replied, an incredulous look on his face. Alice pushed him in the chest.

"Is he now, you arsehole? Well he ain't anymore, so stay away from him, yeah? Joey's a good lad, once he's not near the likes of you, so piss off" Alice said. Muggser knew that he was beaten. His eyes panned up to his old friend's bedroom.

"You and that poxy X-Box Burrener! I'll see you, never fear. You can't hide in your room forever" Muggser warned. Alice pushed him again, forcing him further away from her home.

"You lay a hand on my son and I'll bleedin' kill you, you hear? I'll swing for you Muggser, I fuckin' swear" she yelled. Muggser turned and walked away sharply. He shoved his hands deep inside the pockets of his red hoodie and disappeared around the corner.

CHAPTER TWENTY-SEVEN

A NEW BURIAL

Tony Lee flew home from California that same evening. He knew that he faced the anguish of having to deal with Jan again when she followed him to Ireland. He was mentally prepared for that ordeal when the time came. Tony decided that he could not stay at number eighty-eight while the baby's remains were still at his house. As he sat impassively on the plane, his mental planning was punctured by a smiling stewardess who offered him coffee on the evening flight home. Tony smiled back and turned down the offer before returning to his private thoughts. His plan was to check into a hotel, once he was satisfied that his house was still secure. All around him on the jumbo jet, people did their best to catch some sleep. Tony's mind was buzzing with fears and worries. Baby Martin flashed before him, as did Fergal Carrie. He struggled with his conscience as to what to do for the best. There could be no rest for Tony on the flight. Too much was still unresolved. Until he had closure for his half-brother, Tony Lee felt that he might stay wide awake forever.

Tony phoned Stacey from his hotel room. He could not bring himself to tell her of his discovery. Stacey would surely never set foot in number 88 St. Oliver's Road again if she knew the truth, nor could he blame her.
"Hi Stacey, how's your Mam now?" he asked. They had exchanged text messages several times during his trip to The States. Never once did Tony indicate that anything was amiss. Stacey had her own troubles, and he was not about to add to them.
"She's fine Tony. Much, much better in fact. Dad is back at work, so I'm lending a hand around the house. I want to get home for next weekend. Dad had some

holidays coming, so he's taking two weeks off next Friday. I can't wait to see you again" Stacey said in a happy voice.

"Great! We'll do something special, eh? Maybe go out for a nice meal or something" Tony replied. Stacey thought for a moment.

"To be honest Tony, all I want to do is relax and be with you. I want to get back to work and do ordinary things, you know, like see Angie and Gina, go shopping, and chill out" she said.

"Yeah, sure Stace, we'll take it as it comes. I can't wait to see you too" he said.

"Any word from Jan? Has she been bothering you?" Stacey asked. Tony bit his lip.

"Jan? Nah, I've almost forgotten all about her!" he said with a confident chuckle. He hated to lie to Stacey, but it seemed the right thing to say at the time. Ultimately he would have to admit everything to her, but his feelings were still too raw at the moment.

"And what about this Fergal Carrie man? Has he been in touch?" Stacey continued. Tony sighed before answering.

"No, I've heard nothing for a couple of days Stace. It's hard for me to make contact to be honest. I still have my doubts, you know? The test results are due in the next couple of weeks. Until then, we just have to be patient" Tony said.

"It must be difficult for you. What's your gut feeling?" Stacey asked. Tony almost said that he was sure Fergal was his father, because Jan had told him. He stopped just in time.

"Oh, mixed, I suppose. I don't really remember my Dad. At least if Fergal turns out to be my real father, I might get to know him" Tony replied.

"Oh my God Tony, how awful for you. I can't imagine what you're going through. If that was me, I don't think that I could sleep until I found out the truth" Stacey replied. Tony smiled to himself at the irony of what she was saying. Sleep had been fleeting over the past few days.

"It has kept me awake Stacey, but I'll be okay" he answered.

"Well, best of luck with it anyway. I can hardly believe this has happened. I'll text you later, okay? Mam is calling me again. She's lying down upstairs. She's still a little weak, but I'm sure that she will get stronger as the days pass" Stacey said.

Tony lay on the bed in his hotel room and tried to sleep. He had barely closed his eyes since uncovering the child's body in his partitioned room. Earlier that day he had visited his house briefly. It had been difficult to enter the bedroom, but he felt compelled to check that everything was as it should be. The wooden board was in place, blocking off Tony's horrendous discovery. The honest citizen in him knew that he should report the matter, yet had he done so, he might never have gotten the answers from Jan and Howard which he needed. Once they flew in to Dublin, Tony would carry out the second part of his planning.

His mind wandered back to his two aunts. Both apparently knew more than he ever realised. Now it was too late to quiz either of them. Somewhere in Aunt Ethel's brain lay memories of her nephew Martin. She would have cuddled the child, kissed him, perhaps even babysat while Delores went out. It might have been different for Auntie Mary. Perhaps she never forgave Delores for her affair with Fergal Carrie. She may never have known about Howard. But then it struck Tony at Mary's reaction to the photographs he had shown her. She could barely bring herself to study them. Tony sat upright in the bed.

"Of course! Auntie Mary had to know! That's why she could not stomach seeing Howard's picture! Sean Lee must have told Auntie Mary everything. She was sparing my embarrassment by never mentioning it" he thought. Tony sank back down on the soft bed. He looked to his phone on the bedside locker.

"What if Howard and Jan refuse to come to Dublin?" he thought, questioning the wisdom of his ultimatum to them.

"They have to. They just have to" his brain said.

The next day Tony Lee made his way back to St. Oliver's Road. He had had a fitful night's sleep. Tony felt drowsy and on edge. Once inside the house he decided to text Stacey. Within seconds the message came back.

"O.k. 2 day. She's up & about. Dad's at work. Wish I was! R u working on the house still?" said the text message. Tony smiled as he read it.

"Yeah. Up since early. Hope u like what I've done" Tony replied. He glanced around the new kitchen, wondering if it all had been in vain. They surely could never live there now, yet in his heart he still harboured hope.

Late that afternoon, Tony's house phone rang, startling him somewhat. He had decided not to have either the radio or television on, feeling that it would not be appropriate. The ringing tone seemed to echo louder than ever around the silent house.

"Hello?" Tony said, holding his breath. It had to be The Williams'. He waited for the reply.

"This is Jan. We just got in. We're at the airport now. What should we do? We need to book into a hotel and rest. Can we meet up tomorrow?" she said. Tony felt his temper rise.

"Are you crazy or something? Didn't you understand any of what I said? There's a child lying dead in my home. You two get over here and deal with it-now!" he said firmly. Tony listened as Jan passed the telephone to her husband.

"Look Tony, both of us are exhausted. What difference is one day gonna make?" Howard said in a cheerful tone.

"I'll tell you what difference. The difference between me going to the authorities or not. How does that sound? Now Howard, you and your wife get over here to 88 St Oliver's Road immediately, you hear? You have one hour, hear me? One hour, no more" he said. Tony hung up and paced the hallway. Suddenly there was the sound of the doorbell ringing. Tony knew that it could not be Jan and Howard. It had to be someone selling something. He brusquely opened the door to get rid of them.

"Hiya mate, just dropped by to see how you are getting on. I want to see the outcome" Erik Ngombiti said cheerfully. He had a beaming smile and was wearing some old work clothes. Instantly Tony realised that his workmate had come to help him finish off installing the fireplace. He had to think fast.

"Well, everything is going fine Erik. I've done all of the donkey work. The back garden is full of rubble. I'll have to hire yet another skip. That skip company are making a fortune out of me! All I have to do is slip the fireplace into position" Tony said casually. The smile quickly vanished from Erik's face.

"You mean that it's not even installed? But you're at it days now. I came around to help finish it off, but I expected you to be nearly there by now" Erik said, his ready smile replaced by a disappointed look on his face. He had now joined Tony in the hallway, and was inching towards the stairs.

Tony's mind was racing with excuses. He had to come up with something believable.

"I know, I know. Listen, something came up. Stacey flew in yesterday from England. We went out for a meal, and one thing led to another..." Tony said, a bashful grin on his face. Erik's familiar laugh started in the bowels of his stomach.

"Huh-huh-huh-huh! Have you been up to naughties, Tony Lee?" he asked, pointing accusingly at his friend.

"You know how it is Erik! We haven't seen much of each other lately. Besides, there's no hurry. It's the final thing that I have to do with the house. Anyway, we can hardly start hammering at this time of the evening, can we? I'll finish it off tomorrow" Tony reasoned. Erik looked dejected. Within seconds, his expression changed.

"Yeah, I suppose that you're right. Well, now that I'm here, I might as well take a look at your handiwork" he said, making his way up the first few steps. Tony had to think fast.

"Hold on Erik, there's something else. My sister has just flown in from The States. She's on her way here now" Tony blurted out. Erik stopped in his tracks. "You mean Jan? The one you call Mrs. Crusty Knickers? You said that you two weren't getting on" Erik replied. Tony's head was fit to explode.

"We weren't. That is, we still aren't. Look, It's Jan's birthday tomorrow. Her husband has flown her in to patch things up" Tony said. His white lie was a last desperate effort to save himself. Erik looked down the four steps to his pal and shrugged his shoulders.

"Okay. Let me have a look at the fireplace you bought anyhow Tony. Let's see if it meets with my approval" Erik said with a smile. In an instant he was at the top of the stairs. Tony followed him at pace. By now Erik had entered the bedroom. He eyed the flat board nailed hastily to the wall.

"Jeez! You must have been in a hurry to get your leg over man! Those nails are all over the place!" Erik said with a knowing grin. Tony passed him and stood over the black metal fireplace on the other side of the room near the window, hoping to divert Erik's attention away from the boarded-up wall.

"It will do until tomorrow Erik. Here, what do you make of this little beauty?" he said, hunching down beside the fireplace. To Tony's relief, Erik slowly made his way across the room. He too stooped down next to the fireplace.

Erik whistled sharply as he studied the old, intricate cast iron fireplace and mantelpiece.

"She's superb all right, a right find. They don't make them like that anymore, my friend, no sir! How much did you pay for it?" Erik asked. Tony was happy with the distraction, but still wanted to ease his work colleague from the room.

"I t was a steal! I nabbed it for seventy quid. Do you fancy a quick coffee before my visitors get here?" he replied, rising to his feet. Tony stood with his back to the blocked-up wall, awaiting Erik's reply. Erik Ngombiti looked thoughtful.

"Nah, I had better not. Your guests will be here soon. Another time maybe Tony. Now, you've put a strong lintel in to support that wall?" Erik asked. Tony managed a smile.

"Of course! I took in everything that you said Erik!" Tony said with a forced laugh.

"You make sure that you do a nice job on that wall, you hear? Give me a bell if you need me. And don't leave it on the long finger, do it tomorrow morning, first thing" Erik replied.

Tony grinned. It always amused him how much slang and Irish terms that Erik used. It was as if the man studied such things in his spare time. Tony considered Erik's parlance was almost more Dublin than his own.

"It will be fine Erik, I promise. I'll have it in place by tomorrow afternoon" he said. Erik led the way back downstairs, much to Tony's relief.

Erik had a quick look around the newly refurbished house, admiring the new conservatory and kitchen. Within a few minutes he had left, still uttering last-minute instructions to Tony as the two walked to Erik's red Ford Focus car. "The finish is the most important thing Tony. Nice plasterwork and a simple paint job. Make the fireplace look as though it was always there" Erik said. "I will Erik. Thanks. I'll see you when I get back to work" Tony said. He sighed with relief as Erik finally drove away.

Sometime later, Jan and Howard arrived. The atmosphere was strained, to say the least. Howard tried to make small talk, telling Tony how the flight was delayed for almost an hour. Tony said nothing as he led them inside to the sitting room. Jan and Howard stood around awaiting the words that they dreaded from Tony Lee. They had not long to wait.

"Right, we all know why we are here. I suggest that we say a prayer before we begin" Tony said quietly. Jan looked startled.

"Is that really necessary? Come on Tony! Really?" she asked, looking from Howard to Tony.

"Yes" Tony replied deliberately. Howard patted his wife's hand in his.

"Come on honey, let's just do it" Howard said.

Tony prayed out loud with his head bowed, while Jan and Howard murmured half-heartily. When he had finished, Tony spoke a few words.

"Dear Lord, please take Martin Lee into your sacred Kingdom. We pray forgiveness for our sins. Keep Martin safe always. Amen" Tony said. He then made the sign of the cross on his body. Howard and Jan stood impassively across from him.

"Okay, this has to be dealt with. It's nine o'clock. It shouldn't take you two more than half an hour. The cemetery is within walking distance, but we'll grab a taxi. I want to make sure that you get there safely. Remember, I want him buried at the foot of Mom's grave. It's been raining, so the clay will be soft. Here" Tony said, handing Howard a small gardening spade and a torch. Howard looked scared.

"Do you really want to go through with this Tony? This is morbid. What if we bury him in a park or somewhere like that?" Howard said, realising that the moment of truth had arrived. Tony Lee shook his head.

"No. He will be buried in consecrated ground. That's the least that he deserves" Tony replied. Howard looked to the floor in defeat. Tony Lee continued with his instructions.

"I left some fresh flowers on Mom's grave today. When you've buried Martin, place the flowers over the spot. That will cover any signs of digging. Not that anyone would notice a small disturbance of clay anyway" he said. Jan was still searching for a way out.

"But how will we get into the graveyard? Isn't it locked at night?" she asked. Tony managed a faint smile.

"This is Dublin, not California. There's hardly a railings in Ireland that isn't broken! There's a gap right at the entrance on Newry Road. It's a secluded area, with an old factory across the street. No one will see you go in" he said. Jan looked terrified.

"Won't you come and help Tony? How will we know where to go?" she asked. Tony shook his head.

"No. This is something that you must do yourselves. I'll go with you in the taxi, just to show you where to go. Mom's grave is just inside the railings. It has the big white cross. Jan, you've been to visit it when you were home last. Let's just stop waffling and get on with it. As I said, I'll go there with you. After that, you're on your own" he replied. Howard seemed to finally accept their fate.

"Okay, have you put the baby in a box or something?" Howard asked. Tony looked ruffled for the first time.

"No. That's your job. Martin is still where you left him". Tony's words were halted by an interjection from Jan. She gasped and then cried out in disbelief.

"Jesus Christ Tony! You could have at least done something to help!" she whimpered. Tony Lee looked at her steely-eyed.

"It's your mess, both of you. Now, I left a small suitcase and a wooden box upstairs. I suggest that you put the child into the box, and then into the case. It will look less conspicuous. We'll get out of the cab just on the corner. After that it's a short walk to the cemetery" he said calmly. Howard and Jan looked at each other for a moment.

"Come on, I'm ready" Howard said.

Upstairs, Tony prised the sheet of wood away from the wall with a small claw-hammer. Jan stood by the door trembling and crying softly. Tony lifted the wood away. The stench was overpowering. Tony Lee tossed the small white industrial mask that he had used to demolish the wall, into Howard's hands. "Here, put that on" he said, dragging the wooden board away to the opposite side of the room. Howard squatted down on the floor. He shone the torch which Tony had offered him earlier, into the darkness. The white mask covered Howard's nose and mouth, yet Tony could still hear his words of disbelief. "Sweet mother of God. Oh my God! How could I have done this?" Howard's muffled voice said. Jan turned her back and sobbed into her hands. Tony Lee watched impassively from across the room. Howard Williams reached unsteadily into the open gap in the wall, his hands trembling noticeably. Slowly he pulled the tattered blue baby blanket towards the light. Tony looked away and whispered a prayer. The skeletal features of the child's head were all that were visible. The filthy, ragged blanket covered the rest of the baby's lean remains. Tears of despair and pain flowed from Howard's eyes. He tried not to look at his son, yet felt compelled to do so.

"Forgive me, please forgive me" he sobbed. Jan refused to look around. Tony wiped away tears with his open hand.

Howard managed to place the remains inside the mahogany wooden box. Delores Lee had used the small wooden chest to store old photographs. There were never any pictures of Martin Lee in the family snaps. Photos that were taken of the unfortunate boy had been destroyed long ago. Tony felt that it was apt to inter the infant with his mother, and in one of Delores's treasured possessions. Many evenings he had witnessed his mother trawling through the hundreds of old family snaps. In later life, it was when Delores was at her happiest. Now Tony wondered what his mother had been thinking on those private occasions. Had Martin Lee featured in her memories, he wondered? Did she wish that she had given Fergal Carrie another chance to share her life? Tony would never know. Now he felt that he was doing what was best for what remained of his ravaged family.

Tony still felt hopeful that he and Jan could come through this. They were still family of a sort. Perhaps Jan and Howard might even thank him in the long run. Their minds would be free of their demons at last. Maybe all three could build bridges. Tony hoped so. All he ever wanted was to have a proper family, something that he had been denied all of his life.

Howard shut the wooden box gently and closed the two metal clasps on the outside. He lifted it carefully inside the grey suitcase, placed open on the floor. Once he had shut the lid of the small case, Howard lifted it carefully onto the bed. Tony Lee covered the open hole in the wall with the large wooden board once more.

"It's done" Howard said, whipping off the white mask. He looked to Jan, who still stood with her back to him. Tony took the case and led the way downstairs.

"I'll phone for a taxi" he said. Neither Howard nor Jan spoke. They followed him dutifully to the hallway, where Tony placed the grey case near the front door. Both stood and listened as Tony telephoned the local cab company. Howard placed the torch and small spade inside the small grey suitcase and waited.

When the cab arrived, all three hurried from the front door.

"We're just going to Newry Road. You know the junction with Manson's Square?" Tony said cheerfully to the cab driver. The driver nodded impassively, offering to take the small case from Howard. A startled Howard quickly rebuffed his offer.

"It's just a short journey. I'll be okay" Howard said. The taxi man seemed surprised by the foreign accent.

"American?" he asked. Howard nodded and smiled.

"Yeah, I'm Irish originally, just home to see the folks" he replied. The cab driver nodded again, accepting his explanation. They set off on the short journey in silence.

Tony paid the fare and climbed out of the car to join Howard and Jan.

"Okay, we just walk along casually up this street" Tony said, nodding up towards St. David's Cemetery. They set off at an even pace, Tony constantly looking back to check that nobody was about.

Within minutes they had reached the gap in the black railings. The street was eerily quiet and deserted.

"No one comes up here at night. It leads nowhere. Only during the day is it busy. There's an industrial estate at the top of the road" Tony said.

Still Howard said nothing, his mind focussed on the task ahead. Tony stopped at the railings. He could see his mother's grave in the distance. A single streetlight shone a faded yellow beam of light inside to the cemetery.

For the first time it struck Tony that Delores and Sean Lee were buried in different cemeteries. It was such an obvious fact, yet something that he had never considered before. Delores had bought her plot many years ago, stating that she had always liked St. David's Cemetery. Tony now realised that his mother must have felt it inappropriate to be interred with Sean Lee. It was just another piece of the jigsaw sliding into place.

"Off you go. It shouldn't take you more than a few minutes. I'll meet you back at the house. You can book into a hotel once this is completed" Tony said in a businesslike manner. Howard nodded and squeezed the grey suitcase in through the broken railings. He eased his considerable frame inside, never letting go of the suitcase. A slimmer Jan quickly followed.

"Right. See you back there" Howard said. Jan said nothing. She had the look of a frightened child, unsure what was happening around her.

Within seconds Howard was at the graveside of Delores Lee. He pulled the short spade from the suitcase and began to dig furiously at the foot of the grave. The clay was soft, just as Tony had said it would be. A trembling Jan squatted beside him, whimpering like a puppy dog.

"Oh God Howard, oh my God" she whispered through her tears.

"Sssh. Let's get this done Jan" he said.

Tony Lee stopped further down the road. There was yet another gap in the railings. He quietly wondered should he trust Howard and Jan. What if they buried the infant in the wrong grave? What if it wasn't buried deep enough? They might even panic and not go through with it. Tony's impulse was to check on them. He climbed through the open gap and crept back along the railings. Further down he doubled across the deserted graveyard away from the road. The darkness enveloped him, yet he knew his way back to where his mother's grave was. Tony circled around behind the white cross. The light from the road was dim, but he could see the two silhouettes of Howard and Jan ahead of him. He crept even closer. A hedge divided one row of graves from another. Tony used this as a buffer, and crept along in the darkness. He could hear Howard's digging now.

"Jesus Howard, that has to be deep enough" Jan's pleading voice said.

"Just keep hold of the torch Jan" Howard said, wiping beads of sweat from his high forehead.

"I'm scared Howard. Please hurry" she whimpered.

"Nearly there Jan. We have to be sure that it will never be found" Howard replied in a low tone. Tony listened quietly, pleased that Howard was doing as he had been instructed.

"Once this is finished, we can get back to The States. I won't be sorry either" Howard continued. Jan was next to him, almost clinging to his body.

"What about Tony? Will he leave us in peace now?" she said.

"He had better. I came within inches of killing the bastard. I want nothing to do with that brother of yours. I forbid you to have any contact with him Jan from this day onwards. When we get home, I'll change the phone number. We'll have to think about moving, just in case the asshole doesn't get the message" Howard said vehemently.

Tony Lee crept away silently. His heart sank. It was the final insult. His hopes of building bridges with Jan were doomed.

Outside the cemetery he reached for his phone. He was about to do what he had wanted to do in the first place. All along he had wrestled with his conscience. Burying Martin next to his mother should have been enough, but it was not real justice.

"Hello, police? I want to report a crime" he said. Tony went on to describe two people digging at a grave in the local cemetery. He told the emergency operator exactly where it was happening, and urged them to be quick.

At the bottom of the road, Tony watched as a police car raced by him. His eyes were teary, but he knew that he had done what was right by Martin. Perhaps tonight Martin Lee would not be laid to rest after all, but at least sometime in the future it would happen. Tony made his way home and waited. There would surely be a knock at the door. He would probably go to prison. Tony Lee flopped down on the sofa. He was ready to accept whatever fate befell him.

A bewildered Howard leapt to his feet as the police car screeched to a halt. The blue flashing lights darted across the graves in an even, symmetrical line. Jan clung to Howard in terror.

"What's happening Howard, what will we do?" she wailed. Howard grabbed the torch from her and switched it off. A look of panic spread across Howard's face. He scanned around the cemetery for a way out. Already two policemen were through the broken railings. One was on the phone calling for back-up. A torch from the second policeman shone its beam onto the couple. Howard Williams tried to think fast.

"Whatever happens, we must say nothing, you hear? Admit nothing, tell them nothing. Let them figure it out for themselves. Don't mention Tony. It will lead them to the truth. I'll get us a decent lawyer" Howard whispered, tossing the small spade away. He placed his hands above his head, as he had witnessed criminals do in hundreds of detective programmes on American television. Jan sank slowly to the ground and wept uncontrollably.

Tony stayed awake all through the night. When nothing happened, he began to suspect that Jan and Howard had escaped somehow. Yet Martin's remains still occupied his mind.

By late morning he decided to install the fireplace. He had to cobble together some sort of story in case he was arrested. Tony hired yet another skip to dispose of the rubble. He then scrubbed out the recently excavated hole in his bedroom. Tony poured disinfectant into the opening, scouring the gap in the old wall several times. It appeared that the stench had finally vanished.

Tony put the lintel in place to support the wall. Each task helped to take his mind away from the awful reality of the situation. It was as if he was suspending the inevitable. The day dragged on, with Tony constantly listening for the dreaded knock at his front door which could change his life forever.

Tony Lee slowly dragged the fireplace into position. With some cement and bonding agents, Tony finished the job by late evening. He polished the old grate and fitted the mantelpiece above it. Then Tony applied a fresh lick of paint to the area surrounding the newly-installed black fireplace.

Later he had some coffee, but could not face eating. He sat for some time in his new kitchen, pondering what had happened to Jan and Howard. Eventually he returned to his bedroom to examine the fireplace again.

"It looks as though it has always been there" he remarked. Yet he knew that he would never feel comfortable sleeping in the room. Tony decided to switch bedrooms. He moved his furniture into his mother's larger room, confining the new bed and wardrobe from Delores's room to his. The irony that Delores Lee's bed now sat beside the fireplace was not lost on him. Perhaps it was a final statement to his dead mother. Even in the splendour of his new surroundings, Tony refused to relax. He would again spend a second night on the sofa, fading in and out of sleep. By morning he began to hope that Jan and Howard had indeed slipped the net.

At a city centre police station, Howard and Jan were being questioned separately. Both had refused to make any comment since their arrest. The odd story had not been released to the press, with the police unsure what charges to prefer. They had established the identity of Jan and Howard through their passports, which Howard had unwittingly kept in his jacket pocket. The U.S. police were running a check on the two American citizens, which was delaying the investigation. By now The Williams' had acquired an Irish solicitor to help with their defence. The time spent alone had given Howard a chance to put together a story in his head.

On the second day in custody, the police had afforded The Williams' a room to meet alone with their solicitor. It was to prove a fatal slip by a junior policeman. Howard was surprised and pleased with this development. It offered him the chance to brief Jan on his story. As they waited for their solicitor to arrive, Howard began to fill Jan with as much information as he could.

"We'll say that the baby had been buried in a different part of the cemetery. All we were doing was given it a proper burial next to your mother. That way it doesn't sound so bad. Saying that the child had been interred in a wall in the house sounds horrible. This way we might gain the sympathy of the public. Tony Lee will hardly go against us. Why would he want to become involved? If he admits to anything, he will be in trouble too" Howard said in a whisper. Jan looked as though she had aged way beyond her years.

"Won't they want to question Tony? Won't they search the house?" she asked. Howard nodded furiously. He knew that they might have little time together. "Sure they will, but we can only hope that they find nothing. If Tony has any brains, he will have cleaned out the house thoroughly. He must have seen the police car speed towards the cemetery that night. It's our only hope Jan. You have to trust me. The rest of the story we can tell them as it was. Like when your mother shook Martin to death. They can't charge a dead woman. We can say that we knew that Delores had buried the baby in the cemetery, but that we were too terrified to do anything at the time. When we buried the child a second time, we can say that we were only giving it a Christian burial" Howard said in a rapid, confident tone. Jan looked puzzled. Her eyes took in every word that Howard said, yet still she felt uncertain.

"But Howard dearest, won't they want to know where we dug the remains up from? There has to be a second grave Howard" she reasoned. Howard had already considered this.

"Yes, yes! Listen, you can say that I went to retrieve the body, while you dug the hole at your Mam's grave. That way you are off the hook. In other words, Delores only told me where Martin was buried. I'll say that it was somewhere in another part of the graveyard. Unless they actually lead me around the place, they will never prove it. And if they do walk me through the cemetery, I'll say that I am confused. I'll claim that I filled in the hole, and that an embedded white stone which I had tossed away, had marked the spot. It's a long shot Jan, but it might help" Howard whispered.

Jan Williams nodded slowly. Howard was always right. Whatever he said must make sense. Yet again she would back him, as she had always done.

A tall detective rushed into the tiny room. His heart sank as he realised what had happened. Howard and Jan were conversing. He left quickly, slamming the door behind him.

"Magee! Magee! What were you thinking of?" the detective screamed. Howard realised that the police had messed up. Without making a prior statement, Jan and he should have never been allowed to see each other. A lower ranking policeman had bungled badly. Their solicitor arrived moments later, just as Jan and Howard were being isolated again. The solicitor would only get to see them separately, but by now their story would at least be very similar.

It was Friday morning before the police had connected Jan   Williams with her old address at St. Oliver's Road. The work on the case had been painstakingly slow. That morning Howard and Jan Williams had made a statement confirming the re-burial of baby Martin.

When Tony answered the door to the two policemen, he looked genuinely shocked. Tony had come to believe that his sister and brother-in-law had managed to flee back to California without being caught.

The police questioned Tony about his sister. They gave him no information about her being in custody. Tony said that he and Jan had really never got on, and that there had been minimal contact since his mother passed away.

"You've been busy doing some house improvements then?" said the senior detective. Tony glanced around the kitchen. He nodded a few times before responding.

"Yeah, Mam didn't like change. It's only now that the old house is having a bit of a facelift" he joked. The second detective eyed him suspiciously.

"Mind if we take a look around?" he asked. Tony shrugged his shoulders.

"Sure, but what is this? Has something happened to Jan? If so, you should tell me" he said. The senior man stared Tony in the face.

"No, Jan Williams is safe. She's in custody now as it happens" he replied deliberately. A look of shock spread across Tony's face. He tried to remain in control.

"What? What's she charged with?" he asked in a surprised voice.

"All sorts. Cecil, go and have a look around the house" Detective Byron said. Tony felt the hairs on his head stand up. He wanted to blurt out the full story. Yet part of him wanted to save his own skin. He said nothing and waited for the next question.

"When did you see Jan last? Was she here? Have you been in contact with Howard Williams?" the detective asked. Tony decided to flex his muscles.

"If you're not prepared to tell what Jan is charged with, then I'm not going to answer your questions" Tony said firmly. The detective paced the room. He peered out into the new conservatory to the rear of the kitchen. Earlier that morning a skip had removed all of the rubble from the back garden. Tony held his breath.

"A brand new kitchen and a conservatory? My, you have been busy!" the policeman said sarcastically. Before Tony could speak, the second policeman returned from upstairs.

"Nothing of note" the detective said as he entered the kitchen.

"Would you object to us having a look around outside?" Detective Byron asked. Tony eyed him for a second.

"We can obtain a search warrant" the detective added. Tony shrugged indifferently.

"I've nothing to hide" he replied. The two men looked at each other. Detective Cecil Appleby set off through the new conservatory and opened the back door. Instantly he made for the small shed. Minutes later he returned, shaking his head at his senior colleague.

"I repeat my question Mr. Lee. When did you last see Jan Williams?" Detective Byron asked.

"I need to see my solicitor" Tony replied.

"Why? It's a simple question?" the middle-aged policeman replied dryly. Tony said nothing.

"Very well, we'll have to ask you to accompany us to the station" said the detective. Tony rose wearily to his feet. It seemed that his worst nightmare was about to come true.

CHAPTER TWENTY-EIGHT

WHEN FRIENDS FALL OUT

Howard stuck rigidly to his story, as did Jan. They maintained that they felt guilty after the death of Delores, and had decided to move the body closer to its mother. At all times Howard let it be known that he had nothing to do with the child's death. Through their solicitor, the married couple were careful as to what they said. The detectives in charge of the bizarre case seemed unsure how to proceed.

"What do you reckon Cecil? It all sounds too far-fetched to be true. A couple fly in from The States to bury a dead child in another grave. They're not telling the truth" Jim Byron said grimly. Cecil Appleby smirked at his senior partner.

"Of course not! The wooden box alone tells us that. It was never buried in the ground. It's too clean. The mud on that box is from the grave of Delores Lee" Appleby replied.

"What about the brother? This Tony Lee chap has very little to say for himself. I get the feeling that he's in on it. Yet he appears not to get on well with his sister. They hardly seem close" Jim Byron said.

Jim Byron sat at his desk, his hands stretched behind his head. Opposite him, Cecil Appleby sipped tea from a blue and white mug.

"We've gotta bring Mr. Williams out to the graveyard. Let him show us where the first grave was" said Cecil Appleby. Jim Byron laughed heartily.

"There was no first grave Jim, not in that cemetery anyway!" he answered. Cecil Appleby grinned back at him.

"I know that! He's saying that a white stone marked the baby's grave. Our boys have been out there. Guess what? There's no white stone unearthed anywhere. My guess is that the child was buried somewhere in that house, or in the back garden" Jim Byron replied.

"I agree, but if we get forensics out there, the press will have a field day, plus we might never find anything. That goddamn house has been redecorated from top to bottom. It would be impossible to accurately say where they hid the remains" Appleby said.

"My guess is that it was in the ground where that new conservatory stands" Detective Byron remarked. Cecil Appleby nodded his agreement.

"Okay, let's go through the motions. Let's discreetly take the Williams' back to St. David's Cemetery and see what we come up with. Their solicitor is demanding that we either press charges or release them" Detective Byron said.

"Right. In the meantime, why not put Lee under a bit of pressure? Why not tell him what his sister is being questioned about, and see how he reacts?" Cecil Appleby suggested.

"Agreed Jim. I'll tell you this though. If we have to cordon off that house for forensics, the world press will be on our door! This could be huge" Cecil Appleby replied tersely.

"So Mr. Lee, you flew all the way to California to see your sister, and then flew back immediately? Then the following day she and Mr. Williams arrive in Ireland. Isn't that a bit odd, don't you think?" Detective Appleby asked. Tony Lee sat upright on his plain, wooden chair and sighed loudly.

"I've already told you. My sister and I don't really get on. I flew over to try and make the peace. It didn't work out. We argued. How was I to know that she flew back here? Maybe she had a change of heart and wanted to patch things up" Tony replied.

"So she never came to see you at your house?" Appleby asked. Tony shook his head.

"No, not this time. Perhaps she called while I was out, I don't know. I went out cycling that evening, I often do. Maybe she called while I was away" Tony answered.

"Where did you cycle to?" Appleby asked, leaning over the simple table which separated him from Tony Lee. Tony sighed again and inhaled.

"Up to a spot near Johnny Fox's Pub in the Dublin Mountains. It's a favourite of mine. You can see out over the whole city from there. It helps me think" Tony replied with distain. Appleby ignored his reply.

"Does Jan Williams have a key to your house on St. Oliver's Road?" Appleby asked. Tony shook his head. Appleby rose from his seat and paced the room slowly.

"What if I told you that we arrested your sister and brother-in-law at St. David's Cemetery while they were in possession of the body of a dead child?" Appleby said, turning sharply to gauge Tony Lee's reaction. Tony tried to look surprised.

"That's daft! I don't believe you" he said.

"It's true Tony. Gospel. The thing is, we believe that you know all about this. In fact, we suspect that you insisted on them moving the body from its original resting place. Was that what you rowed about with your sister?" Appleby said, leaning over Tony Lee in a threatening manner.

"Ridiculous! Maybe I should see my solicitor now" Tony replied. Detective Appleby ignored his response.

"You see Tony, that child was never buried in that graveyard, although Jan Williams insists that it was. The child's body was somewhere else for all of those years. And it was never interred in the ground. It was probably somewhere dry and safe. Somewhere like, oh, I would say in a house" Cecil Appleby said suggestively.

"If you are accusing me of some crime, I definitely want to see a solicitor. I'm saying nothing else on the subject. I've told you everything that I know. Look, there was a rumour that my Mam had a baby, and that he was taken to live in America. I was just a kid at the time. Now what exactly am I supposed to have done?" Tony replied angrily.

"And where do you think that child is now Tony?" Appleby asked.

"Don't know" Tony said bluntly.

"Is this the same baby? The same child that you claim your mother gave birth to all of those years ago? Appleby inquired.

"No comment. From now on, every question that you ask will be answered the same until I see a solicitor" Tony replied firmly.

At the same time, Detective Byron was escorting Howard and Jan Williams around St. David's Cemetery. Two plain-clothes policemen followed behind discreetly.

"Where did you dig up the child from Mr. Williams?" Byron asked. Howard put on a show of panic and confusion.

"I can't remember. I've told you about the stone. I tossed it away. Some kids might have picked it up and moved it somewhere. This place is wide open to vandalism. Look, there's a couple of beer cans lying there. There are probably syringes about too" Howard said.

He knew the implications of what he was saying. The crime scene may have been tampered with. The police had failed to cordon off the old graveyard, fearing that it might draw unwanted attention. There was no way of proving or disproving for certain that there had not been a white stone.

"You see, what I can't understand is where you got the wooden box from. Did Tony supply it? We know that that box was never in the ground. It hasn't aged you see Howard. If that box was in the clay for all of those years, it would be rotting and falling apart. It's brand new. And then there's the empty grey case.

411

We've checked footage of you at Dublin Airport. Neither of you are carrying luggage" Detective Byron said.

"I understand that. We were only planning on staying for a short while. I bought the suitcase in the city. I knew that we might need it to move the baby. You see, like you, I figured that the remains might not be in the best possible state. I intended on burying poor Martin in the suitcase. I was amazed at how well preserved the wooden box was" Howard said.

For the first time, Jim Byron looked annoyed.

"Jesus Christ! So now you say that you never opened the wooden box? You never actually saw the remains? What about the ragged blue blanket? You never saw that either? And the preservation of the wooden box is some kinda miracle?" Byron said, halting suddenly in his tracks. The detective stood ahead of Howard and Jan now, blocking their path. Howard Williams actually managed a smile.

"That could be it Detective. It is sacred ground after all. Yeah, I never considered that thought. Perhaps God lent a hand. He wanted to see to it that little Martin had a decent burial, so he looked after him until we came along" Howard replied. Byron looked to the ground in despair. Inside he was fuming, but he had to act professionally. He turned to the two trailing policemen.

"Get them back in the car. This has been a total waste of time, just as I predicted" he said. Howard and Jan Williams walked silently back to the unmarked police car. Byron stared across to Delores Lee's grave.

"The secrets of the past. Dear oh dear! It's not just this generation who have marriage problems, it's been going on forever" he whispered.

Jan Williams and her husband were released on bail. Their passports were confiscated, and they were ordered not to leave the country. Howard had managed to telephone home while in custody. His parents were worried, having heard nothing for days, but Howard insisted that everything was fine. He said that he was delayed in Ireland, and would be home soon. On release, the pair checked into a city hotel.

"What will happen now Howard?" Jan asked fearfully. Howard went to hold his wife in his arms. He embraced her for a few moments before speaking.

"I don't know darling. It's up to the police. You should phone Tony and ask him what he knows. It's best to keep our story straight" Howard replied.

"Really? What if his phone is tapped? Don't the police do that sometimes?" she said. Howard laughed heartily and hugged his wife.

"Not for something like this sweetheart! They're hardly gonna bug his house! If it makes you feel better, phone his cell-phone" Howard said.

Tony Lee sat at home in his front room, staring out the large new bay window. Stacey would be home in a couple of days. He was sure that it would be her on the phone.

"Number withheld" had lit up on his mobile phone. Hearing Jan's voice had given him a start.

"Yes Jan, where are you?" he asked. Jan explained what had happened, and that they had been released without charge for the moment.

"Yeah, me too. I get the feeling that it's not the end of things though" Tony replied. Howard took the phone from his wife and outlined what he had told the police.

"What did you tell them Tony?" Howard asked.

"Nothing. I said that we argued a lot, which is true. I half expect them to come and do a thorough search of the house. The fireplace is in place now, but I suspect that it won't take them long to figure it out. I think that it's just a matter of time before they tear the place apart. Don't worry, whatever happens now, I won't be bothering either of you again" Tony said. Howard tried to make light of Tony's remarks.

"Look Tony, we're all feeling a little fraught. Once the dust has settled, we can work things out" Howard said with a false laugh. Tony Lee did not feel much like laughing. He kept his answers short and clear. Once Howard had checked that Tony's story did not affect him, he appeared content.

"Okay Tony, we'll keep in touch. Jan will phone you later, yeah?" Howard said. Tony listened as the line went dead. He did not wish to have any further contact with either Howard or Jan. They had made clear their feelings for him. Tony did not need to be around people who did not want to know him. He had reluctantly accepted that he had lost the final part of his immediate family. All that remained now was Aunt Ethel.

Tony rambled up to his bedroom and stared at the newly-installed fireplace. He sat on the bed and wept openly. How could he ever live in this house again, he wondered? He cried for his family, and for Martin, a brother that he had never known. Then he wept for his lost mother, and what she had done to destroy his life. He felt all alone, and at his lowest point ever in life.

Suicide suddenly appeared to be an option again. He thought of Harry Brand, and how the young man had ended his life. Tony stopped his sobbing and walked out to the landing. How easy it would be to open the attic door and do it. His eyes gazed to the small trapdoor. So much had happened since he discovered Fergal Carrie's love letters up there. He recalled the broken pram belonging to himself and later to Martin, his mother's old handbags, and smashed-up furniture from almost a half-century ago. Then Tony realised that Stacey would return home the following day.

Suddenly there was something worth living for. It was like opening a new book. His life did not have to centre on the past. He could move on. He could start afresh, just like number eighty-eight had. If need be, he could sell the house and begin his life again. Once he was sure that Stacey Boyd wanted to be with him, that is. That was the crucial ingredient to beginning again. There and then Tony decided to propose to Stacey. Not in a week's time, not next month. He would propose the very moment that he saw her again.

Detective Jim Byron went to see his supervisor.

"A messy one this Jimmy. The U.S. are involved now. International diplomacy has to be considered. Our internal office has been on at the highest level, and the implications of the press getting hold of this could be catastrophic. My hunch is to shelve the whole sorry episode. What are your thoughts?"Inspector Ian Clarkson said tersely.

"I agree sir. The evidence is sketchy, although we did catch them red-handed with the body. If we want to believe that they were simply re-burying the infant for their own peace of mind, well then it could be classed as a matter for leniency. But the press would crucify us on this if it gets out. It happened days ago, and we have failed to prosecute so far. I've never charged anyone with a crime like this one. My instinct would be to let them off with a stern warning. Get them back to The States as soon as possible" Detective Byron said.

"My sentiments entirely. What about this Tony Lee fellow?" Ian Clarkson replied, a furrow appearing on his high forehead. He was a man in his early sixties, with several folds of skin beneath his grey-blue eyes. The last of his grey hair circled the back of his head in a perfect semi halo-type ring. Ian Clarkson had worked his way up through the ranks over a period of thirty five years. He was nearing retirement, and was tiring of his desk job. Jim Byron continued his assessment of the case.

"This Lee chap seems decent enough. He's lived as a carer to his mother for many years, while also holding down a job in I.T. Whether or not he was in on this episode is debatable, but my gut feeling says that he was. Anyhow, it would be difficult to prove anything. It appears that he and his sister don't really get on. Perhaps this child burial was the source of their dislike for each other. I guess that we will never really know. I also suspect that that house holds some dark secrets. The only sure way of knowing is to seal it off and make a thorough search of the building. There's a new conservatory which might hold the key. It would have to be demolished. It might take weeks, and then the media are sure to get wind of it!" Jim Byron replied tersely. Ian Clarkson looked physically sick.

"What? Heavens no Jimmy! I want this investigation wound down today. We've already wasted far too much time on this. No. Our men could be used much more effectively in other more serious crimes. See to it Jim. I want this kept quiet. Get those people out of the country as soon as possible and get the case shelved immediately" Ian Clarkson replied.

Detective Byron nodded obediently. He was not sure that he approved completely. It was difficult for him to see anybody get away with a criminal act, but he understood that it was often a necessary evil. It would not be the first crime that had been hushed up to save face, and to protect diplomatic relations. Jim Byron would obey his orders without question, just like many times before. But he needed clarification on procedure from the very top. He was not about to allow this botched case to fall back on him.

"Sure boss, but what about the burial? Where shall it be, and who should attend?" Jim Byron asked. Ian Clarkson looked agitated with the attention to detail. He wished that senior members of his staff would learn to deal with matters themselves.

"Well, let the Williams' couple and Mr. Lee attend by all means. It goes without saying. I want the burial done well away from prying eyes. Why not in the grounds of a maternity hospital? All three should agree to this on the understanding that we won't press charges. I don't want any headstone with notification of the year of death or suchlike. A simple plaque or cross with the child's name should suffice. Use a priest from the hospital to conduct a quick, quiet ceremony. See to it today Jimmy" Ian Clarkson said. Jim Byron nodded and stood up to leave.

"If this file was to disappear from the records, it might not be any harm Jimmy" Inspector Clarkson said pointedly. Jim Byron said nothing and closed the door quietly behind him. He would do as required, just as he always had done.

"Ma! I'm just going down the chipper!" Joseph Byrne called out from the hallway. He listened for his mother's reply.

"Don't be long son. It's late. Here, get me a bag of chips" Alice Byrne replied. Burrener went inside the cramped living room. His father lay asleep on an armchair, much the worse for drink. Alice Byrne sat in the opposite armchair sipping on a can of lager.

"Is your sister still asleep upstairs?" Alice asked. Joseph had just come down from his room, having failed to reach the next level of his X-Box game. Once he had something to eat, he would try again to master his latest game.

"She's out to the world Ma! No doubt she will have us all awake during the night!" Joseph replied. A slow grin slowly spread across Alice's pudgy face.

"Not your old man son! Look at him! A marching band won't wake him tonight! It will take all my strength to get him up the stairs!" Alice smirked.

"Ah sure I'll give you a hand when I get back" Burrener said, turning to leave.

"You're a great lad Joey, I'm proud of you! You're one in a million" Alice Byrne said with a grin. Joseph Byrne stopped in the doorway and turned back suddenly towards his mother.

"Ma, I love you and me Dad" he said, planting a peck on Alice's chubby left cheek. In an instant he was gone, the front door closing softly behind him.

"Well, there's a first! He hasn't kissed me since he was little!" Alice muttered, wiping the kiss from her cheek with a smile.

Hey Burrener! Giz a chip!" the voice said in the blackness. Joseph Byrne's eyes scanned the darkness for a face. The street lamp had been broken for almost a week now. Once out of range from the lights of the local chip-shop, it was difficult to see very far. Muggser came into view, a sneering smile on his face. The two had not seen each other since the day Muggser was released from prison.

"Sure Muggser, here, have the bag. I'm not hungry anyway. I just stepped out to get some for the Ma" Burrener replied, offering the white wrapped-up paper containing his supper to his former pal. Muggser punched the wrapping from below, sending a cascade of chips across the pavement.

"Fuck you and your lousy chips. Who do you think you are now Burrener? Mr. fucking Big! You won't come out with me anymore, eh? Well fuck you and your poxy family! I do all right on my own anyway. Three purses I got tonight, three! One hundred and eight-five euro in my pocket! And what did you make? I'll tell you, you made level two of some poxy Playstation game!" Muggser said mockingly. He stood ahead of Burrener, blocking his path.

"I play X-Box, not Playstation, and leave my family out of it!" Burrener said weakly.

"I couldn't give a shite what you play! People with half a brain play that crappy stuff! I'll bet your brain-dead sister could play them!" Muggser sneered. Burrener dared to take a threatening step forward.

"What did you say about me sister, you fucking toe-rag?" Burrener yelled. He was in a furious rage. Burrener had helped to take care of his handicapped younger sister since the day that Muggser went to prison. He pushed Muggser in the chest, forcing him backwards.

Muggser was quick to react.

"I'll say what I fucking-well like Burrener. Now move aside, before I do something that I might regret" Muggser said, stepping forward once more. His body width was now spread out to its maximum, daring Burrener to advance again. Muggser widened his shoulders and spread his hands out from his lower body in readiness. Joseph Byrne tried to brazen out the row.

"I'm not scared of you Muggser; I could always beat you when we were at school. I was stronger than you, I still am" Burrener replied, now feeling more confident about defending himself. He moved forward again, defying Muggser to block him off.

"I don't want to fight you Muggser, just leave me alone. My Ma's chips are getting cold" Burrener said, clutching the second bag of hot chips under his arm. As he took another step forward, Muggser refused to yield. Burrener made another attempt to push him to one side. Before Burrener could react, he saw the flash of the steel blade in the darkness. Muggser lunged forward, planting the knife firmly into Burrener's chest. He jabbed it into the flesh of his old friend three times before stepping backwards. A look of utter surprise and disbelief spread across Burrener's face. He tried to speak as the white wrapping fell to the wet ground below, Chips scattered across the grey pavement. Burrener clung unsteadily to Muggser's torso. His grip slackened as the blood oozed from his chest and stomach. Burrener tumbled slowly to the ground in a crumpled heap, his left arm caught beneath him as he clutched his chest.

Muggser dropped the flick- knife before quickly picking it up again. He always carried a knife when out mugging or breaking into houses. This was the first time that he had ever used it. Panic set in as he tried to think straight.

A passing taxi drew slowly to a halt up ahead. The headlights caught the scene full on. A truck going in the opposite direction screeched to a halt. Muggser tried to run, but his feet refused to obey him. He stood trembling on the path, trying to decide what he should do. The taxi driver phoned the emergency services. He described the scene from the safety of his cab. The two doors of the truck opened slowly. Two burly men stepped out of either side. The two construction workers were on their way home from a job in Navan, about ten miles away.

"Drop the knife son. Come on, don't try anything foolish" said the driver of the truck. The two approached the scene, slowly inching forward.

"Let us see to the chap before he bleeds to death" said the second man. Muggser looked to his old pal as if he was seeing him for the first time.

"He's my mate, he'll be all right. It's Burrener. He's gonna be okay" Muggser said, trying desperately to reassure himself. He dropped the knife a second time and knelt down beside the limp body of Joseph Byrne. Muggser cradled his friend in his arms as the driver of the truck kicked the knife away. The taxi man climbed from the cab and walked slowly forward. The siren from the ambulance could be heard in the distance. It was too late for Joseph Byrne. The reformed criminal was already dead.

Muggser was taken away by the police still pleading that it had been an accident. The knock would soon come to Alice Byrne's door to inform her that her son would never come home again. Some years ago Alice might have had such a horrific evening in the back of her mind, but lately she had begun to believe that her son would turn out all right after all. All she faced now was a life of struggle, as she tried to raise her daughter almost single-handed. Her alcoholic husband would be of little help, citing the death of his only son as yet another reason for self-pity and endless drunken nights.
The law would not be so lenient with Muggser this time. Muggser faced a long sentence for manslaughter, the court ruling that the charge of murder could not be proven. The prosecution would settle for the lesser charge of manslaughter, Muggser claiming that his old friend had instigated the argument.

On Saturday morning, Tony Lee arrived at the grounds of the maternity hospital alone. He knew that Jan and Howard would be there, but had made no specific arrangements to meet up with them. So far, everything had been done by telephone through the police. Now he had to face Jan and Howard for the first time since that fateful night at the cemetery. Mentally Tony was prepared. He knew that Jan did not really want anything to do with him in the future. Whether it was her own choice or borne out of a duty to Howard, mattered little. Tony had already accepted the inevitable. Today was all about laying Martin to rest properly. Tony Lee vowed to forget that Jan and Howard Williams would have happily left his half-brother interred behind a cement wall forever, if they had their way. Today he would act with dignity and compassion. He had to remember that his mother was also a part of the gruesome pact. And so he would swallow his pride and say nothing for the sake of everybody.
Tony strolled through the sunshine in the small field to the rear of the hospital. In a secluded area in a type of dog-leg stretch of land, Tony noticed some people standing among the tiny white crosses. As he grew closer he recognised both Jan and Howard. There was a priest dressed in black. Tony had expected white robes, but quickly realised that discretion was the order of the day. It had been explained to him by the police what the rules were to be. Tony had agreed to go along with everything. All that mattered to him was for Martin to be buried in consecrated ground. Tony noticed two gentlemen standing away

at a respectable distance. He realised that it would be the police. They would have to witness that everything was done in accordance with the agreement. Jan eyed Tony as he approached in his black suit and tie. Both she and Howard were dressed casually. Jan wore a grey trouser-suit, while Howard wore dark trousers and a navy-blue jacket. Tony decided that they had purchased their new clothes, as they had travelled to Dublin without any luggage.

"Good morning Tony" Jan said solemnly as he came to stand opposite them. The tiny dark coffin lay to the left of the small opening in the ground, resting on some green felt over a wooden board. Howard stood silent, staring down into the open hole.

"Morning" Tony answered in an even tone.

"Shall we begin?" the middle-aged priest asked.

Tony stood silently as the priest read from The Bible. The young, innocent-looking priest's words wafted over Tony's head as he tried hard to forgive his mother. He tried to put himself in her position. Nothing made sense. In his wildest dreams Tony Lee could never imagine doing such a thing. Forgiveness came hard for him, even for his devoted mother. Sometimes during the short ceremony, Tony would catch some meaningful words from the priest. He would soon drift back to his soul-searching and struggles, lost in a world of his own. Martin lay just feet from him, and that was at least a comfort. At last his young brother could be free of torment. It was the only good thing to come from the sorry mess.

Tony realised that he had not had any nightmares since he discovered the body on that awful day. He wondered if he had set Martin's soul free in some way. Tony looked up to the bright blue sky and wondered if his mother and her son were reunited. Could Martin forgive her? Tony certainly hoped so, for he found it almost impossible to do so himself.

"Let us pray" said the priest. Tony bowed his head again. He prayed with all of his might for everyone involved.

Jan stared across at her brother, wondering what he was thinking. Never did it cross either her or Howard's mind that it was Tony who had phoned the police that night.

They could see no possible reason for that. After all, it was Tony who had instigated the whole mission. She was not to know that the words that they uttered that night had finally ended Tony's faint hopes of being at least a tiny part of her little family.

"Let us give each other the sign of peace" the priest said. He closed his Bible and offered a handshake to all. If it was not such a poignant moment, Tony Lee might have burst into uncontrollable laughter. The simple Christian custom meant that all thee would have to make physical contact without ever wanting

419

to. An awkward moment followed as Jan hesitated to offer her hand to Tony. He instigated it, and then shook Howard's hand warmly. It meant nothing to Tony. It was a goodbye rather than a hello.

"We're heading home tonight Tony. I'll phone you during the week" Jan said as they walked from the tiny graveyard. Tony stopped and looked at both his sister and Howard. It was no use. He had to have his say.
"Let's not kid ourselves, eh?" he replied. Howard patted Tony on the shoulder. "Listen Tony, this is all behind us now. Don't you see? This was driving a wedge between Jan and you. Now that it's in the past, we can get on with our lives" Howard said with a friendly smile. Tony eyeballed him for a second. The two policemen passed by, their work complete. They glanced sideways at the three, but said nothing. A simple white cross now marked Martin's tiny grave. The only proof that he had ever been on this earth was the name of Martin Lee inscribed on the tiny cross. There would be no date of birth, and no year to signal his passing.
"Yeah Howard, it's all behind you. You can sleep well again, eh? Your conscience is clear once more. You've done the right thing. God! I would hate to be like you two! You have everything in this world, yet you have nothing. You have no morals, no understanding for what you did, and certainly no guts. You are just two people floating through life in your own little bubble. You got away with what you did, but there is a higher judge, remember that" Tony said. Jan clung to her husband's arm. She could not let it pass.
"And what about you Tony? All of the sacrifices Mam made so that you could be happy. We have had to live with this terrible secret, not you. It was Mam's wish. Don't you see that? She needed to be there to raise you. What kind of life would you have had if Mom went to prison? We only did it for her" Jan said, sobbing out the words as her emotions took over. Tony shook his head in frustration.
"You still don't get it, do you Jan? Whether it was her wishes or not, it was wrong. It was heinous what the three of you did. Evil. I don't care what Mam thought, what Howard feared, what my Dad believed. It really is irrelevant. We're talking about another human being here, no matter how old or young he was. Now, I'm going to disappear from your lives for good. I have things to do. I suggest that both of you go home. Go back to your life of making money, of living the dream. Forget about me, because I certainly intend to forget all about you two" Tony said. He turned briskly and walked off towards the exit, leaving Jan and Howard behind.
"Will he be all right Howard?" Jan asked. Howard patted her shoulder. He stood with his right arm around his devoted wife.

"He will be fine honey, just fine. Come on; let's go back to the hotel. I need to catch a nap before flying home" he said.

"Yes Howard. I'll do a little shopping for presents, if that's okay?" Jan said. Howard nodded and chuckled softly.

"Yeah, Jan, that's fine. You have those two kids spoiled! Give me a couple of hours. Then you can wake me with a nice cup of coffee. The coffee in that hotel sure don't taste like at home though!" Howard replied.

"Right Howard, that's what we'll do" Jan said obediently.

Tony Lee took a taxi to the airport to meet Stacey Boyd. It was a sunny Autumn Sunday afternoon, and Stacey was due home on an early evening flight. Tony was going to surprise her at Dublin Airport.

Stacey knew of Tony's dislike for travelling anywhere unnecessarily. Unless his destination was within easy striking distance of home, Tony tended to make excuses for travelling. If the journey could not be made by his trusty silver racing bike, Tony preferred not to go. Of course, when they went on a date, Tony would never complain about using a taxi. That was different. That involved both parties. However, for Tony Lee to actually hire a cab by himself, it would definitely need to be a special occasion. And this time it was. Stacey was coming home at last.

Tony stood at Arrivals in his grey jacket and navy trousers. He wore a red tie and white shirt. Checking again that his tie was in place, Tony craned his neck above the crowd. He carried a bunch of red roses and smiled as he saw Stacey's blonde hair in the distance. Tony eased his way to the front of the crowd. Stacey saw him immediately and looked surprised. He had never said that he would be there to greet her. Stacey's intentions were to go to her apartment and meet up with Tony later that evening.

She waved her hand in the air, pulling her small pink case behind her. They were now face to face, and Stacey planted a kiss on his lips.

"What a lovely surprise Tony! I didn't expect you to come all of this way!" she exclaimed.

"That's because I have something to ask you" Tony said nervously.

He slowly knelt down on one knee and pulled a small red velvet box from his jacket pocket. Gasps could be heard all around in the gathered crowd. People coming through Arrivals stopped in their tracks. The sound of hand luggage wheeling along the tiled floor ceased. Stacey tried to put both hands to her mouth in shock. Tony clung to her left hand. The fingers of her right hand rested flat against her open mouth.

"Stacey Boyd, I love you so much. Will you marry me?" Tony asked. He opened the red tiny box and slipped the engagement ring onto her middle finger. The crowd cheered. An airport worker shook his head wryly as he passed by the couple. People around Stacey stood motionless as they awaited her reply.

"Say yes!" a man shouted from the crowd. It was only then that Stacey realised that Tony's question required an answer.

"Yes, yes please!" she said, almost stumbling over her words. The crowd was larger now, as other folk in the airport quickly rushed over to witness what was happening. People cheered again, this time much louder. Tony Lee stood up sheepishly and kissed her on the lips. He embraced her gently, holding her in his arms. Stacey kissed him back, lost in the moment.

"Get a room!" someone yelled from the crowd. Some laughter filled the hall for a moment. A gentle, spontaneous round of applause ensued. The couple kissed again, this time more slowly. The crowd began to disperse. Tony led Stacey through the smiling crowd. Folk were now losing interest. The airport was a busy place, and people quickly realised that they had places to go to.

"What brought all this on?" a smiling Stacey asked, accepting the bunch of red roses from him. Tony grinned back at her.

"Nothing-well, everything really I suppose! Let's just say that it was ever since I realised that life is too short!" he replied.

"Do you mean because what happened to my Mam?" Stacey asked. Tony shook his head.

"No Stace, other things. Come on. Let's go home" he said.

CHAPTER TWENTY-NINE

A HOMECOMING FOR STACEY

Tony lifted Stacey's case from the boot of the black taxi. He paid the cab fare
as Stacey Boyd eyed the house. It looked pretty, yet still she had her
misgivings. The gleaming white frontage seemed to mask a darker mode
inside. Could she ever settle at number eighty-eight St. Oliver's Road, she
wondered? Tony turned to her with a beaming smile on his face. He could see
the doubt in her eyes. It was perhaps understandable. The most important
thing for Tony Lee now was for Stacey to be happy. Soon he would tell her all
about Martin. She ought to be told about Jan and Howard's plotting and
scheming. Yes, Tony vowed that he would tell her everything, but not just now,
not today. This was a happy time, and he did not want to spoil it.
"Come on love, it will be okay. Wait until you see what I've done with the
place" he said cheerfully. Stacey managed to smile back at him. She followed
him inside into the garden, in through the gate with its tight spring. The gate
was now painted white, to match the new windows and door. Bright flowers
bloomed in the new snow-white window-box outside the downstairs window.
The lawn was newly-laid, and a row of flower beds decorated the edge along
the pavement. Tony held the gate open as Stacey took in the changes. Even the
unkempt hedge at the bottom of the garden had vanished.
"You've done loads!" Stacey said. Tony beamed proudly back at her.
"This is nothing! Wait until you see inside!" he replied.
Tony turned his new key in the front door. Stacey gasped as she peered inside.
The house had changed beyond all recognition. The internal doors were new,
as was the flooring. She almost floated down the hallway into the kitchen,
trying to take everything in.
"It must have cost a fortune Tony!" she whispered. Tony laughed nervously.

"A few bob Stace, but it was well worth it, don't you think?" he answered.
"Yeah, definitely!" she said, running her hand along the new kitchen units. She gasped as she noticed the door leading to the bright and airy conservatory. Tony Lee held her gently in his arms.
"I hope that we can be happy here" he said. Stacey looked nervous.
"I…I'll try Tony, I will, honestly. But not straight away. I want to live at my apartment for a while, okay?" Stacey replied. She kissed him gently on the cheek. Tony smiled back at her again. He understood completely.
"Of course Stace, I just want it nice for when you can stay over" he said. Stacey Boyd grinned at him and hugged him tight.
"Like tonight you mean?" she asked. Tony's eyes lit up.
"Yeah, like tonight" he said. Stacey broke away suddenly.
"What's upstairs? What have you done to the bedrooms?" she asked. Her tone was almost child-like, wanting to explore the whole house. Tony smiled confidently at her. It was time to be strong, to be assured.
"Lots Stace. The first thing is that I now sleep in the master bedroom. We have an en-suite in two of the bedrooms. I did up my old room, but we can use that for guests" Tony said. Stacey bolted upstairs. Tony took a deep breath before slowly following her. As he climbed the newly-carpeted stairs he felt confident that he could mask his true feelings.
"This is perfect! We have a brand-new giant size bed!" she said, flopping down on the soft mattress. Tony stood in the doorway of what was formally his mother's room.
"I hope it meets with your approval! Come on, this is the en-suite" he said, opening the white door leading off the bedroom. Stacey gasped again as she wandered inside. She held her hands to her face in surprise.
"Oh God Tony! This is brilliant! It's like a new house" she whispered. Her words made it all worthwhile for Tony Lee. He had spent over €45,000 on the house, but Stacey's reaction made everything seem value for money.
They spent some time in their new bedroom talking before Stacey realised that there was more to explore.
"Oh! Your old room! Come on, let's see it!" she said in a cheerful voice. Tony braced himself. He barely had the heart to enter the old bedroom in the last few days. Tony Lee followed her out onto the landing, past the old spare room, and into the place where he had discovered the remains of his half-brother.
"Oh my God! Oh my God, a fireplace! It looks as though it had always belonged there! And Jodie suggested it Tony, didn't she? Oh my God! She was so right!" Stacey said in a gushing tone. Tony swallowed hard. He had almost forgotten about Jodie Callaghan lately.

"Yeah, I wasn't sure that you would approve. You know, with Jodie and everything..." Tony replied, trailing off at the end of his sentence. Stacey's face was aglow with happiness. She ran to put her arms around him.

"Of course I do! I love it! I always want to remember Jodie. She was mad! Every time I think of her, I smile. We should never forget her, promise?" Stacey whispered. She kissed Tony softly on the lips.

"I promise" he replied.

They sat downstairs in the conservatory drinking coffee. Stacey had phoned Angie and Gina to tell them that she was home from Wolverhampton and had just become engaged. She had one more day off work before returning to her old job. Tomorrow she would be reunited with her old friends again.

"What about those tests Tony? When are the results out?" Stacey asked. A furrowed row of lines appeared on Tony's high forehead.

"Sometime early this week I've been told. It's not something that I'm looking forward to" he said tersely. Stacey looked surprised.

"I thought that you would want to know" she said. Tony Lee nodded several times.

"Oh I do Stace, but it's just so...so final I suppose" Tony answered. Stacey sat beside him on the small new leather two-seated sofa. Tony had bought it specifically for the new sunny room, figuring that they would spend a lot of time there. A new flat screen television stood in the corner opposite. Stacey patted his hand for reassurance.

"And this, this Fergal Carrie, have you been in touch?" she asked. Tony smiled and nodded again. He stood up and walked to the new French doors leading to the back garden.

"Almost every day Stace. He phones me on my mobile to see how I'm getting on. I run out of things to say to him, you know? He doesn't really know me, and I certainly don't know him! It's weird. I don't know what he wants from me. He doesn't feel like my father at all, and yet..." Tony's thoughts were left hanging in midair as Stacey struggled to find words to comfort him.

"Maybe when it's all sorted you'll feel different" she suggested. Tony turned to face her with a smile.

"Yeah, maybe. Who knows? I still go to see my Dad's grave, you know? He feels like my real father still. It's funny; I've probably had more contact with Fergal Carrie than I ever did with my Dad. I still call him my Dad because it feels right. I'm so confused Stacey" Tony said. Stacey stood up and went to him. She took him by the hand

"Come on you! Let's go to bed before you get all morbid on me!" she said. Tony kissed her gently on the lips.

"That will never be the case with you around. You're the best thing that ever happened to me Stacey Boyd" he said. Stacey smiled and hugged him to her.

"I want to say something Tony. I promise that I will never mention it again. I made a huge mistake when I went back to Alex Woods" she started. Tony quickly interrupted her.

"Stace! There's no need" he pleaded.

"There is. I just want you to know that I'm sorry. I thought that I was doing the right thing. I was totally wrong. Sometimes you don't know what you have until you lose it. I love you Tony, I really do" she said. Tony kissed her back and then led her upstairs. Upstairs to their new bedroom.

Alex Woods watched outside as the light lit up the bedroom. He sat in his car opposite the house at number eighty-eight. Alex had watched as the couple had returned from the airport. It had been a routine spying exercise for Alex until the taxi had suddenly pulled up. An alert Alex could barely believe what he was seeing. All along he had hoped that Stacey would never return to Dublin. As the weeks had ticked by he had convinced himself that such would be the case. In his daydreaming Alex had imagined that one day he would follow her to England and that she would take him back. His very reason for stalking Tony was in the hope that he might find a way to kill him off without raising suspicion. Once Tony Lee was out of the picture, Alex figured that he could finally sell the business and retire.

Alex stared at the bedroom window and watched as the new white blinds were closed tight. He lowered the throbbing music on the radio and wound down the window. The evening air wafted into the car. Alex leaned his elbow on the open window and tried to think of a strategy. His Stacey was getting into bed with Tony Lee. He felt powerless. Every second was a wasted second. He tried to think of a way of stopping the inevitable happening. Sheer despair set in as he realised that for once he was not in control of his own destination. The girl who he still considered his girlfriend was with another man. Worst of all, she was with Tony Lee, his sworn enemy.

The light went out in the bedroom suddenly. Alex thumped his fist on the outside of the car door as his free hand hung loosely from the window. The other hand gripped the steering wheel in frustration.

"Bastard! Fucking bastard! I'm gonna kill him. I am, I'm going to fucking murder the swine. My Stacey-mine! She's my Stacey. Always was, always will be" he muttered deliberately.

Alex turned the key in the engine. He slammed the car into gear and released the hand brake. Suddenly he swerved out of his parked space, forcing an oncoming car to break with a loud squeal. The irate driver tooted the horn loudly in temper. Alex never even noticed. He shot off, unsure where he was going. His mind was swamped with thoughts and ideas about how to end Tony Lee's life.

Alex drove on in the evening traffic, swerving in and out of side streets. He shot up through Leinster Road, and out onto the main Rathmines Road. The traffic was heavier now. The giant clock over the town hall chimed out ten o'clock. He seemed to calm a little as he was forced to slow down. Alex eased his way up towards the canal bridge, which was one of the main streets into the city centre. The heavy traffic seemed to have a calming effect on him. Alex crossed the bridge, but then changed his mind. He was in no mood to hit Dublin City, not in the temper he was in.

A side street caught his eye. Alex turned off, and then did a u-turn. He shot back out into the main street forcing several cars to screech to a halt. Alex laughed out loud at the sight of the irate drivers tooting and yelling at him. "No balls, none of you! Why not keep going? Call my bluff! See who brakes first!" he screamed back. He was now completely lost in his own world. The normal, calming other side of his personality had vanished. Alex shot up along the canal in the direction of Leeson Street. The canal lay on his left, a row of shops and businesses on his right. Now and then some houses or flats would appear. Alex cruised now, trying to imagine some way of salvaging the situation. Suddenly he sat up at the wheel, now more alert than ever.

"Well, well, well!" he said with a grin. Sitting next to him in a car on the inside of the two-laned road was someone he recognised. Alex dropped off and slipped in behind the yellow vehicle. He followed the car for about two miles until it swung off to the right. They were in Donnybrook on the south side of the city. It was an affluent area, and Alex new the district well. The car ahead slowed as it turned off onto a leafy side-street. Alex watched the brake lights light up as the vehicle drew to a halt. Before the sole occupant could get out, Alex was at the driver's door. Already he knew that the man was alone. As the younger man removed his seatbelt, Alex hauled the startled man from the car.

"Remember me punk? Remember? What was it you called me? An areshole was it?" Alex snarled. By sheer coincidence he had come across the blonde man who laughed at him outside Tony Lee's place of work. While Alex had been losing the plot in traffic that day, the young man had made a laugh of him. Now it was Alex's turn for revenge.

Alex grabbed the startled man by both shoulders and aimed his right knee into the blonde man's solar-plexus. The younger man crumpled to the ground in pain. Alex dragged him back to his feet by the hair. He head-butted him in the nose and pushed him back hard against the car. The look of shock on the stranger's face amused Alex.

"By fuck are you in the wrong place at the wrong time" he growled.

"Look, I never meant any harm" the young blonde man panted. Alex barely heard him.

"Here dickhead, taste some knuckle!" he sneered, punching the man violently in the mouth. Blood oozed from the petrified man's nose and lips. The white shirt worn by the blonde man was now splattered in blood. Alex waded into him again, a flurry of punches stunning the petrified youth. The man's face was a mess, and Alex gave him one final punch to the stomach. The man collapsed face down onto the quiet street.

"You're lucky that I'm in a hurry, shithead. Have a nice day! If I was you I would stay well away from the cops. Don't forget, I know where you live now" Alex said. His breathing was a little heavy now, and he slowly returned to his car. The blonde man made one token effort to climb to his feet. His hands clutched at the ground vainly before passing out on the narrow road. Alex sped off; narrowly missing the man's outstretched fingers.

Tony Lee lay awake. It was the early hours of the morning and still dark outside. He shifted a little in the big bed. Stacey moaned and turned away from him on her side. Tony stared at the ceiling, a feeling of guilt nagging at him. He would have to tell Stacey the truth about what he had discovered. Yet he knew that once he did this, Stacey could never live in his home again. The temptation to say nothing was great. They could at last settle down to live a normal life, just like plenty of couples that they knew.

It had always been what Stacey craved most. A normal life. Children. A pretty home. They were simple things, but Stacey Boyd had always felt that she had missed out. Tony remembered the look of envy on Stacey's face every time that they went to a friend's christening, or when they saw a young child with their friends. Tony always knew what she was thinking. Stacey had dreamed of one day becoming a mother, but felt that she had missed out on the chance. She had wasted many years with Alex Woods, and also with Tony. Tony had often tried to reassure her that all was not lost.

"It's not too late Stace. We'll have kids someday" he would say. That was when Delores Lee was alive. At that time, Tony could never propose to her. They could never dream of settling down and having children. Now it was probably too late. In those heady days Stacey would always smile and say that it did not matter. Tony knew that it did. He was never very paternal back then. Life was too busy and hectic to consider becoming a father. The experience over the last few weeks had forced him to reconsider. He too dreamed of starting a family of his own, and he wanted desperately for it to be with Stacey.

Perhaps Stacey was correct though, Tony thought as he lay there quietly that morning. Maybe it was too late. They were both in their thirties. Marriage was probably still some distance away. Time was against them. And once he told Stacey the truth, she might even finish with him again.

Tony closed his eyes. Martin Lee suddenly appeared. His sunken face and distorted features stared back at Tony. It was no use. He could never go back to sleep now. Tony slipped quietly from the bedroom and tiptoed downstairs. Tony sat sipping coffee, trying to imagine how he could tell Stacey about his ordeal. He looked around the sparkling, high-spec kitchen and wondered again if it all had been in vain. Tony Lee had all but cleared out his bank account in an effort to finally win Stacey over.

"I should have left the bloody bedroom alone" he thought aimlessly. Tony Lee shook his head. It was an idle thought. He came to the conclusion that smashing down the bedroom wall was probably the finest thing that he had done in life. He had set Martin free from his concrete prison and afforded him a decent, humane burial. If he never achieved anything else in life, at least he would leave that fact behind him. Martin's burial was a testament to his belief in justice. And a big part of that was down to Jodie Callaghan.

Tony wandered out through the glass conservatory towards the new French doors which led to the back garden. The garden appeared a lot smaller now. Tony looked to the sky. If there was a heaven, Jodie was surely up there, he imagined. She would be exercising, stretching, maybe even jogging around. Tony grinned at the thought. He whispered a prayer for Jodie, before returning back to his bed.

Later that morning, Alex Woods parked his car outside Stacey's apartment. He had been to work early, but had left telling Michelle that he would again be away on business. Alex tried to figure out what had happened with Stacey and Tony Lee. He guessed that they had been in touch all along. Alex cursed himself for not realising what had been going on. His presumption that Stacey might never return to Ireland had been proved wrong.

"Fool! You damn fool! Those two took you for a mug! Well no more. This time it's war. This time there will be only one winner" he muttered.

He watched as first Gina and then Angie set off for work. Alex Woods fiddled with the key to the apartment which he had found in Angie's coat. One thing bothered him. Had Stacey stayed over in Tony Lee's house overnight, he wondered? Alex guessed that she had.

His plan was to enter the flat and hide out in the attic once again. He would spy on Stacey when she finally did return to the apartment. Never did he consider that she might decide to permanently live at eighty-eight St Oliver's Road. Stacey had often told Alex how much she detested Tony's old house.

Today was not some routine spying mission by Alex Woods. His plan had some substance. Alex figured that Stacey might now have a spare key for Tony Lee's address. If he could just get hold of that key, he could really take revenge on the couple. To murder Tony Lee in his home would indeed be very satisfying. Alex figured that if he let himself into number eighty-eight St. Oliver's Road with Stacey's spare key, he could possibly set a death-trap for Tony. Alex knew a little about electricity. His plot was to wire the new shower in the en-suite so that Tony would electrocute himself. During the renovations, Alex had spoken to a workman and discovered the extent of the work at Tony's home. Alex had decided that the accident would be blamed on the builders who had worked on Tony Lee's home. Weeks of surveillance on Tony's old house had given Alex plenty of time to work out several ways to end Tony's life.

Alex waited some twenty minutes before exiting his car. He moved quickly now, anxious to set up a base in the attic space. With him he had a sleeping bag, extra clothes, some food, a couple of bottles of drinking water, and some miscellaneous goods. Over the next few days he could come and go when the coast was clear. This time he was determined to wreak revenge on Tony Lee. This time he would hunt his adversary down until its conclusion.

Alex had no set time for his plan. It was still too early in his thinking process to have a cast -iron view of what to do. But he felt that Stacey's apartment held the key-literally. He would stake out the place and see what occurred. Something would present itself in the coming hours or days to forge an opportunity for the final revenge on Tony Lee. He had to believe that, for his own sanity. Something might be said by any one of the three girls to spark an alternate idea of revenge. If not, Alex would carry out his original plot.

He slipped silently into the hallway and listened intently for any sound. With the key still in his hand, Alex purposely closed the front door firmly. Still nothing. He was now sure that no one was at home, but still he tiptoed along the hallway checking each room. When he came to Stacey's old room, Alex felt a tingle of anticipation. Even if she was at home, Alex was not sure that he could turn back now. He carefully opened the bedroom door and peered inside. Her bedroom was as he remembered. Stacey's clothes and personal items were on show. It seemed to have a calming effect on Alex Woods.

Alex checked out the rest of the apartment. It was pretty much as he recalled it. There were no visual signs of a masculine presence, and a disappointed Alex opened the door to the attic space.

"So the girls have been on their best behaviour! No new boyfriends on the horizon!" he mumbled as he hauled his frame upwards into the loft space. Alex placed his sleeping bag directly over Stacey's bed. He peeped down through the tiny hole to the bedroom below.

"Perfect! Now all we do is wait for dear Stacey to come back home!" he thought.

Alex climbed back down into the apartment and looked around. He sat on the armchair and considered if he had forgotten anything.

"Let me see. Food, check. Water, okay. Phone and torch, yes. Sleeping bag and clothes, okay" he said quietly. Alex considered if he might need something to read. He could play games on his phone to pass the time, but it rankled with him that he might get bored. He would be spending a lot of time in the attic space over the next couple of days. It might take a while to come up with a master plan.

Alex decided to slip out and buy something to read. Perhaps a book or some magazine might suffice. All that he could find in the apartment were women's literature and glossy gossip publications. They certainly were not to his taste. Alex closed the attic door and set off for the nearby newsagents. It was less than five minutes away. He was back in the small car park in minutes, checking for anything unusual.

If Stacey was going to return that morning, it would probably be by taxi. He noted that her car was nowhere to be seen. Alex figured that she would be in no hurry to leave Tony Lee's home. He made a quick call to work, telling Michelle that he might be away all day.

Alex slipped quietly back inside the flat. It was as he had left it. He carried a paperback thriller and some sports magazines under his arm. He decided that he would have a quick cup of coffee before retiring to the loft. It might be his only warm beverage that day. Upstairs he had a basin for his toiletry needs, but he would have a coffee and then use the bathroom before leaving the apartment for his base camp in the loft.

Alex switched on the kettle and then checked the fridge for milk. He toyed with the thought of switching on the television, but decided that it was too risky. If Stacey returned home unexpectedly, he had to be ready to move.

Alex sat down and haphazardly browsed through a golf magazine. Lately it had become one of his favourite television sports, although he had barely played the game over the last year. Suddenly he heard a noise. He jumped to his feet, spilling the magazines onto the carpet. He tried to pinpoint the sound. It appeared to be coming from inside the apartment rather than the front door. Alex switched off the kettle and listened. He heard a door open.

A startled Angie O'Rourke stared back at him. She had come from the bathroom, holding her head in her hands in pain.

"Alex?" she said questioningly. She looked at him in surprise, not wanting to believe what she was seeing. Alex stood silent, frozen on the spot. His brain tried to engage, desperately seeking an explanation to why she was there.

"How...how did you get in?" she asked. Alex tried to smile.

"I want to surprise Stacey. We're getting back together. Did she tell you? We talked over the phone last night" Alex said, his words disjointed and erratic. Angie shook her head.

"You're wrong. Stacey's with Tony. He asked her to marry him yesterday at the airport. How the hell did you get in here Alex? I want you to leave now!" Angie said, daring to raise her voice. Alex took in the shock news. Stacey was to marry Tony Lee. He felt his blood boil with rage. His brain sought answers, assurances and logic. Things did not sound right. It was never meant to be like this.

"What are you doing here? I saw you leave for work" Alex raged. He stepped towards Angie in a threatening manner. Angie looked terrified.

"I...We went out for a drink last night, myself and Gina. We were celebrating the engagement. I might have had one too many. I had to return to the flat to get sick. My stomach was upset Alex. I'm sorry, I'll go now. I should be all right. I feel a little better" she said.

Angie's main objective now was to escape. She sensed danger. If she could just get away, she could phone the police on her mobile phone. Angie backed away. Her handbag was still in the bathroom. She tried to think clearly. The handbag did not matter. She could use a public phone, or even call to a neighbouring flat. The main thing was to get out. Angie thought to scream. She feared it might panic Alex into drastic action. Angie O'Rourke continued to back away, keeping her eyes fixed on Alex Woods at all times. She inched along towards the exit, down the corridor, getting nearer and nearer to safety. Alex followed her at a steady pace, eyeing her, trailing her. He seemed unconcerned that she was escaping, mimicking each step she took with one of his own.

When she reached the front door, Angie felt for the latch behind her. She dare not take her eyes off Alex. The door latch was high up, almost head height. She fumbled behind her again as Alex came nearer and nearer.

"Get back Alex, this is not funny. If you don't leave quietly now, there will be big trouble. I mean it. Go now and nothing will be said, I promise" she stammered. Alex smiled and leaned his right palm on the front door, just over her head.

"It's too late Angie, I can't trust you. Just as I could never trust Jodie, or Philip" he whispered. She could feel his breath on her face. Angie heard his words, but they did not make sense. They were jumbled, irregular. The names jumped out at her. Why did he mention Jodie Callaghan and Philip Westbourne, she wondered? Slowly a terrifying thought entered her head. It was incredible, unfathomable, preposterous.

Just as she tried to take in his meaning, Alex placed a hand around her slender neck. He pressed slowly and firmly, tighter and tighter by the second. Angie's eyes began to bulge. She suddenly reacted, grappling with his hand with both arms. He pinned one of her arm back against the door with his free hand. A spluttering, choking noise came from Angie's throat. Her contorted face stared back at him in disbelief. Slowly her eyes closed. Her body gave up the struggle. Alex kept her pinned to the door until all of the fight had evaporated. He could smell the stale alcohol on her mouth. Then he released his hand and watched as she sank to the floor.

"Bitch! Fucking bitch! Why did she have to spoil everything? Think Alex, think. We have to move fast now!" he said, pacing the hallway. Alex looked at the crumpled body lying behind the front door. He sought a quick solution, but nothing sprang to mind.

"I have to get that bitch out of here. My Stacey will be here soon. I can't have her finding that drunken dead bitch" he muttered.

It was broad daylight outside. Alex decided that he had to move Angie's body. He could bury her later that night, but it was too risky to leave her in the apartment. A kernel of an idea entered his head. He remembered the sleeping bag in the attic. Perhaps he could somehow smuggle Angie out to his car. Most people in the apartments were at work. His car was not very far from the main entrance. Alex decided to back his car right up to the main door in the foyer of the building. It was a no parking zone, but he would only be a couple of minutes.

The first thing that he did was to retrieve the sleeping bag. He unzipped the side all of the way down and hauled Angie's limp body onto the quilted sleeping bag. He placed her head to the bottom, so that her feet would be to the top of the brown sleeping bag, which he then zipped up all of the way. Alex fetched a length of twine from a drawer and tied the top of the sleeping bag roughly, shoving Angie's feet inside. He then retrieved Angie's handbag from the bathroom and took it with him to back his car up to the main entrance. Alex hid the black handbag behind the driver's seat before quickly returning to the building.

The elevator groaned as its doors slammed shut. As he again reached the apartment, Alex checked that everything was as he had found it. He entered the bathroom from where Angie had suddenly emerged. There was nothing out of place. Alex dragged the sleeping bag through the open front door and then went to press the button for the elevator.

When the lift arrived, Alex used one of his shoes to stop the doors closing. He then hauled the sleeping bag into the lift and went to lock up the apartment. Deftly he then slipped his shoe back on, breathing a little easier again.

"Drinking was always your downfall Angie!" he sneered as the elevator jolted shut. He hoisted the heavy sleeping bag onto his shoulder and waited. Even if he met someone now as he exited the elevator, he would be past them before they realised that anything was amiss.

The doors slid open and Alex smiled with relief. He had got away with it again. He lowered the brown quilted sleeping bag into the open boot and slammed it shut. Alex drove away, happy that he had won another small battle.

"No one messes with me. No one!" he grinned as he cruised slowly through the late morning traffic. Alex returned to him home in Blackrock by lunchtime. He made coffee and considered what he should do with Angie O'Rourke, whose body now lay lifeless in the boot of his white Ford Mondeo car.

Stacey stirred in bed. She looked around, bleary-eyed from her long sleep. Tony lay quietly beside her. She stretched and yawned, forcing him to stir. "That's the best sleep that I've had in ages!" Stacey said. Tony opened his eyes slowly. He smiled on seeing her beside him.

"That makes a change! The last time that you were here you were freezing all night, remember?" he said, kissing her gently on the lips. Stacey Boyd smiled and nodded.

"Yeah, and you had a nightmare! Do you still have those dreams?" she asked. Tony tried to retain a happy demeanour.

"No, not so much lately. Come to think of it, it's ages since I've had a bad dream. What about you? How come you haven't been sleeping well? Did you miss me?" he asked, cosying up to her. Stacey kissed him again.

"Of course I missed you, but it wasn't that! I was up and down all night checking on my Mam. You have no idea what a relief it is that she's doing okay" Stacey said.

"Should we get up and have some breakfast?" Tony said. Stacey's eyes met his. "Let's not. Why not just stay in bed for a while. It's not often that we get the chance" she replied.

Alex lifted the covered body of Angie O'Rourke from the boot. His house was not overlooked by neighbours, so he took his time. The front door stood open, and Alex negotiated the steps up the house carefully, with Angie's limp body flung across his right shoulder inside the brown sleeping bag. Once inside the house, he dropped her body casually onto the leather sofa.

"Whew Angie! You're putting on a bit of weight there! Better lay off the burgers for a while, eh?" he said, catching his breath. He undid the string on the sleeping bag and then flopped down on the armchair opposite.

"I'm tempted to bury you right here in the garden Angie, but that would be sloppy. I'm afraid that it will have to be in The Dublin Mountains again! You know, that place is like an open graveyard! I reckon that there are all sorts of criminals buried up there! Once you find the right spot, it's as safe as houses! Now take my Isobel. She's buried there, and not once have I heard her complaining!" Alex said with a hearty laugh. He stared at the crumpled heap opposite him. It was just another tiresome inconvenience that he would have to deal with.

Now the reality of what he had done hit home. He began to consider who would miss Angie O'Rourke. Obviously Gina and Stacey would, plus her friends at work. He recalled that both Angie's parents were still alive, so her family would question her whereabouts also.

"Damn! I should have thought this through a bit better" he muttered.

Alex paced the room, occasionally stopping to sip on his cup of coffee.

"She would have left a note if she was going anywhere, but where would she go? At least a note would buy me some time though. By the time the police began looking for her, the trail would be cold" Alex thought quietly. He began to delve into Angie's black handbag, and quickly found a little notebook. Alex scanned through it. It contained phone numbers and addresses.

"Ha! Angie, your handwriting is appalling! I could easily copy that" he sneered. Alex thought for a few moments before pulling a pen from Angie's handbag. Tearing a single page from the yellow-covered notebook, Alex began to write in a thoughtful manner.

"Gina\Stacey, feeling very down. Missed work today. Thought that I might go home to stay with my folks for a while. Please don't worry or phone. Will get in touch when I'm feeling better. I want to get off the booze for a while. It's ruining my life. Love, Angie xxx"

Alex examined the short note. He was pleased with his handiwork.

"Yeah, that sums you up Angie, an old broken-down drunk! Tomorrow I can phone your job and say that you're very ill. That will buy me some time. I'll pretend that I'm your father. Yeah, that will satisfy your workmates for a while" he whispered. Once again Alex felt that he was back in control.

"I'll be right back, darling! I have to drop this note off at your flat. Don't go anywhere, you hear?" he cackled.

Alex drove away in his car, first making sure to lock up properly. Once Stacey had not come back to the apartment, he would be all right, Alex reckoned. If she had returned, that he would simply slip the note in through the letterbox. Either Stacey or Gina would find it anyway.

Alex rang the doorbell to the apartment and quickly moved out of sight. He waited a few moments before returning to the front door. The key turned easily in the lock, and he quickly slipped inside.
"Good, I like things done perfect. By the time they realise that old Angie is missing, the cops will presume that she was depressed. It will be weeks before a formal search begins. They'll be dredging The Liffey and The Grand Canal for her fat body!" Alex cackled. He placed the note on the coffee table and double-checked the apartment once more. Alex noticed the literature that he had purchased lying on the floor. It shocked him to think that he had overlooked such an obvious piece of evidence.
"Fuck Alex, you're slipping!" he whispered, angry with himself. Alex then remembered the stuff that he had left in the attic. In his hurry to move Angie's body, he had forgotten his other personal belongings.
"Come on man, these are stupid, childish mistakes" he muttered, irritated at what he saw as a lack of professionalism. He gathered up everything, throwing them into a plastic bin liner. Slowly his confidence returned, forgiving his earlier carelessness.
"Good! Another perfect job!" he thought, closing the front door behind him.

Tony Lee looked at his watch. He did a double-take on the time.
"Shit! Stacey, it's after twelve o'clock! Wake up!" he said, gently shaking her. Stacey slowly awoke, a startled look on her face.
"Why? What's wrong? Where have we to go?" she mumbled. Tony grinned at her drowsy expression. Her blonde hair was tossed and her eyes were barely open.
"Well, nowhere I suppose, but don't you want to get settled back at your flat? I mean, you want to be there when Gina and Angie arrive back from work, don't you?" Tony reasoned. Stacey yawned and snuggled back down under the duvet.
"But I'm comfy here! There's no hurry Tony, honest!" she said, closing her eyes again. Tony Lee grinned and slowly lay back down.

"You don't really have to go you know. You could simply just move in here. Tell the girls that you changed your mind" he said, slipping an arm beneath the duvet. Stacey wriggled and let out a knowing laugh.

"Stop you! You've taken advantage of me twice already!" Stacey said. The smile slowly vanished from her face.

"No Tony, I'll go home to my apartment all right. Let's take our time to set up home, yeah? We'll be together soon, okay? For now though, just give me a half-an-hour's rest. I'll get up then, I promise" she said. Tony turned and lay on his back. He had never stayed in bed so late in his life. In a matter of moments, Stacey was snoring gently again. Tony figured that it was all of those weeks of looking after her mother that had taken its toll. He was pleased to finally have Stacey back beside him. Yet something continued to nag away at his conscience. He had to come clean with Stacey, and soon. She might never forgive him if he kept his dark secret much longer.

CHAPTER THIRTY

HILLCREST

Alex returned to his home in Blackrock. He eased his car slowly along the white pebble stones, observing all around him. He liked things to run smoothly. Soon it would be dark. He could think about disposing of Angie's body. Although he had not selected a burial place, Alex was pretty confident that he would find a suitable spot. He sat in his car now with the engine turned off as he plotted his next move.

"Yes Angie, it's the mountains for you I'm afraid! You see, where the criminals go wrong is that they don't bury the bodies deep enough. Perhaps they don't care if the bodies are found. I do you see. Without a body, there is no crime. That's the golden rule in my book. Who's to say that you did not simply disappear to start a new life? Even a fat old alco like you might find someone to love! Let's say that's what happened to you Angie, just for the sake of romance. You were on your way home to stay with your folks, feeling a bit sorry for yourself! You met this guy on a bus. The two of you got talking and one thing led to another. He persuaded you to begin a new life say, in Spain. Gina and Stacey would soon tire of looking for you. The police have nothing to go on. End of story!" Alex said with a self-satisfied grin. He climbed from his car and slammed the door.

"I like a nice happy ending! I'm not all bad!" he sniggered.

Angie O'Rourke woke up slowly. Complete darkness engulfed her. She began to panic as she clawed at the dark sleeping bag. It was difficult to breathe. She could feel that her feet were free. Slowly she remembered Alex Woods at her apartment. Terror filled her head as she realised that he had tried to kill her. Angie's first thought was to scream, but then she realised that it would alert Alex. It was best to try to free herself initially.

She started to struggle from the tight sleeping bag in a worm-like manner. In her effort to be free, she rolled from the sofa onto the floor. All of the time Angie listened out for any noise, any sound, that would indicate Alex's presence. She was encouraged by the silence around her. Still she wriggled, inching her way slowly backwards to freedom. Her blue jeans emerged slowly from the sleeping bag, and then her lower torso. All of the time Angie listened for any noise that might signal her captor was returning.

Alex opened the front door and strode deliberately towards the sitting room. The window blinds were drawn down almost all of the way. The darkened room was large, with almost too much furniture about. Tom Woods had a liking for antiques, and his large collection filled the house. Alex planned to eventually sell off his father's items, and replace them with things more in keeping with his bachelor lifestyle.

Angie could hear her captor approaching. Her mind was spinning. Inside the sleeping bag she had drifted in and out of consciousness. Now she was alert. Suddenly she remembered Alex talking about killing his wife. Had she imagined it, she wondered? Her alert brain told her no. It was real. His chilling words ran through her head, terrorising her. She could hear the footsteps approaching. It was too late to climb back inside the musty-smelling sleeping bag. She flung the brown sleeping bag aside and breathed in fresh air. By now Alex was at the open door. His face looked disbelievingly at Angie as she struggled to her feet. "I thought that you were...I thought that I had killed you" he stammered. Angie stepped backwards away from him.

"I don't want trouble. Let me go. I won't say anything" she said quietly, panting for breath. All of the time Angie's eyes were scanning the room for a weapon. Alex advanced menacingly, stepping over the quilted sleeping bag. Angie backed away further, knocking over a brass lamp. Alex displayed an evil grin as he watched the glass shade shatter on the floor.

"That was one of my Dad's favourite pieces Angie. Lucky for you I don't share his appreciation for the finer things in life. My tastes are much simpler, like the love of a good woman. You didn't help there Angie, did you? After all that I did for you, you slapped me in the face. Yeah, I sorted Philip out for you, didn't I? Yeah Angie, it was me who ran him over. It was me who killed him in the shower. But what thanks did I get, eh? I'll bet that you encouraged Stacey to get back with that Lee fellow, didn't you? Don't deny it Angie, you're a drunken bitch, that's all that you'll ever amount to" Alex said. His caustic words sounded ever more threatening as he backed her into a corner.

Angie shook her head continuously. She was taking in his words, but still trying to plan some way of escaping. Slowly she continued to back off until she could go no further. Her body shook with fear and shock at what she was hearing, and what was happening to her. Angie O'Rourke felt the wall behind her. It felt cold and final. There was nowhere else to go.

Alex made a grab for her. She screamed with all of her might. Alex laughed as he gripped her by the throat with both hands. She could feel the rawness of her neck from the previous assault.

"Scream all you want bitch! This is my Dad's home. There's no one here. You see, out here where civilised people live, we like a bit of room! The next house is almost a mile away!" he said in a sarcastic tone. Angie's brain was in overdrive. There had to be a way of escaping. She saw her only opportunity in a flash.

Instantly she brought her left knee up between Alex's legs. It was something that Jodie Callaghan had thought her. Jodie had been forever talking about self-defence, and what a girl should do in certain circumstances.

Alex crumpled to his knees, his hands releasing his grip on Angie. She fled in a blind panic, unsure where she was going. She found herself in the hallway. The front door was within feet of her. Nothing else was in her sights. Her eyes homed in on the large wooden black door. She had to get away. The door was her only hope.

"You cow, you fucking fat cow! Oh, you'll pay for this Angie, never fear! Come here bitch!" Alex screamed. She could hear his footsteps behind her. It scarcely mattered. She was by the door now, fiddling for the latch.

"It's locked, the frigging door is locked" she said, her voice trembling. All of the time Alex's footsteps grew louder. She looked around in panic. He was within yards of her. Angie felt her heart thump even louder. She felt that it would explode in her chest.

I suppose that I had better give the girls a call. I have no key to get in" Stacey said with a loud sigh. Tony Lee laughed from across the table.

"What are you like Stacey Boyd? You are the most disorganised person that I have ever met!" he replied. Stacey looked embarrassed.

"Well, I packed in a hurry when I left for England, didn't I? The key might be in my suitcase somewhere" she countered. Tony grinned back at her.

"Yeah, or in Wolverhampton, or in your car. Or you might have lost it anywhere in between!" he said mockingly. Stacey looked at him haughtily.

"I parked my car in the underground car park in work for safety. It can't be in my car, because I know for a fact that I had my set of latch key after that" she replied. Tony shook his head again and smiled. Stacey's way of justifying her actions always amused him. She had an answer for everything, and nothing was ever her fault.

"Okay, why take your key off your key ring? You have your car keys, don't you?" Tony asked earnestly. Stacey looked a little embarrassed.

"For safety. I knew that I would need it when I returned to Dublin. I think that I put it somewhere safe in the pocket of one of my jeans when I left the flat" she replied. Tony looked to the ceiling and suppressed the laughter.

"I despair for you Stacey, I really do! Oh, just phone Gina, I'll go with you by cab" he said. Stacey looked at her watch and thought for a moment.

"No, Gina can't take calls at work. Angie will be on her lunch break. I'll call her" she answered. Tony stood up and strolled to the window. Tomorrow he would return to work. He wanted to find the time to tell Stacey everything. The longer he put things off, the worst it got.

"It's ringing" Stacey whispered. Tony stared out into the back garden. It looked a picture with the new lawn and the shed varnished in a dark brown colour. The walled garden had been painted white, and a wooden trellis ran all of the way around the garden. Tony planned to grow plants, and new shrubs already adorned the edges of the rejuvenated garden.

Angie darted for the stairway as Alex made a desperate grab for her. She took the stairs two by two, her heart pounding in her chest. Alex ran behind her, a confident look on his face.

"There's no way out Angie, trust me. It's just you and me" he said. Angie made for the bathroom and slammed the door. The tiny, flimsy bolt looked like it would offer little protection from her assailant. She forced the bolt across anyway, and stood with her back to the door. Tears streamed down her face as her eyes scanned the square room. The window was tiny, and if she went to call for help, Alex would surely smash in the door. There was nothing to use as a barricade, and so she stood trembling with her weight behind the cream door.

Suddenly she heard a phone ring. She recognised the ringtone too. It was her mobile phone. Angie's trembling right hand reached down to the pocket on her blue jeans. Her phone had been in her pocket all of the time. She pulled it out and stared at the screen. Stacey's name lit up the white screen. Angie was barely able to believe her luck. Alex realised what was happening. He shouldered the door with all of his might. Angie began to cry again as she watched the small silver bolt come loose. She pressed back hard against the door.

Angie's index finger flicked on the green button to accept the call.

"Angie, it's Stacey. Listen I'm..." Stacey had barely got the first few words out when she was interrupted by her beleaguered friend.

"Stacey? I'm at Alex's father's house. Please call..."

Alex grabbed the phone and flung it down the stairs as he burst through the door. Angie stumbled back against the white bath. She fell to the floor cowering, her hands held up for protection.

"Bitch! Who phoned you? Who was it? Another boyfriend? I wouldn't be surprised! You like to put it about, don't you Angie?" he said in a mocking voice. Angie could take no more. She began to weep uncontrollably, fearing that her final chance of escape had vanished.

"Strange! Either Angie is drunk, or she's gone completely nuts! Listen to this Tony, I said hello, and before I could say any more, Angie said that she was in Alex Woods' home. No wait, she said that she was in his father's house! What the hell does she mean?" Stacey asked. Tony walked casually over to her and glanced at the blank mobile phone.

"It's gone dead. Phone her again Stace. She's in one of her giddy moods!" he said. Stacey dialled Angie's number again, but got no response.

"There's no tone. Either she's switched off or her battery needs charging" Stacey said. Tony chuckled and sat down next to her.

"She will be having a good laugh at your expense! This is her way of welcoming you home!" he replied. Stacey shook her head.

"No, you're wrong. She sounded...well, panicky. It was as if she was afraid of something" Stacey said. Tony looked bored with the conversation.

"Aw, come on now, this is stupid. I mean, what would she be doing with Alex Woods?" Tony grinned. Then an awful thought occurred to him.

"You don't think that Angie and Alex have, you know, hit it off?" he asked. Stacey looked horrified. She phoned her friend for the third time. There was still no answer.

"No way! She wouldn't do that! Tony, I get a terrible feeling about this. I'm going over to the flat. Something's not right" Stacey said.

Tony pointed out that she had no key to get in.

"Well, I'm gonna get my car and drive out there to Alex's father's house. Hey! I'll bet that he's living there now. His father died, so what's to stop him moving in?" Stacey said.

For the first time, Tony Lee looked concerned.

"You don't think that she's really with him, do you? Perhaps they are going out together and they've had an argument" Tony said. Stacey stared back at him, daring to believe that he might be right.

"Oh my God! What if they're fighting about me? We should phone the police!" Stacey said in a panicky voice. Tony chuckled nervously.

"Don't be silly! What would we tell them? It could still be some silly prank, dreamed up by Gina and Angie. Phone Gina and see does she answer" Tony suggested.

Stacey did as he asked. Again she got no reply. Stacey jumped to her feet.

"I'm getting a taxi to my work. I'm picking up my car and then I'm going to drive out there. I have a horrible feeling that something's not right. Are you coming with me?" Stacey said.

Tony Lee thought for a moment.

"Well, I'm certainly not letting you go there alone. Do you know where this house is?" he replied. Stacey nodded several times.

"Yeah, that is, I hope that I can remember. The house was called Hillcrest. It's on one of those posh roads. I went there with Alex when we first started dating. He drove, but I'm sure that I can remember where it is" she answered.

Alex dragged Angie O'Rourke back downstairs and flung her onto the sofa. As she fell backwards, he slapped her hard on the face.

"Sit there bitch and don't move. You're more trouble than you're worth. No wonder no man would put up with you, you drunken cow!" he said, his eyes wide now with anger. Angie sobbed into her hands. She tried to clear her brain of fear. It was time to try and think rationally. She needed to stay alert, just in case she had a second opportunity to run.

"I...I'm sorry Alex, really I am. I promise to behave. Please don't hurt me" she said, her voice straining almost beyond recognition.

"Hurt you? Didn't you hear me fucker? You are dead-dead, do you get it? I'm gonna bury you where no one will ever find you. Fuck! Why did you have to come home? It was Stacey and that Tony Lee bastard that I wanted. You are just small fry. You are only a bleedin' nuisance. Once it's dark you'll be dead, just like Isobel, and just like that pervert Harry Brand. I killed him for you, did you know that? Hung the bastard from a tree I did. I hammered that Philip swine too, but what thanks did I get? None, you ungrateful cow!" he screamed.

Alex stood over her, yelling at the top of his voice. She knew that she had to calm him down. Her brain began to clear. Angie put a plan in place which might benefit her in the near future. She would gain as much information as possible in case she had a chance to pass it on. Even if she did not survive, she would make sure that Alex Woods saw justice.

"What...What did you do to Philip? What do you mean?" she said in a whimper. Alex looked at her as if he was seeing her for the first time.

"Oh pure innocent Angie! You really don't get it, do you? I killed Isobel so that I could be with Stacey. I would have murdered my own father, except that two assholes messed up my plans. Jesus, you were even going to be part of my alibi! When I heard about Philip knocking you about, I genuinely felt sorry for you. What a fool I was! This is how you repay me. You help Stacey get back with Tony Lee!" Alex said angrily.

"No Alex, I don't even like him. I told Stacey to marry you, remember? I was to be the bridesmaid at your wedding. I was as shocked as you were at the time. I pleaded with her to go through with it" Angie said convincingly. Alex stared at her, wondering if he should believe her.

"Yeah, she let everyone down that day. Her parents, the guests, but above all, me. Well, she has to pay, you hear Angie? She must pay" Alex said. Angie nodded.

"You're right, for every action there is a reaction" she said, plucking the saying from her memory. Alex leaned nearer to her.

"No Angie, for every action there is a consequence" he replied. She nodded again, lost for words. Her body was trembling. She dare not take her eyes off of him.

"Tell...tell me about Harry. What did you do?" she said, surprising herself with her forthrightness. Alex reeled his neck in. He turned around and sat opposite her on the big armchair. He said nothing for a few moments, lost in his own private world.

"I suppose that I can tell you. You're gonna die anyway" he said coldly.

"I think that it's this turn here" Stacey said. Tony was becoming bored. They had been driving around Blackrock for almost an hour.

"Why don't we just go back to the apartment Stace? Angie's probably home by now. Anyway, what will we say when we knock on his door? Alex Woods won't be too happy to see us" Tony said. Stacey was almost too busy finding her way to listen. She peered inside every driveway in the hope of recognising something familiar.

"Alex should be at work. We won't knock if his car is in the driveway. I'm just curious" Stacey said. Tony blew out air from his lips at a rapid rate.

"Jeeezz Stace, that's just great! We come all of this way, and we don't even call to the door! This is crazy! Look, I'll try her number again. If there's still no reply, I think we should go. The traffic is going to be mad at this time of the day. We really should be getting back. On top of that, I'm back in work in the morning" Tony said. He dialled Angie's mobile again. There was still no ringing tone.

"There it is! That's the house right there! Look! Hillcrest!" Stacey said. Tony looked up at the large gates. To the side, the house name "Hillcrest" was written in black letters into the white wall.

"Phew! They really have got a few bob! This place must be worth a couple of million!" he said. Stacey drove slowly through the open gates, and up along the winding track.

"Are you sure about this Stace? Perhaps we should park outside" Tony Lee said; now looking worried for the first time. Stacey grinned without taking her eyes off the winding driveway ahead.

"It's all right, if his car is there I'll turn back" she replied confidently. Tony sat upright in his seat. He felt uneasy at what they were doing. His eyes were on full alert as they passed the heavy bushes on either side of the long narrow drive.

"So you see, Harry was easy. He was scared shitless! Hardly a man at all! What a wimp! He was sobbing when I strung him up-sobbing like a baby! Jodie on the other hand, she had balls!" Alex said with a faint grin.

"Jodie? You...you murdered Jodie Callaghan?" a distraught Angie asked.

CHAPTER THIRTY-ONE

SHOWDOWN AT BLACKROCK

Alex went through his catalogue of murders and schemes as Angie listened with a total sense of shock. It was hard for her to fathom that a seemingly normal man was in fact a monster. Alex sounded proud of what he had done, and almost justified each episode as if he had been left with no alternative. A disconsolate Angie felt more vulnerable than ever. Her own death now appeared imminent rather than a possibility. There was something unerringly brutal and inevitable about each death that Alex described.

"You killed Jodie, but why?" Angie asked as Alex explained again with relish about the hit and run. She wanted to keep him talking for as long as possible.

"Don't you see Angie? She took sides against Stacey. She betrayed her pal by stealing her boyfriend. It's obvious that she had to pay the price" Alex replied. Angie knew it was dangerous to challenge his views, but figured some mind games might confuse him.

"But if Jodie had lived, she would have stayed with Tony. Stacey and Tony would never have got back together if that was the case. That means that you and Stacey might have had a chance" Angie reasoned. Alex looked confused. He tried to speak, but her words mixed up his thinking.

"Shut up bitch! It doesn't work that way! People have to pay for their sins! You can't wait around for things to happen. Sometimes you have to take action!" Alex yelled.

Angie could tell that she was having an effect. She decided to push on.

"You're not God. You can't decide who lives or dies. You messed up by killing Jodie. It just brought Stacey and Tony closer together" she said defiantly. Alex saw red. He dashed across the room and grabbed her violently.

446

"Shut up! Shut up!" he screamed, shaking her with all of his might. Angie defied him again.

"No! It's the truth. Just as you messed up by coming to the flat today. The police will be out looking for me. They'll get you Alex, you'll see. They know where you live" Angie said. It was too much for Alex to take. He released his grip with his right hand and smashed a punch into her face. Angie's head shot backwards. She watched as Alex Woods' face faded into blackness. He pushed her limp body back against the sofa and stood over her.

"See bitch? No one gets the better of Alex Woods" he said, panting for breath.

Outside, Stacey quickly reversed the car back around the bend in the long driveway.

"He's home, that's his car. What do we do now?" she said. Tony shrugged indifferently.

"Go home? Like we should have done in the first place?" he said with a smug smile. Stacey shook her head several times.

"No Tony, something's not right. You didn't hear Angie's voice. She was scared. She definitely said that she was at Alex's father's house. This is too weird to just ignore it. I mean, Alex is at home on a work day. Something doesn't add up" Stacey said. Tony exhaled breath slowly from his puffed cheeks.

"Well, maybe they have something going on together! I mean, it is possible" he reasoned. Stacey was not about to be fobbed off.

"Tony, for Christ sake listen to me! Her phone is dead. Why did she not call me back that time? He's done something to her, I just know it. I'm calling the cops!" Stacey replied firmly. A look of despair spread across Tony's face.

"Ah that's ridiculous Stace! Look, I'll tell you what. I'll go and have a quick glance around the back of the house. It's a dull day. I'll make sure not to be seen. What if I sneak in and have a look around? I'll peep in the windows and see if I can see anything amiss. You go and park the car outside on the road, just in case he wants to leave in a hurry" Tony said. Stacey looked at him, taking in his words carefully.

"Okay, it's a deal. Only just look around mind. Don't go playing the super hero!" she replied.

Suddenly Tony's phone rang. He reached into his jacket pocket and retrieved the large black iphone. He saw Erik's name light up the screen.

"Hello Tony? You'll never guess what happened. Old Ted Matthews, you know the guy in administration? He's only popped his clogs over the weekend! That means his job is up for grabs! I reckon that either you or me will be in the frame. Great news or what?" Erik said in a jocular tone. Tony shook his head wryly.

"Jesus Erik, a man has died! That's an awful way of looking at things!"Tony replied.

"Yeah, I know, but it's good news for someone!" Erik said, his rumbling laugh starting in the pit of his stomach. Tony tried to suppress the infectious laughter.

"Yeah, if you say so! I never liked the old fart either! Listen, I have to go, I'm doing a bit of detective work with Stacey!" Tony said with a rueful grin. Stacey shook his arm in protest.

"Don't say anything!" she mouthed silently. Tony Lee could hardly resist.

"Listen to this Erik. You know that chap that I told you about? Alex Woods, the fellow that Stacey nearly married? Well Stacey reckons that he's holding Angie O'Rourke captive in his father's house out in Blackrock! And guess where we are now? Right outside the bleedin' place!" Tony laughed. Stacey looked cross. Tony realised that he might have overstepped the mark.

"Sorry Erik, I have to go. Inspector Boyd is looking very annoyed" Tony said. He ended the call and slipped his mobile phone back inside his grey jacket pocket.

"What?" Tony said to Stacey, trying to look as innocent as possible.

Erik Ngombiti sat silently looking at his computer screen. Something about what Tony had said played on his mind. He decided to Google the name of Alex Woods' out of sheer curiosity. After a number of searches, Erik narrowed it down to one man. His mouth went dry. He moved his seat closer to the computer. Erik could scarcely believe what he was seeing. The hair on the back of his neck tingled as he read the profile. Next, Erik googled Wood's Motors. A photo of Alex Woods popped up straight away.

"Oh my sweet Lord!" Erik whispered.

Alex Woods walked idly around the room. He had tied Angie's hands and legs with some rope. Once it was dark, he could finally be rid of her forever. He stopped to examine his security camera, focussed on the grounds outside. Alex knew of Muggser's and Burrener's fate, so was less concerned of late with his safety. He had read the story of the stabbing in the local paper with great relish.

Suddenly Alex noticed a shadowy figure on the camera. There was someone to the rear of the house near a window. Alex used the state-of-the-art button to zoom in on the character. He could scarcely believe his luck. The man bore a striking resemblance to Tony Lee.

"Well, well, well! So that's who was calling you Angie! Well done! Two for the price of one! Today might just well be the best day of my life!" he sneered.

Alex moved quickly now. He grabbed a golf club from his storage press in the hallway and placed it by the front door. Angie O'Rourke woke to find herself bound and gagged. Her arms were tied tight behind her back, while a strip of common plaster covered her mouth. A piece of blue twine bound both of her legs together as she lay lengthways on the leather sofa in the sitting room. Alex quietly checked that the back door was locked. He then slipped silently out through the front door, grabbing the golf club as he went.

A meeting was scheduled for five-thirty at Erik's job. It was his usual time to finish work, but staff were being asked to stay behind for a briefing. Erik guessed it would be to do with Mr. Matthews' death, and to advertise the promotion position which was now vacant. Such gatherings had happened before, and the company liked to move fast to fill vacancies at the top level. Erik knew that he could not hang around. Not this evening. He sought a word with his immediate boss, Mr. Carrington.
"Erik, you realise that you will be ruling yourself out of the running by not attending?" Mr. Carrington said crossly. Erik desperately wanted the higher position, something that he had worked for since joining the firm.
"If that's the way it has to be sir. I have a prior engagement as I have already explained. This is something that cropped up over the weekend" Erik replied. A stern-looking Mr. Carrington was far from impressed.
"Staff should be available at all times in a crisis, Mr. Ngombiti" Mr. Carrington retorted. Erik noted that Mr. Carrington had suddenly gone from first name terms to his surname. He suspected that his shot at promotion had already vanished. Erik looked disappointed, but was now resigned to losing out. He valued his job, but hardly considered the matter of promotion a crisis. Erik knew that he had to act on Tony Lee's behalf. That was his number one goal.
"I'm sorry again Mr. Carrington. I'll be in tomorrow" he said, grabbing his jacket.
"Yes, quite" Mr Carrington muttered, turning his back on Erik.

Alex Woods crept quietly along the side of the house. He had identified the exact spot where Tony Lee was lurking. Alex inched along right up to the back garden. By now the light was fading fast. He could see the shadowy figure peering through one of the kitchen windows. Alex gripped the golf iron even tighter He moved forward once more, the golf club raised skywards in his right hand.

Tony Lee pulled the mobile phone from his pocket. He dialled Stacey's number and crouched down on the ground. Stacey answered and he spoke in a whisper.

"Stace? I'm around the back of the house. There's no sign of life in the place. I can't see a trace of Angie or him. This has been a complete waste of time. See you in a bit" Tony said. He ended the call before Stacey had a chance to speak. Tony was peeved. In his eyes, his day off had been totally wasted. Just as he shoved the phone back in his pocket, Alex bludgeoned him with the club. It came down hard on Tony's head, knocking him unconscious instantly.

Erik climbed into his car wondering if he had just scuppered any chance of progressing at the IT company. He also questioned if he was heading off on a wild goose chase. His evidence was sketchy at best, but something at the back of his mind was urging him to follow through on his hunch. He telephoned home, telling Eileen that he was delayed at work. Erik explained about Mr. Matthews dying, saying he had to attend a meeting. At least if his hunch was wrong, he would not look so foolish in his wife's eyes.

Alex dragged Tony's body in through the kitchen door at the rear of the house. He had overheard Tony's brief conversation with Stacey.

"Everything is coming together nicely! I should have guessed that she would be around. I should have realised that stupid Tony can't even drive after all! Stacey will be outside waiting. I only have to send a text message on dopey Tony's phone" he grinned.

Alex retrieved the mobile phone from Tony's pocket and typed out a simple message.

"Stacey, I've tripped on some wire in the back garden. Can't untangle my leg. Need ur help. Don't phone, it might alert him –Tony" he wrote.

"All I do now is wait" Alex said quietly.

Alex Woods bound Tony's hands and legs and left him lying on the kitchen floor. He watched the monitor closely awaiting the imminent arrival of his ex-girlfriend.

Stacey read the message on her phone. She glanced in towards the dark driveway. Cars drove by with headlights on as the rush-hour reached its climax. She would rather do anything than enter Alex's property. Yet she had to help Tony. She had no choice but to go to his aid. Stacey locked her car and entered the long driveway cautiously.

Erik Ngombiti sat in the stationary line of traffic on The Merrion Road. His car had barely moved in ten minutes. The stretch of road was notorious at peak time. He was losing patience fast, but there was little that he could do. "Come on, come on! The lights are green man!" Erik muttered. Up ahead he watched as the traffic lights turned from green to red without him moving forward an inch. He had researched Tom Woods address through the internet and phone book. Erik knew where he wanted to get to, but it was proving impossible.

Stacey crept along the driveway. Darkness was fast falling on the autumn evening. She was terrified with every step that she took. Her eyes strained into the blackness, hoping that Tony would appear. With every few feet, her heart seemed to beat faster. She clutched her phone in her hand, daring not to phone Tony in case she alerted Alex Woods. The house suddenly came into view. Stacey stopped to check the surroundings. A pale yellow light shone from one window in the front of the house. Hillcrest was not quite as she remembered. The big imposing premises did not look so welcoming now as it had on her first visit there. Stacey recollected meeting Alex's father on that initial journey. He had been courteous, though had asked a lot of questions about her social standing. It was as if Tom Woods had been weighing up her suitability to date his son. It seemed like a lifetime ago now to Stacey. She blinked it from her memory and inched onwards once again.

"Come on, sweetheart, come on a bit more!" Alex whispered as he watched the monitor. His driveway and grounds had security cameras everywhere. It was a legacy from Muggser's and Burrener's threat to his privacy. Alex zoomed in on Stacey's face. He watched her, almost in awe.

"It could have been so different darling, so very different. We could be having the time of our lives together. Instead you chose that arsehole" Alex said quietly, looking to Tony Lee's body lying prostrate on the floor.

Alex Woods slipped quietly out of the back door. He sidled along towards the entrance to the rear garden. Stacey would have to negotiate that corner in her search for Tony Lee. Alex waited patiently. Within minutes he could see her dark shadow on the ground, highlighted by the early evening moonlight. Stacey inched nearer. She whispered her boyfriends' name, almost in a panic.

"Tony? Tony! Where are you?" she hissed. Alex smiled smugly to himself. As she neared the corner, he made a sudden grab for her, placing a hand over her mouth, another around her neck. Stacey struggled momentarily, but it was only a token effort. Alex overpowered her easily and pulled her nearer to him. A startled look on Stacey's face soon turned to horror as she realised who her assailant was. Alex shook her violently and swung her around. He pressed her up against the wall.

"Well my pretty, we meet again. Nice of you to drop in!" Alex said with a beaming grin. Stacey suddenly felt very woozy. She struggled to keep her balance. Alex caught her in his arms and hauled her towards the back door as she fainted.

Stacey awoke to an eerie scene. She found her arms and legs tied as she sat on an armchair in the living room. Ahead of her, Tony Lee lay on his back on the leather sofa, his hands tied firmly behind his back. His feet were bound by a length of rope and a thick strip of plaster covered his mouth. Tony's eyes were open, and they showed a look of despair. A trickle of blood ran down from Tony's head onto his forehead. To her left, Stacey could see Angie O'Rourke. Angie was also tied up. She, like Stacey, was seated in a big leather armchair. Angie also bore a length of skin-coloured plaster across her lower face and mouth. Her eyes told Stacey that she had been crying, her dark eye-shadow smearing her cheeks. It struck Stacey that her own mouth was free. For some reason, Alex had omitted to gag her. Out of the corner of her eye, Stacey suddenly saw Alex Woods. He had been standing almost behind Stacey, waiting for her to regain consciousness.

"So you decided to join us Stacey! Isn't this nice? We're all together again! When was the last time all four of us met up? Don't tell me! It was our wedding day, wasn't it Stacey?" Alex said. The smile quickly vanished, to be replaced by a scowl.

Stacey tried to speak. She opened her mouth but nothing came out. Alex crouched down beside her, staring her directly in the eyes.

"So you think that you can just dump me and go back to that tosser over there?" Alex said with a gesture of his head. Stacey's eyes fell on Tony. His eyes pleaded for a chance to help Stacey. Tony felt hopeless and weak as he watched Alex from across the room. Stacey summoned up the nerve to speak.

"Why are you doing this Alex?" she asked nervously. Alex moved even closer to her and smiled.

"Because I can!" he replied. The smile vanished as his mood changed.

"I can do anything I want. Who's gonna stop me? You? That weakling tied up over there? I don't think so!" Alex crowed.

"You won't get away with this Alex. People will be looking for us" Stacey said defiantly. Alex laughed in her face.

"Like who? Gina?" he cackled. Stacey said nothing.

"Well, we can soon fix that!" Alex said. He had already retrieved Stacey's phone from where she had dropped it in the back garden. Stacey watched in horror as he began to compose a text message to Gina.

"Gone to stay with Tony for a while. Talk to you soon. P.S. Spoke to Angie. She's fine" Alex said, reading the message aloud. Stacey tried to brave it out.

"It's not just Gina, there are others who know we're here" Stacey said. Alex was growing tired of the conversation.

With you three dead, I'll soon get rid of Gina Stynes. That will be the final piece of the jigsaw. It will be months before anybody really misses any of you" he sneered.

"You're crazy Alex, it will never work" Stacey replied. Already Alex Woods was tiring of the conversation.

"It won't matter in a little while anyway. All three of you will be lying face down under a pile of clay, just like Isobel! Oh, I'm sorry Stacey; you never knew about Isobel, did you? Well, why not let Angie tell you all about her-and the others!" Alex said, his face lighting up at his latest idea. He strode across the room and ripped the sticky plaster from Angie's mouth. She grimaced as he freed her mouth. Alex then pulled a fresh strip of the skin-coloured bandage from his pocket and placed it sideways across Stacey's trembling mouth.

"Now sweetheart, you just listen to Angie's little story" Alex said. He walked from the room laughing, leaving a sobbing Angie to tell the other two her tale of evil.

Erik Ngombiti was approaching The Frascati Centre in the heart of Blackrock. The traffic was less intense now as the evening rush hour abated. He only had a sketchy idea of the area. Blackrock was on the coast, and on sunny summer weekend days, Erik had often taken the family for a trip to the seaside. However, Alex Woods' address was on a road which he had never heard of.

"Right, let's try this way" Erik said, cursing himself for never investing in a sat-nav system.

Stacey's eyes bulged as she listened to Angie relay Alex Woods' claim to have killed so many people that they knew. Tears streamed down her face as the name of Jodie Callaghan was added to the list. Tony could scarcely believe what he was hearing. It made no sense to him. His head throbbed with a dull aching pain from the blow of the golf club. Yet Tony Lee was not about to give up. He struggled to undo the knotted rope binding his wrists, but seemed to be fighting a losing battle. Alex had made certain that the knot was tight and secure.

Suddenly Alex Woods strode menacingly into the room. He had backed his car up to the front door, leaving the boot open.

"Time to go guys. I apologise in advance for the cramped conditions, but the boot in the Mondeo is really roomy. Count yourselves lucky that I don't drive a Mini!" Alex remarked. He scooped up Stacey first, as she was the lightest of the three. Within seconds he returned and homed in on Tony.

"Right, you're next. You see, we have to go, girl, boy, girl!" he said, laughing at his attempt at humour. He eased Tony's bound body up onto his shoulder and carried him to the boot of the car. Tony was lowered down next to Stacey. He could see the tears of fear in her eyes. Tony lay helpless next to her, his long legs cramped up. The single yellow bulb in the boot of the car offered a little light. Tony could hear Stacey's whimpering. The terror that he had felt when discovering Martin's body was nothing to what Tony felt now. At least with Martin, Tony could do something about it. Now he felt powerless. Alex was calling the shots. Tony tried to stay calm, to wait for an opportunity to escape. Yet he felt that Alex was so in control and focussed, that a chance might never arise.

Angie's trembling body was soon placed next to Tony in the boot of the car. Alex slammed the big door of the car's boot without speaking a word. The yellow light vanished instantly. They heard the engine start seconds later. Angie began to talk. It was mostly gibberish until she realised that she was the only one who could speak. Her mind cleared in the darkness as she considered that she would have to help her friends to stay calm.

"It's okay. We'll be all right. Keep a level head Stacey. Tony, we might get one chance. We have to be ready. On the journey I'm going to yell out every time the car stops. Someone might hear me, you never know" Angie said. She could feel Tony's head nodding next to her. Suddenly the booming of the radio could be heard. The thump-thump-thump of bass music echoed through the car.

"Oh my God! He has the stereo on full! No one will hear me over that noise!" Angie wailed. She descended into uncontrollable sobbing. Tony Lee tried to stay strong. He could feel both women weeping either side of him in the dark clammy boot of the car. Tony's mind was focussed and clear. Even before the pep talk from Angie, Tony already knew that he would have to be ready for any half-chance at freedom that might arise. Yet Tony felt utterly useless. And as he remembered Jodie Callaghan, he blamed himself for her needless death.

Erik Ngombiti arrived at Alex's home thirty minutes after they had left. He parked outside on the street and went to investigate. Once he had established that no one was at home, he had a decision to make. He should either contact the police, or break in. Erik decided on the latter. His information was not conclusive, and Erik had some experience at house-breaking.

"Right! The first thing to do is to disable the alarm" he muttered. He found a ladder at the rear of the house and set about his task.

"God! I'm so rusty at this game! I wish that I had gone to the gym more!" Erik muttered as he scaled the silver aluminium ladder. Within seconds he was back down. Wires hung limply from the white alarm box below Alex Woods' bedroom window. Erik carried the ladder on his shoulder back around to the rear of the property. He had noticed a small window open upstairs. He placed the ladder up against the wall of the house in the back garden.

Seconds later, Erik was in a small bedroom. It looked like it was used for storage. He went downstairs, having first checked each bedroom.

Alex Woods drove up through Templeogue towards The Dublin Mountains. The traffic had eased, and he was calm and alert. He watched ahead of him, checking that there was nothing untoward. Police check points were a rarity at that time of the evening, but he was still very wary. The music throbbed against the roof of his white Ford car as he drove steadily on in the dark early evening. Alex glanced at his watch. The news would be on in two minutes. Perhaps it was best to listen in, just in case, he thought. Alex was confident that his kidnapped victims had not alerted anyone, yet it was no harm to double check. Once through the set of traffic lights at the junction leading towards the M50, Alex switched radio stations. The news channel had just started its bulletin.

"Hear that? He's lowered the music. We must have reached the destination. Remember, if any of us get a chance, be ready. We might only have seconds" Angie said to the other two. She had calmed down considerably, and tried to remain positive for everyone's sake.

Alex listened intently to every item of news. He was feeling ultra confident and smug. Only when the newsreader reached the end of the bulletin did his mood change.

"Motorists are advised to take extra care on roads in the Templeogue and Tallaght areas of Dublin. Police are on the lookout for two dangerous criminals who have escaped from custody while attending Tallaght Hospital earlier today. Road checks are in place, and police are warning people not to approach these men" said the female newsreader. She went on to give a description of both men, and details of their crimes.

"Shit! Fucking shit!" Alex yelled, thumping hard on the steering wheel.

"Of all the fucking nights for that to happen…" he ranted, pulling over to the hard shoulder.

"Think Alex, think. All right, stay calm. Okay, we can always go back to the house. No, wait a minute. It's nearer to the garage than it is to Blackrock. Yeah! Clever thinking, my son! I'll use the garage as a stopgap until they catch those gobshites. They're bound to scale down the road checks later on. Yeah, I'm in no hurry. I can wait!" Alex thought quietly to himself. He hired the music again and drove on. Turning off at the next junction to his right, Alex headed in the direction of Walkinstown. He drove down Templeville Road, and on through Greentrees Road. He was now just minutes away from Wood's Motors.

Gina arrived home to an empty flat. She saw Angie's note on the coffee table. The contents surprised her, but Stacey's text message earlier had already put her mind at ease. Angie had been drinking heavily since splitting up with Philip, but Gina never thought of Angie O'Rourke as depressed. She did not question the situation further. Her plan was to cook a meal, and enjoy the novelty of having the apartment to herself. What should have been a girlie night, with all three friends reunited, suddenly meant that she could relax and have an early night in bed.

Erik began to fear the worst as he examined the sitting room of the big, imposing house. Scraps of twine and rope fibres littered the carpet. Tell-tale signs for the trained eye told him that his intuition had been correct. He found the discarded plaster, used to cover Angie's mouth, thrown in the bin. Lipstick smudges covered the sticky felt side of the skin-coloured wound-dressing. Erik could smell perfume, another sign that something was amiss. It was time to act. But time was against him. And he could only guess where Alex Woods was heading next.

Alex drove his car inside the rear entrance of the huge garage and showrooms. The glass cage which dominated the main part of The Long Mile Road, gave way to a more mundane and practical premises at the rear. This was the area where the mechanics and other staff worked. Alex parked up and closed the big blue gates behind him. His office would suffice as a holding cell for the next couple of hours.

Alex clicked the switch which popped open the boot of the car. He then entered the garage and turned off the alarm and the CCTV system so that no footage of the three would exist. Tony gulped in fresh air as the boot opened. He lay helpless on his back. Tony then watched in despair as Alex Woods delved into the boot. Alex carried Angie away first. He left her on a simple office chair and returned to remove Tony from the boot. Dragging him roughly out onto the tarmac, Alex ignored Tony Lee and instead lifted Stacey up onto his shoulders. Tony lay helpless as he watched Alex's black shoes stride away towards the building. His eyes searched the darkened grounds for something to use as a weapon. There was nothing within reach, and anyway, Tony had no way of holding it. Utter despondency engulfed him as he strained to remain composed.

Stacey saw Angie sitting opposite her as Alex dropped her carefully onto a similar chair.

Alex bent down to speak to Stacey.

"It's not too late you know. Just say the word and you and me could still make up" he said. A serious, questioning expression now masked his face. Stacey nodded silently, anxious to gain her captor's trust.

"Really?" Alex asked, ripping the plaster from her mouth. Stacey grimaced in pain before speaking.

"Yes Alex, I think that we could still make a go of it. I made a big mistake in not marrying you" she said convincingly. Alex threw back his head and laughed loudly.

"Oh Stacey, Stacey! You almost had me believing you!" he said. The smile quickly vanished, to be replaced by a scowl.

"Too late now bitch! You had your chance, but you chose that prick instead. Well now it's my turn to have the last laugh" he said, a look of hatred etched on his face. He suddenly seemed to remember Tony Lee. A faraway look developed in his eyes as he stared towards the tiny window overlooking the yard.

"Feel free to talk. No one can hear you now. Scream if you like girls. We own all the land to the back of the building. There's nothing out there except industrial units" Alex said. Alex then returned to the rear yard, leaving the two terrified women alone.

Tony was busy chafing the twine that bound his arms, on the underside of Alex's car. A rough metal corner beside the exhaust pipe was gradually eating away at the blue twine.

"Got it!" Tony whispered as his binding finally gave way. If he could just undo his feet he might have a chance, he thought. The length of rope was tight against his ankles. Tony knew that it would only take a matter of seconds to open the knot. All too quickly he heard the sound of Alex's heavy shoes approaching.

"Shit! I just needed another minute" Tony said under his breath. Tony quickly lay back down with his hands behind his back. This might be the chance that Angie had talked about. He waited until Alex Woods was within feet of him.

Tony suddenly lashed out with his bound feet, sweeping Alex to the ground. In seconds Tony Lee was climbing upright, using the parked car as a crutch. Alex began to clamber to his feet too, a little stunned by what had happened. Tony flung himself at him, fists flailing. Punches rained down on Alex's shocked face as he fought to defend himself. Tony Lee was on top of him, punching, gouging, and biting his opponent. It might be his only chance, and Tony knew it. He had to do all in his power to save Angie and Stacey.

His bound legs restricted him as Alex Woods fought back. Tony was on top of his rival, trying his utmost to dominate Alex Woods. Tony landed punch after punch on Alex's face and upper body. Suddenly Alex wriggled to the side, forcing Tony off of his chest. Tony's bound feet meant that he had little leverage, and Alex gained the advantage. Still Tony fought with all of his might, landing blows on Alex around the head and face. Alex grabbed Tony's head and thumped it against the concrete ground several times. Tony battled on, his punches becoming weaker.

"Die, fucker, die" Alex yelled, landing a heavy blow of his right fist into Tony's face. Tony's vision faded away as the blackness took hold. His eyes watched as a shadowy figure of Alex's sneering face floated away into the darkness. Tony passed out, blood trickling slowly from his mouth.

CHAPTER THIRTY-TWO

THE GLASS CAGE

Erik Ngombiti pulled up outside Wood's Motors on The Long Mile Road. The police were already there to the front of the building. They had seen the footage at Alex's house in Blackrock of the three captives.

"Are they inside?" Erik asked. The detective in charge shook Erik's hand. "Thanks for your help Mr. Ngombiti. We suspect so, but we can't confirm it right now. There's a light to the back of the premises. An officer who I sent to scout the building thinks he saw some activity. The rest of the place is in darkness, but there's a car matching the suspect's vehicle parked in the garage area. I don't want to do anything that might endanger any of the captors. We'll play this nice and easy until we have my men in place" said Detective Dave Valentine.

Erik stared at the giant glass building. The showroom was vast. The latest car models peeped out through the darkness onto the busy road. His own car was parked discreetly further down the road, as were the three unmarked police vehicles. The police used a parked articulated truck on the opposite side of the road as cover, avoiding any direct contact with the building for the time being. Erik took the time to call his wife.

"Eileen? I've been delayed longer than expected at this damn meeting. Forget about dinner love, I'll have something later" he said. His wife was far from convinced.

"I know well what your game is Erik. You will order a takeaway meal again, won't you? It's any excuse with you to eat that rubbish. How did the meeting go anyway? Will you get the promotion?" she replied. Erik grinned privately to himself.

"I'm afraid not love. Let's just say that things conspired against me. Don't fret, there will be another chance soon" Erik said with a loud sigh.

"Yeah? Pigs might fly Erik! That company never appreciated you and you know it!" Eileen countered. Erik shook his head wearily.

"Goodbye Eileen, I'll see you later. We can talk about it" Erik said.

Tony Lee slowly came to in the square office belonging to Alex Woods. His mouth felt sore and he was a little light-headed. All three were seated on plain straight-back chairs below the small window. Tony's face looked a sight. Sticky blood had dried into his lower face. A concerned Stacey eyed him from her left side. She was seated in the middle of the three. Alex opened the door and smiled at his three captives. He himself had a cut below his left eye and some scratches on his face. Otherwise he looked untroubled by his tussle with Tony Lee. Alex immediately checked that their hands and feet were still tied securely.

"Well, isn't this cosy? Don't worry; I've just heard the news. Those two criminals have just been recaptured. We will soon be on the road again. Oh sorry Tony, how is your face? Gosh, that's a nasty cut on your lip. Cut yourself shaving, did you?" Alex sniggered. Tony Lee was the only one whose mouth was not gagged now.

"You crazy bastard! You will never get away with this. The police will be after you" Tony said forcefully. Alex seemed to relish the opportunity of a verbal battle.

"Ha! And how would they connect me with you three? I'm a respectable businessman, for Christ's sake! You three vanishing might look suspicious for a while, but you will soon be forgotten about, just like Jodie!" he sneered. Tony struggled in his chair in frustration, wriggling from side to side.

"Careful Tony, you might topple over and hurt yourself!" Alex cackled.

"You bastard, I'll have you, trust me. I'll get you if it's the last thing that I ever do!" Tony roared. Alex grinned apathetically.

"Yeah, yeah, whatever. Do I look scared of you?" he said, leaning into Tony's face. Tony Lee spat full in his face. Alex reeled back, slightly stunned by Tony's reaction. He wiped the spittle from his face with his sleeve.

"You're not worth it, arsehole. I'll enjoy getting rid of you. In fact, I'm gonna bury you alive, just to watch you squirm like the worm that you are!" he sneered. Alex then turned to Stacey and Angie.

"Don't worry girls; I'll strangle the two of you first. You'll be well dead before I deal with this twat!" he said with a leering grin. Tears appeared in Angie's dark eyes. Her head shook in spasms as she took in Alex's threat. Stacey closed her eyes and tried to keep her composure. Alex glanced from one to the other before announcing his latest decision. He suddenly whipped off the bandages from both Stacey's and Angie's mouth.

"I'll tell you what, you three might like to say goodbye to each other. Be my guest. We'll soon be off, so make it brief" he said. Alex stood in the doorway for a few moments watching all three. When none of them chose to utter a single word, he quickly turned and exited the room. Alex left the white door open as he went to check the building again. Tony was the first to speak.

"Can anyone think of anything? There has to be a way out of this" he whispered. Angie shook her dark hair, the despair showing in her damp eyes. Stacey Boyd looked thoughtful.

"He seems a bit indecisive. How many times has he gagged us and then undone it to allow us to speak?" she said.

"I'm not sure Stace, but I'm convinced that he will try and kill us. Pray for one last chance. If I get the opportunity to grab him, you two run and don't look back" Tony replied.

"We could scream for help. You never know, someone might hear us" Angie suggested. Stacey seemed unimpressed.

"You heard him, this is an industrial area. He would hardly have taken off our gags if he thought that there was any danger. No, we'll have to come up with something else" she replied. Utter despair seeped into Angie's trembling body. She began to weep openly once again.

Alex Woods checked the yard to the back of the building once more. Soon he would have to open the gates again. Only when he had the three bodies loaded into the boot could he do that. His method of not taking unnecessary chances meant nothing could be taken for granted. Security and caution was paramount. Yet Alex did not expect any problems. He had often left the showrooms at a much later hour. Cars coming and going in such a busy area was the norm. He foresaw no hitches, and was confident that he would soon be finally rid of Tony Lee. Alex loaded his spade and shovel into the rear of his car and covered them with black bin liners and an old coat.

Unknown to Stacey, Angie and Tony, Alex Woods intended strangling both of the girls before placing them inside the trunk of his car. Alex had reasoned that it would be easier to quickly bury them if they were already dead. It would mean less time spent in the open, although The Dublin Mountains were a desolate and lonely place at night. By transporting Tony Lee in the boot with the two dead girls, it would be a last mocking shot at the man he now hated more than any other. Alex vowed that he would bury Tony Lee alive as he had threatened, for he considered Tony his greatest enemy. He could already visualise piling shovels of clay over Tony's struggling body. Alex looked to the sky. It was a clear night and the twinkling stars above seemed to bring a certain serenity to him.

"I'm sorry Nan. I have to do this. I promise you that once this is over, I will change my ways. I'm going to sell this business and move abroad. No one will ever suspect me. I will live a peaceful life far away from here" he whispered.

A noise from somewhere near the large gates shook Alex back to reality. He shone his torch in the general direction of the blue heavy gates and walked guardedly towards them. A man dressed in black and wearing a dark helmet lay flat on the roof to the right side of the gates. Alex's torch light scanned across the shadowy figure. The policeman lay perfectly still, but Alex was already suspicious. He said nothing and hurried inside.

Alex was now on high alert. He dashed to the office and began to gag each of his captives with some white bandages once again.

"You think that you can really do this Alex? Kill two innocent women for no apparent reason?" Tony Lee said. Alex said nothing, his mind racing. He finished gagging both Angie and Stacey, and then started to wrap the long white cloth around Tony's mouth.

"Yeah arsehole, I can certainly do it, no problem. If I was you, I would start saying my prayers. You are in for a particularly bad end to your useless life" Alex said. He stared at the small window, wondering if he had actually imagined seeing something on the low roof of the workshop. His active mind was racing now. How could anybody else possibly know of Tony Lee's whereabouts, he wondered?

Tony Lee's imminent death was secondary now. Alex had to find out if anyone really was outside. Was it one of Tony Lee's friends, he silently questioned his mind? Had he really seen a shadowy figure on top of the wall? If so, Alex knew he had to kill that person too.

Alex crept out into the showrooms at the front of the building. He checked the view on all three sides of the huge glass showrooms. With the one solid wall to his back, Alex began to rationalise coldly. Alex peered out onto the busy road. He used a gleaming black Nissan Note in the showrooms as cover. Everything looked normal. Cars whizzed by on each side of the extra-wide road. The giant yellow skip to the side of the building caught his attention. Rubble, metal girders and old furniture from his father's office lay inside. Alex dismissed it from his mind. The large articulated truck parked across the street caught his eye. Alex homed in on the gap between the front and rear wheels. He thought that he detected shadows on the pavement, but was not positive. Alex backed away towards the small open door again.

"I can't take a chance. There might be someone waiting out there. I need to be sure that it's all clear. Was that my mind playing tricks on me? Did I really see someone out back? Come on Alex, you're beginning to imagine things! Yeah! There's no one out back! Come on Alex, stay cool. But just to be certain, I'm going to check out there again" he thought quietly.

Suddenly a phone rang. Alex looked startled. He did not recognise the ringtone. Immediately he realised that the sound was coming from another office. He had left all three phones that he had taken from Angie, Stacey and Tony, in his old office. It had to be one of their mobile phones ringing. Alex figured that it would be Gina calling. It made sense. She was bound to be concerned for Stacey and Angie. Alex identified the tone as coming from Tony Lee's phone.

"Withheld" appeared on the screen to indicate that the caller did not want to be identified. Tentatively Alex pressed the green button to accept the call. If it was Gina he would simply hang up and shut off the phone.

"Hello?" said the male voice.

"Yeah?" Alex replied quietly.

"This is the police. I want you to come out through the main front door. The building is surrounded Alex. If you have any weapons, put them on the floor and leave now with your hands on your head" said the voice.

Panic set in instantly for Alex Woods. He had to think fast. Alex tiptoed back towards the showrooms again and looked outside. He checked on all three sides of the glass building. There was nothing untoward or out of the ordinary to see. The big yellow skip stood to one side of the showrooms. He could see no movement there. Again he focussed on the huge truck opposite.

"Who is this?" Alex demanded. The policeman leading the operation nodded to his colleagues gathered around him.

"This is Detective Dave Valentine. Alex, there is nowhere for you to go. It's best for everyone if you give yourself up peacefully. No one needs to get hurt" said the detective. Alex strained to identify the shadows across the road. He decided to chance his luck.

"I can fucking see you behind the truck, dickhead! What sort of fool do you take me for? Now, you're not dealing with some amateur here. If anybody tries to enter this place, I will slit the throats of these three. The doors are all booby-trapped. Now back off you shithead" Alex ranted. He ended the call in a panic. Alex ran to check the back of the building. He scanned the yard outside. It looked quiet. His eyes homed in on the big bolt on the rear metal gates. It was still in place. There were bars on all of the windows. No one would get through from the back of the well-fortified building.

"What did he say?" Detective Valentine's second in command asked.

"He said that the doors are booby trapped. He sounds determined. He's pumped up all right. We had better take things slowly" Valentine replied. George Kelly nodded slowly.

"Phone him again. Keep the pressure on" his sidekick suggested.

Detective Valentine phoned again on Tony Lee's phone. Erik had supplied the number, guessing that Alex Woods' would have taken his workmate's phone from him.

"Alex? There's no escape. We don't want to use force, but we will if we have to. This is no idle threat. We have trained marksmen out here. The sensible thing to do is for you to surrender" Dave Valentine said in calm, even tone.

Alex Woods paced the small office. His captives were in the next room. His plan was suddenly going completely wrong. Alex considered himself smarter than the average person. He found it hard to admit that things were going awry.

"No. I can still get out of this. Think Alex, think" he murmured to himself, clutching Tony Lee's phone to his chest for a moment. He listened to the caller again.

"Do you hear me Alex? We know all about you. We know where you live, about you and Stacey. Don't make this any worse than it is. All we're looking at so far is a kidnapping. Now, why not simply come out quietly and give yourself up?" Detective Valentine said.

Alex's brain searched for some speck of hope. The police knew nothing of his other crimes, yet his three captives knew everything. He was trapped. The only way out was to try and negotiate.

"It's too late detective, I'm going all of the way with this. You need to consider the outcome, not me. I have three people captive here. They're all going to die, unless you back off now. I mean it. I will slit their throats one by one, and their blood will be on your hands. Do I make myself clear?" Alex said in a menacing voice.

In the next room, Tony, Stacey and Angie heard his chilling words. They sat silently, each eyeballing the others. Tony Lee had been grappling with the heavy twine since he had been tied to the chair. He continued to rub it frantically against the sharp corner at the back of the wooden seat. Tony felt that he was getting nowhere, but carried on anyway.

Detective Valentine looked grimfaced as he listened to Alex's response.

"We can't just back off Alex. Why not set the two girls free as a goodwill gesture? Then we can talk. You'll still have Tony Lee. What do you say?" the policeman said. Alex was in no mood to bargain.

"What the fuck is this? Don't you hear me? There will be no deals done. Listen to this, you prick, I want a helicopter outside with just the pilot on board. I want enough fuel to get to Britain. I have a gun, so no funny business. I want safe passage out of here. I'm gonna take Stacey with me, so no marksmen need try and have a pop at me, you hear? Now, you go and organise that a.s.a.p. I mean it. You have one hour to act, after that I slit Lee's throat" Alex said in a loud voice.

"These things can't be done just like that Alex. We might need more time. At least let Angie go, eh? Just to show good faith" Dave Valentine said in a convincing tone. Alex screamed his next words down the phone with derision.

"Stupid fuckin' prick! Don't try to humour me! This is not some television programme where you wear the bad guy down with promises. This is for real, asshole. I'll say this one more time. You have one hour to meet my demands, after that, God help you!" Alex said. He ended the call and strode back to where Tony, Angie and Stacey were.

Alex eyed up all three. There seemed little point in having them gagged now. Alex did not like the silence. He whipped off the white bandages from their mouths.

"Did you hear what I said? So help me Stacey, it's gonna happen" he said, homing in on his ex-girlfriend. Stacey swallowed hard before speaking.

"It's insane Alex, how far do you think you will get? They're hardly going to give you a helicopter, are they? Even if they did, you can't get far. And what will you do for cash?" she reasoned. A trace of a smile spread across Alex Woods' face.

"Oh, I have cash Stacey, plenty of it too! I've moved money abroad, and I also have a substantial amount in the safe. Don't worry, they'll give in. Once I reach England I will disappear. Money goes a long way to getting you what you want. I could be in South America by the weekend. You better pray that I don't have to kill the three of you first. Either way, those clowns outside will never take me alive. I ain't going to prison, that's for sure" Alex said confidently.

"Have…have you really got a gun Alex?" Angie asked. She was still petrified, and her words were barely audible. Her body visibly shook as she spoke. All eyes followed Alex as he paced the small room, his brain still searching for a way out.

"What? A gun? Well, sort of!" he said. Alex went back to his office and then quickly returned. He was carrying what looked like a small black pistol.

"See this? It's an airgun. It only shoots pellets, but they're not to know that! It will put the shit up them when they see it! It certainly convinced that wimp Harry! In the right hands, this could kill a man dead" Alex said with a grin. The phone rang again and the smile vanished from Alex's face.

"Hello Alex? I've talked to my supervisor and we're doing the best that we can. In the meantime, why not let me send someone in with some food and coffee?" Detective Valentine said. Alex laughed out loud, holding the phone away from his face.

"You really are watching far too much television, dickhead! You want me to open the doors to some special branch tosser? Get real! Those doors are packed with explosives. Do you hear me fuckface? Anyway, this is a working firm. We have enough food and coffee in this building to last a lifetime. The canteen here is bigger than your house! The explosive on these doors won't be moved for no one! Now get on with organising things. Don't phone again unless you have some news. Fifty minutes and counting" Alex replied.

Detective Valentine looked around at the faces gathered before him. The phone had been on speaker now, so each person was in no doubt of the gravity of the situation.

"You have to do something. Why not smash in the back door? There's only one of him" Erik Ngombiti suggested. Detective Valentine looked ruffled. He was inexperienced in such a situation. He specialised mostly in white collar crime, and spent most days at his computer in the police station.

"Listen Ngombiti, you've been very useful up to now, but I'll take it from here. One move by us at the back of the building, and someone inside might lose their life. This calls for painstaking negations. He will wear down eventually. By tomorrow morning he will be exhausted and desperate. Don't worry; I'll get all three of your friends out alive" Dave Valentine said with a steely, confident grin. Erik Ngombiti did not agree.

"At least get someone down here that knows him. He has friends or family surely? Bring someone here to talk to him" Erik said, a pleading tone in his voice. Valentine looked around and selected a police officer.

"Dolan, take Mr. Ngombiti home. We won't need him again tonight" the detective said. Garda Dolan stepped forward and placed a hand on Erik's arm. Erik Ngombiti pulled his arm away.

"I don't need an escort, thanks" he said, turning to walk away towards his car.

Alex Woods dragged each prisoner, still bound to the wooden chairs, one by one into the showroom. He placed all three in a line facing the glass window to the front of the building. Alex then switched the lights on full.

"Oh my God! Sweet Jesus! Look what he's doing!" yelled a policeman.

Detective Valentine stared open mouthed at the scene. Alex held the gun to Tony Lee's head, a sneering expression on his face. It had been forty minutes since he had issued his ultimatum. Before Detective Valentine could react, Alex suddenly vanished once more, switching out the lights as he went.

"Shit! What's he up to?" Valentine asked his number two. George Kelly stubbed out a cigarette.

"I dunno. Maybe he's getting desperate. But that was a gun in his hand-unless I'm very much mistaken" the younger man answered.

"Block off the street. Close both ends of this road. I don't want the public witnessing this. Shut the whole friggin' place down" Valentine yelled. Instantly Dave Valentine's phone rang. Alex was phoning on Tony Lee's mobile phone.

"You see them tosser, do you? Do you see all three of them out there? I'm gonna kill them now. I'm not waiting. You've had almost an hour. I can see nothing happening-nothing! Where's that copter? I wanna be out of here tonight, you hear? Not when you say so, not when your boss thinks so-now! Three minutes and counting" Alex said in a rage.

"Three minutes Alex? Come on, be fair. The helicopter is on its way. Really. It's in the air right now. Your pilot is a civilian, I swear. Don't do anything crazy. Please" Detective Valentine pleaded.

Alex was back in his office. He peered out his window to the rear of the premises. The yard was silent, the main gates still secure.

"I'm losing patience fast here, arsehole. What have you been doing for the last hour? Sweet fuck all, that's what. You have five minutes-five. You hear? After that I won't be responsible" Alex said, terminating the call.

"He sounds like he means business" Valentine's number two said warily. Dave Valentine shook his head confidently.

"Nah! He's an amateur. It's all bravado. He's no more a killer than I am! Malone, you're our top marksman. I want you to take someone around to the back of the place. See if you can get a clear shot at him" Valentine said. George Kelly looked nervous.

"Shouldn't we make sure that he's armed? That might not be a real gun sir" he said. Valentine appeared edgy.

"That goes without saying. Yeah, Malone, make sure he's armed first" he replied.

"How...how will I gain access? The guys say that there's a twelve-foot metal gate back there" Malone said. Dave Valentine seemed more edgy than ever.

"Well climb the goddamn thing, that's what you're paid for! I don't care how you get in, I want him taken out. People's lives are at risk for Christ's sake!" Valentine snapped back. A young uniformed policeman stepped forward almost reluctantly.

"With respect sir, it was me who cased the rear of the building. The windows are barred, and the door into the building is a heavy steel, locked door. There is no way in to the rear" he said. Valentine appeared desperate. He looked to Malone again.

"Do it Malone. If he appears at the back of the building, take him out" Dave Valentine demanded.

Malone and a colleague took off, creeping along the narrow slip-road that led to the rear of the glass building.

Erik Ngombiti had rejoined the group unnoticed. He stood among the thirty or so force. By now the police had parked openly on the sealed-off road. Police vehicles stood abandoned, a road block at either end of the main street.

Diversions were in place for any night travellers still on the streets. It would appear as just a small inconvenience to them. Most would assume that it was road works or a burst gas pipe. No member of the public could ever imagine the gravity of the situation.

The giant showrooms glistened in the moonlight. Across the street, every policeman was on full alert. The faces of the three captives were barely noticeable in the semi-darkness.

Erik took in Valentine's words. He was becoming more disillusioned with the detective's leadership by the second. He pushed his way back through the bodies to face Dave Valentine.

"There's something else that I have to tell you" Erik said. Valentine stared back at Erik in astonishment.

"I sent you home ages ago. What are you doing still here?" he demanded. Erik stepped even closer to the man.

"You have to listen to me. That man inside tried to kill Tony Lee at our place of work. At first I wasn't sure. Now it all makes sense. Only for I intervened, he would have pushed him to his death. This man is clearly a lunatic. You can't wait and hope that he doesn't carry out his threat. He's dangerous. Alex Woods means every word that he says" Erik said forcefully. Dave Valentine eyed him for a few seconds.

"I think that I know what I'm doing Ngombiti. Thanks for your advice. You can go now" Valentine replied. Erik refused to back down.

"With respect sir, I don't think that you do. I suggest that you get a more experienced man down here to lead this operation" Erik said calmly. Dave Valentine moved forward. He was inches from Erik's face now.

"You do, do you? I've tolerated you for long enough. Get out of here now before I have you locked up" he yelled. He pushed Erik with both hands, forcing him backwards against the grey and black articulated truck. Erik shoved back and suddenly several officers were busy trying to separate the two men. A shot rang out, bringing calm to the situation. It came from behind the garage area, and all eyes looked towards the slipway leading to the huge metal gates.

Malone and another officer dashed back across the wide road. Malone was breathless, but managed to speak.

"He's armed all right. I was almost over the top of the gate when he took a pot-shot at me through a window. He missed my leg by inches. I fired back, but missed him. There's no way in back there. The place is as fortified as a prison sir" Malone panted.

Valentine's phone rang again.

"Hey dumb ass, I'm about to do it. You've had every chance. Where's the chopper, you lying bastard?" Alex yelled.

"It's almost here Alex. Honest. Two more minutes, yeah? Just give me a couple of minutes" Dave Valentine pleaded.

"Send another copper around the back, I'll fucking shoot him too, I swear!" Alex screamed.

"That officer acted without authority Alex. That won't happen again" Valentine replied in a subservient tone.

"Two minutes, that's it. Hey, I changed my mind by the way. I won't slit their throats" Alex said.

"Good boy. That's it, you stay calm Alex" Valentine said, interrupting Alex Woods.

"Let me finish, dickhead! I won't slit the girls' throats. I'm gonna shoot them both in the back of the head. But Tony Lee is going to get slit all right. He's last. When you see the blood running down those big glass windows out front, remember that it was your decision that caused this" Alex yelled.

"No Alex, wait. Listen to me. You have to stay with me on this. What difference will a few minutes make? Give me some more time, yeah?" Dave Valentine pleaded.

"Time's up!" Alex said, ending the call.

"What are we gonna do?" George Kelly asked. Valentine avoided eye contact. He was running out of ideas.

"I'll get some more people down here. Maybe we should call in the army?" Valentine replied, his voice shaky and unsure. Valentine paced back and forward in deep thought.

Erik managed to get George Kelly to one side. Valentine was now busy telephoning his superior on his own private phone.

"Listen, I have an idea. I need your help. Valentine is going to blow this situation. We need to do something" Erik said. George Kelly listened to what Erik had to say. He too was losing faith in his boss.

"It sounds a bit hairy! Are you sure that you can pull it off?" Kelly said when Erik had finished explaining his plan.

"What have we got to lose? Woods will slaughter those people in the next few minutes. Just give me a couple of your men to help me. By the time Valentine realises what's going on, it will be too late" Erik said. George Kelly nodded slowly. It was against his better judgement, yet Erik's idea just might work. "Okay, but I never gave permission" Kelly replied. Erik smirked back at him. "Understood! Have your men ready. Once inside we can secure the prisoners, and take the front of the building, then let Malone lead a team in towards the rear" Erik said.

Erik Ngombiti raced away towards where his car was parked. It was time to move without Valentine. Erik had to act fast. It would take all of his past experience and knowhow to rescue his friend.
Erik watched as the two burly policemen quietly lifted the two long metal girders from the yellow skip and set them at a forty-five degree angle to the ground in a ramp-like fashion. They were at least twenty foot long and flat on the upturned side. The width of the long metal girders worried Erik. Less than a foot wide meant that there was little room for error. He sat in the driver seat of his car and waited until everything was in place. George Kelly stood a fair distance away across the street. Valentine sat in a police van, talking to his immediate superior. The two burly policemen signalled to Erik that everything was ready. They slipped away back into the darkness. Erik looked to George Kelly who offered him a thumbs-up. Erik grinned and patted the dashboard. "Time for a new car anyway!" he said with a nervous chuckle. Erik started the engine and revved up. He reversed suddenly before shooting forward. The lights on his red Ford Focus were full on. Valentine looked up in surprise. "Sweet Jesus!" he remarked, holding the phone away from his face. He watched in amazement as Erik's car sped forward.
Erik hit the bottom of the girders at full speed. The red car flew up the home-made ramp and shot skywards. George Kelly held his breath.
"Holy shite!" he exclaimed as the car sped off the top of the heavy grey parallel girders. Erik gripped hard on the black steering wheel. He lowered his face towards the dashboard for protection. The vehicle shot onwards catapulting towards the huge glass walls to the side of the building. George Kelly readied his men.
"Malone! Get your men in place! Six of you lead the way in. Secure the three prisoners first before moving on!" he yelled. Steve Malone nodded and spoke concisely to his team.

The front of the car smashed through the glass, shattering all four giant panes to the side of the showrooms. Glass flew in every direction across the black-

and-white tiled floor. The noise was deafening. Shattered glass spewed through the air, clinking and chiming all around the quiet street. Stacey and Angie screamed in terror. The squeal of the engine on Erik's car filled the glass room. Erik braced himself as the car crashed to the ground in the tiled showrooms. It landed unevenly on its two left wheels before screeching forward again. Smoke bellowed from the engine and from the tyres. The car hurtled onwards as Erik pressed hard on the breaks. Noise and smoke filled the air. The screech of the brakes was deafening as the car hurtled across the floor. A sparkling navy Volvo car blocked Erik's path. He braced himself once more as his red Focus car smashed against the passenger door of the brand new Volvo. "That's gonna cost!" Erik said with a grin as his Focus car shuddered to a sudden halt.

A startled Alex rushed into the showrooms. He tried to take in what was happening. It was hard to figure out where the threat came from amid the smoke and chaos. Alex waved the small airgun wildly, unsure what he should do. Erik seized on his opportunity. He pulled his gun from his inside pocket and aimed a shot at Alex Woods. Alex leapt back in surprise as the bullet whistled into his upper right arm. Erik tumbled effortlessly from the driver seat to the tiled floor outside. He rolled forward several times before taking up a safe position. By now Alex had turned and fled back to his office.

Within seconds a team of police were inside the building. They crashed through the opening made by Erik's Ford Focus, knocking away the remnants of the shattered glass with their truncheons and black shields. The first batch of policemen pressed on, passing Erik's shattered car. They made their way towards the glass frontage, quickly securing the three prisoners.

The elite force of policemen surrounded Stacey, Tony and Angie, quickly cutting away their bindings and pulling the three gently to the floor.

"This way!" said the leader of the second team. He led his team of six men on towards the rear offices. Steven Malone held his gun at the ready.

Alex Woods stood with his back to his office door. He had fled back towards the office area, blood seeping from his arm into his white shirtsleeve. It had all happened so fast that Alex could barely think straight. The commotion out in the showrooms was like a scene after a bomb attack. Alex could see no way out now. He picked up his airgun and put his finger on the trigger.

"I can't face jail. I can't. It's all or nothing. I'm ready; I'll get at least two of the bastards" he thought to himself. He felt for his knife in his jacket pocket. Alex took up position behind his desk, facing the door. He crouched down, ready to fight to the end.

A policeman kicked in the main office door which had once belonged to Tom Woods. The room was empty. Alex heard the crash in the next room as the office door smashed against the wall in the newly refurbished room. Alex knew that his old office would be their next port of call. Tears ran down his face. Suddenly he did not feel so brave.

"I'm sorry Nan, truly I am. If you can save me now, I promise that I'll change" he whimpered.

Steve Malone readied himself a second time. He looked to his colleague to let him know that he was ready. Once again the heavy-set policeman nodded to Malone before smashing in the door. Alex Woods stood up as he heard the crash and took aim. He held the air gun to his chin and pointed it at the open door.

"Drop the weapon now!" Malone yelled. Alex pulled the trigger, aiming directly at the policeman. Two further shots rang out. Alex fell backwards against the wall. Malone hit him in the chest with both shots. Alex dropped slowly to the floor. He released the small air gun and clutched his chest.

"Stacey...sorry. I loved you" he whispered. His eyes were wide open as he lay dying.

"Call an ambulance" Malone yelled.

"I think that it's too late" one of his colleagues said in a whisper.

Tony Lee winced as he heard the shots ring out. Stacey flinched beside him, her head automatically ducking down further. The silence that followed told the experienced policemen that the operation had come to a conclusion.

Erik crawled along the floor amid the glass until he was face to face with Tony Lee.

"Man, that was some entrance!" Tony said with a relieved grin. Stacey hugged Erik. He smiled at Tony who then put a comforting arm around his girlfriend.

"Thank you so much Erik. How did the police allow you to do something like that?" Stacey asked. Tony Lee wondered the same thing.

"Yeah, who gave you permission to do that stunt? I thought only policemen or Special Forces could do that sort of thing" Tony remarked. Before Erik could answer, George Kelly and Dave Valentine joined them.

"Well done Ngombiti, thanks for saving the day" Detective Valentine said with a begrudging tone. George Kelly smiled as he crouched down beside them.

"You'll be moving on again so?" he said to Erik. Erik frowned as the smile vanished from his face. He looked from Tony to George Kelly before replying.

"Yeah, I guess" he said slowly. Tony looked puzzled.

"Moving on? What do you mean? What's he talking about Erik?" Tony asked.

"It's a long story Tony mate. You're right of course. Only someone from Special Forces could do what I did. You see, when I told you that I settled in Dublin for Eileen and the children's sake, it wasn't strictly true. The truth is that I'm here as part of a resettlement programme. You see, a few years back I busted a drugs cartel in London. We uncovered millions of pounds worth of heroin and cocaine. Anyway, I had to testify against Mr. Big. He was the top man in Britain at the time. After he went down, I was more or less a dead man walking. I had to get out of there and get a new identity. They offered us a house in Australia, or in The States. We persuaded them that we would be safe in Dublin. The crime gang would never expect us to set up home here. Until now, it worked perfectly" Erik explained.

"So, you're really an English policeman? You're not an IT worker at all?" Tony asked. Erik laughed and shook his head.

"Oh, I was always very useful on computers. Once I knew that I had to go undercover, they put me through a crash course. I passed my exams. Don't worry; those diplomas on my wall at work are real. I put them up to back up my story. I guess that I'll have to find another career now" Erik said.

"He wasn't just an ordinary copper, were you Erik?" George Kelly whispered. Erik shook his head.

"I suppose it won't hurt to tell you now Tony. Yes, I was with an elite group when all of this drugs raid stuff happened. I knew the risks. We all did. I lost a good friend during that time" Erik said. Angie inched forward next to Erik.

"You were in the S.A.S?" she asked. Erik smiled politely at her.

"I'm afraid I can't say. I'm sworn to keep my identity private" Erik said. Tony Lee had an incredulous look etched on his bloodied face.

"So that's not even your real name? And all of that tosh that you told me about Africa was part of your cover too?" he said in a disappointed voice. Erik shook his head.

"Okay, Erik Ngombiti might not be my real name, but the rest is true. I would never deny my roots Tony. I did come to Britain as a refugee. It was not easy to get into the police force. It took years of training to accomplish what I did. I saw what damage drugs did in the area of London where I grew up. I was determined to make a difference" Erik said.

"And what about Eileen? Did you really fall in love with her, or is she part of your cover too?" Stacey asked. Erik threw back his head and laughed his special laugh.

"Of course we fell in love! Eileen was a policewoman too. You cannot expect two young children to act as stooges! My marriage is real, my kids are ours, and I'm still very much in love" Erik explained.

Detective Valentine was anxious to get everybody to safety.

"Come on folks, we have to get you out of here" he said. Stacey looked towards the door leading to the offices.

"Is he...is Alex...dead?" she asked. Dave Valentine looked over to Steven Malone. The police marksman nodded slowly back at him. The detective glanced down at Stacey Boyd.

"Yeah Miss, I'm afraid that he is" he replied.

At the police station, Tony had the chance to talk privately with Erik.

"What made you suspicious Erik? I mean, how did you know that we were in danger?" he said. Erik shrugged his shoulders as he sat sipping on a cup of coffee.

"Intuition I suppose. My job thought me that-my former job that is! You see, when you told me over the phone about Stacey suspecting him of holding Angie captive, I just had to check it out. His photo popped up when I googled that garage. Straightaway I realised that he looked very similar to that guy who called to our workplace. Never forget a face, you see! Alex Woods might well have pushed you to your death that day Tony!" Erik said.

"Phew Erik, you saved my life-twice!" Tony said with a relieved grin.

"Stay away from windows my friend-especially on the fourth floor!" Erik answered, his rumbling laughter starting once again in the pit of his stomach. A senior detective entered the room and began to whisper to Erik Ngombiti. He broke away to talk to Tony for the last time.

"I'm being shifted out. Eileen's outside with the children. Another safe house for now, and then it's off for destinations unknown" he said with a frown.

"God Erik, I'm so sorry. I've messed up your whole life" Tony remarked.

"No mate, it was always a risky business. You take care, you hear?" Erik replied.

Tony, Stacey and Angie spent the night in hospital under observation. No one had any serious injuries, just minor cuts and bruises to their bodies.

The next day all three made statements to the police. Angie relayed what Alex had told her.

Her statement was met with shock and incredulity by the police officers. However, everything would soon be verified.

Isobel Woods had indeed lived in Ireland and was reported missing by friends in England, but under her maiden name. She had phoned to say that she was returning home, but of course never did.

Isobel's body would never be found. She would remain one of many dead or missing women unaccounted for, and presumed buried somewhere in The Dublin Mountains.

The news of Harry's murder offered his family some small comfort. His brothers had always doubted that Harry was capable of committing suicide. At least the cause of death on Harry's death certificate could be changed from suicide to murder. A small crumb of comfort for his loved ones.

For some time, Karen Westbourne did mourn her estranged husband, Philip. However, after a year or so she would meet someone else and settle down happily with her new man. It would be left to Philip's brother, William, to tend his grave in later years.

Margaret Thompson would never meet someone new. She would return to work as a schoolteacher, her parents becoming her permanent baby-sitters. Margaret would of course be told that Terry's death was probably murder, but it would make little difference to her. Every day would be a struggle in an effort to care for her two children.

Tony insisted that he and Stacey Boyd stayed at a hotel for the next few days. By the third day, Stacey was becoming bored.

"We'll have to go home sometime Tony. We can't live like this forever" she said. Tony looked at her earnestly across the breakfast table in the hotel.

"Stace, I can never live in that house again, I'm sorry. It holds too many bad memories" he said quietly. Stacey looked surprised.

"You mean Jodie?" she asked. Tony smiled and nodded back at her.

"Yeah, Jodie and other things. It doesn't matter. I'm selling up and we're going to buy a new home. One without a history, a brand new house on some quiet estate, but not on the outskirts of town. I need to live somewhere near to where I grew up. I fancy a fresh start, somewhere where we can build a life together. What do you say?" Tony said with a beaming grin. Stacey squealed with delight. People at nearby tables gave her an odd look. Stacey Boyd covered her mouth with embarrassment. She leaned forward to speak.

"Oh Tony, that's brilliant! I never thought that you would agree to move! I can't believe it! I was afraid that I would have to live at number eighty-eight for the rest of my life!" she said in a whisper. Tony laughed across the table at her.

"I thought that you were warming to the place?" he said. Stacey shook her head several times.

"Never! I hate the house, but I would have done anything to keep you. I love you Tony Lee" she said. Her eyes fell on her engagement ring. Tony followed her stare.

"And I love you too Stace" he whispered, kissing her hand gently.

The next day Tony went to his house alone while Stacey visited her old apartment. His test results were due by post. Tony knew that it was time to face the truth. He opened the front door and collected up the mail that had gathered behind the new white door.

"Bills, junk! Rubbish!" he said as he flicked through the envelopes. Tony stopped as he reached the one letter that mattered. He fell silent as he ripped open the long white envelope. The door was wide open, and Tony Lee glanced out into the sunshine. His trusty bicycle stood locked to the gleaming railings. Beside it, a "for sale" sign stood sturdily in the front garden.

Tony reached for the phone once he had read the contents of the letter. He phoned Fergal Carrie's number and waited.

"Did you get the results this morning?" Tony asked.

"I did son. I tried to phone you earlier" Fergal replied.

"I was out. I've been busy for the last few days" Tony explained.

"Well, its official I suppose. What do we do now?" Fergal replied.

"I'll call around to see you straight away" Tony said.

Tony stood on the top step of the large Georgian house in the heart of Dublin City. He was carrying a large brown paper envelope, and waited patiently for Fergal Carrie to open the black imposing door. Fergal greeted him with a warm smile, beckoning him inside with a sweep of his left hand. Tony remained stoic as he entered. He took a seat in the luxurious living room opposite to Fergal's armchair by the fireside.

"I'm so sorry to have had to put you through all of this Tony, but we had to know, didn't we?" Fergal said. Tony nodded his head twice.

"Yeah, I suppose so" Tony replied.

"Sorry, can I offer you something to drink? It's a bit early for me..." Fergal said as an afterthought. Tony shook his head.

"Look, I don't want to be rude or anything, but can we just sort this out?" Tony said. Fergal arched his grey eyebrows and nodded his head several times. He stood up and walked to the window, placing both hands behind his back. He then turned to face Tony Lee.

"What can I say lad? I was so sure that you were my son. I'm sorry. All of those wasted years thinking that one day you would learn the truth" Fergal said. Tony eyed him up and down.

"That's why I'm here. The tests were negative. I want to know for sure who my father was" Tony said. Fergal ambled back and sat opposite him again.

"Oh, there's no doubt about that now. Sean Lee was your father. He and your mother were still sleeping together while…well, while we had an affair" Fergal said.

"I always felt that he was my Dad, in fact, I was positive" Tony replied. Fergal Carrie nodded in acceptance.

"And you were right. I suppose that it was wishful thinking on my behalf. When your mother ended our affair, I clung to the hope that she might relent when you came along. I believed that we could be a family" Fergal said. Tony Lee leaned forward in his chair.

"You've put me through hell in the last few weeks, not knowing who I was. I hope that you don't mind me saying this sir, but you have everything in life. Success, wealth, a nice home. Why on earth could you not simply get on and enjoy life?" Tony said. A flicker of a smile crossed Fergal's lips.

"I apologise again for putting you through this. The answer to your question is simple really lad. I never got over Delores. I was in love with her, in fact, I still am. When she became pregnant, I honestly believed that I was the father. So did she. I suppose that outsiders might consider me a sad, warped old man. In a way I probably am. Don't get me wrong Tony; I have tried to move my life on, oh yes! But I never found anyone to equal your mother. Never" Fergal said, his voice almost breaking.

Tony said nothing for a moment. He wanted to tell Fergal about Martin. He would have, had Fergal proved to be his biological father. Tony felt that telling him such a horrific story would shatter the old man's fanciful dreams of Delores. He decided against it.

Tony looked to the large brown envelope that he had being clutching close to him.

"I think these are yours" Tony said. He stood up and spilled the coloured envelopes onto the fancy square table in the centre of the room. Fergal eyed the old love letters and nodded. His deep blue eyes filled with tears.

"Aye, they were mine. I often wondered if Delores ever read them" he whispered. Tony Lee managed a wry smile.

"Oh, she read them all right. Each one was opened when I found them" he said.

Tears streamed down the old man's face.

Tony felt that there was no more to be said. In a way he was glad that the old musty letters belonged to Fergal. Had they been written by Howard Williams, it might have been too much to bear for Tony.

"I must be going Mr. Carrie. I just needed to confirm the truth" Tony said. Fergal Carrie's had a sad, defeated look in his eyes.

"If you really must Tony. Can we keep in touch? I see a lot of Delores in you. It would be nice to meet up from time to time" Fergal said, stretching out a hand. Tony shook the old man's hand warmly.

"Sure, I have your number" he said with a smile.

Jan Williams returned home from her part-time job at lunchtime. Sometimes she might go shopping, but today she had no need or inclination to do so. As she exited the family vehicle, she was surprised to see Howard's car parked ahead of her in the driveway. This was odd, but not unique. Mostly Howard would spend his entire day at the store, but on occasion he had returned home for a break, or to collect some paperwork. What caught Jan's eye was the fact that the door on the driver's side of the glistening Mustang was wide open. Howard always closed and locked his bright blue vehicle, having once had a car stolen from outside of his workplace.

Jan turned the key in the back door and called out.

"Howard love, are you home?" she asked in a gentle voice. There was no response. Jan searched the downstairs section of the property. She was now becoming concerned. Jan made her way upstairs towards the master bedroom, calling Howards' name as she went. Passing the open family bathroom door, Jan pressed on, her steps more hurried now. Her voice emitted a more urgent tone, feeling that all was not well.

"Howard? Are you okay?" she called.

Jan opened the door to her bedroom, half fearful of what she might find. The sight of Howard crouched on the floor beside their bed greeted her. Howard Williams was sobbing childlike into his fists, a look of foreboding etched on his round face.

"Howard?" Jan said questioningly. Howard did not acknowledge her. His blubbering continued, a thin, wailing noise escaping from somewhere within his throat.

"Howard? Are you okay love?" Jan asked, moving closer to him. She stooped over him, pulling his fists away from his red glassy-looking eyes.

"No, no, no! I'm not all right! God help me, how could I do it? How can we go on? It's a sin. It's wrong, what we did was so wrong" he mumbled incoherently. Jan knelt down beside him, holding him gently in her arms.

"What brought this on? What are you saying Howard? Ssssh. Don't go upsetting yourself" she whispered. Howard stared back at her as if noticing her for the first time.

"Jan? Oh Jan, what have we done? The children will never forgive us. We made a pact with the devil. It's over. We're going straight to hell. It's the end, the end of everything" Howard said. His red-rimmed eyes had ceased crying now, but yet he sobbed intermittently through his broken semi-sentences. His words were disjointed, almost abstract. Howard Williams spoke in a faraway tone, yet his voice sounded convincing and believable. For the first time Jan was frightened. She was scared for her husband, and for her close family.

"Hush Howard love, don't talk like that. We're over the worst. The children need never know about what happened in Dublin. Come on, let's have a nice cup of coffee together" Jan said. She started to climb to her feet, offering to help Howard up at the same time. He immediately pulled away.

"No! Don't you see? The kids have to know. The spies are everywhere. Whispering. It's all doom Jan. There's no way out. But you might escape. Yeah! That's it! If you go now you just might make it. Go on, you run Jan-run for your life" he said, rocking back and forward on the spot. Jan Williams looked appalled.

"Stop Howard, you're frightening me. Run where? Where could I go? My place is with you and the children. Please Howard, snap out of this...this trance" she pleaded. A flicker of a smile crossed Howard's worried face. He pointed to the bedroom window, his finger jabbing animatedly. All of the time he continued to rock gently back and forward on the floor.

"The men Jan, those special men in suits. It's the only way. They might take you. I saw one as I came home. Hurry! No need to pack. Go as you are" he whispered.

Howard began to cry again openly. His words were confused now. Gibberish spouted from his lips, filling the bedroom with useless, incoherent words. Jan sank to her knees again and held him, a terrified look on her lined face.

Since returning home from Ireland, Howard had become very subdued. Gone was the brash, upbeat man that Jan had idolised and admired. Lately he had become confused and introvert. Jan had supposed that it was the result of events in Dublin. She imagined that it would eventually pass, and soon her Howard would again become the bubbly optimistic man of old.

This would never be the case. Howard was heading for a nervous breakdown. Soon he would be admitted to a psychiatric home, where he would stay for several years. Jan would be forced to sell his beloved business at a knock-down price. Howard's family would of course rally round, helping to push both Josh and Amy through college. But Howard would never return to the man he once was. When eventually released from hospital, Howard would barely know Jan or his children. Jan Williams would see out her days taking care of the man she loved. Eventually Amy and Josh would move away, there calls and visits home becoming less and less frequent.

Erik Ngombiti and Eileen were ushered to the semi-detached house on a quiet street on the outskirts of Brisbane. They had been in Australia almost a week now, living under guard in a downtown hotel. Two days earlier they had viewed the property, which was to be their new home. The three-bedroom house was modest, but definitely adequate for their small family. Erik held his son's hand as they stood in the empty living room. Eileen cradled their youngest in her arms.
Erik nodded at the two special branch men to let them know that it was okay. They left without saying a word.
"So this is home now. Better make the most of it" Eileen said quietly. Erik released his grip on his son Simon's hand and embraced Eileen.
"Yeah, I'm sorry love. I messed up" Erik replied. Eileen managed a half-hearted smile.
"No, you didn't Erik. You did what I always expected you to do. Once a policeman, always a policeman!" she whispered. Erik kissed her on the left cheek.
"Yeah, I guess. By the way, my name is Wesley, Wesley Johnson. Remember that Sandra" he smiled. Eileen's brow furrowed a little.
"Sandra Johnson. Yeah, that's me now. I hope that there are no more new names. Our kids will become so confused!" Eileen said with a smile.
"Huh-huh-huh! No, this is it now. No more new starts!" Erik said as his customary laughter echoed around the empty room.
"You said that in Dublin" Eileen replied. Erik held her in his arms, their youngest nestling between them.
"I hope Tony Lee appreciates what I did for him. He had better marry that Stacey!" Erik said.
"We'll probably never know" Eileen answered.

Tony Lee had felt the need to get away from the hotel and think for a while. He returned to number eighty-eight St. Oliver's Road to get a change of clothes. On the spur of the moment Tony decided to go for a spin on his silver racing bike. He donned his cycling clothes and headed off. He was feeling particularly energetic that morning.

Heading up along the canal and out through Templeogue, Tony took the winding roads leading towards the mountains. It was a steep climb, one that Tony Lee had done many times before. He wound his way up towards the mountains, and onwards past Johnny Fox's Pub, advertised as the highest public house in Ireland. Tony cycled on, sometimes pausing for breath. On certain stretches of steep road, he simply walked with his bicycle.

Once he reached his favourite spot, Tony finally halted. The sweeping view over Dublin always took his breath away. He could see his beloved city spread out across the landscape, right down to the sea and beyond. Tony stared down from his mountainous position in silence. His mind was awash with thoughts and mixed feeling.

Tony Lee questioned who he really was, and what would become of him. In the last few months, his family as he knew it had been torn to shreds. Even his best friend at work was not the man who he had claimed to be. Tony smiled wryly. He could at least forgive Erik Ngombiti for his deceit. Already Erik had said goodbye, ready to move on to a new life far away. Tony Lee could never imagine such a fate.

Tony decided that he could forgive Fergal Carrie too. He began to consider Jan and Howard. It was hard to absolve what they had done.

"And what about Delores Lee?" his brain asked. Tony stood tight-lipped, clutching the handlebars of his bicycle in both hands.

"Maybe in time, but not just yet" he answered. Tony thought of Jodie for a moment. Had he not fallen in love with her, she might still be alive today.

"So many if's and buts' "he thought. Tony then recalled the news that Alex Woods had buried his wife Isobel somewhere in the vast area where he now stood. It was indeed a sobering thought.

The tooting of a car horn snapped him from his daydreaming. Tony looked around in surprise to see Stacey waving frantically from her car window.

"How did you find me?" he yelled. Stacey smiled back at him and climbed from her car. The sun shone down brightly on the spring-like day.

"It was easy. When I went to the house, your bike was gone. I figured where else would you go on such a nice day? This is your favourite spot in the whole world, isn't it? Apart from number eighty-eight, that is!" she laughed.

Tony Lee kissed her gently on the lips.

"No, this is my favourite place in the whole world. And you are my favourite person" he replied.

"What about number eighty-eight?" she asked, in an almost teasing voice.

"What about it? It was only a house" he said, kissing her again.

"Yeah, but you loved that old place. I'm sorry that I could never settle there, Tony" she sighed.

"That's okay; we'll buy another house soon, but not too far away. I like the area, and it's handy for work" he replied casually. Tony kissed her again softly on the lips.

"You're such a home-bird Tony Lee! Don't you ever want to be adventurous?" Stacey said with a giggle. Tony shook his head.

"I've had enough adventures to last a lifetime!" he grinned.

"AN INCREDIBLE CHAIN OF EVENTS" IS THE FIRST BOOK PUBLISHED BY FRAN O'REILLY. IF YOU ENJOYED "88 SAINT OLIVER'S ROAD" YOU WILL LOVE HIS FIRST OFFERING. SET IN DUBLIN, THIS ORDINARY WORKING-CLASS MAN'S LIFE IS THROWN INTO CHAOS BECAUSE OF ONE CHANCE MEETING.

SYNOPSIS

JOE SWEENEY FACES HIS DREAD OF FLYING TO TREAT HIS DEAR SARAH TO HER FIRST EVER FOREIGN HOLIDAY, LITTLE KNOWING WHAT AN INCREDIBLE JOURNEY IN LIFE IT WOULD LEAD TO.
WHAT BEGINS AS AN ORDINARY TRIP SUDDENLY TAKES A CRAZY TURN WHEN JOE MEETS SOMEONE WHO HE CONSIDERS AN OLD FRIEND. HOWEVER, THE PERSON IN QUESTION CLAIMS TO HAVE NEVER MET JOE, NOR EVEN TO SPEAK ENGLISH.
COULD JOE HAVE MADE AN EASY MISTAKE, OR HAS THIS PERSON SOMETHING MORE SINISTER TO HIDE? WHAT ENSUES LEADS JOE ON A ROLLERCOASTER OF TWISTS AND TURNS, AND EVENTS THAT WOULD CHANGE HIS LIFE FOREVER. IT ALSO UNEARTHS A SHOCKING SECRET FROM JOE'S PAST....

ON RETURNING HOME, JOE FINDS IT IMPOSSIBLE TO LET THE CHANCE MEETING GO. IT NAGS AWAY AT HIM, FILLING HIS DAYS WITH INQUIZITIVENESS AND DOUBTS. SOON HE RECRUITS HIS BEST PAL TO HELP SOLVE THE MYSTERY, BUT THIS ONLY SEEMS TO THROW UP MORE QUESTIONS THAN ANSWERS.

DESPITE HIS DREAD OF FLYING, JOE IS SOON ON THE TRAIL OF THE MYSTERY MAN, LITTLE KNOWING THAT THE STRANGER ALSO HOLDS A KEY TO JOE'S OWN PAST. JOE'S OBSESSION AND DOGGEDNESS CAN ONLY LEAD TO ONE OUTCOME. A FINAL CONFRONTATION WITH HIS ADVERSARY, WHICH WILL SET THE RECORD STRAIGHT ONE WAY OR THE OTHER.

Made in the USA
Charleston, SC
13 November 2014